THE BREATHING SERIES

BOOKS 1 & 2

Rebecca Donovan

SKYSCAPE

The characters and events portrayed in this book are fictitious. Any similarity to
real persons, living or dead, is coincidental and not intended by the author.

Text copyright © 2013 Rebecca Donovan

Published by Amazon Children's Publishing
PO Box 400818
Las Vegas, NV 89140

ISBN-13: 9781477816950
ISBN-10: 147781695X

For my intuitively perceptive friend, Faith,
~ we were friends before we met ~
you helped me discover who I have always been...a writer

For my gifted friend, Elizabeth,
~ my search for words led me to you, where I found the perfect
partnership and a beautiful friendship ~

REASON TO BREATHE

1. NONEXISTENT

Breathe. My eyes swelled as I swallowed against the lump in my throat. Frustrated with my weakness, I swiftly brushed away the tears that had forced their way down my cheeks with the back of my hand. I couldn't think about it anymore—I would explode.

I looked around the room that was mine but had no true connection to me—a hand-me-down desk with a mismatched chair against the wall, and next to it a three-tiered bookcase that had seen too many homes in too many years. There were no pictures on the walls. No reminders of who I was before I came here. It was just a space where I could hide—hide from the pain, the glares and the cutting words.

Why was I here? I knew the answer. It wasn't a choice to be here; it was a necessity. I had nowhere else to go, and they couldn't turn their backs on me. They were the only family I had, and for that I couldn't be grateful.

I lay on my bed, attempting to divert my attention to my homework. I winced as I reached for my trigonometry book. I couldn't believe my shoulder was sore already. Great! It looked like I'd be wearing long sleeves again this week.

The aching pain in my shoulder caused horrific images to flash through my head. I felt the anger rising, making me clench my jaw and grit my teeth. I took a deep breath and allowed a dull wash of nothingness to envelop me. I needed to push it out of my head, so I forced myself to concentrate on my homework.

A soft tap at my door woke me. I propped myself up on my elbows and tried to focus in my dark room. I must have been asleep for about an hour, but didn't remember dozing off.

"Yeah," I answered, my voice caught in my throat.

"Emma?" the small, cautious voice called out as my door slowly opened.

"You can come in, Jack." I tried to sound welcoming despite my crushed disposition.

His hand gripped the doorknob as his head—not much taller than the knob—peeked in.

Jack's wide brown eyes scanned the room until they connected with mine—I could tell he was nervous about what he might find—and he smiled at me in relief. He knew way too much for his six years.

"Dinner's ready," he said, looking down. I realized it wasn't the message he wanted to be responsible for giving me.

"I'll be right there." I tried to smile back to assure him it was okay. He walked back to the voices in the other room. The clatter of platters and bowls being set on the table could be heard down the hall, along with Leyla's excited voice. If anyone were to observe this routine, they would think this was the picture-perfect American family sitting down to enjoy dinner together.

The picture changed when I crept out of my room. The air became thick with discord, with the crushing reminder that I existed, a blemish to their portrait. I took another deep breath and tried to convince myself I could get through this. It was just another night, right? But that was the problem.

I walked slowly down the hall and into the light of the dining room. My stomach turned as I crossed the threshold. I kept my gaze down at my hands, which I twisted in anticipation. To my relief, nobody noticed me when I entered.

"Emma!" Leyla exclaimed, running to me. I bent down, allowing her to jump into my arms. She gave me a tight embrace around my neck. I released a breathy grunt when the pain shot up my arm.

"Did you see my picture?" she asked, so proud of her swirls of pink and yellow. I felt the glare on my back, knowing that if it were a knife, I'd be incapacitated instantly.

"Mom, did you see my drawing of *Tyrannosaurus rex*?" I heard Jack ask, attempting to distract her.

"That's wonderful, honey," she praised, her attention drawn to her son.

"It's beautiful," I said softly to Leyla, looking into her dancing brown eyes. "Why don't you go ahead and sit for dinner, okay?"

"Okay," she agreed. She had no idea that her affectionate gesture had caused tension at the dinner table. How could she? She was four, and to her I was the older cousin she idolized, while she was my sun in this dark house. I could never blame her for the added grief her fondness for me caused.

The conversation picked up, and I thankfully became invisible once again. After waiting until everyone was served, I helped myself to the chicken, peas and potatoes. I could sense that my every move was being scrutinized, so I kept my focus on my plate while I ate. What I'd taken wasn't enough to satisfy my hunger, but I didn't dare take more.

I didn't listen to the words coming from *her* mouth as she went on and on about her trying day at work. Her voice raked through me, making my stomach turn. George responded with a comforting remark, attempting to reassure her as he always did. The only acknowledgment I received was when I asked to be excused. George looked across the table with his ambivalent eyes and drily granted my request.

I gathered my plate, along with Jack's and Leyla's, since they'd already left to watch TV in the living room. I began my nightly routine of scraping plates and placing them in the dishwasher, along with scrubbing the pots and pans George had used to prepare the dinner.

I waited for the voices to move into the living room before I returned to the table to finish clearing. After washing the dishes, taking out the trash and sweeping the floor, I headed back to my room. I passed the living room with the sounds of the TV and the kids' laughter in the background. I slipped by unnoticed, as usual.

I lay on my bed, plugging in the earbuds to my iPod, and turned up the volume so my mind was too preoccupied with the music to think. Tomorrow I would have a game after school that would keep me late, missing our wonderful family dinner. I breathed deep and closed my eyes. Tomorrow was another day—one day closer to leaving this all behind.

I rolled on my side, forgetting about my shoulder for a moment, until painfully reminded of what I was leaving behind. I shut off my light and let the music drone me to sleep.

———

I grabbed a granola bar on my way through the kitchen with a duffel bag in hand and my backpack slung over my shoulder. Leyla's eyes widened with delight when she saw me. I went over and kissed the top of her head, making a conscious effort to ignore the penetrating glare I was receiving from across the room. Jack was sitting next to Leyla at the island eating cereal—he slipped me a piece of paper without looking up.

"Good Luck!" was written in purple crayon with an adorable attempt at a soccer ball drawn in black. He glanced at me quickly to catch my expression, and I flashed a half smile, so she wouldn't pick up on our interaction. "Bye, guys," I said, turning toward the door.

Before I could reach it, her cold hand gripped my wrist. "Leave it."

I turned toward her. Her back was shielding the kids from witnessing her venomous glare. "You didn't ask for it on your list. So I didn't buy it for *you*. Leave it." She held out her hand.

I set the granola bar in her palm and was instantly freed from her crushing grasp. "Sorry," I murmured and rushed out of the house before there was more to be sorry for.

"So…what happened when you got home?" Sara demanded in anticipation, lowering the volume of the fast-beat punk song when I entered her red convertible coupe.

"Huh?" I responded, still rubbing my wrist.

"Last night, when you got home," Sara prompted impatiently.

"Not much really—just the usual yelling," I replied, downplaying the drama that had awaited me when I got home from practice yesterday. I decided not to divulge more as I casually rubbed my bruised arm. As much as I loved Sara and knew she would do anything for me, there were some things I thought best to save her from.

"So, just yelling, huh?" I knew she wasn't completely buying it. I wasn't the best liar, but I was convincing enough.

"Yeah," I mumbled, clasping my hands together, still shaking from her touch. I kept my eyes focused out the window, watching the trees fly by, broken up by the oversize homes with their landscaped lawns, feeling the crisp late-September air whip against my flushed face.

"Lucky for you, I guess." I could feel her looking at me, waiting for me to confess.

Sara turned up the music, recognizing I wasn't going to give her more, and started yelling while thrusting her head to a British punk band.

We pulled into the school parking lot, receiving the usual turning of heads from the students and shaking of heads from the faculty. Sara was oblivious, or at least acted like she couldn't care less. I ignored it, because I really couldn't care less.

I slung my backpack over my left shoulder and walked across the parking lot with Sara. Her face beamed with an infectious smile as people waved to her. I was barely noticed, but I wasn't bothered by the lack of recognition. It was easy to be overshadowed by Sara's charismatic presence with her mane of gorgeous fiery hair that flowed in layers to the middle of her back.

Sara was every high-school boy's fantasy, and I'm sure some of the male teachers' as well. She was startlingly attractive and had the body of a swimsuit model, filled out in just the right places. But what I loved about Sara was that she was real. She may have been the most desired girl in school, but it didn't go to her head.

"Good morning, Sara," could be heard from just about everyone we passed as she walked with a bounce of energy through the junior halls. She'd return these welcomes with a smile and a similar greeting.

There were some greetings thrown my way as well, to which I would respond with a quick glance and a nod of my head. I knew the only reason they even acknowledged me was because of Sara. I actually wished I wasn't noticed at all as I slunk through the halls in her shadow.

"I think Jason's finally coming around to realizing I exist," Sara declared while we gathered what we needed for our first classes from our adjacent lockers. By some miracle, we were in the same homeroom together, making us practically inseparable. Well, that was until our first class, when I headed to Advanced Placement English and she was off to Algebra II.

"Everyone knows *you* exist, Sara," I responded with a wry smile. Some too well, I thought, holding my smile.

"Well, it's different with him. He barely looks at me, even when I sit right next to him. It's so frustrating." She collapsed back against her locker. "You realize guys notice you too," she added, picking up on my emphasis, "but you can't look up from your books long enough to notice *them*."

My face turned red and I looked at her with a questioning scowl. "What are you talking about? They only notice me because I'm with you."

Sara laughed, her perfect white teeth gleaming. "You have no idea," she scoffed, still smiling in amusement.

"Enough. It doesn't matter anyway," I replied dismissively, my face still hot. "What are you going to do about Jason?"

Sara sighed, holding her books to her chest while running her blue eyes along the ceiling, lost in thought.

"I'm not sure yet," she said from that far-off place that kept the corners of her mouth curled up. It was evident she was picturing him and his swept-back blond hair, intense blue eyes and drop-dead smile. Jason was the captain and quarterback of the football team. Could it get any more cliché?

"What do you mean? You always have a plan."

"This one's different. He doesn't even look at me. I have to be more careful."

"I thought you said he finally noticed you?" I asked, confused.

Sara turned her head to look at me, her eyes still sparkling from that place she was slowly returning from, but the smile was lost.

"I don't get it, really. I made sure to sit next to him in Business class yesterday, and he said hi, but that was it. So he knows I exist. Period." I could hear the exasperation in her voice.

"I'm sure you'll think of something. Or maybe he's gay." I smirked.

"Emma!" Sara exclaimed with wide eyes, punching my right arm. I forced a smile while gritting my teeth, hoping she hadn't noticed my shoulders tense with the impact of her harmless blow. "Don't say that. That would be devastating—for me at least."

"Not for Kevin Bartlett." I laughed, causing her to scowl.

To see Sara so distracted by this guy was amusing and disarming at the same time. She had a way with people—the results almost always ended in her favor, especially with guys. It didn't matter who she was trying to persuade, she would put an endearing spin on what she wanted so that the person was actually eager to accommodate her.

Sara was obviously flustered by Jason Stark. It was a side of her I almost never saw. I knew this was new territory for her, and I was interested to see what she was going to do next.

The only people who have given her a greater challenge were my aunt and uncle. I kept assuring her that it had nothing to do with her, but it only made her more determined to win them over. In doing so, she hoped to make my personal hell a little more livable. Who was I to stand in her way? Even though I knew it was a lost cause.

We parted after homeroom. I entered AP English and sat in the back of the room as usual. Ms. Abbott greeted us and began the class by handing back our most recent papers.

She approached my desk and looked down at me with a warm smile. "Very insightful, Emma," she praised as she handed me my paper.

My eyes met hers with a quick, yet awkward smile. "Thank you."

The paper was marked in red pen with an "A" at the top, and positive comments were written in the margins throughout the paper. It was what I anticipated and what my peers expected of me. Most of the other students were leaning over to see what the person sitting next to them had received. No one looked at my paper. I tucked it into the back of my binder.

I wasn't embarrassed by my grades; I didn't care what other students thought of my high marks. I knew I had earned them. And I also knew that they were going to save me someday. What no one understood, besides Sara, was that all I really cared about were the days I counted down until I could move out of my aunt and uncle's house and go to college. If I had to put up with the whispers behind my back as I received the highest marks in the class, then so be it. They weren't going to be there to save me if I did anything but succeed, so I didn't need to get involved in the gossip and typical teenage tripe.

Sara was the closest I was going to get to any semblance of the high-school experience, and she definitely kept it entertaining. She was admired by most, envied by many, and could discreetly seduce a guy with a grin. What mattered most to me was that I trusted her with my life—which was saying a lot, considering the unpredictability that awaited me at home each night.

"How's it going?" Sara asked when we met at our lockers before lunch.

"Nothing new and exciting here. Any progress in Business class with Jason?" This was Sara's class right before lunch, so it usually gave her enough to talk about until we reached Journalism after.

"I wish!" she exclaimed. "Nothing—it's so frustrating! I'm not being overly aggressive, but I am definitely putting the obvious signals out there that I'm interested."

"You don't have what it takes to make him interested," I teased with a grin.

"Shut up, Em!" Sara looked at me with stern eyes. "I think I'm going to have to be more direct. The worst he can say—"

"I'm gay," I interrupted and laughed.

"Laugh all you want, but I am going to get Jason Stark to go out with me."

"I know you will," I assured her, still smiling.

I purchased lunch with my weekly stipend from the money I'd earned during the summer—money that was strictly regulated without allowing me direct access. Just another irrational rule I had to live with for the next six hundred and seventy-three days.

We decided to have lunch outside at the picnic tables to take advantage of the Indian summer day. Fall in New England is very unpredictable. It can be frosty and cold one day, and warm enough to pull out the tank tops the next. But once winter hits, it sticks around for longer than it is welcome.

As most of the other students were shedding clothes to take advantage of the warmth, I could only push up the sleeves of my shirt. My wardrobe revolved around the colors of the healing bruises on my arms, and had nothing to do with the temperature.

"What did you do to your hair today? It looks good. It looks straighter. Very chic."

I looked at Sara sideways as we headed outside, knowing the only reason my hair was in the ponytail was because I'd run out of my allowed five minutes in the shower this morning, and couldn't rinse the conditioner out of my hair before the water was turned off. "What are you talking about?" I asked incredulously.

"Forget it. You can never take a compliment." Changing the subject, she asked, "So will you be able to go to the football game tomorrow night?"

I just looked over at her with my eyebrows raised, taking a bite out of an apple.

Realizing I wasn't going to answer the obvious, Sara picked up her soda, stopping with the can raised to her lips.

"Why is he torturing me?" Sara whispered, slowly lowering the can with her eyes fixated on something behind me.

I turned to see what had captured her attention. Jason Stark and another well-built senior had their shirts off and tucked into the backs of their jeans as they threw a football back and forth. The attention he captured was painstakingly obvious. I watched him for a minute as Sara moaned behind me. Oddly, he seemed oblivious to all of the girls drooling over him—interesting.

"Sara, maybe he doesn't realize he's as wanted as he is," I observed objectively. "Have you ever thought of that?"

"How could he not know?" she questioned in disbelief.

"He's a guy," I said with a resigned sigh. "Have you ever seen him out with anyone other than the two years he was dating Holly Martin? Just because we think he's a god, it doesn't mean he puts himself on the same pedestal."

We looked over at the tall figure with the defined muscles and playful smile. Even I couldn't help but get lost in the details of his tanned body. Just because I was focused on school, it didn't mean I was dead. I still noticed—well, sometimes.

"Maybe," she considered with a devious smirk.

"You guys would make an amazingly beautiful couple," I said with a sigh.

"Em, you have to go to the game with me tomorrow!" she pleaded with an edge of desperation.

I shrugged. It wasn't like it was my choice. I had no control over my social life; hence, I had no social life. I was holding out for college. It's not like I wasn't participating in the high-school experience. I just had my own version—three varsity sports, editor of the school paper, along with participating in the yearbook, art, and French clubs. It was enough to keep me after school every day, and sometimes into the evenings when I had games or deadlines with the paper. I needed to create the ideal transcript for a scholarship admission. It was the only thing I felt like I had control over, and it was honestly more of a survival plan than an escape plan.

2. FIRST IMPRESSION

While Sara and I walked to Journalism, I could tell the lunch performance was still lingering in her head. She looked enchanted, and it was a little eerie. I paced alongside her in silence, hoping she'd snap out of it.

Upon entering class, I went straight to the computer with the oversize monitor and pulled up the latest draft of this week's *Weslyn High Times*. Focused on the screen, I zoned out the scraping of chairs and murmuring voices as everyone found their seats. I had to get this edition to the printer before the end of class so it could be distributed in the morning.

Faintly, I heard Ms. Holt gather everyone's attention to review the progress of the assignments for next week's paper. I blocked out the conversations. I continued scrutinizing the formatting, moving ads to accommodate article space, and inserting photographs to complement the featured articles.

"Is it too late to consider another article for next week's paper?"

The voice distracted me. I didn't know this voice. The guy spoke without hesitation, with a sense of purpose and confidence. I stared at the computer screen without seeing what was in front of me, waiting. The room was silent with anticipation. Ms. Holt encouraged him to continue.

"I wanted to write an article about teenagers' self-image and whether they're able to accept their flaws. I'd like to interview students and hand out surveys to find out what part of the body they're most self-conscious about." I turned my chair around, interested in who would think of such a controversial topic. "The article could reveal that despite a perceived social status, everyone's insecure about something." He glanced over at me during his explanation, realizing I was paying attention. Some of the other students also noticed I was no longer working on the computer and were watching me, trying to decipher my pensive expression.

The voice belonged to a guy I'd never seen before. As I listened to him finish, I was irked by his request. How could someone obviously without flaws think it would be okay to interview emotionally vulnerable students to reveal something they didn't like about themselves, probably confiding an insecurity they had a hard time admitting to themselves? Who'd want to openly discuss their embarrassing whiteheads, or admit that they wore an A cup, or that they had the muscle structure of a ten-year-old? It sounded cruel. The more I thought about it, the more irritated I became. Honestly, who was this guy?

He sat in the back of the class wearing an untucked sky-blue collared shirt and a pair of perfectly fitted jeans. His sleeves were rolled up and the buttons undone enough to reveal his smooth skin and a hint of a lean, muscular frame.

The shirt complemented his steel-blue eyes, which moved across the room, connecting with his audience. He appeared relaxed, even though everyone in the class was staring at him. He probably expected people to take notice of him.

There was something else about him that I couldn't quite put my finger on—he seemed older. He definitely looked like he was either a junior or senior. He had a youthful face with a strong jaw that extended to the angles of his cheekbones, complementing his brow line and the straight nose that pointed to his perfectly defined lips. An artist couldn't have chiseled a better bone structure.

When he spoke, he easily captured everyone's attention. He obviously got me to stop and take notice. The projection in his voice made me think that he was used to talking to a more mature audience. I couldn't decide if he seemed distinguished or just arrogant—he was so confident. I leaned toward arrogance.

"Interesting idea—" Ms. Holt began.

"Seriously?" I interjected before I could stop myself. I could feel fourteen pairs of eyes shifting toward me. I even caught a couple of mouths dropping open out of the corner of my eye. My gaze remained focused on the source of the voice. I found perplexed smoky eyes looking back at me.

"Let me get this straight—you want to exploit the insecurities of a bunch of teenagers so that you can write an article exposing their flaws? Don't you think that's a little destructive? Besides, we try to write news in our paper. It can be entertaining and witty—but it should always be news, not gossip." He raised his eyebrows in what appeared to be shock.

"That's not exactly—" he began.

"Or are you planning to write an exposé on how many girls want bigger breasts and the number of guys who want bigger"—I paused and heard a few shocked inhales—"um, muscles? Superficial and sleazy may work for tabloids, or maybe that's what you're used to where you come from. But I give our readers the benefit of assuming they have brains." There were a few muffled laughs. I didn't flinch—I stared intently into the unwavering blue eyes. There was a slight smirk on his face. Was he amused by my verbal assault? I set my jaw against his attack.

"I take my assignments seriously. I'm hoping my research will uncover how much we all have in common, regardless of our popularity or perceived attractiveness. I don't think the article will exploit anyone, but assure us that everyone has insecurities about their appearances, even those who may be considered perfect. I respect the confidentiality of my sources, and I understand the difference between a puff piece and actual news." His voice was calm and patient, yet I thought it was patronizing. I could feel the heat rising in my cheeks.

"And you think you will get honest answers out of people? They will really talk to *you*?" There was a bite in my tone that I was not used to hearing, and judging by the silence in the room, it was a surprise to everyone else as well.

"I have a way of getting people to open up and trust me," he said with a smile full of conceit and narcissism.

Before I could rebut, Ms. Holt interrupted, "Thank you, Evan." She looked at me cautiously. "Emma, since you seem to have reservations about this article, as the editor of the paper, would you be willing to permit Mr. Mathews to write the article, and then you can have the final say as to whether it makes the cut?"

"I can agree to that," I stated methodically.

"Mr. Mathews, is that acceptable to you?"

"I'm comfortable with that. She is the *editor*."

Oh, he was pompous, wasn't he?! I couldn't stand to look at him any longer. I turned back to the computer.

"Great," Ms. Holt replied with relief. Then she directed her attention back to me. "Emma, are you just about done with the computer? I'd like to begin today's discussion."

"I'm sending it to the printers now," I confirmed without looking back.

"Wonderful. Would everyone please open your textbooks to page ninety-three, with the heading 'Journalism Ethics'?" Ms. Holt attempted to redirect the attention to the front of the class.

I took my seat next to Sara, feeling the shocked stares linger upon me. I kept my eyes glued to the book, unable to concentrate.

"What was that about?" Sara whispered, just as surprised. I shrugged, not looking over at her.

After what felt like the longest fifty minutes, the class was finally over. When we were released into the hall, I couldn't hold back any longer. "Who does he think he is? How completely arrogant can a person be?!"

Sara stopped when we rounded the corner, heading to our lockers. She gawked at me as if she didn't recognize me. Not acknowledging her confounded stare, I went on. "Who is he anyway?"

"Evan Mathews," his voice said from behind me.

My back tensed, and I stared at Sara, mortified. I slowly turned toward the voice with a reddened face. I couldn't say anything. How much had he heard?

"I hope I didn't upset you too much by suggesting the article. I wasn't trying to offend you."

It took me a moment to compose myself. Sara stood beside me, unwilling to miss out on a front-row seat for this confrontation.

"I wasn't offended. I'm just looking out for the integrity of the paper." I tried to sound aloof, as if the interaction in class hadn't bothered me.

"I understand. That's your job." He actually sounded sincere, or was he patronizing me again?

I changed the subject. "Today your first day?"

"No," he said slowly, appearing baffled. "I've been in class all week. Actually, I'm in a few of your other classes too."

I looked to the floor and quietly said, "Oh."

"I'm not surprised you didn't notice. You seem pretty intense in class. It's obvious school's important to you. You don't seem to pay attention to anything else."

"Are you accusing me of being self-absorbed?" I shot my eyes back up at him, feeling my entire face flame up.

"What? No." He smiled in amusement at my reaction.

I stared at him in offense. He held my glare, his cold grey eyes unblinking. How had I ever thought they were blue? He was full of himself, and it repulsed me. I shook my head slightly in disgust and walked away. Sara could only stare with her mouth ajar, as if she'd witnessed a horrific car wreck.

"Where the hell did that come from?" she demanded, her wide eyes glued to me as she strode alongside me. "I've never seen you act like that before." I couldn't get over her astonishment. She almost sounded disappointed.

"Excuse me?!" I shot back defensively, unable to look at her for more than a second. "He's a conceited jerk. I don't care what he thinks of me."

"I thought he was just concerned that he'd offended you in class. I think he might even be interested in you."

"Yeah, right."

"Seriously, I know you're extremely focused, but how did you not notice him before today?"

"What, do *you* think I'm self-absorbed too?" I snapped, regretting it as soon as I said it.

Sara rolled her eyes. "You know I don't, so stop being stupid. I get why you shut everyone out. I know how much you need to get through high school, like every breath depends on it. But I also get how it looks to everyone else.

"It's just accepted that this is who you are, so no one really pays attention anymore. Your lack of"—she hesitated, looking for the right word—"*interest* is expected. I think it's amazing that a guy who's only been here a week has picked up on your intensity. He's obviously noticed *you*."

"Sara, he's not that perceptive," I accused. "He was just trying to recover from the blow he took to his ego in class."

She let out a quick laugh with a shake of her head. "You're impossible."

I opened my locker, then looked over at Sara before putting my books away. "He's really been here all week?"

"Don't you remember when I mentioned the hot new guy during lunch on Monday?"

"That was *him?*" I scoffed, shoving my books in my locker and flinging the door shut. "You think he's good-looking?" I laughed like the thought that he could be attractive was insane.

"Yeah," she responded emphatically, like I was the one who was insane, "along with, like, every girl in school. Even the senior girls are checking him out. And if you try to convince me that he's not gorgeous, I'm going to slap you."

This time, I rolled my eyes. "You know what—I really don't want to talk about him anymore." I was oddly exhausted by my outburst. I was never out of control, especially in school—with witnesses.

"You know everyone in school will be talking about it. 'Did you hear Emma Thomas finally snapped?'" Sara teased.

"Nice. I'm glad you're finding this funny," I shot back before walking past her down the hall. Sara jogged to catch up, still smiling.

As much as I wanted to forget it, I couldn't help but replay the entire scene in my head while we walked to study period in the cafeteria. We continued through the caf, where I could already hear the whispers, and out the back doors that led to the picnic tables.

Seriously, what happened? Why did this guy bother me so much? I shouldn't care enough to be this upset. Honestly, I didn't even know him. Then my overreaction sank in.

"Sara, I'm an idiot," I confessed, feeling truly miserable. She was lying down on the bench, absorbing the warm rays, peeling back the straps of her tank top to avoid tan lines—messing with every guy within eyeshot. She sat up curiously and took in my agonized expression.

"What are you talking about?"

"I have no idea what happened to me in there. Really, why should I care if this guy writes an article about the imperfections of being a teenager? I cannot believe I acted like that and then made a scene in the hall. I'm completely humiliated." I groaned and put my face down on my folded arms.

Sara didn't say anything. After a moment, I looked up at her, questioning. "What? You're not even going to *try* to make me feel better?"

"Sorry, I've got nothing. Em, you were pretty crazy in there," she remarked with a smirk.

"Thanks, Sara!" I connected with her smiling eyes and couldn't hold back. We simultaneously burst out laughing. It came out so loud that the table next to us stopped midconversation to stare. I definitely looked like I'd lost my mind now.

It took a full minute for me to break through the hysterics. Sara tried to stop, but small bouts of laughter would escape whenever she looked at me.

She leaned toward me and lowered her giggling voice. "Well, maybe you can redeem yourself. He's on his way over here."

"No way!" My eyes widened in panic.

"I hope the laughing wasn't about me." It was that same confident, charming voice. I closed my eyes, afraid to face him.

I took a calming breath and turned to look up at him. "No, Sara said something funny." I hesitated before I added, "I shouldn't have gone off on you. I'm not usually like that."

Sara started laughing again, probably replaying my mortifying moment in her head. "Sorry, I can't help it," she said, her eyes watering from trying to hold it in. "I need to get some water."

She left us alone. Oh no—she left us alone!

He responded to my indirect apology. "I know." His perfect lips curled up into a soft smile. I was surprised by the casualness of his response. "Good luck in your game today. I heard you're pretty good." Without allowing me to respond, he walked away.

What just happened? What did he mean, *he knows* I'm not usually like that? I stared at the spot where he stood for half a minute, trying to comprehend what just played out. Why wasn't he upset with me? I couldn't believe I was so worked up, especially over a guy. I needed to shake it off and be over it—stay focused.

"He's gone? Please don't tell me you insulted him again!" Sara's voice startled me. I hadn't even noticed her return.

"No, I swear. He wished me luck in the game today and walked away. It was…strange." Sara raised her eyebrows, grinning.

"Oh, and I guess you could say he's decent looking," I mumbled. Sara's face lit up with a huge smile.

"He's so mysterious, and I think he likes you," she taunted.

"Come on, Sara. Now you're being stupid."

Somehow I completed the homework due the next day, despite glancing around and searching for Evan every other minute. I couldn't get to the longer-term assignments. I saved them for the weekend. It's not like I had anything else to do.

"I'm going to the locker room to get ready for the game."

"I'll be down in a minute," Sara replied from her meditative spot on the bench.

I gathered my books and walked through the cafeteria.

I did everything I could to stare straight ahead so I wouldn't look for Evan—unsuccessfully.

3. DISTRACTION

You will never believe who just asked me—"

I wasn't able to throw my varsity jersey over my head in time. I closed my eyes and took a breath in preparation for her reaction.

"Shit," Sara whispered, still frozen at the door of the locker room.

I didn't turn around. I couldn't bring myself to say anything. I knew the large circular bruises that covered my right shoulder and continued to the middle of my back said more than enough.

"It's not as bad as it looks," I mumbled, still not having the heart to face her.

"Looks pretty bad to me," she murmured. "I can't believe *that* was for forgetting to take out the trash." We were interrupted by voices and laughter as a few girls entered the locker room. The girls brushed past Sara, who remained unmoving in the doorway.

"Hey, Emma. We just heard about you telling off the hot new guy," one of the girls exclaimed when she noticed me.

"He must have totally pissed you off," added another as they began to change.

"I don't know. I guess he caught me on a bad day," I mumbled, my face changing color. I picked up my shoes, socks and shin guards and left the room before anyone could say anything else, especially Sara.

I sat at the top of the steps leading to the fields behind the school and proceeded to put on my shin guards and shoes. I needed to gather myself after everything that had happened in under two hours. This was not how my days were supposed to go. This was the place where everything was supposed to be safe and easy. No one tried to get involved with me, and I kept to myself. How could Evan Mathews unravel my constant universe in just one day?

That's when I heard his voice again. What was with this guy? First I didn't notice him for almost a week, and now I couldn't avoid him. He exited the guys' locker room below the steps, talking to another guy I didn't know about giving him a ride to the football game the next night. I caught his eye, and he nodded in recognition. Why wasn't I invisible to him like I was to everyone else? To my relief, he continued to jog toward the practice fields, a small black bag in his hand. From his attire, I realized he was heading to the guys' soccer field. Great, he played soccer.

The sun danced off the glints of gold in his tousled light brown hair as he jogged farther away. The lean muscles along his back brushed against his over-worn T-shirt. Why did he have to look like he just stepped out of an Abercrombie bag?

Sara exhaled looking after the same image. "Nice." I turned with a start, not realizing she was next to me. Heat spread across my cheeks, fearing she could read my thoughts. "Stop it—he's hot. It's just taken you way too long to notice."

Before I could defend myself, a bus pulled up along the dirt road that circled the school, separating the fields from the building. The open windows carried the synchronized chanting and hollering that were indicative of a high-school sports team.

"Who are we going to beat?" several boisterous voices screamed.

"Weslyn High!" the bus rumbled in response.

"Don't think so," Sara stated. I smirked and jogged with her to the field.

"Omigod!" Sara screamed as we drove home. "Stanford! Emma, this is so amazing!"

I couldn't find the words to say anything. The stunned smile on my face said it all. I was soaring from our win, then taken to a different level when I discovered that four colleges had been scouting the game in which I happened to score three out of the four goals.

"I can't believe they're going to fly you out there this spring," she continued in a rush. "You have to take me with you! California! Can you imagine?"

"Sara, he said that they'd be *interested* in setting up a visit, depending on next quarter's transcript."

"Come on, Emma. That's not going to change. I don't think you've received less than an A your entire life."

I wanted to be as confident, but then we pulled into my driveway. I was immediately grounded—the win and the scouts dispersing as if I'd woken from a dream into a nightmare.

Carol was strolling up the driveway from the mailbox, pretending to get the mail. She was up to something, and my heart sank into my stomach. Sara glanced over at me, just as concerned.

"Hi, Sara," she said, completely ignoring me as I got out of the car. "How are your parents?"

Sara smiled her dazzling smile and replied, "They're wonderful, Mrs. Thomas. How have you been?"

Carol sighed her exasperated, pathetic sigh. "I'm surviving."

"That's good to hear," Sara returned politely, not falling for the woe-is-me bullshit.

"Sara, I feel terribly uncomfortable asking you without speaking to your parents directly." I froze in anticipation. "But I was wondering if it would be a bother to allow Emily to stay the night tomorrow night. George and I are going out of town, and it would be easier if she were with someone who was responsible. But I don't want her interrupting your plans." She spoke of me as if I weren't standing next to the car, listening.

"I don't think that'll be a problem. I was planning to go to the library to work on a paper. I'll check with my parents when I get home." Sara smiled, playing along.

"Thank you. We would be so appreciative."

"Good night, Mrs. Thomas."

Carol waved back as Sara drove away. She turned her attention to me in disgust.

"You have no idea how humiliating it is to have to beg people to take you just so that your uncle and I can spend some time together. It's a good thing Sara pities how pathetic you are. I have no idea how she can stand to be around you."

She turned and walked back to the house, leaving me standing in the driveway. The words slipped from her tongue with ease, slicing barbs leaving a vicious sting.

There was a time when I'd thought she was right. That Sara was only my friend because she felt bad for me. Honestly, all you had to do was look at us standing next to each other to easily conclude the same thing: Sara, in all her gorgeous brilliance, compared to me in my ordinary plainness. But I learned that my friendship with Sara was probably the only thing I could really trust.

I entered the house to find life waiting for me, the sink full of dishes and pans from dinner. I set my bags in my room and returned to clean up. I didn't mind the monotony of washing the dishes, especially tonight, as I engrossed myself in scrubbing to keep from smiling.

———

When I woke the next morning, I felt more optimistic than I had in a long time. I had my backpack over one shoulder and a tote bag full of clothes in my hand.

Then reality came crashing down with a jolting tug of my hair. "Don't embarrass me," seethed into my ear. I nodded, my neck tense, resisting getting any closer to her as she tightened her hold on my hair, her hot breath scorching my skin. And just as quickly as it happened, she was gone—calling sweetly to the kids to come down for breakfast.

Sara was giddy when I entered the car. She gave me a hug and exclaimed, "I can't believe you're going to the game tonight!"

I pulled back, still shaken by the threat. "Sara, she's probably watching. We'd better get going before she changes her mind and locks me in the basement for the night."

"Would she do that?" Sara asked, concerned.

"Just drive." *Yes. She would*, was the answer I couldn't say out loud.

Sara drove off. The top was up; the brisk fall air was finally catching up with us as we headed into October. The leaves on the trees were beginning their yearly change to the vibrant hues of red, orange, gold and yellow. The colors looked brighter to me today, maybe because I was actually paying attention. Despite Carol's threat, I was still floating from our team's win along with the positive comments from the Stanford scout. And knowing I was going to the game with Sara tonight eased a smile onto my face that actually felt comfortable. This would be my very first football game—it had only taken me three years.

"I've decided that before we go tonight, I'm going to pamper you a little."

I looked at her cautiously. "What are you planning?"

"Trust me, you'll love it!" Sara beamed.

"Okay," I gave in. I feared my idea of being pampered was going to be completely different than what Sara had in mind. I preferred to hang out, watch movies and eat junk. While that might seem very predictable and boring to most teenagers, it was a true luxury to me. I decided not to worry about it. She knew me, so I trusted her.

"I'm going to ask him out tonight after the game," Sara declared while we walked to the school from the parking lot.

"How are you going to do it?" I was finally able to ask after tunneling through Sara's entourage and their gleeful morning acknowledgments. I couldn't believe how matter-of-fact she was about putting herself out there. But then again, who would say no to her? No didn't seem to be in Sara's vocabulary, whether it was receiving it or saying it.

"I was thinking…but only if it's okay with you"—she gave me an apprehensive glance—"after the game we'd go to Scott Kirkland's party, and I'll ask Jason to meet me there."

A party?! I'd never been to an actual *party* before. I overheard the gossip about them in the halls and locker room, and even saw photographed moments displayed in lockers throughout the junior and senior halls. It was a rite of passage I hadn't been privy to, and wasn't sure I was ready for. A wave of panic surged through me just thinking about walking through the doors and having everyone stare at me.

Then I looked into Sara's anxious blue eyes and knew this was important to her. I could make meaningless small talk with people I'd been in school with for the past four years, yet knew nothing about. This would definitely be interesting.

"That sounds great," I said, forcing a smile, falling in line with all the others unable to disappoint Sara.

"Really? We don't have to go to the party. I could figure something else out. You looked pale when I mentioned it."

"No, I want to go," I lied.

"Perfect!" Sara exclaimed, hugging me again. She was very affectionate today; it was throwing me off. I think she realized it too because she pulled back. "Sorry, I'm just so excited that you're going with me. I don't think I could go through with it if you weren't there. Besides, we hardly ever get out-of-school time together, so this is going to be the best."

I smiled awkwardly, my stomach still twisting with thoughts of the party. It was for Sara. I could get through it. What was the worst that could happen? Well…people might actually try to talk to me. My stomach turned again just thinking about it. This was going to be terrible. I swallowed hard.

More than ever, I needed to retreat to Art class to recover from these panicked thoughts. Art was the rotating class that moved through my schedule. Today it took the place of English, my first class—thankfully. I was desperate to escape in my work.

I walked into the open space of the Art room, inhaling the calming scents of paints, glue and cleaning chemicals with a gentle smile. The room was inviting and warm, with its tall yellow walls covered with art projects and its oversize windows that glowed with natural light. I breathed easier in this room. No matter how my day was going or what I'd left behind at home, I gained control over it in here.

Ms. Mier greeted us as we sat at our stools at the tall black worktables. Ms. Mier was the sweetest, kindest person I'd ever met. Compassion exuded from her, which made her an amazing artist and an inspirational teacher.

She invited us to continue working on our assignments, replicating a picture we'd torn from a magazine that portrayed movement. There was some murmuring, but it was fairly quiet, as our attention was primarily focused on the art. The quiet was another reason I loved this class so much.

My heart skipped a beat—among the murmurs, one stood out. I didn't want to look but was drawn to the smooth voice. There he was, standing at the front of the class, talking to Ms. Mier while holding a camera. She flipped through a book of what appeared to be photographs, making comments. He glanced up and grinned when he saw me. I shot my eyes back to my canvas. I wished I really were invisible.

"So I guess you *are* pretty good," Evan said from beside me. I looked up from my canvas. My heart was behaving insanely, beating at a pace that didn't coincide with sitting still. *Calm down*—what was wrong with me? He continued, since I could only stare up at him blankly. "Soccer. That was quite the game yesterday."

"Oh, thanks. Are you in this class too?" I felt the heat rise in my cheeks.

"Sort of," he responded. "I asked to switch to this class if I could work on photography projects instead. Ms. Mier agreed, so here I am."

"Oh," was all I could mutter. He grinned, which sent more color to my face. My body was betraying me—between my hyperactive heart and my fiery face, I had no control. It was not like me, and it was driving me crazy.

To my relief, Ms. Mier interrupted us before the possession could completely humiliate me. "So you know Emma Thomas? That's wonderful."

"We met yesterday," Evan replied, glancing at me with a smile.

"I'm happy to see that you've made some connections. Emma, would you mind showing Evan the photo-lab supplies and the darkroom?" My heart went from being on speed, to a dead stop, but my face kept beaming red. It must have been radiating heat by now.

"Sure," I said quickly.

"Thank you." Ms. Mier smiled in appreciation. Why was she, of all people, torturing me?

Without looking at Evan, I stood and walked to the back corner of the room. I slid open one of the cabinets that hung above the counter.

"This is the cabinet with all of the photo supplies. There's paper, developer, whatever you need." I slid the door shut, with my back to him.

On the counter below I pointed to the paper cutter and sizing equipment. We crossed the room to the darkroom, where I explained the developing light and the switch on the inside wall to turn it on.

"Do you mind if we look inside?" he asked.

I stopped breathing for a few seconds. "Sure," I replied, glancing at him for the first time.

We walked into the small rectangular room. In the center was a long metal table lined with trays for developing pictures. There was a sink in the back right corner. Cabinets lined the long wall on the right, and to the left were two rows of wires with black clips for drying the developed pictures. Even though the developing light wasn't on, the space seemed unnaturally dark—not a place I wanted to be alone with Evan Mathews.

"Here it is," I declared, holding my palms up to present the room.

Evan walked past me toward the cabinets and started opening them, examining their contents. "Why don't you talk to anyone besides Sara?" I heard him ask from behind the cabinet door. He closed it, anticipating my answer.

I remained frozen. "What do you mean?" I shot back, sounding defensive again.

"You don't talk to anyone," he stated. "Why not?"

I didn't answer. I didn't know how to answer.

He recognized my stalling. "Okay," he said. "Why don't you talk to me?"

"That was direct," I accused.

He smiled, causing my heart to attempt another escape from my chest. "Well…" he pushed.

"Because I'm not sure I like you," I blurted without thought. He looked at me with that devious, amused grin. What kind of reaction was that?! I couldn't stay in the confined space with him any longer. I turned abruptly and walked out of the room.

Concentration evaded me for the remainder of class, so my art piece remained unfinished. Evan left to take pictures of whatever he took pictures of, but his presence lingered. This class was supposed to be my sanctuary, and leave it to Evan to turn it upside down.

Sara noticed my agitation when we were switching books at our lockers.

"Are you okay?" she asked.

"Evan Mathews is in my Art class," I fumed.

"And…" Sara looked confused, waiting for me to continue.

I shook my head, unable to find the words to explain how disruptive he was to my predictable day. As much as Sara understood me, I wasn't ready to talk about it. My blood was still surging; I was having difficulty collecting my thoughts.

"I'll talk to you later," I said in a rush and walked away. I couldn't make sense of what was happening to me. I survived by keeping my emotions in check—by maintaining my composure and tucking it all away. I managed to stay under the radar, skating through school without anyone truly remembering I was here. My teachers acknowledged my academic successes, and my coaches depended upon my athletic abilities, but I wasn't important enough to make a recognizable social contribution. I was easily forgettable. That's what I counted on.

There were times when people tried to befriend me by talking to me or inviting me to a party, but that didn't last long. Once it was obvious I wouldn't accept the invitations, or provide more than one- or two-word answers, I wasn't interesting enough to acknowledge any longer—making my life easier.

Sara was the only one who'd stuck by me when I first moved here four years ago. After six months of Sara persistently inviting me over, Carol finally said yes. She wanted to go shopping with a friend and didn't want to take me along, so the invitation was convenient for her. That serendipitous moment sealed our friendship. I was permitted to go to Sara's every once in a while, and I got to sleep over on rare occasions when it suited Carol's social schedule. It helped that Sara's father was a local judge, so Carol relished the prestige through affiliation.

Last summer I was even allowed to go to Maine with Sara and her family for a week. It coincided with a camping trip George and Carol had planned with the kids. When Sara's parents invited me, they made it sound like they were inviting the entire soccer team and were obligated to include me, which made it easier for Carol to agree. I ended up paying for it when I returned home—I guess I wasn't grateful enough.

But the bruises couldn't take away the best week of my life. It was during that week I met Jeff Mercer. Jeff was a lifeguard at the beach that was walking distance from the lodge. His family owned a summerhouse on the lake, so he stayed for the season.

For two days, we went to the beach and drooled over him. After his shift on the second day, he invited Sara and me to a bonfire at a private beach.

When Jeff introduced us to his friends, I lied and said I was Sara's cousin from Minnesota. That lie developed into a more elaborate story that Sara and I prefabricated before the party. My false life revealed itself comfortably, allowing me to be anyone I wanted, and no one knew the difference. I didn't have to be invisible, because I really didn't exist.

Swept up in my story, I allowed Jeff to get close to me. I was able to talk and laugh with ease. Jeff and I ended up having a lot in common—he played soccer and we listened to a lot of the same music. He was an easy person to like.

At the end of the night, while everyone was sitting around the fire either coupled off or involved in conversations, Jeff sat next to me on the sand, leaning against a large log intended to be a bench. In the midst of the calming mood, with the sound of a few guys playing guitar in the background, he put his arm around me, and I leaned against him. It was oddly comfortable being with him, considering this was the closest I'd ever been to a guy.

We talked and listened to the music. He shifted his body to face me and casually leaned down to kiss me. I remember not breathing for a minute, paralyzed with fear that it was obvious I hadn't kissed anyone before. He was gentle as his soft, thin lips touched mine.

It wasn't easy saying good-bye, with false promises of e-mailing; but it wasn't hard either. Not for Emma Thomas from Weslyn, Connecticut—the overachieving, self-contained shadow who roamed the halls of Weslyn High. It wasn't hard because that girl didn't truly exist to Jeff.

That's what was bothering me so much about Evan Mathews. He knew I existed. He was determined to pull me out from the shadows, and I couldn't get away from him. He wasn't deterred by my one-word answers or abrupt responses. He wasn't supposed to be paying attention to me, and I was trying, without success, to ignore him. But he was getting to me, and I think he knew it—and it seemed to amuse him.

I took a deep breath before entering AP European History, prepared to see him as I walked in the room. He wasn't there. I looked around in surprise and felt my heart sink. That was another problem. My heart was beating, stopping and sinking like it had a mind of its own, not to mention the absurd flushing that was overtaking my face. I was beyond annoyed!

Evan wasn't in my Chemistry class either. Maybe he wouldn't be everywhere, as I feared. Distracted while retrieving my home-work assignment during Trig, I tensed at the sound of his voice, which incited rapid beating in my chest.

"Hi."

I continued opening my notebook for today's lesson, refusing to look at him.

"Not talking to me at all now, huh?"

Angered by his antagonism, I couldn't contain myself any longer. I turned to face him.

"Why do you want to talk to me? *What* could you possibly want to talk to me about?" I snapped.

He raised his eyebrows in surprise but quickly replaced the look with his taunting, amused grin.

"And why do you keep looking at me like that?!" My face flushed as I tightened my jaw.

Before Evan could answer, Mr. Kessler walked in to begin class. I stared at my book and the front of the classroom throughout the period. I could feel Evan looking over at me every so often—it kept me on edge the entire class.

As I was gathering my books to head to Anatomy, I heard him say behind me, "Because I think you're interesting."

I slowly turned around, my books clutched firmly to my chest.

"You don't even know me," I replied defiantly.

"I'm trying."

"There are so many other people in this school—you don't have to know me."

"But I want to," he replied with a grin.

I walked out of the class, confused. He never said what I thought he should. What was I supposed to say? I started to panic.

"Can I walk with you to Anatomy?" I was too distracted to realize that he'd followed me out of the room.

"You are not in my Anatomy class too, are you?!" Seriously, the world was conspiring against me, along with my rapidly beating heart. I tried to take a deep breath, but I couldn't fill my lungs.

"Didn't notice me at all this week, huh?" People stopped to look at us as we walked down the hall. I'm sure their universe was getting tipped upside down too, to witness Emma Thomas walking down the hall with another student, who was also a guy—the same guy she'd made a scene with in the hall yesterday. Let the gossip begin.

It didn't take long to reach the classroom due to my escaping pace. I stopped outside Anatomy and turned to face him. He peered down at me in anticipation.

"I get that you're new, and I must seem intriguing to you. But I assure you, I'm not that interesting. You really don't need to get to know me. I get good grades. I'm decent at sports, and I keep myself busy. I like my privacy. I like my space, and I like being left alone. That's it. You can get to know everyone else in this school who's dying to know you. I'm not. Sorry."

He grinned.

"And stop looking at me like I'm entertaining you. I'm not amused, so leave me alone." I rushed into the classroom. I thought I would feel better, relieved—but I didn't. Instead, I felt defeated.

I had no idea where Evan sat during Anatomy, but it wasn't next to me. Actually, no one was sitting next to me. The seat where Karen Stewart usually sat at my table was empty. Karen was always lost during the lessons and constantly asked me questions to try to keep up. Today, I finally had the silence I kept pushing everyone away to get, but it wasn't comforting.

By the time the bell rang at the end of the day, I was over it. Knowing I was staying over at Sara's and didn't have to return home helped—as did not seeing Evan again.

"Hi!" Sara greeted me as we gathered our books from our lockers. "I feel like I haven't seen you at all today. How are you? You didn't get to tell me—"

"Don't mention it. Later, okay? I'm finally feeling better and just want to have fun tonight, alright?" I pleaded.

"Come on, Em. Don't do this to me. I heard you and Evan walked together to Anatomy. You *have to* tell me what's going on."

I hesitated, not wanting to say anything where we could be overheard. I scanned the halls, stalling to make sure I wasn't going to add to the already circulating gossip.

"He keeps trying to talk to me," I explained to Sara. I thought this might be enough, but Sara shrugged her shoulders, waiting for me to continue.

"You were right yesterday. He told me he thinks I'm *interesting*, whatever that means. Sara, he's in all of my classes, or at least it feels like it. I can't get away from him—he's always *right there*. I finally told him that I wasn't interesting and to leave me alone. That's what the walk to Anatomy was about. I don't get this guy."

"Em, he's interested in you. Why is that so bad?" Sara asked, genuinely perplexed. I was surprised she didn't understand the problem.

"Sara, I can't have anyone interested in me. You're my only friend for a reason." Her eyes lowered, beginning to understand my dilemma.

"I can't go out. I don't go to the movies. Tonight will be the first and probably only party I'll ever go to. I don't want to have to lie. And if anyone ever got close enough to touch me..." I couldn't finish the sentence. The thought of being afraid to be touched because I might cringe in pain made me shudder.

I wished I didn't have to be so convincing, but until I said it, Sara hadn't put it together. For just a moment, she saw the world through my eyes, and her sorrowful expression made my chest tighten.

"I'm so sorry," she whispered. "I should've realized. So, I guess you shouldn't talk to him."

"It's okay," I assured her with a tight smile. "I have six hundred seventy-two days left, and then *anyone* can find me interesting."

She smiled back, but not as big as usual.

The pity in Sara's evasive eyes reflected the pathetic-ness of my life; it was hard to take. It was harder to escape—literally.

I couldn't remember a time when my life wasn't a disaster. I had images of a smiling child stored in shoe boxes, but my father was in most of those pictures. When he was taken away, I was left with a mother who didn't know how to be one. I did everything I could to get by with as little parental interaction as possible. If I was perfect, then there wasn't anything to regret or distract her from the replacements she sorted through, who would never live up to my father.

I was still too much—a burden. I hoped my academic drive would help my aunt and uncle accept me as an addition to their family. Unfortunately, the reception never warmed beyond the frigid steps when I'd crossed their threshold four winters ago. Guilt opened the door that night, and I couldn't be perfect enough to earn their forgiveness for what they never wanted. So, I mastered evasion and overachievement. Neither as deftly as I would have preferred, since Carol was right there to brand me with my lack of worth at every opportunity.

4. CHANGE

Sara was quiet when we drove away from school. I knew she was thinking and hoped that it had nothing to do with me. But of course it did.

"There's a way around it, you know."

I sighed, afraid to encourage this train of thought.

"You don't have to cut yourself off from everyone to get through high school," she continued. "We just have to anticipate the questions and have answers ready. There are so many guys who would love to ask you out, but have no idea how to approach you. Em, we can figure this out."

"Sara, you're not making any sense. Besides the obvious—I can't go out."

"What's the obvious?"

"Honestly, who do you know who's interested in me? Be specific."

"Evan already told you he found you interesting," she said with a grin. "Let's start with him."

"Let's not," I groaned.

"Oh! Did you hear that Haley Spencer asked him to homecoming?" she exclaimed.

"Of course I didn't. You're my source of gossip, remember?" Something in my chest twisted. "Isn't homecoming a month away? And she's a senior—what's that about?"

Sara examined me with narrowed eyes. "Honestly? It's only *three* weeks away. Anyway, I heard he turned her down. I told you the senior girls were looking at him too. But, Emma, he's into *you*."

"Sara, let's put this into perspective," I corrected. "I amuse him. He thinks I'm *interesting*. He didn't ask me on a date. He just probably thinks I'm a freak or something."

"Well, you are," Sara said with a playful smile. "Who else can live with pure evil while still maintaining a four-point-oh, play three varsity sports, be in what seems like every club, and to top it all off, be scouted by four colleges. That is pretty freakish."

Before I could respond, she continued, "Okay, let's just say we don't know his motives. He already knows you're a private person. It sounds like you made that perfectly clear. Why can't you give him what he wants and just talk to him? He's either genuinely interested and will ask you out, and we'll deal with that when it happens. Or he ends up becoming a friend, which isn't a bad thing. You have nothing to lose. Come on, the worst thing that could happen is he moves on and everything's back to the way it was before he got here."

She was so compelling. Besides, I thought, talking to him could get him to leave me alone, especially once he realized there's not much to know—which would be the best thing that could happen, not the worst.

"Fine, I'll talk to him. So what's the story? And I don't want to lie." I figured she'd already concocted something during her silence.

"No lying, sort of. You just leave most of it out, so it's omission," she said smugly, confirming my suspicion. "You tell him you were adopted by your aunt and uncle after your father died and your mother became ill. That's pretty accurate. You can tell him anything you want about Leyla and Jack, since that won't affect anything. Explain that your aunt and uncle are very busy with work and the kids, and that will hopefully be reason enough why they don't go to your games.

"He's definitely going to want to know why I'm your only friend and why you don't talk to anyone."

"He's already asked that," I admitted. "I didn't answer him."

"Well, tell him you and I became friends when you first moved here. That's true." She hesitated for a moment to think about the second part of the question. "Say that you're the first in your family to go to college—which is technically true—and that you have a lot of pressure on you to get a scholarship."

"That's not bad, but why don't I have more friends?" I challenged.

"How about, your aunt and uncle are very overprotective and have no idea how to raise a teenager, so they tend to be strict. Then you can admit that because you're so involved in school activities and sports, and with the early curfew, you don't get to go out much. That should work.

"Besides, that'll be like one conversation, and then you can talk about anything else. Almost all truthfully—you know, music, sports, college. You may have a hard time with pop culture, but I can bring you magazines so you can catch up during the rides to school if you want."

I laughed. "Why is this so important to you?"

"I don't know." She paused, considering the answer. "These past two days, I've seen a fire in your eyes that I never have before. Granted, it's mostly anger and frustration, but it's still emotion. You keep everything locked up so tight—I'm afraid some day you're going to explode.

"This guy's found a way to get to you unlike anyone else. You're different, and I like it. I don't like seeing you upset, but I like seeing you *feeling* something. I know you put your guard down a little with me, but you refuse to show me the hard stuff. You never get angry or scared, or let me know when you're hurt. You don't want me to see you that way, but I know you have to feel it, especially with everything Carol puts you through.

"In the past two days, you've been angry, frustrated and humiliated. I was actually relieved you didn't turn into dust or a mass murderer. So if it takes this guy to annoy you to let some of it out, then I want you to keep talking to him. Sound crazy?"

"It does actually," I said. She scowled, not pleased with my honesty. "But I understand what you're saying."

After we pulled into her driveway, she shut off the car and turned to me in expectation.

"What if I like him? That would be horrible. You're the only one who knows my secrets, and I can't risk letting anyone else in right now. Not while I'm still living with them. It's too complicated." I took a deep breath before continuing, "But I'll try to talk to him." This caused a smile to spread on Sara's face.

"Besides, he'll probably continue to frustrate me, and I'll end up strangling him. If I murder him, you're my accomplice for encouraging it."

"Do you promise to tell me everything?" Sara asked, glowing.

"Of course!" I replied with a grin as I rolled my eyes. "If I don't tell you, then it's like it never happened. And besides, who's going to help me bury his body when I bludgeon him for patronizing me?"

She laughed and hugged me again. Feeling my body tense, she pulled back. "Sorry."

I followed Sara into her enormous house. Her family lived in a newer home compared to the historic colonials and Victorians in the center of town. The development used to be farmland at one point and was now broken up into expansive lots to showcase huge homes.

I could never get used to Sara's setup as we neared the top of the stairs. Sara was an only child, so she had a lot of room to herself in the three-story house—actually, she had the entire third floor. The bathroom was larger than my entire bedroom, with its granite double sinks, Jacuzzi tub and separate shower. To the right, the landing opened into a game room with cathedral ceilings and white walls accented by a hot pink racing stripe around the perimeter with black electric guitars mounted on it.

There was a plush white couch with a matching recliner and love seat in front of a home-theater system that included a giant flat-screen mounted to the wall on the far side of the room. It was hooked up to several gaming systems that were set on a console beneath it.

Behind the couch was a reading area with built-in bookshelves that extended to the ceiling, with a sliding ladder attached to reach the higher shelves. Oversize pillows lined the floor beneath the bookcases, creating the perfect place to get lost in the pages. In the corner, opposite the library, were air hockey and foosball tables.

Sara touched the screen of the built-in music dock on one of the walls, selecting an indie artist declaring what she expected from a guy. The rhythmic guitar strums filled the entire floor through the inset speakers in the ceiling. I followed Sara into her bedroom on the other side of the stairs.

"Are you ready to be pampered?" Sara asked, jumping onto one of her two queen-size beds, adorned with pink and orange pillows.

"Sure," I answered, hesitantly walking past the door that opened into her office, with its walls covered with pictures of friends, record covers and celebrities. The room was small, but still large enough to squeeze in a full-size black vinyl couch. I sat down on the identical bed next to Sara's.

"I have the perfect sweater for you to wear with the best pair of jeans," she declared, bouncing off the other side of the bed and entering her walk-in closet.

This room—and I say room, not closet—was as large as my
bedroom, with two long walls lined with shelves and bars storing
folded and hung clothes. At the end of the closet were racks of shoes
in every color and style. Visiting Sara was like taking a break from
reality—everyone's reality.

"Sara, you're five-ten—there's no way I'm going to fit into your
jeans," I argued.

"You're not that much shorter than me," she retorted.

"You have a good three inches on me. Besides, I brought a pair
of jeans."

She paused, trying to decide if my jeans were acceptable.

"Okay. You can take a shower up here, and I'll use my parents'
bathroom," she instructed, handing me a scoop-neck white shirt,
paired with a light pink cashmere sweater with a square neckline.

"Two shirts?" I inquired.

"Well, it's supposed to be cold tonight, and you can't wear a
jacket that will hide the sweater, so…layers," she explained simply.

I raised my eyebrows and slowly nodded. It was obvious that
she was loving this, and my lack of fashion savvy was not going
to keep her from treating me like a life-size Barbie doll. I couldn't
imagine what else she had in store, or maybe I didn't want to.

"Listen," she said, trying to put me at ease. "I know you never
make a big deal over clothes or any of that, but it's because you can't,
not because you don't want to. I know they don't let you shop, so let
me do this for one night, okay?"

Of course she knew that I appreciated the latest trends, as we
often flipped through the fashion magazines together during lunch.
But I was only allowed to go shopping twice a year—at the beginning of the school year and again in the spring. I had to get the most
out of my biannual clothing stipends and buy items that could easily mix and match, so it wasn't obvious when I rotated them every
few weeks. This practicality didn't allow me to shop in the trendy

stores in the mall or the boutiques in the city like most of my class-mates. It meant going to the discount chains in the plazas. I never let it mean that much to me—it wasn't worth it.

However, to have access to Sara McKinley's wardrobe for one night would be any girl's dream, so I wasn't about to refuse it. I knew she had clothes in that closet that still had tags on them. I took the tops, grabbed my tote, and headed to the bathroom. Sara ran out of her room before I closed the door.

"Oh, I have this lotion I bought last week that I think you'd like. I was going to save it for a Christmas gift, but you should use it tonight," she said, handing me a bottle of lotion with pink flowers drawn on the label.

"Thanks," I said, taking the bottle before I closed the door. It was great to take a long, hot shower without fear of *The Knock* on the door, signaling the end of my allotted five minutes. It gave me time to think about the past couple of days and how different today felt. I was actually looking forward to the game, despite how awkward it was going to be. I thought if I could get through the game, then I would be able to get through the party. I shut off the water with a new conviction—how long it would last was another story.

I flipped the top of the bottle and took in the soft floral scent. After dressing, I opened the door to find Sara on the stairs, with a towel wrapped around her head. She wore a flattering light blue angora sweater. Sara had no problem with tops that hugged her modelesque body. Sara looked amazing, even with the towel on her head. Conversely, I tugged and pulled at the pink sweater that felt like a second layer of skin, despite the layer beneath.

"Oh. That sweater looks great. You should wear more clothes that fit you like that, instead of hiding your figure." I dismissed her with a shrug. She smiled before asking, "Are you ready for the next step?"

We were interrupted when her mom called up that the pizza was here.

"We'll eat and then finish getting ready," Sara decided, and turned to descend the stairs.

"I heard you scored three goals yesterday," Anna said from the refrigerator where she was pouring us glasses of diet soda. "Sara also told me about the scouts. You must be so excited, Emma."

"I am," I replied with a small smile. I was horrible at carrying on a conversation with my peers—forget about trying to say something worthwhile to an adult. The only adults I spoke to on a regular basis were my teachers, my coach, and my aunt and uncle. I only discussed my assignments with my teachers; Coach was all about soccer—so that was easy. George hardly said a word, or maybe he couldn't get a word in over Carol's rambling about how difficult it was to be her. And of course the interactions I had with Carol were one-sided, usually reprimands about how useless and pathetic I was. So I didn't have a lot of practice. Anna recognized my conversational ineptitude, so she didn't push.

"Congratulations," she added, walking toward the stairs. She paused to tell Sara, "I'm going upstairs to change for dinner. Your dad and I are going out to eat with the Richardsons, and we've invited the Mathews to come along, since they're new in town."

"Okay, Mom," Sara said, only half-listening. My heart had stopped when Anna said their name.

"Your parents are going to dinner with Evan's parents?" I whispered in disbelief.

Sara shrugged, "My parents have to know everyone in town. You know, they're like Weslyn's unofficial welcoming committee. My father is the ultimate politician."

Then she added with a grin, "Do you want me to get some dirt on Evan and his family for you?"

"Sara!" I exclaimed in shock. "Of course not. I'm really not that interested in him. I'm just going to talk to him so he'll leave me alone."

"Sure," she said with a knowing smile. I tried to ignore her and took a bite of a pizza slice.

"What's next?" I asked, needing to not talk about Evan anymore.

"I was hoping you'd let me cut your hair," she said with a cautious smile. My hair was all one length, hanging past the middle of my back. There was no way I could get it cut every eight weeks or whatever was needed to maintain a style, so I kept it simple and trimmed it myself a few times a year. I usually wore it up out of my face in a clip or ponytail—again, simple.

"What do you want to do?"

"Nothing crazy," she reassured me. "Just shorten it."

"Whatever you want to do is fine with me."

"Really?! This is going to be so great!" she exclaimed, practically jumping off the stool and dragging me back up the stairs.

She opened the middle drawer of her vanity, which displayed every shade of lipstick and nail polish on the market, and took out a comb and pair of professional shears. She invited me to sit as she laid a towel on the floor to capture the clippings, and attached another around my shoulders. "No one's going to recognize you tonight."

That wouldn't be a bad thing.

Sara drew the comb through my hair and clipped portions of it up. I felt the weight begin to fall and decided it was best to keep my eyes shut and let her concentrate—or keep me from panicking as more hair fell to the floor. Sara sang along with the music as she combed, clipped and cut. Before I knew it, she was plugging in the hair dryer and running it over a round brush as she styled my hair.

"Keep your eyes closed," Sara instructed as she spread eye shadow along my lids with her cool fingers.

"Sara, please don't make me look ridiculous," I pleaded.

"I'm barely putting any on. I promise." The bristles of a brush streaked across my cheeks. "What do you think? Em, open your eyes!" she demanded impatiently.

I peeked between my lashes to view the transformation. My dark brown hair gently rested on my shoulders, and layers of bangs softened my heart-shaped face. I found myself smiling.

"I like it," I admitted. She hadn't put much makeup on, to my relief—just a slight shimmer on my lids and a hint of pink on my cheeks, which wouldn't be needed if I was anywhere near Evan.

"Here," Sara said handing me a tube of lip gloss and mascara. "I thought it would be easier if you put these on yourself. I'm going to get ready in the bathroom, I'll be right back."

While Sara was drying and styling her hair, I sat on one of the beds and flipped through the latest women's magazine, full of articles on how to be more aggressive and the fastest way to lose ten pounds. When she glided back into the room, she was radiant, with loose curls of shiny red hair and just enough makeup to show off her blue eyes and pouty red lips. It deflated me a little.

"What's wrong?" Sara asked, reacting to my sunken shoulders.

"Are you sure you want me to go with you? I don't want it to be awkward for you having me tagging along when I know everyone will want to talk to you."

She scowled and threw a pillow at me. "Shut up. Of course I want you to go with me. Why should this be any different than any other day? If people talk to me, and I want to talk to them, I will. It's never bothered you before."

I looked at the floor, recognizing my nerves were getting the better of me—and it really had nothing to do with Sara's popularity. "You're right. Sorry, I'm just getting a little paranoid about going."

"We'll have fun, I promise." Sara's teeth sparkled between her shiny red lips. She went back into her closet and threw something out in my direction. "This white scarf goes perfectly with that sweater, and it will keep you warm, so you won't miss not having a jacket."

"Thanks." I grabbed the fuzzy scarf and wrapped it around my neck as I stood in front of the mirror. Sara was right—I did look different.

"This is going to be the best night," Sara reassured me when we got into her car to drive to the school. She was so excited she could barely contain her energy, which made me smile. I made an effort to let go of the anxiety that had been building. I could do this. I could be social. Okay, let's not go that far. I would not be completely pathetic—that sounded better. Who was I kidding?

5. FADING

When we pulled in, the parking lot was filling with cars, and spectators were making their way to the ticket booth in a steady drove. A jolt of panic rushed through my body. I knew I was being ridiculous—this was only a high-school football game—but I might as well have been walking to school naked. Sara jumped out of the car and yelled to a group of girls who were lost in a giggling conversation while heading toward the stadium.

"Sara!" they screamed in unison and ran to her, receiving her with hugs and gleeful babble. I followed behind her, suddenly feeling overly exposed in the fitted sweater—the fashionable scarf doing little to conceal the low neckline.

"Emma?!" Jill Patterson exclaimed in shock. Everyone turned to gawk at me. The fire ignited in my cheeks. I knew the artificial color would be unnecessary.

I forced a smile with my lips pressed together and waved casually.

"Wow, you look great," another girl declared in disbelief. The rest of the girls offered similar gushing compliments.

"Thanks," I mumbled, wishing I were invisible again.

Sara linked her arm through mine and led us to the ticket booth with a proud smile. I took another deep breath and prepared myself for whatever the night presented. Unfortunately, there were many more reactions of astonishment and gawking.

There were a lot of stares, whispers and comments about my presence and transformation, but not a lot of conversation. It was evident no one knew what to say to me, any more than I knew what to say to them. So I sank into the metal bleachers and engrossed myself in the football game. Sara cheered for Jason and watched as much as she was allowed. She was often drawn away by just about everyone passing by, including some of the parents who were there to support the local high-school football team or their son who was on the field—or bench. I couldn't get over how many people Sara knew and how effortlessly she'd come up with a witty remark or a kind sentiment. I should've taken notes.

During the third quarter, I decided to get a hot chocolate while Sara walked off toward the school with Jill and Casey to use the restroom, talking and giggling about something. While I waited in line, I scuffed the ground with my foot, lost in the booming voice of the announcer calling the last play as Weslyn continued to move the ball down the field.

"Not a bad game, huh?" His voice carried through the cheering crowd and the deep baritone of the announcer. I turned to find Evan behind me, holding his camera.

"No, it's a pretty good game," I replied, struggling to find my voice. The sweater suddenly felt stifling as my cheeks were set aglow once again, ignited by the frenzied beating in my chest. "Are you covering the game for the paper?" As soon as I said it, I knew it was a dumb thing to say. Of course he was covering the game—I'd assigned him the coverage!

"Yeah," he said, holding up his camera, dismissing my ignorance. "I thought I heard you didn't go to the games?"

"I'm staying over at Sara's tonight," I answered, thinking that would be enough of an explanation for him, as it was for everyone else. But he appeared confused. I paused to recall the answer Sara had prepared.

"I'm usually so busy with school and everything that I don't get out much. It worked out that I could tonight."

The line continued to move forward, and I stepped up. Evan followed.

"Oh," he replied. I could tell he still wasn't satisfied with my answer. "Are you and Sara going to the party after the game?"

"I think so," I said tentatively. "Are you?"

"Yeah. I'm supposed to follow some of the guys from the soccer team over there."

I nodded, not knowing what else to say. I turned toward the counter, thinking this would give him the opportunity to escape and go back to taking pictures of the game. I remained facing forward, not looking back to see if he'd walked away. I ordered a hot chocolate and turned to find him still waiting for me.

"Do you want to walk around with me while I take a few more pictures?" My heart stopped again. I wished it would decide if it was going to pound out of my chest or stop beating altogether. The stopping and starting were beginning to wear on me.

"Sure," I heard my mouth say, before my brain registered what I'd agreed to do. He smiled, and my heart thrust to life. "So, you've decided to talk to me," Evan observed, looking at the ground as he walked next to me.

"I shouldn't. But it's only a matter of time before you see that I'm not that interesting, and you'll let me fade into the background like everyone else."

He laughed and studied me, uncertain if I was serious. I was bewildered by his reaction.

He drew his eyebrows together with a smile and said, "I actually think you've become more interesting now that you've decided to talk to me, whether you *should* or not." I groaned. He smiled bigger and added, "Besides, I don't think it's possible for you to fade. Well, at least not in that sweater."

All of the blood in my body rushed to my face. "It's Sara's sweater," I confessed, looking at the ground to conceal the drastic color change.

"I like it," he admitted. "It's a good color on you." Maybe talking to him wasn't such a good idea after all. This was way more than I'd bargained for. What was I supposed to do with a comment like that? I took a sip of my hot chocolate and sucked air between my teeth as the scalding liquid soaked into my tongue.

"Too hot?" he observed.

"Yeah—I don't think I'll be able to taste anything for a week."

He smiled again. I decided my heart had been tortured enough by his smile and stared back at the ground.

"I have a bottle of water in my bag by the team's bench, if you want."

"No, that's okay, thanks. The damage is done." Before I knew it, we had circled back around and were walking in front of the bleachers, where the cheerleaders encouraged the crowd to spell W-E-S-L-Y-N. I glanced up into the stands to locate Sara. She waved to me and pointed to Evan, her mouth open in disbelief. I shrugged in return, turning away before he noticed.

"Have you met many people yet?" I asked, trying to sound casual. It occurred to me that maybe he kept harassing me because he didn't know anyone else. Why he chose me was another mystery.

"Actually, I have," he answered sincerely, to my dismay. "It helps to be on the soccer team and involved with the paper. It gives me an excuse to talk to people. Someone's always eager to fill me in on who's who. That's how I learned more about you—which was harder than I thought it was going to be."

Before I could question what he'd found out, he continued, "So your name's actually Emily, huh?"

I nodded with a slight shrug.

"Then how come everyone calls you Emma?"

It had been a while since anyone needed this explanation, but I found myself being more honest than I had with the others. "My dad used to call me Emma."

I left it at that, and so did he.

We'd passed the bleachers and were standing in their shadows along the track. The cheering and announcing drifted away with the quickening of my pulse as panic raced through my body. I needed him to tell me what he'd found out, but at the same time I was afraid to know.

Unable to stop myself, I finally asked, "What else could you have possibly learned about me?"

He smirked and replied, "Besides the obvious—your perfect GPA, involved in three varsity sports, and all of that?"

"Yes, besides that." I held my breath. No one besides Sara knew about my life, right? There was no way he could know. Then why was I so paranoid?

"Well, you intimidate most of the guys in the school, so you never get asked out. The girls think you're stuck up, and that's why your only friend is the most popular girl in school. It's assumed that no one else is good enough for you." My eyes stretched wide as he continued. "Your teachers feel bad for you. They think that you put too much pressure on yourself to be perfect and are missing out on what high school's all about. And your coach thinks he's lucky to have you, and is confident the team's a shoo-in for state champions this year as long as you don't get injured."

He became serious, noticing the awed look on my face. "But you've only been here a week," I whispered. "People actually told you this?"

Evan paused in confusion before he asked, "You didn't know any of this?" I could only stare at him. "I figured the reason you keep to yourself was because you were so confident, and you didn't care what anyone thought of you. You really had no idea what they say about you?"

I shook my head. "Honestly, I never gave it much thought—it wasn't important to me. I just need to get through high school."

"Why?" he asked slowly.

It was the question I couldn't answer, and the reason I shouldn't talk to him. I was saved from having to lie when the crowd erupted as the announcer declared a touchdown for Weslyn. I looked up at the scoreboard to see Weslyn's numbers change to 28, as the visitor's remained 14. The clock held steady with less than two minutes remaining in the fourth quarter.

"I should go find Sara," I said. "I'll see you later." I walked off before he could respond. There was so much to take in, and I didn't know how to absorb it all.

I located Sara along the sidelines, behind the rope that separated the field from the track.

"There you are!" she exclaimed. "Did you see Jason run in that last touchdown?"

"I didn't have a good view," I confessed. She clapped and yelled for the defense to stop the ball.

Then she pulled me aside, away from the crowd. "First," she said intently, "you are going to repeat every word of the conversation you had with Evan before we go to sleep tonight. Everyone's been talking about you two. I think half the school already assumes you're dating." My mouth dropped open.

"I know, it's stupid," Sara huffed with a shrug. "No one's ever seen you talk to someone besides me so much before. So most of the girls hate you, and the guys don't get what's so great about him. It's actually kinda funny."

"Great," I grumbled, rolling my eyes.

"Anyway, after the game, I'm going to wait outside the locker room for Jason to ask him to go to the party. Will you wait with me?"

"Sure, but I'm not waiting by the locker-room door. That's all you. I'll sit on the stairs, okay?

"Okay." Her eyes sparkled. "I can't believe I'm doing this!"

"He's going to say yes," I assured her.

"I hope so."

The air horn blared to declare the end of the game. There was a final cheer from the home crowd, congratulating the team for their win. The guys on the field celebrated with chest bumps and shoulder-pad punches as they headed to the locker room.

Sara and I lingered while the crowd filed out through the gates. A few people asked if they'd see us at the party. Sara enthusiastically assured them we'd be there. She began silently wringing her hands as we got closer to the locker room. It was almost entertaining to see her this nervous. I'd never seen her so uncertain before.

"Wish me luck."

"I'll be right here," I promised, climbing the steps to observe from above.

Sara paced back and forth in front of the open double doors. Every so often she'd glance up at me anxiously, and I'd return an encouraging smile. Before long, the guys started coming out of the locker room, showered, dressed and carrying their gear bags over their shoulders. Most of them greeted Sara as they exited. It was evident a few of the guys hoped she was waiting for them, only to be disappointed when she responded with a casual greeting.

Then the damp golden hair of Jason Stark walked through the doors. I held my breath in anticipation as Sara said, "Hi, Jason." Her voice didn't project its signature confidence, but her smile made up for it.

"Hi, Sara," he replied. She'd definitely taken him by surprise. I listened intently.

A second passed. He was about to walk away when she finally asked, "Are you going to Scott's party?"

He was caught off guard again. "Um, I don't know. I didn't drive, and I think Kyle wanted to go home."

"I could drive you if you want to go," Sara blurted.

I gasped. What was she thinking? She only had two seats in her car. She glanced up at me quickly and cringed in apology.

"Ah, I guess I could do that," he agreed slowly. "You don't mind?"

"No," she answered casually. "I think you should celebrate your win."

"Okay, let me find Kyle to let him know. I'll meet you back here in a minute." When he walked into the locker room, Sara looked up at me, jumping up and down, and opened her mouth to release a silent scream. I laughed.

"It sounds like you'll need a ride to the party," a confidently charming voice concluded from the bottom of the stairs. Startled, I whipped around to discover Evan looking up at me.

"Sorry. I didn't mean to scare you."

"How do you do that?" I shot back.

"What?"

"Appear out of nowhere. I don't even hear you coming, and then all of a sudden, there you are," I accused.

"I guess you just don't pay attention. I think you're too busy attempting to fade." He chuckled. I scowled back in annoyance. "Well, do you want a ride to the party? Unless you're going to sit on Jason Stark's lap?"

"You saw that? Do you usually go around eavesdropping?"

"I was taking victory shots after the game for the story and was heading to the locker room to get the rest of my things. I happened to notice they were having a moment, and waited here until it was over," he said, defending himself. "Besides, it looks like you're the one spying from up there."

"I'm being supportive," I snapped.

"Sure." He laughed. I clenched my jaw, trying to contain my aggravation.

"Well, do you want a ride?" Evan persisted.

"Fine," I said through my teeth. This only fueled his laughter before he walked toward the locker room. Why did he find me so funny? It annoyed the hell out of me. Then why was I driving to the party with him? Especially after hearing the latest gossip. If I showed up with him, it was only going to make it worse.

What did it really matter at this point? According to Evan, I wasn't well liked by just about everyone—so who cared what they said if I pulled up with him? But I did care. Not being liked was so much worse than being invisible. I took a deep breath and blew it away before it could hurt. I didn't need to know what people thought about me.

Before I could think too much more about it, Sara ran up the stairs. "Em, I am so sorry. It came out before I had time to think about it."

I could see Jason waiting for her by the locker room.

"It's okay. Evan's giving me a ride," I assured her.

"Evan? Really?" She narrowed her eyes and examined me.

"Don't worry, I'll see you there. Okay?" I forced a supportive smile.

"Okay," she said, still hesitating.

"Really. Go. I'll be right behind you." Sara gave me a quick excited hug and skipped back down the stairs to Jason. I watched them walk off toward her car, already in conversation.

"Ready?" Evan asked from the bottom of the stairs. I jumped again. "You honestly didn't see me coming from the locker room?"

"I guess I wasn't looking for you," I bit back.

"Let's go." He held out his hand, inviting me to take it. I creased my forehead in disbelief and walked past him. My rejection didn't seem to faze him as he walked alongside me to the parking lot. Nothing about Evan made sense. But for some reason, I kept finding myself with him.

He approached a black BMW sports car. I never really paid attention to the cars in the lot. Most of the residents in town could afford luxury cars to complement their ginormous houses—so of course their kids also drove cars that reflected their parents' success. Diversity in Weslyn came down to what you drove, not your ethnicity. So I was a minority, especially since I didn't have a car. Forget that, I didn't even have a license.

Evan opened the passenger door for me, making me pause before I entered, unaccustomed to the chivalrous gesture.

"Do you know where we're going?" he asked as he closed his door.

"No, don't you?"

He laughed. "I just moved here. I don't know where anyone lives. I thought you would at least know that much." I didn't respond.

Evan rolled down his window and hollered to someone he recognized, "Dave, you going to Scott's?" I couldn't hear the answer. "Do you mind if I follow you?"

Evan started the car and drove around to get behind a silver Land Rover.

"I didn't ruin your night, did I?"

"No," I answered casually, removing the scarf from around my neck. "But if you don't mind, I'd rather not talk about what other people think of me anymore, okay?"

"Never again," he promised. "So what are the parties like in Weslyn?"

I snickered. "Are you seriously asking me?"

"Okay," he said slowly. "Well, I guess we'll both find out tonight, won't we?" I didn't answer.

"If you want to do something else, I'm up for anything," he offered. I looked over at him, my lungs paralyzed.

"No, I want to go," I lied, almost choking on my words. "Besides, I'm meeting Sara there, remember?"

The Land Rover pulled away from the school, and we started down unfamiliar back roads. Evan turned on the radio. I wasn't expecting to recognize the voice of a female singer bellowing about how life sucked to the strums of a heavy guitar. He turned it down so he could talk. What else could he possibly have to say to me?

"Where did you live before you moved here?"

I hesitated to decide if I could tell him without backing myself into a corner.

"A small town outside Boston," I replied.

"So you've always lived in New England?"

"Yup," I answered. "Where in California are you from?"

"San Francisco."

"Have you lived anywhere else besides here and San Francisco?"

Evan let out a short laugh. "We've moved just about every year since I can remember. My dad's a lawyer for a financial conglomerate, so his job takes him wherever he needs to be. I've lived in New York, different parts of California, Dallas, Miami, and even in several countries in Europe for a few years."

"Does it bother you?" I asked, relieved to be talking about him instead of me.

"It didn't used to. When I was younger, I'd get excited to go somewhere new. It didn't bother me when I left my friends behind because I was convinced that I'd see them again, eventually.

"Now that I'm in high school, it's not as easy. I made some decent friends when we moved to San Francisco two years ago, so it was harder to leave. Also, I don't want to keep fighting for a position on the sports teams. My parents offered to let me stay there to finish, but I decided to give Connecticut a chance. I can visit my friends during the breaks. If I don't like it here, I'll move back."

"By yourself?" I asked in amazement.

He smiled at my reaction. "I'm pretty much by myself as it is anyway. My father works all the time, and my mother is on every fund-raising committee from here to San Diego, so she travels a lot."

"I'm sure Weslyn doesn't even compare to San Francisco. I'd choose California in a second."

"Weslyn's interesting." He looked over at me with his infamous grin. I was glad it was dark so he couldn't see my scarlet cheeks. I looked out the window, still having no idea where we were.

"I hope you're paying attention to where we're going, because you have to figure out how to get yourself home," I warned.

"What, I'm not driving you back to Sara's?"

I wasn't sure if he was serious.

"This isn't a date," I blurted, knowing I shouldn't have said it as soon as it came out of my mouth.

"I know," he said almost too quickly—instantly making me regret saying it. "I figured Sara would drive Jason home."

"Oh," I whispered. I felt like an idiot.

"I can offer to drive Jason so you and Sara can leave together," he suggested. "That may be easier for everyone."

We were quiet as we followed the Land Rover down a long driveway lined with cars—or it could have been a private road, as long as it was. Evan pulled in behind the Land Rover and shut off the car.

"If this is going to be weird for you, I can go in by myself so no one knows we came here together," he offered. I must've really offended him.

"No, it's okay," I said softly. "I shouldn't have said that about it not being a date. I haven't been as filtered as I usually am, especially when I'm around you for some reason."

"I've noticed," Evan teased. "I never quite know how you're going to react. It's one of the things that makes you so interesting." His flawless smile reflected in the soft light of the driveway's lanterns.

"Let's get this over with," I said under my breath as I opened the car door.

"Do you really want to do this?" Evan asked as we approached the house.

I took a deep breath and replied, "Yes, it'll be fun." I forced a smile. It wasn't convincing, but he didn't call me out on it.

6. DIFFERENT PLANET

A s we neared the front steps, we spotted Sara and Jason sitting off to the side along a stone wall. They were deep in conversation with red cups in their hands, oblivious to the party happening inside.

"Hey, Sara," I said as I walked over, breaking her entranced attention.

"Emma, I was waiting for you!" she exclaimed as she jumped up from the wall and went to hug me, but restrained herself when she saw my body tense for the embrace.

Sensing Sara wasn't quite ready to give up her moment with Jason, I declared, "We're going in. Find me inside later."

"Okay," she replied with a beaming smile that could only mean that I wasn't going to see her for a while.

I was so wrapped up in my anxiety that I didn't realize Evan had grabbed my hand upon entering the loud crowded space—not until he was leading me through the entanglement of bodies. I didn't pull away as we squeezed through the bodies, afraid that I would be stranded if I let go. Wide eyes followed me through the crowd—evidently not everyone who was here had been at the football game or had received the circulating texts.

The house was the typically huge Weslyn estate, with an open floor plan that was conducive to throwing a large party. There were only two rooms at the front of the house enclosed by walls—the formal dining room and another room with a large wooden door, which appeared to be locked.

We squeezed through to the back of the house, where we found the kitchen. The island in the kitchen was lined with different-colored liquor bottles and soda, ending with a large stack of red plastic cups next to a tap handle.

"Want something to drink?" Evan yelled, still holding my hand.

"Diet whatever's fine," I yelled back.

He left me standing on one side of the bar to get our drinks at the other end, instantly consumed by the crowd within the few feet it took to reach the sodas.

"Holy shit! Emma Thomas?!" I heard someone yell from across the room. I froze, afraid to look. The exclamation caught the attention of a few other people; they evidently were among the few who hadn't heard that I was at the party, since they couldn't stop staring at me. I spotted a guy from my Chemistry class as he fought his way through the crowd, parting the bodies with his red cup.

"Hi, Ryan."

"I can't believe you're here!" he exclaimed, throwing his arms around me in a tight embrace with alcohol rolling off his breath. Great, he was drunk. I tensed, unable to react to his breach of my personal space until he finally let go.

"Wow, this is so great," he said with a ridiculous smile on his face. "I was hoping to see you tonight. I heard you were at the game. Do you want a drink?"

"Hey, Ryan," I heard Evan say from behind me. I turned toward him with a panicked expression, but he didn't pick up on it. Instead he handed me one of the cups he was holding.

"Evan!" Ryan hollered, in a volume too loud for how close we were standing to him. He put his arm around me and zealously pulled me toward him, making me spill my drink—he was oblivious. "Evan, you know Emma Thomas, right? She is the coolest person." I gave Evan my wide-eyed look of despair—he raised his eyebrows, finally getting it.

"Yes, Ryan, I know Emma," he said, grabbing my hand and pulling me carefully away from Ryan. "We actually came here together."

Ryan appeared confused and then shocked as he released me. "You did? Oh, man, I am so sorry. I had no idea."

"It's okay," Evan assured him. "We're going outside. We'll see you later." Evan turned toward the sliding doors that led to the deck.

It was a little less crowded and definitely quieter, leaving the music behind in the house. We found an empty section of railing and leaned our backs against it, watching the craziness inside.

"I'm sorry about that," Evan finally said, leaning on his forearm to face me. "I had no idea why you'd given me that look. I didn't know Ryan liked you."

"Neither did I," I confessed quietly. "Thanks for getting me out of there. I'm way out of my comfort zone with all of these people."

"Really?" Evan shot me a teasing smile. "I don't think I noticed when you could barely force yourself through the front door."

"Okay, so I'm here for Sara," I admitted with a sigh. "She's wanted to ask Jason Stark out since the beginning of the year, and this was the perfect opportunity. I'm here for moral support."

"It looks like Sara's doing just fine without you." Evan noted wryly. "I think you're the one needing the support."

I scowled up at him, then said, "Thanks a lot," with a mocking smile.

"Mathews!" a male voice yelled from the doorway.

"Hi, Jake." Evan greeted the voice with a shake of his hand.

"It's good to see you," Jake said. "No way, is that Emma Thomas?" I smiled awkwardly and nodded.

"Wait, did you come here together?" he asked, looking at Evan with a sly grin.

"I brought her here to meet up with Sara," Evan explained.

"Wow, I can't believe you're here." Jake shook his head, looking me over. "Can I get you something to drink?"

I raised my cup. "Thanks, I'm all set."

"Maybe I'll see you inside, and I can refill it for you," he said, flashing his teeth. I froze, trying to understand what was going on. I swore I was on a different planet. And on this planet, people noticed me. Some noticed me too much. I desperately wanted to be on the other side of the locked door at the front of the house.

"Did you guys see the fire pit they have around the side of the house?"

"No," Evan replied.

"It's pretty cool, you should check it out," Jake encouraged. "I'll see you later." He winked at me before he turned away. I stood there, stunned.

"Did he really just wink at me?" I asked, completely astounded.

"I think he did," Evan confirmed with a small laugh.

"You're enjoying this, aren't you?" I suddenly realized. "I'm so glad I'm finding more ways to entertain you. This is horrifying for me. I don't think you quite get that."

Evan looked at my distraught face, straightening out his smile. "I'm sorry, you're right. I can tell you're not enjoying this. Let's go check out the fire pit; it's probably less crowded."

"Evan, you don't have to stay with me. You should go in the house and meet people. It looks like the entire junior and senior classes are here. I'll be fine." I tried to assure him with one of my forced smiles. He looked at me doubtfully. I really did have to work on faking it, didn't I?

"How about this—I'll walk down to the fire pit with you, and then I'll make a round inside the house before coming back to check on you?"

"Okay," I agreed reluctantly. As much as I hated the thought of being alone at this party, I wasn't going to ruin Evan's night by making him feel obligated to babysit me. I was used to being invisible, and I could sink into the shadows again—even on this planet.

The deck became more crowded as we moved toward the stairs that led to the backyard. Evan grabbed my hand to lead me through.

"Evan!" a female voice exclaimed. Although he was still holding my hand, we were cut off by a person between us, so I couldn't see the owner of the overly excited voice. "I've been looking for you."

I squeezed through in time to find Haley Spencer with her arms flung around Evan's neck, pulling him into her well-developed body. One of his hands was holding mine and his cup was in the other, so he didn't return her embrace. An unwelcome heat turned in my stomach. I quickly shook off the insecurity and attempted to release his hand—but he held on tighter and pulled me closer.

Haley stepped back, keeping her hands on the back of his neck. "We were just going inside to get another drink. Join us." Her eyes met mine, then traced along my arm. Her eyes tightened when she realized that my hand ended in his.

"Oh," she said, quickly dropping her hands from his neck. "I didn't know you were here with someone." She eyed me up and down cynically.

"Sorry, Haley," Evan said sympathetically, "we were just heading down to the fire pit." He pulled me a little closer, wrapping his arm around me. My breathing stopped as I remained immobilized by his side.

"I guess I'll see you later then," Haley sulked. She flipped back her hair before strutting into the house, followed by two aghast girls who'd been standing next to her.

Evan turned to face me, his hand still on my back, drawing me in so we could talk as people squeezed by us. It remained difficult to breathe while looking up at him, my heart still pounding through my sweater.

"Still want to go to the fire pit?"

I nodded with wide eyes.

As he turned to head down the stairs, I missed his hand, and we were separated. In that brief second, I was aggressively pulled in the opposite direction, with the exclamation, "Emma Thomas! I heard you were here." The tug dragged me right into the large frame of Scott Kirkland.

"I can't believe you came to my party. This is the best night ever," he declared in slurred speech. Perfect—he wasn't just drunk, he was obliterated.

"Thanks for having me, Scott." I tried to step back from his strangling embrace. "It's a great party."

He peered down at me with half-closed eyes and breathed heavily in my face. "Would you go out with me?"

"Um…that's really nice of you." I struggled to find the words while pushing him away with a little more force. "But—" The panic rose in my stomach and spread into my chest. I started breathing faster as I remained trapped against him. I needed to get away from him, but he didn't show any signs of releasing me.

"Hey, Scott." Evan greeted Scott with an overly emphatic pat on the back. "This is a great party."

"Thanks, Evan," he slurred. "Evan, this is Emma Thomas." Scott captured me against his body with one arm. I had no idea he was so big, or strong, for that matter. I almost fit entirely under his arm. I looked up at Evan in despair, trying to squirm away—I wasn't making much headway.

"Yeah, I know—" Evan began.

"Emma and I are going to go to homecoming together," Scott declared, interrupting Evan. "Right, Emma?"

I was finally able to back out from under his arm. My face was bright red, and my hair clung to my cheeks. Scott lifted his arm in confusion, searching for me.

Evan took my shaking hand and gently guided me next to him. I tried to regain my breath, overcome with the sudden need to sit down.

"Emma, I think Sara's looking for you." Evan scanned my face in concern. "Scott, we'll be right back."

Before Scott could respond, Evan held my hand tightly and led me down the stairs. My knees buckled slightly, but I recovered and kept my feet moving beneath me. We went around the corner, and I collapsed on the stone wall under the deck.

Evan crouched in front of me and looked up, trying to meet my eyes. "Are you okay? That was crazy. I'm sorry I lost you."

I took a deep breath and tried to will my hands to stop shaking. I couldn't understand why I was so worked up. Evan gingerly took my hands in his and looked at me intently, trying to get me to focus on him. I stared straight ahead, desperately needing to pull myself together. I barely noticed he was there.

There was something about the crowd, the smell of liquor rolling in the air swirled with cigarette smoke, that transported me to another place—a place I could barely remember, but I had a feeling I didn't want to return there. There was no space among the bodies. No space to breathe or move without being touched and jostled. The confinement and groping had created a storm that erupted before I knew how to contain it. I shivered, not wanting to remember what was beginning to stir.

"Emma, look at me." His voice was soothing. "Are you okay?"

I found his blue eyes and began to focus. My face became hot when I realized what I must have looked like to him. I tried to stand up, and he backed up to give me space, but my legs weren't as ready as my mind. I wobbled—he caught me by my elbows and pulled me into him to steady me.

I felt his breath against my face as he peered down to examine me. "Maybe you should sit down again." But he didn't move to let me go.

My pulse quickened with the warmth of his body against me as my hands rested on the hard curves of his chest. I looked up at him, but he was too close. I panicked and backed away. He let me go easily.

We stood still for a second, until I finally said without looking up at him, "I'm fine, really." But my quivering body betrayed me. I was mortified—I must have appeared so pathetic.

"This was probably not the best first party for you," Evan said gently. "Maybe you should try something with about ten people before you jump to a hundred."

I pressed my lips into a smile and shrugged. He offered a warm smile in return.

"Do you want to leave?"

"No, you stay," I encouraged, determined to regain my composure. "I'm fine. I'm going to sit by the fire."

We continued to walk around the corner, where a cut stone patio lay next to the dark silhouette of trees along the perimeter of the property. In the center sat a wall encasing a blazing fire. There were two dozen chairs around the fire, but only half were occupied. I sat down in a chair on the far side of a small group talking and giggling in low voices.

"Evan," I pleaded, "go have fun. I'll wait here for Sara. Thank you for bailing me out tonight, but I can take care of myself. I swear." His delving eyes tried to read my face, making me wish I could disappear and erase the whole night. I stared into the fire, unable to bear his silent inquisition.

"I'll be right back," he assured me. "I'll find Sara and get us something to drink, okay?" The careful tone of his voice fueled my embarrassment. I still couldn't look at him as he walked back toward the house. I couldn't believe I'd let him see me like this, unable to fend for myself. I fumed in disgust at my vulnerability. I didn't want Evan to think I needed protecting. I pulled back my torment and let the numb blanket envelop me, pushing away the stirred memories, the noise of the crowd and the trembling that still lay beneath the surface. I stared at the flames licking at the darkness, and everything was lost as I sank deeper into nothingness.

"You know it's raining, right?" Evan asked from the seat next to me. I looked around, snapping back from my empty place. I was the only one sitting in front of the dwindling flames. A steady cold rain pasted my hair to my face, causing me to shiver. Evan stared at the few defiant flames that remained, ignoring the rain while holding his black camera case.

"Are you going to stop talking to me?" Evan asked quietly.

A smile spread across my face, turning my head toward him. "No." I started to laugh.

"What?!" he asked, surprised by my reaction. A half smile crept across his face as he tried to get the joke.

"I get accosted by a drunken bear and completely freak out, humiliating myself, and you're afraid I'm not going to talk to *you*?!" I laughed again.

Evan smiled lightly, still not getting the humor in my explanation. "Why were you humiliated?" Serious once again.

I shrugged—hugging my knees into my chest, trying to suppress the shivering. I wasn't sure if I wanted to explain my vulnerability to him. He waited patiently for me to find the words. I took a deep breath.

"I saw the way you looked at me, and I know how I must have come across, reacting like that." I looked down. "I hate that you keep seeing me at my worst. This really isn't me."

"Emma!" Sara hollered from under the deck before Evan could answer. "You're crazy. Get out of the rain!"

I suddenly realized I was wearing Sara's cashmere sweater and jumped up to join her.

"Sara, I am so sorry. I completely forgot I had your sweater on."

"I don't care about the sweater," she replied. "What are you guys doing out there? You must be freezing." Evan joined us under the deck.

"Getting some fresh air," Evan answered with a smile. He was rubbing his arms, registering the cold.

"You're a bad influence on her." Sara scowled at Evan, but it melted into a smile. She wasn't good at being mad—probably as bad as I was at delivering my forced smiles.

"Ready to go?" she asked me.

"Where's Jason?" I asked, not sure if I should be concerned.

"He rode home with one of the football players," she explained with a twinkle in her eye. I knew I was going to get a good story in the car.

"Let's walk around the house," I suggested. "I'd rather not go back inside."

We ran to Sara's car, trying to avoid being in the rain as much as we could. When we got in, Sara started the engine and turned on the heat full blast. Evan leaned against my door, remaining in the rain while waiting for me to roll down the window.

He bent down to peer in through the opening. The water ran down his artistically structured face, dripping off the tip of his nose over his shivering blue lips. My breath escaped me as I took in his smoky eyes.

"Can I call you tomorrow?"

"You can't actually." I grimaced. He looked confused. "It's complicated. I don't exactly have phone privileges." I hated to say it out loud, but I didn't want him to think I was rejecting him.

The questioning look didn't quite leave his eyes, but he tried to respond understandingly, "Okay, then I'll see you Monday."

"Yeah, Monday."

He lingered a second too long, and I couldn't breathe again.

"Good night," I finally said, exhaling. "Get out of the rain before you freeze to death." He stood up and casually raised his hand to wave as I rolled up the window. He ran back into the house.

"No way! Was he going to kiss you?" Sara shrieked, breaking my lingering stare. "Emma, I swear if I wasn't in the car, he would have kissed you."

"No, he wouldn't have," I said dismissively. My heart collapsed at the thought of Evan leaning in just a little closer. I shook it off.

"You need to share details," she demanded as we pulled onto the road.

"You first," I insisted.

Sara didn't hesitate. The entire ride home, she gushed about her time with Jason.

It was dark inside her house when we walked in.

"I think we beat my parents home."

"What time is it?" I asked, having no idea how much time had passed since we left the house earlier in the evening.

"Eleven thirty."

It was earlier than I thought. That meant I'd only been at the party for a little over an hour. It seemed so much longer. But now that I looked back at it, I hadn't really done much. Evan and I hadn't had a real conversation the whole time we were there. I was too busy trying to avoid being grappled by drunken idiots.

I got ready for bed and scrubbed off the makeup that the rain hadn't already washed away. If I were caught wearing makeup, I would probably need it to hide what Carol would do to me.

Last year, Sara had given me a few samples of lipsticks she didn't want. I tried them on, but ended up wiping the colors off with a tissue. When I returned from practice that evening, Carol confronted me with the tissues removed from the bathroom trash, accusing me of trying to sneak around wearing makeup behind her back after she had already told me it wasn't allowed. She called me a whore and other derogatory names as she squeezed my cheeks together so tightly in her hand that my teeth ground into the soft tissue until they bled.

So I'd rather have raw skin than face a second round over the makeup issue.

As we lay in the dark, Sara insisted, "You have to tell me what happened with you and Evan tonight."

I'd hoped that Sara would be so lost in her night with Jason that she'd have forgotten all about me, and we could avoid this conversation. No such luck.

I stared into the darkness above me, not certain where to begin. "I talked to him," I confessed. I was quiet for a moment.

"Please don't make me drag this out of you."

"I found out he's from San Francisco and that he may move back if he doesn't like it here." I added, "I can only hope."

"What do you mean?" She sounded confused. "It looked like you guys really connected from where I was sitting—you know, his almost kissing you." My cheeks warmed at the mention of the close proximity of his face to mine when we had said good night.

"Sara, I can't do this." My voice grew stronger. "I barely talked to him. He spent most of the night rescuing me from drunken hormonal gorillas. It was pretty pathetic. I don't want to like him. I don't want there to be any more moments where he may kiss me. I need to stay away from him."

"I am so confused," Sara confessed. "I thought we had a plan. And who was hitting on you? Now I feel bad that *I* wasn't there."

"Don't," I said with an edge to my voice. "That's just it. I don't want to be protected or looked after. I should be so much stronger than to need you or Evan Mathews to stand up for me. I don't know how I'm going to be able to look at him on Monday."

"That's not what I meant," Sara said quietly. I heard the hurt in her voice. "I know you don't want me protecting you, you've made that clear way before tonight. But I feel bad because I knew how hard tonight was going to be for you, and from the sounds of it, it was pretty horrible. I should've been there as your friend, that's all."

"But it shouldn't be horrible, Sara. It was just a stupid party, and I freaked. I could barely function." I sighed in frustration. I was glad it was dark so she couldn't see the tears welling in my eyes. I clenched my jaw and swallowed the lump in my throat. I took a calming breath to be rid of the dizzying emotion, wiping my cheeks dry. Safe again, I turned away from Sara.

"I'm sorry, Sara," I said softly. "It's been a long day, and I'm being ridiculous. We have to get up early so I can get home to do my chores. Let's just get some sleep, okay?"

"Okay," she whispered.

I was afraid that sleep wouldn't come easily, but with all that my psyche had fought throughout the day, I was exhausted.

7. REPERCUSSIONS

It took me a few blinks to remember where I was when I woke up in the queen-size bed, with the sunlight beaming behind the shaded skylights. I rolled over to find Sara in the bed across from me, still asleep with the down comforter pulled up around her. She groaned as the alarm beeped to wake us so that I could get home in time to do my weekend chores.

She grumbled, flopping her hand down on the snooze button. She revealed her blue eyes reluctantly, peering over at me with her head still on her pillow. "Hey."

"Sorry you have to get up so early," I said, my head propped up by my elbow.

"I know how it is," she replied with stretched arms above her head. "Em, I'm really sorry I bailed on you last night."

I shrugged, not wanting to think about it. "It's not like I'll be going to another party any time soon."

"True. So, Evan, huh? This is really happening, isn't it?" Sara ran her fingers through her long hair as she sat up in the bed, fluffing a pillow behind her.

"Not really," I contradicted her. "I mean, I'm talking to him, or was. Who knows what he'll think of me after last night."

"I'm pretty sure he's still interested. Please don't give up on him. I don't know all that happened last night, but I still think he's good for you. Give him a chance. Try to be friends, or at least use him as an emotional punching bag. He seems to be able to handle the backlashes that you can't unleash on anyone else." She said it like being reprimanded by me was a privilege. She studied my face with a soft smile to make sure I understood.

I returned a half smile, trying to digest her words.

Knowing I wasn't going to say anything, she flipped back the covers and swung her feet to the floor. "Well, let's get you back to hell before the devil realizes you're not home." It would have been funny, except that it was too close to the truth for me to laugh.

When I walked in the back door, the house was strangely quiet. George's truck was not in the driveway; he and the kids were getting the Saturday-morning donuts and coffee. That meant she was here, somewhere. My stomach dropped. I focused on getting to my room without having to see her.

Just outside my door I was abruptly stopped in my tracks by a sharp pain shrieking through my head. I winced as her claw dug deeper into the fistful of my hair, tugging my head back so that my neck snapped awkwardly. She hissed in my ear, "Did you think I wouldn't find out that you went to the game last night? What did you do, screw the entire football team?"

With an unexpected amount of force, she thrust my head forward without giving me a second to resist. The front of my skull collided with the doorframe. A thunderous bolt shot through my head as the hall blurred around me. Black dots filled my eyes as I attempted to focus. Before I could find center, her viselike grip tore the hair from my scalp and drove my head into the hard wood again. The corner of the frame connected with the left side of my forehead. The stinging burn above my eye gave way to a flow of warmth that ran down my cheek.

"I regret every second you're in my house," Carol growled. "You're a worthless, pathetic tramp, and if it wasn't for your uncle, I would have shut the door in your face when your drunken mother abandoned you. It says a lot when even *she* can't stand you." I slid down the wall, collapsing on the floor with my bags by my side. Something landed on my knees. I made out my navy blue soccer jersey from Thursday's game crumpled on my lap.

"Clean yourself up before they see you, and get rid of the stench in the basement. You'd better be done with your chores and out of my sight by the time I get back from grocery shopping," she threatened before disappearing.

I heard the truck pulling in to the driveway and the doors closing, followed by excited voices nearing the back door. I didn't want them to see me either, so I clumsily tossed my bags through the open door of my room and pushed myself to my feet. I stumbled into the bathroom, using the wall to hold myself up, as I heard Leyla announce, "Mom, we have donuts!"

I pressed my shirt against the left side of my head, trying to stop the bleeding as the cut pulsed under my hand. My head pounded as I tried to regain control of my balance. The sensation that I was about to lose consciousness seized me. I gripped the sink, fighting to focus, as I took deep, even breaths. A minute passed before I was able to stand up straight. The dizziness subsided, but the claw of pain dug into my head.

I slowly let up pressure. The side of my face was covered with blood that ran down my neck, seeping into the collar of my turtleneck. I couldn't quite tell where the opening was. I took a few tissues and exchanged them with the shirt so I could run the shirt under cold water.

I wiped the drying blood from my face with the damp jersey and revealed a small incision above my left eyebrow. It wasn't very big, but it didn't want to stop bleeding. I applied more pressure with the shirt as I searched in the medicine cabinet for bandages. I pulled out two butterfly bandages and applied them to the gash, pulling the sides together so it could heal—hopefully leaving a minimal scar.

In the center of my forehead, along my hairline, a large lump was already turning purple. I couldn't bring myself to touch it—the unwavering pain was making my eyes water. I knew I needed to put ice on it, but I couldn't figure out how to do that without being seen.

I leaned against the wall across from the mirror and closed my eyes. I couldn't hold back the tears that rolled down my cheeks. I struggled to maintain a steady breath so I wouldn't cave in to the full-out cry that the lump in my throat yearned for. The images of what had happened flashed through my head. I hadn't heard her come up behind me. She was obviously waiting for me.

As hard as I tried to be invisible, Carol was inescapable, and her wrath was crushing. I wanted nothing more than to destroy her. My seeping eyes were aglow with fury as I stared into the mirror.

I looked down at the bloody jersey in my hand. Her blitz attack had nothing to do with the football game, or my dirty laundry; it had everything to do with me. I knew all I had to do was make one phone call, or walk into the school psychologist's office and utter one sentence, and this would all be over.

That's when I heard a squeal of laughter in the kitchen from Leyla, accompanied by a chuckle from Jack as *she* said something to make them laugh. It would be over for them too, but in a way that would damage them forever. I couldn't ruin their lives. Carol and George truly loved them, and I wouldn't take them from their parents. I swallowed hard, determined to compose myself, but the tears refused to stop.

I opened the cabinets under the sink and pulled out the cleaning supplies. With my lips quivering and hands shaking, I scrubbed the tub, swallowing against the sobs. The built-up pressure from keeping the cries contained infuriated the pain in my head. My whole body ached.

I was back to my numb, emotionless state by the time I finished cleaning the sink. I blankly stared at the water running down the drain, rinsing away the chemicals and blood. My raging thoughts were quiet.

"I'll be back in a couple of hours," I heard Carol announce, closing the door behind her. The kids were watching TV in the living room. I couldn't hear George.

I looked at myself in the mirror and mindlessly wiped the remaining dried blood from around the bandages before I opened the bathroom door. I stepped into the hall to retrieve the broom and mop from the hall closet when George rounded the corner. He stopped, and his eyes widened. But his shocked expression quickly dissolved.

"Bump your head?" he asked casually.

"That's what I get for walking while reading," I droned, knowing he would convince himself of anything except for the truth.

"You should put some ice on it," he recommended.

"Mmm," I agreed, and walked back into the bathroom to complete my task.

After my chores were completed, I returned to my room to find a bag of ice waiting for me on my desk.

I gently put the bag of ice on the lump and watched Jack and Leyla chase after George in the backyard through my window— sworn to silence in my hell.

———

I awoke in a panic around midnight. I stayed pressed to my pillow, my eyes fervently searching the room. I was breathing heavily; my shirt was damp with sweat. I tried to detach myself from the nightmare that had awoken me. It was hard to push away the urgency of the dream that had me pinned beneath the water, drowning. I took in a deep breath, confirming that I was still alive as the air passed easily through my lungs. They weren't burning for oxygen as they had been in my dream. I had a hard time falling back to sleep after that. Sleep finally found me just before the sun rose.

I was awoken by a hard knock on the door. "Are you going to sleep all day?" the voice barked from the other side.

"I'm up," I mustered in a rasp, hoping she wouldn't come in. I looked at the digital clock next to my bed that read eight-thirty. I knew I had to take a shower before nine o'clock or do without. I slowly sat up with the throbbing pain, a reminder of my living nightmare. I needed to find a way to ice it again so the lump would be gone by the time I went to school tomorrow. I knew there was nothing I could do about the dark purple bruise. Thankfully the area around the cut wasn't bruised. Sara's new hair-style was going to come in handy with covering up most of it.

I gathered my clothes together and slipped into the bathroom without being seen. Washing my hair was more painful than I antic-ipated. I hadn't realized how sore the back of my head was from her iron grip of my hair. I felt blood scabbed over where some of the hair had been forcefully removed. I had been so focused on the con-tusion that the back of my head didn't register until now. I gingerly used my fingertips to rub the shampoo into the front of my hair, but it still felt like a form of torture. I turned off the water before *The Knock* and proceeded to dry off and get dressed. After gently drying my hair with a towel, I discovered that brushing my hair was worse than washing it. Tears filled my eyes with each stroke of the brush. There was no way I was going to be able to blow it dry. Reluctantly, I made the decision not to wash my hair the next day despite how atrocious I knew it would look after sleeping on it. I wasn't willing to go through the pain again.

"Does she know we're taking the kids to the movies this after-noon?" I heard Carol ask George from the kitchen as I sat at my desk engrossed in my trigonometry homework.

"Yeah, I told her yesterday," he replied. "She's going to the library and will be back for dinner."

"And you believe she's going to the library?" she asked doubtfully.

"Why wouldn't she?" he questioned.

I didn't hear a response from Carol.

"I'll be back around one," she finally said. Then the back door opened and closed.

"Want to go outside and play with Emma?" George asked the kids.

"Yeah," they screamed in unison.

"Emma," George bellowed through the closed door, "do you mind taking the kids outside?"

"Be right there." I grabbed my fleece jacket and was greeted warmly by jumping, cheering kids.

The rest of my day was actually fairly pleasant. I kicked the soccer ball around in the postage-stamp backyard with Leyla and Jack. George and Carol's house was modest, puny compared to Sara's. The section of town we lived in was typical middle America, but compared to the Pleasantville of the rest of Weslyn, it might as well have been the other side of the tracks.

I rode my bike to the library while George and Carol took the kids to the movies. I spent the remainder of the afternoon hidden in the stacks, completing my assignments, or in the computer room, typing my English paper. I avoided human interaction at all cost, fearful of the reaction I'd receive on being seen. I finished with a few minutes to spare before I had to start home, so I called Sara from the pay phone.

"Hi!" she exclaimed, a little too overzealous for someone I had just seen the day before. "How are you calling me?"

"I'm at the library, on the pay phone."

"Oh! I'll be right there."

"No," I blurted before she could hang up the phone. "I'm leaving in a minute, but I wanted to prepare you for when you pick me up tomorrow."

"What happened?" Sara asked with concern, almost panic.

"I'm okay," I calmly assured her, trying to downplay her reaction. "I *fell* and hit my head, so I have a bandage and a little bruise. It's really no big deal."

"Emma! What did she do to you?!" Sara yelled, a mix of fear and anger in her voice.

"Nothing, Sara," I corrected. "I *fell.*"

"Sure you did," she said quietly. "Are you really okay?"

"Yeah, I'm okay. I have to go, but I'll see you in the morning."

"Okay," Sara replied reluctantly, before I hung up the phone.

8. BAD LUCK

I woke up to the same routine as any other morning, until I looked in the mirror—and was reminded that there was nothing routine about my life. I took in my nightmare of a hairstyle and knew there was no way I could get away with not washing and drying it. I was already going to draw attention—I didn't need to look like I'd slept on the streets as well.

My head still throbbed, but the golf ball had significantly reduced, now almost flush with my forehead. I was able to tolerate showering and brushing my hair, and my eyes only watered slightly when I dried it.

I thought maybe I'd be able to survive the day after all—until I slid into the car and Sara's jaw dropped. She didn't say anything to me, and I couldn't read her expression with her oversize sunglasses covering most of her face. She handed me a bottle of water and aspirin. Then again, maybe today was going to be one of the longest days of my life.

"Thank you," I said as I dumped a couple of pills in my hand and swallowed them down with several large gulps of water. I tried to act natural, despite the tension.

She barely glanced at me. I flipped the visor down to examine my cover-up in the mirror, trying to figure out what was making her so withdrawn. My bangs were swept across my forehead to conceal my bruise, and the bandages were barely noticeable under the fan of hair.

"Okay," I demanded. "Why aren't you talking or looking at me?"

"Emma," she breathed in exasperation, "look at you!"

"What?" I said defensively, glancing back up at the mirror. "I think I did a pretty good job of covering it up."

"That's what I mean." Her voice was shaky. It sounded like she was going to cry. "You should never have to cover anything up. I know you won't tell me what happened, but I know you didn't *fall*. Will you at least tell me what it was about?"

"What does it matter?" My voice was small, not anticipating the strength of her reaction. I wasn't expecting her to act like nothing happened, but I didn't want her to cry.

"It matters to me," she choked. I watched her blot her eyes with a tissue under her glasses.

"Sara, please don't cry," I pleaded. "I'm okay, I swear."

"How can you be okay with this? You aren't even angry."

"I've had the weekend to get past it," I admitted. "Besides, I don't want to be angry. I don't want to let her get to me. I'm not okay with this," I said, pointing to my head, "but what other choice do I have? I'll deal with it. So please don't cry. You're making me feel horrible."

"Sorry," she murmured.

We pulled into the parking lot, and she slid off her glasses, blotting her eyes while looking in the rearview mirror.

"I'm okay," she said, trying to produce a smile.

"How bad does it look? Be honest."

"You actually did a decent job hiding it," she admitted. "I'm having a hard time because I know the truth." And then again, she didn't know the half of it.

"If anyone says anything, because I know they will, tell them I slipped on the wet floor and hit my head on the coffee table." She rolled her eyes at my lie.

"What, do you have a better one?" I countered.

"No." She sighed. "Keep the aspirin. I know you'll need them."

"Ready?" I asked tentatively. I didn't like seeing Sara upset, especially over me. The anger and sadness were in complete contrast to her personality. It was uncomfortable to witness.

She released a heavy breath and nodded.

I received a few questions about my injury from some of my soccer teammates and other brave gossipers, but most people just stared. I should've been used to the stares after Friday's disaster. I wished I was invisible once again—or at least ignorant of the gossip that was always happening around me.

I found my way to English class without having to explain my *fall* to more than two or three people. I sat in my usual seat, pulling out my paper to pass in.

"Does it still hurt?" Evan asked from the chair next to mine. At that time, Brenda Pierce approached the seat she'd been sitting in since the first day of class and scowled to see it occupied. He smiled politely and shrugged.

"Well, there's one person who's not going to like you," I said wryly, trying to avoid the question.

"She'll get over it," Evan stated with little interest. "So, do you still have a headache?"

I drew my eyebrows together and reluctantly admitted, "I took some aspirin this morning. So, it's better, as long as I don't turn my head too quickly."

"That's good," he said casually. Though some people had asked what happened, no one had bothered with how I was feeling—until Evan.

"How was the rest of your weekend?" Evan whispered.

"Okay," I answered without looking over at him.

Ms. Abbott began with the class discussion, handing out our newest reading assignment after we passed in our papers. She also assigned us a short story and allowed us to begin reading it in class after she'd given us our writing assignment.

"Are we talking, or not?" Evan whispered when Ms. Abbott stepped out of the room.

"We are." I glanced at him, confused. "Why?"

"I can never figure you out. I want to make sure I'm on the same page today."

"I'm not much of a talker," I confessed, turning back to our assigned reading.

"I know." His answer drew my attention—he had that amused grin spread across his lips.

Not in the mood to inquire about his antagonizing grin, I didn't give him another glance for the remainder of class. I wasn't allowing myself to be dragged into the mystery that was Evan Mathews, not today. I just wanted to get through the day with as little attention paid to me as possible. I wished it could have been that easy.

Evan escorted me to Ms. Mier's Art class. He didn't try to talk to me, but he'd inspect me with a concerned flip of his eyes every so often as I walked blankly through the halls, not looking at him or anyone else. I had to sever my emotional cord to escape the anger and shame that silently slithered through my head, disconnecting myself from the stares and whispers that followed me down the hall.

"Today you are going to take a walk around the school property and snap pictures of scenes that inspire you for the calendar entry next month," Ms. Mier announced. "The final pieces will be displayed along the wall of the main entrance, where the students and faculty can view them. A vote will decide the twelve pieces to make the calendar. The artistic creation that has the most votes will also be the cover of the calendar. Does anyone have any questions?"

The class was silent. Ms. Mier asked a couple of students to pass out the cameras from the storage cabinet.

"Are you submitting an entry?" I asked Evan, who was standing behind me with his own camera in his hands. I glanced back to catch him raise his eyebrows, surprised to hear my voice.

"I'll submit a photograph."

"Please meet back in the class in forty minutes to return the cameras," Ms. Mier instructed.

The class emptied into the halls, heading toward the stairs that led to the back of the school. I opted to take the side stairs that led out to the football field and tennis courts.

"Do you mind if I come with you?" Evan asked from the top of the stairs. I looked up at him from the middle of my descent and shrugged. He followed me in silence.

When we exited, the cool air blew against my face. The refreshing breeze sent a chill through me, waking me from my stupor. Observing the brilliant colors of the foliage, I headed for the football field.

"Did your parents say anything when you came home soaked the other night?"

"They weren't around," he replied dismissively.

"Does that bother you—not having them around?" I asked the question without thinking, not expecting an honest answer, since it really was none of my business.

But he responded. "I've learned to cope. It was easier when my brother was still here. You live with your aunt and uncle, right?"

"Yup." I bent over to take a picture of the field through the fence, twisting the lens of the camera so it produced a blur of color. I stood up and continued toward the wooded area behind the bleachers.

"Not easy?" Evan asked casually, like he already knew the answer.

"No, not easy," I agreed. I wasn't finding the need to lie—yet. We were walking a delicate line of disclosure, without revealing too much.

"Tight reins?" Another question that sounded more like a statement.

"Definitely," I answered, still taking unfocused pictures of the green foliage mixed with hints of red and orange. "And you don't have any reins."

"I guess not."

The wind blew my hair from my face, and Evan winced. I flushed, realizing he hadn't noticed the bruise on my head until now.

"Prone to bad luck?" he asked, nodding to my head.

"Depends on where I am," I answered without answering. I tried to brush my hair back across my forehead with my fingers, concealing the purple reminder of my bad luck.

"How many brothers and sisters do you have?" I inquired, switching the focus back on him.

"Just the one brother, Jared. He's a freshman at Cornell. And you?"

"No brothers or sisters—just my two younger cousins. Is he anything like you?"

"Nothing. He's quiet, more musically inclined than athletically, and is really easygoing."

I smiled at the comparison. Evan smiled back, and my heart woke up from its two-day slumber.

He continued with the questions. "Where are you considering going for college?"

"Several schools in California mainly, along with a few others in the New York–Jersey area. I'd love to get into Stanford if they'll have me."

"I heard they were here watching your game Thursday."

I nodded, now focusing the camera on the brush and zooming in to capture the details of the fallen leaves.

"Where are you looking?"

"Cornell, obviously, but I have friends going to different schools in California, so I may head back. I have time to figure it out."

We continued our delicately balanced conversation until it was time to return to the classroom.

"You have a night game on Friday, right?" he confirmed as we climbed the stairs.

"Yes."

"What are you doing after school, before the game?"

"Probably staying at school and doing homework or whatever."

"Do you want to get something to eat?" he asked, hesitating on the landing before opening the double doors leading to the hall. I stopped, and so did my heart.

"And yes, this would be a date, so that we're clear," he stated with a smirk. I stopped breathing too.

"Okay." I exhaled, still unable to move. I really just agreed to go on a date?!

"Great," he said, producing a brilliant smile that caused my heart to catapult to life at such a frantic pace that it left me light-headed. "I'll see you in Trig." He continued down the hall past the art room.

I returned my camera to the supply closet and walked in a daze to my locker.

"What is that grin for?" I heard Sara ask from what sounded like a mile away. I brought her into focus, not realizing that I'd been grinning.

"I'll tell you later." The grin turned into a smile.

"I hate it when you say that," she groaned, but knew she didn't have time to interrogate me between classes. I grabbed my books and headed to Chemistry.

Class went by so slow. I took notes automatically and worked on the lab assignment with my chemistry partner. I kept looking at the clock to find that only five minutes had crept by. Finally, the bell rang.

"I hope you feel better," my partner said. My forehead crumpled. "You seemed kind of out of it today." I grinned, which only made her more confused.

When I arrived at my locker, Evan was waiting for me.

"Sorry, decided not to wait for you in class," he explained with a grin.

Sara walked up to her locker. "Hi, Evan." She gave me a suspicious look from behind his back. I looked into my locker, pressing my lips together to fight the urge to smile.

"Can you tell me what you're allowed to do?" Evan asked as he walked alongside me.

"Not much," I answered seriously, my grin deflating.

"But you can do anything that involves school, right?" he confirmed, trying to put the pieces together.

"Pretty much. As long as I have a ride and am home before ten o'clock."

"Would they know if you weren't doing the school thing that you said you were doing but still followed the ten o'clock rule?"

I sank onto my seat with my stomach in my chest. I could guess where he was going, and it was a place I was too afraid to even consider.

"I don't know. Why?" I tightened my eyes to try to read his thoughts.

"Just wondering," he said, still thinking. My attention was snapped to the front of the room when as we were asked to pass our homework forward.

Evan continued with the inquisition on our way to Anatomy. "Have you ever purposely done something you knew you weren't supposed to do?"

"Like what?" Again, not liking this line of questioning.

"Like sneaking out of the house, or saying you're at the library but going to the movies instead?" I looked at him with wide eyes. I swallowed the lump lodged in my throat at the thought of it.

"I guess not," he concluded by my speechlessness, and probably audible gulping.

"What are you thinking?" I finally asked.

"I'm just trying to figure this out."

"What out?"

"Us," he said as he entered the classroom and took his usual seat.

I stumbled to my seat, not breathing again. He was so confusing. I wished I had warnings when he was going to say things like that.

"Mr. Mathews," Mr. Hodges instructed, "would you please join Ms. Thomas at her table? It appears her partner is no longer in this class, and there is no point in having two single tables, especially when we have our dissection labs."

Upon hearing this announcement, I stared down at the black surface of the table to conceal the blood that was rushing to my face.

Evan sat next to me and said, "Hi," like he was introducing himself to me for the first time.

I released a blushing smile and quietly replied, "Hi."

After Mr. Hodges began his lecture on the bones in the hand, I scribbled on a blank piece of paper, *Are you already assuming there's an us?*

Evan wrote in response, NOT YET.

I still didn't understand what that meant and drew my eyebrows together, so he wrote, I'M GETTING READY FOR WHEN THERE IS.

My heart felt heavy, as if it had just fainted. There was a huge grin on Evan's face. I wasn't as amused. His questions and comments were making me dizzy. I tucked the paper in the back of my folder and stared at my notes, trying to conceal my bright red cheeks with my hair.

"See you later," Evan said after class as he walked away. I was left looking after him, baffled. I knew there was a motive behind his line of questioning and the insane statements that followed, but I was so lost.

Sara was waiting for me, leaning against our lockers when I arrived. I opened my locker to return my books without saying anything. I knew what she was expecting.

"Do not do this to me," she demanded impatiently.

I attempted to redirect her attention. "How was your date with Jason this weekend?"

"Not this time you don't," she scolded, still way too serious for Sara. "We'll get to me later—talk."

I paused, trying to digest what I was about to tell her.

"We're going on a date after school on Friday, before our soccer game. We're getting something to eat," I confided. I wasn't sure what else to say.

"Wow," she responded with a smile that made me flush with color once again. "That's really great. I really like this, Em. I have a good feeling about him."

"I'm glad *you* think so."

She flashed her eyes toward me, not understanding my reaction.

"I still don't get him, Sara," I admitted with a heavy sigh as we trod downstairs to the cafeteria. "He asks these questions and makes these cryptic remarks. I feel like I'm trying to read between the lines, but I'm still coming up blank. And then when I have an opportunity to ask him what he means, he disappears."

"I know he's been collecting his surveys from people and has a couple more interviews for the article that's due tomorrow. He's interviewing me at the beginning of Journalism. Maybe that's where he keeps disappearing to."

"I'm not really worried about where he's going," I corrected, knowing she was trying to put me at ease. "He always leaves just after he makes some remark or asks a question that I need him to explain. That's what's driving me crazy."

"Like what?" she inquired.

"I don't even know where to start."

"Do you like him?" We pulled the chairs out at our table in the back corner of the caf.

"I'm still trying to figure him out. But I'm getting used to being with him in class and walking down the halls together. I don't have the urge to push him away like I did before. So maybe he's wearing me down."

"Or maybe you like him," Sara countered with a devious smirk.

Before I could answer, Jason approached our table with a tray of food.

"Hey, Sara," he greeted, hesitating before sitting next to her.

"Hello, Jason." She beamed, shifting in her chair to face him. I suddenly felt like I was witnessing something that wasn't meant for a third pair of eyes.

"I'm going to get something to eat," I announced to ears that were deaf to my voice.

On my way back to the table with my lunch, I caught Sara and Jason smiling absurdly at each other. I hoped I didn't look at Evan that way. I'd feel like an idiot if that's what everyone saw whenever he was around me—although it looked nauseatingly adorable between Jason and Sara. The excessive flirting was enough to deter me from returning to the table, so I went to the Journalism classroom instead to get a head start on my article.

Since the class was in the computer lab, no one came into the room besides Ms. Holt, who grabbed some things from her desk and checked on my progress. She didn't have a class after Journalism, so I stayed during Study as well. I buried myself in my homework to avoid thinking about Sara's reaction that morning or Evan's persistent interest. But my mind drifted toward those unavoidable thoughts anyway.

I was overwhelmed by the whirlwind that had forced its way in, turning everything upside down in such a short amount of time. I was losing control, and it was making me panic. I was having a hard time staying focused on what had always come so naturally before. The end was within sight, and I couldn't jeopardize everything and let it all slip away now.

If I was going to make it to college in one piece, I had to avoid panic-inducing situations like the party—or anything else that distracted me, for that matter. That included...dating. My heart sank in my chest at this realization. But I knew it was what I had to do. I had too much to lose.

"There you are," Evan declared as he entered the room. "I was wondering where you've been."

"Hi," I responded, looking down at the keyboard.

"It's definitely quieter in here," he observed, then noticed my avoidance. "What's going on?"

"I can't go on a date with you," I blurted in a rush. "I need to stay focused on school and my responsibilities. I can't afford distractions. I'm sorry."

"I'm a distraction?" he asked in bewilderment.

"Well...yes, you are. The fact that I think about you at all is a distraction, and I can't commit myself to any more extracurriculars." That came out way worse than it did in my head.

"Are you comparing our date to Art club?" I couldn't tell if he found it insulting or amusing.

"No." I sighed in frustration. "Evan, I'm not good at this. I've honestly never been on a date in my life, and I'm just not ready. I said it. Is that good enough for you?" My faced turned crimson with the spontaneous confession. I continued to reveal too much to him, and that was a part of the control I needed back. There was too much he couldn't know, and I couldn't keep slipping up.

He tried poorly to suppress his signature grin. I grunted in annoyance and threw a paperback book at him from atop my pile.

"I always bring out the best in you, don't I?" He released a short laugh as he avoided my throw. "Okay, no date. But we can still hang out, right?"

"As long as you promise not to ask me on a date, mention *us* as if we were an entity, and no comments about sweaters," I insisted. I realized my demands were ridiculous, but it was what my insubordinate heart would need to survive a friendship with Evan Mathews.

"Okay, I think." He nodded slowly. "But you're still talking to me, and I can sit next to you in class and even walk with you in the halls, right?"

"Sure," I replied after hesitating.

"Can we hang out outside of school?" he pushed.

"When would we possibly do something after school?"

"Friday—no date, I promise. But you can come over after school, and we can hang out before the game," he suggested. "We can even do homework if you prefer."

I examined him with narrowed eyes, trying to decide if he was serious. More importantly, I needed to decide if I could handle the offer. A small voice was screaming at me to say no, but I didn't listen.

"Alright," I conceded. "But just as friends."

"I can do that," he replied with a mischievous grin. "For now."

"Evan!"

"Kidding!" He held up his hands in defense. "I can be friends with you—no problem."

The bell rang declaring the end of the day, and the halls started to fill with the voices and footsteps of students anxious to leave.

"Good luck in your game today," I said, gathering my books.

"Thanks," he replied. "I'll see you tomorrow in English?"

"I'll be there."

He smiled as he walked away.

I remained in the seat, absorbing the results of my attempt to put my life back in order. It hadn't gone exactly as I planned. I was supposed to cut him out completely, and a part of me was furious that I hadn't. I knew I was taking a big risk involving someone else in my life. I tried to convince myself that I could be friends with him, not allowing him to get too close, while still remaining focused on school. But I wasn't as confident as I should have been.

I fell back into my routine for the remainder of the day. My head hurt from running around during soccer practice, but I got through it. Sara was gushing about Jason and her date, so I was convinced that she was over the emotional trauma from earlier that morning.

The rest of the week fell into a familiar pattern as well. The only difference was that most of my classes, along with my journeys to them, included Evan. He respected my reserved disposition, keeping conversation within the boundaries of school topics. I continued breathing and my heart kept beating, although at times it still acted insane and sped up at the sight of one of his mesmerizing smiles—or when he'd look into my eyes a little too long. But even that I could push into the pocket of acceptance. I had my safe place back, and that helped when I had to cross the threshold of instability at home.

I avoided Carol as much as possible, although her slicing tongue always found an insult to carve into me every time she saw me. I had an away game on Tuesday and worked on the newspaper layout on Wednesday, so I was able to stay away until after dinner. On Wednesday night I even felt brave enough to sneak into the fridge at two o'clock in the morning to take a filet of cold breaded chicken back to my room to quiet my rebelling stomach. I was back to focusing on surviving the next six hundred and sixty-seven days however I could.

9. NOT A DATE

The grey skies did little to quash my excitement for the night game when I left for school Friday morning. It was also the day I was spending the afternoon with Evan. The thought of being alone with him shot a current of thrilling terror throughout my body. What a strange contradiction of emotions: feeling exhilarated and terrified at the same time.

I double-checked the calendar on my way out to make certain my game was written on it. If it wasn't on the calendar with plenty of notice, then I wasn't allowed to do it. That included going to the library, which I marked for every Sunday afternoon. I was surprised I didn't have a tracking device inserted into my heel—but that would mean spending money on me, and that was laughable.

"Good morning," I almost sang when I entered the car.

"Good morning," Sara replied, looking at me curiously. She began to say something, then thought better of it. Instead, she turned up the radio and we drove off to the drumbeats, guitar riffs and angst of a singer bellowing about being misunderstood. I let the music soak in with a grin on my face.

"Are you still going to Evan's after school?" Sara asked, turning down the music.

"As far as I know," I replied, trying to sound casual, like it wasn't the only thing I could think about.

"Then I'll see you at the game tonight."

"I'll see you in Study, right?"

"I have a note from my parents allowing me to get out early. I'm going to Jill's house for the afternoon. You could probably get out early too if you wanted. The study-period teachers don't always expect you there since you work on the paper or whatever."

The thought of breaking the rules and leaving school early without permission made my stomach turn. Or perhaps it was the thought of spending an additional hour with Evan.

Sara eyed my distressed expression. "It was just a suggestion; you don't have to do it."

"I'll think about it," I muttered. Another surge of thrilling terror flashed through my body with a shiver.

"I expect details," Sara called over her shoulder upon exiting homeroom. She was about to continue to class when she noticed the dazed look on my face and stopped. "Are you nervous?"

"I'm pretty freaked," I whispered, oblivious to the buzz of bodies passing us.

"You have nothing to worry about. You made it clear you just want to be friends. But if you're really that afraid to be alone with him, I could give you an excuse to bail."

"No, I want to hang out with him. It's just something I've never done before, and I'm not sure what to expect. It's not like hanging out with you."

"Why don't you pretend that it is?" Sara gave me an encouraging smile. "Details," she repeated as she walked toward the stairs.

Evan was seated in English when I slipped into the desk next to him.

"Hi," he said, his mouth twitching, trying not to smile.

"Hey," I returned, without looking over at him.

"Do you want to skip study period and get out of school early?" My heart stopped as a million excuses not to leave ran through my head.

"Sure," I heard my mouth say, glancing at him quickly. Panic overtook my body. I'd never broken the rules before. I fumbled with my notebook and pulled out the completed assignment to pass in. I thought I noticed Evan smiling out of the corner of my eye, but I stared intently at my notes.

"You're quieter than usual today," he observed after the bell rang, as we gathered our books to leave.

"Distracted by the back-to-back tests later," I lied. I wasn't truly concerned about the tests awaiting us in Trigonometry and Anatomy. I'd studied the test material and was pretty confident that I knew it inside and out. Why couldn't I be as confident about everything else?

"I wouldn't have expected you to be nervous." He knew me better than I wanted to admit.

"It was a lot to study. You're not worried?" I asked, trying to deflect the attention.

"Why should I be? I've studied; there's nothing else I can do." Great, he was confident in school *and* everything else. "I'll see you in Trig."

History, Chemistry, and my two tests distracted me enough to keep from completely obsessing about the end of the day and being alone with Evan—until it was unavoidable.

"How'd you do?" Evan asked as we walked out of Anatomy.

"I think I knew what I was doing," I admitted. "And you?"

"I got through it," he said with a shrug.

I noticed he was walking with me instead of going in the opposite direction, as he usually did.

"Where are you going?"

"To your locker," he stated bluntly.

"Why?" I asked, not catching on.

"What? You don't want to have lunch with me?" He sounded almost offended, but then again, I knew him better than that and dismissed the possibility.

"You never have lunch with me, I don't get it."

"There's a first for everything. Sara left to go to Jill's, so I thought you could use the company."

"That's right," I remembered. "I'm actually not that hungry. I was going to pick up something small and get started in the art room."

"Would you prefer to be alone?"

"Doesn't matter to me; do what you want." I shrugged, attempting to sound disinterested.

"That's not possible," he responded casually. I narrowed my eyes, trying to read between the lines. Before I could demand an explanation, he asked, "Will you ignore me if I have lunch with you in the Art room?"

"I don't have to." How was I possibly going to survive the afternoon with him? Maybe I should make up an excuse and stay at school instead. My heart skipped at the thought of bailing. I could be friends with him—I just had to keep reminding myself that's what I wanted.

I placed my books in my locker, and Evan slipped his books on the top shelf as well. My mouth dropped in disbelief.

"What?!" he said defensively. "We're leaving together after Art. I'll take them out. I promise." We walked in silence to the cafeteria.

Before we entered, he said quietly, "You know that the latest rumor is that you and I are dating, right?" I stopped to stare at him with wide eyes, my arms crossed.

"It's just a rumor!" he said with his hands in the air and a half smile that made me fume.

"Do you really want me to come over today?" I snapped.

"Of course," he answered eagerly.

"Then don't share things like that with me. Remember, I don't want to know what people are saying about me."

"I didn't realize our friendship had rules," he replied, grinning.

"I'll be sure to point them out when you don't follow them. Try to keep up." I was hoping to sound severe, but he continued grinning at my reprimand. I huffed and walked into the cafeteria at an exaggerated pace.

"Are you this strict with all of your other friends?" he inquired with a chuckle while keeping up with me.

"Sara is my only other friend, and she plays by the rules. She doesn't need lessons." I glared at him so he'd take me seriously, but he still seemed more entertained than offended.

"All you're getting is a granola bar and an apple?" He nodded toward the food in my hands as we made our way through the lunch line.

"I told you I wasn't very hungry. Besides, aren't we eating in a few hours?"

"Yeah, but you're an athlete, and you have a game tonight—you need more sustenance than that." He almost sounded concerned.

"Fine." I caved and grabbed a banana. Evan eyed me disapprovingly, shaking his head.

"So much better," he commented with sarcasm.

I walked away, leaving him to catch up after he bought his lunch.

When we entered the art room, he settled on the stool next to me to eat while I gathered my project, which currently consisted of shades of green sweeping along the bottom of the predominantly blank canvas. I removed the picture of the early October foliage taped to the back and set it on the table next to me.

"Are you having a hard time liking me?"

I figured he was messing with me until I turned on my stool to find that he looked seriously concerned.

"I'm not having a hard time liking you," I assured him. "I don't understand you. You say things that don't make sense or could mean more than they do. I'm trying not to let you get to me—that's all." I turned back to my painting and began squirting different shades of green on the palette.

"But I get to you?" he confirmed, his signature grin creeping on his face. I rolled my eyes.

"Not if I can help it. But enjoying my discomfort is always a great way to win me over," I retorted, flashing my eyes at him.

"Sorry," he said with an insincere smile.

"I'm sure you are," I huffed. I proceeded to mix colors and apply them to the canvas in blotches and heavy strokes. I concentrated on painting while he sat behind me, silently watching. Flustered by his presence, I couldn't summon anything to say to lighten the awkwardness, so I kept my back to him.

"I think I'll go outside and work on my assignment," he finally announced. "I'll meet you at your locker after class."

"Okay," I answered without looking. After he left the room, I put down my brush and took a deep breath. He *was* getting to me, and my defensive retorts bothered me, despite how much they appeared to amuse him. I made the conscious decision to be friends with him—that I could handle it. So far, I was failing miserably, trying so hard to keep him at a distance that I was practically cruel. If I kept this up, he'd probably decide not to have anything to do with me at all—and I wouldn't blame him.

Evan was waiting for me at my locker after class, as he'd promised.

"Hi," I said with a gentle smile, hoping he wasn't regretting inviting me over.

"Hi." He smiled back.

"Come back for more punishment?" I asked quietly, leaning against the locker to face him. I kept glancing at the ground, having a hard time looking him in the eye.

"I can handle it." He tilted his head down, forcing me to look into his riveting blue eyes. "Besides, I'm getting used to your reactions, so they don't really bother me. You can actually be pretty funny." His lips relaxed into a vibrant smile.

"Great, here I am feeling horrible for how I've talked to you, and you think it's hilarious. I guess you bring out the best in me, don't you?" I jeered, turning toward my locker.

"That's why I'm here," he murmured in my ear. I froze.

I inhaled quickly when his shirt brushed against my back as he reached over my head to grab his books. My heart began its ritualistic dance in my chest, sending a surge of blood to my cheeks. I closed my eyes and slowly let out the captured breath when he backed away.

"I just have to get a few things from my locker before we go, okay?"

"Sure," I whispered, still distracted.

The halls were vacant when we walked to Evan's locker so he could stuff a few books into his backpack. I was relieved not to have witnesses when we left together. I really didn't want to fuel the gossip—or get caught skipping class, even if it was just study period.

I looked around nervously as we exited the school, expecting a voice to stop us and ask where we were going. But nobody stopped us. We didn't say anything as we walked to his car under the stubbornly grey sky. Evan held the car door open for me again, a gesture that still caught me off guard. "This should be an interesting game in the mud tonight, huh?" he noted as he started the car.

"It slows the game down," I admitted, "but I actually like sliding in the mud."

"I know what you mean."

I relaxed into the leather seat as we talked the entire ride to his house. My guarded tension was finally melting away by the time we pulled into his driveway.

Evan lived in one of the historic homes in the center of town. The extended driveway pulled the white farmhouse with black shutters away from the road, revealing a perfectly manicured front lawn with a large maple tree that was turning a magnificent red. A wide porch wrapped around the house, accented with white rocking chairs and a hammock—a three-dimensional Norman Rockwell painting. At the end of the driveway, behind the house, a two-story barn had been converted into a garage. Beyond was an expansive field surrounded by trees, without a neighboring house in sight.

We entered through a door on the side of the porch that led into the kitchen. The house may have been historic, but the big eat-in kitchen had every modern amenity. The space still held a rustic farmhouse charm, with exposed beams and rough plank walls stained a warm brown.

"Do you want something to drink? I have soda, water, juice, and iced tea," Evan said after placing his backpack on a chair. A peninsula separated the cooking space from the dining area, which was sunken into the floor, with three long steps leading to a large dark-wood dining table.

"Iced tea would be great." I sat in a chair along the peninsula while he filled two glasses with iced tea from a glass pitcher he removed from the refrigerator.

"I like how you set up the newspaper," he said, handing me my drink over the counter. "The paper at my other school was rougher-looking, since the printing was done in-house. It was more of a flyer than a newspaper. The *Weslyn High Times* actually resembles a newspaper."

"Thanks. Have you received any comments about your article—you know, since it made the first page?"

"Yeah, I have," he admitted with a grin—knowing that was the only acknowledgment he'd get from me that it was a well-written article. "Mostly questions about my sources, trying to pair up an insecurity with a person. It's kind of annoying, but I should've expected it."

After a moment, he added, "I never did get to interview you. I thought it would be a conflict of interest."

"I don't think I would have let you interview me," I replied. "But if I had, what would you have asked?" As soon as I said it, I regretted it. What was I thinking putting myself out there? Telling Evan my physical insecurities was not on the top of my list.

"Name one part of your body you're insecure about. How would you change it?" His expression was calm and attentive, which surprised me. I thought this topic would definitely have evoked one of his wide smiles.

I hesitated.

"Okay, I'll tell you mine first, if that'll help," he offered, still serious.

"You're insecure about your body?" I scoffed.

"I hate the size of my feet. They're huge," he confessed.

"Your feet? What size are they?"

"Fourteen, and the average size is ten. It's not easy finding shoes I like that fit." Oddly enough, he remained genuine.

"I can honestly say I've never noticed, maybe because you're tall. Or maybe because your feet are not what most people look at." I realized, with a blush, that I shouldn't have made a comment that he could misinterpret.

"Really?" he grinned, confirming my fear.

"You know what I mean," I retorted, my whole face reddening.

"What's yours?" he prodded.

"My lips," I admitted cautiously. "I've always wanted them to be smaller. I've even practiced tucking them in, in front of the mirror." Revealing more than I intended, as usual.

"Really? I love your full lips," he said without hesitating. "They're perfect k—"

"Don't say it," I shot back at him, turning redder by the second.

"Why?" There was a crease between his brows.

"Do you want to be friends with me?"

"Yes," he answered quickly.

"Then you can't say things like that. It's one of the lines you don't cross. Remember the rules I set if we're going to be friends? You are not playing by the rules," I explained firmly, hoping this time he'd take me seriously.

"What if I don't want to be friends with you?" he challenged, grinning again, staring directly into my eyes. Obviously taking me seriously was an impossibility for Evan.

Despite not being able to breathe, I connected with his taunting gaze and refused to look away. "Then we won't be friends," I said flatly.

"What if I want to be more than friends?" He grinned wider, leaning his forearms on the counter, shortening the distance between us.

"Then we won't be anything at all." Now not only could I not breathe but my heart had stopped as well, making it harder to keep up my defiant stare when he leaned in closer; but I was determined not to back down.

"Okay, then friends we are," he declared, suddenly standing up straight, taking a gulp of iced tea. "Can you play pool?" I couldn't say anything for a few seconds—my head was spinning as I tried to reel my heart back from across the counter.

"I've never tried," I floundered.

I took a deep breath to clear my head before I stood up. Evan was waiting for me patiently, holding the door open.

We entered the large white barn through a side door and walked into a space that could easily fit two cars. A door to the right of the stairs led to another unrevealed area.

Hung on the opposite wall were shelves displaying tools and other typical garage items. But what caught my eye was the recreational equipment stored beneath the stairs. There were snowshoes, skis, two surfboards, a couple of wakeboards and everything in between. There were bins of basketballs, soccer balls, volleyballs—it looked like a sporting goods store.

"Can't say you're bored," I commented as we climbed the stairs. He let out a short laugh.

I followed him into a full rec room. Along the far wall was a dark wooden bar with a flat stone top, fully stocked and furnished with matching stools. There was an oversize dark brown leather couch and recliner set in front of a large flat-screen television on the wall to the left. Abandoned on the floor were several video-game components and corresponding gear. I wondered if all of the wealthy kids at Weslyn High had setups like Sara's and Evan's.

A pool table lit by suspended chrome canisters stood on one side of the room, with plenty of space to maneuver a pool stick without bumping into a wall. A dartboard hung on the wall to the right of the door, and to the left were two foosball tables. There was another closed door behind the tables. The deep red walls and the exposed wooden beams along the pitched ceiling lent the room a masculine vibe that was accentuated with framed rock-concert posters, showcasing a variety of bands over a span of a few decades.

"This is my mom's way of trying to get my brother to come home more," Evan explained as he crossed the room toward the bar. "So this room is more for him than me. My stuff is in the other room." He nodded toward the closed door.

Music erupted through strategically placed speakers when Evan turned a sound system on from behind the bar. He lowered the volume so that we could hear each other.

"I've never heard this band before," I remarked, listening to the reggae-influenced rock band. "I like it."

"I saw them at a concert in San Francisco and really liked them. If you give me your iPod, I can download them for you."

"Sure."

"Darts first?" he suggested, heading to the corner where the dartboard hung. I sat on one of the stools dispersed along the dark wooden bar running the length of the wall while he pulled out the darts.

"I think I've only played once before, and I sucked," I warned. He handed me three darts with silver metallic wings, keeping the darts with the black wings. He stood behind a black line painted on the dark hardwood floor and threw each dart with ease. He made it look so simple, but I wasn't convinced.

"We'll warm up first and then go from there." I approached the line, and he demonstrated how to hold the dart for the best control. I attempted to followed his example. "Getting used to the weight of the dart is the hardest part, to determine the angle and speed you want to throw it. Then aim, and toss with a quick, steady hand." He threw the dart firmly, and it stuck easily into its intended target.

"You may not want to be anywhere around me when I attempt this," I advised him. He smiled and sat on a stool, giving me my space. My first shot was weak. I missed the dartboard completely. The dart landed low, embedded in a black board that covered the length of the wall behind the circle.

"Oops, sorry," I said, scrunching my face. This was going to be a long game, especially if I couldn't even make the board.

"That's what the black board's for. You're not the first, and won't be the last, to miss," Evan assured me. "We won't play an actual game until you feel comfortable. Try it again." I threw the last dart with a little more force and it hit the number 20—not in the points area, but the actual number.

"Well, at least I hit the board," I said optimistically. Evan smiled and retrieved the darts.

We threw three more rounds until I was consistently hitting within the colored ring. Not exactly the areas I was aiming for, but I was getting closer. Even with all of my near misses and extreme misses, I wasn't self-conscious about my lack of dart experience. Evan made it easy with his patience and advice. I was actually enjoying myself.

We played a round of cricket. I made Evan take two steps back from the line, in attempt to make it slightly more even. He still won—it wasn't even close. During the game, we talked about sports and what we'd tried or, in my case, never tried.

"So you're great at everything, huh?" I confirmed, after he shared surfing and kiteboarding experiences he'd had in different parts of the world.

"No, I'll try just about anything, but I'm only really good at a few things. My brother's better at pool and darts than I am. I'm decent at soccer, but I'm not the best player—the same with basketball. I think I'm best at baseball. I have a consistent swing and pretty good reaction time at shortstop.

"I bet if you were exposed to more experiences, you'd find you're better than I am at most of them. You're definitely a better soccer player. I haven't seen you play basketball, but I heard you have an impressive outside shot." The heat made itself known across my cheeks as he spoke of my athletic abilities.

"I love soccer, I really like basketball, and I run track just for something to do in the spring. Since I play a sport, I don't have to take Gym, so I haven't attempted anything else for a long time. I'm not sure how I'd do."

"Do you want to find out?"

"What are you thinking?" I asked cautiously.

"Tomorrow I'll meet you at the library, and then we'll go from there." My stomach twisted at the thought of lying. "Or maybe not," he corrected after observing my pale face.

"I can't tomorrow," I said quietly, but before I realized what I was about to say, I finished with, "but I could on Sunday." Evan's eyes lit up. My heart leapt into its high-speed patter.

"Really?" he asked, not convinced.

"Sure," I confirmed with a smile. "What did you have in mind?"

"Batting cages?"

"Why not," I replied with a shrug.

"Noon?"

"Noonish."

"Great." His full-fledged smile left me light-headed with the rush of blood to my face. "Ready to eat? You must be after that sad lunch."

"I could eat," I said casually, ignoring his antagonizing remark as he turned off the music.

I watched from a stool at the peninsula in the kitchen while he pulled items from the refrigerator and cabinets and started cutting up celery, mushrooms, chicken and pineapple.

"What are you making?" I asked, not anticipating the huge production. I'd expected something from the typical food groups of pizza and subs.

"Chicken and pineapple stir-fry," he replied. "Sorry, I didn't ask you if you were a picky eater. Is this okay?"

"Sure," I said slowly. "You cook?" I didn't know why I was so surprised. I should have been used to the unpredictability of Evan Mathews, but I still couldn't help but follow in amazement as he measured, mixed and chopped with ease.

"I have to fend for myself a lot, so, yeah, I cook," he explained without looking at me. "You don't, I take it?"

"Not since eighth-grade Home Ec."

"Huh, that actually surprises me." He didn't say anything more, and I wasn't about to try to explain the rules of Carol and George's kitchen.

"Can I ask you something?" I blurted, without really thinking through what I was about to say. This was becoming a habit that was causing my heart and head more distress than I could handle.

Whenever I was with Evan I found myself revealing, asking and agreeing to things that were sending my brain into shock.

"Go for it." Evan stopped what he was doing to lean his back against the counter, still holding the knife in his hand.

"Do you always get what you want?" He looked at me with uncertainty, so I attempted to clarify. "I mean, are you as forward with everyone as you are with me?"

He chuckled, not the answer I was looking for.

Evan paused long enough to make me wish I hadn't asked the question. He smiled before he replied, "No. Normal girls wouldn't be able to handle it. They tend to respond better to subtlety and flirting. I know that whatever I say to any other girl would be passed on to her friends and eventually to the rest of the school, so direct doesn't work in most situations. But this is not most situations, and you are far from any other girl." He turned to continue his preparation.

His answer left me baffled. If this was direct, then I would hate to be a normal girl, because I had no idea what he meant by half of what he just said. I decided not to even attempt to understand it, fearing it would only make me more confused.

"Okay," he said, still with his back to me as he dumped the contents of the cutting board in the wok on the stove, "I have a question for you." Now look what I started—I sighed and braced myself.

"How come you've never been on a date?" Evan turned to look at me, anticipating my answer.

"Why would I?" was the first thing that came out of my mouth.

He laughed and went back to tossing the contents of the wok. "I wasn't expecting that," he said with a smile. I shrugged, fiddling with a string on my sweater. I had to change the subject, but I was coming up blank.

"Have you ever been kissed?" he asked suddenly. My face flashed with the familiar warmth as my mouth dropped open.

"Well, that was *definitely* direct," I accused. "And I don't think I'm going to answer that question."

"You have," he concluded, glancing back at me with a smirk. "Good to know."

"Let's change the subject," I insisted as the heat on my face spread to my ears. "Where was your favorite place to live?"

He didn't respond.

"Evan?"

"What? Sorry, I didn't hear the question," he confessed, absently pushing around the ingredients sizzling in the wok. "I was trying to figure out if I know who the guy is. But if it was someone from school, I'm sure I would have found out by now. Is he in college?" He leaned against the counter to examine me, trying to pluck the answer from the mortified expression on my face.

"You're forgetting The Line," I reminded him with wide eyes.

"What? This isn't about you and me," he said in defense. "I thought friends shared this kind of stuff. I'll tell you who my first kiss was, if that will make you feel better."

"No, not really," I stated emphatically. "I'm not interested, and I'm not going to answer your question about my private experiences. We're not that good of friends."

"But you have been kissed—I was right, wasn't I?"

I gaped. "So? What does it matter if I've been kissed?"

"But you've never been on a date," he mused, like it was a mystery he was attempting to solve. If he thought that the answer was going to reveal something surprising, he was definitely going to be disappointed. He set two filled plates on the counter.

"This is really good," I said after taking a bite, anxious to change the subject. But I wasn't being dishonest, the stir-fry *was* good. I wasn't sure I liked continuing to find things about Evan that impressed me.

"Thanks," he said absently, still thinking about my responses.

"Can we please move past this?" I pleaded.

"Sure, but you'll tell me eventually."

"I don't understand why you want to know." I realized, after I spoke, that I was feeding into the same topic I was trying so hard to get away from.

"I'm still trying to figure you out."

"There's nothing to figure out. I'm not that interesting." Evan didn't respond. He looked down with his mischievous grin and pierced a piece of chicken with his fork.

As we ate, I was finally able to redirect the conversation toward different places he had lived. He described each country or city and what he liked and didn't like about it. I breathed easier, having escaped the ever too-revealing inquiries into my personal life. I helped with the dishes while we continued talking about a skiing trip he'd gone on with his brother in Switzerland a couple of winters ago. I was enthralled by his travel stories and the many experiences he'd had in only seventeen years, especially in contrast to my sheltered life within the confines of New England.

"Do you have your license?" Evan asked as we sat back at the counter.

"No, I don't have my permit yet," I admitted.

"How old are you?"

"Sixteen."

"You're sixteen?" He seemed surprised.

"Oh, something you didn't know about me?" I taunted. "I skipped a grade early in elementary school. My birthday's in June, but I've been too busy to get my permit and take classes."

This, of course, was a complete lie. In order to get my permit, my guardian was required to take two hours of parent classes—that was never going to happen. Carol and George weren't burdened with having to drive me from place to place—so why would they care if I had my license? Besides, what good was a license if I couldn't afford a car?

"Do you know how to drive?"

"Sara's tried to teach me the basics in empty parking lots. She wants to take me on the road, but I'd die if anything happened to her car. If we ever got caught and she lost her license, it would suck for both of us."

"Does she have an automatic or manual?"

"Automatic."

"I'm surprised that her car's an automatic. Want to learn to drive a stick?"

"Not today," I replied bluntly.

"A library day," he determined with a grin.

"Maybe," I said hesitantly. How many of these library days was he planning? The thought of getting caught made my stomach hurt. It was bad enough I had agreed to go to the batting cages on Sunday. There was no way I could risk more excursions.

"Do you want to give me your iPod, and I'll download that band for you?"

"It'll be hard to be without it for the weekend, or actually even for the game today." I reached in my backpack, trying to decide if I should give it to him.

"You can borrow mine," he offered without hesitating. Trading personal property already? This simple gesture felt so much bigger than just exchanging music. Or perhaps I was reading too much into it. *Relax.* It was just music.

"Okay." I handed him my lime green player in exchange for his black one. It may have been just music, but my heart was pounding so hard it might as well have been a ring.

"I should get ready for the game. Can you show me where the bathroom is so I can change?"

"Sure."

I followed him into a soft yellow room that was elegantly furnished with a Victorian-style couch and chair set, upholstered in light blue velvet and framed with carved white wood. A small but stunning crystal chandelier was suspended above the antique coffee table. I looked across at the picture window, which allowed a full view of the front yard. The room opened up into a receiving area at the main entrance with a small table against the wall, where a colorful arrangement of flowers was set next to a picture of four people, who I presumed to be the Mathews family.

"The light switch is inside on the right," Evan explained when we stopped at a door along the long hallway, leading away from the elegant sitting room. "I'll be in the kitchen."

"Thanks," I replied, before closing the door. I collapsed against it, looking at the girl in the mirror smiling back at me with flushed cheeks. She looked…happy.

10. NIGHT GAME

When we pulled into the parking lot at the school, I assumed Evan would drop me off and come back later for the varsity game. The junior varsity team didn't draw many spectators besides their parents. But he shut off the car and proceeded to get out.

"You're staying?" I asked, grabbing my bags from his car.

"Is that okay?"

"Sure," I replied. "There aren't a lot of people here, but it's up to you."

"Can I sit with you and Sara?"

"We usually sit with the team, but I don't see why you can't. I have to warn you, I listen to music to block everyone out so that I can get focused. I'm not going to talk to you."

"That's fine. I'll find something good for you to listen to." He took the iPod from my hands and started scrolling through the music selections.

"Hey, Sara," I called when we neared the first row of the bleachers. With her attention on the game and talking to one of the girls, she hadn't noticed us approaching.

"Hi," she exclaimed excitedly when she caught sight of me. "How did—" Then she noticed Evan, and her question turned into a smile that lingered a little too long. I knew she had a thousand questions about my afternoon, so I was relieved that Evan was here, allowing me to avoid them until the drive home. "Hi, Evan," she said warmly.

Evan sat next to Sara so that they could talk, and I zoned them out while listening to my—well, Evan's—music. He'd selected a band I was familiar with, allowing me to get lost in the high-energy beats while I silently watched the game on the field. I didn't look over at Evan or Sara and kept the volume up so I couldn't hear them.

The bleachers started to fill with the remaining members of the varsity team as the first half of the game came to an end. They'd acknowledge me with a wave, and I'd nod back in recognition. My teammates were familiar with my ritual and didn't bother trying to interact.

Every so often, Evan would reach into my jacket pocket and pull out the iPod to find another selection of songs. When his hand first entered my pocket, my heart faltered—actually, so did my breathing. Once I realized what he was doing, I continued to ignore him and watched the movement in front of me.

The junior varsity teams were having difficulty moving the ball due to the saturated field and the divots created by the last football game. Grass flew, cleats were caught in the grass and bodies slid in the mud. The mist had ended by the end of the first half, but the damage was done.

When the JV game concluded with the Weslyn girls losing 2 to 1, the varsity players gathered on the track to prepare for the warm-up laps. While we ran, the bleachers continued to fill with spectators. I didn't check the stands to see how big of a turnout the cool, damp night had collected—it had nothing to do with the game.

When the whistle blew, I was entranced. My mind was clear of every thought other than where the ball was, where it was going and who was going to be there to receive it. But the ball did not go anywhere very fast. There were a lot of missed kicks and sliding attempts to dribble or pass the ball, along with times when the ball was left spinning in place. By halftime no one had scored, but everyone was covered in mud.

The second half started the same as the first. After a time, it became evident that the best way to move the ball was to get some air under it. There were a lot of collisions between players fighting for position to receive the soaring ball. It developed into more of a physical game than a ball-controlling game, with plenty of yellow-card warnings as a result.

With approximately five minutes left, Weslyn had control of the ball. Our sweeper booted it from the top of the keeper's box, allowing the midfielder to gain possession. She dribbled a few yards, avoiding the defender, before she sent it farther upfield to Lauren. Without hesitating, Lauren sent the ball up the sideline to Sara. The sidelines weren't as muddy and treacherous as the center of the field, so Sara continued the ball along the painted white line. She drew a defender, who came at her with a sliding tackle. Before Sara slipped off her feet, landing on the attacker, she sent the ball sailing.

I was a few yards inside the keeper's box, with the sweeper coming toward me, eyeing the ball that was floating right to me but at waist height. Without considering the success of it, I crouched, forced the balls of my feet into the field, and pushed back up with everything I had, propelling myself into the air. I leaned to my left, concentrating on the ball, and swung my right foot in attempt to make contact. I wasn't aware of where the sweeper was, but I hoped I had sent the ball around her, toward the goal. After connecting with the ball, my shoulder collided with the wet ground, followed by my hip as the mud splashed on my face. I grunted in response to the contact, still focused on locating the ball. I couldn't see anything through the sweeper's feet while I lay on the ground. I lifted my head to hear the ref's whistle declaring the goal, just as I found it resting in the back of the net.

Sara pulled me off the ground, screaming. She embraced me, jumping excitedly. Amid cheers, I raised my arms in celebration as I ran back to midfield to prepare for the kickoff. I was soaring, filled with the rush I sought from the game.

The remaining time ran down without another goal. At the sound of the long whistle concluding the game, the team ran out to the center of the field, hollering and jumping in celebration. When I looked around, I realized that it wasn't just our team on the field. Many of the spectators had come down from the stands to congratulate us. People I recognized and many that I didn't patted me on the back. It was a whirlwind of faces, cheers and hands.

Coming down from the high, I decided I needed to remove myself from the chaos. I told Sara I'd meet her in the locker room, and she promised she'd be right behind me. I slipped away from the crowd and jogged to the school. As I approached the stairs, I saw a tall silhouette leaning against the building.

"Congratulations," the smooth voice said from the dark shadows.

"Thanks," I replied, slowing to a walk as I approached the figure. Evan stood with his hands in his pockets, waiting for me.

"That was an impressive goal."

I smiled, accepting the recognition, while my cheeks warmed.

"Do you want me to wait here for you while you change?" I stopped, not prepared for the question.

"You don't have to wait," I said slowly.

"I was hoping to drive you home." My stomach fell at the thought of him pulling up to my house. I didn't anticipate Carol and George waiting to greet me, but I knew she wouldn't sleep until I was locked within the house. The last thing I wanted was for her to look out of her bedroom window to see Evan's sleek black car letting me out. I didn't even want to think about how that confrontation would go.

"Thanks," I replied sincerely, "but I haven't seen Sara all day. I promised to ride home with her."

"Okay." He sounded disappointed, which kinda surprised me.

After a second, I awkwardly added, "I had a good time today. Thank you for dinner."

"Me too," he agreed, without the awkwardness. "I'll see you on Sunday then?"

"Yeah."

Evan flashed a quick grin before walking back toward the field, where he met up with a few guys from the soccer team and was immediately absorbed in conversation. By this time, Sara was jogging toward me, the mud on her face unable to conceal her enormous white smile. She greeted me with a fierce hug.

"I loved that game!" she exclaimed.

"Yeah." I exhaled. "Sara, I…can't…breathe."

"Sorry," she said, releasing me. "But that game was fricken awesome." Bouncing in her skin, she could barely stand still.

"Yeah, it was," I agreed, but my energy level was nowhere near hers. "Let's get changed. I'm ready to crash."

"Don't think I'm letting you get out of my car without providing details," she added. I groaned. "You two looked really comfortable sitting next to each other tonight. Are you sure you're still 'just friends'?"

"Sara," I stressed, my voice rising an octave, "I didn't even talk to him the whole time he sat next to us." She laughed, and I realized she was playing with me. I shook my head, smiling. "You're such a jerk."

After showering, Sara drove me home, and I provided her with the details she sought regarding my afternoon with Evan. I even told her about his confusing comments, and to my dismay, Sara laughed.

Then she proceeded to catch me up on her situation with Jason. Sara was still enthralled with him, which was good to hear, but she seemed flustered that he'd barely kissed her. Sara wasn't exactly shy when it came to "getting to know" guys. I was hoping she'd finally found a guy who respected her, but instead she was wondering what she was doing wrong.

We pulled up in front of my house. I looked out the car window at the grey Cape. The dark windows didn't reveal any movement inside. I took a deep breath and said good night to Sara before exiting the car.

I dragged my feet along the unlit driveway to the back of the house. When I turned the handle of the back door, I was met with resistance—it didn't move. The door was locked. My stomach dropped.

Sara had already driven away. There was no way I was going to knock; they'd made the conscious decision to lock the door, knowing I wasn't home. My mind raced. What could I possibly have done wrong, to get locked out of the house? My pulse quickened, wondering how much trouble I was in, fearing the worst.

I cupped my hands to the glass to look inside, but my reflection blocked my view into the kitchen. Then the reflection smirked, and the eyes squinted into a glare. I jumped back, realizing I was staring at *her*. I remained frozen, not sure what to do next, waiting for her to make a move. But the darkness remained still.

A light illuminated the kitchen. I expected to find Carol glowering at me, but the kitchen was empty until George appeared from the dining room, where he'd turned on the light. I scrunched my eyes in confusion—questioning if I had really seen Carol. George opened the door, his lips pressed in a tight scowl.

"You're supposed to be home before ten o'clock," he reprimanded.

"I had a game tonight," I said softly, confused by his reaction.

"That doesn't matter. Your curfew is ten o'clock. If you can't get home in time, then maybe you shouldn't participate in the night games." His voice was unsympathetic, and his eyes were hard. I knew there was no point in arguing. If I did, he could take soccer away altogether, and I wouldn't risk that.

"Okay," I whispered. I slipped by him and went to my room without another word.

"I would have left you in the cold," hissed through the dark as I passed the living room. I took in a quick startled breath. I continued to my room, quickly closing the door behind me, fearing what awaited me in the dark if I paused to look.

11. THE LIBRARY

I was bent over with my head in the refrigerator, wiping the back wall, when the air expelled from my lungs and I gasped in pain. I groaned, the force knocking me to the floor. I collapsed onto my side, cradling my stomach. My eyes filled with tears as I tried to gulp in air.

I pulled myself into a ball, not sure if another blow would follow. Carol stood over me with Jack's aluminum baseball bat in her hand. She glared at me as I tried to shrink against the refrigerator.

"You are not important. Nothing you do is important. Don't think that you will ever amount to anything more than the whore that you are." She walked away.

My quick gasps slowed as the air came back in easy breaths. Shaking, I pushed myself off the floor and wiped the tears from my face. I winced when I stood, holding my stomach. Without thought, I replaced the contents of the refrigerator before walking to the bathroom.

Wet red eyes stared back from the mirror. I blankly studied the pale image. Exhaling slowly, I tried to control my shaking limbs. The cold water soothed my distraught face as I gathered water from the faucet. I crushed the anger that was beginning to boil and filled my lungs with another soothing breath. I closed my eyes and reminded myself that I wasn't going to live here forever, before returning to the kitchen to complete my chores.

I breathed in sharply when I sat up in bed the next morning, my hand reaching for my sore stomach, feeling like I'd executed a thousand crunches. Despite the misery of my condition, I was still going to the library. There was no way I was staying in this house all day.

George and Carol didn't think twice about allowing me to go. I was sure they wanted me out of the house as much as I wanted to leave it. I promised I'd be back in time for dinner at six. When I started out, the need to contract my tender muscles was excruciating. I pushed through the discomfort, eventually able to block it out completely—a coping skill I'd mastered over the years.

My heart fluttered faster than the effort needed to pedal the bike when I neared the library. My mouth crept into a smile at the thought of seeing Evan. I knew I should have been paranoid about being caught, but after last night, I knew there was going to be pain whether I did anything wrong or not. I should do something to actually deserve it. I locked my bike at the rack in the front of the building and leapt up the stairs. Before I entered, I discovered him propped against the stone exterior.

"Hi," he said with a grin on his face.

"Hi," I replied, my heart shifting into a higher gear. Seeing him standing there waiting for me only confirmed that this was worth the risk.

"Ready to hit some balls?"

"I'm ready for anything," I declared, following him down the stairs to his car.

"Anything, huh?" he confirmed with a smirk, opening the car door for me.

I hesitated and looked up at him before I crouched to enter the car, "Yeah, anything." The smile spread wider across my face.

His blue eyes sparkled as he returned the smile, having no idea what I really meant.

"Okay," he said, closing the door behind me. "How was your Saturday?" he asked as we drove away from the library.

"Uneventful. How was yours?"

"I went to New York for one of my mother's charity dinners. So it was uneventful too."

"Sounds it," I said sarcastically. He grinned.

When we arrived at the recreation center, the distinct crack of aluminum bats making contact carried across the parking lot. The low thuds of clubs connecting with golf balls came from a different direction.

"Are you cold?" Evan asked.

"No, it's really nice out today," I responded, not knowing why he'd asked.

"I thought you shivered."

"I'm fine," I replied dismissively. I hadn't realized my body had reacted to the sound of the bats smashing their targets.

We walked toward the office to gather our helmets and bats.

"Have you ever swung a bat?" Evan asked, stopping near the slow-pitch softball cages.

"Maybe in elementary school," I confessed.

"Let me show you first, and then you can give it a try." Evan continued to the medium-pitch baseball section. "I'll start here so I can talk while I demonstrate what to do, then we'll move to slow-pitch softball for you."

"I'd like to stick with baseball actually."

"That's fine," he agreed. "Can you hold this for me?" Evan took off his jacket and handed it to me. I couldn't help but take in his subtle clean scent as I folded it over my arm. My heart hummed into action as I inhaled deeply.

Before he inserted the coins to begin, Evan stood in the hitting stance. He explained his position and grip while demonstrating a swing. I listened as best as I could, but kept getting lost in the fit of his shirt along his chest and back, revealing the lean muscles concealed beneath. I shook off my daze and forced myself to concentrate on his words. He paid the machine, and it started sending baseballs flying at him.

Evan made contact with most of the mechanical pitches. I watched as they arced across the net to the back of the enclosed space. He would occasionally miss when he was providing instructions on how to follow through with a steady swing, noting the importance of keeping an eye on the ball. The balls flew toward him at a blurring speed. I didn't know how he could even see the ball, forget about keeping his eye on it.

When his turn was over, we walked over to the slow-pitch baseball cage. Evan came in with me to get me set up. I stood in my best impression of the hitting stance. Evan stood behind me and placed his hands on my hips to adjust my angle. He wrapped his arms around my shoulders and grabbed hold of the bat, covering my hands. I tried to listen to what he said, but all I could hear was my heart thumping in my chest as his breath tickled my neck. He instructed me to keep my elbow up as he eased me into a slow swing, the warmth of his chest pressed against my back. I was entranced by his clean, almost sweet scent.

"Ready?" he asked, backing away.

"Sure," I replied in a daze, not realizing he had finished his instructions.

"I'll stand in the corner so I can correct your swing."

"Are you sure that'll be safe? I would hate to knock you out." He laughed and assured me he'd be fine. Then he pressed the button to begin the pitches. The first few whizzed by me before I had time to react.

"I thought this was supposed to be slow-pitch," I accused.

"Just concentrate on the ball," Evan instructed patiently. I watched as the machine flung the ball at me and swung.

I connected with a piece of it, flipping it in the air right in front of me. The twisting motion ignited a fire in my tender stomach muscles. I kept my face blank, determined not to let the soreness get to me.

"That's it," he praised. After a few more swings and misses, and a few weak connections, Evan adjusted my swing and paid for another round of pitches. This time, he stepped out of the cage and sat on the bench.

I improved with each pitch, finding my rhythm. Soon I was sending the balls through the air. I wasn't covering the distance Evan had, but at least I was hitting them.

"Much better," he said approvingly. I enjoyed the release, feeling my tension and pain slip away each time the ball made contact with the bat.

"That was great," Evan commended while we walked to the fast-pitch baseball cages. "You picked it up quickly, but I knew you would." I didn't say anything.

After a few more rounds each, Evan asked if I wanted to get a burger from the small restaurant that extended from the office.

"What do you want to learn to do next weekend?" Evan asked as he set a tray of food on the table. "Golf?"

"I really have no interest in golf," I admitted. "And I'm not sure we should make plans for next weekend yet."

"If we are able to do something, what do you want to do?" he pressed, but then his eyes lit up. "I know the perfect thing we can do." A devious smile spread across his face as he thought about it.

"What?" I asked cautiously.

"I'm not going to tell you, but you'll love it."

I narrowed my eyes, taking in his smug expression.

"Oh, I have your iPod in the car. You have an interesting selection of music. If I'd looked through the playlists without knowing who it belonged to, I would have assumed it was a guy's. Well, except for that one…"

"That one's good for when I can't fall asleep," I said, quickly defending myself, my cheeks flashing with heat.

"It's very—" Evan hesitated, searching for the right word.

"Soothing," I interrupted.

"Sure." He laughed. "It definitely sets a mood, let's put it that way." The color continued to spread across my face.

When we were in the car driving back to the library, Evan asked one of the questions I'd been bracing myself for. "Why do you live with your aunt and uncle?" My heart skipped a beat, but I knew that avoiding the question would only make him more curious.

"George is my father's brother," I began. "My father died in a car accident when I was seven, so George and his wife, Carol, took me in."

"What about your mother?" I knew that the questions weren't meant to be invasive, but they brought me crashing back from our escape at the baseball cages to a reality that was inescapable.

So I inhaled deeply and answered each question with a truthful brevity that flowed out of my lips as if I were reciting it from a newspaper. No connection, no emotion—truth at its simplest.

"She became ill after my father died and wasn't fit to care for me anymore."

"I'm sorry to hear that," Evan replied genuinely. I forced my lips into a pressed smile, letting his sympathy roll off me. It didn't feel warranted and made me uneasy.

I had accepted long ago that the death of my father and fall of my mother were part of my life—I was unable to give in to the grieving. I refused to feel sorry for myself or receive pity for my circumstances. Besides, I had to focus on the present—which included surviving the wrath of Carol—so I couldn't afford to live in the past. My future was the only thing that mattered now.

"So you have a game tomorrow?" I asked, trying to sound unaffected but needing desperately to change the subject. We continued to talk about the last two weeks of the soccer season until we pulled up alongside the library.

"See you tomorrow," I said casually, not certain what else to say.

"Bye," he replied before I shut the door. I could feel him watching me as I walked toward my bike, but I didn't look back until he drove away.

I rode my bike home, arriving in plenty of time for the grilled cheese and soup that was served for dinner. I was able to hold on to the day with Evan for a little while longer, letting it replay in my head when I sat down to dinner, keeping me oblivious to the stares I received when I took a second helping of soup. I think I was even grinning.

12. BAD INFLUENCE

The next two weeks glided by with the same carefree ease. Evan became part of my routine, accepting all that came along with it—and finding ways to add to it as well.

Remembering my ten o'clock curfew and taking advantage of my after-school activities, Evan easily convinced Sara and me to come over to his house one night after completing the layout of the newspaper with hours to spare before my deadline. Jason met us there, and the four of us attempted to play pool. I should say Sara and I attempted, Evan and Jason were pretty decent. I laughed as Sara made fun of her miscalculated shots, and she teased me for not being able to draw a straight line when I'd hit the cue ball in an unintended direction. Still smiling, I walked in the door before ten o'clock. I was oblivious to Carol and George's presence, consumed by the playback of the day in my head.

Not getting caught empowered me, making it easier to concede each time Evan came up with something else for us to do. I should've remembered I wasn't the luckiest person in the world, but the thrill of getting away with it was addictive.

One of these nights, Sara watched in rolling laughter as Evan taught me to drive his car in the parking lot of the high school. It was late enough that no one was there, and the lot was on the side of the building, not easily seen from the main road since it was lined with trees. I suppose if I had witnessed the car jerking and stalling and heard me yelling in exasperation, I would have been laughing too. Evan was patiently determined, and after what felt like a whip-lashing eternity, I was finally able to smoothly shift from first to second. He tried to convince me to take it on the road to get used to changing gears, but I refused.

That Sunday, I met him at the library again. I told my aunt and uncle I had a huge History project to work on so I could meet Evan earlier, and we'd have more time together. He'd warned me to dress warmly when we left school on Friday. I was glad I did when he pulled into the state park a few towns west of Weslyn.

Evan guided me along a dirt trail through the leaf-encrusted woods with the cool crisp air sweeping across our faces. The warm layers became unnecessary once my blood started pumping. It took some effort to climb the loose terrain as we progressed further into the woods. I removed my gloves and wrapped my coat around my waist, leaving on my fleece.

We didn't talk much as we walked. The quiet was comfortable, and I was relieved to be away from Weslyn and enraptured by the serene setting with the chirping of the birds and the light breeze rustling the leaves. I absorbed the colorful wilderness while following Evan's navy backpack, allowing a grin to rest on my face.

Evan stopped at the base of a tall rock structure that looked like a boulder had crashed into the hillside, exposing one smooth side that was only slightly marred with subtle indentations. It had to be at least a hundred feet tall. "Ready?" he asked, looking up. I stopped and took in his line of sight, eyeing the large structure.

"Am I ready for what?" I asked tentatively.

"We're going to rappel down the face of this rock," he answered, smiling back at me. "It's really not that big, don't worry."

"We're going to do what?!"

"You'll love it, I promise." My reaction did little to deter his huge smile. "I was here yesterday scoping it out. There's a path around to the left that brings us to the top."

Aware that I was unable to move, he added, "You trust me, right?"

I looked at him and shook my head. "Not anymore."

He laughed. "Come on." He hiked along the path that skirted the massive structure. To my dismay, my legs followed.

Looking down from the top, the distance seemed twice as far as it had looking up. My stomach rolled, but instead of succumbing to panic, I was unexpectedly struck with a surge of adrenaline.

Here's to falling to my death, I thought to myself. I joined Evan in the center of the flattened area on top, where he was laying out the equipment.

"Ready yet?" he asked, grinning at me.

I took in a lung full of air and released it slowly through my puckered lips. "Sure."

Before I could change my mind, Evan had me slip my legs through the loops of the harness and fastened it securely. He proceeded to explain the rope system and where I should place my hands and how to release it to let myself down. I listened carefully, knowing if I didn't pay attention, I would never be listening to anything again—even with Evan's promise that he'd spot me the entire time and I had nothing to fear. Easy for him to say.

Once the rope was anchored to a sturdy tree and the figure eight was clipped to me, Evan returned to the base where he held the dropped rope to ensure that I didn't fall—or to get the best view when I plummeted to my death. I backed up to the edge of the rock. The first step was the hardest, especially leaning back into a position that defied gravity. The adrenaline pushed me over the edge, and I was planted on the side of the rock, staring straight up through the treetops toward the sky. I remained still, trying to fight the urge to lean upright.

Evan hollered instructions from below to correct my angle and the positioning of my feet. I tentatively fed the rope with my right hand as my feet slowly crept down. After I got used to the release and footing, my stuttered steps progressed into small hops, until my feet found the safety of the ground. It didn't take as long as I imagined, but I still felt exhilarated to be standing on my own—upright.

"What did you think?" Evan asked with a grin.

"I liked it," I admitted, grinning back.

"I knew you would." I rolled my eyes as he unclipped the rope from my harness.

We rappelled a couple more times, and I felt increasingly comfortable with each attempt. Evan chose to go face-first his last time, which was difficult to watch. The speed with which he ran down the rock caught my breath.

"Show-off," I mumbled as he landed with ease on the bed of fallen leaves.

"Don't worry, you'll be looking for the next rush too after you get used to it."

"I don't think I'll ever want to do that."

"I think I found the perfect place for you to try to drive my car," Evan declared on our way back down. "A road that almost never has cars on it. We can go out after you work on the paper on Tuesday."

"You really think that I should be driving on the road for the first time in the dark?"

"You're right," he agreed. "Let's go out while it's still light after soccer practice. Then we'll go back to the school so you can work on the paper."

"We'll see," I said, without committing.

"Do you think you'll be able to go to the homecoming game on Friday night?"

"No," I said without even thinking twice.

"So no dance on Saturday night either, huh?"

I let out a laugh in response.

"Are you going to the homecoming dance?" I asked, not sure why I wanted to know.

"Don't think so."

"Why not?" I inquired, oddly filled with a sense of relief. "You can't tell me you couldn't find anyone to go with."

"Emma, you and I are dating, remember?" he teased, a slow grin spread over his face.

"Shut up," I snapped back. "You can't tell me people still think that? Haven't you told them we're not?"

"I haven't said anything either way."

"That's stupid." I stopped to look at him. "Why would you want everyone assuming something that isn't true?"

"Why should I care?"

"So you can ask someone you're interested in to go to the dance with you," I replied, not expecting his lack of concern.

"I just did."

"You did not just ask me to the dance." I crossed my arms across my chest in defiance. He smirked and shrugged. I turned and kept walking along the path.

"Whatever happened with Haley?" I questioned, changing the focus. "She's nominated for homecoming queen."

"Seriously?" he scoffed. "Have you ever tried having a conversation with her?"

"I don't think she even knows my name."

"I think she does now," he teased. "You know, now that we're dating."

"Evan! Knock it off," I huffed. He laughed.

"Honestly," he admitted, "I haven't been here that long, and the thought of going to the dance doesn't appeal to me. I'm not that into anyone else." My heart stammered at the last word, but my mind dismissed it before I could think too much about it.

"Is there a way you could stay over at Sara's after your game on Saturday? That way you and I could hang out and watch movies or something."

"That's unlikely. My aunt works for the school system, in their administrations building. She'll know that it's the homecoming dance and will doubt that Sara would give up the dance to hang out with me."

"Why doesn't she like you?"

A spasm shot through my chest, realizing I'd revealed too much. I must have been silent for too long because Evan added, "Sorry. I don't get it, but you don't have to explain." We walked the remaining distance to the car without speaking. I searched for a way to recover.

What was I supposed to say? *No, Evan, she doesn't "not like me," she despises me. She lets me know it every opportunity she can because I invaded her life, and she wants me out. But her marriage to my father's brother keeps me in her house, so it's her mission to make every second of my life torturously miserable.*

I knew those words would never leave my lips, so while Evan loaded the backpacks into the trunk, I leaned my back against the car and blurted, "It wasn't easy to be an instant mother of a twelve-year-old. I'm sure she's just being way too overprotective, not wanting me to get into trouble."

Evan let my words sink in for a moment before responding. "Does she even know you?" he challenged. "You're not the type of person to hang out with the wrong crowd. You're the perfect student, a talented athlete and the most responsible person I've ever met." He almost sounded angry.

I turned to look at him, confused by his fervent reaction.

"I don't understand why they can't see who you really are and allow you to live a little. You know—go to football games, dances or even on a date." His voice grew louder, more agitated, as he completed his thoughts.

"No, you don't understand," I said quietly but firmly. His reaction bothered me. He shouldn't care if they knew me or not. He was just supposed to accept my answers and let it go. "I think I should get back to the library." I turned, leaving him looking after me as I entered the car.

Evan slipped quietly onto the driver's seat and hesitated before starting the car.

"Emma, I'm sorry." I looked out the window, not ready to face him. "You're right, I don't know. If it's none of my business, then I promise not to bring it up again. I didn't mean to make you upset." His voice was quiet and pleading. I heard his sincerity through my defenses.

"It *is* none of your business," I confirmed quietly, still not looking at him. He started the car, and we drove away in silence. "And I'm not mad at you." I looked over at him with a soft smile to convince him I wasn't—he smiled back. My cheeks flooded instantly with heat.

"Do you think you and Sara could get out of watching the JV game to get pizza or something on Wednesday?"

I smiled, recognizing he wasn't ready to give up trying to stretch my boundaries. "I think so."

After that, we continued as if the conversation never happened. He didn't talk about my lack of freedom, and I didn't push him away. We had our driving lesson on Tuesday and pizza with Sara and Jason on Wednesday. My world revolved in a fairly predictable rotation, despite Evan's impulsive persistence—determined to be a bad influence. Miraculously, I was still able to avoid Carol for the most part. Each day, I found it easier to smile.

To top it all off, the soccer team was locked in as the division champions. We had one game left of the regular season before the state championship play-offs. Coach Peña revealed he'd been taping my games to send highlights to college recruiters. I didn't realize he'd been doing this, but the knowledge that more schools were interested made me believe that escape was actually possible. He even warned that more scouts might be attending the first round of the play-offs. For the first time, my life felt livable.

13. REPLACED

You've changed," Sara observed when we drove home on Friday.

"What are you talking about?"

"It's not bad," she said quickly. "I think it's Evan—he's made you…happier. I like seeing you like this." I absorbed her words with my eyes scrunched. She continued, ignoring my reaction. "Why aren't you dating him yet?"

"Are you done?" I asked dubiously.

"*What?*"

"Sara, I cannot date *anyone*," I declared. "Forget about Evan Mathews. And despite your assumptions, he really doesn't want to date me."

"Em, you're seriously blind. Why *wouldn't* he want to date you? He spends just about every second that he can with you."

"We're friends," I stressed.

"Whatever you have to say to convince yourself," Sara said, shaking her head. "But did you know that he's been asked out by several girls and won't even give them the time of day?"

I shrugged, but a smirk crept on my face in hearing this. Sara eyed me with a small shake of her head as she pulled up in front of my house.

"I'll pick you up at two o'clock tomorrow," Sara said as I got out of the car.

"Have fun at the game tonight," I told her, leaning into the car. "All the nominees get announced onto the field at halftime, right?" She rolled her eyes at the thought of being paraded in front of the spectators. I laughed and closed the door.

———

I practically hummed through my chores the next morning. I was looking forward to getting out of the house for the last game before the play-offs and the ice cream Evan, Sara and I were going to try to sneak in on the way home. After replacing the trash bag in the kitchen, I turned to go back to my room to find Carol blocking my path.

"What are you up to?" she demanded.

"I don't understand," I said slowly, recognizing the fire in her eyes. My body tensed, evaluating her stance and checking to see if she was holding anything in her hands. Her hands were empty and set firmly on her hips.

"Are you fucking someone?" she accused in disgust. My jaw dropped open. "I don't know what you're up to, but you don't seem to care about anyone other than yourself—even more than usual. When I figure it out, you'll wish you never treated me with such disrespect."

Confusion swirled with anxiety as the tension continued to build. I couldn't find the words to provide her with the proper answer to her illogical accusations.

"Maybe you should be spending more time at home, so I know what you're up to."

"I'm sorry," I blurted, not knowing what else to say. I was terrified by the thought of being confined within these walls any longer than I was already sentenced, and it was the first thing that came out of my mouth. My head rocked to the right as her closed fist collided with my jaw.

My hand instinctively covered where she made contact as my eyes watered from the force of the blow.

There was a sharp breath, but it wasn't mine. I looked toward the whimpers and found Jack and Leyla staring in shock. Leyla was crying, her sobs muffled by her small hand. Big tears soaked her soft, round cheeks. Jack was silent, but his wide, shocked eyes were more painful than Leyla's uncontrollable sobs. My heart broke as I moved to comfort them. Carol grabbed my arm, stopping me.

"Look what you've done," she growled, glaring at me with her cold hateful eyes. "Get out of my sight." I allowed the heart-wrenching image of Leyla and Jack's terrified faces to brand me before retreating to my room.

I threw myself on my bed and cried into my pillow. My heart ached as their image continued to burn in my head. They were never supposed to see. It was never supposed to touch them. I couldn't contain my spasms as I cried harder, stifling my moans with my pillow. I was supposed to protect them from this. The guilt consumed me until I couldn't cry anymore and I sank into a draining sleep.

My body tensed with a streak of pain across the back of my legs. I shook out of my slumber, not certain if I'd dreamt it. The second lash against my bare skin confirmed my waking nightmare.

"You selfish cunt." I recognized the words through clenched teeth.

I pulled my legs in tight, covering my head with my hands, leaving my back exposed. With each rageful swing, my body recoiled, receiving the sharp burning lashes with a jaw-tightened grunt.

"How could you hurt them like that?" she demanded with a fury that made her almost unintelligible. "I knew I should never have let you set foot in my home—you've destroyed everything." Her hatred streaked across my back as she swung wildly. I could barely breathe. I clenched my teeth harder, tensing with each strike, unable to escape.

"You fucking worthless piece of shit. You should never have been born." She continued hurling expletives, inaudible to my ears. I remained in my protective ball, shutting her off and blocking out the fire emblazoning my flesh—searching for an escape. I retreated deeper until I was no longer in the room with her, blocking out the pain and rage and the tears dripping off my nose.

"I don't want to see you for the rest of the day," she grunted in exhaustion, leaving my room.

I remained still for another minute, listening to my erratic pulse thumping in my ears and my breath quivering with each inhale. I slowly unwrapped myself, my back an inferno. I turned to sit on the edge of my bed, looking down at my trembling hands, embossed with red streaks.

I leaned forward, my forearms on my thighs, forcing the air to pass through my lungs at a slow, even pace. That's when I noticed the thin leather belt coiled on the floor. Anger overtook me, slithering around my heart. I continued to breathe deeply through my nose, my jaw clenched. Consumed by loathing, I allowed the venom to pump fervently through my veins. I didn't have the strength to push it away. Instead, I let it rest under my skin and feed my weary muscles. I stood to prepare for my game.

I slid gingerly into Sara's car, sitting up straight to avoid contact with the seat.

"Hi," she began with a smile, and stopped short, her smile instantly fading. I knew what I looked like, and her eyes reflected back the same image I had seen in my mirror. My face was pale, contrasting with the dark circles under my withdrawn, vacant eyes. I kept my lips pressed together, afraid of being betrayed by a gasp of pain. I couldn't look at her, but I didn't try to be anything different than the person she stared at in horror.

She slowly pulled away, unable to say anything. We drove in silence for a moment until she finally demanded, "I need you to tell me what happened." I kept my eyes focused on the side window without seeing the passing scenery.

"Emma, please." I could hear the desperation in her voice.

"It's nothing, Sara," I said flatly, still unwilling to look at her.

We arrived at the school without saying another word. Absently, I walked to the field, not noticing Sara walking beside me until a few girls greeted us. As we approached the field, I pulled the hood of my sweatshirt over my head, focusing on the ground, ignoring everyone around me. The varsity game was the only game being played, so as soon as the other team arrived, we gathered for our pregame warm-ups.

The first half of the game was an agonizing blur. I couldn't focus, and my legs failed me when I sprinted to a pass. I ended up quickly passing the ball off or was unable to intercept it at all. At halftime, Coach Peña pulled me aside.

"Are you okay?" he asked, concern reflecting in his eyes. "You seem stiff out there. Are you hurt?"

"I think I moved wrong and pulled something in my back," I lied, looking down.

"Do you want the trainer to look at it?"

"No." The word came out in an urgent rush too; shock flashed across his eyes. "I'll be fine, really," I pleaded.

"Okay." He paused. "I'll sit you out the second half, so you don't push it. I can't afford to have you injured for the quarterfinals on Friday." I nodded.

We returned to the team that was gathered around the bench. To everyone's surprise, Coach Peña told Katie Brennan she was starting the second half in my place. I sat with my hood over my head and my hands in my pocket, avoiding the questioning stares.

When the final whistle blew, I rushed to the locker room before anyone knew I was gone. I knew I'd have the locker room to myself since everyone usually went home to shower and change. It was a quick shower with the warm water burning my inflamed skin, making it difficult to breathe. I was getting dressed with my back to the door when I heard footsteps behind me. I should have pulled the curtain shut behind me, but it didn't matter now.

I didn't turn around, and the person behind me didn't say anything. I delicately pulled the turtleneck over my head, covering my marks of disgrace. Unable to avoid the confrontation any longer, I turned to face Sara. She was sitting on the bench across from me, tears running down her cheeks and her jaw tensed. She looked... broken.

"I can't—" she began, but choked on the words. Sara stopped to breathe it away before uttering, "I can't do this anymore." I could only stare at her, watching her crumble. A wall encased me, separating me so I wouldn't break with her. "I can't ignore it; I can't pretend that I don't see what she's doing to you."

Sara's shoulders sank as she slowly lifted her head, revealing the tears streaming down her cheeks. "Emma, you have to tell someone." Her words sounded desperate and urgent. "If you don't, then I will."

"No, you won't," I snapped, my icy tone that made Sara wince.

"What do you mean?" she demanded, even more passionately. "Did you see your back? The blood was seeping through your shirt during the game. Emma, I'm afraid some morning when I pull up to get you, you won't come out. I care about you, and I can't watch her do this to you."

"Then don't," I stated coldly. I was disconnected from my thoughts, and the words dug into Sara like daggers. She recoiled with each jab. This was a confrontation I never saw coming, and my defenses were heightened. I wasn't willing to let her jeopardize everything I'd sacrificed to protect Leyla and Jack.

"You won't tell anyone about me, and I won't tell anyone about how you fuck every other guy that gives you the time of day."

Sara's eyes widened, filled with pain; the mortal blow had been driven. "You're not the only one who's good at keeping her mouth shut. I know exactly who you are, Sara, so don't think for one minute you know what's good for me."

"You bitch," she murmured, the shock settling into her shoulders as she practically disintegrated in front of me. "You fucking bitch." She couldn't look up at me, covering her face to conceal the cascade of tears.

"Stay out of my life. And keep your mouth shut." I took my possessed body and left her fighting to gain control of her breath after my verbal assault. I didn't look back. With my bag in hand, I walked away—not truly comprehending what I'd just done. At that moment, I didn't really care.

Jason and Evan were waiting outside the building when I walked out of the school.

"Sorry about the loss," Evan said. Then he looked at me, taken aback, as if he didn't recognize me.

"Can you drive me home?" I asked before he could say anything.

"Sure," he answered, deciding it was best not to ask the question that flashed across his eyes. Jason remained quiet as we left him waiting for Sara.

I gave him directions in a foreign flat tone when we drove out of the parking lot.

Unable to contain the question any longer, he asked, "What happened with Sara?"

I stared out the window, not wanting to think about what I'd done—letting the question dissipate into the air. He let my silence answer for me and kept driving.

"Do you want to talk about it?" he asked gently. I could feel him looking at me, but I kept staring out the window. I shook my head and held my hands together to conceal the shaking.

We pulled up to my house in tense silence. I got out of the car and shut the door before he could make me face my betrayal with another question.

Dazed, I walked up the driveway to the back door. I looked around, perplexed, when I found it locked. That's when I realized the driveway was empty. I was too entangled in my whirling emotions to care that I was locked out of the house. I sat on the top step of the deck and wrapped myself in my jacket against the cold October evening. I brought my knees up to my chest and let my head fall onto them, releasing my regret. I cried until the muscles in my chest hurt and my sobs were tearless.

When the anger washed away, I was left sad, defeated and alone. The darkness surrounded me while I waited for someone to come home. I shivered against the cold wind whipping against me. I had no idea how long I'd been sitting there, but I was startled from my hollowness when headlights illuminated the driveway. Suddenly comprehending what this might mean, my stomach released a surge of paralyzing fear.

When George walked around the side of the house alone, I released the tension with a long breath.

"Carol and the kids are staying over at her mother's tonight," George stated as he unlocked the door. I followed him in silence. Before I could retreat to my cave, he added, "I don't know what happened between you two today, but I want you to take it easy on her."

The statement threw a shocked look across my face that I knew he saw.

"She's under a lot of stress at work, and she needs to be able to relax at home," he explained. "Do what you can to make it easy for her."

I stared at him for a second before I whispered, "Okay." My stomach turned in disgust as I continued toward my room. He was never around to witness what happened—he couldn't feel guilty for what he refused to see.

I entered the dark room, closing the door behind me—not bothering to turn on the light. I dropped my jacket on the floor and collapsed on to my bed, falling into a restless sleep.

I couldn't breathe. I grasped at my neck, trying to loosen the tightening cord as my feet were pulled off the bed. I couldn't see in the dark, but I could feel my body sway with each jerk of the thin rope. I tried to reach above me to find something to pull myself up on. The line was cutting into my neck, crushing my trachea. I became dizzy with the pressure building in my head and the screaming of my lungs, demanding the air that would never come.

14. HOLLOW

I woke up gasping, drenched in sweat. I slowly rolled onto my side, trying to orient myself as I sat on the edge of the bed, breathing heavily. My turtleneck was sticking to my inflamed back, and all I could feel was the burning. I slipped into the bathroom hearing the sound of the TV in the kitchen, where I'm sure George was drinking coffee and reading the paper.

I slowly peeled off my turtleneck, revealing the swollen red striations of different lengths sprawled across my back. Most of the marks were superficial, with a few scabbed over. The lashes were thin, but the swelling made them appear so much worse.

Pushing away the sorrow, I eased into the shower, wishing I could wash away the pain along with the sweat that still clung to me from my nightmare

I stayed in my room for the remainder of the day, forcing myself to focus on homework assignments I had yet to complete. The work allowed the day to slip by, but my lack of concentration made it take twice as long to finish.

I heard Carol and the kids return in the early afternoon. I stayed out of sight until I was startled by the door opening and found Carol standing in its frame.

"They need to know you're okay, so be happy to see them," she said coldly. "Come eat."

After allowing the paralysis to wear off, I walked to the dining room.

"Emma!" Leyla greeted me with a huge hug. I didn't flinch against the stinging pain when I bent over to put my arms around her.

"Did you have fun at Nanna's?" I asked. Leyla responded with a jubilant recollection of her time at Janet's house.

My eyes caught Jack's, and I smiled at him reassuringly. He cautiously examined my smile, determined it was genuine, and smiled back. I could see the light in his eyes again, and I smiled bigger.

"We went to the aquarium today," Jack announced, adding to Leyla's exclamations about sharks and starfish.

I sat in my seat and focused my attention on their stories while I ate the meal George had prepared. I didn't look at Carol or George throughout dinner. After everyone left the table, I performed what was expected of me. The entire time, I couldn't escape the empty feeling in the pit of my stomach. When I finally went to bed, I lay awake, thinking about what was going to happen in the morning. I tried to remember if I knew where the bus stop was, fearing Sara wasn't going to be waiting for me.

———

Sara wasn't waiting for me. As happy as I was to see his car, it meant that I'd hurt Sara even more than I could have imagined, and that was crushing.

I opened the car door to Evan's warm smile. "Good morning."

"Good morning." I offered a small smile in return. "Thank you for picking me up. I really appreciate it." I was filled with his intoxicating clean scent upon entering the car. Not a bad way to start the morning.

"No problem," he returned casually. After a minute of driving, Evan finally said, "I was hoping to see you at the library yesterday. I had a great plan to cheer you up."

I bit my lip. "I am so sorry. I completely forgot. It wasn't the best weekend of my life."

"I understand," he replied. "You seem a little better today."

"I'm okay," I said quietly. Knowing Sara couldn't be in the same car as me meant that nothing about me was okay. My chest hurt with the thought that she might not forgive me.

"How was the homecoming game on Friday?" I asked, attempting to sound interested.

"Weslyn lost, but it was close."

"Did you end up going to the dance?"

"No, I met my brother and some of his friends in New York. We went to a bar to check out this local band." He told me about his night, and that I'd have to look up the band to download a few songs. I tried to listen to his story, but the closer we got to school, the more distracted I became.

I'm not sure how much of what Evan said I heard, because I was snapped back to the confines of the car when he said, "I have to find a way to get you to New York."

"What?! No—there is no way I'm going to New York." Then I looked over at him, and his lips were pressed into a devious half smile. "Nice. That's exactly what I need in the morning—a heart attack."

"I was just seeing if you were paying attention," he said, still smirking.

After a short silence, he tried to console me. "I promise it will get better." I knew he was promising something he knew nothing about, but I forced an appreciative smile anyway.

The halls seemed so long and crowded today—it felt like it took forever to reach my locker. My heart was thumping loudly when I rounded the corner, but it sank when I saw that there wasn't anyone at the locker next to mine. I gathered my books and slipped into homeroom without looking at anyone. I sat in the first available desk and waited for the daily announcements and attendance so I could begin my excruciatingly long day. I couldn't bring myself to look around the room to see if Sara was there.

I did see Sara as the day progressed. Her vibrant red hair was easy to spot among the other bodies occupying the halls. She was usually walking alongside Jill or Jason. So, I knew she was in school, but she chose to avoid me. I watched her from a distance, wishing she would look at me and see how sorry I was. I couldn't tell her, since she wasn't there to listen.

Evan accompanied me to every class, even the ones he wasn't in with me. My heart would have been fluttering uncontrollably by his constant presence if it hadn't already sunk into my stomach. At first, he tried to distract me with superficial conversation about topics I couldn't recall even if I tried. Once he realized I wasn't listening and was just nodding politely, he stopped trying.

I was too consumed with my own remorse and misery to consider how he must have felt walking alongside a shell of a human being. I wasn't whole; the guilt was eating away at me, slowly devouring my insides.

We left Journalism after spending nearly an hour sitting beside Sara in silent torture.

"Let's get out of here."

"Huh?" I looked up to find Evan standing beside me.

"Let's get out of here," he repeated.

Was it the end of the day already?

"You can't be here anymore. Let's get your things and we'll go to my house and hang out."

Registering what was happening, I asked, "Don't you have soccer practice?" I knew Coach had given us the day off, planning to

work us hard for the next three days before our game on Friday—
but I was pretty sure the guys still had practice since their game was
on Thursday.

"I asked one of the guys to tell Coach that I have a doctor's
appointment."

I couldn't come up with a reason to reject his invitation. I followed him to my locker and threw books in my bag, not paying
attention to whether I needed them or not. Then Evan led me to his
locker where he grabbed his things.

I didn't remember driving to his house. The next moment I
was aware of was when we slowed down to pull into his driveway. I
looked around, dazed, wondering where my thoughts had taken me
in the time it took us to drive here. Had Evan tried to talk to me?
Had I answered him?

"We're here," he announced. The way his voice cut through the
air let me know we'd driven in silence, and perhaps I'd fallen asleep.

I took a deep breath and got out of the car. Before I took a step
toward the house I said, "Evan, I'm not sure you really want to hang
out with me today."

He stopped on the steps of the porch. "Of course I do.
Come on."

I wanted to force myself to put up a pleasant pretense so that
his efforts to cheer me up wouldn't be completely lost. I searched
within the shadows, but couldn't find a persona that was remotely
convincing. I decided to do my best not to appear completely
devestated.

Evan grabbed two bottles from the refrigerator and continued
down a long hall that opened up into a brightly lit space containing
a piano and a built-in bookcase. Besides some large planted trees,
there wasn't anything else in the window-encased room except for a
set of winding wooden stairs that led to a landing overlooking the
perimeter of the room.

I followed Evan upstairs to a door off the landing. The dark room was much smaller than Sara's, but still twice the size of mine—and with its own bathroom. Overlapping images of athletes and musicians covered the wall behind his bed. A simple black desk with a rolling chair was set in the opposing corner, and above it hung a board with snapshots of friends and creased concert tickets pinned to it. A queen-size bed filled the center of the room, complementing the deep espresso stained bureau sitting in the corner across from with with a flat-screen television set on top. Evan set his backpack next to his desk and pushed a couple of buttons on his laptop. Music hummed through the speakers suspended in each corner of the room. Soothing acoustics and rhythmic melodies filled the bedroom.

"Sorry, I don't have anywhere to sit besides the bed," he said, offering me one of the bottles of soda he had in his hands.

I remained still inside the doorway. My heart found a rhythm from within the cave where it was held captive. Sit on his bed, really? I slowly walked over and sat on the edge, not ready to commit to putting my legs up.

Evan propped up one of his pillows against the headboard and sat next to me on the deep red comforter. I knew I had to move further onto his bed to face him. I pushed my shoes off and shuffled toward the foot of the bed, sitting opposite him with my legs crossed beneath me.

"I don't like seeing you upset," he finally said.

"Sorry," was all I could find to say, looking down at my hands.

"I wish I could do something to make you feel better. Can you tell me what happened?" I shook my head. Silence followed for a minute as the comforting tunes continued in the background.

"Sara will talk to you again," Evan said as if it were a fact.

"I don't know if she will," I whispered. My chest ached thinking about why she might not. "I said some pretty terrible things." My eyes brimmed with tears that I tried to blink away.

Evan scooted closer to me and placed his warm hand on my cheek, brushing away the escaped tear.

"She'll forgive you," he said softly. He pulled me toward him and put his arms around me. I buried my head in his chest and released the seeping tears. After a time, I collected myself and pulled away.

"You always seem to see me at my best, huh?" I tried to smile, feeling emotionally exposed.

"It's not a bad thing."

I wasn't sure what he meant, but decided to leave it alone.

"Can I use your bathroom?"

"Sure."

I entered the small bathroom, closing the door behind me. I rinsed the emotions away, splashing my face with cool water. I took in the light brown eyes looking back at me and urged myself to recover. After drying my face with a towel, I inhaled a calming breath before opening the door. It didn't hurt that the breath contained Evan's soothing scent.

Evan was sitting against the headboard again, flipping through channels on the flat-screen TV.

"Still haven't unpacked?" I asked, nodding toward the unopened boxes marked "Evan's room" under the empty built-in bookcase, and another box beneath the only window.

"Getting there," he replied casually.

"How is it that the rest of your house looks like people have been here for years, and you can't finish putting away a few boxes?"

Evan let out a quick laugh.

"We have moving down to a science. My mother plans out in advance where everything is to be displayed, stored and hung; then they hire the same moving company we've used for every move. They not only pack and move us, but then unpack us when they arrive. We walk in, and this is already done. The only thing they don't touch is my stuff."

"And…" I pushed him to explain the reason for his taped boxes.

"Well…I haven't decided if I'm staying." Something shot through me—I couldn't tell what it was, but it felt a little like panic.

"Oh," I murmured.

"Do you want to watch a movie?"

"Sure." I walked around to the vacant side of the bed and propped the other pillow up to sit next to Evan.

He found an action movie he had saved in his digital movie library. I didn't last very long before my eyes became heavy. Being miserable was exhausting. I surrendered to their weight and drifted to sleep.

"Emma," Evan whispered in my ear. It took me a minute to comprehend that his voice was real. "Em, the movie's over." His voice sounded too close.

My eyes popped open. My head had slipped into the hollow of his shoulder, with his arm resting on the top of my pillow. I pushed myself up to sit on my own, still trying to blink the sleep from my eyes.

"Sorry. I didn't mean to miss the entire thing." I stretched my arms over my head, expecting to be sore or stiff—surprised to find that I wasn't.

"It's okay," he said with a laugh. "I think you drooled on my shirt, though."

My mouth dropped open. "I did not."

"I'm just kidding." He laughed louder.

"You're such a jerk," I declared, throwing my pillow at his head.

Evan took the pillow and swung it back at me. I jumped up, standing on the bed, and grabbed the pillow from behind him. I swung it, connecting with his back. He pulled my legs out from under me and I toppled on the bed, igniting my back. He proceeded to pelt me in the face with a pillow.

"That's cheating," I murmured from under the pillow, trying to dismiss my discomfort. "No tackling."

"You can tackle," he argued.

"Fine." I charged, pushing him onto his back with all my force, and sat on his chest, pinning down his arms with my knees. I swung the pillow, and it collided with his face.

"Uh, playing dirty," he grunted as he flipped me over, easily sliding his arms out from under my weight. He held himself above me with his hands on either side of my head, his body still between my knees. He looked down with a smirk. I could feel his warm breath on my face, and the burning along my back disappeared. We both recognized at the same time the close proximity of our bodies and that neither of us was holding a pillow. I stopped breathing, looking up at him with wide eyes, watching his smirk slowly disappear.

"Want to play pool?" I asked, quickly rolling out from under him as he fell to his side. In a continuous motion, I stood and grabbed my shoes before leaving the room. Evan looked after me from his bed, still propped up on his side as I scurried down the stairs.

He sauntered into the kitchen with his cheeks flushed.

"Want a bottle of water?" he asked, casually opening the refrigerator.

"Sure," I said, unable to ignore the fire engulfing my back from the pillow fight. "Do you mind if we play darts instead?" I asked. While his back was turned, I washed down a few ibuprofen that I had stuffed in my pocket.

"Works for me," Evan commented, studying my face for a moment. I grinned before he saw the pain dart across my eyes. He grinned back, and I followed him to the garage.

After a few rounds of practice, my thoughts drifted to the unpacked boxes in his room.

"I thought you liked it here?" I watched him hesitate before throwing a dart.

"What do you mean?"

"You said you didn't know if you were staying, and that's why you haven't unpacked."

Evan stopped before he threw his last dart and turned to face me. "Are you worried you'd miss me if I left?" he asked with a wry grin.

I raised my eyebrows in disapproval, refusing to answer.

"I like it here," he finally said, after tossing his last dart. "Honestly, I've never completely unpacked anywhere. I still had unopened boxes after living in San Francisco for over two years."

"Why?"

"I don't know," he replied, stopping to think about it. "Maybe I was never completely convinced I was going to stay—and look, I was right. You didn't answer my question—would it bother you if I left?"

I shrugged, "I'd survive." I smiled, giving away my inability to be serious.

"Now you're the jerk," he said, grinning back. "Don't worry; I won't throw darts at you."

The rest of the afternoon passed with darts and foosball, allowing my back to cool to a simmer. Evan still won every game, but he appeared impressed when I didn't lose by much. I kept my sorrow at bay while in his company, thankful he helped me escape the rest of my day at school. It was so hard to be there with Sara, knowing she was so angry with me. But it was harder to go home.

My smile faded when I got into his car. Evan noticed my solemn transition, but he didn't say anything to distract me from my silence as I braced myself for the tension that still festered in my house.

"I'll see you tomorrow," he said softly as I opened the car door. I nodded and then stopped to look at him.

"Thank you for today." I offered him a small smile. He lightly smiled back.

"Whose car was that?" Carol questioned as soon as I walked through the door.

"Sara's car is getting a tune-up," I lied. A spasm of anxious nerves shot from my stomach through my chest, fearing she'd see right through it. I kept walking to my room before I could find out.

———

I was greeted with the same mixed feelings upon seeing Evan's car when I walked down my driveway the next morning. The improbability of Sara forgiving me was sinking in. I had been so very cruel; how could I blame her? Besides, why would she want to put up with my insane life anymore? I wasn't sure how *I* was still coping.

I knew I'd never be able to confide in Evan the way I did Sara. I was still struggling with allowing him to be as close as he was. I suppose I'd been selfish to think that Sara would always be there. We came from two completely different worlds, and the reality of these differences was unavoidable. It was only a matter of time.

Evan allowed me to grieve without much intervention. He escorted me through the bustle of the halls to each of my classes, and somehow I got through the day. The teachers' incoherent lessons hummed in my ears. The minutes crept, and the hollowness grew. At some point during the day, Evan disappeared too. I almost didn't notice until I rounded the corner to my locker and saw him standing in front of it with his back to me.

Evan was talking to someone. He seemed really upset. Then I saw the red hair shaking back and forth. My feet kept me moving forward against my will. I couldn't hear their voices, but her face looked so sad. Evan's hands were pleading.

Then I heard, "Sara, please tell me what happened. She's devastated, and I need to understand why."

"If she hasn't told you, then I can't."

Her eyes caught mine. I froze a few lockers away, unable to process what was happening. Sara closed her locker and rushed away. Evan slowly turned to acknowledge me. I examined him with narrowed eyes, trying to understand.

"Why did you do that?" I accused, horrified.

"If you only knew what I've seen for the past two days, you would have done the same thing."

I still didn't understand. His intrusion rocked me, and I needed to get away from him. I turned and dodged my way through the crowd, my books still clutched to my chest.

"Emma, wait," he implored, but he didn't come after me.

I ducked into the bathroom and found an empty stall. I pressed my back against the partition, remembering Sara's sad expression. I allowed the tears to burn down my cheeks while the scene replayed in my head. I didn't know why I wasn't relieved that she hadn't told anyone about my situation—maybe because I never thought she would.

As much as I wanted to, I couldn't be angry with Evan. I didn't like that he had upset Sara, but I knew it wasn't his fault. He really had no idea what he was walking into. Could I continue to allow him to be a witness to my misery without an explanation? Knowing I wouldn't ever tell him what had come between Sara and me, and I could never confide in him if something were to happen to me again left only one answer. I needed to give him up. I struggled with the decision, but it was something I had always known I'd have to do.

15. RELENTLESS

I t's nice to see you using such vibrant colors," Ms. Mier commented as she stood behind me, admiring my painting. "You have always used such deep colors in the past, still with extraordinary results, but this is refreshing. Whatever's changed, I like it."

Then she walked on to the next easel. I leaned back and looked at my nearly completed portrait of the fall foliage. Before Ms. Mier approached, I'd been thinking that it was too bright and unrealistic. The paintbrush in my hand was coated with a burnt orange, to tone down the fiery hues on the canvas. I set the brush down and stared at the colors again. They were blinding to my dull eyes.

I continued to stare at the blur of colors until Ms. Mier asked everyone to begin cleaning up. Startled by the sudden movement, I looked around and clumsily began gathering my supplies. I caught Evan standing in the back of the room, by the photography supplies, watching me with concern. I continued cleaning up my unused paints, ignoring him.

"Do you want to study for the Anatomy test with me?" Evan asked when we left the room.

"Uh…no, I can't," I stumbled. "I have to work on the paper."

"I can go with you."

"No, that's okay," I said quickly, barely giving him a glance. "I think I'd rather be alone."

"Okay," he said slowly and continued down the hall when I stopped at my locker.

I was forced to look after him, reminding myself that closing him out was the right thing to do. The right thing felt horrible—my eyes followed him until he rounded the corner. My heart ached, and for a second I reconsidered my decision, but I shook it off and opened my locker.

Soccer practice was hard not only physically but emotionally as well. Having to interact with Sara without connecting was torturous. When we weren't on the field, she remained as far away from me as she could. When we were on the field, she'd only pass to me when she didn't have any other choice.

"Lauren, would you be able to give me a ride home today?" I asked when we were standing on the sidelines during one of the drills.

"Sure," she answered without hesitation.

I kept walking alongside Lauren after practice, without looking at Evan as he waited for me by his car. I felt his eyes follow me to her car. I reminded myself again that it was for the best. But it didn't help.

"Thank you for doing this," I said to Lauren, ducking into her dark blue Volvo.

I had no idea what I was getting myself into when I asked Lauren to drive me home. She was very sweet, but she talked nonstop the entire drive. I heard about the homecoming dance and how Sara and Jason won homecoming king and queen, but neither had shown up. I tried to conceal my shock. She assumed I knew why they weren't there and tried to get me to confess. She obviously hadn't noticed that Sara and I weren't talking. Why did she think she was driving me home? I played it off and said that I didn't know either.

Lauren went on about soccer and the upcoming game. She was obviously excited to make it to the championships as captain for her senior year. I heard the details of every college she applied to and how she was having a hard time deciding which she preferred. Did most girls talk this much? I tried to figure out how she could breathe between sentences. The topics blurred together like the scenery, and I was almost relieved when she stopped at my house, exhausted by listening to her.

"Thank you again, Lauren," I said as I opened the car door.

"If you want a ride home tomorrow, let me know. It was nice talking to you. I feel like we never get to really talk."

"I may take you up on that," I said reluctantly, knowing I'd rather walk than ask for another ride.

I tried to make it through the kitchen, but was stopped in my tracks by a stinging pain to my right arm. I winced and turned to find Carol with a metal serving spoon in her hand.

"Who the hell was that?" Carol demanded, obviously very agitated. I looked around and realized George wasn't here. From her grip on the spoon, I knew this would not be good.

"That was Lauren. She's one of the team captains," I tried to explain. I was too nervous that she'd see through my lie if I tried to explain why Sara hadn't driven me, so I left it at that.

"You're pathetic. If you're begging for rides and embarrassing me, I will hurt you severely. Sara's finally seen you for who you are, huh?"

The mention of Sara's name stung worse than the red mark on my arm. I remained still, looking for any opportunity to back away to my room before this escalated.

That's when her eyes widened, and the metal spoon walloped the side of my head. I let out a moan and put my hand to my head, backing against the wall.

"You're fucking disgusting," she declared, the storm in her eyes brewing, making me fear what was to come. "How dare you come into my house smelling like that?"

I looked down at my practice clothes and released a breath of defeat. I'd chosen not to shower after practice today, so I wouldn't keep Lauren waiting. Wrong choice.

"Mom," Jack yelled from upstairs, distracting her. "Is Dad back with the pizza yet?"

She had to shake the fury from her brow before she replied in her best mother tone, "No, honey, but he should be here soon. Why don't you and Leyla get washed up?

"Get out of my sight before I make you sleep outside," she snapped. I took advantage of the opportunity to rush to my room.

Shutting my door, I dropped my bags and rubbed the small bump on my head, relieved to have walked away with nothing worse. I was starving, but I knew I'd have to suffer through it.

I tried to focus on my homework instead. I couldn't concentrate to save my life, staring at the words as they blurred in front of me. I only faintly recalled the lessons in class that went with the assignments, and my notes were a scribble of incoherent words. I jumped at the sound of the knock on the door at ten o'clock, the signal to turn off the lights.

I set the trigonometry book at the bottom of my closet and shut off the lights. I waited in bed until I'd heard two sets of footsteps ascend the stairs, then crept breathlessly out of bed and slipped into the closet, closing the door behind me. My closet wasn't very wide, which was fine, since I didn't own a lot of clothes, but it was tall and deep. I had plenty of clearance to sit under my clothes without them touching the top of my head. A small door at the back of the closet led into a crawl space where I stored the things that meant the most to me.

That minute space contained the only pictures I had of my parents, my memories of a time almost too distant to remember. It was certainly a universe away from where I sat now in the confines of a closet. I'd also stored some of my favorite paintings and athletic awards there, along with a small shoe box full of letters that my mother had sent to me after I'd moved in with George and Carol.

She wrote frequently at the beginning, about nothing of importance, just rambling on paper. After a while, the letters arrived less frequently, until finally they stopped coming altogether, about a year and a half ago. I figured she was consumed with her life and couldn't bother with me. She had always been consumed with her life—that's why I was in this house and not hers.

Reading by the pull-string lightbulb suspended above the closet shelf, I pored over my textbook, trying to teach myself what I'd neglected to learn in class. By the time I crept out of my study space, it was after one o'clock in the morning. I collapsed on my bed, never changing out of my practice clothes. Sleep came quickly, but the dreams kept me twisting.

———

I dragged myself to the bathroom in the morning. It would be another day with little to look forward to, but I got ready all the same. I intended to walk to the bus stop, but there he was—relentless. I was determined to keep walking, ignoring his shiny sports car.

As I walked past him, he stepped out of the car and pleaded, "Emma, don't do this."

My eyes widened in panic as I glanced from him to the picture window of the house. He saw my look of terror and glanced to the house as well.

"Then get in," he demanded. With an exasperated sigh, I stomped to his car and slid in. He closed his door and began driving away. I sat stiffly against the leather seat, my arms crossed around my backpack and my lips pressed together, staring straight ahead.

"Are you sulking?"

Insulted, I glared at him. He produced his amused grin, agitating me more.

"You're seriously sulking," he concluded, almost laughing.

"Stop," I shot back, attempting to be serious. But the more I tried, the harder it was, and despite myself I felt my lips curl into a smile. "I am not *sulking*."

Evan burst out laughing.

"Enough," I yelled, but found I was involuntarily smiling.

After he was able to stop laughing, he became too serious.

"Now you have to tell me what's going on. Why are you avoiding me?"

I remained quiet. I struggled for a rational explanation, a way to make him respect my decision to cut him out of my life. I couldn't come up with anything that would make sense to him. Everything I wanted to say would reveal too much. He waited patiently for my response.

"You're not Sara," I finally breathed.

"I don't want to be Sara," he replied in confusion. "I still don't understand."

"I don't know how to fit you in my world without hurting you too." The truth in my words revealed more than he'd ever know.

"Don't worry about hurting me," he replied calmly. "I like being a part of your world, and I understand that it's more complicated than you're willing to share with me. I'll respect that…for now."

He pulled into the parking lot of a drugstore and put the car in park. Evan seemed nervous as he turned to speak to me. He released a quick breath before he spoke. My chest tightened, afraid to hear what he had to say.

"I don't do this." His hands gestured between us. My eyes narrowed, trying to interpret his meaning. He exhaled and looked out the windshield. "I don't stay, and I'm used to that. And I'm always prepared to leave—because I have to eventually."

He stopped again, frustrated with himself. I sat motionless, absolutely convinced I didn't want him to continue—but I couldn't bring myself to ask him to stop.

"I want to stay here," he finally declared. "It would bother me if I left. I mean...unpacked."

Evan looked at me with a small, uncertain smile. We sat silently, looking at each other for an excruciatingly slow minute while he waited for me to say something. I broke his gaze, flashing my eyes around the car, searching for the right words. Disappointed, Evan looked away, his face turning red before he continued driving to school.

The tension was unbearable in the awkward silence. I was still struggling to say something that would make him give up on me, but every time I tried to say it, the words were strangled in my throat. Finally, when he pulled into a parking spot and shut off the car, I looked over at him and said the only thing my heart would allow me to say.

"You should stay." A smile crept across my face. Then I quickly added, "But you'll probably wish you hadn't, when you finally realize I'm not all that interesting." His eyes sparkled, and I watched the tension drain from his face.

As much as I knew it was the right thing to do, I couldn't continue to push him away. I searched for a logical reason to remain friends with him without finding one. It was a risk having him around, and he could never know the truth—but I wasn't ready to give him up.

"Did you really unpack?" I asked skeptically as we walked into school.

"Actually I did—the other night after I got back from dropping you off. I think you guilted me into it."

I laughed. "So that's the secret to getting to you—guilt."

"There are other ways," he replied with his grin.

About to respond to his taunting, I stopped, realizing where we were. From the end of the hall, I searched to see if Sara was at her locker, and I let out a defeated sigh when I saw that she wasn't.

"How do I get her to listen to me?" I murmured, still staring down the hall.

"Maybe you have to make her," Evan answered before walking away.

Crushed with the acceptance that this was going to be another day of avoidance, I slowly sauntered to my locker to prepare for class. I remained hollow, but I was beginning to accept the emptiness as a part of me.

I was able to listen in class and understand the lectures. I walked alongside Evan and heard his words, and even contributed to the conversation. But my eyes still searched for her in the halls, continuously disappointed when she was too far away, or if I didn't see her at all.

I tried to convince myself to give up on her and accept that I was alone in my truth. That's when it hit me—*the truth*. I stopped in the middle of the hall with Evan in midsentence. His words faded when he turned back to find me.

"Are you okay?" he asked hesitantly.

"I think I am." I said each word slowly, contemplating my epiphany—she *knew* the truth. Evan appeared worried. I turned my attention to him and grinned.

This did not change his look of concern, but he didn't say anything as we continued to Anatomy. Once class let out, I hurried into the hall, leaving Evan questioning my retreat. I almost ran to my locker, hoping I'd get there in time. I breathed an anxious sigh of relief when I found her still putting her books away in her locker. I moved to intercept her before she could walk away.

Spotting my approach, Sara attempted to escape in the opposite direction. Thankfully, she was alone. I followed her, and before she could exit through the doors leading to the stairs, I bellowed, "That wasn't me."

Sara stopped in her tracks when she heard my voice, but she didn't turn to face me. I caught up with her and stood behind her, close enough so my words wouldn't draw attention.

"I know I said some horrible things, Sara, and I will always be sorry for what I said," I said in a rush before she could change her mind and keep walking. "But *you* know that wasn't me."

She turned apprehensively, without responding.

"Can we please talk?" I begged. She shrugged and pushed the door open. I followed her down the stairs and out the side door, where we lowered ourselves onto the grass. She rested her arms on her bent knees, staring straight ahead without looking at me.

I slowly sat beside her and let my words float into the air, in hope that she'd hear them.

"I'm so, so sorry for what I said to you. I wasn't myself, and I hope you know that. I was hurting, and angry, and unfortunately you were there to receive it. It wasn't right. But you know that person is not who I am."

Sara tilted her head to look over at me, so I knew she was starting to understand.

"I don't get angry. It feels horrible, and I can't stand to be like that. If I do…If I let her get to me, then she wins. She destroys me along with everything and everyone who's important to me.

"I let her get to me that day. I was consumed by it. I shouldn't have said what I did, but I also couldn't let you tell anyone. I know how easy it would be to end all of this, but I can't. It's not just my life I have to think about. Taking Leyla and Jack away from their parents would destroy them, and I can't be responsible for that. I'm strong enough to handle this. They're still kids, so I have to put up with it for a little while longer. Do you understand?"

Sara's eyes brimmed with tears. She looked away so she could wipe them.

"I know I don't have any right to ask you to be there for me. It's not the ideal friendship to be involved in, but I know I can get through this if you're there to help me. You're the only one who really knows me, and I trust you. I will never ask you to lie for me, and I will never make you be a part of anything you don't want to. But the thought that you may never talk to me again hurts worse than anything Carol could ever do to me. I don't want to lose you too."

My heart stammered at the honesty I spilled at her feet. I had never been this exposed, not even to Sara. I couldn't take back the words. I couldn't hide my vulnerability. I knew I meant what I said more than any bitter, hurtful word I'd spewed in the locker room, and I hoped the truth was enough.

I waited in tense silence. "You haven't lost me, Em," she finally whispered. "You're right, as much as I don't understand it—you're not an angry person. Sad and withdrawn, definitely—but not angry; even though you have every right to be." She paused.

"I knew you didn't mean what you said. The reason I haven't been able to face you is because *I* get so angry when I look at you." I was confused by her confession. "I *hate* this woman for hurting you. It makes me so angry I can hardly contain myself, and I don't like feeling angry either. But you're right, this is exactly what she wants—to isolate and destroy anything positive you have. We can't let that happen. I know you're strong enough to do it without me, but I'm not ready to quit being your friend either." Her eyes glistened as she offered me a soft smile.

I tried to blink away the wetness in my eyes. Sara stood up and opened her arms to hug me. I stood as well, and I let her, without tensing.

She pulled away and smiled, wiping the tears from her cheeks again. "Let's get one thing straight," she said looking me in the eye with all seriousness. "If you ever call me a slut again, I will never speak to you. I know what I'm doing, so stay out of it. Got it?"

"Yes, I get it," I promised. "I am still really sorry about that."

"I know," she replied, grabbing my hand. "And I'm sorry I threatened to expose you. I understand why you're doing this. I hate it—I'm not going to lie. But I'm here for you, no matter what."

This time, I hugged her tightly. "Thanks."

16. THE PLAN

We walked to the cafeteria together. When we neared the entrance, Sara said, "We have to come up with a plan."

"What kind of plan?"

"You deserve to be happy. I've noticed how much more relaxed you've been since Evan's been a bad influence. So let's figure out a way for you to get into college, survive living with your aunt and uncle, and still have fun."

"That sounds impossible," I said, shaking my head.

"We'll be smart about it," she said, winking.

"You did not just wink at me."

"Shut up," she said, playfully shoving my arm. Thankfully not the arm with the fresh bruise.

When we were seated at the lunch table with our trays of food, Sara continued with her thoughts. It was obvious that she'd given this some attention before today.

"Okay, you and Evan have already started doing what I have in mind. You know, with pushing your at-school time, and going to the library. I think we can try to expand it to a Friday or Saturday night so you can stay over at my house. It will definitely work the nights you have basketball games, but the game will take up most of the night and not give us much time to do anything else. I have to figure out an excuse that they'll buy to get you out of their house as much I can."

She was right—I was already stretching the little freedom I had when I claimed to be at school or the library. What was another night? Then I remembered Carol's suspicious interrogation, sending an icy chill down my spine as the doubt settled in. How was I going to get away with this?

"But Emma," Sara stated seriously, "if you ever get caught, I will not let her hurt you. I will tell my parents, or call the police, before I allow you to get hurt for my plan. Okay?" From the stern look upon her face, I knew she meant it.

"Okay," I whispered, knowing I'd never let it happen. "Sara, while we're talking about that—you have to trust me." I could tell she didn't quite understand. "I know what I can handle. Even though it's not right, it's the way things are until I can get out of their house. So you have to trust me when I don't tell you what happens sometimes, okay?"

Sara paused for a moment, absorbing my words. "Emma, always be honest with me." I connected with her penetrating eyes and nodded slightly, again knowing I wouldn't.

On our way back up to our lockers, Sara turned to me and asked eagerly, "Are you and Evan officially dating yet?"

I rolled my eyes. "That still will not happen."

"I don't understand why not," she teased.

Sara's smile got bigger when we found Evan waiting at my locker. His eyes brightened when he saw Sara walking with me.

"Hi, Sara," he said, grinning.

"Hi, Evan," she greeted, still smiling.

"Ready for Journalism?" he asked. "Oh, Em, do you think you'll be able to finish with the paper during class and study period so that maybe we can do something after practice?"

"That's perfect," Sara interjected, before I could answer. "Let's go back to my house and get pizzas and hang out." She was thrilled to have an accomplice in Operation Free-Em. She was almost jumping up and down.

Evan paused and took in her overjoyous response, having no idea what Sara and I had been discussing during lunch.

"Sara's trying to come up with a plan to expose me to the world outside of school and my house, and you're just feeding into it," I explained.

"That's always been *my* plan," Evan admitted. Sara beamed.

"I hope I know what I'm getting myself into," I said with a sigh and a roll of my eyes.

"The chance to live a little," Sara declared, barely able to contain her enthusiasm.

"So *you* say," I grumbled. She laughed. I loved having her back.

After practice, Evan and Jason followed us to Sara's.

While we were in the car, I told Sara, "I'm so sorry you and Jason didn't go to homecoming. I can only assume it was my fault."

Sara scoffed, "Don't even worry about it. I really didn't want to go, and Jason is so shy, he would've been mortified to have to wear the crown onstage." I still felt bad for being the reason she missed out on such a huge moment.

"How was the ride home with Lauren yesterday?" she asked, changing the subject.

"Exhausting." I sighed, which made Sara laugh. "I didn't realize anyone could talk so much or so fast."

"She's so nice, but yeah, she likes to go on and on about anything and everything."

Sara's house was dark when we pulled up.

"My parents went out to dinner *again*," she observed with a heavy breath.

The next few hours epitomized everything Sara wanted for me. We ate pizza, listened to music, played video games, and laughed. The laughter filled up the empty hole, and my heart returned to its proper place in my chest, putting me back together again.

Not wanting to risk it, I decided it was best to leave around nine o'clock. Evan volunteered to drive me home. Sara hugged me good night and said she'd see me in the morning. Evan looked up from putting on his jacket when she said this.

"I liked picking you up," Evan admitted when we stepped outside. "Although you were less talkative than usual, I actually looked forward to seeing you first thing in the morning."

"Sorry. You'll have to be satisfied with seeing me in just about every class instead."

"It's good that you and Sara are okay," he said during the drive to my house. "How'd it happen?"

"I made her listen."

He smiled at my response.

———

The next week continued as if the time without Sara had been just a hiccup. Sara and I were inseparable again. Evan still walked me to class, but became absent during the second part of the day, when I had lunch and study with Sara. I noticed the first couple of days and couldn't figure out why I was bothered by it.

The three of us did things together after school, and occasionally Jason joined. Coach let us watch the second half of the guys' quarterfinals on Thursday, which they lost. Evan was crushed, but he recovered when I told him that I wasn't expected home until nine o'clock. Weslyn won the soccer game that Friday with a score of 4 to 3. I contributed two of the scores, which was fortunate, since three scouts were in attendance. I was assured by Coach Peña that I'd played well and that I'd be hearing from them. I could only hope.

Sara joined Evan and me that Sunday for our library day. I think she was trying to make up for lost time, which made me happy. But I noticed the surprise on Evan's face when Sara pulled up behind his car. I don't know what Evan had initially planned, but once he saw Sara was joining us, he suggested we go back to his place to play pool.

Sara and I were a team and played against Evan. Of course, he still beat us. Despite his initial reaction, Evan didn't show any signs that he wasn't happy to have Sara there. While we played, Sara instigated a plan for the following weekend. She figured I'd be able to sleep over at her house on Friday for the championship game, assuming we won the semifinals on Tuesday. I wasn't convinced, since it was a five o'clock game and wouldn't warrant me having to stay out past my curfew.

Sara wanted to think of a way for me to stay Saturday as well, so we'd have Saturday and then all Sunday together. Evan glanced at me when she mentioned Sunday, but he didn't openly object. I let Sara go on with her pretend plans, because I knew it wasn't going to happen. The only day that had a chance was my usual library visit on Sunday.

Everything changed that night when George told me, "We're taking the kids skiing next weekend. Janet said you could stay with her."

My stomach dropped. Janet lived two towns away, and there was no way I would be able to play in the game on Friday, forget about going to the library on Sunday.

"The championship game is Friday night," I said urgently.

Carol glared at me. "Maybe you'll have to miss it," she snipped. "My mother is kind enough to let you stay with her; you should be more appreciative."

My chest tightened as the fire of nerves twisted in my stomach. This could not be happening.

"Can I ask Sara if I can stay with her instead?" I pleaded, looking directly at George, ignoring Carol.

"That would be okay," George agreed reluctantly. I could hear Carol take in a breath.

"I'll ask her tomorrow," I said, relieved.

"Why don't you let me call her parents tonight," Carol interjected. "I want to be sure this is really okay with them. I don't want them to feel obligated to say yes if *you* ask."

I still wasn't concerned, since I knew Anna and Carl wouldn't care if I spent the weekend. They'd made it more than clear every time I saw them that I was welcome to stay whenever I liked. I tried to look worried and suppress my smile—I had to appear miserable to stay under Carol's radar.

After dinner, Carol called and spoke with Anna. Of course Carol made a case for what an inconvenience I'd be for two nights, but to her dismay, Anna was pleased to have me. I knew Sara was going to be beyond excited to hear that we didn't have to come up with a lie for me to stay the weekend.

I wasn't wrong. When Sara pulled up the next morning, she was a burst of energy. I smiled at her enthusiastic greeting. She was already trying to decide how we were going to spend the weekend. She mentioned a party on Saturday night, but dismissed it as soon as she saw the blood rush from my face.

"I know," Sara exclaimed while we walked down the hall. "Want to have a sleepover on Friday night with some of the girls from the team?"

"I don't mind that idea," I agreed, to her surprise.

Sara was satisfied with Friday night's plan, even though the details still needed to be worked out. That included making it to the championship game and winning.

Sara was still going on about the weekend when Evan met me outside homeroom.

"Emma's staying over my house this weekend," Sara gloated, before disappearing down the hall.

"Really?" Evan mused as we walked to English.

"My aunt and uncle are taking the kids skiing in Maine for the weekend," I explained.

"Then what are we doing this weekend?"

"I think Friday night is going to be a girls' night. But I'm not sure about the rest of the weekend. You'll have to ask Sara. I think the planning's out of my hands."

I was so afraid the week was going to drag now that I had the weekend to look forward to, but thankfully, it sailed by.

Friday night's plans were sealed after we won the semifinal game on Tuesday. It was a close game, and we only just won, scoring two points to their one. Lauren tipped in the winning goal with less than a minute to play, perfecting her senior year.

Lauren decided to have the team over after the game on Friday, regardless of the outcome. Sara discreetly invited five of the girls to sleep over at her place after. I was truly looking forward to the estrogen overload. I knew the girls on the team and didn't mind the idea of spending the night hanging out.

We still hadn't figured out what we were doing on Saturday—that is, until Wednesday afternoon, when the decision was made by…me. I was standing at my locker getting my books for Chemistry when I was approached by Jake Masters—the same Jake who was friends with Evan, captain of the soccer team, and who'd *winked* at me at Scott Kirkland's party.

"Hey, Emma," he said casually, as if we spoke every day. "How are you doing?" He leaned against the locker next to mine, giving me his full attention.

"Good, Jake," I answered, looking around, making sure he was really talking to me. "How are you?"

Ignoring my question, he continued.

"Listen, I'm having a party on Saturday night. It's not going to be big, only about twenty or so people who I really want to be there. And I really want *you* to be there. What do you think?"

Before I could process what he was asking, he added, "Oh, you can bring Sara or whoever with you if you want."

"Okay," I said, without realizing I was answering him.

"Great! Then I'll see you on Saturday." He winked and walked away, leaving me stunned. I stood there for a moment, glancing around, waiting for someone to tell me it was a joke. And what was up with the *winking*? Seriously, it was weird!

As we walked to Trig, I told Evan, "I know what we're doing Saturday night."

Evan sighed and asked, "Great, what has Sara planned now?"

"Actually," I corrected, "I told Jake Masters we'd go to his party." I expected to hear him laugh at the irony of me deciding to go to a party, but he was silent. I examined his pensive expression.

"What?"

"Jake asked *you* to go to his party?"

"Yeah, I was completely surprised, and I still haven't figured out why—but he did. So I kinda agreed."

Evan let out a short laugh. "You don't know why Jake asked you to the party? Does he know that you want to bring me with you?"

"He said I could bring whoever I wanted." I wasn't following along and didn't understand why Evan found this so intriguing.

"Okay, we're going to Jake Masters's party," he finally conceded. "Have you heard about his parties?"

"No. Why?" By the tone of his question, I wasn't sure I wanted to know.

"They tend to be pretty...exclusive," he explained. "I've been to one of them."

"Was it horrible?" I asked when he didn't say more. I wanted to know what I was about to walk into.

"No," he said dismissively. Then he must have realized he was freaking me out and added, "It'll be fine. Don't worry."

Sara was much more excited than Evan when I told her. She had also heard about the handpicked guest list of Jake's parties and was thrilled to finally get to see what they were all about. I was surprised to learn she'd never been to one before. I told her to bring Jason, which I think she had already planned to.

When Friday arrived, I was a bundle of nerves. All I could think about was the game that night. The Weslyn girls' soccer team had always been pretty competitive in the division, but this was the first time in almost ten years that the team had made it to the finals.

My quiet anxiety was mirrored by Sara's exuberant anticipation. Unable to contain her energy, she fidgeted during the car ride to school. Trying to keep our minds off the game, she started to run through our plans for the weekend. I let her talk the entire drive, unable to focus on what she said enough to contribute.

When we arrived at school, we were greeted with homemade banners and flyers along the halls, wishing the girls' soccer team luck in the championship game. Our lockers were decorated with streamers and glittery letters with a message of encouragement, along with our jersey numbers. Instead of groaning, as I had at the sight of the glittery mess, Sara shrieked with excitement.

"I don't know how I'm going to get through the day," she exclaimed. "I can't wait for tonight!" I was trying to figure out how I was going to get through the day as well. It was hard to focus, knowing the game was approaching, and the over-the-top energy wasn't helping—it felt overwhelming and disorienting. I wanted to slip into an empty room with music blaring in my ears to gather myself.

Then it only got worse. During morning announcements, we were informed we'd be getting out of our last class early to assemble for a pep rally for the soccer team in the gymnasium. My mouth dropped as I heard Sara holler with enthusiasm, joined by the rest of the room.

"Looking forward to the game?" Evan asked while Ms. Abbott handed back our latest writing assignment.

"I think I'm going to throw up," I confessed and dropped my head onto my folded arms. Evan chuckled.

"Don't worry, you'll be great," he assured me.

"I wish everyone would treat this like every other game and stop acting so insane," I said, facing him with my head still resting on my arms.

"Not to add to your nausea, but I don't know if I can go to Jake's party tomorrow night."

"What?" My head shot up. The exclamation came out a little too loud, turning a few heads. Ms. Abbott continued handing back papers, unfazed by my disruption.

Evan looked around and waited until no one was looking before he continued.

"My parents are making me go to dinner with them," he explained, annoyed. "It's being hosted by one of the partners, and we have to put in appearances. I don't have a choice—I'm sorry."

The thought of going to a party with just Jason and Sara did not appeal to me. I didn't want them to feel obligated to entertain me when I knew they'd want alone time. That would mean *I'd* have alone time, which terrified me.

That thought must have translated on my face, because Evan said, "Don't worry. I'll see what I can do."

"It's okay," I said, trying not to sound as disappointed as I was. "I understand."

I had to survive History and Chemistry, coping not only with nausea from the approaching game but also with the building anxiety of going to Jake's party without Evan. I decided I needed to shake off the distraction of Jake's party and stay focused on the first hurdle—winning the game.

Evan met me outside Chemistry with a mischievous grin on his face. I approached him cautiously.

"I'm afraid to know."

"I think I've figured out a way to help us both get through tomorrow night."

"How?" I asked, still afraid to hear his plan.

"You can come with me to the dinner—"

Before he could continue, I took in an audible gasp of air. He pressed his lips together at my reaction.

"It won't be that bad," he comforted. "It'll get you warmed up for the party. You can be my excuse to get out of staying the whole time, and then we can go to the party together." I wasn't sure what was more terrifying, going to a party practically alone or meeting Evan's parents and being surrounded by adults who'd expect intelligent, coherent conversation.

"Maybe I'll beg Sara to stay home and watch movies instead," I whispered, trying to breathe evenly.

"I knew it was a long shot," Evan said quietly, looking away. "I hate these dinners—having to pretend to be the perfect son to the perfect parents, while talking to pretentious people gloating about their accomplishments. I thought it might not be so miserable if you were there too."

I didn't say anything as we found our seats for class. Evan sat quietly next to me. I kept glancing over at him throughout class. He looked...sad. I didn't like seeing his drawn mouth and his slumped shoulders. It was obvious that this dinner was Scott's party for Evan. I didn't know how I would have gotten through that night if Evan hadn't been there.

I took a deep breath and swallowed my stomach, digesting what I was agreeing to do. I felt nauseous at the thought of meeting

Evan's parents, but my chest warmed when I looked at him, know-ing I was doing the right thing.

"I'll do it," I said when the bell rang at the end of class.

"What?"

"I think that it's a good compromise." I tried to sound confi-dent. "I'll go to dinner with you, and you go to the party with me." He examined me cautiously, making sure I was serious before he let the smile release on his face.

"You know I'm making out in the deal, right?"

"Whatever," I said dismissively. "I still owe you for Scott's party. But I have to warn you, I'm not great with small talk, so I may end up embarrassing you."

He laughed. "I don't think that's possible. Besides, you'll find you won't have to do too much talking. This crowd loves to talk about themselves, so all you have to do is stand there and nod politely. Don't worry; I won't leave you alone with any of them."

Just before we entered the art room, Evan stopped to face me.

"Are you sure you want to do this?"

I pressed my mouth into the best fake smile I could and said, "Of course I do." When I saw the relief in his eyes, I found that I didn't need to fake it.

I told Sara the revised plan during lunch.

"No way," she gasped. "You're going to meet his parents?"

After thinking about it for a minute longer, she added, "You know, I don't believe you when you say you're just friends. You have a thing for him, whether you're ready to admit it or not."

"Sara," I exclaimed with fiery cheeks, "you don't know what you're talking about!" I couldn't cool my face for the rest of lunch. It didn't help that Sara kept a stupid grin on her face the entire time, fueling the fire.

"You have to promise me that you'll keep your thoughts to yourself when we're around him," I begged.

"Em, I would never say anything about how you feel about him," she promised.

"How *you think* I feel about him," I corrected. But I couldn't argue my point beyond that.

I was so overwhelmed I could barely sit through Journalism. Between Sara's provoking smile on one side and Evan's heart-stopping grin on the other, my head was spinning. I couldn't deny how I felt every time I was around Evan. But I'd convinced myself that being friends was what was best. I knew what was best, right?

I *couldn't* think of him as any more than a friend. I had too much to lose. Why had I let Sara get to me? I didn't have any serious feelings for him, right? There was no way…

I watched while Evan listened to Ms. Holt's review of the current assignments. I traced the profile of his straight nose and his distinct cheekbones, down to his chiseled jaw. His perfect lips were separated slightly as his steel-blue eyes glanced from Ms. Holt down to his notebook, where he would occasionally jot down notes. I followed the tight muscles that extended down his neck, concealed under a blue sweater that hinted at the contours of his chest. I was breathing slowly, unable to redirect my eyes. My heart murmured softly in my chest, releasing a tingling that sent goose bumps along my arms.

Evan glanced at me, and I quickly turned my head, my cheeks warming. I knew he didn't know what I was thinking—*I* didn't know what I was thinking—but I didn't want him to catch me staring. Seriously, what was I thinking? I could not have feelings for Evan! What was going on? My mind unraveled as images of our time together flashed through my head. I finally gave in to what I'd been trying to ignore for the past month. I took a gulp of air as I finally faced the truth—I was in love with Evan Mathews.

"Are you okay?" Sara whispered. "You look freaked."

"Ms. Holt," I interrupted in an unsteady voice. The whole class turned to look at me. "Uh, Sara and I have to leave now so we can get ready for the pep rally."

Before she could answer, I stood with my books in my arms, heading out the door. I turned when I got into the hallway, urging Sara to hurry up as she slowly gathered her things.

"What is wrong with you?" she demanded when we walked into the girls' bathroom. I checked the stalls before answering. Sara followed my actions with a worried stare.

"I *am* freaked," I admitted in a loud whisper. "Sara, I can't believe I like him."

"I'm not following," she replied with narrow eyes. "And why are you whispering?"

"You're right. I like Evan a lot more than a friend," I said, sighing.

"You are just now realizing this?" She almost laughed.

"Shut up, Sara," I snapped, still whispering. "This is horrible. I can't feel this way. And you can't tell me you don't understand why I'm so freaked."

She absorbed my desperate words and took a long breath.

"I know why *you* think you can't date him. But I think you're only hurting yourself more if you try to deny how you feel."

"Besides, how do I know he feels the same? I can't *tell him*. Then it would be so weird, and we wouldn't even be able to be friends."

Sara shook her head and grinned, "You are such an idiot. Of course he feels the same way. I can't believe how blind you are. Are you worried that if you dated him, she'd find out?"

"If she ever found out I was dating someone, I'd lose everything. She would never let me out of the house. And he can never find out what it's like for me! I can't do this."

"No, you can't do it," she agreed firmly. "I'm already going against everything my gut is telling me by keeping your secret. I'm not going to let you risk it more by pissing Carol off if she finds out about Evan."

I wasn't expecting Sara to say this. I knew she was right, but my heart still sank.

"I don't want you to have to give him up, so we'll just have to figure out a way for you to remain friends—nothing more. Maybe you shouldn't spend time alone together."

"I have to this weekend," I huffed, now even more tormented by the thought of going to dinner with him. "But Sara, if I can't be alone with him, then I shouldn't be friends with him. You can't chaperone to make sure he doesn't stand too close. Just help me keep my head on straight, that'll be enough. If I can't handle it, then I can't be around him anymore. It's that simple."

"We can do this," she assured me, unable to contain her grin. "Although I've wished for forever that you guys would hook up."

"Sara, that's not helping," I snapped, no longer whispering.

"You're right—sorry," she said, still grinning.

17. UNEXPECTED VISIT

D o we really have to go to this pep rally?" I moped when we returned to our lockers to get our game jerseys.

"Of course we do," she exclaimed, amazed by my question. "Em, it will get us so pumped to have the whole school cheer for us before the game."

"Can I listen to my music, so I don't have to hear it?" She looked at me with her hands turned up in front of her, unable to process my unwillingness to be a part of the excitement.

"Sara, I need to get focused on the game. I've been distracted all day with this Evan stuff. I can't be swooped up in the chaos of listening to everyone screaming."

"You are so strange." She shook her head. "You cannot get away with listening to music during a pep rally. We have to run in as they announce us, and we sit together at the back of the gym where everyone can see us—so you will have to put up with the *chaos*."

"Are you serious?" I almost yelled. "We get announced and have to sit in front of everyone?"

"Don't you remember the football pep rally?"

"I didn't go."

Sara sighed. "Em, it will be fine. You have the half-hour bus ride to get focused, and we aren't even leaving the school until three thirty. So after the rally we'll find an empty room where I promise not to talk to you. You can listen to music, do homework, or whatever ritual you need to do to get your head ready for the game. Okay?" I nodded, sighing heavily.

The pep rally was worse than I imagined. The band played, the football cheerleaders cheered, there were a ton of balloons and lots of screaming. The worst part was when they "announced" the team. Sara had neglected to mention that we'd be announced individually—I'd thought we would run in together. I was mortified when I was introduced last. It only added to my humiliation when they noted that I was the leading scorer in the state, causing the screams to escalate. I really didn't want to be there.

When it was finally over, I hid from everyone in the art room and worked on my Trigonometry homework while listening to the band Evan had added to my playlist.

I remained quiet on the bus, tuning out the chants and cheers. As we approached the school, I sank further into my seat and closed my eyes.

I felt a hand on the knee that I had pressed against the seat in front of me. I opened my eyes to find Coach Peña sitting across from me, the bus was almost empty. I sat up and turned off the music.

"Ready?" he asked with a confident smile. "You can do this, you know."

"I know," I assured him.

"Let's go." He patted my leg and headed down the aisle to exit the bus. I followed him, turning the music back on.

More and more people flowed into the stadium as we settled into our pregame warm-ups. The air was whirling with the voices and energy of the crowd and the players. I didn't look around, not wanting to see what was at stake. I shut out the cheers, the flashes from the cameras and the announcements over the speakers. I breathed in the cold November air, settling my thoughts on what was about to take place. When I was oblivious to the distractions, I knew I was ready.

The game was better than I anticipated. It was aggressive, with bodies bumping and fighting for possession. It was fast; the ball flew from foot to foot, covering the length of the field and back again within a minute. It was hard, with passes intercepted and goals blocked. It was still scoreless at halftime.

The second half exploded with the same intensity as the first. Neither team wanted to walk away with the loss. Midway through the second half, we were able to charge in tight around the goal. There was a lot of bumping and pushing as the ball shuffled among the feet. The sweeper attempted to clear the ball up the sidelines with a forceful kick, blocked by Jill's braced body. The collision sent the ball sailing back toward the middle of the field. Concentrating on the arc, I took a few hard strides forward, pushing my body into the air to make contact with the ball using my head. The side of my head connected with the ball, redirecting it toward the goal in a single motion. At the same time, my shoulder collided with a body pushing up against me. The hands of the goalie landed on my head a second too late. The ball was already moving in the direction of the net.

I fell to the ground with the goalie, knowing my timing was a fraction of a second faster than hers. The whistle blew to announce the goal and the crowd erupted, something I had never noticed before. Startled, I looked around to take in the lights and the flashes, right before Sara and Jill pulled me off the ground and embraced me, screaming in my ears.

Each team scored one more time, but we came out with the win. When the final whistle blew, the field was inundated with a rush of people yelling and cheering. I received hugs and pats from a blur of faces. Still floating on adrenaline, I was too excited to be bothered by the invasion.

Evan pushed through the crowd to find me, his camera in his hand. Before I could react, he wrapped his arms around me and pulled me to him.

"Congratulations," he said in my ear before letting me go. "You always find a way to make the most impossible goals. I think I got a decent picture of it."

"Thanks," I said with a huge smile.

Before I could say anything more, I was attacked by more hands, hugs and shouts of congratulations. I lost sight of Evan in the crowd, but I kept searching for him. The crowd slowly eased up, and after shaking hands with the other team, I made it back to the bench to gather my things.

The spectators steadily dissipated, filing through the gates leading to the parking lot, Evan somewhere among them. Sara waited for me in the middle of the field. As we approached the exit, I caught a glimpse of someone lingering on the other side. I kept my head down and continued toward the bus.

"Emily!" the figure yelled when I got closer. I looked up and stopped abruptly. Sara hesitated a step ahead of me, following my frozen stare. Her eyes widened.

"I'll tell Coach you'll be a minute," she said quietly, and left me alone.

"What are you doing here?" I asked, my voice not as strong as I wanted it to be.

"A friend dropped me off so I could see your game," my mother replied with a cautious smile. "Congratulations, I'm so proud of you."

Then a slight breeze allowed her signature sweet perfume to burn my nose. "You've been drinking," I murmured, crushed. She hadn't changed.

"I was nervous about seeing you, so I had a couple of drinks. No big deal."

I couldn't say anything. I couldn't move. My body quivered with nerves.

"I've been following you in the papers," she explained. "I had to see you. You look so great."

I stared back.

"What happened above your eye?" she asked, nodding toward the small scar above my left eye.

I shrugged, looking at the ground, afraid she'd see the emotion in my eyes, which were starting to tear.

"I figured you didn't want to hear from me," she said sheepishly, playing with her hands, "especially since you haven't written back in so long."

"What are you talking about?" I asked in confusion.

"You haven't been getting my letters?"

I shook my head.

"I think about you all the time—" she started.

"Don't," I interrupted, beginning to feel anger among the swirling emotions. "Don't say it. I can't hear it again. How much you love me but can't take care of me the way I deserve. Just…just don't, because you have no idea what I deserve." She couldn't look up to meet my watering eyes.

Before she could defend her abandonment once again, a voice hollered, "Rachel, there you are. We've gotta go, babe."

I noticed a guy with a shaved head in a leather jacket and worn jeans approaching us.

"We can't be late," he said impatiently, not giving me a second glance. My mother eyed me apologetically, but I knew I wasn't a choice—I never had been.

"I have to go," I said, slowly back away from them, needing to escape the tension before I was smothered by it.

"Emily, this is Mark," she said, trying to introduce us. He barely acknowledged me with a quick "Hey" as he grabbed her hand with an impatient tug.

I nodded my head, understanding exactly who he was. *He* was her choice.

"It was so great to—" she started to say as he led her in the direction of the running Charger in the parking lot. I turned my back on her and walked away without letting her finish.

The bus was filled with excitement and chatter—no one had realized they were waiting on me. I tried to smile as I received praise from my teammates, making my way down the aisle to sit next to Sara.

"Do you want to sit next to the window?"

"Yeah," I replied, my voice shaky. I moved in as Sara scooted closer to the aisle. I collapsed on the seat and rested my head against the cool glass, trying to fight back the tears. My hand shook as I wiped my eyes with the cuff of my sweatshirt. Sara grabbed my hand and gave it a gentle squeeze. We sat in silence while I stared out the window, trying to regain control.

"Your mom, huh?" she eventually confirmed. "She looks—"

"Nothing like me," I muttered, wanting there to be more than her light blue eyes and thin lips to differentiate us. "After four years, why did she have to choose one of the most important nights of my life to show up?"

"I don't know," she whispered. "If it's easier, we can pretend it never happened. I won't mention it, and you can forget it. We'll have a great time for the rest of the night."

"I'll try," I promised, pushing away my mother's depressing image.

"We'll take showers at the school and go straight to Lauren's," she explained, keeping me distracted. "Let's only stay for an hour or two before we head back to my house with the girls. We're going to have an amazing night." She smiled and squeezed my hand, then added, "But if you ever want to talk about her…after tonight, I'm here."

I nodded slightly, knowing that was highly unlikely. I washed my mother away in the shower—tucking her back in the dark place where I kept her. And that's where she stayed…at least for the rest of the night.

After an hour at Lauren's, surrounded by hyped girls who talked even faster than usual, Sara nudged me—it was time to go. Five other girls joined us, following us to Sara's in their cars.

We listened to music, ate junk food, and eventually the topic of boys came up. I knew it was inevitable, so I chose not to contribute until I was forced into the conversation.

"So, what's up with you and Evan?" Casey demanded.

"We're just friends," I said casually, hoping that would be enough for them to move on.

"Then what's wrong with you?" Veronica accused. "He's totally hot."

"We're just not interested in each other that way," I responded defensively.

"You know that Haley Spencer pretty much hates you, right?" Jill added.

"What?" I asked incredulously.

"She's obsessed with Evan and thinks the only reason he won't go out with her is because of you," she explained. I laughed.

"Emma, are you serious?" Jaclyn Carter accused. "You have to admit he's gorgeous, and smart, and athletic—"

"Basically perfect," Casey finished.

"No one's perfect," I rebutted.

"So, what's his flaw?" Casey demanded. I looked at Sara, hoping she'd change the subject.

"He can be really annoying," I told them, knowing that wasn't going to be enough to satisfy them.

"I think you should date him," Jill said bluntly. "You two would be as perfect together as Sara and Jason." I turned red.

"Speaking of Jason," I said, finally seeing a break, "Sara, what's he doing tonight?"

Sara intercepted the girls' attention and started talking about Jason's perfections. As Sara fed the girls' intrigue about what it was like to be with Jason Stark, I thought I heard something off in her enthusiasm. I couldn't figure it out, but there was something missing.

I let the buzz of voices continue without my participation. I settled back into the recliner, but I couldn't help thinking: What *was* going on between Evan and me?

18. ANOTHER DIMENSION

Wed better hurry," Sara said as we emerged into the diminishing daylight through the doors of the movie theater. "We only have two hours to get you ready."

"How long could it possibly take me to get ready?"

"Well, you have to take a shower, and make sure you shave. Oh, and I bought you more of that lotion."

"I still have lotion left from the first bottle. And why are you concerned if I shave?"

"Well, now you have more. I really like it on you. It's subtle and pretty."

"I like it too, thank you. But you didn't answer the shaving question." She was beginning to make me nervous.

"You're wearing a skirt," she revealed cautiously.

"Seriously?" I couldn't remember the last time I'd worn a skirt. When *was* the last time I'd worn a skirt? Then I tried to remember what my legs looked like. Did I have any bruises or scrapes on my knees from the game? "A skirt?"

"Em, you're going to look amazing." Then Sara quickly added, "But not too amazing. The last thing we need is for him to want to kiss you." She paused, looking at me before sighing. "This is going to be harder than I thought."

"I don't think you have to worry about that," I assured her.

When we got back to her house, the grand production began. While I showered and shaved, Sara went through her closet, rifling through what seemed like everything she owned. She wouldn't let me see what she'd finally decided on until I was ready to get dressed.

Sara dried my hair and rolled it in hot curlers. I was panicked when I saw my head full of the white cylinders. Then my eyes popped at the sight of the ringlets dangling from my head after she unrolled them.

"Sara, you cannot let me go out like this," I pleaded.

"Don't worry, I'm not done," she promised.

She gathered my hair into a high ponytail, allowing my bangs to sweep across my forehead. I decided it was best not to look until she was done, so I closed my eyes as she teased, pinned and sprayed. I opened them to find a large, smooth bun on the back of my head. It looked more sophisticated than anything I could've imagined.

Sara handed me the softest pink sweater I'd ever seen. Once I was dressed, I stood in front of the full-length mirror, admiring the boat neckline of the fitted sweater, which subtly revealed the tops of my shoulders, and the dark skirt that swayed above my knees. It was a classy vintage look, and I loved it. She clasped a thin silver chain with a single diamond around my neck—the diamond sparkling as it settled into the hollow of my throat. Finally, she handed me a pair of black heels, at least three inches high.

"Heels?" I grimaced, imagining falling on my face in front of everyone.

"Yup."

"Sara, I'm going to kill myself," I pleaded. I'd never worn heels and knew this was not the night to be experimenting with my grace or balance.

"You'll be fine. Just take small steps."

I slowly hobbled around the room, my ankles threatening to give way with each step. We wobbled into the entertainment room so I'd have a larger catwalk. I delicately strolled the length of it several times before the doorbell rang.

"He's here?" I panicked. Sara laughed.

"It's not a date, remember?"

"You're right." I took a calming breath.

"It's only dinner with his parents and a bunch of stuck-up old people." She laughed again.

"Emma, Sara," Anna yelled up the stairs, "Evan's here." My heart fluttered into my throat.

"Here." Sara handed me a long white wool coat that hung to the middle of my calves, along with a tote bag with a change of clothes for the party.

"Thanks."

"Em, try to relax. You have nothing to worry about."

I took a deep breath and walked carefully down the stairs, trying not to fall. I hated heels already. They were too much work. Walking shouldn't be something I had to worry about. I had far too many other things to be concerned with, like how to not sound like an idiot in front of a room full of wealthy overeducated men.

Evan waited for me at the bottom of the stairs. I couldn't look up as he came into view, afraid that if I stopped looking at my feet, I'd crumple to the bottom step. When I was finally able to look up, I noticed that his cheeks were flushed and he had a grin on his face that made my breath stop for a second.

"Hi."

"Hi." He smiled.

"Hey, Evan," Sara said, leaping down the stairs. "How'd I do? Is she acceptable?" I widened my eyes, wanting to shoot her for asking him to comment on my appearance.

Evan laughed. "Yeah, she's *definitely* acceptable."

"You met my parents, Anna and Carl?"

"Yes, I did."

"Have a great time tonight, Emma," Anna said, giving me a gentle hug and kiss on the cheek. "You look beautiful."

"Thank you," I replied, blushing.

"I'll see you at Jake's. Evan, I have your cell number in case we get there before you," Sara said.

"Ready?" Evan asked me.

"Sure." We said good-bye one more time and headed out the door.

Evan waited until we were in the car before he said, "You really do look beautiful."

"Thanks," I murmured.

"You're not comfortable, are you?"

"Not at all," I admitted with a small laugh. Evan laughed with me, releasing the tension.

"Well, I'll try not to torture you too long. Let's get this over with," he said, pulling out of Sara's driveway.

"I have to warn you, I suck in these shoes. I could fall and break something very expensive."

He laughed. "I'll be sure to keep you away from anything breakable."

"If there is any way I can sit the entire time, that would be great."

"Let's see what we can do. But I'm afraid we'll be in a room without many options during the cocktail hour."

"The what?" I asked, confused and embarrassed that I had to ask.

"Sorry, I forgot that this is your first time. We're meeting my parents there. They'll wait for us, and we'll all go in together."

"Your parents know I'm coming, right?" I was suddenly nervous that they might not be expecting me.

"Yes, they know you're coming. They may refer to you as my girlfriend when they introduce you to everyone. I keep trying to correct them, but…" He sighed. "Anyway, I'm sorry about that."

"It's okay," I whispered, feeling the fire on my face once again.

"So, Mr. Jacobs and his wife are hosting the party, and they'll be greeting everyone at the door. I think it should only be about twenty people, so that shouldn't be bad." Only twenty people? That meant there were twenty names to forget and twenty hands to shake and exchange meaningless small talk with—not comforting.

Evan proceeded to give me a rundown of the flow of the evening and the expected etiquette.

"I'm hoping I'll be able to excuse us after dinner. I'll say that we have a show to go to or something. Just agree with whatever I say, okay?"

"Okay." This sounded way more complicated than just eating food and making mindless conversation. I knew I was getting a glimpse of Evan's world tonight, but I'd had no idea how much I didn't fit in.

"Thank you so much for doing this," he said, glancing at me as he drove. "I'll seriously owe you after tonight."

"I think we'll be even."

"You may want to wait to say that until after we leave."

A few minutes later, Evan pulled up behind a large black Mercedes that was idling on the side of the road. I realized it must have been his parents when the car merged onto the road, as if it had been waiting for us.

We followed them down a driveway that was guarded by two large stone pillars with corresponding ornate wrought-iron gates that were swung open in expectation. We followed the long, winding driveway, lined with antique lanterns, until it opened up to reveal a spectacular white stone mansion.

The front of the house was dramatically uplit, illuminating its grandeur. It appeared to be two stories, encircled by large arched windows that let out a warm glow of light, giving a hint of the heavy drapery on the inside. The front lawn displayed perfectly trimmed hedges outlining the house. The lawn itself was flat, but raised from the driveway and surrounded by a stone wall.

I swallowed hard, realizing I was in over my head. I was not just in a different world, I was in another dimension. I eyed Evan nervously.

He smiled and said, "Don't worry. It'll be over before you know it."

We pulled up along the circular driveway, where we were greeted by a man with a black jacket and a bow tie. He opened Evan's door.

Evan leaned over before he got out and said, "Wait right there, I'll get you out." I didn't move. I actually didn't want to get out.

Evan walked around the back of the car and opened my door. He offered me his hand. I would have typically looked at him like he was insane, but with these shoes on, I gladly accepted the assistance. Waiting in front of the first set of stone steps were Evan's parents.

His mother was sparkling, with bobbed blond hair and bright blue eyes. She was wrapped in a fur coat and adorned with more diamonds than I'd ever seen on one person. She had soft, delicate features and looked very thin and breakable. She clutched a small black handbag that was sealed with more glitz.

In contrast, Mr. Mathews was a statuesque man, taller than Evan, but with strikingly similar features. He and Evan shared the same light brown hair and grayish blue eyes. His face was angular and serious as he stood in a long black coat concealing a tuxedo.

I took a deep breath before approaching them. I tried my best to smile cordially while I was introduced.

"Vivian and Stuart Mathews, this is—" Evan began.

"Emily Thomas," Vivian finished, holding out her hand. I tried to conceal the shocked look on my face, especially with being called Emily by someone I'd never seen before today. "It's very nice to meet you," I said, shaking her delicate hand. Stuart remained still with his hands by his side, making no attempt to acknowledge me, forget about shaking my hand.

"Well, aren't you lovely," Vivian said, looking me over. "We never get to meet Evan's girlfriends." I knew it was coming, but my heart still leapt when she said it, sending a flicker of heat to my cheeks.

Evan rolled his eyes. "Mom, you met Beth, remember?" His tone was impatient.

"Maybe for a second as you were leaving the house," she countered. "Anyway, it's a pleasure to meet you, Emily. Shall we go in?" There was an air about her that made me stand up straighter. I was afraid to walk, knowing how clumsy I'd appear next to her grace and sophistication. I gave Evan a fearful glance as we approached the first set of stone steps. There were only three, but they might as well have been a flight.

Evan offered me his right elbow to clutch as I concentrated on each step. I don't think I breathed the entire time. His parents glided ahead of us as I carefully placed one foot in front of the other along the stone pathway. At the top of the second set of steps was an enormous wooden door that opened as Vivian and Stuart neared it. They waited for us before entering.

"Stuart, Vivian!" the dual voices of a man and woman sang out. "Welcome. It's so wonderful to see you again." Vivian and Stuart were warmly greeted by whom I presumed to be Mr. and Mrs. Jacobs with a quick embrace that included a brushing kiss on their cheeks and a handshake.

"Evelyn, Maxwell, you remember our youngest son, Evan, don't you?" Vivian offered as they stepped aside to let us enter.

"Of course." Mr. Jacobs greeted Evan with a handshake.

"And this is his girlfriend, Emily Thomas." I smiled politely.

"Thank you for joining us," Mrs. Jacobs said, grasping my right hand between her two cool, soft palms.

"Thank you for having me," I replied.

Evan slipped my coat off and handed it to a formally poised man dressed in a tuxedo.

I was too distracted by the grand foyer, with its huge crystal chandelier and expansive stone staircase with a large red carpet running down the center, to notice Evan staring at me. I glanced over at him with a start.

"What?!" I was afraid I'd done something wrong already.

"Another pink sweater, huh? You're killing me."

I looked at him with wide eyes, my face flooded with color. "Evan!"

He smiled as we followed his parents into a room to the right of the foyer. I wasn't about to admit that seeing him in his dark tailored suit was just as distracting.

We entered a large room that could easily contain the entire first floor of my house within its walls, with a ceiling that was easily two stories high. The windows along the front of the house were framed with heavy ivory scrolled drapes, held open with tasseled ropes. The top half of the walls was adorned with soft coral wallpaper set above ivory wood panels embossed with leafing scrolls. Three of the walls held museum-worthy paintings. A fireplace as tall as I was commanded the remaining wall. As Evan had predicted, there wasn't anywhere to sit. Several oversize antique chairs were set against the walls, but they were obviously for appearances only. The only other piece of furniture was a large stone-topped table with dark wood legs gathered in the center that rolled out into a round base. Set on the round surface was the biggest floral arrangement I'd ever seen. It looked like a tree of flowers with different colors and textures—it was absolutely amazing.

"Are you okay?" Evan asked as my unblinking eyes scanned the room.

"Sure," I replied slowly, nodding my head. He smiled and grabbed my hand to escort me to the corner of the room.

"Evan," a deep, distinguished voice said in greeting. It belonged to a man of average height, much shorter than Evan, with dark wavy hair and a thick black mustache. "How are you? Stuart said you were going to be here this evening."

"It's great to see you, Mr. Nicols," Evan said, shaking his hand. "Mr. Nicols, this is Emma Thomas. We go to school together. Emma, this is Mr. Nicols. He works for the same firm as my father."

"Aren't you stunning," he observed, cupping my hand in both of his as his eyes rolled over me. Taken aback by the greeting, I forced an uncomfortable smile. "Evan, you should bring your girls around here more often." He nudged Evan with his elbow. It took everything I had to keep an even expression.

After a few more exchanges about soccer and Evan's winter travel plans, Mr. Nicols excused himself. I let out the breath I'd been holding while in his presence.

"I am so sorry. I had no idea—well, I was afraid—but I still didn't think anyone would actually be that rude."

"That was interesting," was all I could say.

"Want something to eat?" he asked, eyeing a server dressed in a tux, carrying a silver tray of bite-size food.

"I'm okay."

"This will be over before you know it," he promised.

"You keep saying that," I mumbled. I was beginning to wonder if he was saying it to himself as much as he was to me.

At that moment Vivian approached us with a portly man wearing small frameless glasses. A ring of white hair blended with his pale complexion and contrasted with his ruddy cheeks.

"Evan, you remember Dr. Eckel, correct?" Vivian presented the small round man.

"Of course. It's nice to see you again, Dr. Eckel," Evan said, gripping his hand.

"Dr. Eckel, this is Evan's girlfriend, Emily Thomas."

"It's a pleasure to meet you, Miss Thomas," Dr. Eckel said, shaking my hand gingerly. I produced a small smile.

"Dr. Eckel is a professor of Bio-Chemistry at Yale," Evan explained.

"Oh." I nodded lightly.

"Are you and Evan in many classes together?" his mother asked.

"Evan's in most of my classes."

"So you're intelligent. That's wonderful," she concluded, smiling softly. I wasn't sure what to say to that.

"She's also a great athlete," Evan contributed on my behalf, trying to deflect the awkward comment. "The girls' soccer team won the state championship last night because of her." His acknowledgment didn't help. The sweater became stifling the longer they spoke about me.

"Congratulations," Dr. Eckel stated. "Have you started looking at colleges?"

"I haven't visited any campuses yet, but I've had a few college scouts come to my games. My first choice is Stanford." My voice sounded so small in the huge room.

"Really?" Vivian reacted in interest.

"What do you plan to study?" Dr. Eckel inquired.

"I haven't narrowed it down yet."

"She could choose anything," Evan boasted. "She's in all of the advanced classes and has a four-point-oh."

"Hmm," his mother responded, still intrigued.

"Well, I wish you the best," Dr. Eckel said, shaking my hand once again. "Evan, it's always a pleasure." He and Vivian strolled off to greet another face they recognized.

I turned to Evan, trying to recover my composure. "Don't do that," I pleaded.

"I'm sorry, what did I do?"

"Talking about me like that—it's so uncomfortable."

"But I didn't say anything that wasn't true, and I didn't exaggerate. Sorry if it's hard to hear the truth."

I took another breath. "I'm just not used to this."

"I know," he said, grabbing my hand and giving it a gentle squeeze. He didn't let go as I anticipated he would.

"My parents said you were going to be here," an excited female voice squealed. I watched a stunning girl with long, wavy blond hair saunter toward us, a strapless black cocktail dress hugging her slender figure. I felt juvenile and plain in comparison—despite Sara's best efforts. She wrapped her arms around Evan and gave him a quick peck on the mouth. He released my hand to return the embrace. I became an invisible witness to this intimate greeting, holding my hands in front of me, preferring to look at the floor.

"Catherine, this is Emma Thomas. We go to school together. Catherine is the daughter of Mr. and Mrs. Jacobs," Evan explained.

She turned to me with a start, oblivious to my presence until Evan mentioned me. I understood why as she pressed her body against his side, her arms wrapped around his.

"Nice to meet you," she acknowledged with the slightest nod.

"Catherine attends Boston College," Evan explained, obviously trying to make up for Catherine's disinterest.

"Do you like it?" I asked, thinking I should say *something*.

"I do," she answered shortly, barely glancing at me.

"Evan, I have a surprise for you," she announced, dismissing me completely. "Come upstairs so I can give it to you." She started pulling him behind her. My eyes widened as I realized I was being left standing alone.

Evan slowed Catherine's persistent pace and said something low into her ear. They stopped, and she glanced at me with confused eyes. Evan said something else, and she looked at him with a furrowed brow as she lightly ran her hand across his cheek. Her face dropped to a sulk. She whispered in his ear and took in his expression with a mischievous grin. He shook his head with an apologetic smile. She shrugged, gave him a quick kiss on the lips and glided away. I wanted so much to blend into the wallpaper at that moment.

Evan returned to me, his cheeks flushed.

Before he opened his mouth to say anything, I blurted, "Don't, it's okay. I really don't want to know. It's actually none of my business."

He examined me cautiously and said, "Really? That didn't bother you?"

I drew my brow together. "Why would you ask me that?"

"Because what she did was completely offensive. I was bothered by it, so I can't believe that you weren't."

I shrugged slightly and dropped my eyes to the floor. "I'm really not sure what to expect."

"You should never expect that," he stated, taking hold of my hand and raising my chin with his other hand. I couldn't breathe when I turned my eyes up to him. "Okay?"

"Sure," I whispered, glancing away.

This was the strangest night of my life. I was in the most exquisite house I'd ever seen, surrounded by people who assumed they had the privilege to say anything they wanted, regardless of how distasteful, and Evan was talking and acting ten years older than he was. He was right—Jake's party was going to be easy after this.

I was introduced to more people throughout the longest hour of my life. They'd ask Evan a question and cut him off to talk about themselves. Finally, as I was becoming cross-eyed feigning interest in another mind-numbing story, a bell chimed, and Mr. Jacobs requested that everyone make their way into the dining room.

I found that after all of this stifling drama, I was starving. We entered a long dimly lit room with the same large arching windows framed by dark red drapes that showcased the back terrace. The top half of the walls was covered in antique mirrors up to the ceiling, while the bottom half duplicated the ivory paneling of the previous room. Another impressive stone fireplace centered the wall opposite the windows.

A long, dark wooden table divided the room, with the windows on one side and the fireplace on the other. Complementing the grand table were tall, straight-backed chairs—closer to forty chairs than the twenty Evan had guesstimated. The table was set with delicate china bordered with gold scrolling, along with a collection of elegant glassware and flatware. Small silver cups holding colorful flowers and glowing crystal votives were intermittently dispersed along the center of the table. A stunning crystal chandelier was suspended over us, creating a soft ambience enhanced by a crackling fire.

Evan pulled out my chair for me before sitting to my left. To my changing fortune, Dr. Eckel sat to my right. He was the only person I'd met who had not been self-righteous and rude. Then again, he hadn't said much at all. That was fine by me too.

However, in keeping with the momentum of the evening, on Evan's left was Catherine, who scooted her chair closer to him. She took a sip from an oversize wineglass and leaned toward him.

"What, Evan, not drinking tonight?"

"I'm driving," he explained.

"You don't have to," she whispered, still loud enough that I could hear her. My back straightened, and I tried to distract myself with a sip of water. I didn't dare look over at them.

"Evan, I've missed you," she said breathlessly. I choked on the water, coughing midgulp. I couldn't stop. Everyone stared at me as I tried to contain my fit in my napkin.

"Sorry," I whispered, looking around at the startled faces. My face was red, not only from choking but also from the words I'd just overheard.

"Are you okay?" Evan asked, trying to turn his back to Catherine.

"Yes," I replied apologetically. "I swallowed wrong, I'm sorry."

A line of servers entered the room, holding shallow bowls in each of their hands, which they set in front of every person simultaneously. It was very impressive to witness.

"Start with the silverware on the outside and work your way in," Evan whispered. I looked down at the lines of silver. How much could we possibly eat to need all of this?

"Evan, don't ignore me," Catherine demanded while we ate our soup. It didn't appear that anyone else could hear her whispers over the murmurs of conversation that bounced around the cavernous room. I heard her because I was sitting next to Evan, and Dr. Eckel was as mute as I was.

"I'm not ignoring you, Catherine."

"When are you visiting me in Boston again?" she asked. "We had so much fun the last time. Remember?" She released a high-pitched giggle.

My head cocked in reaction to this artificial sound. Did she really force a giggle? Who does that? I tried to hold in my laughter and ended up coughing again, receiving a few more glances.

"I'm really busy right now," Evan explained, glancing at me. I couldn't look at him.

"But I haven't seen you since I started school in August. Don't you miss me?"

I couldn't wait to hear his response to this one.

"I had a good time."

Nice one, Evan.

"I can promise you a better time. Why don't you come up next weekend?"

"Aren't you on break for Thanksgiving?"

"Then come visit me here."

"My brother will be home. I think we're going skiing."

"Evan," she whined. "Don't make me beg you."

Was she serious? I took another gulp of water, trying to stifle my urge to laugh. I swallowed it without incident, but found I was soon out of water. To my astonishment, my glass was quickly refilled by a server dressed in a tuxedo who appeared out of nowhere with a silver pitcher.

Catherine sulked during the second and third courses. I had no idea what I was eating; the courses didn't resemble anything I could conjure up as food. But I tried them and was pleasantly surprised to discover that I liked them.

"How are you doing?" Evan leaned over to ask me.

"I'm doing just fine, thank you." I grinned. I still couldn't look at him, because that meant I would see her too. I didn't know if I could do that and keep a straight face.

"How are *you* doing?" I inquired, still grinning.

"I'm ready to leave actually," he admitted. A smile broke out on my face with the escape of a small laughing cough.

By the fifth course, which I did recognize as beef, I had consumed three glasses of water and really needed to use the bathroom. The thought of standing up in front of all of these people and slipping out of the room unnoticed kept me paralyzed in my chair, but the settling pressure made taking one more bite unbearable.

"I have to use the restroom," I whispered to Evan.

"I'm not sure where they are," he admitted. "But you can ask one of the servers, and they'll let you know where to go."

Thankfully, the entrance was behind us. I held my breath as I slowly slid my chair away from the table. A loud scraping sound filled the room, disrupting every conversation. I grimaced and looked around apologetically at the same annoyed glares I'd been receiving all evening. I slipped out of the chair, and with as much concentration and grace as I could gather, I walked toward the open door. Next to it was a woman in a tuxedo with her dark hair neatly tied back into a low knot.

"Excuse me," I whispered. "Could you please tell me where the restroom is?"

"Go right out this door, and you will find them tucked on either side of the staircase. It doesn't matter which you use."

"Thank you." I smiled at her and stepped out the door. As I crossed the threshold I caught the heel of my shoe, upsetting my fragile balance. I took several stammering steps into the foyer, trying to prevent myself from falling on my face. I recovered and remained on my feet, but my hard steps echoed like thunder.

Evan came rushing out. "Are you okay?" he asked, prepared to scoop me off the floor.

"I'm fine," I replied, standing up straight. I pulled my sweater taut over my hips and took a quick breath before continuing to the restroom. I remained in the small space for longer than was necessary, fanning my face in an attempt to reduce its scarlet shade to a less noticeable red.

When I returned to the table, my unfinished beef course had been removed, and a plate with small portions of cheese, garnished with a fan of strawberries and tiny grapes, was set in its place. Catherine was hovering over Evan, whispering in his ear while stroking the back of his neck. I fought the temptation to glance over at him when I eased back into my seat.

Whatever Catherine was saying to Evan, she was saying it low enough that I couldn't hear. At the end of the course, Evan excused himself and slid out of his chair. I turned toward him to see his red face before he left the room. Catherine giggled, watching him go. I caught her eye and stared at her, questioning. She smirked with a raised eyebrow before taking a sip of wine. I looked away and placed a grape in my mouth, unnerved.

Evan entered through a door at the other end of the fireplace and leaned over to whisper to his parents, who were sitting near the head of the table with the Jacobses. He tilted his watch and said something else. His mother gave him a quick peck on the cheek. Evan approached Mr. and Mrs. Jacobs to exchange a few words before shaking their hands. He exited the door and re-entered through the one behind me.

"Ready?" he whispered, leaning over the side of my chair.

"Sure," I replied, setting down my glass of water.

He helped pull my chair out without making the bellowing noise I had earlier. We walked into the foyer, and Evan handed a card to retrieve our coats to the same poised gentleman in the tux who had taken them earlier.

"Leaving so soon?" Catherine asked as she sashayed across the marble floor.

"We have another commitment," Evan stated flatly.

"You will come back to visit me, won't you, Evan," she demanded rather than questioned.

I couldn't contain myself any longer. As Evan slid my coat over my arms, I started laughing, at first in spurts, as I tried to hold it in. But then there were tears in my eyes, and I couldn't stop it from erupting.

"Are you laughing at me?" she asked.

"Actually, yes I am," I said, my eyes watering. My face reddened as I covered my mouth to smother another bout of laughter.

Evan smiled wide and said, "Good night, Catherine," before escorting me out.

Once the door closed behind us, I couldn't hold back. I laughed so hard, I had to bend over to support myself, my hands on my knees. I couldn't see through the tears streaming down my face. Wiping the moisture from my cheeks, I tried to compose myself and took a couple steps forward.

Then I thought of her whine and giggle, and lost it again. I collapsed onto the top stone step, holding my stomach as I convulsed with laughter. After it was too painful to laugh anymore, I took a deep breath and wiped my cheeks again. Evan stood at the bottom of the stairs, watching me with an amused expression.

"I'm glad you found that funny," he said, observing me with his hands in his pockets.

"Please don't mention it," I groaned, trying not to laugh. "I can't laugh any more. It hurts. Let's just say we're even."

19. NOT LAUGHING

Ready for Jake's party?" Evan asked from the driver's seat, easily releasing the formal persona I'd witnessed most of the evening.

"After that, I'm ready for anything."

"We'll see." He grinned. "Maybe I'll be the one laughing at the end of the night."

"What's that supposed to mean?" I asked, suddenly nervous.

"Nothing," he replied, continuing to grin.

When we pulled into Jake's driveway, there were already a dozen or so cars lining it, making us the last vehicle to fit before the street. Evan kept watch outside the car while I changed into a pair of jeans and more manageable shoes.

"So much better," I said in relief when I stepped out of the car.

"You still look good," Evan remarked with a half smile. I ignored him.

I kept the same guard while he changed from his suit into a pair of jeans and a sweater.

"Whenever you want to leave, we leave," Evan told me as we approached the front door. "Don't feel bad either. He invited you— this isn't for me. I'm just here because you are."

"Okay," I agreed, trying to read into his warning. He'd been acting strange about this party since I'd mentioned it. But I couldn't figure out why.

I rang the doorbell, since it seemed more appropriate than just walking in. It wasn't the loud scene we'd encountered at Scott's party. Jake answered the door with a huge smile.

"Emma! You're here! Sara said you'd be here soon," he said, opening the door wider for us to enter. His welcoming smile faltered when he found Evan behind me. "Oh, you brought Evan." Evan gave him a quick smirk.

"Nice to see you, Jake," Evan said, patting Jake's shoulder as we passed him to enter. Jake shut the door and turned to Evan.

"Sorry, man. You may be outnumbered tonight," Jake informed him with a snide grin.

"I'm not worried."

I had no idea what they were talking about, but could definitely sense a little tension. I studied Evan's face for a sign, but he just smiled at me.

"You can hang your coats in the closet." Jake pointed to the door next to the entrance.

The small foyer led down a hallway. As we followed Jake, I noticed an entrance on the left that opened into a living room with an over-stuffed couch and a large flat-screen TV. To the right was another room with a long leather couch and a desk, presumably an office.

The rooms were dimly lit by flickering candlelight. There were only a few people in each room, quietly conversing. A soothing jazz tune with a soulful trumpet carried throughout the house. The end of the hall revealed a set of carpeted stairs, and then it opened up into a kitchen. The kitchen was bright. Overhead lights gleamed off the white surfaces.

Sara was leaning against the island, laughing at something Jason had said. She looked up when we entered the room.

"Drinks are downstairs," Jake told us. "Relax and have a good time. I'll be right back." He disappeared down a set of stairs that connected with the stairs leading up.

"Emma, Evan!" Sara exclaimed. "How was dinner?"

"Filling," I replied, with a quick laugh. Evan pressed his lips together and scowled at me.

Sara examined us with her brows pulled together, trying to decipher our exchange.

"I'll tell you later," I said quickly, still grinning. "When did you guys get here?"

"We haven't been here that long," Sara admitted. "I was going to give you a few more minutes before I called."

"Where is everyone?" I asked, looking around, then picking up on the small grin that Evan wasn't doing a very good job of hiding.

"I honestly don't know," Sara confessed, looking around too. "We really did *just* get here. I think everyone must be downstairs, but I don't think there's a lot of people here."

We were interrupted by the ringing of the doorbell. Jake bounded up the steps and strode down the hall. Six more people I didn't know entered the house—they looked like seniors.

"I think everyone's here," I overheard Jake tell one of the guys when they neared the kitchen.

"Emma Thomas?" the guy whispered in shock. I tried to pretend I didn't hear him.

"Don't even think about it," Jake whispered firmly, leading the group down the stairs.

Evan pressed his lips together to keep from laughing. I narrowed my eyes, knowing something was up. He raised his eyebrows and shrugged, looking away to avoid my glare.

"Do you want to go downstairs?" Sara asked, as it was obvious we were the only ones upstairs, except for the few people in the front rooms.

"Might as well," I agreed.

Sara and I walked down together while Jason and Evan followed us, discussing a football game or something.

We entered the shadowy basement with its low ceilings. At the base of the stairs was a long, dark bar, with tall black leather chairs pulled up to it. A few people were sitting on the chairs, talking. When I scanned the wide U-shaped space, I estimated about fifteen people dispersed throughout it.

Besides those at the bar, others were sitting on a sectional couch in front of a suspended television. The rest were clustered around a pool table across from the stairs or sitting on the black leather sofa tucked in against the wall. I was surprised that no one was playing pool or watching TV. The same sultry soulful music piped through the speakers down here

"Want a drink?" Jake asked me as we congregated at the end of the bar.

"Do you have bottles of soda?"

"Sure. In the fridge on the other side of the basement. There's a door over there—help yourself."

I cut through the sectional area, through the door he indicated into the unfinished side of the basement. Against the wall was an old white refrigerator filled with bottles and cans of a variety of sodas. I grabbed a bottle and returned to Evan, Jason and Sara, who were still standing at the bar.

"What do you think?" I whispered to Sara, who was sipping something red from a glass. "Does this feel weird to you?"

"I have a feeling I know what's going on," she admitted. "I've always wondered what Jake's parties were all about, but I had no idea. Guess he never wanted to invite the judge's daughter for a reason."

Before I could ask what she was talking about, Jake approached again.

"Evan," Jake said, beckoning him, "I want you to meet a couple of people I don't think you know."

Evan looked at Jake curiously. He hesitated before saying, "I'll be right back," and walked away. I nodded, not really concerned. I had no idea why he was acting so weird, but this party wasn't nearly as intimidating as the last. I wasn't worried about being left alone. There really wasn't much going on.

"I wish we could play pool or something," I told Jason and Sara. "It feels strange just standing here."

"It's not that kind of party," Sara whispered with a knowing grin.

"What do you mean?" I was so confused—and kinda bored, to be honest.

"Hey!" a small brunette walking down the stairs exclaimed. Sara turned toward her and smiled.

"Hey, Bridgette!" Sara returned enthusiastically.

Bridgette was followed closely by one of the guys from the soccer team. She greeted Sara with a quick hug.

"I didn't know you were going to be here," the petite brunette said to Sara in surprise.

"We came with Emma," Sara explained. "Emma, this is Bridgette."

"Hi," I said softly. She smiled politely, casually eyeing me. The guy's hand slid around Bridgette's waist, resting low so it was practically holding her ass. I looked up at her face, pretending not to have noticed.

Jason started talking to him; apparently they knew each other too. The entire time the guy's hand remained attached to Bridgette. It was almost as if he were claiming her or something.

"Did you just get here?" Bridgette asked.

"Not that long ago," Sara replied.

"I didn't realize you were interested in Rich," Sara whispered, nodding to the guy with the branding hand.

"I figured, why not?" Bridgette declared with a shrug.

Sara tightened her eyes at the response but didn't inquire further. Instead, she and Bridgette began talking about their mothers, who apparently knew each other, and other subjects they had in common that I knew nothing about. I pulled out one of the black leather bar chairs to sit and half listened as I fiddled with the soda bottle.

"We're going upstairs," Sara said after a while. "Will you be okay? I promise I'll be right back."

"Sure." I nodded with a reassuring smile.

"Don't go anywhere," she warned, leaving me even more confused.

I scanned the room but couldn't locate which group Evan was in with the lights so low.

"Left alone?" a voice asked from behind me. I turned to find a dark-haired guy with vibrant bluish-green eyes leaning against the chair next to me. I recognized him as one of the guys who'd arrived after we did.

"For now," I said with a small shrug.

"That's not good."

"How do you know Jake?" I asked.

"We're friends—we're both seniors," he explained. "You're Emma Thomas, right?"

"Yeah," I said slowly, trying to figure out if I should know who he was.

"I'm Drew Carson. I realize you probably don't know me." But something made me wonder why I did. His name sounded so familiar, but I couldn't quite place it.

"But you know who I am?"

"Of course." He laughed. "That was a great game last night. I heard you have scouts looking to pick you up."

I blushed. "Yeah. So you were at the game?"

"Who wasn't?" His sincerity made me smile.

"Why do I recognize you? I know I've seen you," I questioned, struggling, "but I can't place it."

"Basketball, probably," he said. That was it. Drew Carson, captain of the guys' basketball team this season. That made sense with his lean-built frame. How had I not noticed him in school? But then again, it seemed I didn't notice unless he threw himself in front of me.

"That's it. Sorry."

"That's alright. I should have tried to talk to you before tonight," he admitted. "But I'm glad you're here. I'm surprised you're here, but whatever." He revealed a sparkling smile as his cheeks creased with deep dimples. Honestly, how had I not noticed him before? He was beautiful.

"I like your sweater," he said after a few seconds of silence.

"Thanks." I blushed again. I was searching for anything to say that wouldn't sound forced. "Do you ski?" I had no idea where the question came from, but it was the first thing that came out of my mouth. Could I be any more pathetic?

"Yeah, I'm going to Vermont next weekend with my family. Do you?"

"Actually, I don't." We both looked at each other and started laughing at the awkwardness. Our laughter was loud against the murmuring voices, invoking a few annoyed stares.

"Oops." I smiled, covering my mouth. "I didn't realize we were *supposed* to be quiet."

"Don't worry about it," he said, smiling back. "They're just taking this way too seriously." I was confused by what he meant, but most of tonight seemed confusing. I'd figure it out eventually, hopefully.

"Do you do anything else besides play basketball and ski?" I asked, still trying to keep the conversation alive, but not as stressed after our outburst.

"I surf and try to go white-water kayaking when I can." Then he continued to talk about the best waves he'd ever surfed—in Australia. I listened and was soon engrossed in his story.

We continued back and forth until it occurred to me that it had been a long time since Evan, Sara and Jason had disappeared. I glanced around casually while contributing to the conversation but was unable to make out any of their faces in the dark corners.

"I'll be right back," I announced. "I'm going to get another drink."

"I need to run up to the bathroom," Drew said, pointing up the stairs. "Meet you back here?" He actually wanted to keep talking to me?

"Sure," I agreed.

I walked through the space with the sectionals again, discreetly trying to look at the faces to find Evan or Sara. I was shocked to walk in on a few couples kissing—heavily. It didn't seem to bother them that I was there or that there were other couples next to them doing the same thing. I kept my eyes to the ground. Then I heard the heavy breathing and walked faster.

When I was behind the closed door, I tried to figure out how I was going to get through there again. I inspected the other side of the basement, hoping there was a door that connected to the pool-table side, but was disappointed. The only other door was a bulkhead that led to the backyard. Was I that desperate?

"There you are." I spun around and found Jake closing the door behind him.

"Hi, Jake," I responded casually, trying to conceal my anxiety.

"I've wanted to talk to you all night," he confessed while approaching me. "But I didn't really want to do it here." He presented the dingy surroundings, sounding overly cocky. "Let me show you around the house, and we can find somewhere private to—" He paused before adding, "talk." He smirked like it was an inside joke. Everything suddenly made sense. I remained still, catching myself before dropping my mouth wide open in shock.

"Uh, well…," I stumbled, looking past him to the closed door. "Thanks, but I don't need a tour. We can talk at the bar?"

"I was hoping for some place with less people." He winked. No way, again?! I couldn't help myself; the words were coming out of my mouth before I could stop them.

"Who are you?" I questioned, aghast at his boldness.

"What?" he replied in shock.

"This is a hook-up party, isn't it?" It came out more as an accusation than a question. I couldn't believe how long it had taken me to figure it out.

"Whatever happens, happens," he said with a devious smirk. I remained dumbfounded by his arrogance.

"And so you decided to invite *me?*" I questioned, unable to imagine how that made sense.

"Why not?" he asked, not catching on, still overly confident.

"You obviously don't know me." I glowered, unable to conceal my disgust. "Why would you think I'd want to hook up with *you?*"

"Ouch," he replied, not looking pleased anymore.

Before I could say anything else that would make me not want to show my face in school again, I hurried past him to discover that the door was open. Evan stood in the frame, his hand still on the handle. I didn't know how long he'd been listening, but it must have been for most of it, because he greeted me with his amused grin.

"You are so dead," I threatened as I pushed past him. It only added to his amusement as he let out a small laugh.

"Hey, Emma," Drew started when he saw me approaching. Then he looked at my face, which hid nothing, and asked, "What happened?"

"Were you in on this too?" I accused harshly.

I didn't wait for his answer as I rushed up the stairs and found Sara and Jason talking in the kitchen with their jackets on.

"Can we please go?" I pleaded. "This is too weird."

"We were just coming to get you," Sara admitted. "I was wondering how long it was going to take for you to want to leave. Let's go back to my place."

"Sure," Evan agreed from behind me.

I turned sharply and snapped, "I don't think she was inviting *you*." Sara's eyes widened at my attack. I continued down the hall to retrieve my jacket from the closet.

Sara and Jason headed to Sara's car while I paced myself a step ahead of Evan to his.

After he shut his door, he said, "I should have warned you. I'm sorry."

"Evan, you knew, and you still let me come here?" I yelled.

"I knew nothing was going to happen. I wasn't afraid you were going to do anything, and I hoped that you'd let Jake see you're not into him—which you definitely did. I'm so sick of hearing him talk about—" He stopped himself.

"I'm sorry, really." His face was serious and his eyes soft, forcing my anger to dissipate.

"Fine, you can come over to Sara's." I still found it difficult to be upset with him for very long.

After we pulled out of the driveway, my stomach shot out a charge that caused my heart to stammer. "Evan, where were you? *And* you said you've been to one of his parties before. Are you serious? Did you...who...no way." My voice grew louder with each unfinished question.

Evan laughed.

"Forget it, it's none of my business," I murmured quietly, looking out the window. I was tormented by the possibilities.

"Relax. Jake was trying to keep me distracted by introducing me to some girls, so he could talk to you. He hated that I was there. He knew you'd bring Sara, and she'd probably bring Jason, but he wasn't expecting me. So I was just *talking*—like you were with Drew Carson, right?" My heart skipped a beat.

"I've only been to one other party of Jake's, and I didn't know what they were all about when I accepted the invite. I didn't..." He had a hard time finding the words. I turned to look at him, realizing he couldn't tell me what he'd done.

"Really?" I accused in shock.

"It's not what you think." He explained evasively, "I'd rather not get into details." We were quiet for a moment. I stared out the window at the silhouetted trees and the occasional uplit house.

"Does that really bother you?" he finally asked.

"What?"

"That I may have kissed a girl or whatever at one of Jake's parties?"

I hesitated before answering. "I didn't think you were like that," I replied softly.

"I'm not," he claimed emphatically. "That's why I've only gone to the one party, and I didn't do what you probably think I did. That's not what interests me. It's too important of a decision to pick someone at random in someone else's house."

I let out an awkward laugh and tried to catch myself before I let out another.

"What's so funny?"

"I can't talk about this with you." I let out another uneasy laugh. "It's too weird. Sorry."

"You think talking about sex is weird?"

"No. Talking about it with *you* is weird," I emphasized. "Can we please change the subject?"

"So, you've never—" he started.

"Evan!" I yelled.

"Of course not," he concluded quietly.

"And you have?" I asked before I could shut my mouth.

"I thought we weren't talking about it."

"We're not," I said, turning to look out the window again. We didn't say another word until we pulled into Sara's driveway.

"Do you still want me to come in?" he asked.

"Do you still want to?" I asked in return.

"Of course I do."

"Then come in."

We followed Sara and Jason into the house. Sara let her parents know we were home before we headed up the stairs.

"Would you mind if Jason and I watch a movie in my room?" Sara whispered as she and I followed a few steps behind the guys to the third floor.

"Are you serious?!" I asked. She begged with her widened eyes. "Fine." I conceded. She smiled gratefully.

Sara bent over the couch as Jason sat down and whispered in his ear. He grinned and followed her into the bedroom. Evan looked to me, trying to interpret what just happened.

"They want alone time," I explained. He nodded, suddenly understanding.

"What movie are we watching?" I inquired, sitting on the opposite end of the couch.

"Are you going to stay awake this time?"

"Yes," I stressed, acting offended.

Evan selected a movie about a small town where people were inexplicably disappearing.

After a while, the exhaustion started pulling at me, so I grabbed a pillow and curled up in the empty space on the couch next to Evan to continue watching the movie—still committed to staying awake. I began fighting with my eyelids as they attempted to glue themselves shut every time I blinked. Finally, I gave in.

"Emma," Sara whispered, gently shaking my shoulder. She sounded distant as I struggled against consciousness—I was too comfortable. "Em, you know it's two o'clock in the morning, don't you?"

Her whisper was louder now, coming in more clearly. I groaned to acknowledge I'd heard her. Then I felt a weight around my waist and warmth against my back. I blinked my eyes open, attempting to focus. I heard rhythmic breathing behind my ear and felt warm breath upon my neck. My eyes grew wider.

"What are you doing?" Sara demanded. I glanced behind me in surprise.

"Sara," I whispered emphatically, "how could you let this happen?" I carefully removed the arm from around my waist, then slowly slid off the couch. I looked at Sara with huge eyes and my mouth open accusingly.

"Me? I didn't do anything," she whispered firmly. I crept over to the stairs; Sara followed.

"I fell asleep," I whispered vehemently. "I had no idea he was still here; forget about *that*." I pointed to his position on the couch.

Sara tried not to laugh. "Em, you two looked so cute." I swatted at her arm.

"Knock it off, Sara," I demanded, still whispering. "What am I supposed to do now?"

"Wake him up and kick him out."

"Why can't you?"

"He's all yours." She laughed and went to her room.

"Sara," I yelled in a whisper at the closed door.

I sighed, looking over at the couch. He did look so peaceful lying curled up on his side. I folded my knees into me as I scrunched at the end of the couch next to his feet. I watched him sleep for a minute, trying to build up the nerve to wake him.

I kicked the back of his thigh gently with my foot.

"Evan," I called softly. He didn't respond, so I pushed a little harder, rocking him. "Evan, you need to wake up."

"Hmmm," he groaned, peeking out from under his long dark lashes. He peered up at me and grinned. "Hi." He stretched his arms above him and turned onto his back so that he could face me.

"Hi," I whispered.

"What time is it?" he asked with a groggy voice.

"Two in the morning."

"No way," he replied in disbelief, pushing himself up to sit. "Why did you let me fall asleep?"

"Me? I think I fell asleep before you did."

"Yeah," he remembered, "that's right."

"Are you going to be okay to drive home?"

"Why? Would you let me sleep here?"

"No," I admitted. "I was just trying to sound concerned." He smiled—finally fully awake.

"Did I kick you off the couch?" he asked, trying to take in the scene.

"I slept just fine," I admitted, avoiding his question.

Evan stood up and stretched again. He found his shoes and slipped them on his feet.

"Will I see you…today, actually?" he confirmed, grabbing his jacket from the back of the chair.

"I have to be home by four, so I need to be back here by three. Would you rather sleep?"

"No, it's Sunday. It's my day—so I'll pick you up at ten, okay?"

"Can we make it eleven?" I countered, thinking about how late Sara and I would sleep in, and that we still needed to compare stories.

"Really?" he pleaded. "Ten-thirty?"

"Sure."

I stood up to walk him down the stairs. We snuck to the first floor, careful not to wake Sara's parents. I stopped on the bottom step as he went for the door. He turned to look at me without saying a word. I stood with my arms crossed, bracing myself against the cold air seeping in through the open door. His lingering made me nervous, igniting a tingling in my stomach.

"Good night," I finally whispered, trying to urge him to leave.

"Good night," he replied and walked out the door.

I locked it behind him, and quickly ascended the stairs to Sara's room. She was waiting for me in her bed.

"Did he kiss you?" she inquired eagerly.

"No! Sara, you can't ask me questions like that—like you're hoping he has—and then try to tell me we can't date."

"You're right," she admitted with a sigh. "I promise to try to be more consistent. But I really want you to kiss him."

"Then keep it to yourself. Good night, Sara."

I slipped under the covers after preparing for bed, compelling sleep to find me again, so I wouldn't think about whether I wanted Evan to kiss me.

20. THE ROOM

"Are you awake?" Sara asked from the bed across from me.

"Uh-huh," I grumbled from under the covers. "I'm awake."

"You need to wake up so you can tell me about dinner last night."

I rolled over to face her. She was definitely more awake than I was, supporting her head on her elbow, waiting for me. I stretched and yawned loudly. I propped the pillow against the headboard and pushed myself up to sit.

"How was dinner? I can't wait any longer," she insisted.

I told her all about The Other Dimension, describing Evan's parents, the rude guests and how different Evan was around these people. I left Catherine for last. When I was done, Sara was laughing hysterically—not quite as hard as I had when it happened, but she did wipe tears from her eyes.

"I cannot believe you said that to her," she finally managed to say.

"I couldn't contain myself," I confessed. "I guess it warmed me up for Jake's party."

"Wait, what happened at Jake's party, besides everyone hooking up?"

"Let's see—I met Drew Carson, and I thought he was such a nice guy until I realized what the party was all about, and then Jake followed me into the other side of the basement and tried to get me to go somewhere alone with him."

"What did you do?" she asked, looking horrified. "I warned you not to go anywhere."

"Sara, I had no idea what you were talking about. But when I finally got it, I basically told him there was no way in hell I was hooking up with him and came upstairs, where I found you and Jason. Sara, Evan knew what kind of party it was when Jake invited me, and he didn't warn me. He's been to one before."

"Seriously?" she asked in disbelief. "Wow, I didn't think he was like that."

"Neither did I," I agreed. "And he swears he's not and that he didn't 'do anything.' But he couldn't tell me what he did. Maybe I really don't want to know."

"I do," she exclaimed.

"Sara!" I looked at her, astounded. "He can do whatever he wants with whoever he wants. It's none of our business." Needing to change the subject, I asked, "What's going on with you and Jason? How was your 'alone time'?"

Sara sighed and fell dramatically on her back. It was not the reaction I was expecting.

"What?! Tell me!" I demanded impatiently.

"You and Evan did more on that couch last night than Jason and I have. Well, except we've kissed, and even that took forever," she confessed in frustration.

"What do you mean?"

"I know what you think of me." She glanced over at me, and my eyes apologized again. "But I don't care; I like sex. He won't touch me. I don't know what to do. I don't think he's into me." Sorrowful disappointment resounded in her voice. I wasn't sure how to console her.

"Do you still like him?"

"I'm not sure of that either." After a moment of silence, she cautiously brought up a new topic. "So, we never got to talk about what happened the other night with your mom showing up at the game."

"I'd rather not," I blurted. "It's just too much to think about." I didn't want to let myself go back there to that night, or any other that involved my mother. It was too painful.

Sara respected my withdrawn response without a word. She glanced at the clock next to her bed and asked, "What time is Evan picking you up?"

"Ten-thirty," I told her, and then glanced at the clock too. "Sara, he's going to be here in an hour. I need to take a shower. But we're not done talking about you and Jason. We'll talk about it tomorrow, okay?"

"Okay," she sighed.

When Evan arrived exactly at ten-thirty, I was barely ready in time to meet him at the door.

"What are we doing today?" I asked, soaking in the warm November sun when I entered his car.

"Don't worry, I'll show you," he answered before driving away.

When we pulled into his driveway, I was surprised to find a silver BMW parked there as well. I'd never seen another car in his driveway before. Then it struck me that someone else was home. Could I possibly face his parents after my humiliating performance last night?

"Who's home?" I asked, hoping he'd tell me, no one.

"My mom. Don't worry, we probably won't see her."

The words were barely out of his mouth when the kitchen door opened and his mother stepped out to greet us.

"Or maybe you will," Evan corrected in surprise.

Vivian was dressed in wide-legged black pants with a fitted blue turtleneck sweater that flattered her petite figure. I couldn't get over how refined she looked, even without all the glitz.

"Emily," she said with a smile, "it's nice to see you again." I smiled cautiously, not understanding the warm reception. Even Evan was scrutinizing her greeting.

We met her at the bottom of the porch steps, and she gave me a brief embrace. I froze, unable to return it since it happened so quickly, and I honestly wasn't expecting it.

"I understand you and Evan have planned to spend the afternoon together. I think that is wonderful," she said, glowing.

"Mom, what's wrong with you?"

Vivian looked at him disapprovingly.

"Evan, I'm happy to see Emily again, that's all." She smiled at me, apologizing for Evan's rudeness.

"We're going in the garage," he told her, eyeing her suspiciously.

"It was great to see you," she said. "Perhaps you could come over for dinner sometime."

"Um, that would be nice," I answered in shock. I replayed our interaction last night, not understanding why she was being so nice to me.

I followed Evan into the garage, but instead of going upstairs to the rec room, he opened the door leading into the other half of the garage. When we were behind closed doors, he paused, his eyes flickering in deliberation.

"What's wrong?" I asked.

"I have no idea why she's acting so strange, and it's making me really nervous. I'm trying to remember if I said something, or overheard anything, to explain it. I'm sorry if it made you uncomfortable."

"I was actually trying to come up with the same answer," I admitted. "I thought she'd despise me after my humiliating clumsiness last night. Besides, I thought for sure Catherine would've said something."

He smiled, remembering my parting comment.

"Oh, I'm sorry about that by the way," I told him, looking at the floor.

"What are you talking about?"

"I should have helped you out more than I did during dinner, instead of laughing. I really wasn't laughing at you. I felt bad that you had to put up with her. I was laughing at how ridiculous she was."

"Don't worry about it. You definitely helped in the end with that priceless exit." He smiled, and I smiled back.

"Okay, what are we doing?" I asked, looking around the expansive space. There were two ride-on lawn mowers, a jet ski and some other recreational vehicles parked in the otherwise empty space.

Evan walked over to a black dirt bike and handed me a red helmet.

"We're going for a ride," he said, kicking up the stand and rolling it toward the large door at the other end. He pressed a button on the wall, and the door rolled open.

I watched him leave the garage, not sure if my legs could move, let alone about walk.

"Evan, I'm not sure that's a great idea."

"Trust me, you'll love it." He fastened a black helmet on his head. I warily walked out to him and slid the helmet onto my head. What the hell was I doing?

Evan helped me fasten the strap and showed me where to sit and place my feet. He explained that the path was pretty flat, but to expect to bounce a little. Great, not only was this my first time on a bike, but this one could potentially throw me off!

Evan kicked the starter, and the dirt bike revved to life. The explosive rumble caused my heart to falter. It didn't help when he throttled it a few times. He motioned for me to get on. Before I could talk myself out of it, I climbed up and threw my leg over the seat. I slid closer to his back and put my hands on his waist. He grabbed my hands and pulled them around him. Once we started, I understood why.

We sped off through the back field toward the woods. My heart pounded against my chest. I gripped him tighter as we entered the woods and the terrain became bumpier—I could feel the seat give with each divot and root, still too scared to enjoy the experience.

Eventually, I became accustomed to the uneven ride and loosened my death grip. I still kept my arms snugly around Evan, knowing that one unexpected bounce and I'd be airborne. I focused on the trees streaking by and the sun fighting through the tops of the evergreens. It was brighter in the woods than I'd expected, probably because despite the unseasonably warm day most of the trees were bare, preparing for winter.

Evan eventually slowed and allowed the bike to coast to a stop. He shut off the bike and took off his helmet. I sat up and attempted to do the same. I couldn't figure out how to take it off, so I climbed off the bike and asked him to help me. My legs trembled beneath me.

"Well?" he asked, after removing the helmet from my head.

I shrugged. "Not bad."

"What?" he questioned. "You loved it, admit it."

"Not really."

He shook his head and smiled.

I looked out at a glistening clearing with sunlight dancing along swaying, overgrown blades. A brook along the bottom of a small hill bubbled over rocks before disappearing into the woods. "This is nice."

"I've taken some amazing pictures out here."

"I don't think I've ever seen your pictures. Well, except for the newspaper and the one you submitted for the calendar."

"I can show you when we get back if you want."

"Sure."

We walked to the brook and sat at its edge, mesmerized by the water rippling over the stones.

"My mom showed up at the game the other night," I blurted, staring into the water. I wasn't prepared to say that, and honestly, I'd thought I was past it until I inadvertently found my thoughts drifting there again.

"You must have been happy to see her."

I let out an uneasy laugh. "I don't know about that."

Evan remained quiet, waiting for me to continue.

"It was awkward," I confessed.

"I'm sorry," Evan replied, not knowing what else to say. I shrugged dismissively, afraid to reveal more.

He casually took my hand, making my heart trip. We sat in silence, caught up in the glistening flow of the water.

"I'm still trying to figure out what my mother's up to," he finally said. "Or it's possible she could actually like you."

"Thanks," I shot back sarcastically.

"You know what I mean," he said, trying to make me feel better. "It's not like you talked to her very much last night. She's never been this...accepting of anyone before. She's really hard to please."

"I can see that," I recognized with a slight nod. "Speaking of which, you were so different at dinner. It was a little strange."

"How?"

"You seemed...older. You spoke more properly and were almost stiff," I explained, hoping I hadn't offended him. I looked over at him as he considered my words.

"I guess I never thought about it, but you're probably right. It's most likely from years of having to go to those things—they're rubbing off on me. That sucks."

I let out a short laugh.

"I guess you'll have to come to more of them to keep me real," he suggested, gently nudging my shoulder with his. I caught my breath at his touch, my mouth frozen in a shocked smile at the thought of future dinners.

Then I heard a buzzing and a distant chime. Evan reached in his pocket and took out his cell phone. He read who was calling on the screen and grinned at me before answering.

"Hi, Jake," he answered. My mouth dropped open. Evan smiled. He listened for a while, but couldn't keep the smile off his face, occasionally glancing at me.

"Sorry I didn't tell you I was showing up with her. I didn't think it mattered." He listened again for a minute.

"I understand, but I warned you she wasn't like that." He looked at me with a grin. My eyes grew wider—I could only imagine what was being said on the other end.

"No, I don't think you have to worry about either of them saying anything. No, Jason won't—I talked to him about it last night.

"Yeah, I'd say she wasn't interested either." Evan smiled wider—heat flashed across my cheeks.

"Don't worry about it; it's fine. I'll see you tomorrow." He laughed as he pressed *End*.

"You'd better tell me what that was all about," I threatened.

"He was pissed off that I was there, thinking that's why you acted that way. And he wanted to know if I thought any of you would say anything. The parties are handpicked for a reason—no one talks about what goes on there. There are rumors, but no one ever admits to anything. But the good news is that you won't have to worry about him hitting on you—I think he got the hint."

"Well, that's good," I admitted. "He really is so full of himself. I can't believe you're friends with him."

"I wouldn't say we're friends. I met him before I moved here. His mother and mine were on a fund-raising committee, and I met him at the dinner. When he found out I was moving here, he invited me to one of his parties to 'introduce' me to people before I started school."

I really wanted to comment about his "introduction," but the thought of it made my stomach flip. I forced out the stray thoughts.

"Besides that, we have soccer in common, and we've hung out a few times with other guys. But I would never call him up and ask him over. He's a lot to take by himself. I'd hate to be the girl he's focused on—you have no idea what he says..." Then he stopped to look at me apologetically.

"Evan, are you serious?! He's said things about me to the soccer team?" My stomach turned in disgust.

"He doesn't when I'm around because he knows it pisses me off, and I have no problem telling him that. He's an ass—don't worry about it. He's not lying and saying that you've gotten together or anything like that." I knew he was trying to make me feel better, but I was fuming at the thought of being the topic of anything that came out of Jake's mouth.

"We should head back," Evan said, pulling me back from my angry thoughts. I followed him to the bike, where he helped me with my helmet before we climbed on. The return trip didn't seem as long, thankfully. Can't say the bike was my favorite adrenaline rush.

Evan parked the bike in the garage before leading me upstairs. Upon entering, he selected the music of a guy with a smooth voice, strumming a guitar to an easy rhythm, singing about being under the stars—it reminded me of being on the beach.

"Are you hungry?" he inquired. "I can run down and grab us a couple of sandwiches."

"Sure." He left while I sat on the couch, enchanted by the optimistic melodies. I barely heard him run back up the stairs.

"Here you go," he announced. I jumped.

"You don't pay attention very well, do you?"

"I didn't hear you," I countered defensively. He let out a quick laugh. He placed a plate on the table in front of me with a bottle of root beer.

"Is your mom still here?"

"Yeah, she just gave me a hard time about taking you out on the bike. I assured her you weren't that breakable." I tightened my lips to hide a smile. I couldn't imagine his mother being so concerned about my well-being. She barely knew me.

When we were done eating, Evan asked, "Do you want to see the pictures I was talking about?"

"Definitely."

I followed him as he opened the door behind the foosball tables into a rustic room with exposed beams in its walls. There were two small windows on the other side of the room, overlooking the driveway. Two twin beds with navy comforters sat along one wall, and a long desk with pictures and photography equipment sprawled across it ran along the other. There was a simple doorless closet on the same wall as the entrance, with shelves holding clothes, books and photography equipment.

One of the first things I noticed was Sara's white scarf hanging on the back of the rolling desk chair. Evan caught my eye and pressed his lips together.

"Yeah, you left that in my car. I keep forgetting to give it to you." I nodded, not sure what to make of that, so I decided to dismiss it.

Evan started pointing out different pictures of scenic landscapes pinned to the wooden beams above the desk, explaining where he was when he took them. I was easily lost in the detail of each shot, transported to the location as if I were there standing next to him when he took them.

I began flipping through the loose pictures scattered on the desk. Evan commented on some of the shots, then became silent to let me look on my own. I couldn't say anything—I was speechless. I'd known he was talented when I saw the results for the paper, but I had no idea.

I opened a book bound in black, causing Evan to take in a quick breath. I hesitated, uncertain if he wanted me to look through it.

"That's my work for Art class," he explained. It didn't explain his reaction.

"Can I look through it?" I'd never seen him so tense before.

"Sure," he answered quietly, remaining uneasy, standing perfectly still.

I turned the pages and studied the art that he captured through his lens. The portfolio contained scenic pictures, sports action pictures and abstract pictures of unidentifiable objects with smooth lines and intricate curves. Then I flipped the page and stopped. I could sense Evan stiffen even more when the image caught my breath.

I examined the black-and-white angled profile of a girl. The soft lines of her face filled most of the picture, her pale skin in dramatic contrast to the dark background. A thick, wet strand of hair clung to her subtly parted full lips. Drops of water scattered on her smooth skin, dripping from her sloping nose. Her almond-shaped eyes were smeared with black, framing their haunted depths as she focused on a place far removed from the picture. "It's beautiful," I breathed, admiring the powerful emotion and truth frozen in the single shot.

"I love that picture," he admitted softly. "I think it's because I love the girl in that picture."

I turned slowly to face him, confused by his words and feeling my stomach twist.

"What?" The strangling spread to my chest. I could feel my heart beating in my throat.

"You don't remember when I took that picture?"

I stared at him, unsure of what he was talking about.

"You were so quiet for so long. You didn't say anything when I came back to check on you. So I left to get my camera, thinking I could get shots of people at the party and give you time alone, since you didn't seem to want to talk." I was afraid to hear more. My heart beat louder and my head felt light—I could barely breathe.

"By the time I got back, it had started to rain. I saw Sara in the house—I told her where you were, and that I'd meet her outside. You looked so amazing in your stillness, sitting in the rain; at the same time, you looked displaced—like you were a million miles away. I had to capture it. I tried to talk to you, but you wouldn't say anything. So I sat next to you and waited. You finally stirred from wherever you went and realized it was raining."

I heard every word he said, but I couldn't comprehend a single syllable. Then I stared into his stormy blue eyes and saw what he was saying. My knees buckled—I inhaled several fast breaths. I slowly lowered myself on to the chair at the desk, staring at the floor, my breath lost.

After a few minutes of deafening silence, Evan asked, "Are you okay?"

No, I mouthed, shaking my head slowly. I looked up at him. "Evan, you can't say that. You can't mean it."

"That's not quite what I hoped you'd say," he responded, disappointment evident in his tone.

"I'm sorry…" I started.

"Don't be, it's okay," he replied quickly, suddenly trying to downplay the situation. Then he thought better of it, and asked, "Are you really telling me you don't feel the same way?" I held my breath, and my heart ached.

"I…I can't, we can't," I stammered. "You don't understand. It doesn't matter how I feel; it just can't happen." He stared into my distraught eyes and shook his head in confusion.

"I *don't* understand. What are you talking about?"

"Can't we please just stay friends?" I begged.

"But you're not denying that you feel the same way."

"It's so much more complicated than that. If we can't be friends, then—" I couldn't say it. "*Please*, can we just be friends?"

He didn't respond. The silence was disrupted by the vibration of his phone. He pulled it out of his pocket and looked to me. "I've got to take this—it's my brother."

I nodded, and he left the room. Soon after, I heard his footsteps on the stairs.

I became aware that I was strangling my shaking hands and released them, but was unable to loosen the knot in my throat or calm the throbbing in my chest. I took a couple of breaths in an attempt to push it away. My legs felt rubbery when I stood. I took another breath before walking out of the room, closing the door behind me.

21. JUST FRIENDS

W"e can be friends," Evan said when he found me lost in thought on the couch twenty minutes later. He sat next to me and grabbed my hand. The warmth of his hand sent shivers up my arm. I searched his eyes, wanting to believe him.

"I mean, we're already friends, so nothing has to change." The disappointment and confusion were replaced by a comforting smile. He *appeared* to be sincere. "Okay?"

I had no idea what had happened in that twenty minutes, but he was not the same as when he left.

"Yeah, okay," I said slowly. I tried to smile back.

———

I was so afraid of seeing him in school on Monday, expecting an awkwardness between us. However, there wasn't the tension or avoidance I anticipated. Everything was back to the way it was before the weekend—but then again…it wasn't.

I noticed his presence so much more than I had before. Every time he brushed past my arm when we walked down the hall or leaned in close to whisper to me in Anatomy, it sent thousands of sparks flying through my body. I found myself smiling more and caught up in his gaze longer. It was like I was noticing him for the first time, all over again. But this time, I knew he noticed me too.

Evan sat closer, walked nearer, and looked longer. He started storing his books in my locker between classes, placing his hand on the small of my back when reaching over me to retrieve them. These subtle touches would ignite a warmth in my chest, and release tingles up the back of my neck. He didn't hold my hand in school, but he always found a way for the backs of our hands to lightly touch when we were near enough.

We were engaged in a very intricate dance of touching without touching, knowing without saying, and feeling without expressing. We were friends walking along a ledge, a very thin ledge—and I was too caught up in my heightened awareness of his existence to realize how close the ledge was to crumbling beneath my feet.

"What's going on with you?" Sara asked during our ride to school on Wednesday. I hadn't told her everything when I returned from Evan's that Sunday afternoon. I told her about the dirt-bike ride and Jake's call, but I left out The Picture. I couldn't bring myself to say the words out loud, and since we had agreed to be just friends, there was no point in saying them at all.

"What do you mean?"

"You and Evan have been acting really...different the last couple of days. Did something happen that you're not telling me?" She glanced over at my avoiding eyes and declared, "Something *did* happen! Em, did he kiss you? I can't believe you didn't tell me!"

"No, Sara, he did not kiss me," I said emphatically.

"Then what? You two are almost too.... close, or something. I can tell it's not the same. So, what happened?"

"We're just friends," I emphasized.

"Did he say something?" she demanded excitedly. I couldn't conceal my pink cheeks. "Omigod, that's it. He finally told you how he feels about you. You have to tell me what he said."

"Sara, it doesn't matter," I retorted, getting redder as I remembered exactly what he'd said. "We're only going to be friends, so I'm not going to talk about it."

Sara didn't continue her interrogation, but a knowing smile crept over her face.

"Is Carol getting out of work early today?" Sara asked when we pulled in to the parking lot.

"She actually took the day off so she could go shopping with her mother and start prepping everything for tomorrow. I guess her sister and her kids are getting into town tonight, so she wants to be there for that too." The thought of Carol in the kitchen *cooking* was laughable. I knew she wasn't going to measurably contribute to the Thanksgiving meal, but would gladly accept the unearned praise.

"So you can't go home after school, can you?"

"I think I'm going over to Evan's," I replied as casually as I possibly could.

"Yeah, and I'm coming with you," she insisted. I knew there was no point in arguing with her.

"Sure." I smiled slightly, trying to hide my disappointment.

To my surprise, Evan seemed perfectly accepting of gaining a chaperone. When we arrived at his house after a useless half-day of classes, I discovered why. Alongside his mother's BMW was a silver Volvo with New York license plates.

"Your brother?" I concluded.

"He got in late last night."

The side door opened as it had before, and Vivian came out, wiping her hands on a white apron tied around her waist—evidently she *did* cook. She was stunning once again with her hair twisted neatly off of her face. She wore a full black skirt that fell below her knees and a pair of black boots that rose to meet it, along with a tailor-fitted white blouse.

Behind her was a tall male who was obviously her oldest son and the opposite of Evan in just about every way. Jared had shaggy blond hair that flipped out at the tops of his ears. He shared his mother's soft features, with her thin lips and her sparkling blue eyes. Jared was slightly taller than Evan, with a broader, more muscular build.

"Who's that?" I heard Sara whisper in my ear as they approached.

"Evan's mother and brother," I said quickly.

"Emily, how are you, darling?" she asked, giving me the same embrace but adding a peck on the cheek. I still had a hard time returning the gesture due to its brevity.

"It's nice to see you again, Mrs. Mathews."

"Vivian, please. We are already acquainted, so we can forgo the formalities," she insisted, smiling brightly.

"Jared, this is Emma," Evan declared proudly.

"Hi, I've heard a lot about you," Jared replied, extending his hand. I gave Evan a brief questioning glance, and he responded with a quick rise of his eyebrows.

"This is my friend Sara," I introduced, after she'd nudged my elbow for the second time.

"Sara, it's very nice to meet you. I met your parents. They are wonderful people." Vivian shook her hand. Before Jared could say anything to Sara, Vivian turned to me to ask, "Will you be staying for dinner?"

"Mom," Evan stressed, alarmed by the invitation, "it's the day before Thanksgiving. I'm sure Emma needs to get home to *her* family."

"Well, another time then," she said, ignoring his curtness.

"Of course," I promised.

"We're going upstairs to play pool," Evan announced before his mother could make any other impromptu invitations. He grabbed my hand and escorted me to the garage.

"It was nice seeing you again," I blurted as we passed Vivian. Sara and Jared followed behind us.

While Evan turned on the music and got us drinks, and Jared collected the pool balls on the table, Sara cornered me.

"*What* was that about?" she demanded. "His mother is practically gushing over you. Not to mention that he's holding your hand like it's the most natural thing in the world. Forget about dating— are you having a wedding you forgot to invite me to?"

"Sara!" I exclaimed a little too loudly, shocked by her words. Her eyes widened at my volume, and we both glanced around to make certain the guys hadn't overheard.

"Stop being stupid," I whispered. "I met his mother at the dinner, remember? And he grabbed my hand to drag me away before she said anything else that would embarrass him."

"Whatever you say," she replied, not convinced.

"You two ready?" Evan called from the pool table.

Evan and I were a team against Jared and Sara. Throughout the game we engaged in casual conversation about Cornell, soccer, the upcoming basketball season and Thanksgiving plans. I could feel Sara boring holes through me every time Evan leaned over me with his hand on my hip, adjusting my angle for the tougher shots. Then again, the searing heat could have been my heart pressed against my chest.

"So, what's with Mom?" Jared asked when Evan was taking his shot. Evan waited until he knocked the nine ball into the corner pocket before he answered.

"You mean downstairs when we got here?"

"Yeah, that was strange," Jared noted.

"Um, actually, I didn't get to tell you this either, Emma." I raised my eyebrows when he looked over toward me. "I told you that Emma went to the Jacobses' with us for dinner last weekend, right?"

"Yeah, and I am so sorry you had to suffer through that," Jared said. I grinned in acknowledgment, too anxious to hear what Evan had to share to say anything.

"Well, it turns out that quiet Dr. Eckel likes to gossip," he explained, looking at me with a grin. My eyes widened, catching on. "Emma was sitting next to Dr. Eckel, and I guess he overheard Catherine's—"

"Pathetic charm," I interjected. Evan smiled at my choice of words.

"Sara, you know about this, right?" Evan checked. She nodded, trying to suppress a smile that drew color along Evan's neck. "Anyway, he also heard Emma's not-so-subtle reactions to some of the things she said."

"Noticed that, huh?" My face instantly felt warmer.

"I think half the table noticed, but only he knew what it was about, since everyone else was talking. So, when we made our escape, he *happened* to be on his way to the restroom and witnessed your gracious exit."

"No way," I gasped, my mouth hanging open.

"Don't worry; he thought it was pretty funny. He and my mother survive these dinners on gossip, so he told her what happened. My mother can't stand the Jacobses, including Catherine, and she was impressed by how you subtly put her in her place."

"She's impressed with me because I laughed at Catherine Jacobs? That was not very subtle," I stated, dumbfounded.

"Well, you don't know Catherine. She's probably still trying to figure out why you were laughing at her," he said with a quick laugh. "But my mother thinks you showed a lot of restraint, considering." His mother must have misinterpreted my rudeness for something even I didn't understand.

"Huh," Jared mused, before taking his shot.

"Are you two going skiing this weekend?" I blurted out to change the subject.

"Yeah, what are we doing this weekend?" Jared asked, directing his attention to Evan. "I want to get the snowboards out. We can go up Saturday and stay the night."

"Don't we have plans Sunday?" Evan turned to me for the answer.

"We could go out Friday instead," Sara quickly threw in. I almost forgot she was behind me, she'd been so quiet. "Em, you can say you and I have to work on the Journalism assignment together. You can lie and tell them it's due Monday, and since I won't be around for the rest of the weekend, Friday is the only day available. Then we can all go out to a movie or something. Jared, you're welcome to come too if you want."

"You're good with the lying-to-the-parents stories, huh?" Jared observed, sounding impressed.

"I've had four years of practice," she admitted, making me laugh.

"Sure, we can go out Friday," Evan responded tentatively, looking to me for approval. I nodded in agreement.

"That sounds good to me," Jared confirmed.

"Wait, what about Jason?" Evan asked, realizing that he was missing from the plan.

"Yeah, well, we won't be seeing much of Jason anymore," she confessed.

"What happened?" Evan countered.

"Um, he was just so…quiet," she said with a smile. I knew what she really meant and let out a quick laugh.

"He was really nice," she backtracked, "but I need a little more…spontaneity." She smirked at me.

"Huh, I'm sorry to hear that it didn't work out," Evan said.

"Thanks," she replied, uncomfortable with the condolence.

We played a few games of pool and a couple rounds of darts before I realized that I needed to leave, so I could be home before George.

"I'll be right back," Evan told Jared, grabbing his coat.

"Oh, I'll drive Emma," Sara told Evan. Evan stopped with one arm in his sleeve and looked at me, questioning Sara's offer. I shrugged.

"Okay," he said reluctantly. "Then I'll see you Friday."

"I'll call you to confirm the time," Sara replied. "It was great to meet you, Jared." I lingered, not sure if Evan was going to walk us down. Sara noticed my hesitation and grabbed my hand.

"Bye." I managed to wave before I disappeared.

"You are so full of shit," Sara exclaimed when we pulled out of the driveway. My jaw dropped. "If there was any more sexual tension in that room—"

"What?" I interrupted with a laugh. "You are definitely seeing things that aren't there."

"Am I?"

I couldn't straighten the smile from my lips.

"Yeah, I didn't think so," she concluded from my lack of defense. "Emma, just be careful, okay?"

"I don't understand you," I confronted. "You keep saying how cute we are together and antagonizing me with questions about whether he's kissed me—and now that...well, you're not reacting the way I thought you would."

"I was stupid for teasing you about kissing him," she admitted. "I'm sorry. But now that I see your new *friendship*, I'm really afraid for you. If you can't hide it around me, then Carol is going to destroy you if she picks up on it."

"Don't worry, Sara, nothing's going to happen."

I didn't have to sit on the steps very long before George arrived home. It was easy, without Carol around, to ask him if I could stay over at Sara's on Friday. He agreed, reminding me I had to be home first thing on Saturday to do my chores. He had to work for a few hours on Saturday, so he warned me not to upset Carol while I was home alone with her. I promised, knowing that just breathing would upset Carol, and there wasn't anything I could do about that.

I survived Thanksgiving at Janet's by not existing. I blended into the background as best as I could. When it came to cleaning up, Carol glowered at me, prompting me to make myself useful, but Janet wouldn't hear of it. Carol did everything she could to keep from blowing up, so I stayed out of her way in the living room, coloring with the kids while they watched the first Christmas movie of the season.

I drove home with George while Carol and the kids spent more time with her sister and her two daughters, who were visiting from Georgia.

Sara picked me up in the morning so that we'd have the day together before we went to the movies. She wanted to go to the mall, but I begged her not to make me suffer through watching her try on a million pieces of clothes on the busiest shopping day of the year. She relented, but she still had to get a couple of things done before we went to lunch.

We stopped by a jeweler so Sara could buy new earrings, then a seamstress, to pick up new clothes Sara had had tailor-fitted, and finally Sara splurged on pedicures for the two of us. It was Sara's idea of the perfect girl day, minus the clothes shopping. I was just along for the ride, getting a glimpse of what it was like to be Sara McKinley.

We walked quickly to the house in the cold, with flip-flops on our freshly pedi'd feet. Anna admired my light pink toes and Sara's contrasting hot red while we sat and chatted on the couch. She was preparing a list of recipients for Christmas cards, to be sent out the next week. I watched as Sara and her mom discussed their family and laughed about her dad's side. I smiled at their connection, feeling like I was looking through a window at the ideal family. But it also made me ache, knowing how frigid it was on my side of the window.

"What time are the boys meeting you?" Anna asked.

"We're going to an early show at six and then probably getting something to eat. We'll come back here and hang out after," Sara informed her mom, and me as well. This was the first time I was hearing our plans.

"Sounds great," Anna replied.

"Let's go figure out what I'm going to do with you," Sara said, pulling me off the couch.

I sat on her bed as she sorted through her closet.

"Sara," I called nervously. My tone made her stop what she was doing and step out of the closet. "I don't think I can afford dinner and a movie. I've stashed some money, but not enough to do both."

I hated having to admit when I couldn't afford to do the things she had in mind for us. And she knew I hated when she offered to pay for things. It was hard enough borrowing her clothes; forget about having her extend her wallet to entertain me.

"Don't worry about it," she said nonchalantly. "I have movie passes that I have to use, so you can save your money for food. The passes include drinks and popcorn, so it'll work out. I actually have four, so the guys will use them too. Honestly, Em, they'll probably want to pay for dinner, feeling bad that I'm supplying the movies."

"Are you sure?"

"Definitely. I have the passes, so we might as well use them." She ducked back into the closet, continuing her search.

"Do you have any more pink sweaters?" I yelled to Sara when I heard her groaning in frustration through the open door.

"No more pink sweaters for you," she hollered in return. Then she poked her head out and said, "I should make you go in sweats actually." I scowled at her.

"But you know I couldn't do that. I love dressing you up too much," she said with a smile. "Oh, I have it. I have this black shirt that will look amazing with dark jeans and wedge heels." She revealed a scooping black top that looked like it was too small.

"No heels," I protested.

"Uh, that's not going to work," she groaned. "Wait—what about boots? They have a thicker heel, so they won't be so hard to walk in." I shrugged in defeat. "Then I'll pull your hair back in a curly ponytail and you'll be adorable—to go to the movies with your *friends*." I picked up on the sarcasm and stuck my tongue out at her.

My hair bounced in the ponytail as I descended the stairs with Sara. She had her long locks in a high ponytail as well and wore a sapphire blouse that showed off her eyes. She looked like she was going on a date, despite the supposed casualness of the evening.

I met Evan's eyes and grinned back when he came into view at the bottom of the stairs.

"Don't you two look nice," Carl observed from the sitting room.

"Thanks, Dad," Sara said, giving him a peck on the cheek and grabbing our jackets. "We'll be back later."

Jared's silver Volvo waited for us in the driveway. Jared opened the passenger side door for Sara. She was heading toward the back door with me when the gesture caught her by surprise.

"Oh, thanks," she said, slipping into the passenger seat.

Evan opened the back door for me, before he went around to the other side and slid in next to me. He had my hand in his before we even left the driveway. My lips curled up at the warmth of his touch. As we drove, our bodies gradually became closer until the sides of our jeans were gently touching. I couldn't say that either of us moved intentionally, but there was a gravity that drew us together. My heart murmured in contentment.

In attempt to make up for her silence at Evan's the other day, Sara did most of the talking, with Jared being her main audience—although she kept turning around to include us. I knew she was doing it to prevent us from doing anything in the dark of the back-seat. Jared was an endearing captive to Sara's charm. He laughed at the right time and commented intelligently—I was relieved he was with us instead of Jason.

"No more pink sweaters?" Evan whispered while Sara discussed one of her favorite restaurants in New York, which coincidentally was one of Jared's as well.

"I've been banned," I whispered in return, nodding toward Sara. He looked from Sara back to me, his eyebrows pulled together. "Don't worry about it."

"Okay." He shrugged.

"But you still look great," he whispered, leaning in so that his breath tickled my ear. He lingered for a second. I knew all I had to do was turn my head, and he would be right there. I took an even breath, allowing it to swirl in my head before slowly turning to meet him.

"Does that sound good to you?" Sara turned toward us. I quickly faced her, and Evan sat back against his seat. She shot me an accusing look.

"Sorry, what did you say?" I asked. Evan gave my hand a tight squeeze in frustration.

"For dinner," she emphasized. "Is Italian okay?"

"Sure," Evan agreed.

We pulled up to the theater, and Sara practically pulled me out of the car, putting her arm through mine while forcing us to walk together the entrance. The guys followed.

"Em, you are in so much trouble," she whispered. I could only grin in recognition of the truth.

When the guys found out Sara was taking care of the tickets, they insisted on paying for dinner—as Sara had predicted. After getting our drinks and popcorn, we made our way into the crowded theater to see a newly released action movie.

I could tell Sara was angling to sit between me and Evan, but I slipped in behind him before she could enter the row—so Sara sat next to me, and Jared was next to Evan. Evan easily found my hand again once the lights dimmed. I don't know if I could've recalled a single scene from the overly explosive flick. Not with Evan slowly brushing his fingertips along the inside of my hand, tracing delicate circles that made my entire body tingle.

Every so often Sara tried to distract me with a comment about an unrealistic leap, or saying that the action star should have been dead within the first five minutes of the movie. When I leaned in to rest my head on Evan's shoulder, she finally gave up, shaking her head in frustration. I couldn't concentrate on anything except for his breath next to my ear and his cheek against the top of my head as he casually breathed me in. The star could've died in the first five minutes—I would have had no idea.

When we stood up to leave, my legs were weak and my head was spinning. Evan kept his hand on my waist, holding me next to him while we made our way up the crowded aisle. I placed my hand over his, securing him to me. As soon as we were in the main hall, Sara caught my arm.

"We'll be right back," she announced, pulling me away from Evan and toward the bathroom.

As soon as we entered, Sara whipped around to face me. "What are you doing?" She didn't pause to let me answer. "If you tell me one more time that you're just friends, I'm going to kill you. Do you want this? Because all you have to do is tell me, and I'll leave you alone. But you were the one who convinced *me* this couldn't happen, and now look at you—you can barely see straight.

"Just think about it clearly for one minute and let me know if you want more from Evan than just a friendship. Forget about what you're *feeling*—*think* about it. Think about Carol."

I shuddered at the mention of her name.

I stood there for a minute, taking in her passionate expression. I was overwhelmed. I couldn't think. My body was so mesmerized by the trance of Evan's touch that my mind wasn't working. I couldn't answer her.

"I don't know what to do," I confessed quietly, "but don't worry about me Sara; it will be okay. I promise."

"You know you can't promise that."

I shrugged.

"Do you want me to interfere, so you can decide what to do?"

"Maybe," I agreed. I recognized her logic, but the swirling in my head was not allowing rational thought to penetrate. "But don't be so invasive, okay? You and I can sit in the backseat together, but let me sit next to him in the restaurant, alright?"

"I can do that."

The guys were waiting for us patiently. I took Evan's hand and walked to the parking lot.

"I'm going to sit in back with Sara, okay?" I whispered as we neared the car.

"Sure," he said, pausing to look at me. "Are you okay?"

"Yeah." I smiled back, putting him at ease. "It's a girl thing." He raised his eyebrows and nodded to indicate that he understood. I wished I did.

After a talkative dinner, we headed back to Sara's, still in the agreed-upon seating arrangement. I was intoxicated by him as I gazed at the back of Evan's neatly trimmed hairline and the linear muscles that ran down his neck to his back. I'd stopped fighting against the pull of him anymore, and it felt so invigorating. I didn't want to pretend I didn't feel my pulse quicken every time I was near him. I wanted to feel it—I deserved that much, right?

"Sara, would you be okay with Jared if Evan and I watched a movie in your room?" I whispered in her ear. Her mouth dropped open, and for the first time, Sara was speechless.

"Are you sure?" she asked cautiously.

"Yeah, I'm sure." I smiled, the glow radiating from my cheeks.

She smiled back and whispered, "Okay." Then quickly added, "I want details." I laughed, and Evan turned to find out what was so funny.

I looked at him and smiled, biting my lower lip. "Nothing," I assured him. Then I heard Sara gasp.

My eyes followed hers, and I froze, seeing exactly what had caused her to breathe in so sharply, looking past Evan toward the Jeep parked along the road.

"Oh no, Sara…it's *her*." In that one breath, the ledge disintegrated from under my feet.

22. REVEALED

G et down," Sara instructed fervently, pulling me on to the
seat.

"What's wrong?" Evan inspected our sunken silhouettes with concern.

"Evan, turn around," Sara demanded. He recognized the terror on my face and did.

Still facing forward, he asked, "What is going on?"

Before she could redirect him, Jared pulled into her driveway. Sara unfastened our seat belts so we could slide to the floor behind the front seats.

"Shit," she whispered and pulled out her phone. "Jared, shut off the car. Hi, Mom. Listen. Jared—please listen to this, Jared—is going to come to the front door, and you're going to answer. He's going to look like he's asking if we're home, and you're going to shake your head and look like you're telling him we've already gone to bed.

"Jared, please go."

Jared, definitely perplexed by the situation, obeyed.

Anna said something to Sara. I clutched my knees, staring at her as my body shook and my stomach turned.

"Mom, I promise I'll explain when I get home. Keep the back door unlocked. Bye."

She hung up the phone and watched the exchange at the door from between the seats. From my position on the floor behind the passenger seat, I was unable to see what happened, but it was brief. Jared was back in the car within a minute, awaiting further instructions.

"Pull out of the driveway and drive back to the main road at the end of my street," Sara instructed. "Take a right on the road, and then the first road on the right. Jared, let me know if that Jeep follows you."

After a stomach-wrenching eternity, he said, "No, it's still parked across from your house."

Sara let out a sigh for the both of us. I couldn't tell if I was actually breathing.

"Are you going to tell me what's going on?" Evan demanded, growing more frustrated.

I couldn't bring myself to talk. I could only stare at Sara and shake my head.

"Who's in the Jeep?" Evan inquired.

"My aunt," I whispered, finding my voice. The admission of her presence made me feel faint. What was she doing here?

"Are we on the other street yet?" Sara asked.

"Yeah," Jared answered.

Sara sat back up on the seat, but I couldn't bring myself to move.

"It'll be okay," Sara consoled, pulling me up by my hands and urging me to sit on the seat. I slid on to the leather and sat with my head in my shaking hands. "There's no way she saw us. We noticed her from the top of the hill, before she could see into the car."

Evan turned around. "Are you not supposed to be out?"

"I'm *never* supposed to be out," I said, my voice quivering. I couldn't look at him. I leaned against the window and nervously pulled at my lower lip with my fingers.

"Stop at the blue house that's still under construction." Sara leaned over the seat to point it out to Jared. "Do you have a flashlight that I can borrow?"

"Sure, it's in the trunk."

They got out of the car, leaving Evan and me alone.

"What's going to happen?"

"I don't know," I whispered, shaking my head.

"You're going to be okay, right?" he asked, the concern resounding in his voice.

Before I could answer, Sara opened my door and pulled me out by my hand. Evan opened his door to follow. I fought to find my feet beneath me, and leaned into Sara for support.

"Sara, what's going to happen?" Evan questioned.

"We have to go. I'll talk to you later," Sara blurted over her shoulder, escorting me along the dirt path that would eventually be a driveway, heading toward the construction site.

"Emma!" Evan yelled. But I didn't turn around. I allowed Sara to hurry me along into the darkness.

I didn't remember our trek through the woods from the back of the unfinished property to Sara's expansive backyard. Fear had a way of making time disappear, and the images came in flashes. I remember walking through the downstairs door, the sight of Anna's concerned face, and Sara laying me in the bed. I couldn't close my eyes, staring blankly at the dark sky through her skylights.

My head spun rapidly, trying to figure out how she knew. Had she followed us all night? Eventually, the fear subsided into a manageable place. I sensed Sara sitting next to me, watching me nervously.

"Did she leave?" I whispered.

"Right before we came into the house, my mom said."

"Do you think she knows?"

"I can't see how. My mom said that she called around seven and asked to speak with you. She told Carol we went to get something to eat and asked if you should call her when you got back. Carol said no. My mom doesn't remember when the car showed up across the street, but noticed it about fifteen minutes before I called her."

"What does your mom think?"

"She knows, Em. She doesn't know everything, but she knows how impossible your aunt and uncle are. She would never say anything, I swear."

I believed her.

"Does *he* know?"

"He's called a couple of times. All he knows is that you're really freaked. I wouldn't tell him why, and he got angry with me. He wanted to come back over, but I told him he couldn't, so he asked to come by in the morning. I convinced him that there wasn't enough time, since I had to get you home by eight.

"She won't do anything, will she?" For the first time since we saw Carol's car, Sara sounded scared.

"No, I'm sure she'll just accuse me of whatever lie she decides on, insult me a lot, and send me to my room." I looked up at Sara and realized I couldn't let her know how truly terrified I was to go home. I pushed the fear away so I could put on a reassuring face for Sara's sake.

I propped myself up to sit against the headboard.

"I really freaked out, huh?" I tried to let out a laugh, but it sounded wrong.

"Em, you were so pale, I was afraid you might pass out."

"I thought for sure that she saw us, that's all. I was expecting her to confront me and didn't know if I could face her." I was hoping to downplay my paralyzed reaction in the car.

"My mom offered to try talking to her," Sara said tentatively.

"You know that won't work," I replied, trying to control the panic in my voice.

"I know," Sara agreed with a defeated breath.

"I can't believe I reacted like that," I blurted, replaying my horrified reaction in my head. "Evan's probably wondering what the hell's wrong with me."

"He's just worried," Sara tried to soothe me. "He doesn't think any less of you, honestly."

I took a deep breath, trying to regain control over my quivering body before Sara noticed. What I couldn't tell her was that if her mom called, it would be the worst thing that could happen. What I couldn't show her was that I was petrified and didn't know how I was going to walk into that house in the morning. I knew Carol didn't need proof that I'd disobeyed her. She just had to believe I had.

———

I sat straight up, heaving and covered in sweat. I looked around the room, trying to place where I was. I recognized Sara and eased my fists from their white-knuckled grip of the blanket.

"You sounded like you couldn't breathe."

"Just a nightmare," I explained, trying to relax my tense posture. "What time is it?"

"Six thirty," she reported, still concerned by my appearance. "Do you want to talk about it?"

"I really don't remember it," I lied. "You should get some more sleep. I'm going to take a shower, okay?"

The smell of the earth still lingered in my nose, as did the burn in my lungs from the weight of the dirt on my body, pressing the air out of my chest. I shivered and pushed the nightmare away.

Sara didn't go back to sleep. She was on her bed, waiting for me with a silver box in her lap.

"This was supposed to be a Christmas gift, but I can't wait another month." Her face was too serious to be presenting a gift.

"It's not as big a deal as you think, but I really need you to have it before you go home today."

Her choice of words struck me. I glanced at the silver package with apprehension. Sara handed it to me with a stiff smile.

"Thanks." I tried to smile back, but couldn't get past her odd behavior.

I opened the box and unwrapped the tissue paper. A silver cell phone fell into my hand. Why was Sara so uncomfortable giving it to me?

"Thank you, Sara. This is so great. Is this a prepaid phone?" I asked, trying to sound as happy with the gift as I was.

"It's actually on my family's plan. Don't worry; it didn't cost anything to add you."

"Wow, that's perfect. I'm not sure how often I'll be able to use it, but this is so great." I was genuinely appreciative, but her cautious tone kept me from being able to express it. Then I found out why.

"You have to promise to call me when you get home and let me know that you're okay," she requested hesitantly. "If I don't hear from you by the end of the day, I'm calling the police."

"Sara," I implored, "don't do that. I promise you, I'll be fine."

"Then call me," she pleaded. "I have phone numbers already programmed." She showed me how to quick-dial her cell and her home phone. There were two other numbers set in the memory as well.

"Nine-one-one, really, Sara?" I questioned incredulously. "You don't think I could manage that one on my own?"

"One button is faster than four," she explained with a slight grin. I pulled up the fourth number and looked up at Sara in disbelief. She shrugged with a small smile.

"I set the ringer to vibrate so no one will hear it in your room. There's a charger in the box too."

"Sara, I'm not having it on in my house," I stated emphatically.

"You have to. I swear I won't call you, and no one else has the number. You have to promise me that you'll have it on." Her request sounded so desperate, I couldn't argue.

"Okay, I promise." I decided to keep it in the inner pocket of my jacket so it wouldn't be accidentally discovered. "We should get going."

I don't know how I convinced my body to cooperate and walk down the stairs with my bag in my hand. But my legs failed to move when I opened the front door and saw the Jeep parked on the side of the street.

"Oh, Emma," Sara whispered in alarm behind me.

"Hi, Sara," Carol bellowed with sickening charm. "I was driving home from my mother's and thought I'd pick up Emily on the way. Thank you for letting her stay with you." I felt Sara squeeze my arm, her panic obvious. I kept staring at the woman with the wide smile, unable to breathe.

"Come on, Emily, don't just stand there." I stumbled down the front stairs, afraid to look back at Sara, but feeling the weight of the cell phone in my jacket pocket. I let the car devour me as I shut the passenger door, staring straight ahead. My body tightened and shrank away from her, trapped in the confined space.

Silence stung my ears as I waited for her words, her accusations and insults. But there was nothing. Then again, she didn't need words. My head collided against the side window with a sudden thrust of her hand. My head rang with an involuntary grunt of pain.

"You don't breathe unless I tell you you can. You seem to have forgotten whose house you're living in. You've pushed it too fucking far, and it's over. Don't go behind my back again."

We were pulling into the driveway before I could let her words sink in.

When we entered the kitchen, Amanda, our thirteen-year-old neighbor, said she had left the kids playing upstairs and went home.

I continued down the hall and stopped, staring at the door leading to my room. The door was closed, and it was never closed when I wasn't home—one of Carol's irrational rules. I approached slowly, and cautiously pushed the door open, letting out a defeated breath. I faltered through the doorway, looking around in horrified dismay.

The closet door stood ajar, and the crawl space in the back was a vacant hole. Remnants of what it had once protected were strewn at my feet.

"You think you're so smart," Carol accused. My back tensed as every nerve hummed beneath my skin. I turned to find her leaning against the doorframe with her arms crossed, and I instinctively took a couple steps back, my bag sliding from my shoulder, dropping to the floor.

"I can see right through you, and you're not going to divide us." I was perplexed, unable to make sense of her accusations. "He will always choose me. I wanted to remind you of that."

"Carol?" I heard George yell anxiously from the back door.

"I'm here," Carol hollered back in a distraught voice. She backed away from my door and caught George in an embrace. I watched the drama unfold, unable to predict the ending.

"George, I don't know what got into her," Carol said, flailing her arms, burying her head in his shoulder. George attempted to peer around Carol to see into my room. "She burst in yelling that she's tired of being here, and how horrible we are to her. Then she locked herself in her room. That's when I called you. She was scaring me and the kids."

What?! What was she doing?

"I finally convinced her to open the door and…well, you can see for yourself." Carol released him from her desperate grasp, allowing George to enter. His concern changed to anger as he viewed the repercussions of *my rage*.

He looked from the destruction of my things to my stunned face and back down again. I thought I caught him wince when he saw the shattered glass and torn picture of him and his brother crushed on the floor. I couldn't move as I watched his anger grow.

"What did you do?" he bellowed. "How could you do this?" My mouth dropped, shocked by his reaction. How could he think I did this? His face turned red as he scanned my torn canvases, along with the shreds of smiles and small chubby baby hands and feet strewn everywhere.

George moved to me before I could react. He grabbed my arms and started shaking me. He struggled with the words between his clenched teeth, gripping my arms tighter. The tears flowed down my cheeks as I tried to speak.

"I didn't…" I wept.

I was interrupted with a startling sting on my cheek. The force knocked me to the floor. I grabbed the spot where his hand had connected and looked down at the floor, stunned.

"If you weren't my brother's daughter, I'd…" he began. I tilted my head up toward him. His face was so red it was almost purple as he shook with fury. Behind the rage, I thought I recognized sadness in his eyes. "You are not going anywhere for the next week. No sports, no newspaper, nothing. I cannot believe you did this!"

His sorrow broke through when he murmured, "He was my brother." Carol watched him leave in confusion, or perhaps it was disappointment that his reaction wasn't as severe as she'd intended. As soon as he disappeared, she peered down at me and grinned in contempt.

"This is not over," she threatened. "Clean this up, and get your chores done before I get home."

She shut the door, leaving me with the destruction of her hate. Everything I had that was mine—that was truly mine—was in pieces around me. I picked up the images of my parents and baby pictures of me and tried to find a way to fit them together. I let the broken pieces fall through my fingers and collapsed in tears. This pain was sharper than any slap or blow. She had taken the evidence that there was a time when I was happy and obliterated it, leaving only the memories.

I sat up when I heard a knock and looked to the door, but the sound wasn't right—it was more of a tapping. I looked around and realized that it was coming from the window.

No, please don't tell me.

I closed my eyes as something tapped the window again. I wiped my face and rushed to open the window before the tapping repeated and they heard it.

"You can't be here," I whispered desperately.

"What happened? I wanted to make sure you're okay."

"Evan, leave." My voice was urgent as I pleaded with him to go.

"Why is your face red? Did he hit you?"

"You can't be here," I stressed. "Please, please just go." Tears rolled down my cheeks as I frantically looked from his face to the door, expecting it to open at any minute.

He gazed past me, extended onto his toes, to see into my room.

"What happened, Emma?" he gasped at the devastating scene.

"You're only going to make it worse. *Please* leave." I tried to position my body between his eyes and my room.

"I'm picking you up Monday so that you can tell me what this is all about," he insisted.

"Fine, just leave," I begged.

Evan finally acknowledged the pleading in my eyes and the urgency in my voice and backed away from the window. He hesitated, but I closed the window and pulled down my shade before he could say anything else.

I turned back to my broken world and knelt among its remains. I heard Carol say she'd be back soon, and knew I didn't have time to mourn. I found a backpack in which to place the fragments of my pictures and letters from my mother, refusing to throw them away. I tossed the broken frames and sliced canvases in a trash bag.

I mindlessly performed my list of chores. I was secured in this desolate state when I retreated to my room later. I slid onto the floor with my back against my bed and stared at the blank wall across from me. The ache in my chest was curtained behind the numbness.

If I hadn't been able to admit it before now, I knew in this moment that I hated Carol. I clenched my jaw, pushing away the destructive screams that raged in my head. My nails dug into the palms of my hands, wanting so much to release the emotion. Instead I gasped and collapsed into chest-heaving sobs.

Her malevolence threatened to penetrate the only sanctity I had left, and I moaned in pain at how close she had come to crushing me. Was I really strong enough to not let her break me? Six hundred and nine days suddenly felt like a life sentence. Would I be able to recognize myself when I was finally released?

I sat in the closet and dialed Sara's number.

"Em, are you okay?" Sara asked in a single breath.

"Yeah, I'm fine," I whispered.

"You sound so sad. What did she do?"

"I can't talk about it right now. But I wanted you to hear from me like I promised."

"Evan came over this morning."

I didn't say anything.

"He was really upset and wanted to know what was happening, and if you were being hurt. He was basically screaming at me to tell him. I didn't, I swear, but he's insisting on picking you up on Monday. I wanted to warn you. I can be there too, so you can go with me instead if you want."

"No, it's okay," I mumbled. I knew I'd have to face him eventually.

"Emma, whatever happened there this morning, I am so sorry," she said softly.

"I'll see you Monday," I whispered and hung up the phone.

I didn't leave my room except to sneak out to use the bathroom. I heard the murmur of voices and the glee of the kids in the dining room. Not too long after, singing carried through the wall from the television and was followed by a quick rap on my door.

Carol appeared in my doorframe. "Your uncle and I would like to speak with you." Without another word, she walked away.

I stared after her as I sat at the desk, hovering over my Chemistry book. I pushed the chair back and allowed my legs to carry my shell to the kitchen.

George and Carol stood on one side of the island, waiting for me. The remnants of grief remained in George's eyes, while a glint of victory reflected in Carol's.

"Your uncle and I wanted you to know how heartbroken you made us when you chose to act up and destroy your things. We are sorry you don't feel happy here, since we've done everything to provide you with whatever it is you've asked. You play sports and are part of the school's clubs. We think we've been very accommodating.

"I thought we should ban you from all of your privileges for the remainder of the year." My eyes widened, and my throat closed.

"But your uncle has decided to be generous and allow you to be a part of the school activities, hoping it will make you a better person. But you will not be doing anything at all for the next week. You'll have to find a way to explain this to your coach and other teachers, and we'd better not hear that you've blamed us in any way. This is your own doing, and you need to own up to that.

"Since we aren't able to trust you to be home by yourself, you'll go to the library after school. You can have whoever it is who's chauffeuring you around these days drop you off at the house. You can ride your bike to and from the library. I arranged this with the head librarian, Marcia Pendle, this afternoon. She will sign you in and out every day. She has a desk for you to use, so you're in her sight the entire time. Don't even think about trying anything. If we hear that you weren't there or didn't cooperate, you *will* lose basketball for the season. Do you understand?"

"Yes," I murmured.

"Your destruction has hurt your uncle a great deal, and we think it's best that during the next couple of weeks, you allow him to find a way to forgive you. So you should stay out of sight while you're in the house. I'll let you know when we're done with dinner, because you are not getting out of your obligations. We'll have a plate set aside for you to eat before you do the dishes. But other than that, you will stay in your room. Understood?"

"Yes."

"Now, what do you have to say to your uncle?" She pursed her lips to try to conceal her triumph. I tightened my eyes in disgust before I could mask my loathing. "Well?"

I whispered, "I'm sorry you were hurt."

I wasn't lying, but I wasn't apologizing for something I hadn't done either. He only nodded.

I was banned to my room for the remainder of the weekend. As uneventful as it was, it was better than being anywhere near Carol. It gave me time to think about what I was going to say to my basketball coach and the other teachers. I couldn't come up with anything other than a vague explanation of obligations at home that I hoped they wouldn't question too much.

I couldn't think about Evan and what I'd say to him on Monday. Every time I thought of him, and what he'd seen on Friday night, and then again on Saturday morning, I felt miserable. He'd seen a glimpse of my world, and I didn't like how it reflected back in his eyes.

23. SILENCE

I remained silent in the passenger seat. I couldn't even bring myself to look at him.

Evan drove to the end of my street before he asked, "How are you?"

"Humiliated," I answered, looking out the window.

The quiet settled in again for a few minutes before he asked, "Are you mad at me for checking on you?"

"You shouldn't have," I answered honestly.

"You're not going to tell me what happened, are you?"

"I can't. You saw more than enough."

He pulled into the same drugstore parking lot as before, and stopped the car.

"Evan, I really don't want to talk about it," I insisted, finally looking at him.

"That's what's bothering me. Why can't you trust me?" His troubled eyes searched mine for an explanation.

"That has nothing to do with it."

"That has *everything* to do with it," he said emphatically. "I thought we were past that."

"I'm sorry you thought that," I said stoically. He pulled back as if my words burned him.

"So you don't trust me to know what's going on with you at home?" After hesitating for a moment, he added, "You never planned to let me in, did you?" His voice grew stronger as he spoke, almost angry.

I couldn't find the words to agree with him, knowing it would only make him more upset.

"What was I thinking?" he asked himself in a whisper. "I thought you were stronger than this." His words bit, and my heart flinched. "I can't believe you let them treat you like this."

After a minute of unreturned response, Evan murmured in sinking disappointment, "You're not who I thought you were."

"I knew that," I whispered.

"So I don't really know you, do I?"

I shrugged. He exhaled quickly and shook his head, frustrated with my unwillingness to answer.

"Does Sara?" he asked. "Do you trust Sara more than me?"

"Leave her out of this," I shot back.

"I don't get it," he said to himself, looking at the floor. Then he turned to me and asked, "Does he hurt you?"

"George?" I questioned, shocked by the accusation. "No, George wouldn't hurt me."

"Then, she just doesn't like you, is that it?" he pushed.

"Evan, I can't and don't want to talk about what happens behind the closed doors of my house. And you're right, I'm not that strong, and I'm not the person you thought I was. But I've been trying to tell you that all along. I'm sorry that you're disappointed now that you finally figured it out. But I'm never going to be able to tell you what you want to know."

His face turned red, but I wasn't certain what emotion fueled the heat.

"I'd really like to get to school now," I murmured.

Evan pulled out of the parking lot, and we drove the rest of the way in silence.

The silence lasted for a long time.

Sara tried to talk to me about it, but it took a week before I could repeat the words said in the car that day. She never brought it up again, and tried not to mention him at all.

We coexisted within the halls of the school and the walls of our classrooms. We didn't speak to each other, even in Anatomy, where we sat a few feet apart. In the rest of our shared classes, we sat at opposite ends of the room.

This didn't mean I didn't notice him. I noticed him until I convinced myself that I couldn't anymore. I accepted the truth that I'd been avoiding all along—it could never work. It never had a chance. My aching heart had a hard time giving up hope, but I found a way to tuck that deep inside as well. I faded into the walls as I had before Evan Mathews walked through the doors of Weslyn High—except I didn't completely disappear.

The week after Thanksgiving, when I was caught up in being angry and disappointed with Evan—angry that he'd forced his way in and disappointed that he didn't like what he saw when he got there—I was taken by surprise.

"I know what you probably think of me," Drew Carson said, joining Sara and me at our lunch table that Wednesday afternoon.

I glanced from Sara to Drew, not understanding what he was talking about or why he was sitting at our table.

"At Jake's party," he explained. "I saw how you looked at me before you left. I'm not like that."

"Really? Then why were you there?" I was too annoyed by thoughts of Evan to hold back. "Isn't that what all the guys were there for? You even admitted you're friends with Jake."

It was obvious he wasn't expecting my biting words either, but he didn't give up.

"You're right, I knew what went on. But whether you want to believe me or not, that was the first time I'd shown up at one of his parties." I let out a skeptical laugh. Sara remained still, as if she were watching a movie, her wide eyes shooting back and forth between Drew and me.

"I swear I only knew about them because Jake kept asking me to go. But I didn't give in until that night. But only because I heard you were going to be there."

He saw my eyes cringe in disgust, and quickly added, "I just wanted to *talk* to you, honest. Like I told you that night, I should've talked to you before then." I didn't respond.

"I was hoping to convince you to give me a second chance, that's all. I don't want you to think I'm 'That Guy.' "

Before I could say anything, he got up from the table. Sara was left staring at me with her eyebrows raised. I read her thoughts, sighed in exasperation, and left the table as well. It wasn't worth discussing.

I missed the fall awards night because I was officially grounded. Sara let me know that she, Jill and I were next season's captains of the girls' soccer team. She also told me I was chosen as the team's MVP, along with making the All-State and All-American teams. There was a dinner in January recognizing the athletes. I knew I wouldn't be attending that either.

Soon after, the letters from the colleges started to arrive. I suspected there would have been phone calls as well, but our number was privately listed, and only a handful of people in the world were privileged enough to have it. Carol dropped the pile of packets on the floor of my room each day. There were letters from coaches and athletic directors, hoping to set up a time for me to see their campuses and meet with them in the spring. I didn't know most of the colleges were interested in me until I received the letters.

This burst of mail gave me that something I needed to keep me looking forward instead of continuing to be mired in the present. As long as I had the hope of escaping, I was convinced I could recover from Carol's glares and Evan's avoidance. I had to have something to hold on to as I hung from my ledge.

I didn't receive as much grief as I expected from my basketball coach or other teachers for taking a week off. I was technically supposed to try out for the basketball team before being placed on the roster, so Coach had me "try out" during a couple of study periods during the week, and deemed that it qualified me to start as point guard. I was expected to fill the position, so it wasn't a controversial decision.

Sara played volleyball during the winter, so Jill drove me home on the nights Sara had practice after us. Jill was happy to drive me; however, I got more out of our time together than I was prepared for. She was a little too up-to-date on the latest gossip, eager to contribute to its circulation. I really didn't want to hear it.

"Did you know that Evan went on a date with Haley Spencer on Saturday?" Jill asked after my first official practice with the team on Monday—perfect example of why I didn't want to hear it. "I really thought you and Evan were going to be together. What happened?"

I shrugged, unable to speak. Haley Spencer, really? A hot flash of anger and jealousy streaked through my body. I forced it away as fast as it made its appearance.

———

When Sara picked me up the next morning, I confronted her. "You knew about Evan and Haley, didn't you?"

Sara pressed her lips together and exhaled, contemplating what to say.

"I didn't think it was worth getting you upset over. Let me guess—Jill told you, right?"

"Sara, I was going to find out eventually, and it would have been so much easier coming from you."

"You're right. I'm sorry." Then she glanced at me, trying to read my face. "I bet he did this to get to you."

"He can do whatever he wants," I huffed. "I really don't care."

"Sure, whatever you say," Sara said, mocking me. "Em, even *I'm* upset that he went out with Haley Spencer. Come on, *Haley Spencer*—could he have picked anyone more shallow and superficial? She's the exact opposite of you." As soon as the words left her mouth, she bit her lower lip. Sara knew as well as I did that Evan couldn't stand to be around me, so he chose to date the worst possible alternative.

I snapped my head over to gape at her. Her eyes softened as she offered a silent apology. She and I both understood the truth in her statement, and that truth turned in my stomach the entire ride to school. That was the day I finally returned Drew Carson's peace offering.

Drew had been persistently but subtly trying to get me to talk to him again since that day in the cafeteria. During lunch and at the end of the day, he made sure our paths crossed. He'd glance at me and say, "Hi, Emma." I would ignore him and keep walking.

Until the day I finally responded, "Hi, Drew." The sound of my voice stopped him midstep, causing the person following him to the cafeteria to walk right into the back of him. I let out a small laugh and kept walking. I didn't see him again until I was walking up the stairs from the locker room to go to the gym.

"Good luck in your game today."

I hadn't seen him at first. I was too consumed by my thoughts of the game to notice anything. Hearing his voice snapped me back to the halls with the sound of sneakers squeaking and the dribbling of basketballs coming from the gym. That's when I saw Drew standing by the entrance. The guy he was talking to said he'd see him later and left us alone.

"Thanks," I responded. "What are you guys doing for practice today?"

"We're practicing tonight after your game," Drew explained. "I'm thinking about showing up early so I can watch."

I wasn't sure what to think about his interest in our game. Was he coming to show support for our team, or was he coming to watch me?

"How do you think you'll do? I heard you've missed some practices."

My face turned red at this acknowledgment. "I was able to go over the plays with Coach Stanley, so I'm pretty sure I'll be fine."

"I believe it," he said with a smile. "I'll see you after your game." I smiled back.

It was impossible to deny that Drew was incredible looking, with his boyish face and deep dimples. It was easy to get lost in his breathtaking tranquil green eyes. They peeked out from under his black hair, which always looked like he'd just come from the beach. Knowing how much he loved to surf, he probably had. I stood in the doorway staring after him, even after he was out of sight.

"Emma, you ready?" Jill asked as she walked past me, snapping me out of my daze.

"Yeah, ready."

Just as he promised, Drew was waiting for me after I'd grabbed my things from the bench.

"Good game," he congratulated me. "You have a great outside shot."

"Thanks." I took a swig of my sports drink before gathering my gear from the bench.

"I'm glad you're talking to me."

"I figured everyone deserves a second chance." I grinned, and he smiled back.

"I should get to practice." He nodded toward the court, where some of his teammates were dribbling and taking shots. "I'll talk to you tomorrow?"

"Sure."

With that second chance, Drew Carson would change everything. The rest of that week, I found that our paths crossed more often. I invited him to sit with us during lunch, which I thought was going to cause Sara to fall out of her seat. We found a few minutes to talk before or after our practices. Then I discovered he was actually assigned to my study period. As a senior privilege, if any of the students had study as their first or last class, they could opt to come in late or leave early. I never saw Drew in study, because he hadn't been there. But after we started talking, he decided to show up.

Sara didn't say anything about my sudden interest in Drew. She was friendly and accepting of his presence during the times she and I usually had alone. I hoped she found his company as refreshing as I did. Drew was charming, helping me to recover my smile.

When I saw Drew at the end of each day, it was a way to recuperate from being exposed to Evan's evasive presence all day. It was easy to carry on conversations with him about almost everything, but never anything too personal. He didn't push me to reveal more about myself than I was willing to share, which was a relief. When I was with him, I found myself laughing—really, honestly, enjoyably laughing. He was a breath of fresh air after the heart-wrenching storm that had engulfed me.

When I was with Drew, I wasn't thinking about Evan. I couldn't keep the two images in my head at the same time, so I pushed Evan's out. I started not to notice where Evan was, and I didn't flinch at the sound of his voice as often. I wasn't allowing space for him anymore.

Instead, I found myself focusing on Drew, who responded with full attention. I didn't expect it to be the same, and it wasn't. My heart didn't flutter or murmur whenever Drew sat next to me. It stayed deep within my chest, thumping at its consistent pace. I wasn't disappointed—I was relieved.

I didn't talk to Sara about Drew, and she didn't ask. But I wasn't expecting her reaction when I asked if we could meet him at a bonfire on a private beach after the game that Friday.

"Em, I don't think that's a good idea," she objected. "Maybe we should stay in and watch movies. It's only been a few weeks since the incident with Carol. You're lucky she's letting you stay over again."

I knew there was something more to her hesitation than she was admitting.

"Sara, are you telling me *you* don't want to go to this bonfire? I've heard who's supposed to be there, and it's a pretty decent list."

"Yeah, me too," she admitted reluctantly. "Em, you promise you won't do anything stupid, right?"

"What is that supposed to mean?" I asked, offended.

"I haven't said anything because I think you really *do* like him, but I'm worried about where you're headed with Drew."

"I don't know what you mean," I said, but I had a feeling I knew where this was going.

"Just don't do anything you wouldn't if you weren't trying to get over Evan."

I didn't say anything. She knew I understood what she meant. Sara agreed to go to the bonfire after my basketball game Friday night, and I convinced myself that I hadn't done anything that weekend that I didn't want to do. That was until I heard the accusations of what I'd done out loud.

———

"You *kissed* Drew Carson?!" Evan practically yelled.

It took me a second to believe he was standing next to me, forget about talking—well, yelling—at me. His face was flushed, and his jaw was tight. He glared at me from behind my locker door, holding it open with his hand. I glanced around the empty halls to see if anyone had heard him.

"How did you hear about that?" I asked. Not only was I stunned to see Evan at my locker, but I was shocked that Drew had said anything.

"Don't worry, I didn't hear it from Drew—he doesn't talk. But his friends do." He was fuming, and seeing his reaction only ignited my anger. What gave him the right to be upset with me?

"I'm surprised you could hear with Haley Spencer's tongue in your ear," I shot back. His face turned a different shade of red as the surprise reflected in his eyes. "Yeah, I heard about that too."

"It's not what you think," he explained, still angry, but the bite was absent from his tone. "We went out once."

"Oh, is that why I saw you together at the bonfire?!" I yelled back. Now, I was the one infuriated recalling the image of Haley nuzzling into Evan's arm across from me at the bonfire.

"You were there?" he asked, dropping his attack.

"I left pretty much after I saw the two of you. So don't you dare try to make me feel anything remotely like guilt for kissing Drew." The heat spread across my face as I abruptly closed my locker, holding my backpack and duffel bag in my hands.

"But you hardly know him," he rebutted. "What, you've talked to him for a week, and that makes it okay to kiss him the first time you see him out?" His voice escalated again.

"Oh, and you're so much better?! Had you ever talked to Haley before you did whatever you did with her at Jake's party that first weekend?"

His eyes widened as he leaned back from my blow, confirming what Haley had told me earlier that day.

"Yeah, it was really great to hear it from her too, Evan," I snapped, trying to hide the hurt in my voice, while recalling her snide remark about how interesting it was that she and I were both seeing the guys that we had met at Jake's parties. I thought I was going to fall over when the words came out of her mouth. She just walked away with a smug grin.

Evan struggled to find the words. "I didn't do..." His eyes pleaded. "It's really not like that. Can I explain?"

"No." The edge dropped from my voice, releasing the anger with it. I became emotionless, pushing away the pain and sadness that threatened to seep up from where I hid them. "I don't want to know."

I walked past him toward the stairs.

"I trusted you!" Evan bellowed as the distance grew between us. I stopped and turned back around. He walked back to me until we were only a foot apart. "I trusted you, and you couldn't trust me."

I stared back, watching the hurt reveal itself in his eyes. My heart ached in return.

"I unpacked for the first time ever—for you. I was honest with you about *everything*—even with the truth about how I felt about you. I've never been that honest before. I trusted you." His voice drifted into a whisper as he leaned closer to me. "Why couldn't you trust me?"

I swallowed the lump in my throat, tears welling in my eyes. My heart reached for him, begging me to touch him, as I absorbed the pain in his stormy eyes. The seconds lasted for what felt like minutes, and then I tensed my body and walked away.

I went through the doors leading to the stairs and hurried down them.

"I'm still in love with you!" he yelled from the top step. I froze as the first tear rolled down my cheek. "Please don't walk away from me."

The tears streamed silently down my face—I couldn't move. My heart thumped forcefully in my chest, and for a second, I almost turned around. Then the image of Evan and Haley together in front of the bonfire, with his arm around her shoulder, flashed through my head, and I found my feet moving in a rush down the stairs.

I made it through practice that afternoon, although I don't remember much about it. Forcing myself to dribble, pass and shoot kept me from replaying the confrontation with Evan. By the end of practice, I was too exhausted to think about anything.

As I was heading to the locker room, the junior varsity guys started warming up on the court for their game. Drew waited for me at the end of the bleachers, in front of the entrance to the guys' locker room.

"Can you stay for my game?" he asked.

"Sorry, I don't think so," I admitted with a frown. "Good luck, though."

"Will I see you tomorrow night after your game?"

"Yeah, I'd like that. I just have to check with Sara to make sure she doesn't have anything planned."

"One of the guys from the team is having a few people over, and I'd like it if you and Sara came too."

"I'll see," I promised, but I was pretty sure I wouldn't make it since I had to be home by ten.

Before I realized what he was doing, he leaned over and kissed me softly on the lips. My body stiffened, and I remained stunned, unable to breathe for a brief moment. Drew looked up and said, "Hey, Mathews."

"Hi, Drew," Evan returned with a bite. I only caught a glimpse of the bag over Evan's arm as he walked past us toward the locker room.

My heart crashed into my stomach. Had Evan just seen Drew kiss me?

"I'll see you tomorrow." Drew smiled and brushed his hand along my cheek.

I nodded and forced the faintest hint of a smile. He walked through the doors to the locker room after Evan.

I knew what Evan had just witnessed between Drew and me, especially after what had happened at my locker, was worse than anything I'd seen between him and Haley. I suppressed the twisting storm of guilt that threatened to consume me. I waited until I was alone in my room that night before I unleashed it and cried myself to sleep.

24. FALLEN

Emily!" Carol hollered from the kitchen. My hand hovered above my duffel bag, grasping the sweater I was about to pack. Panic set in as I tried to think of what I could've done. My chest felt tight when I entered the kitchen.

"Yeah?" I responded cautiously, my voice getting caught in my throat.

"Do you know who I just got off the phone with?" she yelled, revealing the strained vein along her temple. I glanced around, realizing that George and the kids were gone. Fear gripped my heart, and my head felt tight. I shook my head.

"Of course you don't, right? Because you *never* do anything wrong, do you?" I was past trying to understand her illogical questions, and braced myself for her wrath. "That was someone from Stanford—"

Oh no! My eyes shot up at the sound of the school's name.

"Oh, you *do* know what this is about?" she accused, still boiling. "Do you know how stupid I felt when this man was going on about your visit in the spring, and I had no idea what he was talking about?! Why did he have our phone number?!" I remained quiet. "You didn't really think we were going to let you fly to California, did you? How the hell did you convince him to invite you—did you blow him?"

Shock splayed across my face.

"You think you are so much better than me, don't you? That you can do whatever you fucking want?!"

"No," I whispered.

"That's right—not in my house! You drove your mother to drink, and now she's a useless whore. I'm not going to let *you* destroy my family too. You're fucking worthless. What school would possibly want *you*?"

Carol's face was scarlet while her voice grew louder. "How did you ever expect to pay for these schools? You're not that special that they're going to let you in for free." She waited, as if expecting an answer. "Well?"

"They have scholarships," I said nervously. She scoffed. "And I was thinking I could use my dad's social security money."

"Huh. Did you think I was going to let you live here and not get anything out of it?" She let out a spiteful laugh. I glowered at her; the hate slowly crawled under my skin. That money was because my father died too soon, and she was going to strip me of the last connection I had to him?! I was so furious, I couldn't see straight. I turned to walk away, my jaw clenched.

Then I heard the scraping of metal and her amplified rage. "Don't you turn your fucking back on me!"

A piercing flash of light screamed through my head as something hard hit the base of my skull. I stumbled forward and reached for the support of the wall, but I couldn't find it in time. My legs gave out, and I collapsed on the floor.

"You are ruining my life," she grunted through clenched teeth. "You will wish you never set foot in this house." I pressed my shaking hands against the floor to push up while attempting to focus through the blur. I let out a breathless grunt as my chest was forced back down against the hard wood, and my arms collapsed beneath me when she swung again. The repeated impact left me fighting for my breath, as the sharpness settled between my shoulder blades. The room teetered and blurred around me as I searched for the direction of my room, knowing I needed to get there to escape her. Still gasping, I groped at the floor, urging my body forward while sliding on my elbows and pushing onto my knees.

Her enraged grunts and muttering were incoherent. Then I heard her growl, "You will learn to respect me. You owe me your life for everything I've given you. For everything you've destroyed."

The force of her swing ripped through my lower back—I screamed out in agony. The searing bolt of pain wrapped itself around my spine and spiked through my head. I released a broken moan before sprawling on the floor. The room dimmed in a blur of light as I fought for consciousness.

I didn't know how long I'd been on the floor. I became aware of a loud stomping above me as she muttered to herself. I blinked my eyes open. The floor rippled before me. I closed my eyes to fight against the dizziness so that I could push myself up on my hands and knees. The tender muscles between my shoulder blades twisted into a burning knot as I strained to get up. I peered through my lashes and reached for the wall to steady myself on my knees. I tried to focus through the haze, my head bobbing heavily and my body swaying. With a grunt of effort, I lifted myself up to stand, leaning against the wall. I remained pressed against the wall, breathing heavily as I waited for the room to settle and listened for her movements. A severe sharpness shot up my spine, leaving me breathless.

I took a deep breath to settle the nausea, determined to get out of the house before she came downstairs. I stood still for a moment with my eyes closed, steadying the spin of the earth. Convinced I had control of my equilibrium, I crept into my room and gingerly closed the door. The flight instinct kicked in, and the blood raced through my body, overriding the pain. My heart pounded in my chest as I threw a few more items in my duffel bag. I opened my door to listen. She was quiet; the only sound I heard was my rapid pulse. Deciding to take a chance, I left my room, cautiously taking each step that brought me closer to the back door. My ears hummed, anticipating the slightest sound.

I held my breath as I turned the handle and didn't release it until the door was closed behind me. I hugged the side of the house so she couldn't see me from her window. Once I reached the end of the driveway, adrenaline shot through me and I ran. The pain in my back and head didn't exist while the road passed under my feet. I kept running until I was in the coffee shop a few blocks from the house.

I could only imagine what I must have looked like to the patrons and staff of the intimate café when I entered with the duffel bag over my arm, covered with sweat and gasping for breath. I slid onto a chair at a small table in the corner and pulled out my phone. I pressed Sara's number and listened to it ring, hoping she'd pick up.

"Emma? What's wrong?"

"Come get me," my voice cracked.

"Omigod, are you hurt?"

"Sara, please come get me as soon as you can." My voice quivered as I fought to hold back the tears.

"Where are you?" she inquired urgently.

"At the coffee place near my house." I took a calming breath to keep from losing the little composure I had left.

"I'll be there as fast as I can."

I hung up the phone.

I spent the time it took Sara to arrive staring at my hands, willing them to stop trembling. My breath shook with each pass through my quivering lips. I didn't dare look around the shop; instead I stared out the window, searching for Sara's car. When I saw her pull in, I rushed to meet her before she had a chance to get out.

I winced as I settled onto the passenger seat, the pain streaking up my entire back. I closed my eyes and let out a shaky breath. The tears found their way down my cheeks as I swallowed against the lump in my throat.

"Where are you hurt?" Sara asked, her voice unsteady.

"My back," I quivered, with my eyes still closed.

"Do you need to go to the hospital?"

"No," I shot back quickly. I attempted to release the tension in my shoulders and opened my eyes. I wiped away the tears and searched for my voice. "No hospital, okay? Just…do you have anything to help, aspirin or something?"

Sara rummaged around in the compartments of the center console, then handed me a white bottle of Advil. I spilled some pills into my hand and swallowed them dry. Her forehead creased, mirroring the pain that was evident on my face. "Do you want to go back to my house?"

"Can we just stop there so you can get me a bag of ice? Then let's go somewhere where I can walk around."

"You want to *walk*?"

"If I stay still, I'll get stiff. I need to keep the blood flowing through my muscles so that I can play tonight."

"You think you're going to play basketball?! Em, I'm still trying to decide if I should take you to the hospital. You're pale, and you can't hide how much pain you're in. And if *you* can't hide it, then it must be pretty bad."

"It's because it just happened and my body's still in shock. I'll be fine, I promise." But I knew I was lying. I was far from *fine*.

Sara drove to her house, and I waited in the car until she came out with a small cooler filled with ice, some storage bags and a couple of bottles of water. She handed me a water when she got into the car.

"Let's go to the high school, and we'll walk the track," I suggested before taking several long gulps from the bottle. "I only have to waste a couple of hours before the JV game."

"Are you sure?" Sara asked, still uncertain with my decision.

"Sara, I swear, I'm okay."

I eased my body into a controlled place where the quivering hid beneath my skin. There was a deep ache in my head that trailed all the way down my back, but the piercing pain was gone—as long as I kept still.

We drove to the high school and parked near the football field. The parking lot only contained a handful of cars, since it was still too early for anyone to be here for the game.

I took the cooler with me as I delicately lifted my body out of the car, gritting my teeth through the searing pain that made my stomach flip with nausea. Sara followed me to the field. I filled the bags with ice and lay on my stomach. Sara placed the bags along my back and sat next to me on the grass. We were silent for a few minutes as I lay with my eyes closed and my head resting on my folded arms, while Sara plucked the grass from the frozen field. I barely registered the cold December air with the ice on my back.

"You're shivering," Sara noted.

"I have ice covering my back, and it's freezing out here."

"How long do you want to keep the ice on?"

"Fifteen to twenty minutes, then we'll walk around for a while before we do it again."

After another few minutes of silence, Sara asked, "Are you going to tell me what happened this time? Em, I promise not to say anything."

"I'm not sure if I should. I don't want you to feel guilty if you need to lie to your mom or anyone else for me."

"I'll find a way around answering," she promised.

"Stanford called—" I started.

"Oh no," she gasped. "You didn't tell her."

"No, I didn't tell her. Then she told me I didn't have access to the social security money from my dad for college, that it was her compensation for letting me live there. I got so pissed off that I had to leave the room. That's when she hit me."

Sara's jaw tightened. She demanded with an icy tone, "What did she hit you with?"

"I'm not sure. Probably whatever she could get her hands on." I recalled the hard object crashing into my back and shivered.

"You can't go back there," Sara insisted.

"I really don't want to think about that right now. I just want to focus on being able to play in the game tonight."

"Em, I'm not sure that you should.""Sara, I have to. She's taken everything else from me, including what I had left of my dad. I'm playing in this game tonight," I stated firmly. Sara didn't argue.

We walked briskly, until I couldn't handle it anymore. Of course, I didn't tell Sara this. Then I'd lie back down to be iced. I was desperate to defeat this pain. I was going to play in this game—nothing was going to stop me.

When cars started showing up for the JV game, Sara followed me into the building. We stood by the bleachers and watched until halftime, when I had to change. I blared my music so loudly in my ears, I couldn't concentrate on anything else. Every so often, I'd pace in the hall to keep the blood flowing through my muscles, mostly because it hurt too much to stand still, and I needed to escape it any way I could. I swung my arms over my head and turned my neck side to side to keep my muscles from stiffening.

None of the girls questioned Sara when she followed me into the locker room. She snuck into a curtained shower stall with me to help me change. She carefully pulled my shirt over my head, and I clenched my teeth. My entire back screamed when I raised my arms. Sara questioned my well-being again, but I ignored her. I was counting on adrenaline to make me oblivious to the pain once the game started.

The adrenaline did tunnel my focus when I was finally on the floor, helping me disconnect from the pain. I refused to concede to my burning muscles and the lightning storm in my head as I dribbled down the court, calling out the next play. Passing to the open teammate, squaring up to take a shot, following through with a rebound, and charging back to switch to defense, where the bodies bumped to gain position: that was all I concentrated on as the time ticked away.

I was surviving on adrenaline, and that would only carry me so far. As the second half progressed, it became harder to concentrate. I wasn't reacting as quickly to passes or charging for the steals as I usually did. I passed off the ball more, instead of taking the shot. During a time-out, Coach Stanley asked if I was okay. I explained that I'd fallen on some ice earlier, and it was bothering me a little. He suggested taking me out of the game. I adamantly assured him that I was fine and could keep playing.

It was a close game. Probably closer than it should have been, and I blamed myself for that, knowing I had no right to be on the court. But I was afraid to find out what would happen if I stopped.

There was under a minute left in the game, and the lead kept changing by one with each possession. After a time-out and with about thirty seconds on the clock, we had possession of the ball and were down by one point. I dribbled down the court, sending the offense in motion. I passed to Jill at the top of the key, who dribbled to the center of the paint and bounced it to Maggie along the baseline. Maggie noticed my clear shot from behind the three-point line and popped it back out to me, where I squared up to the basket, jumped, and let the ball roll off my fingers. The defender jumped alongside me, swiping at the ball, which barely sailed over her fingertips. Her arm landed on my shoulder hard, knocking me back so my heels were no longer beneath me when I came down to land.

My breath rushed from my lungs when the floor made contact with my back. My head bounced back, colliding with the waxed surface. The cheers faded, and the images on the court blurred. I blinked my eyes as the colors ran together until there was only black.

I was moving quickly, but my legs were still. There was something around my neck, and I couldn't move. I heard the murmuring of voices but no words. My eyes wouldn't open. The cold air hit me, sending a shiver through my body. I was enveloped by a piercing bolt that ran along my back and into my head. Then I fell into the darkness again.

"Emily, can you hear me?" a soothing male voice asked.

I pulled back from the blinding light as I felt a cool touch on my eyelid.

"Emily, can you open your eyes for me?" the voice requested.

I blinked my eyes open, squinting to keep them protected from the bright light above me. I glanced around at the faces above me. There was something beeping over my head, and a hum of voices surrounded my space.

"Emily, I'm Dr. Chan," the soothing voice said. I focused on the gentle, round face of the man leaning over me. "You're in the hospital. You took a fall during your basketball game and hit your head."

I groaned, admitting to the pain.

"My back," I whimpered.

"Your back hurts?" he confirmed.

"My back," I whimpered again, the tears rolled across my temples. I couldn't turn my head with the brace holding it in place.

"We're going to take some X-rays to see what's going on," he informed me.

"Sara?" I searched for her among the faces.

"Who's Sara, honey?" a rosy-faced nurse leaned over to ask.

"My friend, Sara McKinley," I whispered between moans. "I need Sara."

"Your aunt and uncle are on their way," she assured me.

I groaned louder.

"Sara, please," I begged.

Her voice was comforting. "I'll see if I can find her."

There were more voices, and then I was moving. The fluorescent lights blurred above me as I was wheeled through the maze of corridors. There was a figure at the end of my bed, but I couldn't see a face. Tears continued rolling down the crevices of my eyes and into my ears. I made an effort to contain the moans, but they escaped every so often on their own.

A team of bodies wearing blue and white lifted me onto a hard platform. As I was rolled onto my back, I screamed out in agony. Nothing could hold it back. A nurse gently turned me onto my side to examine the source of my torturous cries and let out a breath.

"Her back is badly bruised," she reported.

"Prop her on her side," Dr. Chan directed from my feet.

I slid into a tube and closed my eyes, concentrating on breathing evenly to cope with the suffering. The corners of my eyes were raw from the never-ending seeping of tears. I remained in that area of the hospital for a time I could not judge, with the rolling, and the clicking, and the doors opening and closing.

Eventually, the hands of the team eased me back onto the forgiving cushion of the bed, supported on my side to provide some reprieve from the torment that had overtaken my body. Exhausted, I closed my eyes.

"We're waiting on the results of her X-rays before we know if there's any damage," Dr. Chan explained to someone. "You're welcome to stay with her, and I'll be back when I have the results."

"Sara?" I whispered through the grogginess. I opened my eyes when we rolled to a stop. A curtain was pulled around me, concealing the people on the other side.

The soothing voice of the nurse greeted me. "Hey, honey, your aunt and uncle are here." I averted my eyes, not finding the comfort she hoped that news would provide me.

"Sara? Did you find her?" My tone was anxious, and concern reflected on her face.

"She's right outside," she promised. "I'll go get her."

"You can't keep me from seeing her," an irate voice yelled. "She's my daughter."

My heartbeat accelerated, picked up by the quick beeps on the machine above my head.

"Relax, Rachel," George instructed firmly.

"What's wrong with her?" she demanded heavily. I recognized her slur. My jaw tightened. What was she doing here? How did she even know?

George responded, "I don't think this is the right time to be talking to you."

"You can't keep me from her. She's my daughter," my mother declared. Then she went on to berate George and Carol about how they didn't love me, using expletives only my drunken mother could come up with.

"Ma'am, I need to ask you to come with us," a deep masculine voice demanded.

"Get your hands off me. You can't touch me. I need to stay here with my daughter. Get off me." The angered voice trailed away, until it was cut off completely when a pair of doors closed farther down the hall.

"Emma?" Sara whispered, peering in through the curtains. My flittering eyes found Sara's pale face and her red-rimmed eyes.

"Sara!" I wept, lifting my head. The movement forced me to moan in pain, causing Sara to wince.

"Ow. Try not to move," she whispered, pulling up a chair to sit beside me. She pressed her lips together, and the line between her eyes deepened as she searched my agonized face. "I'm so sorry."

Her eyes filled and she quickly swiped away the tears with the hand that wasn't holding mine.

"I'm glad they finally let me see you. It felt like I was waiting forever." Her voice quivered. "You scared me." The tears welled in her eyes again, and she looked away to conceal them.

"I'll be okay," I assured her, but I knew seeing me on a hospital bed wasn't very convincing.

"You didn't look okay when you were lying lifeless on the floor of the basketball court. I don't think I've ever been so scared in my entire life."

"I slipped on ice and fell down the stairs at my house," I told her quietly.

"What?" Her forehead crumpled, not understanding.

"How I hurt myself," I explained. "I fell down the stairs on some ice."

"But Em, everyone saw you fall during the basketball game—I mean *everyone*," she explained, still confused.

"Look at my back."

Sara walked around to the other side of my bed and gently lifted my basketball jersey. She gasped upon seeing the bruising. "Oh! I knew you shouldn't have played. Have they given you anything for the pain?" She returned to the chair to hold my hand, her face paler than when she entered.

"Unh-unh," I said through pressed lips, trying to hold back the groan that would give away just how miserable I was.

"Okay, Emily," Dr. Chan declared, pulling back a section of the curtain. He introduced himself to Sara. "Hi, I'm Dr. Chan."

"I'm Sara McKinley," she said in return.

"Is it okay if she stays in the room while I go over this with you?" he asked me.

"Yes."

"Well, it looks like you've had a couple of injuries today, huh?"

"Yes," I whispered.

"The good news is that there's nothing too serious. You do have a concussion on the back of your head, but there isn't any bleeding. The X-rays of your spine came out clear, but you've bruised your tailbone. Unfortunately, there isn't anything we can do for that, and the best thing to do is to let it heal on its own. We're going to take the neck brace off, and give you something for the pain. You'll need to stay inactive for the next two weeks at least."

My eyes widened, not prepared for his prognosis.

"Sorry, but that means no basketball during that time. You won't be up for it anyway. We'll give you something to manage the pain, but you should schedule an appointment with your doctor in two weeks to follow up.

"Do you have any questions?" he asked.

"No," I whispered.

"Now, can you tell me about the bruises on your back?"

I hoped the machine wouldn't start beeping profusely when I lied, "I slipped on some ice outside my back door and fell down the stairs."

"Did you fall on your back?"

"Yes."

"How many stairs did you fall on?"

"Four or five."

"Okay." He sighed. "Sara, could I please have a moment alone with Emily?" I panicked when Sara left the room.

Dr. Chan sat down in the chair so that he was at my eye level.

"I'm concerned with your bruising," he said solemnly. "The images showed that you have a recovered contusion on the front of your head as well.

"Emily, I want you to please tell me the truth, and know that I will hold this information in the utmost confidence. How did you get the bruises on your back?"

"I fell down the stairs." I tried to sound as convincing as I could. I didn't know if it worked, but he nodded and stood up.

"You could have received those injuries in a fall, and I can't dispute that. But if you didn't, I hope that you would be able to tell someone.

"You're going to stay here for the night so that we can keep an eye on you and give you something for the pain to help you rest. If you need anything, or feel like talking, have the nurses page me."

"Can you please send Sara back in?"

"Sure. I'll have the nurse get her."

Sara came back into the room not long after the nurse removed my neck brace and cut off my clothes so she could slide on a hospital gown. I tried to get her to slip my game shirt over my head, but the movement caused me to holler, so she opted for scissors.

"Someone will be down shortly to transport you upstairs for the night," the nurse explained. "I'll be right back with something to help ease the pain."

"Thank you," I whispered, finding some relief already with the brace removed.

After she left, I noticed Sara appeared nervous, like she wanted to tell me something, but she kept stopping every time she opened her mouth to speak.

I watched her struggle through her silent debate until I finally demanded, "What aren't you telling me?"

She pressed her lips together and looked around for the words. "Um, Evan's outside. I didn't know if I should tell you while you were still coherent or wait until you were drugged."

I remained quiet.

"He wants to see you."

"No, Sara," I shot back urgently. "He can't see me."

"I knew you'd say that, but I promised I'd ask. Just so I can say I did, no Drew either, right?"

"He's here too?"

"There are a lot of people here, actually. Well, except for your aunt and uncle, who left after the doctor told them you were staying the night."

"No visitors," I pleaded. "*No one*, okay?"

"Got it," she affirmed.

"Sara, what happened when I fell?" I asked, not sure if I wanted to hear this but also surprised by the multiple visitors in the waiting room.

Sara looked at the ceiling, trying to force back the tears.

"Um, after you took the three-pointer and it went in—"

"It went in?" I tried to remember the moment, but I couldn't get past the pounding in my head.

"Yeah, it did. The crowd was so loud, it was crazy—but in an instant it went dead silent. You were lying on the floor, and you weren't moving. Coach went out with the trainer to wake you, but they couldn't." Sara paused to take a calming breath, trying to control her trembling voice. "They called for the ambulance. The gym was so quiet while we waited for you to wake up. I tried to get down to the floor, but the coaches and some other teachers were keeping people back.

"You still didn't move when they put you on the stretcher. Em, I was so scared. I got to the hospital as soon as I could, but they wouldn't tell me anything, no matter who I asked. Between Evan and me, I think we asked every person in a white jacket or blue scrubs who walked through the waiting area. Then everyone else started arriving to wait with us—first Drew with some of his friends, then your coach and other girls from the soccer and the basketball teams—I'm not sure who else.

"Your aunt and uncle finally arrived, and they were let in to see you. I was going crazy because they got in, and I couldn't, until the nurse finally came out and said you were asking for me."

I listened to her words, unable to account for a single second of that time, until I was in the hospital. It was surreal thinking of my unconscious body on the floor of the gym, with everyone staring at me. The fear and concern that came through in Sara's voice tore at me. I glanced at Sara's hand shaking on her lap. I hadn't realized that the hand holding mine was trembling, since mine was as well.

"I'm sorry I scared you," I whispered.

"I'm just relieved to see that you're awake and moving," she said with a small smile, but the sadness lingered in her eyes. "I should go let everyone know how you are, and that you're staying the night, so they can leave. I'll be back before they move you."

The nurse entered with a syringe. Soon after she administered the clear liquid into my IV, the pain subsided, and the room swum around me as I drifted to sleep.

25. INEVITABLE

I didn't return home to George and Carol during the two weeks of intense recovery. I didn't spend Christmas at home either. My only disappointment was not seeing the kids' faces on Christmas morning. I had always loved writing the letter to Santa and setting out the cookies with them, and watching them open their presents. I wondered what they were told when they asked for me.

Staying with Janet was…quiet. She didn't ask questions about what happened to me, or about anything at all, for that matter. She gave me my space in her spare room, periodically checking on me to make sure I was comfortable and had plenty to eat and drink.

The first week was excruciating, and the slightest movement was debilitating. I relied upon the prescription pain pills to cope, which usually meant sleeping. As the second week crept by, the sharpness subsided and the aching dwindled. My muscles were stiff from underuse, and my tailbone still reminded me of the impact whenever I'd sit—but at least I had some relief. I spent my days reading, sleeping and texting Sara.

Over the school break, I received daily texts from Sara checking in on me, then providing brief accounts of her day and updates on the basketball team. I missed seeing and talking with Sara despite our daily communication—it wasn't the same. I finally got up the nerve to ask Janet if Sara could visit the Saturday before we returned to school. Janet didn't even hesitate to say yes, so I probably could have asked her sooner. It was strange how unlike Carol she was.

Sara tentatively entered Janet's small one-story house. She was not her usual overly exuberant self, although I could tell by the spark in her eye that she wanted to be. Janet found the need to go to the store soon after Sara arrived. I knew it was her way of giving us time alone to talk.

"It's so great to see you!" Sara exclaimed, giving me a gentle hug. "You look good. So, do you feel better?"

"Yeah, I'm fine—just bored out of my mind." I allowed a smile to relax on my face—it had been so long since I'd felt the tightness in my cheeks. "Tell me what's been going on. I could only get so much from the abbreviated texts, and some of it I didn't understand at all."

Sara let out a quick laugh. "Okay, so you know about basketball, right?"

"Yeah, I read about it in the paper too. That sucks about the two losses, but at least they won the other two."

"They're looking forward to having you back, especially Coach Stanley. I went skiing with my parents, Jill and Casey, but you knew that. What else?" Sara flicked her eyes toward the ceiling, thinking of other news she needed to catch me up on. "Oh, um, I guess Drew gave me flowers to give to you. But…I forgot them. Just make sure you thank him so he doesn't know I failed."

"Oh," I said quickly. Having had this time alone, I had the opportunity to consider what was happening between Drew and me. It was a whirlwind relationship, and it was difficult to recall how we had gotten to the point where he'd want to give me flowers. I could have convinced myself that we were friends, except for the kissing part. I couldn't get around that.

"He asks about you whenever I see him leaving practice. We haven't had practices after them for a while, so the guys are gone by the time the volleyball team gets on the floor. But he waits for me just so that he can check on you."

"That's sweet," I replied honestly. "I feel bad I haven't been able to talk to him."

"Are you still interested in him?" she inquired, doubt lining her voice.

I let out a guilty breath, avoiding Sara's eyes.

"What?!"

"Something happened, and I didn't have a chance to tell you, because I got hurt," I confessed. She raised her eyebrows, vehemently urging me to continue. I took a second to decide where to start. It was a scene that I'd been tormented with for the past two weeks—only second to the nightmares that made sleeping through the night impossible.

"Evan found out that Drew and I kissed." I hesitated to allow her to react.

"I figured," she replied with a slight shrug. "Everyone else in the school knows too."

"Seriously?" I groaned.

"His friends have big mouths. That's something you really haven't been a part of yet, huh?"

"What do you mean?"

"Gossip. Everyone knows what you've done before you do. I've heard enough about what I've supposedly done over the years—it's so stupid. Funny thing is, they don't know the half of it. Anyway, there was talk about you and Evan before, but since no one knew anything to keep the rumors going, the fascination died. But you and Drew are a Big Deal for some reason." My stomach turned. Hearing this only added to my guilt.

"That's not something I needed to hear," I sulked.

"Sorry. Why, what happened?"

"Evan and I were yelling at each other in the halls after he found out about Drew, and then I was yelling at him about Haley. He didn't realize I knew about them, and he wanted to explain, but

I wouldn't let him. He shouted down the stairs that he still loved me, and I kept walking. To make it worse, he saw Drew kiss me after practice that night."

"Wow, I missed all that?" Sara digested my story and shook her head. "That explains the tension in the waiting room, I guess."

"What are you talking about?"

"When we were waiting for you in the hospital, Evan and Drew stayed on opposite sides of the room. Evan kept glaring at Drew, until Drew finally called him out on it."

"Please don't tell me this happened in front of everyone?" I sank into the couch and put my head against the floral printed cushion, looking up at the ceiling.

"Sorry." Sara cringed. "The guys didn't *say* anything specifically about *you*—it was more that Drew was fed up with Evan's unwarranted hostility, and it gave Evan the chance to get in his face."

I groaned. This was difficult for me to imagine. Neither guy seemed the type to pick a fight. I knew Evan was mad at me, and unfortunately Drew was the conscious one he could yell at.

"So, what are you thinking?" Sara asked, examining my guilt-ridden face.

"I feel horrible about Evan seeing Drew kiss me, especially after what happened right before that. But I was just so angry at him for trying to hide the fact that he was doing the same thing with Haley."

"What do you mean? He and Haley aren't seeing each other." Sara sounded so sure of her words. My heart skipped a beat.

"Sara, I *saw* them at the bonfire." I was adamant. "Evan had his arm around her. That's when I walked away with Drew, remember?"

"Em, you were on the other side of the fire. I was near Evan, and he did *not* have his arm around Haley. She came over to him, said something stupid, like usual, and hugged him. He patted her on the back, humoring her, and then walked away. She went off and started flirting with Mitch. You must have only seen part of it."

That couldn't be true, could it? If it was true, then I would have never walked down the beach with Drew, and I wouldn't have been so distracted that I allowed him to kiss me. This whole mess was unraveling around me, and I knew I was at the center of all of it. What *did I do?!*

"But she said she was seeing him," I whispered. "I was so pissed when she told me at my locker that day."

"I would have a hard time believing *anything* she has to say. You know she hates you, right?"

"But, why?"

"Please don't make me say it."

"Sara, did I totally screw this up?" The aching returned, but it was inside my chest instead of my back.

"What do you want? You know that you and Evan stopped talking before Drew and Haley ever came into the picture—it had nothing to do with them."

"But I didn't help it any." I sank further into the couch.

"What about Drew?"

"I don't know, Sara." I was so confused about what I wanted and what was best, I couldn't think straight. "He's so nice and, come on, just *look* at him."

Sara smirked in agreement. "But?"

I didn't say anything for a minute. I was tormented by the thought of never talking to Evan again, but that wouldn't change until I told him the truth—and that would never happen. So where did that leave Drew? For some inexplicable reason, and without me realizing it was happening, Drew liked me. I couldn't deny that, despite my inability to understand it.

"Being around Drew makes more sense," I finally said.

"That's the strangest reason to date someone that I've ever heard," Sara responded.

"We're *dating?*" I asked in disbelief.

"Em, he's kissed you in public, he bought you flowers and he calls me to check in on you—yeah, I'm pretty sure he thinks that."

"He calls you too?!"

"Oh, yeah, sorry—I forgot to mention that. You're right—he's sweet, thoughtful, and beautiful." She paused.

"But…" I waited.

"I'm not even going to finish that sentence."

"Sara!"

"Why do *I* have be the one to say it out loud?!" Frustrated, she finally exclaimed, "He's not Evan."

I instantly recognized the truth in her words. But I also knew that the truth didn't matter.

"Can we talk about something else?" I pleaded.

"You can't avoid this forever," she warned. "We're going back to school on Monday, and they're both going to be there."

"Sara, Evan doesn't want anything to do with me."

"I don't know, Em," she said, reluctant to say anything more, but I saw it in her roaming eyes.

"Just tell me, Sara."

Sara took a breath, pausing before she revealed, "Evan was really upset at the hospital. I talked to him alone for a while. He was hurt when you didn't want to see him. He thinks he cares more about you than you do about him. I could tell he wasn't comfortable talking to me about it, but I think he just needed to tell someone, if he couldn't tell you. He wished things were the way they were before that weekend we went to the movies."

So did I.

"Emma, he's not stupid. He pretty much knows what's going on at your house. You should have seen the way he looked at Carol and George when he realized who they were. He still cares about you. I think if you just talked to him…"

"I don't think I can, Sara," I whispered. She didn't respond, but when she dropped her eyes to the floor, I knew that she didn't like my decision. I still wouldn't be able to tell him the truth, and I didn't foresee that ever changing. I couldn't hurt him again. We sat silently for a moment.

"Speaking of the unspeakable," Sara murmured, unable to meet my eyes. "Do you have to move back in with them?"

"Yeah."

"We have to stop her," she insisted. "There has to be a way without hurting the kids."

"I don't know—" I started, but was interrupted by Janet slowly opening the front door to give us plenty of warning that she was returning home.

"So, what else do you have to tell me?" I asked overemphatically, to cover up the serious conversation.

Sara shrugged. Then her eyes got big. She hesitated, tormented whether she should tell me.

"Just tell me."

"I went out on a couple of dates with Jared this week," she blurted. She watched for my reaction, anticipating the worst. I wasn't sure what to say.

"Okay," I said slowly. "That's great, right?"

"It was *really* great." She glowed.

"How did it happen?" I asked, trying not to think of our night at the movies and how they'd hit it off, because then I'd have to think about that night with Evan—and how I'd never get it back.

"I called to return his flashlight. We started talking. Then he called me later that night, and we talked some more. He asked me out, and I said yes."

"Leaving out the details?" A vague account of dates wasn't Sara's style.

"I didn't know if it was going to be weird for you since he's Evan's brother. But I had to tell you, or else I was going to burst. I can leave out the other stuff if you'd rather not hear it."

"No, I want to hear everything," I replied honestly.

Sara went on to talk about their dinner date in Boston and another in New York. Her eyes sparkled as she gushed about her time with Jared. As much as I was happy for her, this strange hollow sensation filled my stomach. Was I jealous? I pushed away the selfish emotion and smiled.

"And the second night, he kissed me. It was the most amazing kiss ever. I thought I was going to fall over." Sara beamed as the memory danced across her eyes.

"What are you going to do now? I mean, he's going back to New York, right?"

"Yeah, he left this morning," she said with a sigh. "It was the best time I've ever had, but he goes to college in New York." She shrugged, smiling contentedly.

"That's it?"

"Yeah, that's it. Honestly, I didn't expect anything else. I knew when I went out with him that that was probably going to be it."

"Then why'd you do it?" I questioned in confusion.

"Why not?!" she answered enthusiastically. "I'd rather have these incredible memories of the two nights I spent with him, knowing that I probably won't go out with him again, than not to have had them at all."

"Huh," I pondered, intrigued by Sara's perception. Her words sat with me long after she left that afternoon.

I continued thinking about what she'd said when I lay in bed that night. Was it better to get as much out of a moment as possible, knowing it could slip out from under you in a second? Did the actual experience outweigh the inevitable conclusion? I guess I had to decide if the conclusion was a broken heart, or a broken bone, in order to weigh the risk.

I didn't sleep well that night. My dreams swirled together in an incoherent jumble of images. I'm certain my restlessness was provoked by the conversation with Sara. Then again, I knew George was picking me up in the morning.

———

George and I sat in silence for the first part of the car ride—I stared out the window, and he kept his eyes glued to the road.

"It would be best if you weren't around Carol very much," he finally said. His voice drew my attention. I wasn't surprised he refused to look over at me. "She's been under a lot of stress, and the new medication she's on is affecting her moods. You can stay in your room and eat after we do, like you did before, but I'll take care of the dishes. You just worry about getting your Saturday chores done while she's out shopping.

"I spoke with the McKinleys. They're willing to help us out by letting you spend Saturdays there, after you do your chores, and any Friday nights when you have a basketball game. They're sympathetic to Carol's stress and are very thoughtful to have offered. So please don't make this any more difficult. Sundays you can spend at the library, like you have been. Emma, I don't think I have to remind you that what happens in our house, stays in our house."

I didn't react to his subtle threat. He had just taken away the remnants of the only family I had—regardless of how dysfunctional. I wouldn't be able to spend time with the kids, and he'd speak to me even less now than he did before. It sank in that I was truly alone.

My world was delicately balanced, but the scales never hung even. When something improved, something else had to crumble. Accepting this would be the hardest thing I'd ever have to learn, and even when I came to know it as true, it still crushed me.

26. BROKEN

You bitch," Haley Spencer sneered from beside my locker. "What did you say to him?"

"I don't know what you're talking about." I knew she was obviously talking about Evan, but I had no idea what was going on.

"You must have said something to him to make him leave," she insisted.

I heard her words, but I couldn't comprehend what she was saying. I stared back, stunned.

"He left!" Haley exclaimed. "He moved back to San Francisco, and I know it was because of you." Before I could respond, she stormed away.

I stood in her wake, unable to move. My books slipped from my hands and fell to the floor. Was she telling the truth?

"Here you go," a voice said, handing me my books.

"Thank you," I murmured, absently taking them without looking at the face.

There's no way she could be telling the truth. He had to be here. He just wasn't in school today. That was evident by his absent seat in English class. He couldn't have moved.

"Em, I just heard," Sara said from behind me. "I am so sorry. I didn't know."

"It's true?" I asked, turning to meet her sympathetic eyes.

"Yeah, I heard it from one of the guys on the basketball team."

Sara stood in front of her locker, contemplating my expression. She waited for me to react. But I couldn't. I didn't want to believe it. How could he be gone?

Then something broke. Sara saw it the second it happened and rushed alongside me, guiding me to the girls' bathroom. The halls were relatively empty since everyone had already gone to class, so there weren't many witnesses to the dramatic scene.

The pain crushed my heart. I sank to the floor, sliding down the cool tile wall, completely numb to the pain I should have felt along my back. I didn't cry, and my eyes didn't fill with tears, although my insides felt like they'd been shredded. I stared straight ahead, unable to focus on the wall across from me. We sat in silence for a time. I heard Sara breathing next to me, quietly witnessing my slow acceptance of the truth.

"He's really gone?" The words were caught in my throat, and I breathed them out in the faintest whisper.

Sara remained by my side without a word, holding my hand. The truth sank in deeper, and my heart released an aching sob. I collapsed onto Sara's lap and gave in to the grief. My chest heaved as I gasped for air. Sara stroked my hair to soothe me while I cried into my folded arms.

"He can't be gone." I wept, wishing that saying it out loud would make it true. I released another cry of pain.

Exhausted and raw, I laid my head still against her legs while the tears dried upon my face. My eyes stung and my throat ached. My mind swirled with thoughts of why he'd left and how he could have done it so suddenly. The more I thought about it, the more the pain turned to anger.

"I can't believe he left without saying anything." I pushed myself up to sit, the tension drawing back my shoulders. "He couldn't even say good-bye? Who does that?"

My rapid succession of emotions left Sara speechless, unable to find the words to answer. I stood up and began pacing, clenching my fists as I fumed at the thought of his selfish escape.

"Did the thought of being around me infuriate him so much that he couldn't even return to school? He had to run away to the other side of the country just to avoid me?! He's the one who stopped talking to me! Was I not supposed to get over him? Did he really want me to continue waiting for him to forgive me for something I didn't do? I'm sorry if he didn't like seeing me with someone else—but to pick up and move because of it!"

I grunted in frustration. My mind raced while I continued my pacing, unable to release my closed fists. I huffed, failing to find words for my rambling rage. I breathed in, considering his actions with my heart strangled in my chest. The ire slowly subsided into a begrudged acceptance.

"Fine, if that's how he felt, then he should've gone. He obviously couldn't stand to look at me, so why should I care if he left?! Now I don't have to worry about him yelling at me, or making me feel guilty for my decisions. I don't care if I never see him again."

This was almost convincing, but my heart stuttered in panic at the thought of not seeing his face in the halls.

"Do you really believe that?" Sara asked tentatively. I blinked at her, realizing that she was in the room. "He didn't hate you, Emma."

"You don't know that, Sara," I shot back. "I hurt him. I couldn't trust him enough to let him in. Then I accused him of things he didn't do. To top it all off, I shoved it in his face by kissing another guy right in front of him. Of course he hates me, and maybe he should. He couldn't even be around me anymore. He absolutely hates me."

Sara remained silent as I convinced myself of this. The words stung, and the anger settled. It was no longer directed at Evan but at myself. I looked at my reflection in the mirror above the sink. The pain and anger flickered in my eyes as I realized that it all circled back to me. Now I was left holding the pieces of my heart, crushed by my own hands.

I shook my head in disgust at the image in the glass. I stared at the dark eyes, my jaw tightening, allowing the anger and revulsion to grow. I accepted the blame for forcing him away. He had every right to hate me, just as I hated myself at that moment. My stomach turned to ice, and I looked away from the accusing eyes.

Taking a deep breath, I pushed the pain deep down, but I let the guilt and self-loathing fester as a punishing reminder. I took another quick breath before facing Sara. She remained a silent witness, concern etched in her eyes. Exhausted, I couldn't feel anything anymore.

"I pushed him away, so he left," I confessed quietly, submitting to the final truth. "I don't have anyone to blame but myself—and now he's gone." I shrugged. Sadness settled in Sara's eyes.

"Don't worry," I assured her. "I'm okay."

"No you're not," she whispered with a small shake of her head. After a brief silence, she said, "I think this period's about over. Are you going to your next class?"

"Sure," I answered devoid of emotion. "Why not?"

We walked back to our lockers. My locker stood open, my books casually tossed in the bottom. I grabbed what I needed as the bell rang.

"I'll see you back here before lunch?" Sara confirmed quietly, the worry still heavy in her eyes. I nodded.

I lingered at my locker for a second after Sara headed to class. I knew what was waiting for me, and as much as I tried to convince myself I was ready, I knew better. Smothered by anxiety, I couldn't loosen the tightness in my chest as I walked to Anatomy.

I sank onto my seat at the black table. The empty chair next to me screamed at me the entire class. I couldn't concentrate on the lecture; I kept glancing over at the crushing reminder of his absence.

By the end of class, I was irritated with my sorrow. I didn't have any right to grieve for Evan. I was the reason he was gone. But it didn't matter how much blame I took for forcing him to leave, or how much effort I made to push it away—I was broken.

"Are you still in pain?" Drew questioned when he sat next to me and Sara at lunch.

I'd almost forgotten he was joining us until he pulled out the chair. The guilt of being distracted by Evan washed over me with Drew's words. I obviously was not concealing my misery very well.

"No, I'm fine," I assured him with a forced smile. "It's just weird having everyone staring at me all day, that's all."

This wasn't completely a lie, although it had nothing to do with my pained expression. Everyone had been staring at me since I arrived at school that morning. I expected some stares and whispers, especially after Sara's account of the last time they saw me at the basketball game. But I wasn't expecting so many gawking faces. It was as if I'd returned from the grave. It was unsettling.

Drew's relief was evident when I saw him in the parking lot that morning. I was too preoccupied with searching for Evan's car to notice him approaching with a huge smile on his face. I suddenly caught sight of him and found his greeting too contagious not to return. He startled me when he wrapped his arms around me and held me gently against him. I hesitated before hugging him back. Sara watched in amusement, knowing I was freaking out on the inside.

I was more concerned that Evan might see us than I was about being in Drew's arms. It wasn't really a horrible place to be. I glanced around at the eyes that turned our way as they walked by. I was still trying to accept that Drew really did care about me. More importantly, I was trying to figure out how I felt about him.

So, as he sat at the lunch table asking me if I was still in pain, I decided I wasn't going to think about it anymore.

I leaned over and kissed him firmly on the lips, saying as I pulled away, "I feel much better, thanks."

A grin emerged across his face, and a subtle flush rose to his cheeks. Behind me, Sara started choking. I turned toward her convulsions.

"Sorry," she whispered, her face bright red. "Some bullshit caught in my throat." I raised my eyebrows at her words, hoping Drew hadn't heard.

"Are you playing in your game Wednesday?" Drew asked.

"It depends on how practice goes today and tomorrow," I replied. Drew moved his chair closer and rested his arm along the back of my chair. I could feel his heat radiating along my side, but the proximity of his body didn't ignite the tingling I was searching for.

"I'll definitely play Friday," I said, casually leaning closer so my shoulder touched his. I urged my heart to take notice, but it was too busy moping and wasn't about to be forced to flutter.

"Do you want to come over after the game to watch a movie?" he asked. Suddenly realizing Sara would be there too, he looked at Sara to include her in the invitation. "Or hang out or something?"

"There's a party Friday night at Kelli Mulligan's beach house," Sara informed him.

"Oh, you have plans?" Drew recognized in disappointment.

I shrugged apologetically, unaware of Sara's plans for us on Friday night. I was still trying to get used to the idea that I *had* a Friday night. When Sara found out that I was going to be staying with her on the weekends, all of her worries about my returning home rushed away. In their place was the realization that she'd finally be able to bring me to all the things I'd been missing out on. So my schedule defaulted to hers on the weekends—which was a little overwhelming.

"I have computer class with Kelli during second period; she invited us this morning. We're probably staying over," she informed us.

I raised my eyebrows in surprise. Not only did I have plans on a Friday night, but my sleepover had a sleepover? The thought of a party sent a familiar sensation surging through my veins—panic.

"She mentioned something about it to me last week after our basketball game. I didn't really consider it at the time. Is she letting anyone sleep over?" Drew asked.

"I don't know," Sara answered. This was not what she expected him to say, and I could tell she was bothered. I grinned.

"Do you want to go to the party?" My invite caused Sara to kick me under the table.

"I'll make sure it's still okay with Kelli. I have class with her next actually."

"Great." Sara forced the word out. Her false enthusiasm was glaringly obvious to me, but Drew didn't appear to notice.

The lunch bell rang, and Drew walked us into the hall.

"I'll see you before we leave for our game?" he asked.

"Yes," I replied with a small smile.

Drew put his hands on my waist and pulled me to him. The chatter of voices and shuffling of feet surrounded us, but I didn't resist his advances. His soft lips were warm against mine as he held them there for a prolonged moment. My heart refused to flutter, but I couldn't deny the warmth that spread through my stomach and the swirls that danced in my head. I decided I could live without the rush; kissing him was by no means uneventful.

"Bye," he whispered with a small smile before walking away, leaving me looking after him.

"Ready?" Sara asked, snapping me back to the noise of the hall. She stared at me with wide eyes.

"Don't look at me like that."

"What are you doing?" she demanded incredulously.

"I don't know what you mean. Aren't we supposed to be *dating*?"

"I just sat with you for an hour in the girls' bathroom—"

"Don't, Sara." I turned at the top of the stairs to face her. "This has nothing to do with *him*. I like Drew."

Sara raised her eyebrows, challenging my statement.

"Really, I *do* like him," I insisted, and continued walking toward our lockers.

"Fine, maybe you like him," Sara conceded. "But it still doesn't feel right to me. I don't care how amazing you think Drew is, he's not—"

"Don't say it, Sara," I threatened. "Stop mentioning *him*. He decided to leave, and I have to move on."

"Just like that?" she challenged. I shrugged. "Don't do anything stupid, okay? You can't kiss your way through this." I rolled my eyes and left her at the lockers to go to Art class.

This ended up being harder than Anatomy. Ms. Mier asked us to create an art piece depicting an emotion. She challenged us to unleash an emotion that could be felt through our artistic interpretation. A thousand different emotions surged through my head. I was fearful of exploring any one of them individually. Anxiety set in as I gathered a canvas and tried to select some colors to begin.

"Having difficulty deciding?" Ms. Mier inquired. "Or are you afraid of tapping into that emotion?" I glanced at her, recognizing her knowing words.

"I'm sorry you have to feel it," she continued, "but I think you can create something amazing if you let yourself explore it. It may not help you heal, but it may help you process it."

She paused, gently placed her hand on my shoulder, and whispered, "It's okay to miss him," before walking away.

I swallowed hard, pressing my lips together. I grabbed shades of red and orange and returned to my easel to begin *processing*.

During the two weeks of that assignment, I allowed myself to tap into the raw pain and drip it onto the canvas. I was true to myself with each stroke. It was a draining process, but the release was therapeutic. On several occasions, I fought to focus through blurred vision as I added layers of color, developing the pain with each shade. When I cleaned my supplies, I forced it all back into the shadows. By the time I returned to the halls, nothing remained— except for the aching murmur that had taken over my heart the day he left.

I moved on. I returned to playing basketball, only sitting out half of the first game after my return. I continued focusing on my academics, and found it easier now that I could escape to my room each night without the suffocating tension. I had the attention of a great guy, who easily distracted *my* attention whenever he was within sight. And I had guaranteed time with Sara. I was surviving as I promised I would.

27. WARMTH

I caught a glimpse of his tousled golden-brown hair in the sea of people. I followed after him, squeezing through the bodies, forcing myself to move faster. No matter how fast I tried to move, I couldn't reach him. The bodies became solid, and I was pushing through branches that raked my skin. I could still see him up ahead, but he didn't look back. My legs refused to cooperate and run faster. It took every effort to propel myself forward. I couldn't let him get away. My heart raced as I feared losing sight of him.

Suddenly the ground slid beneath me, and I couldn't see him anymore. The rocky surface continued to roll away. I tried to stop, but it was too late. I tried to hold on but only came up with handfuls of loose dirt as my legs scraped along the rough terrain. My fingers curled around the edge and my legs hung suspended above the darkness. Panic enveloped me as I tried to pull myself up. The ledge started to break apart, and that's when I saw him standing above me. I tried to reach for him, but as soon as I lifted my hand, the ground beneath the other hand gave way. I didn't see his face when I fell. Just before I hit bottom, I shot up in bed.

I was greeted by the familiar residuals of my active sleep—the racing pulse, heavy breathing and sheen of sweat—but this time, there were tears running down my cheeks. I fell into my pillow and cried, giving way to the ache in my chest until, too exhausted to hurt anymore, I drifted back into a restless sleep.

"You look tired," Sara observed when she picked me up the next morning.

"I haven't been sleeping very well," I confessed, pushing away the unsettling images of the nightmare that still clung to me.

"Are you going to last for the party tonight?"

"I'll be fine," I promised. The thought of spending the night at Kelli Mulligan's beach house was enough to jolt me to attention. I wasn't concerned I was going to fall asleep—I was more concerned about going to my first party with Drew since the bonfire.

"Ready for the party tonight?" Drew asked when he met me in the parking lot.

Seeing him brought a smile to my face—as it had every morning that week when he found me at Sara's car. Although Sara wasn't blatantly rude, she wasn't making any attempt to accept Drew. It was uncomfortably out of character for her. I mindfully ignored her and fell under Drew's arm as he wrapped it around my shoulder.

"Yeah," I responded with a forced hoorah in my voice. Why was I stressing over this party so much?

"It's going to be a good one," Drew said, pulling me against him.

Before we parted ways in the hall, he quickly brushed his lips against my cheek and whispered, "I'll see you at lunch." I smiled at his touch.

"Maybe that's what happened," Sara concluded as we walked to our lockers. "Your concussion must have left you confused and delusional."

"What are you talking about?"

"The fact that you continue to ogle Drew like he is The Guy."

"What's wrong with you?" I couldn't understand her bitterness.

"I just don't like *you* with Drew."

"What? You think I'm different? What have I done wrong?" I questioned in alarm.

"You haven't done anything wrong, really. You're just not the same, like something's missing." She shook her head slightly in deliberation. "I don't know how to explain it."

"Sara, why are you making this so hard? If there's something I'm doing that I don't know that I'm doing, please tell me so I can fix it. But if I'm not doing anything wrong, then I don't understand why it's so difficult to see us together. I'm *trying* to be happy, and Drew makes me happy. I'd be a lot happier if you weren't so critical of me. I want to have a good time this weekend. We're finally getting to spend weekends together without fear or having to lie. Aren't you excited at all?"

"I am," she replied quietly, then forced a smile on her face. It was a start. "I'm sorry. A lot has changed lately. I think I'm having a harder time adjusting than you are. I'll try to be happy for you."

She hesitated, like she wanted to add something, but thought better of it. I waited, letting her gather her words.

"I won't second-guess you anymore. I trust that you know what you're doing, and I'll support you. So, yes, I promise by the time we leave today, I will be excited. Okay?"

"Thank you." I flashed her an appreciative smile before she headed to class.

By the time we met for lunch, Sara didn't show any visible signs of having reservations about Drew and me, and she was her exuberant self once again. She talked about Kelli's party and who was supposed to be there, noting who was sleeping over. Since the house was just twenty minutes from Weslyn, only a few had been invited to stay the night, and they were exclusively girls.

Sara's good mood held up for the remainder of the day. She even had an actual conversation with Drew. He talked to her as if there hadn't ever been anything wrong, but her efforts didn't go unnoticed by me. I was grateful that she was finally giving in to the idea that *he* was who I was with.

I knew that being with Drew was going to be different, and I wasn't going to feel the same. I shouldn't, right? So when he pulled me into the vacant trainer's office before I left for my game, I wasn't expecting his send-off or how he'd make me feel.

"I'll meet you at Kelli's around eight?" he confirmed.

"That's about right," I said, recalling the details.

I knew he was going to kiss me when he leaned over, but I was surprised when he slid his hand behind my neck and wrapped his arm around my waist to pull me to him. His warm breath released into my mouth as he parted my lips with his tongue. The connection ignited a heat in my stomach. I released a shocked breath of excitement. Our bodies pressed firmly together, and our wet lips slid over each other's urgently. When he released me, I exhaled a quivering breath.

"Wow," he exhaled.

"Yeah," I responded softly.

My entire body was pulsing, a sensation I'd never experienced before. I needed to steady my breath and the swirling in my head before I could move.

"I should go," I whispered, pressing my lips together. They still lingered with the remnants of our kiss.

"Okay," he replied with a grin. He met me with another kiss, initially meant to be a soft kiss good-bye. But as soon as we touched, we fell into the same frenzied passion. Before I could completely lose myself in the moment, I pulled away.

"Yeah, I really have to go," I said, trying to breathe.

He smiled back before I slipped out the door.

"Why are your cheeks so red?" Jill observed as we walked together to the bus.

I put my hand to my face, registering the warmth with a smile.

"I had to run to get here in time," I lied. "I was talking to Ms. Holt about the paper."

The warmth and pulsing lingered for most of the bus ride. I sat in the back, resting my head against the window, staring at nothing. I barely heard the music blaring in my ears as I replayed the kiss in my head. My lips turned up at the corners as I inhaled deeply.

"What's going on with you?" Jill questioned curiously from beside me.

I removed an earbud so that I could hear her.

"You don't look as focused as you usually do before a game," she noted. "Are you okay?"

I shook off the buzz.

"Yeah," I stated soberly. "I'm fine. I was just caught up in something else."

"I'm sure I know *who*." She grinned. I ignored her and put the earbud back in, forcing my mind to prepare for the game.

Sara picked me up at school after we returned from the game.

"You win?" Sara asked.

"Of course," I confirmed with a smile.

"My mom has dinner in the oven for us when we get home, so we'll get ready to go to Kelli's after we eat. I've already picked out your clothes."

I smiled, having expected nothing less.

"Should I be nervous?"

"I think you may be."

I groaned.

I groaned again when I saw it.

"A dress, Sara?!" I groaned in dismay, staring in shock at the flirty blue and green strapless dress paired with a blue cardigan.

"No heels this time," she pointed out, hoping it would make up for the lack of material, but I couldn't take my eyes off the dress.

"Just go take a shower and let me worry about the clothes," she demanded.

I obeyed.

I started buttoning the sweater, wanting to conceal the fact that nothing was holding up the dress. Sara removed my hands from the buttons, shaking her head. I examined the dress; it swayed a little too far above my knees in the mirror, and I gave Sara a worried glance. The dress kept me from being concerned with the large curlers in my hair.

"Relax, it looks great," Sara assured me. "I promise it isn't going to fall down. It fits perfectly."

"I don't understand how, considering how much bigger your chest is than mine."

"That's why I never wore it," she confessed. "Don't envy having a bigger bra size. It's more of a pain in the ass than you realize."

I let out a short laugh, skeptical of her self-criticism.

Sara removed the cooled curlers and released soft waves of hair that she tousled with her fingers. It was more volume than my hair had ever seen, and took me the entire car ride to get used to it.

"Stop playing with your hair," Sara reprimanded as we pulled into Kelli's driveway.

The Mulligans' beach house was spectacular. A modern two-story structure set on a cliff, it shone like a beacon at the top of the long inclined driveway when we pulled up. The entire ocean side of the top floor was lined with windows that let off a distinct glow against the darkened sky.

Sara and I gathered our overnight bags and followed the stone driveway to a narrower walkway, our shoes clicking along the hard surface. My stomach turned in anticipation of what awaited us behind the large white doors when Sara rang the bell.

"Hey, Sara! Emma!" Kelli yelled in excitement when she opened the door. "Come on in."

We entered a small foyer, illuminated by a large spiny light fixture suspended above our heads. We followed Kelli up a short flight of stairs that opened into a space so expansive it made my jaw drop. A sleek white-and-chrome kitchen with a massive cooking island and bar connected to a spacious living area that had an amazing view of the ocean. A fire flickered in the large stone fireplace along one side of the open room, and a chic chrome table with a glass top was centered along a wall of windows. Another sitting area focused around a sophisticated entertainment unit on the other side. I recognized most of the forty, maybe fifty, people scattered around.

We followed Kelli through the kitchen and down a long hall. She opened the last door, and we walked into a bright white bedroom with another glass wall looking out at the ocean. There were two full-size beds adorned with white and blue pillows, a small fireplace across from a chaise and a private bathroom.

"This is where you'll be staying for the night," she announced as she walked in. She handed Sara a key. "So you don't have to worry about anyone wandering in here later." She grinned. "Come out whenever you're ready and help yourselves to anything."

"Nice, huh?" Sara said after Kelli disappeared down the hall.

I gaped, watching the dark waves crash against the rocks. "Unbelievable."

After abandoning our bags in the room, we joined the party. This party was very different from the other two parties I'd been to. Everyone here was dressed as if they were going out to an expensive restaurant, or maybe a nightclub. The girls had made a point to show off skin, accented by something sparkly dangling from their ears or necks, while the guys had made an extra effort to wear fitted clothes and style their hair with more product than I owned. Sara's dress now made sense, except that I was covering it up with the sweater, which I wasn't about to take off.

"How was your game?" Drew asked, sliding his arms around my waist and giving me a quick kiss on the lips. Warmth rushed in at the touch of his lips, instantly reminding me of our connection earlier in the day.

I responded with a smile, accented by the red of my cheeks. "We won."

He took my hand and escorted me to the kitchen. Sara was already there greeting everyone as we made our way through. She picked up a glass of champagne, and Drew grabbed a beer. An uneasy twinge passed through my stomach.

"What do you want?" Drew asked, pulling me toward him so he could talk in my ear.

"I think I'm okay for now," I responded nervously. I glanced around and noticed that most people were holding some type of glass, presumably containing alcohol. A flood of anxiety surged through me at the thought of more awkward exchanges with inebriated people. This was going to be interesting.

"Are you sure?" Drew questioned. "I don't need to drink if it makes you uncomfortable."

I didn't know what to say in response. Of course it made me uncomfortable. I'd witnessed too many moments when my mother failed to function while intoxicated. Even though alcohol seemed to be at every party I'd been to so far, that didn't change my aversion to it. Could I really ask him not to drink?

"Are you driving?" was the first thing that came out of my mouth.

"No. I'm staying in the guest house tonight with a couple of the guys."

He was staying over? I held my breath at the thought of having him here all night, especially after the kiss we'd shared earlier. I could handle this, right?

"I don't drink." I shrugged apologetically.

"That's fine," he said, setting down the bottle. "I don't have to either." Then he kissed me softly on the lips, and whispered in my ear, "I don't need the alcohol to give me a buzz." My face grew hot. I let out a quick breath, not convinced I could handle it anymore.

I didn't know where Sara had disappeared to, so I followed Drew to the sitting area, where a few of his friends were talking about surfing. I stood next to Drew, who had his arm around my waist, listening to their animated stories—which were more entertaining than I'd anticipated.

I spotted Sara with a few girls from soccer near the kitchen, so I told Drew I'd be right back.

"Hi," I said as I approached the small group.

"Hi, Emma," Katie said in welcome. "You look really great."

"Thanks," I replied awkwardly. "So do you." I noted her strapless white top, form-fitting black pants and strappy black heels—with more inches than I could manage, but she pulled them off as if she wore them every day.

"Where's Drew?" Sara asked.

"Talking to some friends." I nodded toward the group of laughing guys.

"Are you two officially together?" Lauren asked.

"What does that mean, exactly?" I questioned, not understanding the "officially" part. Dating had rules that I evidently was not aware of.

"Are you seeing other people?" she clarified.

"I'm not," I answered, then glanced over at Drew, who was completely engaged in a story. Did Drew want to see someone else? If he did, would that be okay? The thought of it triggered an unexpected twist in my stomach.

"We haven't talked about it," I confessed.

"Em, you should ask him what he expects," Sara advised. The other girls nodded.

"You don't want to assume anything and then get burned later," Jill added. "Drew doesn't kiss and tell, but you never know what he may have going on on the side." My eyes flashed toward Katie, who'd lowered her eyes, her cheeks flushing a slight pink.

"That's why I was surprised when I heard he kissed you," Lauren noted. "I never hear about Drew."

"I think it's because it was her," Sara concluded. "It was a bigger deal, so I'm sure he couldn't keep that to himself."

The conversation about Drew and me was making me uncomfortable. I really wanted to change the subject.

"Are you staying over?" I asked the girls, but they were too entrenched in analyzing my relationship with Drew to hear me.

"I know how his friends are," Katie finally added, "so don't assume he's as innocent as you think." She wasn't talking to me directly, but I still heard the warning in her tone. I studied her suspiciously—she still refused to look at me.

Sara picked up on the intonation as well. "Katie, what do you know?"

"Nothing—I've just hung out with them before when they went surfing in Jersey. I watched them *all* flirt with the girls there. I went with Michaela once when Jay invited her, right after they hooked up. When we got there, he barely paid any attention to her. He was too busy hitting on another girl from the city. He didn't even think twice about it, and then he didn't understand why Michaela was upset when he came back around and wanted to get with her later that night."

"That doesn't mean they're all like that," Jill argued. Katie shrugged. I recognized she wasn't telling us everything.

"Em, come with me," Sara requested. "I need another drink."

I pulled a bottle of sparkling water out of the refrigerator while Sara refilled her glass, waiting for the real reason she'd pulled me away from the girls.

"I think Katie may have had something with Drew," she warned. "Or still does."

"You think so?"

She shrugged. "Maybe. There's something definitely up. I know he's been with at least two girls here."

"Don't tell me," I pleaded.

Knowing Drew's history of girls was more than I could take; the thought of it caused my stomach to twist tighter. I glanced over at him again, but the guys had dispersed. I scanned the room and found him talking to Kelli and another girl I didn't know. The twist morphed into an unwelcome streak of jealousy. I forced myself to dismiss it, convinced I was overreacting. The girls had gotten to me, and I needed to shake off the insecurity.

"Just talk to him, so you're on the same page," she insisted. "Do you want to date him exclusively?"

It was a question I hadn't given much thought to. I'd allowed Drew to slip in when I wasn't paying attention, and now that I *was* paying attention, I didn't know what to think. I took seeing him every day for granted, unconcerned if he had an interest in anyone other than me. But looking around the room and seeing the options, I understood the temptation, and it made me question what was happening between us.

"I don't know," I answered honestly. "I've never really thought about it."

"I didn't think so." I was prepared for her to say more, but she didn't.

"Hey, Sara." Jay approached us. "It's cool to see you here."

Sara acknowledged him with "Hi, Jay."

"Are you two up for going surfing with us this spring?"

The invitation to be a part of Drew's future was suddenly too overwhelming. I really had been living in the present. All the talk about declaring my intent with Drew and surfing with

him and his friends months from now was too much to absorb
at once.

"We'll see," I remarked with a casual shrug.

"Come on. You'll love it," he insisted.

"A lot can happen between now and then," Sara answered, reading into my abbreviated response.

"True," Jay agreed. "But no matter what, I'd love to get you on
a board—or see you in a bikini." He laughed. I stared at him with
widened eyes, while Sara rolled hers.

"I was just kidding," he said in defense.

"Hey," Drew said, coming up behind me, slipping his arms
around my waist.

"I was just talking about taking them surfing with us this
spring," Jay told Drew.

"Really? You want me to teach you how to surf?" Drew came
alongside me so he could see my face.

"Maybe." I shrugged, not wanting to mislead him about our
potential future.

"She doesn't think you guys will last until the spring." Jay
laughed.

"Jay!" Sara exclaimed, hitting his arm.

"Ow!" He flinched, holding the spot where she made contact.
"What?!"

"She never said that," she bit back. Then she looked to Drew,
rolling her eyes. "He's an idiot."

Drew observed me cautiously, trying to read my face.

"Are you ditching me already?"

"No!" I declared. "I never said anything like that. Thanks a lot,
Jay!" Jay put his hands up in defense, which was obviously a common pose for him.

Drew took my hand and led me down the hall, away from the
noise. My stomach turned, nervous to have this conversation right now.

"What's going on?" he asked.

"Nothing," I assured him, but my voice lacked the confidence needed to set him at ease.

"I'd rather not talk right here." I glanced toward the voice-filled room, with its attentive ears and subtle glances in our direction as we attempted to isolate ourselves.

Drew's eyes tightened. I must've said something wrong. This wasn't going very well, and I couldn't figure out what I was saying that kept upsetting him.

He led me across the room, down the stairs and out the front door. I shivered, wrapping my sweater around me against the cold wind.

"Where are we going?" I asked, continuing alongside him across the driveway.

"Some place we can talk."

Through a break in the trees was a small cottage. He took out a key and unlocked the door. The small house was one large room with an eat-in kitchen, a sitting area, two queen-size beds on the far side, and a ladder leading up to a loft bed. It was decorated in a typical New England nautical theme, with shells and pictures of sailboats—in complete contrast to the chic modern design of the main house.

Drew shut the door and turned toward me. I was not prepared for the concerned look on his face. The misunderstanding evidently had gotten to him. Now I was worried about what to say next.

"Tell me what that was all about?" he requested anxiously.

"I'm sorry." Panic streaked across his face. Wrong words again! What was I doing wrong? "The girls were trying to give me advice, and I let it get to me. It was stupid, really." I hoped he would find some comfort in my dismissive tone, but he remained tense.

"What did you want advice about?"

"I didn't," I said quickly. This was harder than I thought. "They asked me if you and I were *officially* together, and I said we hadn't really talked about it. So they told me I should, that way I'd know in case you were seeing someone else. It was ridiculous, and I shouldn't have listened to them."

"Huh." I waited as he processed what I said. The tension let up in his shoulders, but his eyes remained uneasy.

"So, are we together?" he finally asked.

Not what I was expecting.

"What does that mean, exactly?"

Wrong question again. His eyes flinched in alarm.

"Do you want to be with anyone else?" he inquired cautiously.

My heart stammered at the question. I couldn't force the words out to tell him that there wasn't anyone else, so I shook my head. My pulse raced at the untruth.

"Do you?" I replied anxiously, having already considered the reasons he may not want to be exclusive.

"No," he said quickly. "So why don't you think we'll last until the spring?"

We were back to this question again? I took a breath, stalling.

"I never said that."

"Do you think we will be?"

Now how was I going to answer that without it coming out wrong? I looked into his distraught bright green eyes and grinned. I decided to do the only thing I could to avoid answering. I took a step toward him and put my arms around his neck, pulling him closer to me. He didn't resist when I kissed him.

Drew smiled softly, revealing his dimples. He leaned in to find me again with his soft lips, causing a warmth to surge through me. His mouth rushed to find mine over and over again as he pulled me closer. I could hardly breathe, the pulsing heat capturing the air in my lungs.

His firm body pressed against mine. Small excited gasps escaped from my mouth as he tightened his hold around my waist. We slowly moved across the room, keeping up the frantic kissing and breathing until my legs bumped up against something. He guided me onto my back on one of the beds. My head was caught up in the swirl of quick breaths, unable to process where this was leading. Then his hand slid along the back of my thigh and he pulled my leg around him. A sobering flash tried to register in my head.

Drew ran his lips along my neck, sending another whirl of excitement through my body, crushing the warning before it developed. The warmth of his tongue traveled down my neck as he proceeded to peel my sweater back to reveal my bare skin. I let out a small moan of pleasure as the swirl consumed me. He made his way back to my mouth and began running his hand along my outer thigh, then slid it between my legs.

A sobering crash resounded in my head as a cold draft caught me.

"Whoa," a voice said from the door.

"Jay, get out!" Drew yelled, still pressed against me his head turned toward the door.

I shot up from under him, pulling my dress down and adjusting my sweater. Drew was forced to sit next to me on the bed.

"Sorry, man," Jay said with an annoying smile. "I didn't know."

"Just get out."

"See you inside." Jay laughed, closing the door behind him.

"Shit," Drew whispered, falling on his back. "Sorry about that."

From a distance I could hear Sara's voice. "Jay, have you seen Emma?"

I jumped up from the bed and proceeded to straighten my dress.

"She's in there." Jay laughed again.

"What's wrong?" Drew questioned in alarm, propped up on his elbows on the bed.

"Sara's looking for me," I explained, smoothing my hair in the mirror.

"Do you want to go back inside?" he inquired, disappointment heavy in his voice. He stood up as Sara as knocked on the door.

"Emma, you in there?" Sara shouted from the other side.

"Come in!" Drew hollered, slightly annoyed.

Sara peered in cautiously. I rolled my eyes at her suspicious entrance. She looked from me to Drew and back to me again, then glanced at the rippled bedding. I knew I was in for a drilling later.

"Um, we were going to..." She faltered. "I was just looking for you."

"I'll be right there," I promised, unable to leave just yet; I could feel the heat from the bright red blush running from my cheeks down to my chest.

"Okay, I'll see you inside," she responded slowly, closing the door behind her.

"Sorry," I said to Drew. "But we should go back in before *everyone* starts looking for us."

"I could lock the door," he suggested, pulling back the sweater and kissing the top of my shoulder. Before the swirls regained their momentum, I laughed nervously and backed away, covering my shoulder with the sweater. Drew conceded reluctantly. "Fine, we'll go back in."

We were welcomed with suspicious glances and knowing smiles that made my chest tighten when we entered the house. Maybe my face was still flushed, so they knew what we were up to just by looking at me. I searched the room for Sara and found Jay with the dumbest smile. I was overcome with a strong desire to smack it off his face.

"I'm going to get something to drink," I told Drew, heading toward the kitchen area.

He walked straight to Jay and had him in a corner in conversation before I made it to the kitchen.

"I guess you're official now," Jill said with a laugh.

"What?!" My worst fear was realized as she gave me a knowing grin. The heat crept along my neck to my cheeks.

"Come on," she hinted. "Jay has a big mouth, remember?"

"Great." I shook my head in humiliation. "I'm sure it was so much worse coming out of his mouth."

"I don't know if it could get any worse."

"What are you talking about?" I demanded, now confused.

She didn't respond for a second, and then she nodded for me to walk over to an empty corner next to the cabinets. My heart skipped a beat in panic.

"He said he walked in on you and Drew having sex."

"What?!" I yelled, much louder than I should have. I grabbed the counter to support me so I wouldn't fall over. The people closest to us stopped to listen.

"We were kissing," I assured her in an agitated whisper. "That's it. What an ass!" My stomach turned, suddenly realizing why we'd received so many stares when we came back.

"Sorry." She shrugged. "Jay likes his stories." I shook my head in disbelief.

Sara had slipped in beside us while I was explaining what Jay had *actually* seen.

"I knew you wouldn't do that." She sounded relieved.

"Of course not!" I declared adamantly. Drew seemed to be having a very similar conversation with some of the guys on the other side of the room. Jay continued to shake his head while turning his hands in the air in his infamous defensive pose.

"Please tell me there is something more interesting to talk about than what Drew and I *didn't* do," I begged, trying to settle the nausea in my flipping stomach.

"Um, well, Katie disappeared with Tim somewhere," Jill revealed.

"Really?" Sara asked, intrigued.

If trying to guess what two people were doing alone together was a form of entertainment, then I didn't want any part of it—especially after I had been one of the people providing the entertainment. I slipped past Sara and Jill while they continued to draw outrageous conclusions and found an empty space on the couch in front of the fireplace to stare at the flames. I was struck with an unsettling déjà vu.

"I had him once," Kelli said, breaking my entranced gaze. I watched her scoot toward me, greeted by the sweet burn of liquor. I let out a heavy breath, preparing myself.

"You are sooo lucky," she slurred. "Drew is the greatest guy."

"Mmm," I agreed, humoring her.

"I only fucked him once," she confessed. My back tensed. "We never dated or anything." She shared this information as if it should put me at ease. "But he's amazing, isn't he?" I couldn't move.

"I'm so glad you and Sara are here," Kelli murmured, laying her head on my shoulder. "You are the nicest people I've ever met." I glanced over at her short brown hair, which flipped up in just the right places, and her fitted cocktail dress exposing her cleavage.

Great, so he'd been with her, and probably Katie. Who else in this room had the privilege of a Drew experience? I knew I wasn't the first person he'd dated, as he was for me. But from the sounds of it, dating wasn't necessary to get to know him. I felt sick with the thought of the girl next to me in a compromising position with Drew. I knew I shouldn't allow it to get to me. But whether it *should* or not, it did.

Trying to stay preoccupied to avoid thinking about Drew's past, I eventually lost track of time. I talked to random people about nothing in particular. I even watched a couple of guys arm wrestle, which was ridiculously entertaining—especially when one guy kept cheating by standing up out of his chair. Sara checked on me a few times, but she became preoccupied with a local guy who Kelli had invited. By the time Drew found me, most people were starting for the door or going to their rooms.

"Sorry it's been so long since I've seen you," Drew said, sliding next to me on the couch and wrapping his arm around my shoulders. I was ready to go to bed, and I had hoped to slip into my room without being noticed. Still not recovered from the thoughts that had plagued me most of the night, I was hesitant to lean against him. "You okay?"

"Just tired." I played it off by stretching my back, feeling horrible that he had picked up on my evasion.

"Too tired to be alone with me?" he whispered in my ear. I grinned; the warmth of his breath erased every insecurity that had disturbed me throughout the night. I turned my head, and he met me with a gentle kiss on the lips.

"Well?" he urged. I continued grinning, allowing the warmth to rush through me. He kissed me again, lingering a little longer while wrapping his arm around my waist to pull me closer.

Someone cleared her throat behind us. I pulled back and looked toward the noise to find Katie standing a few feet behind us. I sat up in surprise.

"Drew, could I talk to you a minute?" Katie asked innocently, swaying slightly, her hands on her hips and a flirtatious grin upon her face.

Drew sighed and looked at me. I shrugged, allowing him to decide if he wanted to talk to her.

"Sure," he said slowly and got up to follow her to a vacant spot, leaning against the window in front of the dining room table.

I sank into the couch; my twisting stomach kept me from watching. After a few minutes Drew returned, looking bemused.

"Everything okay?" I asked, not really wanting to know the answer.

"Just wasn't expecting that," Drew admitted with a distant look in his eye.

I couldn't ask him to explain, but his answer was unsettling. Now I *did* want to know what Katie said. He noticed when I tensed, and reached for my hand.

"It's a long story," he said dismissively. That didn't help. "I think a few people are going in the hot tub downstairs. Are you interested?"

"Not really," I replied, wanting more than ever to put the discomfort behind me and go to my room.

"You really just want to go to bed, don't you?"

"I do," I confessed. "Sorry."

"That's fine. It's really late." Then he hesitated before he asked, "Could I lie down with you?"

I stopped breathing. I definitely wasn't expecting that.

"I don't think that would be a great idea."

"You're probably right," he conceded. "Can I at least tuck you in?"

I grinned at the offer. "I think that would be okay."

Drew followed me to find Sara so that I could get the key. She looked at Drew behind me and raised her eyebrows. I rolled my eyes and shook my head, dismissing her silent insinuation. I knew that anyone who saw Drew follow me to the room would assume the same thing. With everything that had already happened and been misinterpreted tonight, I was beyond caring about it anymore.

Drew sat in a white chair in the room while I prepared for bed in the bathroom. I emerged with my teeth brushed, face washed, wearing a pair of striped boxer shorts and a fitted tank top. Drew grinned, probably because he was seeing more of me than he'd seen so far.

I slipped under the covers of the bed as he locked the door.

"So no one walks in and assumes anything," he explained in response to my inquisitive look.

"You're just tucking me in, remember?"

Drew smirked.

"Good night," he whispered, leaning over to kiss my lips. He hesitated ever so slightly before his lips touched mine so that I could feel the heat of his breath. I inhaled softly as the tickle of his breath started to rouse the swirls in my head. His soft lips pressed against mine, and he kept them there long enough for my head to fill with the whirling sensation before he pulled away. I kept my eyes closed and breathed the slightest audible moan, unaware that I'd released the sound.

Before I could open my eyes, he was there again, finding me, but with much more energy and need. I returned the enthusiasm, wrapping my arms around his neck, pulling him closer. He lowered himself over me on top of the blankets, continuing to find my urgent lips. He kissed down the slope of my neck, and I arched to meet him. My body was so caught up in the intoxicating warmth and hunger that I couldn't think. I could only respond to the pulsing that pulled me to him.

My breath escaped in gasps as he slipped under the covers, and I could feel him so much closer. I tasted the salt along his neck, my lips finding the spot below his ear. His breath accelerated, and he pushed harder against me, sliding his hand under the back of my tank top. A sobering shock roused me from my trance when his tensed body pressed into me, warning me to slow down.

Drew ran his other hand along the back of my thigh and stopped under my knee, hitching it around him. The excited warmth racing through me collided with the sobering alarm going off in my head. I pulled away and took a breath, trying to listen. He held himself over me, looking down in an attempt to understand my withdrawal. He leaned in to kiss me again, but I turned my head.

"Need a minute," I explained.

"Yeah." He sighed, pushing off me and sitting on the edge of the bed.

He turned toward me and asked, "Do you want me to leave?" His green eyes searched mine eagerly. I grinned and shook my head.

I interrupted him as he was about to pull back the blanket. "But you should." He nodded slowly, his eyes dropping in disappointment.

"Good night," he said, leaning forward to kiss me.

"I think you did that already," I replied with a grin, stopping him before he got too close. "Good night."

Drew slowly stood and went to the door. He looked back at me one final time, hesitating long enough for me to consider changing my mind, before he closed it behind him.

Just as I was finally falling asleep, a thud on the door stirred me. Sara was saying good night, presumably to the local guy she'd just met. I wanted to slink under the covers when I heard her sliding against the door with heavy breaths and moans. After a few more low thuds, Sara finally entered with a promise to call him. With my back turned to her, I feigned sleep. I'd heard enough of the details of her night and really didn't want to talk about mine. Eventually, sleep found me.

———

In the early hours of the morning, I was confronted with the same images of Evan on the cliff. This time I saw his face before I fell, and he looked so angry. I pleaded with him as he drifted away.

"Em?" Sara groaned, half asleep. "Are you crying?"

The room was dark, the morning light hidden behind custom blinds. I lay in the bed, my eyes wide open as I frantically searched the unfamiliar room. Tears slid along my temples, and sweat pasted the sheet to my body. I eased up to sit, my heartbeat slowing to its intended pace.

"You called out his name," Sara said, rolling onto her side to look at me.

"Whose name?"

"Evan's."

The sadness of the dream returned to me. I wiped the tears from my face.

"You miss him, don't you?"

I didn't say anything.

"You could always call him, you know."

I shook my head. "No, I can't," I whispered. I got out of bed and entered the bathroom, closing the door behind me.

28. THE TRUTH

S omehow I lived through the rumors of what didn't happen between Drew and me. I was mortified when one of the girls from the basketball team asked in front of everyone in the locker room if Drew and I had had sex at Kelli's. Jill tried to defend me, and it worked for the most part with my teammates, but it didn't have the same result with the rest of the school. No one else asked me to my face, but I heard the whispers when I walked down the halls. Sara's urging me to "just ignore them" only confirmed what they were whispering about.

I wasn't invisible anymore, and there was no point in trying to fade away again. More people recognized my promotion in the social hierarchy and were bold enough to try to talk to me. At first it was just small talk, to which I awkwardly responded with short answers. Then I was invited to parties and out with a group of people I would never have known if they hadn't approached me. I always deferred to Sara to plan our weekends.

I remained trepidatious with my comings and goings through the house. I didn't know how long my absence would be accepted without an explanation. My stomach still dropped at the sound of Carol's voice, anticipating the moment she'd notice me again. But as the month progressed, I was still just an occupant in her home, without any expectations other than my Saturday morning chores.

I missed seeing Leyla and Jack. I heard their voices in the distance, but rarely saw them. I convinced myself that this was better
for them so that my world wouldn't disrupt theirs again. It made the
hurt more bearable, especially when I'd hear Leyla's excited stories
from behind the closed door of my room.

During the first week of February, Anna and Carl announced
that during our school break they were taking Sara and me to California to visit colleges. My coach arranged meetings with a few
schools that were interested in me. Carl spoke with George, and he
approved the trip, which I'm sure raked under Carol's skin. I hoped
retribution wasn't waiting for me when we returned.

Sara was beyond excited with thoughts of us going to college
together in California. I was thrilled as well, doing everything to
ignore the fact that we were going to be in the same state—actually
staying in the same city—as Evan.

His nightly hauntings became less frequent. I would think I'd
finally escaped him, just to cry out in the night, propelled back to
the dark bedroom, sobbing. Sara stopped asking about the nightmares. She'd silently watch me recover from the bed across from me.

It was hard to heal when I saw my brokenness displayed in
streaks of red and orange on the wall of the Art room. Ms. Mier
praised it, saying it was my best piece yet and that she was proud of
my honesty. I absorbed her words without reaction. I'd hoped that
releasing it on the canvas would help me move on, but I knew I was
never going to put him behind me.

I allowed my heart to remain silent. It continued to ignore
Drew's touch. But I embraced the warmth he ignited within the
rest of me and the enrapturing swirls of excitement that clouded my
head whenever we had a moment alone together.

It was easy to get lost in the breathing and kissing. But over
time, the urgency increased. His hands wandered more, seeking

REBECCA DONOVAN

the touch of my skin, gradually inching up or down. I felt like I was constantly redirecting his creeping hands and trailing lips. He wouldn't say anything, but I knew he was hoping I'd just give in. Instead of talking about it, I started to avoid being alone with him.

My evasiveness roused a wave of guilt. I tried convincing myself that it was because I wasn't ready, and it had nothing to do with Drew. We didn't have another conversation about our relationship after Kelli's party. We never discussed our feelings or expectations.

I took what we had at face value. We liked to be around each other. We easily found something to talk about, and he still made me laugh without much effort. The public affection and the moments of breathlessness confirmed our attraction to each other. So what was there to talk about?

"You still like me, right?" Drew asked while we sat on the couch in Sara's entertainment room. Sara and Jill had gone to the store, and we were waiting for a couple of Drew's friends to arrive for a night of horror movies. Sara and I had decided to stay in, since our flight left for California first thing in the morning.

"Of course I do," I answered in alarm, my stomach dropping at the unprovoked question. I gently pushed his foot with mine as I sat facing him on the couch with my back against the arm. "Where did that come from?"

Drew shrugged, but remained serious. I tried to connect with him, to make him smile, but he avoided looking at me. I was so confused.

"So, why don't you want to be alone with me anymore?" he asked after a moment of silence.

I sat up straighter, suddenly fearing where this was going.

"I don't know what you mean."

"You seem to always find an excuse. If you like me, then why don't you want to be with me?"

I didn't respond, knowing what he was really asking.

Drew leaned forward and grabbed my calves, pulling me across the couch, draping my legs over his. He put his arms around my waist and inched me closer until our faces were less than a foot apart. The entire move happened so quickly, I didn't have time to react.

"I want more from you," he stated softly, gently brushing his lips against mine. "I want you to want me too. I want you to need to be with me as much as I need to be with you."

He pressed his lips to mine, lingering. I could feel his breath quicken. I listened in shock to what he was really asking me, too panicked by his words to feel his lips.

"I know you want me," he whispered, our lips inches apart.

When I still didn't kiss him, he pulled his head back to look me in the eye. Concern washed over his face.

"You don't?" he asked cautiously, slowly sitting back against the couch.

I couldn't answer. My hesitation caused him to narrow his eyes, examining my stunned face. He looked away, not liking what he saw.

"Hey!" Jill exclaimed when she and Sara reached the landing.

I quickly pushed myself off Drew's lap and scooted to the other side of the couch, while Drew forced a smile to greet Sara and Jill. Jill began loading the small upstairs fridge with beers. I stood from the couch and offered to help get things together in the kitchen. Sara tossed Drew the remote and told him he was in charge of picking the first movie.

"What happened?" she asked, sensing my mood change.

"He pretty much just asked me to have sex with him," I responded quietly as I dumped a bag of chips in a bowl.

"No way!" Sara exclaimed in shock. "What did you say?"

"I couldn't answer him," I confessed guiltily.

"You didn't say *anything*?"

"I was trying to figure out what the answer was when you two arrived."

"So now he thinks you don't like him at all, right?"

"I told him I liked him," I explained. "But he said he wanted more from me."

"Are you ready for this? With him?"

"I like him. But…" I shrugged.

Sara smirked. "I know."

"What should I do?"

"Just treat him like you normally would, and try to avoid being alone with him for now. But you have to talk to him about it eventually. He's going to see right through you anyway when you keep rejecting him, and it won't matter."

I was confused. "What do you mean?"

She smiled. "If you don't know what I'm talking about, then I can't tell you."

"Sara," I pleaded, "you're not making any sense. What are you talking about?"

"Here, bring these bowls of chips upstairs, and kiss him or something so it's not awkward all night."

Jill entered the kitchen, and I hesitated before grabbing the bowls from Sara's hands, still trying to decipher her message. I climbed the stairs slowly, figuring out how to approach Drew. I decided aggressive and direct was best.

I set the bowls of chips on the table and intercepted Drew's view of the television screen while he flipped through movie titles. Reluctantly he looked up at me. I moved closer and straddled his legs, hovering above him. He raised his eyebrows at my forwardness.

"I want to be with you," I whispered, looking down at him. I placed my hands on the back of his neck, running my fingers into his hair. "But I'm just not ready…"

He looked at me in confusion, obviously expecting a different answer. He was about to slide out from under me when I quickly added, "right now…but…soon." I didn't know why I lied to him. It was easier than admitting the truth.

I leaned down and firmly pressed my lips against his. Before I could pull away, he had his hands on my waist and quickly flipped me over onto my back so that his body was on top of mine and my legs were wrapped around him. He continued to search for my lips as my breathing quickened. He tried to roll me on my side, but the momentum forced us to roll off the couch and onto the floor.

I started laughing, deflating the intensity, as he groaned in frustration beneath me. He looked up at me and smiled. I pushed myself off of him and slid back onto the couch as the voices of the guys with Sara and Jill neared the top floor.

During the movies, Drew and I lay on oversize pillows on the floor in direct sight of everyone, so he couldn't get away with too much. Everyone else was scattered on the couch and loveseat, making comments about the pathetic girls wandering alone in the dark and warning the guys to look behind them right before they were slaughtered. I had my head propped against Drew's taut stomach while he played with my hair. I fell asleep during the middle of the second movie.

"Evan?" a voice asked, instantly crashing me back to reality, releasing me from the vivid nightmare.

I shot up and looked around the dark room. I was on the floor under a blanket and tried to place where I was. I was in Sara's entertainment room, I realized—then I remembered watching the movies.

I felt him sit up next to me. I knew in that moment what had happened, and I was afraid to turn around. I wiped the tears from my eyes and slowly faced him. He looked exactly how I feared—hurt and confused. But he also looked pissed, and I wasn't expecting that. I stared at him, trying to calm my quickened pulse, but it remained heightened with the silent confrontation.

"Nightmare?" he finally asked.

I nodded, preparing for what was about to happen.

"About Evan?" he snapped. I looked down, unable to meet his eyes.

"I get it now," he whispered in agitation. I glanced at him as he shook his head slowly.

"Drew," I pleaded. He stood to put his shoes on and grabbed his jacket. I couldn't find the words to make him stay. The truth was...I didn't want him to stay.

I remained on the floor, watching him disappear down the stairs. That's when I noticed Sara on the couch wrapped in the arms of an unconscious guy. She peered over the arm of the couch with sympathetic eyes, having heard everything. I looked away.

———

"You did much better than I thought you would while we were in San Francisco," Sara said on our flight back from California. "I was waiting for you to lose it."

I was relieved I'd been so convincing. In actuality, I'd searched the face of every guy we passed, hoping to see him.

"I almost called him," I confessed, unable to look at her.

"I'm not surprised, but he wasn't there." My mouth dropped open as I turned to stare at her. "He's snowboarding in Tahoe with some friends for the week."

"How do you know?"

"I asked Jared," she confessed. "I called him when I found out we were staying in San Francisco for a few days, thinking maybe we could bump into Evan so you could get some closure. Don't worry; Jared promised not to tell him."

I didn't know what to say. When I thought about it, I wasn't exactly surprised that Sara did this.

I'd tried so hard not to think about him, but it was impossible not to when we were right there. It ate at me that he was so close, and I could possibly see him at any moment. I picked up my phone probably a million times and hit 5. Every time I saw the pre-programmed *Evan* displayed on the screen, I'd hit *Cancel*. Now those agonizing moments of trying to decide if I could push the *Send* button didn't matter at all. He hadn't even been in San Francisco.

"Speaking of closure," Sara continued, "what are you going to say to Drew?"

"I have to say something, don't I?"

"Yeah, you can't avoid him forever. The school isn't that big." After a pause, she asked nervously, "You are over, aren't you?"

I let out a short laugh. "Don't worry, Sara, I won't continue torturing you. You don't have to pretend to like him anymore. It's over."

"I did like him," she said, then thought better of it. "You're right, I didn't like him. Mostly because I didn't—"

"Like me with him," I finished for her. "I know."

"He wasn't right for you."

"I know," I answered honestly. "Drew is That Guy. I'm pretty sure he would've broken up with me when he realized he wasn't going to get anything. I think it's pretty obvious we're over."

"You still need to tell him," Sara urged. I didn't know what I was going to say. The unavoidable Talk was weighing on me more than I wanted to admit.

But as it turned out, there was no need to worry after all. The whole school knew we were over before we'd even returned from California. I found out when I heard, "I can't believe Drew dumped you for Katie," as soon as I walked into school on Monday. Jill stared at me, waiting for my reaction. She wasn't expecting me to laugh.

It took a few weeks, but the rumors simmered, and I was able to return to my evolving world without any more distractions. Although the rhythm had changed since the beginning of the year, I was content with its predictability, and part of that was being alone—which I readily accepted. I also accepted the silence in the house when I retreated to my room each night.

I kept waiting for Carol to react in some way to my trip to California. But all I heard when I returned from Sara's was about the trip George had surprised her with to Bermuda. I had a feeling George hadn't told her about California. I had no problem putting up with her gloating; it didn't leave bruises.

I concentrated on my classes, continuing to push myself to meet my overachiever expectations. I performed on the basketball court, helping our team finish the regular season with only one other loss. I laughed with Sara more than I used to now that we were "weekend sisters," as she liked to refer to us.

Even the pain that murmured in my chest and the nightmares that continued to wake me became a predictable part of my existence. I accepted them, and I moved on—I was still surviving.

29. FLUTTER

S till not doing a very good job fading," his voice said from behind me.

The paintbrush froze in my hand midstroke and started shaking. My heart stopped in my chest. I didn't know if I could turn around to face him.

I forced my legs to swing to the other side of the stool.

"Hi." He smiled. My heart released a brief flutter.

"Hi," I whispered, forcing myself to breathe.

"When you weren't in the caf, I figured you'd either be here or in the Journalism room."

I could only nod, searching for my voice.

"What are you doing here?" I forced the words from my mouth. My question was barely audible, since I still wasn't breathing properly.

"Looking for you," he answered with his familiar grin. My heart picked up its pace, filling my cheeks with a rush of color. All I could do was stare into his blue eyes, afraid that if I looked away, he'd be gone. *Please convince me I'm not hallucinating.*

"Sorry to hear that the basketball team lost in the semis," he said casually. *He's talking about basketball?* I definitely wasn't hallucinating.

"Thanks," I said, forcing my lips to resemble a smile. *Come on, brain, don't fail me now—say something!*

"Not sure what to say, huh?" He smirked, amused by my inability to form a coherent sentence.

"I'm glad I can…" I threw my hands in the air, forgetting that I was holding a paintbrush, and flung green paint across his grey T-shirt. He looked down at the streak with wide eyes. I held my breath, pressing my lips together. A stifled laugh escaped from behind my pursed lips. Then I couldn't hold back and burst out in laughter.

"That's funny, huh?"

I bit my lower lip, still smiling.

"Let's see if you think *this* is funny." He leaned over my table and rubbed blue paint on his hands. Realizing his intention, I jumped off the stool to escape retaliation.

"Evan, don't," I pleaded.

I'd rounded the corner toward the darkroom when he caught me around the waist, leaving blue handprints on my shirt. When he grabbed me, he didn't let go. He turned me to face him. Still smiling, I connected with his blue eyes, unaware he was pulling me closer. Just before I registered what was happening, my heart ignited, fluttering frantically. My head swirled in a rush. He placed his damp hand on my cheek and leaned down toward me.

A paralyzing charge flashed through my body when his firm lips touched mine. I inhaled his clean scent, allowing the tingling to run through my head. When he slowly pulled away, his eyes searched mine cautiously. I blinked through the buzz, trying to steady myself.

"Emma?" Ms. Mier's voice rang from around the corner.

Evan raised his eyebrows in surprise, then slipped by me into the darkroom. I attempted to sober up before responding.

"Hi, Ms. Mier." My voice cracked. I stepped around the corner to meet her. My face was hot with embarrassment.

"Oh, hi," she said with a smile of surprise. With the smile still lingering, she gathered some papers from her desk. "I needed to get a few things. Could you please lock up when you leave today?"

"Sure," I agreed quickly.

She smiled wider.

"That's a good color on you," she acknowledged.

My face grew even hotter, if that was possible. I looked down at the handprints on my white shirt.

"No, the red I mean."

My eyes widened. I watched her walk to the door and turn the lock.

Before closing the door behind her, she glanced at me and said, "Tell Mr. Mathews I said welcome back."

I nearly fell over. I stood there for a moment, uncertain what to do next. I decided not to think about it anymore and to do what I should have done three months ago.

I walked into the darkroom. Evan was drying his hands next to the sink. I closed the door behind me and leaned against it, unable to move. He threw the paper towel in the basket and looked up, hesitating for a second.

My chest moved with an exaggerated breath. My heart beat frantically against my shirt. He read exactly what I wanted him to in my widened eyes and stepped toward me. I wrapped my arms around his neck, and he pulled me into him. I stood on my toes, extending myself to find him. He held me closer as his lips parted, and I felt the warmth of his breath. My heart released a surge that caught my breath when I felt his soft tongue. His lips were firm but gentle, pressed against mine in a slow, breathless rhythm. Tiny sparks flew through my head and down my spine—my legs trembled beneath me.

I lowered my head to his chest before my legs gave out. He kept his arms wrapped around me, resting his chin on the top of my head, while I listened to his accelerated heartbeat and deep breaths.

I wiped an escaped tear from my eye, trying to remember how to breathe.

"That was worth waiting for," he whispered and then added with sarcasm, "Missed me, huh?"

I looked up at his perfect smile and replied with a smirk, "I survived."

"I heard."

I pulled away and eyed him suspiciously.

"I still have friends here." He shrugged. Just then, the bell rang, declaring the end of the school day. "What do you want to do? Do you have to go home?"

"I'm actually staying over at Sara's tonight."

"You are?" Evan confirmed, raising his eyebrows with a deliberate grin. "Do you think Sara will mind if I kidnap you for a couple of hours?" He casually leaned against the doorway as I went to the sink to scrub his handprint from my face.

My heart faltered.

"Um, I think she'll be fine," I replied, turning to face him. "What are you thinking?"

"We have to talk. I mean, I couldn't have asked for a better way to be welcomed back, but I have some things I need to say before there are any more misunderstandings."

I winced. Couldn't we have left it at the perfect welcome? My stomach twisted, fearful of what he needed to say. I could only imagine, although it couldn't be worse than what I'd been saying to myself since he left.

"So you're back?" I confirmed cautiously.

"Yeah." He grinned. "We'll talk about it."

"Great," I huffed, zipping my sweatshirt to conceal the blue handprints and smear of green paint from his shirt.

Evan laughed. "Don't be so nervous. I'm here, right?" He grabbed my hand, and the warmth from his touch spread up my arm.

The halls were sparsely occupied, since most people had already left. The shocked eyes of those remaining followed us as we traced the familiar route to my locker.

"Mathews!" a few guys yelled out in recognition. Evan nodded in acknowledgment, continuing to walk beside me. I think I was as shocked as everyone else to see him next to me. His firm grasp of my hand was the only thing keeping me from believing that I was dreaming the entire thing.

"So, he found you," Sara observed when we neared our lockers. "I was getting concerned that you'd thrown each other out the window or something—but I can see that didn't happen." She eyed our interlocked hands with a small smile.

"We're going…" I started. "Where are we going?" I looked to Evan for the answer.

"We need to talk," he explained. "So, can I bring her back to your house in a couple of hours?"

"My parents are going out *again*. You can stay and hang out with us tonight if you want. That is if you don't say anything that's going to devastate her more than she's already been for the past three months."

Evan's shoulders shot back as he received the blow. I stared at Sara with my mouth open, shaking my head in disbelief.

"What?!" she shot back. "I'm just saying—"

"Enough," I finished. "*More* than enough!"

I glanced at Evan; he looked pale. I turned to my locker to gather my books before he could read the truth of her words on my face.

"I'll see you later then?" Sara confirmed in her pleasant voice.

"Sure," I replied dismissively, still shocked by her honesty.

Sara walked down the hall, leaving Evan and me alone.

"What did she mean by that?" Evan asked slowly.

"She's just being ridiculous." I wanted him to dismiss her words, but they lingered uncomfortably.

He exhaled in contemplation. "Huh. I guess it wasn't any better for you here."

I didn't understand what he meant and looked to him for translation.

"We'll talk about it," he assured me. "Ready?"

"Sure," I said, closing my locker, his assurance filling me with dread.

Evan took my hand again and escorted me to his car. I didn't say much during the ride, too consumed with the pending 'talk.' I wasn't completely surprised when we pulled into his empty driveway. I couldn't think of another place to give us the privacy we needed for our confessional.

I turned to him in the car before he opened his door.

"Can't I just enjoy that you're here for one day before we make it uncomfortable?"

Evan found my plea amusing. Of course he did.

"I need to do this. I've had three months to obsess over this conversation, so I need to say what I have to say." He flashed a reassuring smile. "Don't worry; it'll be better once we talk."

I wasn't convinced.

I followed him into his house. I was confused when he kept walking down the hall and up the stairs to his room. I hesitated before entering his bedroom. Evan stood at the end of his neatly made bed, waiting for me.

"I wanted you to see that I'm really here."

I glanced around the room and noticed that the shelves were full of books and other personal belongings. I didn't see any taped boxes.

"I'm completely unpacked."

With that, Evan walked out of the room. I continued to follow him through the house and into the barn. My stomach was tangled in nerves when I sat down to face him on the couch. I slid my shoes off and leaned back against the arm of the couch, resting my chin on my knees. I hugged my knees to my chest, prepared for whatever it was we had to talk about.

"What I have to say goes beyond the three months I was gone," he began, playing with the seam of the cushion nervously. "I should have said something the month we weren't talking before I left." He hesitated and then focused on my eyes. He let out a breath and pressed his lips together. I waited anxiously, barely breathing.

"I love you."

My heart pounded loudly. I'd never been told those three words.

"I didn't handle things right. I shouldn't have gotten mad at you like that, and I'm sorry. I said some things I didn't mean, and I pushed you away. I practically hand-delivered you to Drew Carson, which killed me."

I opened my mouth to disagree, but he continued before I could get a word out.

"I know I did, Emma. Don't feel bad about it. But what was worse than that was when I was waiting in the hospital, not knowing. I can't get the image of you motionless on the gym floor out of my head."

I shifted my gaze, unable to look into his pained eyes. I mindlessly picked at my jeans with shaking hands.

"It was the worst moment of my life. And then when you wouldn't see me..." Evan paused to take another breath. I glanced up at him, watching him run his finger along the seam of the couch again. "I knew I'd really screwed up. If I couldn't be there for you... if you didn't *want* me to be there for you, then I couldn't be here at all. So I left.

"But I couldn't do it. I'd still talk to some of the guys, and you'd come up every once in a while when they talked about what happened over the weekend. They'd mention they saw you at a party or they'd talk about basketball. They knew we were close, so they'd bring you up—and I wanted to hear about you. Well…except for that one time."

My eyes shot up, and my stomach turned. He didn't look at me.

"Are you over him?"

"Drew?" I confirmed in disbelief.

"Yeah."

I released a brief humorless laugh, to his surprise. "Yeah, I'm completely over Drew."

"Didn't *he* end things with *you?*" Evan questioned, still perplexed.

"I let people think what they wanted," I confessed, meeting Evan's blue eyes. "Like someone else I know."

He obviously didn't understand what I meant.

"I ended things…well, actually you did," I stated, thinking better of it. I knew Evan still wasn't following. It was my turn to explain. "It became obvious I wasn't over you."

"So you didn't…" Evan examined me cautiously, not knowing how to finish the sentence. My eyes widened in shock, knowing exactly what he was asking.

"Have sex with him?! No!" Color rushed to my face.

"Sorry," he said with a relieved smile. "I just heard…"

I sighed. "Yeah, along with the rest of the school. That was horrible."

Evan let out a brief laugh.

"It's great that you can still find humor in my social catastrophes," I snapped.

"Sorry. I was just imagining your face when you found out what people thought you'd done," he said with a chuckle. "It probably looked a lot like what I just saw, actually."

He let out another quick laugh. I tried to force a scowl, but I was having a hard time keeping a straight face.

"He wasn't your fault," I said softly, suddenly more serious than I wanted to be. Evan quietly listened. "I was angry. I assumed things. I thought I saw more than there actually was between you and Haley…"

"I—" Evan started.

"I know," I interrupted, "and *I'm* sorry for ever thinking you were interested in her. So much wouldn't have happened if I hadn't…I thought you hated me."

Evan's eyes got wider, alarmed by my words.

"I thought I forced you away when you saw me with Drew. I thought you couldn't stand to be near me," I whispered, fiddling with my jeans again. "I hated what I'd done, and I was so furious with myself. I could only imagine what you must have felt. I'm so sorry." I blinked away the tears welling in my eyes, recalling how my rage in the bathroom had festered internally since that day.

Evan slid down the couch and drew my bent knees across his lap. He forced me to look into his reflective blue eyes.

"I didn't hate you," he stated softly. "I could never hate you."

He leaned in and gently pressed his lips to mine. It took me a moment to find my breath after he pulled away.

"So what now?" I whispered.

"I'm here, with you…if you want me," he said with a soft smile. I shoved his arm. "What?! I just wanted to be sure."

"Of course I want you," I shot back.

He smiled.

"Then there's just one more thing." His tone became serious. "I know that you won't tell me what happens at home. I was wrong to try to force you, and I was wrong about what I said to you. You are so much stronger than I ever thought you were. I get why it's hard for you to talk about it. Sara told me that you don't even talk to her about it most of the time. But I know…"

I was having a hard time listening to his words. Ice began to build up in my stomach. I wished he hadn't brought it up.

"And even if you won't, or can't, tell me—I know. I do have to tell you that I can't ever sit in a hospital waiting room again."

"I fell—" I tried to explain.

"Don't," Evan urged. "I know. Without you or Sara telling me, I know. So, even if you can't tell me the truth, don't lie. Don't defend them like it's okay. Because it's not. I won't let them do that to you again. I'm just warning you, I'll make you leave with me if I think that—"

"Evan," I interrupted, "I'm okay. I promise. It's been pretty tolerable since that day, actually. They barely even notice me anymore, and I get to spend the weekends at Sara's. It used to be Saturday nights, but it's evolved to Fridays as well. It's not the same, so don't talk like that. Okay?"

He didn't respond.

"Okay?" I repeated, forcing him to look at me.

"Yeah," he whispered.

I put my hand on his cheek, wanting him to believe me. He took my hand in his and kissed my palm, sending shivers up my arm.

"So we're better?" I confirmed.

A warm smile spread across his face. "Yeah, we're better."

Evan leaned toward me again. This time, when he pressed his lips to mine, he stayed there. He slid me onto his lap as I put my arms around his neck. My heart convulsed in a flood of flutters, capturing my breath. His mouth slowly slid against mine, parting my lips in a gentle motion. I felt his hot breath against my lips and an urgent need shot through me. I straddled his legs and gripped him tighter against me. He pulled away and examined me with a smirk.

"What?" I exclaimed, shocked by his withdrawal.

"It's only my first day back."

I bit my bottom lip with a guilty grin, and color flooded my cheeks.

"Yeah," I said quietly, looking down. "Sorry." I flipped my leg over and sat on the couch next to him again.

Evan laughed at my embarrassed retreat.

"Stop it," I said, sulking while gently kicking his thigh with my foot. "I've waited for forever to kiss you."

He laughed again. "You just surprised me, that's all." He continued to grin as he looked at his watch.

"We should get to Sara's before she believes we *did* push each other out a window. That reminds me—"

"Don't," I begged, not wanting to reflect on Sara's earlier reference to my devastation. "Not now, okay?"

"Okay," he agreed hesitantly, studying me more intently than I was comfortable with.

"What do you want to do tonight?" I asked with bright eyes, trying to deflect the serious moment. "A movie at Sara's?"

"Are you going to fall asleep again?"

"Probably."

I was asleep an hour into the movie. I didn't remember falling asleep with Evan lying behind me on the couch, his arm wrapped around my waist and my hand in his. I was actually convinced that I was going to make it through the entire drama when it started.

"I'm right here," he whispered in confusion.

I shot up at the sound of his voice.

"Emma?"

I sat with my feet on the floor, gripping the cushion on either side of my legs with my heart racing. His hand gently brushed along my back.

"Are you okay?"

"You're here?" I whispered in relief, squinting to look at him.

He examined my face in concern, gently wiping the tear from my cheek.

"Yeah, I'm here," he soothed. A pained realization flashed across his face. "I'm not going anywhere."

Still dazed from my abrupt awakening, I stared at him, uncertain if I was truly awake.

"Come here." He pulled me down to lie on his chest, wrapping his warm arms around me as I drifted back to sleep.

———

I awoke the next morning in the same clothes as the night before. I sat up in a panic.

"Relax," Sara urged from the bed next to me. "We're going to see him tonight. I convinced him to go to a party with us."

I lay back down with a relieved smile, her words confirming that I hadn't been dreaming.

"I don't remember going to bed."

"You had some help," Sara explained with a grin. "I couldn't wake you when I got home, so he carried you in here."

My heart thrust to life as the image of Evan carrying me to bed flashed through my head.

"How was Maggie's?" I asked Sara, rolling on my side to face her.

"Good," Sara replied dismissively. "So…what happened? I've been waiting for you to wake up for a half hour. I was going to jump on your bed if you didn't wake soon. Did he finally kiss you?"

"Sara!" My mouth dropped open.

"Finally!" she grinned wickedly, not needing my confirmation. "How was it?"

"Stop it," I insisted.

"That good, huh?"

"Would you stop assuming things without my answers," I demanded with wide eyes.

"Are you going to answer?"

I smiled, deliberating on whether I could say it out loud.

"Stop beaming and give me *details*. You swore a million years ago that it never happened if you didn't tell me."

She got me there.

"Fine," I conceded with a sigh, sitting up against the pillow and crossing my legs. "Yes, we kissed. Actually I think he kissed me before I completed a sentence."

"No way!" Sara exclaimed. "And…"

"I don't think I can find the right words to describe it," I said pensively. "It was better than I could have ever thought possible."

"Figures," Sara stated with an exaggerated breath. "It only took you forever to give in to it. If you'd listened to me, you would have found out before the soccer season was over."

"Thanks, Sara," I shot back sarcastically, throwing a pillow at her.

"What was the talk about?" Sara inquired, determined to hear everything.

"Basically both of us taking blame for his leaving," I replied. Then I continued to sum up the details, not wanting to think about the awkwardness of the conversation too much.

Sara laughed when I told her how I'd reacted when he'd asked about Drew—and what we *hadn't* done.

"What is it with the two of you, finding humor in my horror?"

"I guess we both know how you react in awkward situations, and it can be pretty funny. Sorry." She smirked. "What's going to happen now?"

"Well, we agreed that we're okay, and he's staying. We didn't have the *relationship conversation*, if that's what you mean, and honestly, I don't think that's something I need to have with Evan."

"Because he's already told you he loves you, right?"

My face reddened as I suppressed a smile.

"Right," she confirmed.

"So what did you say we were doing tonight?" I asked, stopping her from answering her own questions.

"You and I are going shopping today," she explained. I groaned. "Stop. My mother's given us both gift cards for the mall. I figured it was time you owned your own pink sweater."

I grinned in agreement.

"And then we're going to Alison Bartlett's party. It's supposed to be pretty big, just to warn you."

"Great," I grunted, but I was slightly comforted when she confirmed that Evan was picking us up so that we could all go together.

As Sara was contorting my hair into a loose, curly knot at the base of my neck, I asked, "Sara, you haven't mentioned an interest in anyone lately. What's going on with *you*?"

"I don't know," she remarked with a sigh. "I'm tired of the games, I guess. I don't think I'm going to find a guy in our school. That reminds me, we're going to New York next weekend. We're staying with my cousin at Rutgers and driving to Cornell for the day on Saturday to view the campus and meet with their coach. So who knows, maybe I'll meet a college guy!"

"We're what?!" I choked.

"Sorry, I forgot to mention it. Your uncle thinks my parents are coming. They're not, so don't say anything to get caught in a lie."

I gawked at her in disbelief.

Sara added with a heavy breath before I could even think it, "Don't worry. Evan's meeting us in the city Saturday night. I asked him last night."

"I didn't say anything," I said with a smile.

"You didn't have to," she said, rolling her eyes. "Em, I'm glad Evan's back—you know that, right?"

"Yeah," I replied cautiously, concerned by her tone.

"I want to make sure that you're going to be okay if Carol and George find out."

"I dated Drew without them finding out," I stated, not understanding what she was worried about.

"That was different," she tried to explain. "It's harder for you to hide it when you're with Evan. It'll be obvious to anyone who sees you that there's something going on with you—you're glowing. So, I need to know that it's going to be okay?"

Sara's nervousness caused me to hesitate before answering. It was going to be okay, wasn't it? I had to believe it would be.

"I hope so," I answered honestly. "Sara, I listened to what you told me that time at Janet's, about why you decided to go out with Jared, and I think I need to do the same thing. I'd rather be with Evan, knowing it may cause me some stress at home, than to never have this chance to be with him."

"It's different for you," she responded, still concerned. "You're risking a lot if Carol finds out."

"I'll survive," I promised. She didn't appear satisfied with my answer but remained silent.

"You're not going to fight this and make it hard for me, are you?" I questioned.

"No," she said with a warm smile. "I'm happy for you—honestly. So, let's go. Let's let everyone know Evan's back and that you two are *finally* together."

"Yay," I groaned, as we walked down the stairs. "That's exactly what I want tonight to be about."

30. LIFE OF THE PARTY

A vibrant smile emerged on Evan's face when we neared the bottom of the stairs. I couldn't help but smile in return.

"That's definitely my favorite sweater," Evan confessed when I reached the bottom step.

"I told you!" Sara exclaimed, reminding me of my hesitation to purchase the pink sweater with a swooping neckline and a just-as-revealing back. The heat on my face crept to my ears and down my neck.

While we were putting on our coats, Evan asked Sara, "Do you mind if Emma and I go for a quick walk before we go? I have to ask her something."

Sara flashed me a glance and answered, "Sure. Come get me when you're ready."

My heart was paralyzed in my chest, unable to think of what else he might want to know. My fear was justified when the question left his mouth.

"So, the nightmares..." he remarked quietly. "That's what Sara was talking about yesterday, huh?"

I avoided his eyes, following the ground as we walked.

"I'm sorry," he said, forcing me to look up into his troubled eyes with a tilt of his head.

"It's not your fault," I whispered.

"I'll make it up to you, I promise," he said with a soft smile.

Evan put his arms around my waist as I reached up on my toes and pressed my lips against his. He held me tighter, and sparks ricocheted through my body. I breathed him in with each slow, deliberate pass of our lips. My head buzzed as his rhythm quickened and our lips parted. I let out a quick breath, pressing against him. He lifted his head with a grin.

"Why do you keep doing that?" I demanded in frustration, not wanting it to be over.

"We're in the middle of the street," he noted, glancing around. I slowly sank to my feet, releasing my hold with a sulking breath.

He wore an amused grin as we made our way back to Sara's. I examined him curiously, silently demanding an explanation.

"Just not what I expected from you," he explained. My eyes tightened in concern, to which he quickly blurted, "Oh, it's not bad, believe me. It's just…you *are* interesting."

We parked in a large field across from Alison Bartlett's house, which was already filled with cars. Her house was about a mile in from the road, with no neighbors in sight—probably why it was such a popular party. The noise of conversation and music carried across the field as we stepped out of the car.

"I'm not going to be the third wheel," Sara declared. "So I'm going in by myself, and I'll meet you in there."

"Are you sure?" I asked, surprised.

"Yeah, definitely," she laughed. "Besides, I want to see everyone's reaction when you walk in."

I shook my head in disbelief as she walked toward the noise.

I nervously looked at Evan as he came around the car to meet me. He stopped in front of me and took both of my hands in his.

"Ready?" he asked with a half smile.

I shrugged. "Sure."

He leaned down and delicately grazed my lips with his. The tease left me breathless, burning for more.

"I keep having to remind myself that I can do that," he smirked. "I've been programmed that it was off limits for so long; now it's going to take some getting used to."

"You definitely have my permission," I said breathily, reaching for him again.

Just before we were able to connect, I heard, "Holy shit! Evan Mathews?"

I sank back to my flat feet with a groaning sigh.

"Wait. *And* Emma Thomas? This is crazy."

I turned to face the annoyance. Of all the people to find out first!

"Hi, Jay," Evan said casually. I clenched my teeth together before I turned to face him.

"Hi," I said quickly, feeling the burning cover my cheeks—so much for subtle entrances.

"When did you get back?" Jay asked Evan.

"Yesterday."

Jay raised his eyebrows and looked back and forth between us, "Wasting no time, I see."

My eyes widened as my mouth dropped open. "Jay!"

"Just saying," he said, with his all-too-familiar feigned innocence.

"Going in?" Evan asked, ignoring his comment.

"Yeah."

Evan took my hand, and we walked alongside Jay into the house. There were people scattered on the front lawn and steps as we approached. The open door released a blare of music and voices that became practically deafening as we got closer. I pushed out a quick breath through my pursed lips before we entered. Evan squeezed my hand and glanced at me with a grin. Jay squirmed his way in ahead of us.

It was as bad as I feared. There was gawking, whispering and even some pointing as we made our way through the crowd toward the kitchen. The guys welcomed Evan back with enthusiasm, while the girls just stared in shock, whispering to each other as we passed. Why had I thought coming here was a good idea?

"You made it!" Sara praised as we squeezed into the kitchen. "Well, *everyone* knows you're here now. Jay was seriously the first person you saw?" She shook her head in amazement. "You couldn't have made a quieter entrance, could you?"

Evan laughed while I groaned at her sarcasm.

"This is crazy," I yelled to Sara as I took in the shoulder-rubbing mass of bodies that continued to the deck. Sara nodded in agreement.

"Do you want something to drink?" Evan leaned in close to ask in my ear.

I nodded.

Evan went in search of the bar, and within a few feet was completely devoured by the crowd.

"Emma!" Jill exclaimed as she wiggled through to get to us. She looked around. "Where's Evan? I heard you came here together." Sara laughed.

"He's getting drinks," I shouted back to her, resigned that this was probably going to be the topic of the night.

"I am so excited for you," she shrieked. "Finally! I heard he came back once he heard about you and Drew."

"What?!" I yelled, shocked by the latest rumor. "Where does this stuff come from?!"

Jill shrugged.

"You're together, right?" she confirmed cautiously.

"Yeah," I said slowly, and then added emphatically, "but Drew has nothing to do with it."

"Let the stories begin," Sara declared with an amused expression. I eyed her disapprovingly.

"Hi!" Lauren shouted with a huge smile on her face. "You and Evan, huh? That is so amazing!"

"Hi, Lauren," I said with a sigh.

"Where is he?" she asked looking around.

"Getting drinks," Jill shouted back.

"Is there anywhere we can go that doesn't require yelling?" I asked.

Jill pointed to the porch. I debated whether I should wait for Evan, but being jostled by the crowd and having to holler to be heard was wearing on me. Convinced he'd find us, I nodded to the girls to head out the door. We held on to each other's arms so we wouldn't get separated as we maneuvered through the human maze.

I took a breath of the cool air, relieved to be away from the confines of the house.

"Great," Jill said facing me, "now we can hear all about it. When did he get back?"

I knew this was coming, but it didn't make the grilling any less uncomfortable.

"Yesterday."

"And..." Lauren encouraged. "What happened?"

I wasn't sure what to say as I looked at their eager faces.

"There you guys are," Casey exclaimed. The girls opened the circle to welcome her.

"Emma was just telling us about what happened with Evan," Lauren explained.

"Evan's back?" Casey asked in disbelief.

They laughed at her cluelessness.

"Where have *you* been?" Jill gawked.

Casey shrugged sheepishly.

"So..." Lauren pressed, looking back at me.

"Um...he apologized, I apologized, and that's it. We're...better." They looked confused, not pleased with the lack of detail.

"That's it?" Casey asked, still not understanding what was going on.

"What do you mean?" I asked innocently.

Lauren moaned in frustration. "I wanted to hear how he swept you in his arms, begging for you to take him back, and kissed you for hours." Her dramatization caused us all to burst out laughing.

"Sorry," I shrugged, still smiling. "It's not going to happen."

"Does he know about Drew?" Jill cringed.

"Yeah," I said quietly.

"Does he know *everything*?" Casey asked in shock. I rolled my eyes, knowing exactly what she meant.

"Casey!" Sara exclaimed swatting at her arm. "You really suck with keeping up. That never happened!"

"Oh," Casey said apologetically.

"Just to warn you, he's here," Lauren said. "And he's not with Katie. They broke up Thursday night."

"That's fine," I shrugged, not really concerned about seeing Drew, with or without Katie.

"They broke up already?" Sara gasped.

"Definitely," Jill murmured under her breath. She looked around, realizing that she'd been overheard and we were all waiting for her to continue.

"Jill, don't you dare hold out," Sara threatened.

"You have to promise not to tell *anyone*," Jill stressed, then continued without waiting for our commitment. "Drew got Katie pregnant."

"No he didn't!" Lauren stated in wide-eyed shock.

"Well, she's not anymore," Jill continued, loving that she was the one revealing the headlining gossip.

"Did she..." Sara started, but Jill shrugged before she could ask.

"Not sure what happened exactly. Either she lost it or her parents made her get rid of it," Jill explained dismissively, not really concerned with the truth. "But I think Drew just dated her because she was pregnant and broke up with her when he didn't have to deal with it anymore."

"Wait," I interjected pensively. "When did she get pregnant?"

The girls turned toward me with sympathetic eyes, wondering the same thing I was.

"Not while you were together," Jill told us. "I guess they hooked up over the holiday break, before you were 'official.'"

"I can't believe she was pregnant," Casey said, mouthing the last word, still absorbing the news.

I felt bad for Katie, and the fact that we were standing in the backyard at a party talking about her most intimate secret made me feel guilty, whether it was true or not.

I wandered away from the conversation, not wanting to hear any more. I scanned the crowd along the deck, looking for Evan. I saw him at the top of the stairs, searching the faces below in the yard. Our eyes connected, and he grinned, making me smile in return.

"Hi," he said, greeting me with a crooked smile as he approached. "I figured you wouldn't want to stay inside."

I shook my head, taking the bottle of soda he handed me. He set his hand on my lower back, escorting me back to the girls. With the exception of Sara, they all looked at us with ridiculous gawking grins. I rolled my eyes.

"Hi, Evan," Jill sang. "Welcome back." Lauren and Casey giggled.

"Thanks," he said politely, giving me a quizzical glance. I just shook my head and sighed.

Our small group stayed outside and talked about the latest gossip, usually inspired by the people passing by. Evan and I stood there quietly, his arm around my waist, forced to listen. There were periodic interruptions when someone recognized Evan and would ask about his return.

"I'm going to the bathroom," I told the girls while Evan was talking to a guy from the soccer team.

"I'll go with you," Sara announced, grabbing me by the arm.

"This party isn't so bad," Sara said in my ear as we climbed the stairs to the deck. I shrugged, agreeing reluctantly.

We made our way through the kitchen and found the line for the bathroom.

"I hope you don't have to go that bad," Sara said, eyeing the wait.

"I'll be fine," I assured her, leaning against the wall.

"Tony Sharpa asked me out," Sara confessed casually.

"When did this happen?" I asked, trying to recall how long she was in here before Evan and I found her.

"Yesterday, during study."

"Why didn't you tell me?!" I asked in astonishment.

"It wasn't that important," she laughed. "Not with Evan coming back and everything. Besides, I said no. He's the 'games' I was referring to earlier."

"Yeah, didn't you like him when he was dating Niki, and then he liked you when you were with Jason?"

She nodded, recalling the bad timing of their interest in one another.

"So, what's wrong now? You're both single finally," I questioned, confused.

"I don't know," she said, sighing. "It feels forced now."

"That doesn't make any sense," I replied in confusion.

"I heard you were here," a voice said from behind me. My heart stopped, and my stomach turned. I stood frozen, unable to turn around.

Before I could pull myself together to face him, Drew appeared beside me, leaning his shoulder against the wall. My nose scrunched at the burn of liquor floating on his breath. It appeared he needed the wall to keep from falling to the floor.

"Had a little to drink, Drew?" Sara accused.

"Hi, Sara," Drew slurred with a smile. "You didn't like me, did you?"

Sara smiled, amused by his drunken honesty.

"Still don't," Sara replied with a malicious grin. "Maybe you should leave us alone."

We were gaining an audience. Everyone around us quieted down to listen. I glanced around, wondering how to get out of this without causing a scene.

"We need to talk . . . in private." Drew tightly gripped my wrist and dragged me stumbling after him into the bathroom, pushing past the person who was about to enter. Sara reached out to grab me, but the crowd closed in around Drew and me, barricading her as we moved past them.

He forced me ahead of him and shut the door behind us, locking it.

"Drew," Sara banged on the other side of the door. "Let her out."

"Leave us the fuck alone, Sara!" Drew yelled back, agitated.

I scanned the large white bathroom, looking for another way out. Drew turned and leaned his back against the door, ignoring Sara's banging.

"What do you want, Drew?" I confronted him coolly, despite the tremors that were overtaking me.

"Just wanted to talk to you," he mumbled, taking a step toward me. I backed away from him, dragging my feet along the tiles.

"Go ahead, talk."

"Don't be like that." He reached for me, trying to take my hand. I pulled it out of reach. The music stopped abruptly, and more people banged on the door, yelling for Drew to open it. It didn't seem to faze him as he slowly approached me. I ran out of tiles beneath my feet, my back bumping into the wall.

"I just wanted you to know that I forgive you." He dragged his hand along my cheek, snagging a few strands of hair with it. A cloud of liquor floated from his parted lips as he continued, "You don't have to be with him just to get back at me."

I was confused by his words and tried to look him in the eye. Except he couldn't focus on anything—his eyes twitched in a drunken dance.

"I'll take you back," he muttered, leaning down toward me. I turned my head—his wet mouth pressed against my cheek.

The weight of his body pinned me against the wall as he trailed his tongue along my neck. I tried to shove him off, but I was his wall now, holding him up. He held me to him, ignorant of my squirming. He groped my breast while grinding into me.

"Drew, stop!" I yelled, pushing him back with all I could. He held tighter, aggressively pawing at me like we were in some impassioned exchange.

There was a crash of splintering wood as the door burst open. Drew was pulled from me and all I could see were faces, staring. There was a group of guys struggling to get in. I thought I saw a glimpse of Evan in the twist of arms and hands before Sara grabbed my arm, and we rushed through the gawking mob.

Scuffling could be heard behind us, with girls screaming and guys swearing. I tried to look over my shoulder before we were out the front door. I could only see bodies pushing in a frantic wave, some to get away, others to move closer.

Not long after we reached the car, Evan caught up with us. He was breathing heavily and his shirt was crumpled. He pulled me against him and held me. I tried not to reveal how shaken up I was.

I pulled back to look up at his face. It was still flushed. Sara was standing to the side, quietly watching. "I'm okay," I assured him. "He was just really drunk. He didn't mean it."

"Don't." Evan stopped me. "Don't make excuses for him. I can't..."

He took a calming breath.

"Let's just go," he urged.

People were still staring at us from the front steps when we got into the car. The party inside resumed, with the music turned up again and the volume of voices steadily increasing. Evan took my hand in silence as he drove away.

31. NOTICED

I begged the week to go by quickly or for someone to do something more catastrophic and humiliating so Evan, Drew and I would be dropped from the headlines. Then Katie returned to school, and I wished I hadn't thought that. Everyone stared, whispered and pointed, avoiding her as if she carried a contagion.

I knew pity wasn't what she needed, but I didn't know what else to offer. If *my* secret were released to the masses, I'd want to drop off the planet. So, whether it was the right decision or not, I left her alone. I didn't avoid her, but I didn't go out of my way to make her feel better either. My ambivalence could've been considered cowardice. Yes, it probably was. I found Katie crying in the girls' room on Friday, and slipped out before she knew I was there.

———

"Things are going to change around here." The threatening voice stopped me from taking another step.

I stood in the hallway motionless, with my backpack over my shoulder and duffel bag in my hand. I had just returned from my weekend in New York with Evan and Sara. Carol met me with a hardened glare. I hadn't heard her hateful voice in so long; I'd forgotten how debilitating it could be.

"No more Friday nights at the McKinleys'. You got away with it for too long and sleazed out of your responsibilities too often. You're not getting away with your shit anymore. You *should* be shoved in a box, but…"

My pulse quickened in anticipation of what she'd say next.

"…your uncle seems to think it would help with the tension in the house if we had one day to ourselves. It's not worth arguing over. *You* are never worth arguing over. So tell Sara she can pick you up at noon on Saturdays—however, you will be in this house by nine o'clock on Sunday morning.

"But not next weekend. You're staying here to rake my backyard and my mother's on Sunday. Speaking of Sundays—"

Please don't say it.

"—you'll only be allowed to go to the library, nowhere else. If I find out that you're anywhere other than where you say you are, you *will* be living in a box until you graduate." My stomach twisted. I remained frozen, hoping she'd slither away without leaving a mark. Not so lucky.

"Am I making myself clear?" she growled, grabbing my ear, making me twist my head to follow the tugging.

"Yes," I whimpered, straining my neck.

I stood in the hall with my hand over my throbbing ear, watching my freedom disappear with her. I threw my bags on my bed upon entering my room and began pacing furiously. Why was she doing this to me? Why couldn't she have left me alone like she had for the past three months? What was the sudden interest in where I was? She hated me. Why would she want me home?

My chest tightened as I fumed at the thought of having to be with her all weekend. And knowing that I wasn't going to see Evan next weekend was more upsetting than spending it with *her*. Well… maybe not.

Unbeknownst to me, Evan and Sara had decided to split my pickups and drop-offs, so I wasn't expecting to see his BMW waiting for me when I walked down the driveway on Monday morning. But I was too distracted by the impending doom of next weekend to be as thrilled as I should've been.

He greeted me warmly when I closed the door. "Good morning."

"Hi," I responded, unable to smile in return.

"Are you ever in a good mood in the morning?"

"What?" His question distracted me from my brooding thoughts. "Oh, sorry. I'm just angry with my aunt right now."

"What happened?" His voice was heavy with concern, more than it needed to be.

"Nothing that bad," I assured, trying to put him at ease. "She's making me stay home this weekend, and I'm pissed. Sorry, I don't mean to be miserable."

"Are you going to the library on Sunday?"

"No, I'm going to her mother's to rake her yard," I grumbled.

"So…" he said, without needing to say any more.

"Yeah," I said with a sigh. "I'm trying to figure out when we'll be able to see each other."

"There's always next weekend," he said to console me.

"You're giving up that easy?" I shot back, questioning his resolve.

"No," Evan replied with a light laugh. "But what other choice do we have, besides you sneaking out of your house?"

A flash of cold nerves streaked through my stomach at the thought of trying to climb out of my window without being heard. But then I was overcome with a spike of adrenaline. *Could I really do this?*

"That may be an option."

Evan shot me a sideways glance. "You want to sneak out of your house?" he confirmed in astonishment.

"I can do this," I declared out loud, trying to convince myself more than Evan.

The repercussions of getting caught sent a wave of nausea through me, but the thrill of getting away with it convinced me that it was worth it. I wasn't going to allow her to control my life any longer. It was more important to try than not to have the chance at all. Where had I heard that before?

"You are insane!" Sara exclaimed when I told her what I was planning to do. "If you get caught, we will never see you again!"

"But, Sara," I argued, "aren't you the one who said that it was better to try and fail than never to have the experience?"

"That's not quite what I said," she corrected. "Em, this is so much different than having a date with a guy I may never see again. You could lose everything."

I looked down at my uneaten lunch, understanding her concern. If I were the same person I'd been six months ago, we'd never be having this conversation. Too much had happened, and I wasn't ready to go back.

"Sara," I murmured, "what do I really have? If it weren't for you and Evan, I wouldn't even exist, or I might as well not exist. I need more than school and sports to keep me wanting to move forward. I can't be that person anymore, not now that I know the difference."

Sara sat silently, breaking off pieces of her cookie without eating them.

"Are you sure there isn't a way for you to move out of their house?" she finally questioned. "If you get caught..." She couldn't look me in the eye.

"I won't get caught," I assured her. We sat in silence for a moment, picking at our food.

"Are you going to the basketball award ceremony tomorrow night?" Sara asked, changing the subject.

"I put it on the calendar, and they didn't say anything, so I think so."

"Are you staying at school, or should my parents and I pick you up at your house?"

"I'll probably stay here. I have to work on the newspaper and my History paper, so there's no point in going home." There was never a point in going home, but it was unavoidable, no matter how much I delayed the return. I didn't have any other choice.

———

"Congratulations," she said as Sara and I walked into the cool spring evening.

I approached her, but not with the shock of our first encounter. I wasn't surprised to see her, but I was surprised by her sobriety. My mother appeared uncomfortably nervous standing on the sidewalk. She had her hands in her jacket pockets, glancing from the ground to my face, awaiting my reaction.

Sara didn't continue to the parking lot but waited a short distance away to give us room to talk. I walked closer to the frail woman whom I barely resembled except for her dark brown hair and the almond shape of her eyes.

"I am so proud of you," she said gently, glancing up at me. "Captain next year, that's great, Emily."

"Co-captain," I corrected. She smiled lightly as she held my gaze with her sparkling eyes.

"I went to some of your games and saw you play." Her smile grew bigger.

"I know," I answered quietly. "I heard you yelling in the stands." My mother's bellows were unmistakable, since she was the only one yelling "Emily" among the cheering crowd.

"I've decided to stop drinking," she declared proudly. "I haven't had anything to drink since December." I could only nod, uncertain if I believed her words. I had no proof of the alleged truth other than her current condition.

"I got a new job too," she continued. "I'm an executive assistant at an engineering firm a couple towns over."

"You moved to Connecticut?" I questioned, shocked by this revelation.

"I wanted to be closer to you," she told me with an eager expression. "I was hoping we could see each other...if you wanted to."

My shoulders pulled back at this request. "We'll see," I replied, unable to commit. She nodded, her shoulders slumped in disappointment.

"I understand," she whispered, looking at the ground. "Are you okay?" She looked up at me again, searching for more than the three words asked.

"I'm okay," I assured her with a tight smile. Her concerned eyes didn't release their scrutiny.

"Would you mind if I went to some of your track meets? I know they're usually during the week, but if you have a weekend meet, would it be alright?"

I shrugged. "If you want." I really wanted to tell her not to come—that I preferred not to see her again. But I couldn't look into her desperate eyes and reject her so blatantly.

"I need to go," I told her, nodding toward Sara.

My mother acknowledged Sara with her charming smile. "Hi. I'm Emily's mother, Rachel."

"Hi." Sara responded with a kind smile of her own. "I'm Sara. It's nice to meet you."

"Well, you girls be careful driving home," she told us. My eyebrows pulled together in reaction to her words. The concern sounded strange coming from her mouth.

"I'm so proud of you," my mother said with welling eyes. I couldn't stand to see the sentiment—it contradicted everything I knew of her. She was the one who hadn't wanted me. Why should she care now?

"Thanks," I said and quickly turned away, striding toward Sara's car. Sara was a few quick steps behind me, not expecting my sudden departure.

"Are you all right?" she asked when we neared her car. "Did she say something wrong that I missed?"

"*Everything* she said was wrong," I declared, slipping into the passenger seat stiffly.

Sara studied me carefully before pulling out of the spot. I knew she wanted to understand, but she couldn't find the words to ask me to explain. So I didn't.

"Do you want to come over to my house for a little while, or do you think they're expecting you home?" Sara asked. "My parents left from here to go to a dinner for my mom's company, so they won't be home."

"I should go home," I decided quietly, looking out the window. "She's acting strange again, and I don't need her saying anything to me tonight. I don't think I could let her get away with it."

I ignored Sara's shocked expression and continued to stare out the window.

———

"So what's the plan for tomorrow night?" Evan asked during our walk to the Art room.

"There's a park a few streets away from my house," I explained, having dwelled on the details all week. "Meet me there at ten o'clock."

"Will they be in bed by then?" I heard the unease in his voice.

"No, but if we wait till then, it'll be so late." I exhaled slowly, recognizing the risk of trying to slip out while they were in the next room watching television. But I also knew that they never came into my room at night, so I was fairly confident they wouldn't check on me while I was gone. "It'll be fine."

"We don't have to do this," Evan said.

"Are you backing out?"

"No," he said quickly. "I just don't want you to get in trouble."

"Don't worry about it," I reassured him with forced confidence.

"Okay." He released a heavy breath before kissing me on the top of my head.

With a promise to text Sara on Sunday as proof that I still existed, I exited her car to begin my gut-wrenching weekend with Carol. The only thing that kept me from festering in fury was the thought of sneaking out to see Evan the next night.

I spent Saturday in the yard raking while the kids jumped in the piles of leaves. Carol was nowhere to be seen, so being outside, surrounded by their laughter, actually made the day enjoyable. George arrived home soon after I was done bagging the last pile. For such a small yard, it was astonishing how many leaves sat under the snow all winter. While I was out there, I moved the trash cans on the side of the house so I had a clear spot to drop to under my window. I figured I could use the metal trash can to climb back through the window when I returned, as long as I remembered to stand on the rims of the can. I was also concerned about moving the heavy can without it making noise. My stomach turned just thinking about it. Of course we were the only family in America who still owned metal trash cans—just my luck.

I had no appetite for dinner. I forced each bite of the lasagna into my mouth. It wasn't horrible, since it was one of the few dishes Carol could handle without disastrous results. Not wanting to draw any unnecessary attention, I finished the food on my plate. I gently pulled down my sleeve, reminded of what Carol's attention felt like.

Was it possible that I'd forgotten what she was capable of? The inflamed skin along my forearm was a brand, a reminder of her seething affection. Carol had played off my contact with the searing lasagna pan as an accident, but I saw her eyes dance when I jumped back with a quick, pained inhale. Did I really dare to test the limits of her loathing by sneaking out my window?

My stomach turned anxiously as I stared at the painted sky while washing dishes. I only had a few more hours to decide whether I was capable of doing this. I thought of Evan and whether I could disappoint him. I knew he'd understand if I backed out. Then I thought of how disappointed *I* would be, and whether I could live with that. I absently rinsed the dishes and placed them in the dishwasher, the movement of my shirt irritating the raw, bubbling skin.

I slipped into my room after taking out the trash, checking the can placement once again. I considered burying myself in homework to persuade time to pass quickly. But I knew I wouldn't be able to concentrate.

I opted to lie on my bed and drown out my nausea with music—it didn't help. A thousand incoherent thoughts raced through my head as I stared at the ceiling. I'd start to visualize my escape route and then get worked up about the potential disasters. Could I drop from the window to the ground without making a sound? Would one of the neighbors see me and say something? What would I say if they discovered I was missing or caught me outside? My stomach turned, and my palms dampened.

I picked up my phone to text Evan that I wasn't going to meet him. With the words displayed on the screen, I started pulling at my lower lip. Could I do this? I wanted to see him so much. I couldn't force myself to hit *Send*. I dug my teeth into my lip and hit *Cancel*. I still had an hour and a half to decide.

The seconds ticked away like minutes—I couldn't keep still.
I tapped my foot rapidly in the air, contemplating my choices.
Should I give in to what I wanted to do, or to what I should do?
But why shouldn't I get to see Evan? Why was I letting them decide
what was right for me? It's not like I was sneaking off to get drunk
or get into any real trouble. They never had to know. I swallowed
hard and bit my lip again.

The last forty-five minutes were the worst. I thought the heat
in my stomach was going to burn through my skin. I shut off the
music and listened to the low talking coming from the TV through
the wall. Eventually, I slid off my bed and walked breathlessly to
my closet with deliberate steps. I removed the stuffed duffel bag
from the closet, placed it on my bed, and folded my comforter over
it. I knew it didn't look much like a body, but I couldn't bear the
thought of having my bed completely flat in my absence.

I examined the facade of the rumpled blankets over the back
for a minute, almost panting with anxiety. I ran through the plan in
my head one more time and inhaled quickly, biting my lip. Should
I leave the window open, or would they notice the cool air if they
walked by my door to go to the bathroom? How would I close it?
I'd have to stand on a trash can. I clenched my teeth and held my
breath in agony just thinking about moving it while they were a
window away. I removed the phone from my pocket and lingered
over the buttons, ready to cancel once again.

Hadn't George just thrown away an empty milk crate that used
to have paint cans in it? That would be high enough for me to reach
the window to close it. I put the phone back in my pocket. I shut
off my light with twenty minutes left to wait. I sat on the floor with
my knees drawn into me, staring up at the window. I watched the
stars blink through our neighbor's swaying trees, allowing the last
few minutes to tick away. *I can do this*—I had to believe it. I took a
breath to calm the pounding in my chest.

My hands shook as I placed my thumb and finger under the ridge of the wooden frame along the cold pane of glass. I held my breath, giving it a forceful but restrained push. The frame gave way slightly, and the first gust of cool spring air blew against my legs. I stopped to listen, my pulse beating in my ears. I could faintly hear voices from the TV continuing to play in the background but couldn't sense any movement.

I held my breath again and pushed the window up farther. I continued inching it up until it was completely open. With my heart beating in my throat, I slid a leg out the window and laid my chest forward to slide my other leg through. I held on to the wooden frame to drop to the ground. I nearly yelled out when I felt the hands around my waist.

"Shhh," he whispered in my ear, lowering me to the ground. I leaned my back against the house, afraid I was going to collapse from heart failure. I stared up at Evan with huge eyes, my hands covering my frantic heart.

"Sorry," he whispered. I covered his mouth, silently begging him not to make any noise.

I searched around for the milk crate. It was difficult to find in the small dark path between the house and the fence, but I finally located the square shape along the fence and placed it under the window. Evan realized what I was doing and touched my arm to indicate that he'd do it. He stood on the crate to lower the window. I pressed my lips together, barely breathing as I watched him ease it into place.

He grabbed my hand after he stepped down, and we slowly made our way along the side of the house until we reached the corner. I heard the television through the closed window above our heads and stiffened. Evan nodded his head, encouraging me to follow him. I hugged the front of the house, under the large glowing glass that peered into the living room. I knew how close they were and held my breath.

Just then, a floodlight lit up across the street, exposing us in the shadows of the house. Evan grabbed my arm and pulled me against him in the dark corner that connected with the wall of the front foyer. I heard his quickened breath, or maybe it was mine. I bit my lip, inhaling quickly when Carol peeked through the curtain to investigate. She let the curtain fall, uninterested when she saw the neighbor getting into his car.

Evan released me when the car drove down the street out of sight. I let out a small burst of air. He smiled. I widened my eyes, shocked by his reaction. He pushed his lips together to keep from laughing. I hit his arm in frustration.

Evan grabbed my hand again and rushed across the front yard. We jogged past a few houses before slowing to a walk. I jumped when I heard his voice.

"You thought we were going to get caught, didn't you?"

"No," I snapped. "But I can't believe you thought that was funny."

"I wouldn't say it was *funny*," he stated. "Well…maybe it was. I've never had to sneak out before, so I did find it…entertaining."

I was still trying to convince myself that I'd made it out safely. I wasn't as amused. Evan put his arm around my shoulder, pulling me toward him. I looked up at his calm, grinning face, and my anxiety melted away. I released a small smile and leaned my head against his shoulder.

"It's been too long since you've been exposed to something new," Evan noted, sitting across from me on the top of the twisted climbing structure in the park.

"This was something new. I've never snuck out before. I guess your bad influence over me hasn't changed."

The white of Evan's teeth reflected in the subtle light.

"I still can't believe you snuck out of your house," he said with a chuckle.

"What other choice did I have?" I said defensively, still not as amused as Evan.

"You didn't have to see me."

"Yes I did."

He leaned forward to kiss me, and my heart skipped in anticipation of the touch of his lips. I leaned in to meet him. Before I could reach him, my legs slipped through the hole that they were dangling in. I fell to the ground, landing on my feet with a thud. I groaned in frustration.

Evan smiled, looking down at me. "Are you okay?"

"Yes," I huffed. He slid down, landing in front of me. Still grinning, he put his arms around my waist and playfully rocked my hips from side to side.

"That was pretty funny." He casually bent down to kiss me.

"Great," I grunted, turning my head away. It was impossible to remain frustrated with his teasing when I felt the warmth of his kiss on my neck. I inhaled as he pulled me closer, and I wrapped my hands around the backs of his firm arms.

The fluttering rushed from my stomach and through my head as I turned to intercept his lips. They delicately slid across mine, inching at a slow, sensual pace, causing a warmth to spread through my chest. I slid my arms around to grip his back and pulled myself closer. He ran his fingers in my hair as his pace quickened with my breath. When he slipped away, I kept my eyes closed, resting my head against him while still holding him tightly. His chest moved beneath me as he attempted to catch his breath.

"What should we do next Sunday?" I asked, releasing my grasp and jogging over to the swings. My sudden departure must have caught him off guard, because he wasn't behind me when I turned around to sit on the plastic seat.

"Um…" he considered, walking toward me. "Let me think about it." Evan sat on the swing next to mine with a contemplative smirk.

"I wouldn't mind going back to the batting cages," I suggested. "But I'm sure you don't want to do that since you play baseball all week."

"I'll come up with something," he promised. "Speaking of going back, I think we're good enough friends now for you to tell me who your first kiss was."

My heart skipped a beat.

"You still want to know?" I questioned.

"He doesn't go to our school, right?" Evan inquired, answering my question with his.

"No." I shook my head. "I met him last summer, when I went to Maine with Sara. He doesn't even know where I really live."

"Nice," he declared with a smile. "Your first kiss is a guy who knows nothing about you."

"Well, I didn't lie about *everything*," I said in defense.

"Poor guy." Evan laughed. "But you just kissed him, right?" I recognized the concern wrapped in his question.

"You know that answer," I replied. "But what about you? I mean, I know you didn't do anything with Haley, but you never said…"

I couldn't come right out and directly ask him if he'd had sex. Did I really want to know? That question left me torn—part of me was curious, while the other couldn't imagine him being with someone else.

Evan was quiet for a moment. I almost asked him not to answer—to forget I'd asked.

"She was my best friend in San Francisco," he confessed before I could withdraw my question. My heart tightened, not prepared for his answer. "We were really great friends for over a year before deciding to date. We trusted each other, and it eventually happened last summer. But it was never the same after. We should have just stayed friends, and both of us knew it—but it was too late."

"Beth?" I whispered, recalling him mentioning her the night I met his parents.

"Yes."

"Oh," I replied, looking down, unable to say anything else.

"Does that bother you?" he asked cautiously.

I shrugged. "I didn't know you, and…" I hesitated. "I guess it's still hard to think of you being with another girl."

"I know," he replied, relating to my discomfort. A twinge of guilt shot through me.

"Do you still care about her? I mean…did you see her when you went back?" The anticipation of his answer caused my stomach to knot up.

Evan stopped his subtle swaying on his swing and turned toward me with a calm, still face.

"I've never felt like I do for you…for *anyone*," he vowed. "Beth and I were friends. I cared about her, but I didn't…It's not even remotely the same."

I swallowed hard, unable to speak.

"She moved to Japan with her family in December, so no, I didn't see her." The silence that followed was more uncomfortable than I could bear.

"I have an idea," I declared a little too loudly as I shot out of my swing. Evan sat up straight in response to my sudden burst of energy.

"Is your car parked here?" I asked, looking toward the street that ran along the park.

"Yeah, it's over there." He pointed to the silhouette of the sports car.

"Do you have a blanket or something?"

"I have a sleeping bag in the trunk," he said suspiciously.

"Can you please get it?" I requested with a smirk. Without inquiring further, Evan ran to get the sleeping bag.

I took it from him and walked to the outfield of the baseball field to open it on the ground. Evan watched curiously.

"I know you're going to think this is strange. Sara and I used to do this all the time, and I love doing it, especially when the stars are so bright."

I stood a few steps away from the sleeping bag and looked up at the sky.

"You focus on a single star," I explained, as I searched for my spot. "Then you spin around, staring at that one star, until you can't stand anymore." I started spinning to demonstrate. "Then you lie down to watch the stars spinning above you while your star remains still."

I stopped, catching my step, searching for Evan. He observed my demonstration with an amused smirk.

"You don't want to try?"

"No, but you can go ahead," he encouraged with a small laugh. He sat down on the sprawled sleeping bag to witness my ridiculousness. After spinning, I lay next to him to watch the stars circling above me.

"You're missing out," I told him, as the earth swayed beneath my still body. He laughed.

My view of the streaking lights became obstructed when he leaned over me. The earth remained whirling beneath me, but it had nothing to do with spinning in circles.

I walked along my dark street, having left Evan a few houses back. The grin on my face felt permanent. The buzz still lingered from our night in the park. I slowly looked around, recognizing I was only a house away from mine. I took a deep breath in attempt to sober up.

The dark windows reduced the fear of being detected as I crept along the shadows to the side of the house where the trash cans awaited me. I held my breath and grabbed the handles on either side of the metal cylinder, lifting it with more force than was necessary. The empty can gave way easily, causing me to stumble backward.

I recovered before bumping into the bags full of leaves set along the fence. I gently placed it under my window and used the milk crate to step on top of the can. In my post-Evan delirium, I neglected to place my feet on the edges—the metal lid popped under my weight. The deep echo rang loudly in the night. I tensed, holding on to the windowsill, listening.

After a prolonged ear-numbing silence, I pushed the window up. My heart stopped. It wouldn't move. I swallowed. My stomach was in my throat. I pushed it again as hard as I could. I nearly fell from the can when the window gave way and slid up. I grabbed the ledge to steady myself. With my hands on the windowsill, I lifted myself and tilted headfirst through the open window. I walked my hands along the floor, then slowly lowered each leg from the sill.

I lay on the floor of my room, panting in relief. After a moment of listening for a stir upstairs, I moved to close the window. I removed the duffel bag from my bed and set it gently on the floor of my closet. I hung my coat on the back of the chair at the desk and slipped my shoes off. I crawled onto the bed, sinking into the mattress with an exhausted sigh and a smile, easily drifting to sleep.

———

"Let's go," Carol declared loudly.

I shot up in my bed, dazed and disoriented.

"Did you sleep in your clothes?" she asked, eyeing me suspiciously.

It took a moment to fight through the lingering sleep to realize that she was standing at the end of my bed with the door open behind her. I lifted the comforter to examine my attire.

"Oh, uh." I stumbled over the words. "I must have fallen asleep reading."

She eyed me suspiciously and glanced around my room. I held my breath, fearing she'd seen through my lie.

"Well, you missed out on your shower," she announced. "We're leaving in ten minutes. You'd better be ready." She walked out of my room, closing the door behind her. I sat in my bed for half a minute, releasing the pressure in my lungs. Then I recalled my night with Evan, and the smile resurfaced on my face.

32. THE QUESTION

That's a pretty nasty burn," Coach Straw observed when she saw me on the stairs leading to the locker room. I pressed my arm to my side to conceal the deep red streak, which still had blisters along it.

"I guess," I mumbled, not looking up at her, wishing I had long sleeves to pull down over it.

Coach Straw paused to look at me. Her scrutinizing glare made my stomach turn anxiously. She slowly nodded her head with a "Hmph."

"I'll see you outside," she declared dismissively, passing me on the stairs.

I hesitated, considering her cool response.

"Are you coming?" Sara questioned, sauntering past me.

"Yeah," I said, snapping back from my paranoid thoughts.

"I cannot tell you how relieved I was to get your text yesterday," Sara announced on our way to the track.

"I told you not to worry."

"Yeah," she teased, "and you saying it makes it that easy too."

I laughed, recalling the years I must have aged in the two minutes it took to escape my room. I shared my late-night adventures with Sara while we jogged our warm-up laps around the track.

She responded slowly. "Wow. I guess I shouldn't be surprised that he's had sex. But were you?"

"Sort of," I admitted. "It shouldn't matter. It's not like he has a list or anything. But it's still strange to think of him with someone else."

"You don't think he feels the same way about you and Drew? And he has to see Drew every day."

"I know," I replied, overtaken by a swarm of guilt. "But I was never going to go *that far* with Drew."

"Do you think you will with Evan?" she asked, grinning in anticipation of my answer.

My face flushed just thinking about it.

"You've thought about it, haven't you?" Sara accused when I didn't respond.

I shrugged and pressed my lips together, fighting to conceal my embarrassed smile.

"We haven't been together that long," I replied when I found my voice again.

"But you've known each other just about all year," she argued. "And even though you wouldn't admit it, you were stupid for each other from almost day one. So even though you've been *dating* for a couple of weeks, you've been each other's person for a lot longer."

I didn't respond. We jogged in silence until the coach blew the whistle to have us gather around for further training instructions. I was distracted for the remainder of practice. Sara's question followed me to bed that night, causing me to lie awake in the dark, contemplating the answer.

———

"Hi," Evan greeted me the next morning when I slid into his car.

"Hi," I said back quietly, my cheeks effortlessly turning a shade of red. I looked out the window when he drove away, hoping he hadn't noticed.

"Bad morning again?" he asked in response to my silence.

"Uh, no," I said quickly, trying to clear my head of the pressing question.

"Okay," Evan replied, baffled. "Did I miss something then?"

"No," I said quickly, trying to bite my lip to keep from smiling.

I forced myself to look at him so he could see that I wasn't upset. My cheeks felt like they were about to burst from grinning. I redirected my gaze back out the side window as the heat crept up my neck.

"I *am* missing something," Evan concluded, examining my comical expression with narrowed eyes.

I let out an uneasy laugh, begging my brain to think of something else, *anything* else.

"But you're not going to tell me what," he added. "Does Sara have something to do with this?"

I laughed again. "Sort of. Don't worry, I'll get over it."

But I couldn't. As much as I wanted to be relaxed and not think about what fate had in store, I found myself staring at him in class, wondering. I was convinced that it wasn't happening soon—but would it…could it…with him? I couldn't deny how I responded to him when we were near each other. I felt his presence in the room even when he wasn't next to me.

Evan didn't kiss me openly in school or hold me in a way that obviously indicated that we were a couple. Our affection was subtle. It didn't mean my heart didn't flutter when he brushed against me or that I didn't shiver from the warm tingling along my spine when he whispered in my ear so closely that his breath tickled my neck. He didn't need to touch me. His attention alone, recognizing my existence, sent a flurry of sparks through my body.

By the time we could steal a moment alone, my body was pulsing with an electric charge, built up from being exposed to him all day. I tried to contain my enthusiasm when I touched his lips or ran my hands along his back. But it was hard to fight the excitement and desire to be closer to him.

So when Sara sank *The Question* in my head, I suddenly found it difficult to breathe when he stood too close to me. I hesitated before touching him, fearing my eagerness would reveal the thoughts that were consuming me. The distraction lingered the entire week, regardless of how much I tried to push it away.

But then I found it was easily forgotten when Carol walked into the room.

"Shut the refrigerator, you fucking moron," she snapped.

"Huh?" I glanced around the kitchen, realizing I had the refrigerator door open in my hand. I quickly grabbed the milk and closed the door.

Carol scrutinized my absentminded action while she leaned against the counter, drinking her coffee.

"Why is the screen open in your room?"

I swallowed hard, trying not to spill the milk as I poured it over my cereal, suddenly remembering that I'd never closed the screen after I snuck out.

"Um," I said, clearing my throat. "I had a spider in my room, and opened the window to dump it outside. I must have forgotten to close the screen. Sorry."

I scooped a spoonful of cereal into my mouth, avoiding her eyes. Besides saying, "You really are an idiot," she didn't inquire about it further.

"I have some boxes in the back of my car that you need to bring in the house before you leave this morning. You can put them in the dining room."

"Okay," I mumbled with my mouth full. I shoveled in more spoonfuls of cereal, needing to escape her presence before she could ask any more questions or read through my lies.

I rinsed my bowl and placed it in the dishwasher before heading out the back door. When I opened the back of the Jeep, I found three large cardboard boxes. I had to use both arms to pick one up. The huge box blocked my view when I lifted it, but it wasn't as heavy as I feared.

"Be careful with them," Carol demanded, supervising from the deck.

I tried to ignore her as I passed by her into the house. She just stood on the deck, watching me struggle with the awkwardly oversize box. By the third one, I thought she'd finally disappeared into the house. I should have been paying better attention.

I stepped up to the second step with my right foot, but when I lifted my left to follow, it was met with the slightest resistance. With the giant package in my arms, it was enough to set me off balance. My right knee buckled beneath me and slammed into the corner of the next step with all of my weight behind it. I collapsed to my knees. The box landed firmly on the board above me, still clutched in my hands.

I clenched my teeth to keep from yelling out as jagged fire shot through my leg.

"You fucking klutz," Carol scolded from behind me. "I hope you didn't break it or else you'll be paying for it."

She slipped past me and entered the house without looking back. I followed her with a seething glare, tightening my jaw to hold back my contemptuous thoughts.

I pushed the box onto the deck and tensed when I pulled myself up by the railing. My knee streaked with pain the moment I straightened it. I yelled out through my clenched teeth, instinctively shifting my weight on to my other leg. I hobbled up the steps, picking up the box to bring it into the house.

I tried to shake off the throbbing pain. I knew Evan was going to be here any minute, and I didn't want him to see me limping.

I grabbed my bags and hobbled out, leaving Carol upstairs getting the kids ready for the day. I was hoping the tenderness would ease up by the time we got to school.

I reached the end of the driveway to find Evan waiting. I made every effort to walk as normally as I could, but my knee wanted to crumble under my weight, and I wanted to scream out in frustration.

"What happened?" Evan questioned in alarm, stepping out of the car.

I shook my head with my lips pressed together, unable to hide my anger. "I'm fine," I replied dismissively, sliding into the passenger seat. He ducked back into the car and closed the door, staring at me with his brows drawn together.

"Em, really. What happened?" Evan demanded. I knew he was worried, but there was an agitation in his voice that made me uncomfortable.

"I fell on the stairs," I explained. "I was carrying a box into the house and couldn't see where I was going. I tripped and hit my knee on the step. I'll be fine. I must've landed right on my kneecap, so it kills right now."

"You tripped?" he confirmed suspiciously, finally driving away from the house.

"Yes. I tripped."

I wasn't lying. I didn't say what or *who* caused me to fall. I wasn't certain he bought my explanation, but I wasn't about to volunteer that Carol had something to do with it. I pulled up the leg of my jeans while sucking the air through my teeth to examine my knee. Evan peered over, trying to see for himself.

There was a red mark at the point of contact, but nothing else—not yet.

"See"—I presented my knee—"I just hit it funny. It'll go away."

But it didn't. I had to grit my teeth to fight through the debilitating pain as the morning progressed. By the time I saw Evan again, I was unable to support my weight on my right side.

"You're not okay," he insisted, examining the pain in my eyes.

"Fine, I'm not okay," I agreed reluctantly. "I'll go to the nurse to get some ice. I think it's starting to swell."

"I'm coming with you."

"Evan, you don't have to. It's not that big of a deal, honestly."

"We'll see," he replied sternly, taking my books from my arms. I knew he would've carried me if I'd let him.

When I gingerly pulled up my pant leg for the nurse to examine it, Evan groaned behind me.

"Ooh, honey, that looks like it hurts," the woman with the short white hair and kind eyes stated at the sight of the large purple circle on my knee. It was so swollen that my kneecap could no longer be identified. "I'm going to have you ice it for a while and keep it elevated."

I raised my eyes to get a glimpse of Evan with his lips pressed together as he stared at the purple nightmare growing on my leg. When the nurse left to retrieve an elastic wrap from the trainer's office, he inquired ardently, "You swear you tripped?"

I looked up to connect with his troubled blue eyes and affirmed, "I tripped."

The nurse instructed me to ice it on and off for the rest of the day. To my horrified dismay, she insisted I keep my weight off of it and use a pair of crutches that she removed from the closet. Evan and I made our way back to catch the end of Trigonometry. Our entrance was, of course, a blush-inducing spectacle with everyone gawking at my condition. I prepared myself for the whispering.

"You tripped?" Sara asked, with the same doubt that I'd received from Evan. My leg rested on a chair next to me at the lunch table, a bag of ice on my knee. Evan sat down across from me with a tray of food for us to share.

"Why won't you two believe me?" I asked in an agitated tone.

"Because, I know you're lying," Sara shot back, just as aggravated. Evan's head shot up, looking between Sara's face and mine.

"You're lying?" he uttered in disappointment.

"Of course she is," Sara answered for me. "She's not *that* clumsy. She usually has help."

"Sara, stop," I insisted, observing Evan's flickering eyes. "I *did* trip. I don't know what I tripped on, because I couldn't see over the box. She was around, but I have no idea what made me fall. I can't say she wasn't thrilled to see me on my knees on the stairs, but I *did* trip."

Evan's jaw tightened. Sara shook her head in frustration.

"You don't have to cover up for her with us," she retorted. "So that means she's paying attention again, doesn't it?"

I shrugged, suddenly unable to eat my lunch.

"Let's see if you can stay at my house tonight since we have to get up so early for the SATs," Sara suggested. "I'll call my mom during study and have her ask Carol."

The thought of seeing Carol gloat as I hobbled in on crutches made my chest tighten.

"You *tripped?*" Coach Straw repeated as she and the trainer examined my purple, almost black, knee.

Why did everyone keep asking me this?

"Yes."

"It doesn't appear to be broken," the trainer concluded after maneuvering it slightly. "The ice should help with the swelling. Stay off of it for the weekend, and if it's still swollen or you can't put weight on it by Monday, go to your doctor to have him order scans."

I *needed* it to be better by Monday. Just the thought of visiting the hospital made me queasy; forget about asking Carol or George to drive me there.

"It looks like you won't be part of practice today," Coach Straw declared. "Are you going home with Sara?" Her knowledge of my life outside of track was a little disturbing.

"Yes," I whispered.

"Well," she thought for a moment, "you can sit on the bleachers and ice your knee while you watch the baseball game if you want."

"Really?" I tried to suppress my grin. I hadn't had the opportunity to see Evan play yet. Our schedules never worked out so that either of us was free on a day the other had a meet or game.

"Doesn't your boyfriend play on the varsity team?" Coach Straw confirmed. How did she possibly know so much about me?

"Yes," I answered quickly. "Thank you."

"So?" Sara demanded when I exited the office.

"I am watching baseball today," I announced with a wide grin.

"Great. But are you okay?" she reiterated impatiently.

"I need to stay off of it, ice it, and see what happens on Monday," I reported.

"You're all set to stay over tonight, but I have some bad news," she stated, pressing her lips together. "My grandfather's back in the hospital, so we're going to New Hampshire to see him after the SATs. That means you won't be able to stay over tomorrow night."

"Oh," I replied softly. "I hope he's okay."

"He's fine," she assured dismissively. "He probably ate the wrong thing and it backed him up or something. It's never anything serious. I'm really sorry."

"That's fine," I returned, trying not to appear disappointed. "At least I don't have to deal with her tonight."

Sara and I continued outside and then went our separate ways. She agreed to find me after practice if the game wasn't over. I hobbled over to the bleachers next to the baseball field. The teams were still warming up when I sat on the first row. I settled onto the hard seat with my leg resting on the metal plank, excited to watch the game.

33. DISCOVERY

You could stay at my house on Saturday," Evan offered when I told him that Sara's wasn't an option. The three of us sat on the bleachers after I'd watched Weslyn win their game.

"That could work," Sara agreed with a smirk. I gawked back at her, unable to believe she was agreeing with him. "My parents won't say that you weren't with me. Your aunt and uncle will never know. Em, you won't have to go home until Sunday morning."

"My parents won't be home, so they won't say anything," Evan added. This revelation didn't make my decision easier—it actually made it harder.

I considered my options and reluctantly agreed to spend Saturday night at Evan's.

"You are in so much trouble," Sara taunted when we drove to my house to grab my clothes for the weekend.

"Shut up, Sara," I shot back. "You're the one who thought it was such a great idea."

"You have to tell me every single detail."

"Stop it. Nothing's going to happen," I declared, trying to convince myself more than Sara.

Sara accompanied me into my house to help carry my bag. I thought it was best not to provoke the situation by using the crutches, so I limped in, trying to creep unnoticed through the kitchen while the family ate in the dining room.

Carol greeted us with a disturbing smile in the kitchen.

"Hi Sara," she said, beaming. It was nauseating to witness. "Emma, the nurse called. She wants to make sure you rest your leg this weekend and continue icing it. So lie low, okay?" Her false concern made me cringe.

"Okay," I said, unable to meet her eyes, continuing to inch toward my door.

"Chores on Sunday morning, alright?" she sang in a sickeningly sweet voice. I nodded.

I didn't know who she was trying to fool. We knew the monster that dwelled under her facade.

"Good luck with the SATs."

"Thank you," Sara replied politely. I turned to escape the bizarre exchange and headed to my room.

We packed silently, the tension thick, knowing Carol was within earshot. I'm sure she was dying to overhear me say something about her to Sara, but there was no way I was going to give her ammunition for her next ambush. I threw clothes on my bed, and Sara stuffed them into the duffel bag.

I breathed easier when I was back in Sara's car.

"She is so strange."

"I don't think that's the right word for her," I grumbled.

"Just you and me tonight?" Sara confirmed. I realized she and I hadn't had much time alone since Evan's return.

"Sounds perfect."

Sara and I watched a movie and ate pizza. I let her paint my toes a horrible shade of purple that resembled the color of my knee. We were in bed early for a Friday night, in preparation for the SATs the next morning.

"Don't even ask." I scowled at Evan, entering the halls after sitting for hours reading questions, writing essays and filling in what seemed like a million little circles. My mind raced through question after question, second-guessing and scrutinizing my responses. My head was spinning and my stomach was upside down, knowing my future was now out of my hands.

"Okay, I won't ask you how you think you did," Evan promised. "Let's get something to eat. Everyone's going to Frank's, if you want to go."

"That's fine," I agreed.

"How'd you do?" Jill asked with way more energy than anyone should have after spending hours on tests that would decide her future. She slid in at the booth across from us, eagerly awaiting my answer.

I dropped my head in my arms and groaned.

"She doesn't want to talk about it," Evan explained.

"Come on, Emma," Jill exclaimed, "you of all people shouldn't be worried about how you did."

"It all ran together," I complained, my voice muffled since I refused to lift my head. "I don't remember any of it. I could have answered anything, and I would have no recollection of whether it was correct or not. I think I'm going to throw up."

"Relax," Kyle urged. I hadn't realized he was sitting next to Jill. "It's over now, so it doesn't matter."

"Easy for you to say," I mumbled, peering up at him from my defeated position. "You've already been accepted to college." Evan flashed his amused grin, which didn't help my anxiety at all. Knowing my angst was entertaining only made it that much worse.

"Please don't tell me you're going to be in a bad mood all day." Evan pleaded as I hobbled on the crutches to his car.

"I'll get over it," I promised with a heavy sigh. "What are we doing today?"

"Not much. You need to stay off your leg. I thought we'd play video games or something so you can keep your leg up."

"Is that going to drive you crazy?" I asked, concerned that my immobility was going to bore him.

"No," he replied with a grin. "I don't always have to be doing something. I can just hang out."

And that's what we did for the rest of the afternoon—hung out on the couch above the garage. I watched Evan play the video games more than I participated. I was too frustrated with all of the buttons and knobs, unable to catch on to what I had to press or turn and when. I opted to prop my leg on his lap, observing his gaming skills while I iced it. It could have been worse.

"Want to watch a movie?" Evan suggested while we sat in the kitchen, eating one of his creations for dinner.

"You know I'll fall asleep."

"I don't mind," he smiled.

"Where do you watch movies?" I inquired, realizing the only televisions I'd seen were in the barn and in his room.

"My room."

A sudden streak of panic made me more alert than I'd been all day. I tried to appear unaffected by his response, but I was hyperventilating on the inside.

"Do you play the piano?" I asked, trying to think of something to do besides go to his room.

"A little," he admitted slowly, not expecting the question.

"Will you play for me?"

Evan's cheeks flushed, making me smile. It was something I didn't see very often.

"Now you *have to*," I taunted after seeing how uncomfortable my request made him.

"I'll try," he said with a deep breath.

After we—or I should say, Evan, since he wouldn't let me help—cleaned up, I followed him to the piano. Evan sat on the bench, and I scooted in next to him. He looked at me hesitantly and poised himself to play. I was truly excited to witness another one of his talents. Before he pressed the keys under his fingers, he looked at me again and shook his head.

"No, sorry—can't do it."

"What?!" I exclaimed disapprovingly. "You have to."

"No." He shook his head again. "I can't. Let's go listen to people who actually know what they're doing."

Without giving me a second to resist, Evan scooped me up in his arms and headed for the stairs.

"Evan, you really don't have to carry me." Being held sent a rush of color to my cheeks. And knowing that he was carrying me to his bedroom didn't help cool them.

"It'll take too long for you to hop up the stairs," he countered.

He nudged the door open with his shoulder and gently laid me on the bed. I quickly pushed myself up to sit, my pulse beating a thousand miles a minute. Evan selected a song with a catchy beat. A distinct voice, singing about being alone with a girl. He turned down the volume so that we could talk.

"I have to ask you something," Evan confessed nervously, sitting next to me on the bed, "and I know you're not going to like talking about it."

I remained still, already not liking it.

"When Sara said, 'She's paying attention again,' was she right?" After a moment of silence, he added, "And please don't lie."

I looked from his desperate eyes to my lap, where I dug my fingernails into my thumb.

"I don't know," I whispered. "I don't understand her enough to even begin to know what provokes her. But I'm not worried, and I don't want you and Sara to be either."

I met his eyes and pressed my lips into the slightest smile, trying to comfort him. It didn't relieve his troubled expression.

"I was serious about leaving with you."

I smiled wider.

"You know that, right?" he confirmed again, more adamantly. "Just tell me, and we'll leave."

"It's not going to come to that," I assured him, still smiling at his commitment to rescuing me. "I can get through this, as long as you promise not to leave again."

"I promise," he vowed and leaned in to kiss me.

I surprised him when I immediately asked some mundane question after his lips separated from mine, not giving us the option to get carried away. He asked me to repeat it, obviously not prepared to talk. I was determined not to give in to the craving. I was going to be in control...or asleep.

"Emma," Evan whispered in my ear. My cheeks tightened as I smiled at the tickling of his fingers along my neck. "You can stay in here if you want, or you can sleep in the guest room."

My eyes shot open. Evan was looking down at me as I lay on his chest with my arm casually draped across him. I sat up and looked around the dark room. The only source of light was from the television, airing a late-night talk show.

"Um," I responded, shaking off the haze of sleep, "the guest room is fine."

"I'll get your bag and crutches," he offered.

"I don't need the crutches. I think I can put some weight on it."

He examined me skeptically.

"Honestly, I think it's feeling better."

Evan disappeared down the stairs, after pointing out a door down the long corridor that led to the guest room. In his absence, I limped to the door, slowly putting more weight on my injured leg. It was still sore, but definitely better.

I opened the door to reveal a delicately decorated room adorned with several paintings of pink, yellow and blue flowers. I recognized Vivian's influence in the white duvet with pink roses embroidered around the edges. The cream-colored walls brightened the space, in complete contrast to Evan's dark room.

"This okay?" Evan checked from behind me.

"Yeah," I replied, limping over to sit on the edge of the bed.

Evan set my bag on the floor and hesitated.

"Um, good night." I wasn't sure what I should have said, but I don't think that was what he was expecting.

"Oh, yeah. Good night." He gave me a quick peck on the lips and walked out the door.

I collapsed onto my back with my arms spread beside me, releasing an aching sigh. I'd done the right thing, right? I *should* be sleeping in here, not in his room. After prepping for bed in the private bathroom, I slipped under the world's softest sheets and shut off the lamp on the white pedestal table.

Eyes, please close.

Willing myself to sleep was not working. I stared into the dark, fighting the desire to go to him. The beating in my chest was loud and steady—I could feel it in my throat. I needed to fall asleep—or at least turn over so I wasn't staring at the door any longer.

"Em? You awake?" Evan whispered. I couldn't help but smile when I turned over to find him peering through the crack of the door.

He smiled back. "Knowing you were right down the hall was way too hard. I couldn't do it," Evan declared, sliding under the covers next to me. "Hi."

"Hi." I smiled wider.

"How's your knee?" he asked, his head on the pillow next to mine.

"You did not come in here to ask me about my knee," I mocked him.

He shook his head with a smirk and pulled me toward him. Although his lips were familiar to me, I still lost my breath when we connected. I became entranced by their slow, soft passes over mine. My mouth parted to his advances with a soft breath. His hands slipped under my tank top, along my back. He stirred a warm tingling within me when he delicately traced his fingers along my stomach. I released a quick breath and pulled him closer—then winced as my knee hit his.

"Are you okay?" he questioned, pulling away—too far away.

"I'm okay," I whispered. He didn't move. "I promise—I'm fine."

Reluctantly, Evan moved closer until we were touching again. I kept my right leg on the bed behind my left, to protect us from another painful interruption. I was easily lost in his warmth again. I slid my hands under his shirt, running my fingers along the smooth curves of his chest and down to his waist. He inhaled quickly. He reached around and pulled his shirt over his head. My heart stopped. I breathlessly observed the silhouette of his defined, lean muscles in the dark and bit my lip. He leaned in to drag his parted lips along my neck.

When I thought we'd stop, we didn't. There wasn't a warning in my head urging me to slow down. All I could hear was our quick breaths. All I could feel was his touch on my heated skin. My head spun, and my pulse quickened, eventually releasing a moan I didn't know I had in my depths. Our discovery of each other left my chest rising with long, drawn breaths. There wasn't quick retreat, just a slow and gradual withdrawal as his arms settled around my waist and I nuzzled into his neck, brushing it softly with my lips.

"How's your knee?" he whispered, kissing the top of my head.

I'd completely forgotten about my injury, but now I recognized the throbbing that kept pace with my heart.

"I'll be okay," I assured him.

"I'm going to get you some ice," he insisted, moving away from me. I instantly missed the warmth of his body, watching him slide his shirt over his head to conceal his defined lines before stepping out the door.

I lay on my back, awaiting his return. My eyes were slowly blinking closed when I heard the distinct clinking of ice. Evan slid a pillow under my knee before setting the bag of ice on it.

"I'm going to my room, so I don't bang your knee while you're sleeping," he stated, easing the down comforter over me before kissing my forehead. "Good night."

"Good night," I murmured with a delicate smile, already drifting to sleep. I knew in that moment, I would never love anyone in my life the way I loved Evan Mathews.

34. PAYING ATTENTION

What did you do?" Sara exclaimed much louder than necessary, when we drove away from Evan's the next morning. "And don't you dare say 'nothing,' because you are glowing."

I pressed my palms against my fiery cheeks, knowing she saw way more than I intended.

"Not what you think," I corrected. "But, it was…interesting." I couldn't hold the smile back. I stared out the window, unable to make eye contact with her.

"Uh, 'interesting' is not details," she said impatiently. "You're not going to tell me, are you?"

"Not today." I grinned. But I would eventually. Not in the explicit detail that she would have liked, but enough so that she knew.

I was so caught up in the mind-buzzing thoughts that fueled my glow when I returned home, I barely registered my discomfort as I limped around on my leg, completing my chores. I was also oblivious when Carol came up behind me while I washed the previous night's dishes.

The knife slipped through my soapy hands with a quick, forceful withdrawal.

I inhaled sharply at the sting of the blade against the inside of my fingers.

"Oh, did I get you?" Carol remarked snidely. "I needed it."

I held my fingers tightly, glaring at her while what I really wanted to say screamed in my head. The blood dripped through my clenched fingers and spread into the water below. She set the knife on the counter, with no intention of using it, and left the kitchen with a malevolent smirk.

I reached across the counter and grabbed a handful of paper towels, leaving a trail of red in my wake. I wrapped them around the padded section of my sliced fingers, right below my knuckles. The blood easily soaked through the papery material.

I cradled my hand and walked into the bathroom, turning on the water to flush out the wound. My fingers pulsed as the blood flowed freely, swirling with the water down the drain. I had to use a towel to apply enough pressure to stop the bleeding. I knew I'd have to do everything I could to remove the bloodstains later.

Within a few minutes of strangling my fingers, the gapes in the fleshy tissue only trickled instead of gushed. I wrapped them with bandages as tightly as I could to allow the cuts to clot. I clenched my teeth, shaking my head in disbelief at her cunningness. I pressed my lips together and flexed my jaw. The anger she provoked was not as easy to push away anymore. I was overtaken by fury, and it lingered long after it should have been tucked deep inside.

———

Sara and Evan both eyed my wrapped fingers throughout the day on Monday, but it wasn't until lunch that Sara said something.

"Are you going to tell us, or what?"

I rolled my eyes at her insistence. "Cut my fingers washing a knife," I responded flatly.

Sara shook her head and folded her arms across her chest. "All four of them?"

"The truth," Evan demanded, not allowing me to get away with the weak explanation. I didn't like the accusing way they were both staring at me. This wasn't their problem. They didn't need to make me feel like *I'd* done something wrong.

"Listen, I'm not going to tell you what happened. If you don't like my explanation, then you can fill in the blanks as you see fit. I'm not going to tell you anything more. You know where I live, and you know who I live with. I don't need to relive it again by telling you." Aggravated beyond what I could contain, I pushed myself away from the table and walked, or slightly limped, out of the cafeteria.

Neither Sara nor Evan said anything to me during Journalism. They allowed me to fester in my own space for the fifty minutes of class. But as soon as it was over, they bombarded me again.

"You can't be mad at us," Evan implored. I kept my back to them while sitting at the computer.

"Emma, you have a tendency to downplay your injuries," Sara added. "You have to understand that we're going to be concerned."

"I can handle it," I snapped, spinning around in my chair to face them.

"Didn't you tell me something similar that afternoon on the track—right before you ended up in the hospital?" Sara's raised voice cracked as she finished the sentence. I remained silent and stared at the floor.

Evan scooted a chair in front of me and gently held my uninjured hand in both of his.

"We know you can handle more than you should," he stated soothingly, "but this is making us...nervous. I really think we should..." I shot my eyes at him, becoming panic-stricken when I realized how he intended to finish that sentence. He didn't finish his thought. The silence said enough.

"You don't understand," I whispered, dropping my gaze. "I can't leave their house. Not yet. I don't want to risk ruining Jack's and Leyla's lives. I could also lose everything I've worked so hard for. Besides, I have nowhere to go."

"You—" they both began.

"Nowhere that I could stay without it causing more problems or exposing my secret," I corrected. "Do you really think they'd let me leave quietly, or live in the same town, wondering what I was telling your parents? I would have to leave Weslyn, and then people would start asking questions. I have no choice."

They understood. I could see it in their broken expressions. I shared with them the thoughts I'd already processed a hundred times before in my head. They finally got a glimpse of the true threat in exposing my situation. We would all lose. I hoped I'd convinced them that the risk of staying was worth it.

"I promise you," I vowed, looking between Evan and Sara, "I will know when I can't do it anymore, and then we can go anywhere you like." I finished my sentence looking at Evan. Sara's eyes flinched in confusion, but she didn't ask for an explanation—she understood enough.

"Besides, I only have four hundred and eighty days left." I smiled, trying to lighten the mood. It didn't work.

The next two weeks passed without incident. It helped that we spent the Easter holiday with Janet, and then I spent most of the week of vacation with Sara. George and Carol took the kids to the theme parks in Florida, leaving me behind, of course. Little did they know, Sara and I escaped to Florida as well, to visit her grandmother for four days on the Gulf Coast while Evan was in France snowboarding with a friend from San Francisco.

———

"I think that would be a great gift for his birthday," Sara confirmed while we lounged on the soft white sand, the warm breeze blowing through our hair.

"You don't think it's too…" I scrunched my face, trying to find the right word.

"No, it's perfect."

"I think Ms. Mier will let me do parts of it in class as an assignment too. You know I'm having dinner with his parents on Sunday, right?"

"No, you didn't tell me that," Sara exclaimed, sitting up to face me.

"Do you remember his mom asking me to dinner back in the fall?"

"Yeah," she recalled eagerly.

"Well, she's insisting it be this Sunday. I can't believe I didn't tell you this," I pondered. "Oh, and the worst part is that she invited Carol and George as well."

"She did not," Sara gaped.

"Well, I actually had to ask them, since I can't give my phone number to anyone besides you."

"So they know about Evan now?" Sara concluded, still unable to close her dropped jaw.

"They were going to find out eventually," I replied with a slight shrug. "You should have seen Carol's face when she found out I was dating someone. I think her irises turned red. It was pretty creepy."

"Are they going?" Sara asked in horror.

"Of course not," I responded, as if stating the obvious. "But George was okay with *me* going, despite Carol."

"Em, this is going to be so bad, isn't it?" I watched as Sara's posture sank with the realization that, after all we'd done to conceal Evan from Carol, she'd found out about him. I'd accepted this inevitability the moment we kissed in the Art room. I had prepared for it until my stomach turned inside out—hoping that I was ready. Sara, obviously, was not.

"What could she possibly do that she hasn't already done?" I said to Sara, trying to put her at ease—without success.

"You're going back home after the track meet on Saturday, right?"

"Yes," I answered suspiciously.

"You have to text me within an hour of being home to let me know you're okay," she demanded.

"Sara, stop."

She silenced me with a stern stare. I knew I had to give in to her demands or risk being ignored for the remaining two days in Florida.

"Fine," I promised with an exasperated sigh, "I'll text you."

Neither of us mentioned it again for the rest of the week. But as Saturday approached, Sara became more anxious. Her nervous energy distracted me from being nervous myself. I focused on seeing Evan at the meet, and that was enough to keep me from thinking of Carol.

35. SABOTAGED

D on't forget to text me," Sara insisted for the twentieth time when she dropped me off after the track meet that Saturday. I waved in confirmation with a roll of my eyes and walked up the driveway.

I prepared myself for whatever awaited me inside as I ascended the steps to the deck. The dining room hummed with little voices. Carol's voice carried through the kitchen, talking to George in a calmer than usual tone.

"Emma!" I was greeted joyfully by Leyla, who attacked my legs before I could bend down to embrace her.

"Put your things in your room," Carol instructed calmly. "We're about to sit down and eat."

The pleasantness in her voice caused me to pause. I glanced around, having a hard time believing that she was actually talking to me. I obeyed warily.

"How was your time with Sara?" she asked, glancing toward me when I sat in my usual seat, where a plate of spaghetti with meatballs was already served.

"Fine," I replied cautiously, still uncomfortable with the attention.

"That's great." She smiled. The expression looked odd on her face; I had never truly seen her smile at me before.

I waited for something catastrophic to happen. But nothing did. Carol redirected the conversation back to George. They discussed a trip to the hardware store the next day to pick out flowers and shrubs for the front yard.

———

There had been so many alarms going off in my head the second I walked through the door the previous night, but there was no way I could have known, or ever suspected her of being so cruel. Even when it became obvious that this was her doing, it was still difficult to understand what had really happened.

"Well, I guess you won't be in any condition to go to your *boyfriend's* tonight, will you?" Carol jeered, poking her head into the bathroom the next morning. She closed the door behind her, leaving me in my misery.

A cold sweat broke out across my forehead and down my back, right before my stomach convulsed. My body quivered at the exertion that had kept me up throughout the night. I collapsed on the floor, pleading for death, or at least sleep. How could I possibly have anything left in my stomach after being in here for an entire night?

"You should call them to let them know you won't be able to make it," Carol bellowed through the door. I glared in contempt at the closed door, wishing she'd fall off a cliff.

I pushed myself up to sit against the bathtub, covering my face with my shaking hands. I lifted myself from the floor and groaned when every muscle in my body screamed in agony. My stomach turned again, and I leaned over the toilet. Nothing happened, so I slowly straightened to walk to the phone in the kitchen.

The effort to move was unbearable. My head was unsteady on my shoulders as I dragged my body through the kitchen, cradling my stomach. When I reached the phone, I realized I didn't have Evan's number memorized. I groaned at the thought of having to

get it from my room. Then I noticed a piece of paper on the counter with "Mathews" scribbled on it, in her writing. Their phone
number was written beneath it. How did she have their number?

I pressed the numbers on the keypad, anticipating Evan's voice
on the other end. The anxiety agitated my stomach; I clutched it
with my free arm as it began to roll again. The phone rang several
times before it was picked up.

"Hello?" Evan answered.

"Evan," I said in a voice I barely recognized.

"Emma?" Evan confirmed, concern resounding in his voice.
"Are you okay?"

"I am so sick," I rasped. "I have a stomach bug or something.
I'm so sorry I won't be able to come to dinner tonight."

"Do you need me to come get you?" he questioned in alarm,
skeptical of my explanation.

"No, really," I pleaded. "I just need to go to bed." My stomach
gurgled in warning, and I knew I couldn't stay on the phone.

"I'll see you tomorrow morning?" he confirmed softly.

"Mmm," I groaned in affirmation before hanging up the phone
and rushing back to the bathroom.

There was nothing left in me, but my body was determined to
purge any trace of whatever it was that had invaded it. The convulsions left me weak and trembling. By the time night came around,
I was finally able to make it to my bed, where I curled up under the
covers and wished I would never wake up again, if this was how I
was going to feel. But I woke up anyway.

I somehow managed to prepare for school the next morning.
I knew that *she* would never allow me to stay home alone, and
the repercussions of having Carol or George miss a day of work
were more than I could fathom. I showered and wrapped my
wet hair in a low knot above my neck. I sipped a glass of water,

hoping it would relieve the trembling, before making my way out the door.

I practically collapsed in Evan's car, wanting so much to be under my covers again. I pulled my knees into me and buried my face in my arms. He didn't say anything for a full minute after we pulled away from my house. But a minute was all it took for my stomach to register that I'd attempted to put something in it.

"Evan, pull over," I whispered with an urgency that he recognized. When the car stopped, I forced myself out and staggered to the back just before my body rejected the fluid. I took a few cleansing breaths, willing the spasms in my stomach to stop while I supported myself on the back corner of his car. I slipped back into the car and put my face in my hands.

"You're not going to school," Evan said in a determined voice. I could only groan. I barely noticed where we were going until the car pulled into his empty driveway.

"Evan, I can't stay here," I argued in a rasp. "I will get in so much trouble for missing school."

"I'll have my mom call in to excuse us."

I gave in and opened the door, setting my feet on the ground and taking an uneven breath before forcing my legs to receive my weight. Evan hovered. I knew he wanted to help, but I shook my head to fend him off. I followed him through the house, allowing him to take off my shoes after I collapsed on his bed. My eyes were closed the second I was enveloped by the warmth of his blankets. His hand gently brushed against my clammy face right before I drifted into a comatose sleep.

My eyes fluttered open in the dark space. I glanced around without moving my head. I recognized the comforting scent and knew where I was. Then I remembered why I was there, and I moaned. Did he really see me throw up?

I peeked next to me and discovered that I was alone in the room. I listened for the warning growls of my stomach, but my stomach was calm, and my head was clear. I pressed my dry tongue to the roof of my mouth, craving water. I pushed myself up to sit, grimacing at the soreness of my abused back and stomach muscles. At least the excruciating body aches had subsided.

I stiffly moved to the bathroom to investigate how horrible I looked. I wasn't disappointed when I observed the ghostly reflection staring back at me—I was a disaster. Was there any way I could slip out and have Sara pick me up without Evan seeing me?

I let down my damp hair and combed my fingers through it, and I immediately put it back in the elastic, horrified by the results. I rinsed my face and mouth, attempting to be recognized as human again. I took a dab of toothpaste and put in on my finger, rubbing it on my teeth and tongue to conceal the aftermath of a day and a half of throwing up.

"Emma?" Evan called from the bedroom.

I peeked out through the bathroom doorway.

"How are you feeling?" he asked cautiously.

"Like someone scraped me off the road." He smiled at my answer, the worry washing away. "Oh, and I look like it too."

"No you don't," he assured, meeting me with open arms when I stepped out of the bathroom. I allowed him to wrap me in his warm embrace. He kissed the top of my head. "You look better than you did this morning. I heard that people could look green, but I'd never seen it before."

I tried to push away with a huff, but he tightened his hold, letting out a quick laugh.

"You still look pale, though," he observed. "Do you want to lie down?"

I nodded. He released me, and I slipped back under the blankets.

"I brought you some tea to try to get some fluids back into you, and it shouldn't upset your stomach—or at least that's what my mother told me."

"Is she here?"

"No, but I had to tell her you were sick, so she would call the school for us. She's called a couple of times to check on you and to give me way too much advice on how to take care of you. I tried to explain that you were still sleeping, but that didn't stop her."

Evan sat on the bed next to me, his back against the headboard. He eased me over so my head rested on his lap, then drew his fingers along my hairline. I closed my eyes, soothed by the tingling that traced his touch.

"What time is it?" I whispered.

"After two."

"I can't believe I slept that long."

"Me either. I had to check a few times to make sure you were still breathing. You never moved."

"I'm still breathing," I assured him quietly, with a small smile.

"I'm glad you're feeling better." He ran his hand down the back of my neck. The warm chills continued down my spine.

I sat up and searched for the tea on the table next to the bed. I took the smallest sip and let the warmth settle in my stomach before I felt it was safe to drink more.

"You still have your state ID from your trip with Sara, right?" Evan asked out of nowhere.

"Yes," I answered slowly.

"Do you have access to your birth certificate and Social Security card?" he inquired further. I drew my eyebrows together and remained silent.

"I think you should try to get them—just in case," he explained.

I knew he was serious, and that's what made it so strange to hear. He really was prepared to escape with me.

"I can tell George I need them to apply to work at the soccer camp again this summer. You're really serious about this?" I asked, studying his face.

"Yes, I am." I dropped my eyes, struck with the understanding of what he'd be giving up too. Going into hiding would mean sacrificing his family and friends, not to mention dropping out of high school.

"Evan, it's not going to come to that. I mean, really—where would we go?"

"Don't worry," he consoled with confidence. "I've given it a lot of thought. Besides, it wouldn't be permanent."

I decided not to question him further in fear of hearing any more of his plan. I refused to admit that it would ever get so bad that we'd be forced to run away. Evan believed in this plan because it was the only thing that he thought he could do to help me. It wasn't realistic, but I wasn't going to tell him that.

———

I did get the documents from George. Evan was relieved. But I wasn't. I couldn't tell him that I was paralyzed with fear at the thought of leaving and that I wasn't convinced I could do it. He just had to believe I could—at least until I was forced to decide.

36. DINNER

Where is it?" she shrieked, startling me as I poured a capful of detergent into the washer.

Stunned, I watched her rush to the laundry area and begin throwing clothes around. The clothes started bouncing off my body. Of course they didn't hurt, but the ferocity behind the throws still made me flinch.

"What did you do with it?" she demanded.

"What?" I asked quietly.

"The fucking towel," she screamed. "The one you ruined. What the fuck did you do with it?"

"I don't know what you're talking about," I lied. I'd thrown away the bloodstained hand towel I used to stop my fingers from bleeding. But how did she know?

"You know exactly what I'm talking about, you worthless piece of shit."

She continued throwing clothes in my direction. She looked ridiculous in her fit of rage, creating a windstorm of clothes tossed about the basement. I straightened up, no longer cowering, and I looked at this pathetic woman as if for the first time. My stomach twisted in disgust and anger. I was fed up with her irrational tirades.

"It's just a towel!" I bellowed over her screams. She froze, shocked by the strength in my voice.

"What did you say?" she hissed. I stared back, unwavering, even when faced with her how-dare-you look. As I stood there, staring her down, I suddenly realized how much taller I was than her. I smirked at the thought of my shrinking cowardice.

"It's just a towel," I repeated calmly, but with a confidence that kept me towering above her. I turned to shut the lid of the washer.

"It's just a towel?" she grunted, shoving the softener bottle right in my gut when I turned around. The air rushed from me, bending me in half as I held my stomach. She raised the bottle again and it came down on my shoulder, crumpling me to the floor. I wanted to run for the stairs, but there was one last blow to my left arm, and I folded against the washer. "Don't ever fucking talk to me like that again."

"Carol," George yelled down the stairs, "you down there? Your mother's on the phone."

Carol walked off, grumbling, "Clean this up," before she climbed the stairs.

I collapsed to the floor, still breathing heavily from getting the wind knocked out of me. My fists were clenched, my nails digging into my palms. I inhaled deeply to calm the fire. It didn't disappear completely, but it was enough that I could pull myself up and begin picking up her mess.

"Emma." George knocked on my door. "Evan's here."

My throat closed—he was *in* my house? What was he thinking?

"Okay," I squeaked, unable to find my voice. "I'll be right there." Something rolled inside me as I grabbed my jacket and walked down the hall.

"Hi," I said with wide eyes. He ignored my anxiety and smiled back.

"It's great to finally meet you," Carol declared with the widest smile. It was torturous to witness.

"You too," Evan returned politely.

"Well…we should go." The words rushed from my mouth in a single breath.

"Ten o'clock, okay?" Carol confirmed in her sweet tone. I winced at the sound.

"Yeah." I tried to force myself to smile, but if felt more like a grimace.

Evan put his hand on my back to escort me out. I stiffened, knowing they were still watching us. I hoped she hadn't noticed that he was touching me.

"What were you thinking?" I exclaimed in a whisper while we walked down the driveway.

"Em, they knew you were coming over to my house," he explained. "I couldn't bring myself to just pull up and honk. It doesn't matter who they are; that's not who I am."

It was unsettling to see him in my kitchen—the place of so much pain. The two images fought in my brain, making the discomfort harder to relinquish.

"You don't have to walk me to the door tonight, okay?" I pleaded.

"Okay," he agreed reluctantly. "But can I at least kiss you good night?" A smile flashed across his face, relieving my anxiety.

"We'll see," I replied with a teasing grin.

When we neared his house, a new anxiety revealed itself. My chest closed in around my lungs.

"Are you ready for this?" Evan asked, pulling into the driveway.

I exhaled, trying to force a composed smile. "Sure." He laughed at my unsuccessful attempt.

Evan took my hand as we walked up the porch steps. I guess it didn't matter to him that his parents saw us touching. This was going to be so strange.

"Emily, welcome," Vivian said in greeting when we entered. She glided over to give me an embrace I was finally prepared for, and I awkwardly returned the gesture.

An enticing aroma floated across the kitchen as we sat at the peninsula. I was still awed by Vivian's grace as she glided around the cooking space, stirring, chopping and mixing. I'd always associated the setting with Evan, but tonight, Evan sat next to me and observed his mother on the other side with his hand affectionately on my back.

"Do you want me to do anything?" he asked.

"No, we're just about done," she announced. "Your father's removing the steaks from the grill, and I'm putting the salad together. Well, you could offer Emily something to drink."

"Oh, yeah, sorry," he fumbled, redirecting his attention to me. "What would you like to drink?"

"You know what I like," I responded. A small grin appeared on his mother's face with my response.

"I'm happy to see you're feeling better," she said. "I understand you were rather ill last weekend."

"Yes, but I'm feeling much better now. Thank you."

"I hope the tea helped."

"It did, thank you," I replied politely, not recalling if I'd finished the cup. Evan tried to conceal his smile, probably realizing I hadn't.

"Steaks are ready," Stuart announced, returning from the grill on the back porch with a platter of small steaks.

"Perfect timing," Vivian declared. "Everything is ready. Evan, dear, would you please help bring the food to the table?"

"Sure." Evan found bowls and serving utensils to pair with the sides and carried them to the dining table. I hadn't noticed the set table with decorative china and sparkling flatware until I turned to follow him. In the center, an intricate candelabra let off a dazzling glow. I wasn't prepared for the formal setting.

"Shall we?" Vivian addressed me as she walked toward the table carrying a bottle of wine.

I picked up my glass to follow her. She and Stuart sat on either end while Evan and I sat facing each other in the middle. Evan shot me a grin when we sat down. I gave him a panicked smile, which made him laugh. His mother looked at him, questioning his outburst. He attempted to conceal it with a clearing of his throat.

My stomach was twisting with nerves; I wasn't sure how I was going to eat. I practically force-fed myself every bite, despite the fact that it was one of the best meals I'd had since…well, since Evan cooked for me.

"How was your visit to California?" Vivian inquired the moment I put a piece of steak in my mouth. My face turned red as she patiently waited for me to swallow so I could answer.

"I loved it," I finally responded.

"Are you still looking at Stanford as your first choice?"

"Yes, I really enjoyed the meetings with the coach and the advisor," I explained. "It's going to come down to my SAT scores and how I perform this coming soccer season. But so far, they seem very interested."

"Have you decided on a major?"

"That did come up, and with my strong science and math background, the advisor mentioned premed."

Evan's eyes widened in surprise. Yeah, I hadn't mentioned that to anyone before this moment.

"That would be wonderful," she acknowledged with a smile. "Evan, have you narrowed down your selections yet?"

"Mom, let's not do this," he begged. "You know where I'm looking. My mother wants me to go to Cornell with my brother," he explained to me, "and my father wants me to go to Yale like he did."

"Oh," I nodded, realizing both colleges were on the wrong coast.

"Well, I suppose California would make sense if Emily were there," Vivian admitted with a slight rise of her shoulder. Stuart cleared his throat. "Stuart, California has some excellent schools."

Hearing our future being planned before me was surreal. It wasn't that I didn't want a future with Evan. I honestly hadn't thought much about it until this moment. However, listening to his *mother* plan our future didn't feel quite right.

"Mom," Evan stressed, obviously just as uncomfortable, "we have plenty of time to discuss it. Let's talk about something else, okay?"

"If you insist," she agreed with an endearing smile. "Are you looking forward to going to the prom next month?"

Evan choked on his water. I stopped breathing.

"What?" She asked, puzzled by Evan's reaction.

"We haven't exactly talked about it yet," he confessed, glancing at me apologetically. I looked down at my plate and moved the asparagus around with my fork.

"Evan," she scolded, "she needs time to pick out a dress. You should have asked her already."

I bit my lip, trying not to smile.

"Well, if you would like some assistance in finding a dress," she said, directing her attention to me, "I would be happy to take you to this fabulous boutique in New York."

"Um...okay...thank you," I stuttered. Evan tensed at the offer. The thought of it horrified me. I could barely survive shopping with Sara at the mall.

"Since I seem to be suggesting the wrong conversational topics," Vivian declared, directing her words toward Evan, "what would you like to talk about?"

Evan looked up, realizing that she was addressing him.

"Dad, how's work?" he asked quickly. Vivian let out an exasperated sigh.

"Emily does not need to hear about his tedious cases," Vivian interrupted before Stuart could open his mouth. I wasn't sure if Stuart had actually intended to open his mouth. "We're supposed to be getting to know her." No, that's not a good idea either.

She offered me a warm smile, which I attempted to return. My stomach churned in anticipation of her impending question.

"What does your uncle do?" she asked politely.

I swallowed hard. We were really going to talk about my family, weren't we?

"He's a land surveyor."

"That's wonderful," she replied. "I understand that your father passed away when you were young. What did he do?"

Evan gave me a worried glance. I took a breath and replied, "He was an engineer for an architectural firm in Boston."

"Mom, aren't you working on a charity event in Boston?" Evan intercepted before his mother could ask another revealing question.

Vivian beamed at the chance to talk about one of her projects. Thankfully, she went into enough detail about the event that the conversation lasted for the remainder of dinner.

"You and Evan should attend it with us," she decided as she set the dessert in front of us. Evan grumbled, not hiding his distaste at the invitation. "Evan, stop that. It's a wonderful cause, and you'll be able to meet so many people in the medical industry since it's for the hospital."

"When did you say it was?" I inquired.

"The middle of June."

"Oh, I'm sorry," I replied, trying to sound disappointed. "I'll be away at soccer camp by then."

"Evan, is that the camp you applied for, as well?"

I turned toward Evan, unaware that he had applied.

"Oh, yeah," he answered, meeting my questioning eyes. "Sara gave me the application a few weeks ago. But I'm not sure if they have a spot open."

The thought of spending the summer with Sara *and* Evan produced a glowing grin. Evan smiled in response to my radiant expression. Vivian asked me to explain the camp while we ate dessert, which was finally an easy topic, since I'd been an assistant coach there for the past two summers.

After dessert, Vivian excused us and escorted me to the sitting room. Evan warily watched us leave while he and his father cleaned up the dishes. When he eventually joined us, I knew why.

"You are not showing her my baby pictures!" He sounded horrified, which made me laugh.

"Come on, Evan," I teased with a laughing smile, "you were adorable."

"I know," Vivian acknowledged, not understanding his reaction.

Evan closed the photo book that was on my lap and placed it on the table. He held out his hand to take me away. "Okay," he announced, "I think you've had her long enough.

"We're going to the barn before I have to drive her home."

"I suppose," Vivian said with a sigh. "It was so nice to finally get to talk with you." She gave me a hug and kissed my cheek. "I look forward to seeing you again."

"Good night," I called to Stuart as Evan led me through the kitchen.

"Good night, Emily," Stuart's bold voice returned.

"Was it that horrible for you?" I laughed while we climbed the stairs.

"I was going to ask you the same thing," Evan returned. When we entered the room, he turned to face me, looking all too serious. "I'm sorry about that. I tried to give her boundaries, but she doesn't listen very well."

"It was fine," I assured him. He wrapped his arms around me and kissed me gently.

"Your birthday's in a couple of weeks," I said, looking up at him from within his wrap. "What would you like to do?"

"Will you be able to do anything on the Friday of my actual birthday?"

I sucked in air through my teeth and shook my head apologetically. "Saturday?" I offered.

"Okay," he agreed. "So, I'll do something with the guys on Friday. Maybe go to the city or something. Then Saturday's just you and me."

"Dinner?" I suggested. Evan considered my offer, then smirked.

"Yeah," he said, grinning. "I have an idea."

"I'm missing something." I was mystified by the look in his eye. I knew he was contriving a plan that he wasn't sharing.

"No," he said quickly. "Dinner is perfect. But can I choose?"

"Sure," I agreed slowly, still not trusting his reaction.

Carol and George were waiting for me when I returned home. Well, they pretended to be sitting at the island talking, but I was pretty sure they wanted to see if Evan would walk me to the door. I was so glad I'd convinced him not to, even when he tried to change my mind on the drive home.

"How was your night?" Carol inquired, with an edge to her tone.

"It was nice," I responded quietly, trying to continue to my room.

"We need to lay down some ground rules," George declared, making me stop and close my eyes. I turned to listen to their determination to destroy my world even more.

"You cannot go to Evan's when no one's home," Carol demanded. "If we hear otherwise, you won't be allowed to see him anymore. And that means when you're at Sara's too."

"He is not allowed to drive you home after school," George added. "We don't care if he drives you to school, but you can only drive with Sara or one of your other girlfriends in the afternoon."

"And lastly," Carol stated with a cutting grin, "if we find out that you are having sex, you will not be allowed to take a step out of this house until you graduate, except to go to school."

I remained motionless while her threat turned over in my head.

"Why are you looking at us like that?" she griped. "Are we not making ourselves clear?"

"I don't understand why you'd assume I'd have sex with him," I replied, my voice more accusatory than defensive. "You know nothing about me, do you?"

"We know enough," Carol snapped. "We know you are naive and can easily be taken advantage of. Don't think for a second he cares about you. He's just like every other guy who only wants one thing."

"You don't know anything about him either," I shot back, my voice growing stronger.

Carol raised her eyebrows at my reaction, while George's face tensed.

"Maybe we should reconsider whether you're ready to date at all," Carol threatened. My heart stopped. "Is there something we should know? Are you already having sex?"

"No," I answered quickly as the panicked heat crept up my neck.

"Then this conversation is over," George finally interceded. "You know how we feel, and that's it."

37. GIFTS

I followed their rules for the next two weeks. Not because I wanted to, but because that's just how it ended up. Evan and I didn't go to his house the following Sunday; we went to the sports complex where he talked me into the driving range instead of the batting cages. I concluded in frustration never to do it again.

I spent time in Art and part of study period preparing Evan's birthday gift. Ms. Mier didn't know exactly what it was for, but she was encouraging as I completed each page. I had a feeling she knew more than she admitted, but then again, she always did.

When it was finally finished, I let Sara look it over to make sure I hadn't stepped over any lines that would make it too...much. She understood its entire content, since I'd told her *everything*, so it was unnerving to watch her reaction as she scanned each page. She smiled at the end and shocked me by giving me a hug.

"Em, it's perfect."

"Really?"

"Definitely—he's going to love it."

"Then why do I feel like I'm going to throw up at the thought of giving it to him?"

"Because it's so personal and thoughtful. He has to love it."

I hoped she was right.

———

My stomach was in my throat the entire ride to school on Friday. I nervously wrung my hands in my lap. Evan finally said something when we arrived at school.

"What's going on?" He turned to face me after shutting the car off.

I took a quick breath. "I didn't know when was the best time to do this, so I'm just going to do it now." I reached into my backpack and pulled out the flat, wrapped square. "Happy birthday."

Evan produced an embarrassed grin. "Thank you."

"You don't have to open it now," I blurted when he started to unwrap the gift. "You can look at it later, when you're by yourself."

He eyed me suspiciously and opened it anyway.

"Evan, really, you don't have to look at it now." Maybe I *was* going to throw up.

"Did you make this?"

I bit my lip and nodded.

To my horror, Evan started turning the pages of the ribbon-bound collection of art. A smile crept onto his face. I held my breath, watching his bright eyes take in each moment captured by the stroke of my brush.

He turned to the page with the image of Sara's scarf and remarked, "I still have this, don't I?" He hesitated at the page with the blue handprint, smiling wider, which sent a warm chill through me. I took in his soft expression while he scanned the lyrics I'd transcribed from one of the songs he'd downloaded on my iPod, and he shook his head with a smile at the image of the Jacobses' exquisite chandelier. Evan ran his fingers along the brook in the meadow, and he let out a light laugh, remembering the cityscape from atop the apartment building in New York. His cheeks flushed at the sight of the pink roses on the last page, and he slowly closed the book with a deep breath.

"This is everything, huh?" he questioned, taking a hold of my hand.

"Only the good stuff," I corrected, my fiery cheeks now crimson.

"This is amazing. Thank you." He leaned over and found me waiting for him. My head was swirling already from not being able to breathe, but with the touch of his lips, the sensation escalated. He left me needing a minute to float back down before stepping out of the car.

Evan met me on the other side of the car and wrapped me tightly in his arms. My heart still hadn't recovered from the kiss and continued to falter when I looked up into his steel-blue eyes.

"That is the best gift I've ever received." He grinned, and kissed me again, but with a little more restraint.

I sighed when he finally released me. "I'm glad you like it."

"That was hard for you, wasn't it?" Evan noted, holding my hand as we walked into school. I hesitated, unsure of what he meant. "Having me look at it with you right there."

"You have no idea," I confessed. He smiled at my honesty.

"So tomorrow night's my turn," he declared with a slight squeeze of my hand, leaving me perplexed as he disappeared down the hall.

Evan wouldn't explain what he meant when I asked later that day. But he did want me to wear his favorite pink sweater, which I agreed to do with a shrug—it was his birthday. He continued to avoid telling me what he meant by his statement, making me nervous. It made Sara giddy. She came up with a thousand reasons he was being so mysterious, but none of them were even close to what he'd actually planned.

"We're having dinner at your house?" I questioned in confusion when we pulled into his driveway. Evan grinned.

"Close your eyes," he requested.

"What?! Why?" I demanded in a rush. "Evan, what did you do? This is supposed to be *your* birthday, right?"

"Yes," he replied with a quick smile, "and this is what I wanted to do for my birthday. Close your eyes."

I swallowed the anxiousness and obeyed. Evan helped me out of the car and wrapped a silky fabric around my eyes.

"Are you serious?"

"I know you'll peek before you're supposed to."

"Evan, I have heels on; I'm going to kill myself."

"No you won't." He swept his arm under my knees, and I fell back, cradled in his arms. I yelled out in surprise and wrapped my arms firmly around his neck.

"That was not necessary," I scolded.

"Don't want you to kill yourself," he remarked, a smile in his voice.

I heard his feet crunching along the gravel that led to the barn and then the squeak of a door. I recognized the scents of the garage as he continued up the stairs. He pushed the door open and effortlessly lowered me onto my feet. I was afraid to open my eyes after he untied the fabric.

When I did, my mouth dropped open. The entire room was shimmering in a soft glow, with lines of candles on every surface. The couch was pushed to the wall to allow room for a small table in the center of the floor, which was adorned with candlesticks and set for two. I recognized the whispery female voice floating through the speakers.

"Is this from my playlist?" I questioned.

"I told you it set a mood." Evan smirked, then examined me intently and asked, "So, how'd I do?"

"It's beautiful," I said breathlessly. He stood behind me with his arms around my waist, bending to kiss the top of my shoulder.

Evan escorted me to the table and pulled out a chair for me. Even though I knew it was part of who he was, the chivalry still felt awkward. I smiled nervously as he sat across from me, a colorful salad in front of us.

"Is this weird for you?" he asked, observing my fidgeting.

"No," I answered reluctantly. "I'm trying to get over that you thought to do this."

"Thanks," he replied sarcastically. "You didn't think I had this in me?"

"It's not that," I corrected. "It's *your* birthday, so it doesn't feel quite right."

"This is exactly what I wanted to do for my birthday. So, relax, okay?"

I nodded in acceptance, summoning the appetite to eat the berries and greens before me.

"We are going to the prom together, right?" he confirmed. "I know I didn't officially ask you. Actually, I think my mother did."

I laughed. "Yes, Evan, I will go to the prom with you."

"Please don't tell me that you're going to go shopping with her," he begged.

"I could never afford any place she'd take me."

"Oh, I'm pretty sure she wants to buy the dress." My eyes widened in surprise. He added, "It would just be too strange having you and my mother alone together. I know she'd tell you things that would freak me out."

"Really?" I teased. "Maybe we *should* go shopping together." Evan shook his head as I laughed at the idea of bonding with Vivian.

After I'd gotten over the initial shock of the romantic setting and recognized that it was only Evan and me, everything felt comfortable again. We talked casually and laughed easily. It was perfect. I'd almost forgotten that we were sitting in the barn. The flickering light transformed the room, hiding the games and tables in the shadows. I was soothed by the candles and the music—lost in the soft light flickering in Evan's eyes. But the anxiety returned when Evan set down a small blue box in front of me, instead of the dessert I was expecting.

I couldn't find my voice or even breathe. He smiled at me from across the table, watching me struggle for words.

"Don't say anything," he insisted. "This is what *I* wanted to do."

I stared at him, unable to bring myself to open the box.

"You have to open it," he pleaded. I looked nervously between him and the box. "*Please* open it. You're killing me."

I took a quick breath and slid the top off the box. I looked up at Evan with wide eyes, still unable to speak.

"I thought you should have one of your own to go with the sweater," he explained. "You like it, right?"

"Yes," I breathed, too overwhelmed to touch the sparkling rock inside the box. Evan stood behind me and removed it from the velvet to place it around my neck. I gently caressed it with my shaking fingertips as it lay against my skin.

I stood up to face him. "Thank you," I whispered. I wrapped my arms around him and stood on my toes to find his mouth. My lips brushed gently against his, lingering for a moment before slowly pulling away.

Evan had his arms around my waist, holding me against him. The music settled in around us and we found ourselves slowly moving to the soothing, seductive voice.

"Are we dancing?" I questioned with a smile.

"I think we are," Evan agreed with a slight nod of his head. "Is that bad?"

"No, just something else I've never done before," I admitted. I laid my head under his chin, allowing him to sway me.

The delicate strums and smooth melodies were mesmerizing, adding to the enchantment of the flickering lights and the warmth of his body. I searched his face as he gazed down at me with a soft smile. My stomach fluttered and my head felt light. I was completely consumed by him.

"I love you," I whispered, the words flowing effortlessly from my mouth.

Evan pulled me against him and pressed his lips to mine. The tender kiss soon turned urgent, sending electric charges throughout my body. His lips moved down my neck and his hands slid along my back under the sweater. I let out an excited breath as I ran my hands along his taut frame under his shirt. He pulled it up over his head. We separated long enough to allow him to drop it to the floor.

We were moving—still in our passionate exchange—in the direction of the room above the garage. I slid my sweater over my head and dropped it behind me. Evan stopped.

"Are you sure?" he questioned with a heavy breath, studying my face for a sign of doubt.

"Yes," I said in a whispering sigh, pulling him toward me again. He eagerly accepted me. I kicked off my shoes and unbuttoned my pants. Evan caught my hands.

"Really, we don't have to do this."

"Evan, I love you. I want to. But if you don't…" I started to zip my pants, and his hands caught mine again. We stood still for a second, staring at each other. Then he slid down my zipper and eased my pants over my hips. I stepped out of them and followed him into the room. He held me against his warm, smooth skin before gently laying me on top of the comforter, his mouth trailing along my shoulders down to my stomach. He stood to remove his shoes and to slide off his pants.

I wrapped my leg around the back of his thigh as he eased himself over me. My mouth found his neck, and I traced my lips along his shoulder. Our frantic breath revealed our excitement as his fingers traced along my stomach, sending a thousand sparks shooting through my body.

Evan froze when the lights flashed through the front windows. My eyes widened in alarm, as I held my breath.

"Oh no," he exclaimed, jumping up to investigate. He grabbed his pants and quickly stuffed each leg into them. I propped myself up on my elbows, watching in shock as he hopped to put his shoes back on.

"Stay here," he instructed as he rushed out the door, closing it behind him.

"Evan, you up there?" I heard a guy's voice yell a few minutes later. *You have got to be kidding me!* The distinct thump of footsteps climbed the stairs.

"Oh," the voice exclaimed. "Are we interrupting something?"

A flood of light shone through the bottom of the closed door. I panicked. Someone was in the other room. My clothes were in the other room! I heard more footsteps and voices. I snuck off the bed and tiptoed to the closet to find something to throw on.

"No," Evan replied uneasily. "Um, I was just cleaning up."

"Had a good birthday, huh?" the voice asked with a laugh.

"Jared, what are you doing here?" Evan finally asked.

"Came here with a few of the guys to surprise you for your birthday. Happy birthday."

"Thanks," Evan responded. Jared didn't seem to notice the tension in his voice.

"Let's turn on the music and play pool or something," Jared suggested emphatically. "Get whatever you want to drink at the bar."

"Sounds good," one of the other voices agreed. "What's with all the candles?"

"It's from earlier," Evan stated dismissively.

In the dim light, I made out a pair of jogging pants and a sweatshirt. I threw them on, folding the waistband down. The clothes hung off me, but it was better than being practically naked.

"I should bring these plates to the house," Evan told the guys. "I'll be right back."

The room on the other side of the door erupted with the bellows of a punk rock band and the crashing of pool balls.

I sat on the bed, having no idea what to do. I knew that there was no way I was going out that door while they were still in the other room.

"Emma?" Evan whispered. I jumped at the sound of the voice coming from the floor. I leaned over the edge of the bed to find Evan peering up through an open trap door in the floor. He was standing on a fold-down ladder that led to the garage.

"You can come down this way. They won't know," Evan explained.

I carefully made my way down the ladder in my bare feet, with Evan waiting at the bottom. He replaced the floor panel before folding the ladder back up. Without saying anything, he grabbed my hand. I followed him out the door into the cool moonlit night.

"I am so sorry," he said while we walked in the damp grass of the field behind his house. "I had no idea he was coming."

"It's okay."

"I hid your clothes in the closet before they came up. I promise to get them back to you."

"I'm never going to see that sweater again, am I?"

"Well, maybe after it stops smelling like you," he responded with a grin. Evan secured his arms around me. "We'll have other moments, I promise. I'm not going anywhere…well, not without you."

"I know."

"Nice outfit," Sara observed with a smile when I walked into her bedroom. "You have a story to share, that's for sure."

"How was your date with Tony?" I asked, trying to delay the inevitable conversation.

"Done," Sara declared casually, with a slight shrug. "Is that a diamond around your neck? Em, start talking."

I brushed over the more intimate scenes—much to Sara's disappointment—and when I was done with my account of the evening, she erupted in laughter. I slowly joined in.

"I can't believe you almost got caught *your first time!*" she exclaimed between fits of laughter.

"Shut up, Sara." I laughed, throwing a pillow at her. "It *wasn't* my first time. It didn't happen."

"You have *the worst* luck," she bellowed, tears rolling down her cheeks.

38. SHATTERED

You little tramp," Carol muttered from behind me while I swept the kitchen floor. I spun around at the sound of her voice.

"What did you have to do to get that?" she demanded, reaching for the necklace. I backed away, out of her clutches. Her eyes widened with shock.

"You can't honestly think he cares about you," she jeered. "He probably had that from the last girl he screwed."

A fire ignited within me as I stared in disgust at this pathetic woman.

"Shut up, Carol," I shot back firmly, towering over her.

"What did you just say?" she demanded, with a ferocity that could have blown the house to pieces. Her hand connected with the side of my face with a rocking force. The broom reverberated off the floor.

I turned my head back toward her. The fire fed every muscle of my tensed body. I raised my fist.

"What, are you going to hit me?" She smirked. "Go ahead and hit me."

My mind snapped back. I looked up at my clenched hand, appalled at what I was about to do. I pushed away the rage before it swallowed me.

"I have no idea why you're so twisted, but I'm not you," I spat. "You disgust me."

Carol stared at me with contempt. My insides twisted, instantly regretting my words. Fear overtook the anger, and my body began to quiver.

She grabbed for my arm, and I shoved her off.

"You fucking bitch," she grunted, coming at me with a force I wasn't expecting but should have been prepared for. She pushed my shoulders to slam me against the door, but I slipped on the broom at my feet. Glass shattered around me, and fire shot through my arm when my elbow crashed through a panel of the door.

I screamed in pain, the jagged edges slicing into me. I cradled my elbow against me. Blood ran between my fingers, dripping onto the floor. I continued to groan through clamped teeth as the shards dug into my flesh.

"What the hell is going on?!" George exclaimed, running up the stairs to the deck. He froze outside the door at the sight of the broken glass and me on the floor, soaked in blood. His eyes trailed up to Carol, and he stared at her in abhorrent shock.

"George," she gasped, "it was an accident. She slipped, I swear."

"Don't just stand there," he yelled. "Get her a towel." Carol rushed to the bathroom, obeying his command.

George opened the door as much as he could with my collapsed body still in front of it, paralyzed with shock. He slipped through and bent down to examine the damage.

"I need to take you to the hospital," he concluded. "There's still glass in the cuts, and you probably need stitches."

Warm tears slid down my face. George lifted me up just as Carol was returning with a towel. Her eyes pleaded with George. He grabbed the towel from her without giving her a glance and carefully wrapped it around my arm to catch the flowing blood.

"George, I'm so sorry," she whimpered.

"We'll talk about this when I get back," he snapped, still unable to look at her. He opened the door for me, and I followed him to his truck wordlessly. He didn't say anything to me either as he opened the passenger door. I climbed in, exhaling with an aggravated grunt as the movement forced the splinters in deeper.

The silence continued until we arrived at the hospital. We were admitted immediately and enclosed by curtains in the emergency room. The doctor examined the cuts before numbing the area to remove the glass and assess which cuts needed stitches.

I sat on the bed mindlessly listening to the chunks of glass clink as they hit the bottom of the metal bowl. I couldn't stop the tears dripping from my chin, as much as I tried to swallow them away. I shivered when the doctor poked and examined the exposed tissue for additional slivers. I eventually surrendered to nothingness while the needle pulled the torn skin together.

George tensed when the doctor asked me to explain how it had happened. My lying had become more convincing over the past couple of months, so the story of slipping backward on the wet floor spilled out easily. I didn't care whether the doctor believed me, but he didn't seem to doubt me. We were there several hours before we were finally on our way home.

"I'm going to take care of this," George grumbled during our drive home. "Just go to your room, and let me handle it, okay?"

"Okay," I whispered.

"There has to be a way for the two of you to live together," he mumbled to himself.

I knew by his tone that he still believed I had as much to do with this, if not more, than she did. I clenched my teeth, clearly understanding that he would always side with her, and as long as he did, she would never stop.

I expected Carol's car to be gone when we arrived home. I don't know why. Maybe I was hoping she would've left. But her blue Jeep sat motionless in the driveway. We pulled in behind it, and I slid down from the passenger seat, careful of my bandaged arm, and lumbered silently into the house.

Carol had swept up the glass and taped a piece of clear plastic to the door, covering the hole the shattered pane left behind. She was nowhere to be seen as I walked to my room, closing the door behind me. My arm was still numb for the most part, but it was already starting to throb. I lay on my bed, staring at the ceiling, too exhausted to succumb to either anger or sadness. I allowed my thoughts to dull, enveloped by numbness that comforted me like a familiar blanket.

I heard a murmur of heated voices upstairs, and the cries of Leyla and Jack. I closed my eyes to block it out. I thought I recognized her sobbing voice, pleading with him. Then there was silence. He came down the stairs and walked into the kitchen. Exhaustion eventually won over, and I drifted to sleep.

I didn't wake until the morning. I blinked, realizing I was still dressed and lying on top of my bedding. I glanced at the clock; my alarm was ten minutes away from going off.

I propped myself up. A sharp fire shot through my arm. I bolted upright, drawing in a quick breath through my teeth. The doctor told me I couldn't get the stitches wet for the first twenty-four hours, and the thought of how I would manage a shower made me collapse onto my back again with a frustrated sigh. Then I thought of how I still had to face Sara and Evan, and I groaned. Wasn't there any way I could avoid going to school today?

I opted for a sponge bath to avoid the impossibility of a one-armed shower, and put my hair up so it wasn't obvious that I hadn't washed it. The house was eerily still when I walked out of the bathroom. I paused in the hall, not hearing a sound except for the hum of the refrigerator.

I cautiously walked into the kitchen, listening intently. There was no movement in the kitchen or the dining room. A small paper bag was set on the island with a note attached to it, next to a key.

This is the ointment to put on your stitches twice a day. Carol is staying with her mother for a few days. She just needs space. Everything will be different. Use the key to lock up when you leave.

I read the note over several times, shaking my head. He really believed it was going to be different? Tears welled in my eyes, forcing their way down my cheeks. I wiped them away and swallowed the lump in the back of my throat.

I put the bag of bandages and ointment on my desk and gathered my books before leaving the house to meet Evan. I locked the kitchen door behind me, struck by the distinct click of the bolt when I turned the key—a sound that I'd never made before. I continued to fight against the tears before clomping down the stairs.

"Is she here?" Evan asked quietly after I shut the car door behind me. I shouldn't have been surprised that he noticed. As much as I was hoping the long-sleeved shirt would conceal my bandages, the bulky wrap left a distinct bulge. I suppose my sunken frame clued him in as well.

"No," I whispered, looking out the window. "She's staying with her mother for a few days."

"You can't stay here anymore."

I know, I mouthed, unable to make a sound. My eyes stung as I blinked back tears, unable to look at him. My mind remained blank, not wanting to think of what his words really meant. We drove in silence the entire way to school.

When we pulled into the school's parking lot, Evan shut off the car and shifted his body to face me.

"Emma?" He beckoned softly, making me turn toward him. "Are you okay?" I shook my head.

His hand brushed along my cheek, and I collapsed into his arms, sobbing against his chest. He held me until I couldn't cry anymore. I brushed the tears from my face and looked up into his glassy eyes. Seeing the pain in them tore at my heart. He kissed me softly, keeping his eyes closed when I pulled away.

"Do you want to go *now?*" he asked, when he was able to look at me again.

"*Now?*" I choked.

"Why not? What are we waiting for?"

The understanding of what he wanted to do suddenly weighed heavily in my stomach. Images of packing my bags and escaping with him ran through my head, causing my throat to close and adrenaline to rush through my veins. It was too much for me to process.

"Tomorrow," I implored, needing one more day to collect my thoughts. "She's not staying at the house tonight. Let me have the night to pack, and we can leave tomorrow, whenever you want."

Evan studied my face as I pleaded with my eyes.

"No one will be home when you leave in the morning, right?" he confirmed.

"Right."

"Then when I pick you up tomorrow morning, have whatever you want to take ready, and we're gone."

My heart skipped a beat as I nodded. Could I really do this? Leave everything behind and risk my entire future to escape her? Allowing her to destroy me didn't seem right, not after everything I'd been through. I needed the twenty-four hours to decide what to do.

Evan and I had missed homeroom, so we had to stop at the office for tardy slips before going to Art class. We were quiet as we walked the halls together. But he never left my side, holding my hand or wrapping his arm around me as I drifted alongside him to each class. His strength kept me moving forward, and it was also tearing me apart.

"You're going to do what?!" Sara asked fervently when Evan told her what we were planning. "How is that going to work? How long will you be gone?"

I could only stare at her; I didn't have the answers. She verbalized the same questions that were running through my head.

"I have a plan," was all Evan would reveal. "I'll tell you later, I promise."

Sara shook her head in amazement at what it had finally come to. She mimicked my every thought with her actions and words.

Before we could discuss it further, there was an announcement requesting my presence in the vice principal's office. Sara and Evan became still as a few heads turned toward me curiously. My stomach wrapped itself around a fiery ball of nerves when I stood to leave. Evan got up to go with me.

"It's okay," I assured him. "I'll see you in Journalism."

My feet felt heavy as they unwillingly carried my body down the hall to the vice principal's office. Mr. Montgomery was standing outside his door, awaiting my arrival. When I entered the room, my chest flickered with nerves as I glanced at the faces seated around the conference table.

"Emily," Mr. Montgomery stated with a voice of authority, "please take a seat."

Still staring from eye to eye, I slid onto the chair at the end of the table. Why were they here? But I knew. Clenching my jaw to fight the lump in my throat, I collected myself before their betrayal could completely break me. My back stiffened, preparing for what would come next.

"We're all here because we're concerned about you." Mr. Montgomery's deep voice boomed across the table, so stiff and diplomatic, without a hint of compassion. "We want you to explain how you get your injuries. Is someone hurting you?"

"No." I shook my head adamantly, my defenses kicking in.

"Emma," Coach Straw said, her approach warmer than his, but still ringing with an accusatory undertone, "We know you're not accident-prone, like you'd like us to believe. We just want to know what's going on."

"Nothing," I snapped back, overly guarded.

"We're not here to make things harder for you," Ms. Mier explained in her melodic voice, empathy pouring from her. "We're here because we truly care about you and want to help you."

Looking into her gentle brown eyes caused the lump to rise in my throat again. How could she have done this to me?! I swallowed hard.

"I swear, there's nothing to protect me from," I protested. My cracking voice betrayed me.

"Is Evan Mathews hurting you?" Mr. Montgomery interrogated. I widened my eyes, appalled at his accusation. Ms. Mier shot him the same look.

"Evan would never hurt me," I growled, infuriated by the allegation. My bite made them all sit back in their chairs.

"I know that," Ms. Mier soothed. "But someone is. Please tell us."

"I can't." I choked on the knot in my throat. I ground my teeth together, trying to fight against the tears collecting in my eyes with exaggerated blinks.

"Emma, I know this is hard," Ms. Farkis, the school psychologist interjected, "but we promise that no one will hurt you because you told us. We'll make sure of it."

"You don't know that," I whispered. They stared at me in silence, waiting. I clenched my fists against the table, needing to escape. "I can't do this."

I stood up and rushed out the door. I heard the screech of chairs when a few stood to follow me.

"Let her go," Ms. Farkis advised.

I ran down the hall in a blur of tears. I wiped my face and tried to breathe evenly when I approached the Journalism room. I didn't care whose attention I got first; one of them had to notice. Sara was staring out the small window of the door, so it was an easy choice. She excused herself to the bathroom and met me in the hall.

"We have to leave," I blurted, rushing toward our lockers.

"What happened?"

"They're trying to figure out what's going on, but I wouldn't tell them. Sara, I have to get out of here."

"Where do you want to go?"

"Let's go back to my house so that I can pack; then I don't care where we go."

"Do you want me to get Evan?"

"Not yet. Not until we can figure out where to meet him. They actually had the nerve to ask if he was hurting me."

"What?! Are they really that stupid?" she exclaimed incredulously.

We grabbed our bags. I didn't bother to put any books in it, not knowing if I would ever need them again. We flew down the side stairs, avoiding the main doors. Sara ran to get her car while I waited for her against the side of the building. My pulse raced and my whole body quivered, unable to keep still while I kept watch for her car.

I ran to the car when she pulled around and sank onto the seat, trying to find comfort now that we were driving away—but I couldn't. This all felt wrong, and it was happening way too fast. My brain couldn't make sense of it, and I was overwhelmed with fear. Was I doing the right thing, or was I overreacting?

Sara remained silent during the drive to my house. I was so lost in my questions and doubting thoughts that I didn't realize when we had turned onto my street. Sara's pocket buzzed, and she looked at her phone.

"Hi," she answered, glancing at me. "Yeah, we're going to her house to get her things."

She listened for a minute and pressed her lips together.

"Evan, I'm still not sure that's the best idea." She listened again. "Okay, we'll meet you there in an hour."

"What did he say?" I asked when she hung up.

"We're going to meet him at his house in an hour. Em, I'm not sure that you taking off to who knows where is the best answer. I still think there's a way out of this without you having to leave."

"I know," I agreed lowly. "But let's at least hear him out."

"Do you want me to come in with you?" Sara asked, glancing at the empty house.

"No, I won't be long."

"Emily?" George's voice hollered after I heard the click of the back door.

I continued throwing things in my bags, ignoring him when he walked into my room. He took in the bags on my bed with confusion.

"What do you think you're doing?! I received a call from the school saying you left upset, and that they wanted us to come in to talk with them. What did you say?!"

"Don't worry, George." I turned to face him, raising my voice. "I didn't say anything to them. But I can't stay here and live like this anymore! I can't live with *her*!"

He flinched at the anger in my voice. The alien tone was as difficult for him to hear as it was for me to project.

"You're not leaving here," he stated sternly between clenched teeth. "Listen, we will straighten this whole thing out, but you are not leaving this house. Do you understand me?"

The underlying threat in his voice knocked me back. Could I walk past him? Would he let me? Should I sneak out the window after he left me alone?

I watched his posture soften and sadness wash over his face. I silently took notice of the resigned transformation.

"I understand you're upset. And I promise you, we'll figure out a way to work this out. None of us can live like this anymore. But leaving right now is not going to help anything. Carol's staying with her mother tonight.

"We'll go to the school together tomorrow and straighten everything out. There's no need for anyone to get hurt by this. Just stay until tomorrow, and if you still want to leave after the meeting, we'll make arrangements. Okay?"

My mind raced. Did he mean it? Would he let me leave tomorrow? I wouldn't have to fly off to wherever Evan had planned to take me—I could stay here? Just one more night.

"Okay," I whispered.

"Why don't you go tell Sara that you'll see her tomorrow."

I slowly walked to Sara's car, still trying to decide if I was making the right decision. Something in the depths of my stomach was begging me to leave.

"I'm going to stay," I told Sara quietly.

"What do you mean?" Sara questioned in a panic.

"She's not staying here tonight. We're going in to the school tomorrow morning to clear everything up, and he said that I could leave if I still wanted to after the meeting."

"You believe him?" she asked, still uneasy.

"I have to," I whispered, my eyes filling with tears. "He's giving me an out without having to hurt anyone or run away."

Sara got out of her car and hugged me. We wiped the tears from our eyes when we finally let go.

"I'll see you tomorrow, okay?" My voice rasped.

"Okay," she whispered, sniffling. "What do I tell Evan? He's not going to be happy when I show up without you. He's probably going to want to come here to get you."

"Sara, he can't," I pleaded. "Convince him that everything will be okay and I'll see him tomorrow. Please, can you do that?"

"I'll try."

"Make him listen. I promise everything will be okay."

39. BREATHE

I tried to move, but there was resistance. Confused, I tugged at my arms—they wouldn't follow. I started to breathe quickly through my nose—my mouth wouldn't open. I frantically looked around in the dark. Where was I?

Then I couldn't see at all. There was something over my face. My heart beat hysterically, like it was going to explode in my chest. I pulled harder at my arms, which were strung above my head. I heard the jangling of metal as the sharp edges of the restraints dug into my wrists.

"I am not losing my family because of you," she seethed.

Panic consumed me. I started squirming, screaming as loud as the restricted covering would allow. The pillow pressed against my face. I shook my head back and forth vigorously, trying to remove it. It wouldn't shift enough to provide me air.

There was pressure on my chest. I tried to twist to get her off. That's when her cold hands gripped my neck. I screamed louder, but my frantic pleas were muffled by the tape. I flipped my body back and forth—the restraints on my wrists and the weight on my chest wouldn't allow me to escape her strangling grasp.

This couldn't be happening. *Please someone hear me.*

I pulled at the restraints—the edges scraping away my flesh. I strained to pull harder, needing to be free of their hold. I couldn't find my breath as her grip tightened. I needed to cough, but the air wouldn't escape.

I pushed against the bed with my feet, arching my back. The strain of our weight pulled at my shoulders, and I heard something pop, then a searing pain catapulted through my shoulder.

One of her hands released its hold. I sucked in a lungful of air, the effort burning my throat. I shrieked in agony when the bones of my ankle crunched with the impact of something she swung into it. I collapsed onto my back, my breath faltering. The darkness swirled as torturous pain overtook me. I fought the pull taking me under.

The cold clutches returned to my throat, squeezing harder. I choked, trying desperately to breathe in. The air didn't come.

I needed someone to hear me. I swung my left leg toward the wall with all my force, pounding against it. Adrenaline and panic shrouded the pain.

The pressure in my head continued to build. My lungs burned. The claws around my neck crushed in deeper.

I pounded on the wall one more time. *Please someone hear me.*

I could feel it pulling me under. I couldn't struggle anymore. The burning was too much. I gave in, collapsing beneath the hands, succumbing to the darkness.

EPILOGUE

In the uneven balance of my life, I experienced love and loss, more loss than I thought I could handle. But the love was unexpected. I almost missed out on it, too afraid and uncertain to give it a chance.

Love helped me live life instead of just survive it. It challenged my resolve, proving I was stronger than I'd ever thought possible. The comfort of it healed my wounds and caressed my scars. It gave me the confidence to stand taller than the inches within my body. In the dark I searched for it, yearning for its reprieve, only finding that I was alone.

I couldn't feel the pain of my broken body. I couldn't hear the beats of my heart fading within my chest. I couldn't listen to the agonizing pleas as he clutched me against him. It was silent. All that was left was…me.

In the silence, there was peace. A peace that came too soon, but I sought refuge in its release. Release from the pain, the chaos and the fear. Finding comfort in the unfamiliar calm would require a sacrifice I didn't want to make, but I didn't know if I had the strength to fight.

I knew time was slipping. I could no longer ignore the dwindling pulse. The thumping struggled to keep pace. The darkness pushed in around me. There was an ease to slipping away—giving in to the quiet and finding the resolution of nothingness. I was drawn to the resignation. I tried to hold on to the memories of my sacrifice—the warmth, the flutters, the truth in his eyes. Was life a choice?

In the balance of love and loss, it was love that made me struggle to...*Breathe.*

BARELY BREATHING

PROLOGUE

Six months ago, I was dead. My heart didn't beat within my chest. Breath did not pass between my lips. Everything was gone, and I was dead.

It's not easy to think about, not existing—no matter how much I fought to be forgettable all those years. So I've chosen not to think of it at all.

My therapist asked me to write down my thoughts and feelings in this journal. After months of avoiding the assignment, I figured I should try it once—then maybe I could finally get some sleep. I'm doubtful, but I'll try anything.

I don't honestly remember what happened that night. I get glimpses and moments of panic in my nightmares, but the details evade me. And I'm not looking to fill in the blanks.

I woke up in a hospital bed, barely able to talk, with dark bruises on my neck. There were bandages wrapped around my wrists to protect the raw skin. A sling supported my dislocated shoulder, and a cast concealed my ankle after reconstructive surgery. I don't know what I went through to end up that way. All I care about is that I'm breathing.

The police asked questions. The doctors asked questions. The lawyers asked questions. Whenever they'd start to talk about the details, I'd close them off, or leave the room. Evan and Sara promised to keep the details from me as well. They weren't there that night, but they were in the courtroom for the entire trial—as brief as it was.

Carol...

It's so hard to even write her name. She pled guilty. I didn't have to see her. I didn't have to testify. I didn't have to listen to the witnesses' testimonies. They summoned Sara and Evan, and I couldn't be there for that either—even though the lawyers requested my presence.

And George…from what little I've overheard, he was there that night. He was the one who called the ambulance. They didn't press charges against him. I begged them not to. Leyla and Jack need their dad. And now…Now I don't even know where they are. ~~I hope they remember how much~~ Sorry. I can't. It hurts too much to think about them.

Sara and Evan have barely left my side since that night. I've tried to assure them that I'm okay, but they just have to look at the circles under my eyes to know that I'm not. In truth, I don't want to be alone.

There was some press coverage, but it was a closed trial, and the records are sealed because I'm a minor (I'm pretty sure Sara's father had some influence over that too)—so there wasn't much for the papers to write about.

The town exploded with news of the attempted murder, and you can only imagine what it was like to return to school, or to be seen anywhere in Weslyn. Whispers. Pointing. Eyes following me everywhere. I've become a morbid celebrity—the girl who survived death.

Even the teachers treat me differently, like they're waiting for me to shatter. The small group who confronted me that day is especially wary. Their interference is what put the whole ordeal in motion. They'd made a call to the authorities before speaking with me, and then called George when I left the school.

Carol must have found out about their call to George, or maybe someone from the state contacted her to look into the allegations. Either way, she was desperate for me to disappear—forever. But it doesn't matter what made her do it. She can't hurt me now.

I do hurt. I'm not going to deny that. Especially since no one will ever see this journal. My ankle will probably never be the same, a con-

stant reminder of what I went through. I fought to recover, and despite the anticipated outcome, I returned to the soccer field four months later. At the beginning, I would cry in the shower after each practice and game. The pain was almost unbearable. But now I barely notice it.

Nothing looks the same anymore. Nothing feels the same. I'm not sure how to explain this to Sara and Evan. I don't know if they'd understand. I'm not sure that I do.

She wanted me dead.

I keep telling myself that she's gone. She's in prison, where she can stay for as long as forever, as far as I'm concerned. But I don't feel safe. Especially when I close my eyes each night, and she's right there, waiting for me.

I need to get out of Weslyn. Away from the stares. Away from the shadows that continue to haunt me. Away from the pain that paralyzes me when I least expect it. Six more months and all of it will be gone. I get to start again, with the two people I love most in the world.

Then again, my life is anything but predictable, and a lot can happen in six months.

1. TRY AGAIN

It's just a dream. I recognized the thought, trying to pull me out of the hands that dragged me to the darkest depths of the water. But panic overshadowed rationality, and I kicked as hard as I could. *It's just a dream,* my voice echoed through my head again, trying to wake me.

I looked down into the murky water, my breath burning in my lungs. The hands were now long, jagged claws, and as I kicked, one claw pierced my ankle, anchoring me under the water. A dark cloud surrounded me as the blood oozed around its nails. I struggled against it, but it only tore deeper into me. A rush of air bubbled around me as I screamed in pain. I was about to inhale my death when something pressed against my face.

It didn't feel like a dream anymore.

I shot up with a gasp, the pillow falling from my face. Disoriented and panting, I searched the room. Sara stood frozen by her bed, her eyes wide and mouth open.

"I'm so sorry," she muttered. "I thought I heard you talking. I thought you were awake."

"I'm awake," I said, exhaling quickly. With a deep breath, I pushed the panic away. Sara remained stunned even after I'd recovered.

"I shouldn't have thrown the pillow on your head. I'm really sorry." She frowned guiltily.

"What are you talking about?" I brushed off her apology. "It was just a dream. I'm fine." After another deep breath to ease the shaking, I pulled back the covers. They clung to the layer of sweat covering my body.

"Good morning, Sara," I said, as normally as I could.

"Good morning, Emma," she finally replied, forced out of her guilt-ridden stupor. And just like that, it was over, thankfully. "I'm going to take a shower. We have to hurry. We're leaving in an hour." She grabbed her things and disappeared.

I'd been trying to prepare myself for this day for over a month. It didn't matter. I was still freaked just thinking about it. And now it was here.

I collapsed back on the bed and stared up at the glowing white skylights that lined the ceiling, the morning sun hidden behind the snow.

I looked around the room, a room that had no true connection to me—the large flat-screen TV hanging on the wall and a vanity in the corner, lined with makeup that had seen way too many makeovers at my expense. There were pictures of laughing friends taped to the mirror, and vibrant art adorned the walls. No reminder of my life before I came here. It was the place where I'd been hiding—hiding from the judgment, whispers and stares.

Why was I here? I knew the answer. If I had the choice, I'd never leave. It's not like I had anywhere else to go, and the McKinleys wouldn't turn their backs on me. They were the only family I had, and for that I would always be grateful. But that wasn't completely the truth. They *weren't* the only family I had.

So when the phone rang while Sara was in the shower, I sucked in all the courage I could gather, put the phone to my ear, and said, "Hi."

"Oh! You're there," my mother exclaimed, completely taken by surprise. "I'm so glad I was finally able to catch you. How are you?"

"I'm fine," I replied, my heart stammering in my chest. "Um, so you have plans tonight?"

"Just a party with some friends," she replied, sounding as awkward as I felt. "Listen. I was hoping we could try, you know...I mean, I live pretty much in Weslyn now, if you ever decide you'd like to—"

"Yeah, sure," I blurted, before I lost my nerve. "I'll live with you."

"Oh, um, okay," she responded in strained excitement. "Really?"

"Sure," I answered, trying to sound sincere. "I mean, I'm leaving for college soon, so better to reconnect now than when I'm across the country, right?"

She was silent, probably digesting that I'd just invited myself to move in. "Uh, yeah, that sounds great. When are you thinking?"

"Since I go back to school on Monday, how about Sunday?"

"Meaning, *this* Sunday? As in, three days from now?" There was no hiding the panic in her voice. My heart skipped a beat. She wasn't ready to take me back, was she?

"Would that be okay? I mean, I don't need anything, just a bed, or even a couch. But if it's too much...Sorry, I shouldn't have—"

"No...no, that's perfect." She stumbled over her words. "Um, I have time to get your room ready, so...sure, Sunday it is. I live on Decatur Street. I'll text you the address."

"Okay. I'll see you Sunday then."

"Yup," my mother replied, the shock still lingering in her voice. "Happy New Year, Emily."

"You too," I returned before hanging up the phone. I stared up at the ceiling. *What did I just do?! What was I thinking?*

I grabbed my things and walked past Sara into the bathroom, trying to control the panic rising inside me. By the time I emerged, I had come to terms with it. It was what I had to do.

"So, I have something to tell you," I began, sitting on the stool next to Sara while her mother, Anna, poured herself a cup of coffee. "I spoke to my mother this morning—"

"It's about time," Sara interrupted. "You've only been ignoring her for like six months."

"What did she have to say?" Anna said encouragingly, ignoring Sara's outburst.

"Well…I'm moving in with her this Sunday." I held my breath as I watched the news sink in.

Sara's spoon clanged inside the cereal bowl, but she didn't say a word.

"What made you decide that was the best thing to do?" Anna asked calmly, diverting attention from Sara's silent disapproval.

"She's my mother." I shrugged. "I'm leaving for college soon, and I don't think I'll have another opportunity to try to fix us. I haven't exactly been fair to her, and she keeps trying to connect, so I thought this was the best way to do it."

Anna nodded, considering my explanation. Sara stood up and briskly walked to the sink to drop her bowl in, still unable to look at me.

"Well, Carl and I will need to talk about it, since we were given guardianship until you're eighteen. And I'd really like to meet her before anything's final. Okay?"

I nodded, not expecting Anna's answer. I wasn't used to having a parent actually care about me, so I didn't really know what to say.

"I understand why you want to do this," Anna assured me with a soft smile. "Let us just talk about it first, that's all."

"Thanks." I smiled weakly. "It would mean a lot to get to know my mother again."

Sara stormed up the stairs without a single word. I exhaled deeply before following her up the stairs.

"Okay, say it," I demanded flatly while Sara shoved items into her overnight bag.

"I don't have anything to say," Sara retorted. But she did; it just took a three-hour car ride to the hotel and a day of primping before it came out.

By the time we returned to the hotel, after being prepped and polished from head to toe all day, I was exhausted—and we hadn't even been to the party yet. Or maybe it was the impromptu decision to move in with my mother that had drained my energy. Either way, I was having a hard time looking forward to tonight.

"I don't understand why you're moving in with her," Sara reprimanded me out of nowhere as she smoothed the brush over my lids. "Couldn't you start with…uh…*talking* first? I just don't like it. She left you, Em. Why go back?"

"Sara, please," I implored her quietly. "I need to do this. I know it seems messed up to you, but it's important to me. It's not like you're losing me or anything. And if it's *horrible*, I'll move back in with you. I feel like I should give her another chance."

Sara sighed dramatically. "I still don't think it's a good idea, but…" She paused a moment, "You're one of the most stubborn people I know, and if this is what you want to do, I know I won't be able to talk you out of it. Um, you can open your eyes now."

I stretched my eyes open and blinked, the mascara sticking along my lashes.

She deliberated, finally conceding with a roll of her eyes, "Fine. Live with her. But she'd better not do anything monumentally stupid like she did when she left you with Psycho."

I grinned, adoring Sara's protectiveness. "Thank you. So…how do I look?"

"Amazing, of course," Sara gloated, taking in her masterpiece. "I'm going to put my dress on, and then we'll be ready to meet the guys in the lobby."

I picked up the note that had been waiting for us when we returned to the hotel and ran my thumb over the elegant script.

Dear Emily and Sara,
I am thrilled that you have arrived safely and hope you enjoy your afternoon together. I am looking forward to seeing you this evening for dinner. I have arranged for the car to pick you up along with Evan and Jared at 6:45 p.m. for our 7:00 reservation.
I have no doubt that you will enjoy all that has been planned this evening!
Sincerely,
Vivian Mathews

"I hope I don't embarrass her," I hollered through the bathroom door.

"Stop being so nervous," Sara returned. "Vivian really wants you there. This is important to her. She even convinced Jared to take me so I could be here with you."

I grinned, knowing that Jared didn't need much convincing.

"What do you think? You haven't said anything about how you look."

"Oh, uh…" I stepped in front of the full-length mirror, and my lips curled up naturally. There was a slight resemblance to the girl who preferred jeans and a ponytail, the girl who still couldn't conquer applying makeup on her own. Her light brown eyes glistened under a shimmer of pink and dark lashes. Those were her flushed cheeks, and her full lips veiled with gloss, smiling back at me.

I turned to the side, and the layers of chiffon flowed around me. My fingers traced the soft pink embroidered design on the corseted champagne top. Sara had chosen the same shade of pink to weave into my hair, creating the effect of an inset headband, and a pile of soft curls was artistically stacked at the nape of my neck. I picked up the finishing touch from the dresser and secured it around my neck, allowing my fingertips to brush the sparkling diamond as I had the day he'd given it to me.

As Sara stepped out of the bathroom, I turned toward the door with my cheeks aglow, ready to thank her for her ingenious transformation, but I was held speechless at the sight of her. The sapphire-blue dress skimmed her body, brushing her curves in a shimmering dance. Large curls of red draped over her right shoulder. She looked… worshipable.

"Jared is in so much trouble," I said, gaping. "Sara, you look amazing." I wasn't sure why I was so in awe. She was the most desirable girl in school for a reason, but I guess I forgot that most of the time—she was just Sara to me. But there was no denying her modelesque figure and Hellenic beauty now.

Sara smiled vibrantly, revealing perfect white teeth behind her glossy red lips. "Maybe he is."

"Sara, please don't tell me you're going to sleep with him," I begged.

"Relax. I won't," she said with a roll of her eyes. "But that doesn't mean we can't have fun."

My phone beeped, distracting me with a text. Spoke with Carl and we called Rachel. She's sweet, and I believe she wants this too. Meeting her on Saturday, but it looks like everything's all set for Sunday.

Sara handed me my jacket and the bag that held Evan's gift. "Your parents are letting me move in with her," I announced.

"Well, then, I guess it's official." Sara held the door open for me to follow.

"I guess so." My stomach flipped with the realization.

I thought my knees might give way when we rounded the corner into the main lobby and I saw the back of his black tailored jacket. My eyes trailed up to find his usually tousled light brown hair neatly swept to the side in a more distinguished look. He was caught up in a conversation with his brother and didn't notice us as we approached.

Evan stopped midsentence when Jared's mouth dropped open. Jared *was* in trouble—it was written all over his face as Sara sauntered toward him.

I couldn't feel my legs moving as Evan turned around. My heart stopped at the sight of his smoky blue eyes, and heat rushed to my cheeks when his mouth formed that perfect smile. It had only been two weeks since he'd left for his skiing trip, but for some reason it was like I was seeing him for the first time all over again.

"Hi," I whispered. He stepped up to take my hand, our connection unbroken from the moment our eyes first met.

"Hi," he responded, still smiling. He tilted his head down to kiss me, but Sara interrupted.

"We need to go, or we'll be late."

"Sure," Evan replied, instantly snapping us back to the bustling lobby of formally dressed people, most likely attending the same event. He helped me slip on my jacket. I slid on black leather gloves in preparation for January's freeze and took his hand again.

"What's that?" Evan asked, gesturing toward the bag.

"A surprise." I grinned. I'd waited so long to give it to him, it was killing me.

"I have one of those too." He smirked, holding the door open for me.

"One what?"

"A surprise," he revealed, smiling wider and sending another rush of color to my cheeks.

I ducked into the limo and slid in beside Sara, since she was sitting across from Jared. Evan was forced to sit next to his brother, leaving my hand empty. I glanced across at him, and we silently exchanged the I-wish-I-were-sitting-next-to-you-too look.

The limo pulled in to a circular cobblestone driveway, and the driver came around to open the door. The restaurant resembled a mansion more than a dining establishment, with multiple eaves and glowing windows on each level.

We were escorted to a private patio that was glassed in for the winter season, offering a spectacular view of the dark, rolling ocean.

"Wonderful! You're here," Vivian greeted us brightly, with open arms. She gripped each of her sons by the shoulders as they bent to kiss her on the cheek, then admired Sara and me after the guys had helped remove our jackets.

"Exquisite," she declared, wrapping each of us in her signature brief embrace with a brush of her lips on our cheeks. "Come. Sit down."

Stuart remained unmoved. He had not given us a glance since our arrival. He stoically gazed out at the ocean, holding a glass of ice, filled with caramel-colored liquor.

At Vivian's insistence, we each found a seat. I made certain to sit next to Evan at the rectangular table, with Jared and Sara across from us and Vivian and Stuart at each end. Evan took my hand under the draped table, instantly calming my nerves.

The polite small talk began. I tried my best not to participate unless a question or comment was directed my way, and of course each time it was, I usually had my mouth full or was in midgulp. Sara pressed her lips together to keep from laughing, which only made me squirm uncomfortably.

After surviving the anxiety-inducing dinner, I excused myself to use the restroom and promised to meet Evan in the foyer.

It was a struggle to hold the chiffon high enough so it wouldn't fall in the toilet. I was standing outside the bathroom door, smoothing the layers back in place, when I heard, "I don't want to talk about this again."

I remained still. Not sure if I should continue around the corner or wait until they were done, I was thankful that I'd decided not to walk in on the next words: "She's not your future, Evan. It's about time you realized that. I won't allow you to pass up Yale to follow a girl, especially *that* one, across the country."

"It's not your choice to make for me, Dad," Evan bit back. "I don't expect *you* to understand."

"Stuart, what are you doing?" Vivian beckoned from afar. "We're going to be late."

I remained still, collapsed flat against the restroom door with my heart pounding and my mind racing. What just happened? I knew Stuart was withdrawn, but I had no idea it was because he didn't approve of me. His reaction sank in, and my lip quivered.

I bit my lip, taking a deep breath to compose myself. Then I walked around the corner and forced a smile when I saw Evan waiting for me with my jacket over his arm.

"Are you okay?" he asked, inspecting my face. I pushed my smile wider with a nod of my head. I slipped my arms into the jacket with my back toward Evan, afraid he could see right through me.

Evan held the door open and allowed me to lead the way to the limo. Sara and Jared were across from us, lost in conversation about who they deemed to be the best guitarist.

Evan took my hand. "Are you shaking?"

"It's cold," I lied, wanting to roll my eyes at my involuntary reaction. Evan wrapped his arm around me to warm me up. I eased away the nerves, nuzzling into him.

"Wow." Sara admired the uplit mansion as the limo slowly crept in line with the others. A streak of nerves twisted my stomach. I felt like I was nearing the head of the line for a death-defying roller-coaster ride.

"They're just people," Evan assured me in a whisper, probably noticing I wasn't breathing. I exhaled to relax my shoulders, squeezing his hand.

Just people soaked in jewels of every color or poised in tailored tuxedos, full of judgment and snide comments. We made our way through the glitz-covered bodies shimmering in the candlelight. The voices swirled in time with the smooth jazz band in the ballroom.

Everywhere I looked, I was struck by more brilliance.

"Mrs. Mathews, this is incredible," Sara said, gawking. "I've never seen anything so beautiful."

"I'm not so sure my sons would agree," Vivian replied with a sparkling smile. My cheeks grew warm when Evan squeezed my hand. "This did turn out more spectacular than I could have hoped. I am so happy to have you all here with me. I need to greet a few more guests, but I will be expecting a dance later, Evan." The corners of her mouth rose as she met her son's eyes, and she glided away in the antique ivory dress that floated around her. Vivian was the picture of sophistication, with her blond hair swept back into a French twist. I admired how collected she always remained, even in a setting that was completely overwhelming to me.

"What was that about?" Sara demanded, looking at Evan. "Do you have some crazy dance moves or something?"

Jared laughed, and Evan shot him a warning glance. "Evan is Mom's *dance partner*. My father refuses to dance, and I failed the lessons…"

"You took lessons?" Sara laughed, interrupting Jared.

"Yes," Evan finally admitted. "My mother loves to dance. And I seem to be the only one who can keep up with her without stepping on her toes." He glared at Jared, who sneered mockingly back at him.

"I can't wait to see this," Sara said with a smirk.

We found a lounge set in a corner away from the stifling conversations, and immersed ourselves in the details of Evan and Jared's
skiing trip in France.

"Oh, Em, did you tell Evan the news?" Sara burst out. It took
me a moment to remember what she was talking about, hoping she
wasn't about to ruin the surprise I had wrapped in the box.

"No," I said slowly, then remembered with a slight nod. "Oh,
I'm moving in with my mother this weekend," I confessed casually,
like I had just announced I was buying a new pair of shoes.

Jared had no idea why this was big news, but Evan narrowed his
eyes. "You're doing what?" he asked.

"Your mother's looking for you," Stuart interrupted from
behind us. Evan turned around to view Vivian scanning the crowd.
She raised her hand when she located him.

"I'll be right back," Evan announced, rising to escort his mother
to the dance floor. I turned toward Sara, but she and Jared were
already making their way through the crowd, not wanting to miss
the spectacle. I was left alone in Stuart's shadow.

Feeling I couldn't just walk away without appearing completely
rude, I fumbled for something intelligent to say. Instead I said,
"This is quite the party, huh?"

He peered down at me as if I'd spoken in a foreign tongue,
shook his head slightly, and walked away.

Okay then, I mouthed, glancing around to see if anyone
had witnessed my humiliation. I pinballed my way through the
crowd to the ballroom. The dance floor was full of couples, but
one stood out among them. They floated around with ease and
grace to the cool rhythms of the Sinatra song sung by a lanky
crooner.

"Omigod," Sara gasped next to me, a glass of champagne in her
hand. "They can really *dance*." My mouth popped open at the sight
of Evan leading Vivian in perfect form, cradling her hand in his.

Her eyes sparkled as they twirled around the dance floor, their feet in perfect unison.

"Told you," Jared interjected. "Kinda scary good, right?"

"Very," I floundered, finding that there were way too many things about Evan I still didn't know.

The song concluded, and there was an overwhelming burst of applause. Evan appeared uncomfortable, while Vivian smiled brightly. At that moment a woman with short white hair in a long-sleeved black dress stepped up to the mic. Stuart joined Vivian, and Evan spotted the three of us on the opposite side of the dance floor.

Wow, I mouthed when he slid his arm around my waist. He shrugged, abashed, and redirected his attention to the speaker.

The woman went on to recognize Vivian's philanthropic achievements over the years, acknowledging her success and dedication to each cause and organization. She'd invested not only time, but her passion. I listened intently, completely astounded by all that Vivian had done. The presentation concluded with a roar of applause, and the white-haired woman handed Vivian an award made of crystal, giving her a kiss on her cheek.

The music picked up again, and we met Vivian, along with every other person in the audience, congratulating her affectionately. Evan hugged his mother, followed by Jared and Sara. I went to congratulate her as well. She wrapped her arms around me tighter and longer than she'd ever done before and whispered into my ear, "I'm so glad you're here with us."

My eyes watered instantly, understanding the intended meaning of her words. She released me and was pulled in another direction, with more words of praise.

Evan took my hand and led me away from the crowd. I was still caught up in the moment, my head buzzing with emotion.

"Let's get out of here," Evan said in my ear.

"What? You want to leave?" I searched his face, baffled.

"Yeah. I want to show you something."

"Okay," I responded, still so very confused. We retrieved our coats, and Evan escorted me out the door without saying good-bye to anyone.

2. FIREWORKS

Evan led me down the long driveway lined with limousines and town cars. We approached the parking lot, and I recognized Evan's BMW.

"When did your car get here?" I asked suspiciously.

"I drove it here earlier," he shared with a crooked grin. That's when I realized this was part of his plan, the "surprise" he'd mentioned when we left the hotel.

He opened the passenger-side door and pulled out a backpack. He unzipped it and handed me a pair of sneakers. I eyed him apprehensively, recognizing the shoes that were supposed to be at Sara's—which meant Sara was in on this too.

"I figured they would be more comfortable than the heels," he explained, tossing his black dress shoes on the floor of the car, along with his tux jacket and tie, and lacing up a pair of sneakers. I sat on the passenger seat, switching my shoes.

I had tried to figure out his plans in the past with little success, so I'd learned just to go along with them without too many questions—unless he walked us to the edge of a cliff and asked me to jump. Then I would have something to say.

Evan found my hand again, and we continued toward the cobblestone street lined with lanterns. My shoulder brushed against him as we walked, the crisp air swirling around us. The sky was clear, allowing the full moon to follow us like a spotlight.

We hadn't walked very far when Evan pulled me between two hedges that lined the bordering property.

"Evan, where are we going?" I demanded in a panic, fearing we were trespassing and about to get caught.

"They're not home," he assured me, our feet crunching in the glistening layer of untouched snow. I looked up to find a tall mansion with dramatic peaks. The windows were dark.

"But I'm sure they have an alarm system or something," I argued, looking around nervously, anticipating the arrival of flashing lights. I continued after him, faltering on the collapsing surface. I was forced to lift my layers out of the ankle-deep snow to keep from tripping.

"Stop worrying," he laughed, supporting me by my elbow. "My mother knows the people who live here—even invited them to the party tonight. They're in Brazil. I spoke with them myself about what I wanted to do, and they couldn't care less. We're not going into their house or anything."

"Really?" I questioned, slightly doubtful.

"Really," Evan confirmed again with a smile. "Trust me."

We walked beneath the long shadows of the mansion to the back terrace. I stopped in my tracks at the sight of a flickering light. "I thought you said no one was home."

Evan laughed again, amused by my overly panicked state. "They're *not*. This is for us. I paid the limo driver to start the fire and bring over our bags."

"Oh."

It was a charming setting, with two Adirondack chairs set before a fireplace on the stone terrace, sheltered by an overhang. A portable Bose system and my gift were set on a small table off to the side. "I like this," I said, beaming up at him.

We walked over to the small fireplace and stood in front of the crackling fire, absorbing its warmth. Evan stepped behind me and slid his arms around my waist, holding me against him. I turned to face him, a ridiculous smile spread across my face. "I've missed you."

"I've missed you too." Evan bent down to find me. His nose was cold against my cheek, but his breath on my lips instantly warmed my entire body. He pressed his firm mouth softly against mine, and lingered there just long enough for me to lose my breath before pulling away. My eyes remained closed, savoring the buzz on my lips.

"I'm glad you came tonight," he said, hovering inches away. "I know it was hard for you. But it meant a lot to my mother."

"I'm glad I came too. I wouldn't have wanted to miss hearing all that was said about Vivian. She's amazing; I had no idea."

Evan leaned over and kissed me, running his hand down the side of my face.

"Do you want your present?" Evan asked when he pulled back. I began to smile, but faltered. Confusion flashed across his face. "You don't?"

All I could hear were Stuart Mathews's disapproving words, and I wasn't so sure I was excited to give him my gift any longer. "Can we wait?" I requested awkwardly.

"Uh, no," Evan responded with his brows pulled together, retrieving the small rectangular box from the table. "But you can open yours first if it makes you feel better."

I took it from his hands nervously.

"Go on, open it," he encouraged me impatiently. I tore the silver paper to find a long rectangular box that looked expensive. I held my breath when I opened it. A gleaming smile spread across my face when I pulled out two concert tickets.

"Evan!" I jumped up to wrap my arms around his neck. "Yes! This is the perfect gift. Thank you."

"You're welcome," Evan replied, hugging me back. "I wanted to be the one to take you to your first concert."

"When is it?" I inspected the ticket for the date. "The end of the month. Great. I won't have to wait too long."

"I almost bought a third one for Sara because I know how much she loves the band, but I decided this was just for us."

I laughed, already hearing Sara's groan in my head when I showed her the tickets to the sold-out show she'd been dying to see.

I put the tickets back in the box and tucked it into the inside pocket of my coat. Evan looked at me in anticipation. I pressed my lips together, fighting the urge to make up some reason not to give him his gift—but I knew I had to.

"So, I hope you like it." I removed the shiny green wrapped box from the bag and handed it to him, holding my breath as he opened it. He took off the lid and looked from what was inside to me, then back down again.

"Does this mean…?" His eyes lit up, and his mouth curled into a stunning smile as he set the box on the chair. Despite my reservations, I couldn't help but smile back—his excitement was too contagious. "You got in!" He swept his arms around my waist and picked me up. I yelled out in surprise, laughing. "Em, I'm so happy for you." He kissed and hugged me again.

"When did you find out?" Evan couldn't stop smiling.

"Ten days ago," I confessed as he set me back on the ground.

"Wow. That must have been hard not to tell anyone," he said, impressed, knowing how much I'd wanted this. "Stanford. You totally deserve this. You didn't even tell me that you'd applied for early admission."

I averted my eyes sheepishly. "It was hard. But I did tell Sara—sorry."

"When I said *anyone*, I didn't count her. She's a given." The excitement continued to seep in. "Now I just have to find out which school accepts me so I can join you."

My smile faltered again.

"What?" Evan asked, his brow furrowed in confusion.

I opened my mouth to speak, but then immediately closed it.

"Say it," he demanded. "Let me into that head of yours before you start thinking things you shouldn't."

"Too late," I confessed with a guilty shrug. I paused again before I admitted, "I heard your dad." Evan opened his mouth, about to spew some not-so-happy words, when I interrupted, "He's right."

He stopped and stared at me. "About what?"

"You can't make one of the biggest decisions of your life based on a girl."

Evan smiled. Not the reaction I expected. "Okay." My eyes widened at his casual response. He continued to wear his infamous amused grin as he added, "Because Stanford and Berkeley are *horrible* schools, and I'd be jeopardizing my whole future if I went to California. You're right. We should just break up now, since there's no point in us considering each other in any decisions we make about our futures."

"Evan!" I balled up the wrapping paper and threw it at him. He laughed and batted it into the fire as if he'd planned it. "That's not what I meant," I huffed.

"I know"—he chuckled, pulling me toward him—"but you can't listen to my father. He only *thinks* he knows what's best for me, when in fact he has no idea who I am." He kissed the top of my head and added, "I would never make such a huge decision based on a girl." He paused long enough for a jolt of panic to make my back tense, before adding, "but you're not just any girl. I'm…*we're* going to California."

I buried my face in his chest and squeezed my arms around him. "Yale's the best law school in the country," I reminded him without conviction.

"And who said I wanted to be a lawyer?" he responded, squeezing me back. Suddenly, he pulled away and declared, "I want to teach you how to dance."

My heart stopped. "You what?"

Evan laughed.

"I can't dance."

He laughed again. "I know. That's why I'm going to teach you."

I groaned and clenched my teeth in dread as he approached the Bose system. I was trying to figure out how to conjure up an ounce of grace as he inserted his iPhone and scrolled through the song selections. I scanned the empty terrace, scouting for potential tripping hazards. Then I took in the puddle of chiffon around my sneakers and exhaled in defeat—this was going to be a disaster.

My head popped up at the sudden strum of a guitar followed by a round of drums. Evan started nodding his head to the beat, walking slowly over to me. He reached for me, cradling my hips in his hands and rocking me to the punk song.

"Ready?" he asked, taking my hand and spinning me around as I laughed. When I turned back to face him, he started bouncing up and down, forcing me up with him. The thumping energy surged through me, and I found myself jumping alongside him. He smiled in approval and proceeded to thrash his head in time with the thumping bass. I rocked from side to side and jumped in a circle, swinging my arms, my skirt swirling around me.

We pogoed around the terrace for another song until I finally collapsed into an Adirondack, giddy and out of breath.

"You're amazing." Evan stood in front of me, admiring me with flushed cheeks.

"I'm sure I don't look so amazing now," I noted, blowing the strand of hair stuck to my nose as a line of sweat ran down my temple.

"That's not what I said," he corrected. "You *are* amazing."

I could feel my cheeks changing color, and my lips stretched into an embarrassed smile. "What did I do?"

"Just you, everything about you—you're amazing," he stated simply.

"You just love that I'm such a great dancer," I teased, making him chuckle.

Evan pulled me to my feet and met me with a kiss that set off a thousand fireworks through my entire body. Wait. Those *were* fireworks. I turned to witness a sprinkling of red sparks in the sky. We stepped out from under the terrace to watch the brilliant spectacle.

"Happy New Year," Evan said into my ear, pulling me around to kiss me before I could say the same.

It was the most dazzling fireworks display I'd ever seen; I could feel my heart beating in my chest with each explosion. The sparks felt like they were going to sprinkle down upon us. Every so often, I'd glance up at Evan to find him watching me adoringly. Then he'd redirect his attention toward the fire in the sky.

When it was over, my toes were numb from standing in the snow, and I was shivering. The fireworks had been so mesmerizing, I hadn't registered that the temperature had dropped until now.

"Let's get going," Evan said, rubbing my arms when he noticed me shaking. "You're about to freeze into a lawn ornament." I followed him to the terrace, where the fire had become a heap of glowing embers. Evan walked to the side of the house and returned with a couple gallons of water to douse the remaining heat in the fireplace. I packed up Evan's package and speaker system while he put the fire out.

When we neared the front of the house, Evan's black BMW was idling in the driveway.

"The limo driver?"

"Is awesome," Evan declared in awe. When we ducked into the warm car, I pulled off my gloves and thawed my hands in front of the blowing heater vent. "Now where?"

"Hotel?" I suggested, trying to sound nonchalant.

Evan grinned knowingly. "Mine or yours?"

The question suddenly made me think of Sara. I wondered how her night had gone, and where she and Jared were right now.

"Where do you think they are?" Evan asked, as if reading my mind.

"You don't think they..."

"He was excited to see her again"—he shrugged—"and she looked incredible tonight..."

"I know, right?!" I agreed emphatically. "But you don't think they would...do you?"

Evan shrugged again. "Let's just pick a room and hope it's empty." He leaned over and found me waiting. What started as a soft kiss pressed into a more urgent one, coated with want. The nervousness that shot through me at the thought of going to the hotel room was quickly replaced with a need to get there as fast as we could.

Evan pulled back, breathing heavily, "Yours." He buckled his seat belt and put the car in gear, speeding out of the driveway. That's when we met the line of slow-moving limos pulling out of the mansion's driveway and were practically forced to stop. "No way," Evan groaned, banging his head against his headrest in frustration. I laughed.

While we patiently waited to move more than twenty feet a minute, Evan said, "I think this is going to be a great year, Em."

"I hope so," I squeezed his hand that rested on my lap and thought, It can't be any worse than last year.

"It's going to be different, that's for sure," he continued, "especially since you're moving in with your mother. Where did that come from anyway?"

I shrugged. "I figured now was a better time than any to recognize I have a mother."

"Okay," he said slowly with a nod of his head. "But this weekend? All in, huh?"

"What do you mean?"

"If you're going to do something, you're going to give it everything you have. You've decided to reconnect with your mother, so why not move in with her?"

I shrugged again. I'd never consciously recognized that this was one of my character traits. But he was right. I was an overachiever, needing to excel in everything I did—so why not this?

"What's your therapist going to say about your decision?" he asked, and then shook his head when I wouldn't answer. "You stopped seeing her, didn't you?" I still wouldn't say anything, knowing how he felt about the therapy. "How come?"

"I'm fine," I said defensively. "I don't see the point. Besides, Sara's a better therapist than anyone with a PhD, and she doesn't force me to write down my feelings."

Evan chuckled. "That's probably true." His laugh tapered off, and he became serious. "You know if you ever need to talk…"

"I'm not much of a talker." I directed my attention out the window, not wanting to stir the emotions I'd made a point of shutting off.

He accepted this. "I know," he said softly. After a moment of silence, he added, "This year will be better at school, too."

I glanced at him skeptically.

"Really," he assured me. "You know something stupid had to have happened over the break. Somebody got a nose job or slept with his best friend's girlfriend. They have short memories." Evan squeezed my hand, and I hoped more than anything that he was right.

My stomach fluttered with nerves when we pulled up to the hotel. While we waited for the valet, Evan said, "Let's not go into this with expectations. We can do whatever comes naturally."

I stared at him. "Are you serious? Of course I have expectations. I've *expected* to have sex with you for about six months now."

"Okay then," Evan replied with a smile. "We obviously have the same expectations." I laughed, easing the nervous tension.

We left the car in the hands of the valet and made our way to the elevator. Evan held my hand the entire time, and my whole body was jittering so much that I couldn't find anything to say.

Before I opened the door, Evan turned me around and said, "Close your eyes." I obeyed. "Deep breath." I inhaled deeply and relaxed my shoulders with the exhale. I awaited my next instruction, but felt his lips upon mine instead. Their touch surprised me. My calm breath faltered and my knees weakened. I opened my mouth to the rhythm of his, feeling the warmth of his tongue on mine. Fumbling in my pocket for the key, I tried to open the door while remaining connected. It didn't work.

I pulled away long enough to insert the key and open the door. Then I tugged Evan toward me, finding his lips again. Evan started to unbutton his jacket as I backed into the room. That's when I heard, "You're here!" I pushed away from Evan midkiss and spun around, slamming the door in his face.

"Sara, hi," I fumbled, trying to catch my breath. I cracked the door to find Evan rubbing his forehead, "So, Sara's here. Umm, I guess I'll see you in the morning."

"Uh, okay," Evan said slowly, looking at me like I was acting weird—only because I was. "I guess I'll see you in the morning." I shut the door before he could even kiss me good night.

"What's wrong with you?" Sara demanded. "You could've let him in."

"No, it's late," I said in a rush, taking off my jacket and tossing it on the chair, my face on fire.

"Oh, wait," she shot out. "You two thought you'd have the room to yourselves. Oh, Em!" She started laughing hysterically.

"Sara," I scowled. "It's not funny."

"Oh, it is," she countered. "For the first time ever, I like a guy and don't sleep with him. And you were finally about to have sex and didn't get to. Oh, that's so fucking funny. Em, I'm so sorry."

I groaned and collapsed next to her on the king-size bed. "This had better not be an indication of how this year's going to be."

Sara rested her head on my shoulder and draped her arm across my stomach, "It's the end of our senior year. Then we're off to college. It's going to be the best year of our lives. Believe me."

I groaned, not sharing her optimism.

3. STILL LOVED

"Can we talk about what happened last night?" I asked Sara after leaving the small restaurant where we had eaten a greasy breakfast with Jared and Evan, surrounded by people who looked like they wished they'd never seen the New Year.

"What? That you were planning on losing your virginity *finally*, but I screwed it up?"

"No, I'm definitely not talking about that," I retorted. "You mentioned *liking* Jared. What happened between you two?"

"I'd rather not talk about it."

Something was off. Avoiding a conversation about a guy was not like Sara at all.

"I'm confused."

"Em, he lives in New York. I'm still in high school, forget about the fact that we're moving to California," she explained, void of emotion. "I can't keep torturing myself. I need to forget about him…again."

I glanced over at her. She kept texting and wouldn't look at me.

"Thanks for driving," she said, slipping the phone into her purse. "I'm going to sleep most of the way, if you don't mind."

"Sure," I responded, concerned by her reaction.

The quiet drive gave me time to think—which wasn't necessarily a good thing. Being trapped in my head for almost three hours could be a bit overwhelming—even scary. But at the end of it, I was content with my internal discussion. Whether moving in with my mother was the right thing to do or not, I was committed to trying.

"Let's just do nothing today and watch movies," Sara proposed as we unloaded our bags from the car.

"Sounds perfect."

Evan had to drive Jared back to school, so it was just Sara and me in front of the television the entire New Year's Day. I forced myself to get sucked into the sappy romantic comedies and awkward teenage humiliation.

Sara responded to a beeping text. "Em, do you want to go to a party tonight?"

"Yeah, I don't think so," I answered without thinking twice.

"Are you ever going to go to another party again?"

"I don't know." I sighed. "I just don't want to hear it if someone gets too drunk and then asks me the wrong thing. I don't want to be the freak anymore."

"They need to get over it, and so do you," Sara argued. "You can't stay locked away forever because you're afraid someone's going to say the wrong thing. Someone *always* says the wrong thing eventually, so fuck them. Who cares?"

I grinned, knowing she was right. "Just not tonight, okay?"

"Okay," Sara shrugged. I knew she was disappointed. I hadn't been to a party with her in over six months.

"But why don't you go?" I suggested. "I don't want to, but there's no reason you shouldn't."

"Are you sure?" she asked cautiously.

"Of course," I replied resolutely.

Sara's face lit up. She went back to her phone and began texting the masses to get the details.

Anna hollered up the stairs, "Girls, we're home. Come down and tell us about the party."

Sara jumped up and ran down the stairs. I followed behind, still not accustomed to this family sharing thing that Sara had going on. Anna and Carl were so patient with me, not prying too much. But even the slightest questions about my day caught me off guard—questions that were so very natural to them.

Sara sat in her usual spot, cross-legged on their king-size bed, and I sat down on the edge of the bed, very much a spectator. Anna was unpacking while Carl flipped through the mail. He pulled an envelope from the stack. "Emma, this is for you."

"Thanks," I replied, as I took it from his hand.

I examined the plain business envelope with no return address while Sara completely re-created every detail of the evening—from the decor to Vivian's award to the fireworks display.

I was running my finger over the "Boca Raton, FL" postmark when I heard, "How did Evan react when you told him about Stanford, Emma?"

I flipped my eyes up on hearing my name. All three were eagerly awaiting my response, making me realize that Sara and I hadn't talked about it either.

"He's excited," I replied awkwardly.

They waited a second longer, and when they recognized that this was the extent of my account, Anna said, "I'm looking forward to meeting your mom in the morning."

I nodded, my stomach tensing at the thought.

"Then I thought you, Sara and I might go shopping after."

"Mom, you should know by now that Emma dreads shopping. But I'm in," Sara answered on my behalf.

Carl looked over at me knowingly and offered, "College football?" I nodded in relief.

"What are you doing tonight?" Anna questioned. "Isn't Marissa Fleming having a party?" I shouldn't have been shocked that Anna knew this. She seemed to know the social schedule of just about everyone in town.

Sara's face flashed with excitement, "Yes, and I'm going with the girls."

"What about you, Emma?" Anna asked, hanging a dress in the closet.

"I'm just going to hang out here and read," I answered feebly.

Sara slid off the bed. "You have to help me pick out something to wear."

Knowing I wouldn't really have any input in this decision, I answered, "Sure," anyway.

I saw Sara off to the party, with several assurances that I would be fine. I was then able to redirect my attention to the mysterious envelope, sitting on the pile of pillows beneath Sara's floor-to-ceiling bookshelves.

I tried to recall whether I was expecting something from Florida. The letter didn't look official enough for college correspondence; it was simply a plain white envelope with small handwriting, addressed to me at the McKinleys'.

When I pulled out the folded paper, my heart stopped. I unfolded it with shaking hands to find it streaked with crayon. On the front was a rudimentary picture of a boy, a girl, a man and a woman with grey hair, standing by a pink Christmas tree. I opened the paper to find, "Merry Christmas Emma. We miss you!" slanted across the page in a child's oversize handwriting. The message concluded on the back with, "Love always, Leyla and Jack."

I stared at the words, tears trailing down my cheeks, and swallowed against the knot in my throat. But the large red smiles and the mountain of presents under the festive tree were comforting. The man was undeniably George, but I couldn't figure out who the woman was supposed to be. I wanted to believe it was Carol's mother, Janet, but she didn't have grey hair.

I dismissed it, thinking it must be a teacher or someone they'd met in Florida. I guess I knew where they were now—it wasn't like I'd ever see them again, though.

That did it. That sent me over the edge. I collapsed into the pillows and cried until I felt a hand brush against my back and raised my head in surprise. Anna was kneeling next to me, her eyes glassy as she offered me a comforting smile. She noticed the picture in my hand and settled in next to me.

"They look happy," she noted, gently tucking my hair behind my ear. "That's all you ever wanted for them, right?"

It became clear to me that Sara had confided in her mother after everything that had happened last May. How could she not? Anna would have insisted on knowing why Sara hadn't come to her, probably feeling betrayed and hurt. So of course Sara had had to tell her that I'd stayed to prevent Leyla and Jack from being taken from their parents. Well…at least they still had one of their parents.

"Yes," I choked, my voice hoarse.

"It was nice that he sent that to you. It means the kids still really love you."

I knew she was trying to take away my pain, but thinking of them missing me tightened my chest, and hot tears flowed freely. Anna pulled me into her arms and hugged me tightly, and I let her without tensing. I inhaled her warm floral fragrance with each gasp of air and allowed myself to miss them.

Once I had control over the pain and was quiet again, Anna released me. I sat up, wiping my wet cheeks.

"I understand why you want to move in with your mother," Anna finally said. "And I want more than anything for the two of you to find the connection you've missed out on over the years. But if for any reason it doesn't work, this is your home first, and we'll always do what's best for you. We're not going to say anything to the social worker, since that will open a whole realm of paperwork that isn't necessary, and you'll be eighteen soon. We'll just let her continue to do her periodic check-ins by phone. Okay?"

I nodded, unable to find my voice.

Anna hesitated before adding, "I love you, Emma. We all do. And I am very serious when I say that we will do anything for you; you only need to ask. Do you understand?"

My breath faltered with her emotional declaration, and I replied, "I understand. Thank you."

Anna's mouth spread into the smile that Sara had inherited, lighting up her kind blue eyes as she instantly defused the seriousness of the moment with, "Let's get some ice cream."

I couldn't help but smile in return, allowing her to help me up from the heap of pillows and following her down the stairs to the kitchen.

———

"Is that everything?" Carl asked, examining the backpack and two duffel bags in the back of Anna's SUV.

"I don't own much," I said.

Anna and Sara got into the car while I turned to Carl. "Thank you for everything."

"It's been great having you here, Emma," he said in return, and without warning, wrapped his arms around me and pulled me to his chest. "I'll keep in touch with Stanford for you, but I'm sure you'll be over before I know it." Then he released me and walked to the house without looking back. I remained still, not having been quite prepared for the departing hug.

"Ready?" Sara hollered from the open car window.

"Sure," I answered, heading toward my car.

As I pulled out of the driveway, I glanced up one more time at the large house with a twinge of sadness. Although I had never felt like I completely belonged there, I certainly felt safe, which was something I hadn't experienced very often in my life.

4. "HOME"

I tried to pay attention to the roads we turned down as I followed Anna in my Honda, knowing I'd need to find my way back to Sara's on my own eventually. At least now I'd be able to drive the car that Carl helped me pick out a few months ago, after I *finally* got my license. There'd been no need to drive when Sara and Evan chauffeured me every day. But now I would be responsible for getting myself to school.

It took about twenty minutes for us to reach the outskirts of Weslyn, where my mother was renting a house. We veered down an interwoven maze of streets within the disorganized neighborhood. Unlike Sara's, with its large homes all neatly lined up on a grid, here much smaller houses lined a tangle of swirling roads. Kids ran from one snow-covered yard to another, since few of the properties were bordered with fences.

Anna pulled in to the driveway of a house at the tail end of the maze. With only one neighbor, it was isolated at a dead end, across from the bare woods that surrounded the neighborhood. I pulled up alongside the curb so Anna could back out when she left.

The small yellow two-story house was quaint, with white shutters framing the windows and a weathered white porch welcoming us. The front door opened, and my mother appeared, propping the screen door open with her hip. She waited for us to each grab a bag, her arms crossed, shivering in the winter air.

I didn't make eye contact as I passed her, fearful that her clear blue eyes would reveal something other than the words that came out of her mouth. "Hi, Emily. I'm glad you're here."

"Thanks for letting me stay with you," I replied awkwardly.

"Of course," she answered, her voice betraying her nerves. "This is your house too now. You even have your own room."

"You have to see it," Sara burst out, taking me by the hand and dragging me up the wide wooden staircase that rose from the middle of the small foyer. Anna laughed, making me suspect that they had done more than shop yesterday.

At the top of the stairs was a small landing. Straight ahead was an open door that led into a bathroom, and two closed doors flanked the stairs. Sara opened the door to the right and flipped the light on. I slowly followed her.

Stepping into the room, I let my eyes trace all four walls, three of them white, the wall where the door stood open solid black. I turned in a circle to take it all in, inhaling the lingering fumes of fresh paint. My lips curled up.

A full-size bed sat across from the door, covered with a black-and-white comforter in a bold baroque design, accented with white pillows bordered in black. Above the bed a three-dimensional art piece made it look like a hundred black butterflies were bursting out of the white wall, tethered by black wires.

Two small windows to the left of the bed were framed dramatically by thick black curtains. A white chest of drawers rested against the black wall, next to a full-length white-framed mirror that tilted on a stand.

On the opposite side of the room was a desk, its glass top stenciled with black flowers and butterflies and set upon two white bookcases. Above it hung a cloth-covered board that echoed the comforter's baroque black-and-white pattern, with one note pinned to it: "Welcome Home, Emma," in Sara's unmistakable scrawl.

"Do you love it?" Sara demanded.

I turned to find Anna and my mother in the doorway, awaiting my reaction.

I gasped. "I can't believe you did this," I said. "Thank you so much."

"Of course," Anna replied.

My mother stood a few steps behind Anna, watching. "Do you want something to drink?" she asked Anna as Sara started unzipping the duffel bags to put my minimal possessions in their places. The two women disappeared down the stairs, Anna's voice drifting away as they neared the bottom.

"Sara, really, thank you."

Sara paused with a stack of shirts clasped between her hands, recognizing the sincerity in my voice.

"I knew you were nervous about moving in with her," she explained, setting the shirts in the opened drawer, "even if you wouldn't admit it. My mom wanted to get to know Rachel too, so this seemed like the best idea. We spent the day together yesterday—shopping, painting and decorating. Emma, I don't think you have anything to worry about. In fact, Rachel's probably more nervous than you are."

I wasn't sure if that was possible.

When Sara was finally pleased with her work—having put away my clothes, arranged my books and set up the laptop and router that I'd received from Anna and Carl for Christmas—she announced, "I think you're all set." Nerves shot through me as I realized she was preparing to go.

I tried to think of a way to delay her, but then Anna hollered up the stairs, "Sara, are you ready?"

The truth was, I wasn't ready to be alone with my mother. And I gathered from her fidgeting that she wasn't ready to be left with me either.

We said good-bye and lingered on the porch until they pulled away, inevitably leaving us alone. As I walked back into the house, the awkwardness hit me in the face.

"So…you can look around if you want," she offered hesitantly, closing the thick wooden door, the pane of glass in the middle rattling when she clicked it shut.

"Uh, okay," I replied, veering right and stepping through the arched entrance of the kitchen. My mother remained outside the room in the foyer, watching me intently.

Besides a coat of soft yellow paint, the kitchen probably hadn't been updated since the house was built. The doors on the wooden cabinets hung slightly askew above a scarred countertop. A deep porcelain double sink sat below a window that looked out on the woods. A refrigerator that was smaller than me hummed loudly in the corner, with a white gas stove sticking out next to it. There wasn't a lot of room for much else in the kitchen except for a small round table with four mismatched chairs. One of the chairs was pinned against the wall to allow room to pass to the entrance.

"Help yourself to whatever," she said from the doorway. The tight space didn't allow two people to avoid each other. I peered into the refrigerator to find condiments and leftover Chinese food that looked like it had been in there awhile.

"Thanks," I replied, closing the door.

"Guess we need to go shopping, huh?" she said with a nervous laugh.

She stepped back with her hands in the back pockets of her jeans, giving me room to walk across the foyer to the living room. I could feel her eyes following me, adding to the mounting anxiety. I felt like I should say something, make some sort of attempt at conversation, but I had no idea where to start.

So I stood in the middle of the living room, playing nervously with my fingers, taking in the brown couch and love seat in front of the television. A spindled rocking chair rested in front of the front window. I paused in my tentative inspection.

It took me a moment before I realized where I knew it from. It had been in my bedroom when I'd lived with her and my father.

The sight of it caused my chest to tighten. I wasn't prepared for the sudden flash of memories. I wanted to go over and touch it, hoping that by running my fingers along the carved arms, I'd be filled with the happiness of the memories stored within its frame. Stories told while wrapped in strong arms, rocking back and forth. Whispered words of love and promises as I drifted to sleep to the thumps of his heart against my ear. I could feel her staring at me as I stood motionless, my eyes locked on the chair.

"I have a ton of movies." Her voice crashed through my reverie, bringing me back to the present. It took me a moment to connect with what she'd said. I nodded at the built-in bookshelf next to the window, which was lined with DVD cases.

"Oh, that's great."

On the other side of the living room, a large sideboard displayed a sound system surrounded by an array of framed pictures. I walked over to them. I couldn't say I was expecting many pictures of me, but my stomach hollowed when I didn't see any at all. I glanced around for any indication that I existed, or that she'd had a life with my father—only to find the room filled with strangers.

"Pictures of my friends," she explained briefly, without going into any further detail. I nodded, fearing that my voice would reveal the hurt.

"So, you have school tomorrow? Ready to go back?" my mother asked as I thumbed through the CDs she had stacked in another built-in nook in the corner.

"Not really," I answered honestly, recognizing that she was trying to have a conversation to which I was doing a lousy job of contributing.

"When's your next basketball game?"

"Friday," I responded, scanning the room.

"Would you mind if I came?" She sounded nervous. The anxiety in her voice drew my attention.

"You can come," I answered, finally looking at her with an awkward smile. The tension in her blue eyes slowly melted away.

"Great. Thank you." That one answer changed everything. The next thing I knew, she was pointing to people in the pictures and talking about where they were and what was going on. She pulled out a couple of CDs, insisting I listen to them because they were "life-altering."

I didn't say much. I didn't think I could have gotten a word in if I'd wanted to. Her nervous chatter flowed without pause as she sat in front of the player and spread CDs across the floor. I tried to relax as I listened to her stories, inspecting the woman before me and trying to connect with her as my mother. It felt like a million years since I'd actually had one. I had no idea how to act around her, or what to say.

"So do you really like your room?" she asked after slipping a CD into the player.

"I really do," I admitted honestly.

"I was pretty useless in designing it. I just let Anna and Sara pick out everything," my mother confessed, her cheeks reddening.

A knock at the door interrupted her search for the song that reminded her of her trip to New Orleans last year. I watched as she answered it. She appeared puzzled. "Um, hello?"

"Hi, Mrs. Thomas. I'm Evan. I'm looking for Emma." I jumped up from my cross-legged position on the floor and practically ran to the door.

"Hi," I greeted him in a rush before my mother could say anything. Evan peeked around the door, and his signature smile crept over his face, causing my heart to stutter. I was beyond relieved to see him.

"Well, come on in, Evan." He stepped into the foyer to allow my mother to close the door. "I'm Rachel. It would completely freak me out if you called me Mrs. Thomas. Mrs. Thomas was Derek's mother, and she didn't like me very much. Besides my last name is Walace, so if anything I would be Ms. Walace, but I really would prefer Rachel." Evan and I were stilled by the burst of information that spewed from her mouth in a single breath. Her cheeks reddened, and she laughed awkwardly when she found us staring at her. "Wow. I have no idea why I just said all that. I'm not usually this nervous. Okay, yes I am." Looking at our stunned faces, she said, "I'm so sorry."

"That's okay," I assured her—all too familiar with being possessed by nervousness. "Why don't I show Evan around?"

"Uh, sure," she agreed, returning to the living room to put away the CDs that were spread over the floor.

I didn't bother showing Evan the downstairs, since all he had to do was turn in a circle to see the entire layout. I took his hand and led him to my room, closing the door behind us.

"Nice room," Evan admired, ducking under the slanted ceiling to sit on my bed. "How's it going? She seems nice."

"Yeah," I said hesitantly, not knowing how to answer him. "It's fine...I mean, she's great."

"You're nervous too, huh?" he acknowledged with a small laugh. "I guess I can see who you get your red cheeks from."

"Funny," I returned sarcastically. Nervous was just the tip of what I was feeling. I couldn't begin to describe the panic slithering inside me. Maybe when it all came down to it, I was afraid she was going to tell me that she couldn't do this—that she didn't want to be a part of my life again. And that thought kept me from being able to relax long enough to appreciate that I was here, with her. "I guess I am kinda nervous."

"You're going to be fine," Evan assured me, giving my hand a squeeze. "Oh, I have something for your room."

Evan reached inside his jacket and pulled out a large envelope, handing it to me. I opened it and pulled out a stack of pictures. I smiled as I flipped through the images Evan had captured with his camera. Action shots of me playing soccer, feral and intense. Moments of Sara and me laughing. Another of me sitting on his front porch, lost in thought, oblivious to his camera. There were even a few shots of the two of us posing, his arm around my shoulder, taken during a picnic last fall.

I leaned over and kissed him. "Exactly what my room needs." I removed the sign from the board above the desk and tucked the pictures under the black ribbon that crisscrossed its surface.

There was a soft knock on my door. Before I could say anything, my mother slowly opened it and poked her head in. "I was going to order a pizza. Are you hungry?"

"That sounds great. Thank you," Evan responded for the two of us. I pressed my lips together and nodded.

I remained silent at the kitchen table as we ate, listening to my mother's nervous chatter. She interrogated Evan about... well, everything. I think focusing on him was her way of keeping the awkwardness between us at bay. If we were both desperately focused on every word that came out of Evan's mouth, we wouldn't have to figure out what to say to each other. Evan handled the pressure calmly, as usual. He didn't give a hint that the atmosphere was heavily laced with anxiety. But after he'd left, the uneasy tension was crushing.

"Do you want to watch a movie?" she asked as I wrapped the leftover pizza to place it in the bare refrigerator.

"I actually have a paper to work on—it's due tomorrow," I lied. She nodded slowly, and I feared she could tell I wasn't being honest.

"Okay," she finally said, looking disappointed. A pang of guilt shot through me as I retreated to my room. But I really needed to be alone.

I lay down on my bed with my arms crossed behind my head and stared up at the freshly painted ceiling. I had so many strange emotions swirling inside me. I needed a moment to sort them out.

I hadn't said more than a half dozen words to this woman in five years, and now I was her roommate. Well, that's what it felt like. She told stories about her friends and the trips she'd taken as if she were sharing them with someone she'd just met, not her daughter. They made me think about what I'd been doing while she was having so much fun, and I felt ill.

While I'd been in the darkest depths of hell, my mother had been traveling, drinking and living a carefree life. I wanted to throw up just thinking about it. She hadn't once mentioned leaving me, or my time with Carol and George and what they'd done to me. It was as if that time had never happened, and we were starting anew— with a big black hole in between. I guess *I* was having a hard time moving past it.

To be honest, I hadn't considered what it would be like to live with her. It's not like I had expected to rekindle a relationship that had never been there in the first place, but I also wasn't expecting to discover that I'd been completely absent from her life both physically and emotionally for the past five years.

I stayed in my room for the rest of the night, finally going into the bathroom—that was pretty much the size of a large closet—to get ready for bed around midnight. The television was on in the living room. "Good night," I hollered down the stairs. I could hear her talking and laughing in the kitchen, evidently on the phone. I shut my door without waiting for her to respond and slipped under the crisp new white sheets, pulling the comforter up under my chin.

My phone chimed next to me, and I picked it up to read, Good night. Hope you sleep well in your new room! from Sara. I didn't respond, just clicked off the bedside lamp.

I stared into the dark, still trying to wrap my head around the fact that I was here, living with my mother. The windows rattled as a gust of wind howled outside. I closed my eyes, but within minutes they snapped open. The boards creaked on the stairs. I tried to relax, realizing it was just my mother. I followed her footsteps as each board gave beneath her, until she shut the bathroom door.

I wish I could say that I drifted off to sleep, but it appeared the boards didn't need anyone walking on them to creak. I was restless throughout the night, continually awakened by the groans of the house. The cold air whistled through the rattling panes of the windows, just like the scattered thoughts that whirled through my head.

5. PEOPLE CHANGE

G ood morning," Evan greeted me from the slick walkway. I closed the door behind me, leaving my mother in the shower, getting ready for work.

"Hi," I replied flatly, adjusting my backpack over my shoulder as I took calculated steps toward his car.

"You have something against mornings, don't you?" Evan teased, opening the passenger door. I smiled slightly before kissing him briefly on the lips and ducking into the car.

When he'd closed his door, I explained, "Sorry, I didn't sleep well. This house is super creaky." Considering my weariness, I was glad he'd offered to pick me up on our first day back after the break.

"What are you doing after practice tonight? Do you want to come over?"

"Sure," I answered automatically, and then quickly countered with, "I can't."

Evan appeared confused.

"I'm going grocery shopping with my mother," I explained. "She's not sure what I eat, so she wants me to go with her."

"Okay," Evan replied. "How was it after I left last night? You two were pretty funny at dinner—she talks when she's nervous, and you don't say anything."

"That was torture for you, wasn't it?"

"I was fine." He chuckled. "I'm pretty sure it was worse for you."

"I...I don't know what to talk to her about," I confessed.

"I think you could just let her do all the talking," Evan advised comically.

I stared out the window in a daze. I didn't realize we had pulled into the school parking lot until the car stopped. A wave of dread consumed me as I watched the students getting out of their cars.

Evan acknowledged this, reading my thoughts. "I know you don't want to be here," he said, "but I'm convinced it'll be different." I didn't say anything as I got out of the car.

I used to look forward to coming to school—not for the social life, but to escape the oppression at home. After everything that had happened, my safe place had become the place I dreaded most.

When I started the school year, I'd kept my head bowed, trying to retract further into my shell—not only in the halls but in the classroom as well. I'd refused to participate other than to complete the assignments. Sara and Evan eventually gave up trying to encourage me, promising that it wasn't as bad as I thought.

I stared at the brick building and took a deep breath before closing the car door. I pulled my backpack over my shoulder, preparing myself for the scrutiny. Evan took my hand, his warmth comforting me. Sara was waiting for us by the back door, smiling brightly as usual, and greeting just about everyone passing her by.

"Good morning," she beamed. Then her brows dipped into a scowl. "You didn't sleep well, huh?"

"Wow," I responded to her bluntness. "Do I look that bad?"

"No," Evan countered quickly before Sara could utter the truthful words on the tip of her tongue.

"Liar," Sara and I chimed in unison. I met her eyes, and we started laughing. The sound of my laughter had the strangest effect, like waking a sleepy village from a curse. All of a sudden I heard, "Hi, Emma."

I turned my head to find Jill standing next to us. "How was your New Year?" Before any of us could respond, or shake off the stupefied looks on our faces, she continued, "Did you hear about the party at Michaela's? Her parents came home in the middle of it, and of course everyone was drunk. But the worst part was when they found Nick and Tara having sex on their bed. Michaela is so screwed."

And just like that, it was as if the past seven months had never happened. Jill and Sara continued talking about the party while Evan and I followed behind. Evan wore an I-told-you-so smile on his face, and I grinned at the sight of it. As we continued down the hall, I realized the stares were gone, and no one was whispering as I passed them. Every so often, someone would acknowledge us with a "Hi" or "Good morning." It was freaking me out. Everyone was letting it go…or pretending to, anyway.

"Good to see you survived over vacation," a voice cut through the crowd. Evidently not *everyone* had gotten over it.

Evan stiffened as the jeering words found us. My chest tightened in response. Evan spun around and pinned a guy against a locker, his forearm across his chest. I looked on in complete shock, and everyone in the hallway froze.

"What did you say?" But it wasn't Evan asking the question. Several other seniors were surrounding the guy, who, judging by the size of him, must have been a freshman. Joel Rederick leaned in closer as Evan kept the guy immobilized. The freshman stared back in complete panic, sweat beading along his forehead.

"Nothing," he said, choking.

"That's what I thought," another senior threatened.

"Don't bother walking down the senior halls again," Evan seethed.

"What's going on here?" an authoritative voice asked from behind the crowd. Evan released the freshman, and the seniors began to part. The guy scurried away in search of the small pack who had abandoned him.

"Dick," Jill snapped from behind me. Everyone continued on their way, and the talking resumed. No one looked twice at me as I remained still, attempting to digest what had just happened.

"Sorry about that," Evan offered, taking my hand once again.

"It's okay," I replied slowly, recovering from my befuddlement. "Thank you."

He studied me with eyebrows raised, not expecting my reaction, then grinned before leaning down to kiss me.

"Ahh, you're in the middle of the hall," Sara said, with an undertone of *Omigod*. Evan pulled back, and I looked at her oddly.

Sara and I continued to our lockers, and I asked, "Since when do you care if Evan kisses me in the hall?"

"You don't like to draw attention, remember?" Sara said from within her locker.

"Sara, is there something wrong?" I sensed that she was still not right.

"No, I'm fine." She closed her locker with a smile.

I watched her walk off, knowing she wasn't being honest with me.

After basketball practice I arrived home to find my mother at the kitchen table, writing down a list of what we needed—which was practically everything, from the looks of it.

"Hi," she greeted. "I think I have some ideas for meals. Is there anything you don't like?"

"I'm pretty open to trying anything…except for meatballs," I told her with an inadvertent shiver. "But you don't have to do anything crazy. Besides, I usually come home late because of basketball."

"We'll pick out some easy things. How's that?" she offered, scanning her list again. "That way you can throw something together for yourself if you come home late or if I have to stay at work."

The thought of preparing anything beyond a sandwich was intimidating. "What?" she questioned anxiously, when she saw my scrunched face.

"Um, I'm not exactly adept in the kitchen," I confessed sheepishly.

"You can't cook?" she clarified in shock.

"Does oatmeal count?" I shrugged in embarrassment.

My mother laughed. "Well...I guess we'll be shopping in the frozen food section, too."

We got into her car and drove to the grocery store in the next town over. She spent the ride reviewing the list and asking for my input. I'd never really had a say before, so I didn't contribute much. When I'd lived with Carol and George, I would write the basics of what I needed on the grocery list—cereal, granola bars and the like—since I wasn't allowed to eat it unless I'd asked for it. But for the most part, I ate what was put in front of me, no questions asked—even when it made me violently ill.

We ultimately decided to make up the list as we went along. Which was pretty much our approach to everything—including our relationship.

"You know I'm not exactly very good at this mother thing, right?" my mother said, picking through a pile of apples and putting a few that met her approval in a produce bag.

I didn't know how to respond. It was the start of a conversation I'd never expected to have in a grocery store.

"I mean, I don't want you to think that I'm expecting to walk back into your life and take charge or anything," she continued, her voice laced with apprehension. "I just want...I think it would be nice if we were...friends. You know, instead of..." She looked at me with her lips pressed together. "I just want to get to know you. Does that make sense?"

My shoulders eased in relief. I had no idea where the conversation was headed, but this was a welcome surprise. I wasn't exactly sure how to be her daughter, any more than I expected her to be my mother.

"Yes." I smiled. "I'd like that."

"So, would you be okay with calling me Rachel?" she asked cautiously. "Mom feels a little weird, to be honest."

I let out an uncomfortable laugh, slightly surprised by the request. "I can try."

She smiled softly and released her nervousness with a quick breath. "Great. Now, what do you eat for lunch?"

I continued behind her, pushing the grocery cart around as she held up items and waited for me to nod or shake my head before placing them in the cart or putting them back. By the time we were done, there was more food in the cart than two people could eat in a month. Thankfully, a good portion of it was frozen.

"Do you want to learn how to cook?" my mother asked as she set the items on the belt. "I could teach you."

I smiled warmly at her offer. "Uh, sure," I replied, not having the heart to tell her that Evan had already made several attempts to teach me, and each had ended disastrously. She seemed eager to be able to do something with me—I would at least *try*.

"So, how long have you and Evan been together?" she asked after we had loaded the groceries into the car and were driving home.

"Officially"—I calculated—"about ten months."

"What does *officially* mean?"

"Well." I fumbled for words, not sure how to explain how we'd felt for each other from pretty much day one, and how due to misunderstandings and hurt feelings, it had taken forever before we'd finally ended up together. "I guess I don't know how to answer that. Let's just say we started dating last March."

"Okay," she said with a confused nod. "He seems really nice."

"Yes," I agreed. My face glowed. "He is."

"I'm still looking," she said with a sigh. "I'll never find anyone like Derek again."

My heart faltered. I knew we had agreed to be friends, but she was still my mother. And having her talk so casually about finding the next best thing to my dead father knocked me back a bit.

"Do you want to help me with dinner tonight?"

"Huh?" I stumbled, still trying to get over her comment.

"Want to start your cooking lessons?" she clarified.

"Can I take a pass on tonight?" I begged. "I think I want to wait a bit before revealing how terrible I am."

She laughed. "You can't be *that* bad."

"You have no idea," I grumbled, making her laugh again.

"Okay. Maybe another night."

I sat in the kitchen while my mother explained what she was doing as she filled pork chops with stuffing. I just nodded like I was paying attention, knowing it was useless. I could figure out the most complex equations, or understand the workings of the nervous system, but asking me to baste or julienne anything caused anxiety beyond explanation.

My mother set the plates down on the table I'd set for two, the one thing I *could* do.

"Thank you," I said, sitting down with a glass of water.

"Sure," she responded, sitting across from me.

When I looked up from my plate to praise her for the meal, I found her watching me. It was like she was examining every inch of my face, so intently that it made me want to sink under the table.

"I forgot how much you look like him." Her eyes were glassy and distant—she was looking at me, but at the same time *not*. I bowed my head to escape her sorrowful gaze.

"So, Sara seems like she's an amazing friend," my mother said, her voice suddenly back to normal. I glanced up as she pierced the cut pork chop with her fork.

"Uh, yeah," I responded, shaking off the haunted look in her eye. "She's my best friend."

"I have one of those." My mother smiled. "Sharon." She let out a laugh just thinking about her. "We've done *everything* together. She usually gets me into trouble, but I have the best stories because of her."

I nodded, trying to remember this woman who seemed to be such a huge part of her life, but came up blank. I realized there wasn't much about my mother that I knew, even from the twelve years she had technically been in my life.

It wasn't the howling of the wind or the boards groaning that drew me from my bed that night. Yes, they were the reasons I was still awake, but I was brought to my feet by the clatter of metal crashing outside my door. I found my mother kneeling on the floor with her back to me, trying to stack framed photographs that were scattered across the hallway.

As I got closer, I could hear her mumbling to herself, clumsily setting one frame on top of the other. When I bent down to help her pick them up, I realized that she was crying.

"Are you okay?" I asked tentatively.

"Huh?" Her head shot up. "Oh, Emily, I'm sorry." She sniffled and wiped her red cheeks with her sleeve. "I woke you up."

She blinked heavily, and I sank to the floor when it struck me… she was drunk. I spotted the bottle of vodka resting next to the top step and swallowed hard against the disappointment that rose in my throat.

"I was…I was just remembering," she stuttered. She was crouching, trying to balance the stack of frames, when she clumsily plopped down to sit.

"Fuck," she muttered, blowing a stray hair from her eye, her arm still wrapped around the frames as she reached for the bottle. It was just out of her reach, so she scooted over to grab it and repositioned herself so her feet rested on the top steps. She took a swig and ran her arm across her forehead, frustrated with the floating hairs that kept falling in her face. She looked like she'd just traveled through a tunnel of blankets.

I held the remaining frames that she couldn't quite manage and settled next to her. I noticed they were all pictures of my father.

My mother shuffled through the stack that teetered on her lap and sent one slipping and sliding down the stairs. "Fuck."

Big, wet tears streamed down her face as she held a photo up. It was of her and my father sitting on a sailboat.

"I know you were looking for these," she blubbered, swiping the back of her hand across her nose. "I had to dig them out of the back of the closet. But I can't…"

She couldn't continue. Her eyes were smeared with mascara, bloodshot and half open. Behind her inebriation was a sadness that was consuming her, and my heart ached at the sight of it.

"You remind me of him."

"I'm sorry," I whispered, not knowing how to comfort her.

"I forgot how much I missed him," she slurred, slouching against the banister. Another frame slid from her lap and crashed down the stairs.

"Fuck!" she screamed. In one sudden motion, she picked up her pile and threw the pictures down the stairs. I jumped at her outburst. Glass splintered along the staircase as the frames collided with each step.

"Why? Why? Why?" she bellowed in agony, crumpling to the floor. I remained paralyzed beside her, my back tense. I took in the destruction at the bottom of the stairs, and then the woman who was disintegrating before my eyes.

"It's okay," I whispered, my heart beating frantically. I doubted she could hear me.

She pushed herself up to sit and reached for the bottle to take another swig. She flopped back against the post, barely able to keep her eyes open. The bottle tilted in her hand as she attempted to rest it on the floor. I grabbed for it, setting it down next to me before it joined the carnage at the bottom of the stairs.

"Let me help you to bed," I offered softly. Releasing the stack of frames that I still gripped tightly and setting them on the floor, I slid closer to her so I could put her arm around my shoulder.

"Huh?" my mother groaned, unable to hold her head up.

"There you go," I encouraged, slowly getting her to her feet. "Easy." She wobbled under my support. I focused on the bedroom door and hoped we'd make it inside before she toppled over. I had a good five inches on her, but if she fell, we'd both go down.

I guided her to her bed, and she collapsed face-first. She drew in heavy breaths with a slight snore as I pulled the blanket over her. Leaving her in her induced peace, I shut the door behind me.

I stood on the top step and surveyed the mess below, exhaling deeply and shaking my head. Picking up the bottle that had instigated this disaster, my jaw tightened. I blinked away the tears, not wanting to feel anything. With a weight in my chest, I trudged down the stairs and dumped the bottle's contents down the kitchen sink. I blew out an exhausted sigh before slowly picking up the shattered pieces.

I hadn't exactly been waiting for it, but I should've known. I'd never been convinced after seeing her sober one night a year ago in front of my school that sobriety was going to take. She may not have had a drink *that night*, but it didn't mean she hadn't every night after. I knew. I knew this was going to happen…I just wanted to be wrong.

I picked up the picture of her and my father on the sailboat, and the lump tightened in the back of my throat. I closed my eyes and took a deep breath to suppress the storm that was brewing in my chest. I breathed out once more before opening them.

After stacking the photos on the stairs, I filled the trash bag with the broken glass and busted frames and swept up the remnants. When I returned from taking the bag to the barrel outside, I brought the memories back to my room, where I tucked them under the sweatshirts on my shelf in the closet. I wasn't ready to face them either.

I slipped back under the covers and lay staring at the ceiling. The tears silently slid along my temples and were absorbed into my hair. I let them flow, but I kept the lump lodged in my throat, pushing away the pain and sorrow I'd seen in my mother's eyes.

6. LIFESTYLES

By the time I stumbled out of bed the next morning, tired and bleary-eyed, my mother had already left for work. There was a text waiting for me. So sorry about last night. You shouldn't have seen that. Dinner tonight?

I responded with, See you tonight.

But when I arrived home after practice, I found her rushing around, slipping earrings into her ears. She wore a short skirt and a flowy blouse, and her dark hair was flipped and curled in an abundance of volume.

"Hi," she said, out of breath, hopping into one of her heels and almost falling over. "Um, I hope you don't mind, but I forgot I had plans tonight. I made them a while ago, you know, before I knew that you'd be here." She stopped, awaiting my reaction with her face scrunched in apology. "But I could cancel them. I mean…I could stay."

"No, go," I encouraged her. "I'll be okay, really."

"Are you sure?" she asked again, battling with her decision.

"Yeah, I have a ton of homework to do," I said, exaggerating in an attempt to make her feel better. "Have a good time."

"Okay," she replied, staggering on one foot to pull up the strap of her heel as she grabbed her purse. "Well, help yourself to the freezer, I guess." She took out a mini Altoids tin and opened it, popping a small white pill down her throat with a toss of her head.

"Don't wait up," she advised, removing her jacket from the hall closet next to the stairs. "I'll probably be pretty late." Before I could even unzip my jacket, she was out the front door. I shook my head in befuddlement and took in the vacant house with a heavy breath.

The door flew open behind me. I turned with a start. "Uh…can you move your car?"

"Oh, yeah. Sorry." I followed her back out the door.

"Sorry that I'm running off so fast," she attempted to explain as we walked down the driveway. "I'm so late, and my friends hate waiting on me."

"It's okay," I replied to…no one. She was already in her car, anxiously waiting for me to back up. I watched her speed away before pulling back into the driveway.

I put my things in my room and went down to the kitchen to prepare something to eat. I pulled out a frozen lasagna and followed the instructions to heat it in the microwave.

As I sat in the silent house, watching television and eating the lasagna, I realized I'd never been alone like this before. As much as I'd felt alone most of my life, emotionally isolating myself from—well, everyone—I'd never really been by myself. Before I lived with Sara, I wasn't allowed to be home alone. But I was usually involved in something at school that kept me occupied anyway. And now that I was alone, I didn't like the stillness. It made the thoughts in my head too loud.

I ventured upstairs a couple hours later, leaving the table lamp turned on at the bottom of the stairs, along with the light on the porch. After getting ready for bed, I kept myself busy with homework as best I could. But with every creak, my head jerked to attention and my heartbeat faltered. When the wind picked up outside, rattling the windows in their peeling wooden frames, I opted to drown out the creepiness with music.

Eventually I crawled into bed, leaving the music playing so I wouldn't be kept awake by every groaning board in the house. I took a deep breath and stared at the black door across from me, hesitating before shutting off the light. The door and the entire wall disappeared with the click of the lamp.

I shot up in bed, gasping and covered in sweat, flipping on the light to disperse the shadowy figure at my door. The black door remained closed, mocking me.

My eyes twitched as I listened for movement. I wasn't sure if I'd screamed out loud, since my mother hadn't rushed into the room. That's when I heard the deadbolt click open at the bottom of the stairs, followed by laughter and a deep voice. It was after two in the morning. I blinked at the clock, wondering where she could've been and who she was with now.

I shut off my light, so she wouldn't think I was waiting up for her, and pulled the covers over me. The wind screeched against the windows, rustling the black curtains with each frigid gust. The old house couldn't keep out the cold that seeped in through its bowed boards. I pulled the comforter up to my nose, waiting for sleep.

———

"That was quite the storm last night, wasn't it, Mary?" the radio personality chuckled, his voice forcing its way into my ears. I rolled over and hit snooze, fighting the urge to pull the covers up over my head and go back to sleep. I lay on my back and stared up at the ceiling, dreading the chill that awaited me once I flipped back the blankets.

My phone beeped, displaying Snow Day! under Sara's name. Good. That meant I could stay in bed until my mother turned up the heat.

Coming to get you in a few hours appeared on my phone a moment later under Evan's name. I responded with an affirmative, feeling much too awake to find sleep again. Footsteps fell across the unforgiving boards leading to the bathroom, and seconds later the pipes thumped and squealed with the sound of water rushing through them. "Fine," I huffed out loud. "I'm getting up."

I threw my hair up in a pile of twists on top of my head and slid on socks to protect my feet from the icy floorboards before plodding down the stairs. Pulling a box of cereal from the cabinet, I poured myself a bowl to take into the living room. I adjusted the thermostat to a warmer temperature so I would no longer have to see my breath.

I flipped on SportsCenter and started eating the cereal. The sound of the door opening and feet banging against the wood on the porch stopped me midbite. I peeked over to find a guy brushing snow from his jacket and shoving off his boots by the door. My heart pounded; I knew what I looked like, and did not want to be seen by whoever was entering like he belonged here.

I watched with wide eyes as a guy with messy dark hair walked into the living room with a bowl of cereal of his own. I pulled my knees up to cover my chest, very aware that I didn't have anything on under my long-sleeved shirt. He had a muscular build and a youthful face, making me question exactly who he was. He didn't look that much older than Jared.

"Hey," he greeted me with a nod, sitting next to me on the couch like he'd known me for years.

"Hi," I replied, not moving a muscle.

"I'm Chris," he offered before shoveling a mound of cereal into his mouth, the milk dribbling down his chin. He wiped it off with his sleeve while his eyes remained glued to the television. He glanced over at me again and said, "It's a shitty mess out there."

I nodded, not really wanting to have a conversation with this strange guy sitting next to me.

"Chris, are you still here?" my mother yelled from the top of the stairs, sounding like she hadn't expected him to be.

"Yeah," he bellowed in return.

"I thought you were leaving to get to class," she replied, sounding confused.

"Got canceled," he answered, still staring at the TV.

"Um…could you start my car for me?"

"Yeah, sure."

Without complaint, Chris put his bowl down on the coffee table and walked out of the room. I listened to the jangling of keys and the click of the door. I'd hoped to disappear before he returned, but I was met with the door flinging open as he rushed in, out of breath, to escape the cold.

"What are you up to today?" he asked, using his toes to remove his snow-covered boots.

"Not sure," I answered, my arms crossed over my chest.

"My friend's having a party tonight, if you and Rachel want to come by."

"Oh," was all that I could find to say.

"Emily, you're up," my mother noted in surprise as she walked down the stairs in a long black skirt, black leather dress boots and a fitted green turtleneck sweater. "I thought school was canceled."

"Don't you look all sexy in your work clothes," Chris interrupted before I could answer. She flashed an embarrassed glance my way and laughed uncomfortably. He grabbed her when she reached the bottom step, burying his face in her neck. She giggled awkwardly and pushed him away, walking past him to the kitchen.

"So, will I see you when I get back from school in a few weeks?" he asked, following her.

"Umm…we'll see," she replied reluctantly, her cheeks bright red. "Want some coffee?" He followed her into the kitchen, and I hopped up the stairs two at a time to escape to my room. I stayed in there until I heard them leave. A few minutes later a text appeared. I'm so, so sorry about that. Thought he'd be gone by the time you got up. I didn't respond. I didn't even know what to say.

I wish I could say that Chris was a fluke and it never happened again. Although she attempted to hide the guys, I could hear her coming home giggling on the nights she stayed out late after work—presumably after drinking a little too much. I didn't usually see them, nor could I confirm that she was in fact drunk—I just had a feeling. Every so often, I'd bump into one of the guys on my way to the bathroom in the morning. I probably wouldn't have known most of them were there at all if I actually slept.

She never provided an explanation or apologized for their presence. Perhaps she didn't realize I knew. They'd come in after I was in bed, and she'd sneak them out early, before I got up. It's not like it happened every night, but it happened enough that I always made sure I had a sports bra on before I left my room.

I hadn't exactly been prepared for her lifestyle. And she hadn't exactly been prepared for mine either.

A creak pulled me from my sleep. I remained still with my eyes closed, listening to the wind push against the house and the groans of the old building fighting against it. I opened my eyes, staring into the dark, my ears at attention. There was another creak, closer to my room.

My unblinking eyes slowly adjusted to the light, as little as there was. But it didn't matter how much I stared at the door, I couldn't see into the black paint. I might as well have been looking into an abyss. I only knew where the door was because a sliver of light seeped in under its uneven edge. Another board let out a creak right outside the door.

I wanted to call out for my mother, hoping it was her. But I remained paralyzed in my bed. The only thing that moved was my heart racing in my chest. I heard the handle jiggle, and the hinges shrieked open. The silhouette stood in the door's frame, unmoving.

I opened my mouth to ask who it was, but I could barely breathe. The person stepped forward, allowing just enough light to make out the angular features of her face and the sneer on her lips. I looked down at her hand and she was holding something long and hard. It reflected the light enough for me to know that whatever it was, it was going to hurt.

"You don't deserve to live," she grunted, raising her arm over her head.

"Emily?!" another voice screamed. My eyes shot open. I remained frozen, breathing heavily, trying to orient myself. The door flung open, and my mother rushed in in a panic. "What's wrong?!" She stood just inside the door, flipping on the light, her hand over her heart.

My shoulders relaxed, and I took a deep breath to ease the racing beats in my chest. "It was just a dream," I explained, from my startled seated position.

"Holy shit, Emily," she declared, letting out a long breath. "You just about gave me a heart attack."

"Sorry." I ran my hand over my brow, wiping away the lingering sweat that clung to my skin. "I'm fine."

She hesitated before leaving, like she wanted to say something. She looked me over again and finally said, "Well…good night," then walked out, shutting off the light and closing the door behind her.

I clicked on the lamp next to my bed to keep out the dark and settled into my pillow with my arms wrapped tightly across my body. The dream lingered. It felt so real, I was afraid to close my eyes again.

My mother came into my room only a couple of times after that night, panicked by my screams. But then she stopped, probably realizing there wasn't anything she could do.

I felt guilty for waking her, especially when I saw her slumped over her coffee each morning. I knew I wasn't easy to live with. I'd often found Sara on the couch of her entertainment room, where she'd gone in an attempt to escape me.

My therapist had prescribed sleeping pills, but they didn't take the nightmares away. They only kept me trapped, thrashing inside them.

"I'm sorry," I offered one morning. My mother looked up from her coffee. "About keeping you awake."

She shrugged. "You can't help it."

We didn't talk about it after that.

7. SOCIAL LIFE

S o, I just started dating this guy," my mother blurted out one morning while I was buttering toast. I paused before turning around, not prepared for the confession—especially after all of the guys she'd hidden in the past month since my "breakfast" with Chris.

I took a breath and turned to face her. "Really?" I tried to remember the last time I'd heard a visitor and narrowed it down to about a week or a week and a half ago.

"Except"—she hesitated with a breath—"he's…younger. *A lot* younger, and I'm not sure how I feel about it." She appeared troubled, clearly looking to me for advice.

"How old is he?" I asked, attempting to fill the role.

"Twenty-eight." She grimaced, waiting for me to pass judgment. I didn't react. He was older than I'd expected, to be honest.

"How old was Chris?" I asked, without thinking.

Her face changed to a hue of red. "He was…young, but I had no interest in *dating* him."

"Right." I nodded, flushing uncomfortably. "So, do you like him?"

"Yes," she answered, her eyes lighting up. "He's *so* nice, and smart, and amazingly hot and confident," she gushed, "but…he's *so* young, Emily. I have no idea what I'm doing."

"Who cares?" I offered with a shrug, taking on my role with a little more gusto. "You obviously like him, and if the age difference doesn't bother him, then…date him. I mean, is it serious?"

"Not really," she admitted. "Not yet, anyway. We've only been on a couple of dates. But we have so much fun together, and he keeps asking to see me again."

"Then do it," I urged her, completely freaking out on the inside that I was encouraging my mother to date a younger guy, or to date at all. She beamed at my acceptance.

"You're going to the concert with Evan tonight, right?" She took a sip of her coffee, unable to keep the smile from her face.

"Yes," I replied, eyeing her jovial expression apprehensively.

"Shit, I'm going to be late," she exclaimed suddenly, glancing at the clock on the microwave and jumping up from the chair. She looked to me and tensed excitedly, and before I knew it, she threw her arms around me and squeezed. I was too stunned to move. "Thank you," she squealed.

As I was walking into school alongside Evan and Sara, my mother texted me. Going out with him again tonight! So excited! I couldn't help but laugh.

"What's so funny?" Evan asked.

"My mother's *dating*," I explained with a shake of my head, "and she's more nervously excited about it than most girls at our school."

Evan raised his eyebrows. "That's got to be interesting."

"You have no idea," I responded, rolling my eyes.

"She has more of a social life than *I* do," Sara added, having heard my spiels about my mother's late nights and the sleepovers she'd hosted.

"Does she go out a lot?" Evan asked, not knowing any of it. I shot Sara a wide-eyed glance.

"Sometimes," I replied casually.

When Evan was out of earshot, Sara stated, "I didn't know you hadn't told him about how much Rachel goes out."

"I was afraid of how it would sound to him," I explained.

"Who cares?" Sara countered. "It's not like it's you who's bringing home strange men."

"Yeah," I explained, "but I don't want him worrying about me being in the same house as the *strange men*."

Sara nodded, understanding how that would rouse Evan's protective side.

"Besides," I continued, "she really seems to like this guy. So maybe the string of one-nighters is over."

"Em, you never saw the guys. Maybe it was the same guy each night."

I flipped my eyes toward her and shook my head. "Don't think so."

"Oh," Sara said with a shocked look of understanding. "Well, let's hope he's a keeper."

The sweat had barely dried from my skin, and my tank top and hair were still damp from exertion when I ran into the house, slamming the door behind me and flying up the stairs. Of all the nights for Coach to torture us with sprints. It's not like we lost by that much in yesterday afternoon's game.

I glanced at the clock as I pulled jeans from the closet and a long-sleeved shirt from the dresser, tossing them on the bed. I had twenty minutes to get ready. From the quiet, I could tell I was alone in the house. She was probably on her date.

I kicked off my sneakers and tore at my socks, then pulled my shirt over my head and dropped my shorts somewhere along the way to the bathroom. My urgency didn't help cool my skin. I turned on the shower and made myself calm down long enough to wash up—and hopefully stop sweating.

Wrapped in a towel, I scampered out of the bathroom toward my room, and I heard the front door open. Shit. I wasn't fast enough.

"I'll be right—," I started to holler, peering down the stairs. At the same time, the guy at the bottom hollered, "Rach—"

We both froze and stared at each other. Neither of us had anticipated seeing the other—especially me in just a towel. I tightened my hold on the fabric wrapped around my body, water running over my shoulders from my dripping hair.

"Whoa," he exclaimed in surprise. "You're not Rachel."

"Uh, she's not home," I answered, but he'd probably already figured that out. I remained still. My instinct was to rush into my room and shut the door, but I couldn't move.

"I knocked." He looked up at me apologetically. "Sorry. I shouldn't have just walked in like that." It didn't seem to faze him that I was dripping wet, half naked. He didn't avert his dark eyes. "I'm Jonathan."

I widened my eyes, dumbfounded by his casualness. "Emma," I uttered.

"Well, it's nice to meet you, Emma," he responded with a smile, still looking me in the eye. "I guess I'll just call her. Have a good night." Before I could say another word, he was out the front door. Within seconds I unglued myself from the floor and was right behind him, securing the deadbolt while exhaling the breath I'd been holding at the sight of him.

It took a moment for me to remember what I was *supposed* to be doing, and I ran back up the stairs, nearly falling on my face as I slid across the wet boards at the top.

I heard the knock on the front door just as I was tying my shoes.

"Hi." I smiled brightly when I opened the door, finally able to get excited about tonight. "Wasn't sure what to wear."

Evan closed the door behind him, examining my selection. "You look great, except you might want to wear short sleeves. It's going to get pretty hot, especially near the stage."

"Right," I concurred, turning back up the stairs. Evan was about to follow me when I noticed my abandoned clothes leading to the bathroom. "I'll be right down." I said, stopping him on the second step. I scooped up my sweaty clothes and brought them into the room with me. I re-emerged from my room, readjusting my ponytail after sliding on a black Newbury Comics T-shirt.

"Much better," Evan pronounced. "Are you ready?"

"Definitely." I bounded down the steps to grab the jacket he held out for me.

When we arrived at the concert, there was a long line on the sidewalk. We walked to the back, awaiting entry with everyone else. Evan stood behind me, wrapping his arms around me to help keep me warm while we waited. I hadn't noticed the cold, too distracted by the anticipation. We continued to shuffle forward until we finally reached the guys in the bright yellow jackets checking IDs. We received large black X's on the back of our right hands, branding us underage. After they'd scanned our tickets and we'd been frisked by blue-gloved hands, we were finally released into the rolling energy of the venue.

Evan held my hand tightly, steering us through the crowd. I let the bottled-up excitement seep in, accepting it with a grin on my face. Evan looked back and smiled when his eyes connected with mine. I knew he'd been concerned about how I'd react, being engulfed by so many people.

This was different. These people didn't know who I was, nor did they care. We were instantly bonded by the music blaring on the stage as the opening act continued its set. They were pretty good, although I'd never heard of them before. A group leaning against the metal barriers along the front seemed to know exactly who they were as they rocked their heads and hollered out the lyrics.

We excused our way to the front, continuing along the perimeter and stopping at the steps that descended into the pit. Those standing directly in front of the large stage were already sweating. Their intertwining bodies jostled for position to get closer. I was instantly captivated by the bare skin, backward baseball caps, tank tops with bra straps revealed, oversize T-shirts hanging over baggy pants as their heads bobbed in unison.

I turned toward Evan and yelled, "This is so great."

"It will only get better," he bellowed in my ear.

And it did. The sea of bodies dispersed slightly in between the opener and the headliner, but as soon as the roadies started tuning the guitars and pounding the bass, the hollering began and the crowd swarmed together even tighter than before. Within a few minutes the band members started filing onto the stage, taking their positions, acknowledging the crowd with a wave. The masses ignited into a trembling roar.

The opening song was recognized by just about everyone. Heads started rocking, the massive crowd cresting with jumping bodies and hands thrust into the air. The storm of energy was contagious, and I found my head nodding in time with the beat. Before I knew it, Evan and I were jumping and screaming out the lyrics along with everyone else. The bass and guitar riffs exploded in my chest.

I was a sweaty mess by the end, but I could've sworn I was floating. The crowd only enhanced the experience, bodies surfing across hands, voices bellowing the words, fists pumping in time—I was addicted. It released me from everything. I was overtaken by every note, until finally, nothing else mattered.

"Thank you," I rasped, my voice lost from screaming. I wrapped my slick arms around Evan's neck and pulled him toward me. I could taste the salt on his lips as I expressed my gratitude.

"Watching you tonight, jumping around and getting lost in the music—you were more entertaining than the band. I'm glad I got to see it." He squeezed my hand as we followed the crowd that was still riding the experience. We were released into a bitter cold that licked at the sweat on our skin, triggering a chill down my spine.

"Don't tell Sara, but I'm happy I went with you."

The buzz of the music echoed in my ears when I found my way to the front door, still floating from the entire night, and his parting kiss.

My mother burst into the room after I released a blood-curdling scream. She appeared disheveled and bleary-eyed when she flipped on the light.

"What is wrong with you?" she yelled. "You'd think someone was killing you or something." Then she slammed the door and went back to her room.

I remained still, staring at the door after she'd left. Her verbal assault swathed me in guilt.

"But someone *is* killing me," I whispered, "every time I shut my eyes."

8. INTENSITY

You survived," my mother declared with a laugh when I walked through the door.

"Um, hi," I replied, surprised to see her. "What was that supposed to mean?"

"Your first time ice-skating with Sara," she explained. "How was it?"

"Cold," I responded, shedding my layers before joining her in the living room. "I wasn't expecting you to be home."

She picked up the wineglass on the end table as I sat down next to her on the couch. My stomach churned as I watched her take a sip.

"And how was the concert?"

"Uh, it was amazing," I responded, trying to conceal my discomfort. "How was your date?"

"He's so incredible, I could die," my mother gushed, instantly transformed into a giddy sixteen-year-old. "He took me to this sushi restaurant, and then we went dancing. He makes me feel like I'm the only girl in the room. And believe me, *every* girl in the room is looking at him. He's so..."

If she said *dreamy,* I was going to laugh.

"...intense."

This description got a raised eyebrow out of me.

I knew she was talking about the same guy who had walked into the house last night. I could feel my cheeks heating up just thinking about how nonchalant he'd been about seeing me in a towel, like it was the most common thing in the world. And of course, I couldn't have been any more awkward. I hadn't told anyone about it, not even Sara. It was not a moment I wanted to relive.

"He sounds great," I replied, distracted again when she took another sip from the wineglass.

"I can't—" She stopped when she saw me staring at the glass. She set it down and adjusted herself uncomfortably. "I really am sorry about what happened a few weeks ago. I wish more than anything you hadn't seen me like that."

I nodded, unable to tell her how helpless it made me feel to watch her drown her pain in vodka.

"I'm okay though, I promise," she reassured me with a hint of a smile. "I don't drink like I used to, really. I know my limit.

"I was hurting that night," she continued. "And I needed to take the edge off. I wasn't ready—"

"For me," I finished for her, knowing that the only reason she'd searched for the pictures was because I reminded her of my father, and that remembering him crushed her.

"No. That's not it at all." She paused, averting her eyes, before explaining. "I've made myself forget him, so I won't hurt so much. It's why you had to..." She couldn't finish the sentence, but I knew she was talking about why she'd left me with George and Carol. "But I'm better. I just had a bad night, that's all. So you don't have to worry if you see me having a drink or two. I have it under control, I swear."

"Okay." I wasn't exactly convinced, but in the month that I'd lived here, I'd really only seen the one lapse. I guess I understood what triggered it, but I hoped more than anything that it wouldn't happen again.

"So, I told Jonathan about you," she said, smiling brightly. "I wasn't sure how he was going to react to knowing I have a teenage daughter. But he wants to meet you!"

She said it like it was the most exciting news ever.

"Really?" I was tempted to tell her I'd already met him—however briefly. "Why?"

My mother drew her brows together, appearing offended that I didn't understand.

"Because he wants to date me," she explained emphatically. "So, he wants to make sure you're okay with us—you know, when he starts coming over."

"Oh," I responded with big eyes, finally understanding. "Great." I feigned excitement, but the thought of seeing this guy again made my stomach flip.

"What's wrong?" she demanded, her smile faltering.

"Nothing." I forced the words through a frozen smile, "That's really great."

"You're such a horrible liar," she stated. "But I understand why you'd be nervous. Don't worry, he's so great. You'll love him."

"So, when am I meeting him?"

"Monday night," she exclaimed jubilantly, her eyes sparkling.

"Great," I repeated as excitedly as I could fake. It seemed to be the only word my brain could form. "Great," I grumbled in dread under my breath when she left to top off her wineglass. "Can't wait."

———

Text me as soon as you get home. I want to hear all about him! Sara sent as I pulled into the parking lot.

I called my mother to make sure she was at the restaurant before I went inside. She picked up on the third ring.

"Hi, Emily," she answered. "Are you there?"

"There?" I questioned in alarm. "You mean you're not here yet?"

"Um, no," she faltered. "I'm still at work."

"What?" I demanded, panic beginning to take over. "So what am I supposed to do?"

"Start without me," she suggested. "It will give you some time to talk without me there, you know, to get to know each other."

I didn't respond. I sat in the car with my mouth open, shaking my head.

"Please," she begged. "You can do this."

"Uh-huh." I stared at the large glass windows, wondering which one of the people in there was waiting for me. "Does he know you're late?"

"I just talked to him. I won't be too much longer, I promise. Just take a deep breath; you can get through this."

The fact that she understood my anxiety wasn't at all comforting. It only gave me another reason to panic.

"Please," she begged.

I filled my lungs with air and blew out quickly. "Okay."

"Thank you, thank you, thank you!" she exclaimed joyously.

"Hurry."

"As fast as I can," she promised.

I walked into the steakhouse, trying to remember what this guy Jonathan looked like. I had been too stunned and embarrassed the other night to really get a good look at him. All I knew was that he had intense brown eyes.

"Can I help you?" the hostess asked as I looked past her into the dining room.

"Umm, I'm meeting someone."

"Emma." A man stood at a table in the middle of the room.

"Found him," I told the hostess, who shot me a curious look. I glanced back a couple of times as I approached the table, finding her still following me with a stunned expression on her face.

"Hi," Jonathan said, pulling out a chair for me.

"Hi," I responded, draping my coat on the back of the chair before taking a seat.

That's when I looked at him—I mean really *looked* at him—and nearly slid off my chair as I pulled it forward. It was hard to believe this was the same guy at the bottom of the stairs. He's not who I remembered.

"I was afraid you wouldn't come in," he said, sitting across from me.

Jonathan definitely looked young. But it was difficult to pin an age on him, except to say he was in his twenties. He was bigger than I remembered as well, but then again, he'd had a jacket on when I'd last seen him.

He had an All-American quarterback look. His dark wavy hair was stylishly unkempt on top, with the sides trimmed tight. But it was his eyes that kept me from speaking. *Intense* was absolutely the word for them. It felt like he could peer right into me, and that kept me a bit on edge.

"Emma?"

"Huh?" I looked up. I'd been fidgeting with my napkin to avoid making eye contact. My cheeks became hot when I realized he and the server were waiting for me to respond to whatever she'd asked. "Sorry. What was that?"

"Do you want something to drink?"

"Um, water's fine."

The tall blonde paused before leaving, looking me over with judgment. Then she turned toward Jonathan and smiled brightly. "I'll be back with your drink."

I raised my eyebrows at her odd behavior and watched her walk away.

Jonathan laughed. "What's wrong?"

I quickly turned back toward him, my entire face heating up again when I realized he'd read the look on my face.

"Wow, I thought Rachel had all the hues of red down," he said, playfully. "But you have a few shades I've never seen before." He chuckled before adding, "Did she do something wrong?"

"No," I answered quickly, my napkin falling off my lap as I adjusted myself in the chair. I bent down to pick it up. While I was out of his sight, I closed my eyes and willed myself to pull it together.

"Everything okay?" he asked in amusement when I sat back up in the chair.

"Just my napkin," I explained feebly.

Jonathan's phone beeped, and he pulled it from his pocket, still grinning at my social ineptitude.

"Looks like she's running later than she thought. She wants us to order, and she'll be here for dessert."

"Great," I muttered without enthusiasm.

"Would you rather not do this?" Jonathan questioned, his bemused expression replaced by one that was suddenly too serious.

"Sorry." I grimaced. "That sounded really bad. I'm just…nervous."

"Because of me?" He sounded genuinely surprised.

I shrugged, reluctantly looking over at him. His brows creased apologetically. I wanted to slink under the table.

"I'm not very good at this," I confessed in a rush. "I guess you could say I'm not the most social person, so even if you looked like that guy"—I nodded toward the overweight, balding man at the next table—"I would still be a fumbling idiot."

His cheeks creased around his broad white smile as he examined me curiously. I closed my eyes and cringed, realizing I'd just inadvertently told him he was hot. This was going *great*.

"You're just like her," he mused, studying me. "I mean, you don't look like her at all, and she talks a lot more when she's nervous, but you're just like her. She spilled coffee on me the first time we met."

"And probably apologized a hundred times while trying to clean you off." I grinned, thankful that he'd skipped right over my comment.

"I don't think I've heard someone talk so fast before." He laughed. "At first I thought she was speaking a different language."

I laughed, easily picturing it. "So you met in a coffee shop?"

"No," he answered. "We met at work. I work for an architectural firm that collaborates on projects with her engineering firm. We met about six months ago, but we didn't go out until just recently. She refused to go out with me for the longest time."

"Really?" The shock in my tone was heavier than I intended.

"The age thing," he explained with a shrug. "She kept saying I was too young."

"Right." I nodded, remembering her dilemma when she first spoke of him.

"But it's not a big deal, right?"

"Nope." I shook my head. "Age shouldn't matter."

He looked right into me and grinned. I could feel my cheeks changing color again, and I wanted to dump the water over my head to cool them off. I felt like an idiot. I still couldn't hold eye contact for more than a second when he spoke to me. I'd never had anyone focus on me so intently before, but I wasn't sure he intended to do it. My mother had said he made her feel like she was the only one in the room when he looked at her—and I guess I didn't want to feel that way.

"Have you decided what you'd like to have this evening?" the server asked, setting Jonathan's drink down. She glanced at both of us, but her bright smile re-emerged when Jonathan looked up at her.

While he was deciding, I glanced around the room and realized she wasn't the only one who couldn't stop staring. I was amused by the women adjusting their chair positions ever so slightly to get a better look.

"And you?" she asked, barely making eye contact with me. Every other glance flipped back to Jonathan to see if he was looking at her, but he was oblivious, his attention was on me.

"I'll have the rib eye, medium rare," I ordered, closing my menu and handing it to her.

"Are you sure you're okay?" he asked, reading me so easily.

"You attract a lot of attention, huh?" I stated honestly.

Jonathan grinned abashedly.

"Sorry," I floundered. "That was internal dialogue that should have stayed inside my head."

"You're funny." He chuckled.

"Unfortunately," I groaned.

"They recognize me from the ads," he admitted, averting his gaze. He was visibly uncomfortable as he took a sip from his glass.

"Ads?"

"I did a shoot for jeans when I was in college, to earn some money for school."

"Oh," I reacted. "You think the reason just about every girl in this restaurant is staring at you is because they saw you in a magazine ad, like what, five or six years ago?"

Jonathan looked up at me with an embarrassed grin.

"Wow, I did it again, didn't I? I can't seem to keep from saying the most—"

"Honest," he interrupted. "You're being honest. It's pretty funny, really."

"I'm an idiot," I admitted, sinking in my chair. "How's that for honesty?"

Jonathan laughed again. I was definitely giving him plenty to laugh at.

"Okay," he said, trying to sound serious. "We're supposed to be getting to know each other. Tell me something about you."

I stared at him blankly, like he'd just asked me to recite the capitals of every country in the world.

"Okay." He contemplated while I remained mute. "Play any sports?"

My shoulders eased up and I nodded. "Yeah, I'm playing basketball right now."

"Are you any good?"

I released a breathy laugh. "I'm decent."

"You're better than decent," he stated, challenging my dismissive tone.

"Why would you say that?" I questioned, my cheeks peaking in color.

"You laughed, so you're not comfortable talking about yourself, meaning you're probably really good."

I shrugged, my cheeks igniting as I adjusted my position in the chair. His ability to read me like a book was a bit disarming.

"Okay, let's put it this way. What would the papers say about you?"

"Umm…I guess they'd say that I'm the co-captain and point guard of the first-place team in our division. That I average twenty points a game and was All-American last season."

"That's impressive," he said with a slow nod. I shrugged sheepishly.

"What about you? Did you play any sports?" I was pretty certain I already knew the answer.

The server arrived, placing our plates in front of us.

"Is there anything else I can get for you?" she asked Jonathan.

"Emma, do you need anything?" He purposely diverted her attention to me.

"No, I'm fine," I answered, trying to keep from smiling. She walked away with her shoulders slumped.

"What were we talking about?"

"What sports you played," I reminded him.

"I played football."

I nodded, having pretty much predicted it, based on his thick neck and broad, muscular build.

"Don't nod like that," he shot back, "like you knew I was going to say that."

"Well, come on," I retorted, "look at you." He rolled his eyes. "Fine." I continued, "What would the papers say about *you*?"

"The papers wouldn't mention me at all; I spent most of my time on the bench."

I laughed. "Really?"

"You don't have to *laugh*." He feigned offense. "I was second-string receiver. I just wasn't as good as the starter." He paused before blurting out, "Okay, fine, I sucked. I couldn't hold on to the ball to save my life."

I laughed again.

"But I swam. Still do when I can."

"Would the papers mention *that*?"

"I guess they would," he admitted modestly. "I swam on the team at Penn State. It helped pay for my tuition."

"So you were really good, huh?" I noted, impressed.

He shrugged with one shoulder.

"Wait, I thought modeling helped with your tuition?" I grinned.

"Yeah, that was a onetime thing, and it really didn't pay that much."

I nodded, taunting him with a smirk on my face.

"Shouldn't have told you that, huh?"

"Sorry." I laughed. "I just think it's funny that you're immune—"

"Hi," my mother greeted us excitedly before I could finish. Jonathan stood up to greet her with a hug and kiss—which made me suddenly interested in the food on my plate. I was still trying to wrap my head around the fact that she was dating, and I wasn't quite ready to handle seeing it. I knew I needed to get over it…fast. Especially when she sat down with us and clutched his hand throughout dessert, dominating the conversation in her nervous rush.

I watched as Jonathan hung on to her every word, every so often calming her enough so she actually sounded coherent.

It was evident that she was enthralled with him, and he really cared for her. By the time we were ready to leave, I was…okay. She was happy. And that was all that mattered.

I pulled out my phone to check the time. "Um, I have to go," I said, interrupting my mother's story about the time she accidentally uploaded a YouTube video of singing cats for a presentation. "Thank you for dinner."

"What do you mean?" she questioned, sounding slightly disappointed.

"Evan's supposed to be meeting me at the house in twenty minutes."

"Do you want to come back to the house?" she asked Jonathan, completely taking me by surprise.

"Sure," Jonathan responded, signing the check.

Hellooo?! What's he like? lit up my phone when I entered the car.

He's nice, was all I texted back to Sara before driving home.

Evan was waiting for me when I pulled into the driveway.

"Sorry," I said, grimacing as I hurried up the walkway.

"I just got here," Evan assured me.

I unlocked the door as my mother and Jonathan pulled in behind me.

"How was it?" Evan asked before they entered the house.

"Okay," I responded with a shrug. Evan eyed me curiously, knowing how nervous I had been about the dinner. "He's nice," I said, providing him with my canned response.

"Evan." My mother greeted him happily. "How are you?"

"Great. Thanks," Evan replied, hanging up his jacket. He paused for a moment with the hanger in his hand when Jonathan walked in. Then he took my jacket from me and hung it up as well.

My mother introduced them, "Jonathan, this is Evan." Jonathan held out his hand with a broad smile.

"Nice to meet you." Evan shook his hand in return.

"You too," Jonathan responded. There was a strange silence while we all just stood there in the foyer, looking at each other.

"We're going upstairs to study," I finally announced, taking Evan by the hand.

"That's him, huh?" Evan said, closing the door behind us.

"Yup," I said, sitting down on the bed. "That's him."

"Not who I was expecting," he stated.

"Who were you expecting?" I asked, surprised by the contemplative look in his eyes.

"I don't know," he said dismissively, sitting next to me on the bed. He leaned down and was about to kiss me when we were interrupted by a knock at my door.

"Hi!" Sara burst in. Then she narrowed her eyes at our frozen posture and rolled them with an impatient breath. "Did I interrupt something?"

"No," I replied quickly, struck by her annoyed tone. I slid up the bed to sit against the wall, distancing myself from Evan. "What are you doing here?"

"I had to see the guy. Your text was pathetic." She shot me an accusing look. "Holy hotness. He is beautiful. I mean truly beau-ti-ful. Like the kind of beautiful they build statues to worship."

Evan looked at her in amusement. I shook my head with a roll of my eyes.

"How old is he, like twenty?"

"No," I replied, like she was insane. "He's twenty-eight."

"Well, nicely done, Rachel," Sara stated enviously. "And just think, you'll get to see him like every day."

I widened my eyes, silently begging her to shut her mouth. Evan's troubled look returned. Obviously he did not share Sara's enthusiasm.

9. JUST NOT RIGHT

I'm not sure what I'm doing." My mother stared out the window while leaning against the counter.

I waited, but she didn't continue. So I prodded. "About what?"

"Jonathan."

I waited again, but she wouldn't say anything else. So I prodded a little more. "What about Jonathan?"

And that opened the floodgates. She spun around and spewed, "I'm not sure I'm ready for this. I haven't really *dated* a guy in a *very* long time. What if he doesn't really like me? What if he's too perfect for me? Look at him. He's so gorgeous; I have no idea what he's doing with me. I notice how girls look at him. They're probably wondering the same thing. I don't think I can do this. I can't do this. Forget it, I'm ending it."

I stared at her, stunned, wondering if she'd taken a single breath during that whole explosive monologue.

"Wait," I said, shaking my head to make sense of her dizzying words. "Did you just convince yourself to break things off with him in ten seconds flat?"

She sighed in defeat.

"First of all, do what feels right. If you're not ready, then you're not ready. But don't end things because you think he's too good for you. Besides, he doesn't give another girl a second glance when he's

with you. It was obvious last night. He's into you. So give him a
chance if you want to, because you like him. And don't walk away
because you're afraid to find out *how much* you may like him."

She exhaled audibly. "Thank you. I can't believe I'm getting
relationship advice from my seventeen-year-old daughter." She
laughed. I couldn't believe I'd just given my mother a pep talk on
dating—apparently I'd taken a page from Sara's book of straightfor-
wardness.

"Okay, so I'm going to do this." She was convincing herself
more than me. "Do you think it would be okay if he spent the night
sometime?"

"Uh, sure," I mumbled, wondering how we'd gone from
whether she should date him to when she was going to sleep with
him.

"That wouldn't be too weird, right? I can make sure he leaves
before you get up."

"It's okay," I answered slowly. Apparently she had no idea I'd
already gone through this *weirdness* more than I cared to remember.

The next night, Jonathan was over watching a movie with my
mother when I arrived home from Sara's. I didn't stop on my way
up the stairs, not wanting to interrupt them.

"Hey, Emma," Jonathan called, despite my best effort to be
invisible.

"Uh, hi," I replied, not looking back.

I stayed in my room for the rest of the night, reading. Without consciously meaning to, I'd find myself listening for the front
door, indicating that Jonathan had left. But I never heard it before
I dozed off.

"Is she okay?"

I froze at the sound of Jonathan's voice. Clamping my hand over
my mouth, I stifled my breaths as I sat upright in bed. I remained

still. He sounded close, like he was right outside my door. My eyes flickered in the dark, waiting to see if he'd actually come in.

"She does that," my mother explained apologetically. "Just come back to bed, okay? She'll be all right." There were a few seconds of silence, and then his footsteps trailed off toward her room. I heard the distinct click of her door, and collapsed back into my bed, feeling terrible that I'd woken them up. Which transitioned into an alarmed recognition that he'd stayed the night.

I stared at the ceiling, waiting for the sun to make its appearance, listening to the wind screech against my windows and finally succumbing to the realization that sleep had evaded me once again. I pulled the covers up to my chin, wishing I were in California, not stuck in this never-ending winter and this icebox called a house.

I finally threw the covers off, resigned to starting the day despite the lack of sun. I slid on a pair of socks and rifled through my drawers, pulling out clothes for the day before dragging my feet toward the bathroom. I paused outside my door when I noticed the kitchen light was on, creating a soft glow in the dark foyer. The coffeemaker gurgled, and the robust aroma drifted up the stairs.

Jonathan emerged from the kitchen with his hair wet and brushed back, creating smooth, dark waves. He was dressed in a shirt and tie. His professional attire made him appear older, a mature look that made me grin. He looked so…grown up, in a *GQ* sort of way. Jonathan stopped abruptly when he spotted me, startled.

"Sorry," I said. My cheeks flushed with color at being caught watching him.

He held his finger to his mouth and pointed to my mother's door. "She's still sleeping." I nodded in understanding. "Did I wake you?"

"No," I whispered in reply.

He continued to the closet to remove his jacket and set the strap of his computer bag over his shoulder. He raised his hand in a wave before slipping out the front door. I watched him leave without a word, finding my hand still frozen in the air long after the front door had closed and his truck could be heard starting up. *Why am I still standing here?* I shook myself out of my daze and continued to the bathroom to shower and prepare for the day.

"Rachel's here," Sara informed me as I was getting ready to run out on the court for our night game. "Oh, and we're going to a party tonight after the game."

I watched her walk into the gym, waving to somebody with an exaggerated smile, mouthing, "Hi." I stared after her in shock. What kind of bomb was that to drop right before a game with our school's rival?!

I could hear my mother screaming my name as I dribbled the ball down the court. I blocked her and the rest of the chanting crowd out as I called the plays to put my teammates in motion. I let the movement on the court keep me focused.

I passed the ball to Jill outside the key along the baseline. She dribbled in toward the net and popped it back to me. Another teammate set up a pick to allow me to dribble down the paint and lay it in. The bleachers erupted, but all I could hear was a buzz of voices.

Weslyn walked away with a three-point win, thanks to Jill's aggressive rebounding and unshakable accuracy on the free throw line. I'd held my own, contributing double-digit points and multiple assists. I was relieved to have the win.

I grabbed my things from the bench and heard someone shout "Emily!" from among the crowd of faces. I turned to find my mother walking toward me, and nearly fell over when I spotted Jonathan a few steps behind her.

She greeted me with a smile. "Hi! So glad we came to this game. It was intense."

I smiled awkwardly, my face fiery as I looked everywhere but at Jonathan. "Nice game," he congratulated me, moving in closer to my mother.

"Thanks," I replied, my pulse racing. I had no idea why I was so nervous to see him. It wasn't like I'd never met him before.

"I was hoping you were going to score more so Jonathan could see your outside shots, especially the three-pointers."

"The defense was tough," I replied with a shrug. "But thanks for coming."

"Are you coming home?"

"Umm, I guess Sara wants to go to a party or something." I wiped the sweat off my chin using my shoulder, scanning the gym for Sara and Evan. But I knew they'd be in the lobby, like they usually were after my games, and nowhere around to rescue me from the awkwardness.

"Have fun," she replied. "See you later then?"

"Yeah." I glanced up to catch Jonathan's eye as he nodded with a smile. My mother took his hand and blended in with the remaining fans exiting the gym.

"*Who* was that?"

I turned to discover Jill and Casey standing behind me, practically drooling.

"My mother," I responded casually, knowing exactly who they meant. That's when it occurred to me why I'd been so uncomfortable. Every girl in the school was ogling him as he and my mother made their way out of the gym. It was kinda pathetic.

"And *he's* her boyfriend?" Jill asked, still gawking after his perfectly placed hair.

"I guess," I mumbled, shaking my head as they practically melted in front of me. I grabbed my warm-ups and stranded Jill and Casey by the bench, staring.

"And why did you tell Evan he couldn't hang out with us at the party?" I asked as we pulled out of the school parking lot.

"I need girl time," Sara explained briefly. "And besides, does he always have to hang out with us?"

"We're going to *a party*," I pointed out bluntly. "If you want *girl time*, then we should do something else. And *no*, he does not always have to hang out with us, and he doesn't. Did he do something wrong? What's going on with you? You've been acting kinda strange lately."

"Nothing's wrong. I'm fine." She sighed impatiently. Her perpetual bad mood was so very confusing, and she hardly resembled my best friend—it was freaking me out. And what, if anything, did it have to do with Evan?

We walked in the side door between the house and the garage. Bass boomed from the basement; laughter and hollering could be heard further down the hall. This house was modest compared to some of the monstrosities in Weslyn. We were on what was considered "the other side of town," closer to where I used to live.

We ventured toward the laughter to find a group sitting around the kitchen table with cards in their hands and red cups in front of them, commanding one another to drink for various absurd reasons. More people were crammed into the small kitchen, either leaning against the Formica counters or passing through to get to the keg.

Sara made her way to the back porch, where the keg rested in a trash can filled with snow.

"Can you stay over tonight?" she asked before taking a cup from the stack.

"Sure," I replied, shrugging, and hugged myself with a shiver. I texted my mother as we walked back through the kitchen, then followed Sara down the shag-carpeted stairs to the basement. I stopped at the bottom when I saw Evan playing pool to the right and hesitated long enough to wave and apologize with a grimace as

I continued after Sara in the other direction. We walked into a small wood-paneled space with a beat-up couch covered in multicolored afghans and a console television pushed into an unused fireplace.

Mandy Cochran smiled at the sight of us and started weaving through the bodies to get to where we stood, while Sara inspected the scene. I didn't really know Mandy; she played volleyball with Sara. But this was her house, so I knew we should at least make an effort to say hi.

Sara scanned the room, not thrilled with what she saw. "Back upstairs," she insisted, completely ignoring Mandy. My face twitched in confusion, but I followed after her anyway. I held up my hand to wave in apology when I saw Mandy's smile fade as she watched us disappear up the stairs.

By the time we were back in the kitchen, Sara needed a refill. Instead of following her out to the deck like a pathetic sidekick, I took a seat on a wooden stool next to the kitchen counter. I watched the card game, trying to figure out the rules and whether there was a point to the absurdity. I quickly discovered there really wasn't a point—it was all about getting drunk and making people do stupid things in the process. I sighed and shook my head.

"Hey, I didn't know you were going to be here," Jill exclaimed when she and Casey walked into the kitchen with pink bottles in their hands. "Where's Evan?"

"I don't know," I replied, making a face—finding it strange that that was the first question they asked. "I'm here with Sara."

"Ooh, are you fighting?" Casey asked, leaning in like she was about to hear a secret.

"No," I answered, drawing out the *o* and looking at them like they were crazy. "I think he's downstairs, playing pool."

"So what do you know about your mother's hot boyfriend?" Jill drilled.

"Not much," I replied shortly, annoyed with the question.

"I think he may be hotter than Evan," Casey interjected.

"No," Jill argued, then paused and said, "Okay, maybe."

"Seriously?!" I finally interrupted, wanting to put an end to the conversation.

"I was just saying," Jill retorted defensively.

"That's messed up," I shot back. "You don't compare my boyfriend with my mother's. That's so very twisted."

"True," Casey agreed, "but he is—"

I walked away before she could finish. Unfortunately, this wasn't a big enough house to lose them, so I slipped into the bathroom when I saw the door open. This was the first party I'd been to in Weslyn since last May. Apparently, I hadn't missed much.

I looked around for Sara upon exiting the bathroom and found her in a corner talking to a tall blond with dark eyebrows. They were laughing and leaning toward each other, her hand occasionally brushing his arm—all the signature flirting moves.

"That's Neil's cousin," Jill explained from beside me. She had apparently been waiting for me to get out of the bathroom. "He's visiting for the weekend from New Hampshire."

"Oh, great." I groaned. This was not going to go over well. And right on cue, Sara's smile faltered. She turned abruptly and stormed out onto the deck. The guy was left dumbstruck, looking around to see if anyone had noticed. The girls giggled next to me, indicating that not only had they witnessed the ditching, but now everyone at the party would know about it as well.

I sighed and followed after Sara.

"Hey."

She continued to pour the beer into her red cup, not looking up.

Before I could find the words to make her feel better, which wasn't something I was used to doing, I heard, "I dare you to jump."

I looked over, and a guy with a dark-green flannel shirt and a backward baseball hat was standing on the top railing of the deck.

"Is he serious?" I asked Sara. She just let out an amused laugh.

Then he was gone. I rushed to the railing. All I could see was his baseball hat. The rest of him had disappeared into the mountainous snow bank below the deck. He thrust his arms out of the snow and tilted his head back, releasing a guttural holler of triumph. I was stunned to see him emerge in one piece.

That's when the insanity took over. More guys leaped into the snowdrift, yelling and whooping as they jumped off the railing.

I had no interest in watching these guys break their necks, so I went back inside, discovering Sara already there. I passed Evan as he and a few guys made their way to the deck to watch the recklessness. I caught his eye, and he brushed his hand along mine. That subtle connection sent a current through my body with a warm shiver.

Sara slammed her red cup down, redirecting my attention. "Let's get out of here."

As we pulled down the street, two police cars drove past with their lights on. I wondered where they were going. Then it hit me that the neighbors must have called them. There weren't acres of land or trees separating the houses on this street, so the noise in the backyard had probably carried, disturbing the neighborhood.

I glanced over at Sara to say something about the busted party, but she remained still, staring out the window. I wanted to cheer her up, but I had no idea *what* to say. Just as I was about to break the silence, she exclaimed, "New Hampshire! He was from fucking New Hampshire!" She clenched her fists. "Are you kidding me?! This is so not funny!"

My mouth dropped open. She continued to rant about how well they'd gotten along. He had even asked her to go out this weekend before he'd finally told her where he lived—indicating that they'd probably never see each other again.

"Sara, you have to tell me what's going on with you," I demanded emphatically. "And don't say 'nothing,' because I know there is. It can't just be this guy."

"There's nothing wrong with me," she snapped, practically biting my head off.

"Really?" I countered defensively. "I think there is, because you're acting like a bitch."

And just like that the car was silent, and I was filled with remorse. "I'm sorry. I didn't mean that," I said as we pulled in to her driveway. "I'm just frustrated because I don't understand what's going on."

"I'm fine," she huffed, slamming the car door after her.

Snow started to fall when I stepped out of the car. Perfect. We'd just finished shoveling after the last storm. This winter was as miserable as Sara.

I walked up the stairs after Sara, who refused to even look at me. My phone beeped as she shut the bathroom door. Meet me out front when Sara passes out.

I remained as patient as I could, staying in the bathroom, pacing, while I waited for her to groan herself to sleep. Fifteen minutes later, I slipped out and poked my head into the bedroom to hear the sound of deep breaths.

I crept down the stairs and out the front door. Evan was sitting on the front steps, snow coating his knit hat. He stood when I stepped out.

"Finally." He pulled me toward him, my hand still on the doorknob, barely closing it behind me. I breathed him in as he pressed his firm lips against mine. I melted in relief, needing this connection more than he realized. "That bad, huh?" Then again, maybe he did realize.

"You got out just in time," Evan said, sitting next to me. "The cops showed up and broke up the party."

"Yeah, we saw them," I muttered, still feeling guilty about what I'd said to Sara. I sat down on the top step, not caring that I was sitting on a layer of snow.

Evan sat down next to me. "Are you okay?" He nudged my shoulder with his and took my hand.

"I have no idea what's wrong with Sara. She's miserable." Then I considered it. "She's been a little off for a while, but it wasn't that bad until now. Something happened, and she won't tell me what."

Evan breathed in contemplation. "I think I know what to do."

I looked at him hopefully. He pulled out his phone and looked at the screen.

"What? What should we do?" I demanded desperately.

"Oh, sorry," Evan replied, distracted as he texted. "It's Jared."

Then he put his phone back in his pocket and said, "Maybe we can at least make her smile."

"I'll try anything."

Evan leaped down the stairs, sinking into the snow up to his shins.

"What are you doing?" I asked, like he was insane.

"How about we make a snowman?"

I laughed. "You *are* crazy."

"True," he agreed with his infamous smile, "but that's why you love me."

"You're probably right." I smiled wider and joined him in the snow, sinking up to my knees.

I fell over several times, losing my footing while rolling the large ball around the front yard. Evan kept chuckling at my inability to stay upright. Sara probably would've been rolling with uncontrollable laughter if she'd seen me. I hoped this ridiculous semblance of a snowperson would at least crack a smile.

As Evan was lifting the head to place it on the other two body parts, I slipped for the millionth time and slid down the small incline on my back. I let out a loud yelp and began laughing when I finally slid to a stop. Instead of helping me up, Evan opted to lie down next to me. From above our heads, light spread across the second-floor windows, and a curtain pulled back.

Anna spread the curtains wider and opened the window.

We remained still, hoping she wouldn't notice us. She squinted, "Emma? Is that you? And...Evan?"

"Good evening, Mrs. McKinley." Evan waved from our flattened position on the snow-covered lawn.

"What are you..." She stopped herself when she saw the snowman beneath her window. "Come in soon, Emma. It's late. And try to keep it down, please."

"Sorry." I cringed guiltily.

She shut the window as Carl asked, "What are they doing?" A moment later, the windows darkened and all was still.

That's when I realized the snow had stopped. I looked up at the wisps of clouds quickly passing over us, weaving through the stars. Evan lay quietly beside me, our hands clasped between us.

"I'm not sure I can feel my legs," I shivered as the cold ground seeped into me, but I still didn't make a motion to get up.

Evan sat up, and just when I thought he was going to pull me up too, he leaned down and found my lips, melting the crystals of snow that had landed on my face. His mouth moved gently along mine, warming my entire body.

"You make me forget how much I hate the cold," I breathed, my eyes still closed.

"Let's finish the snowman," Evan finally said, pulling me to my feet. I looked down at my snow-caked jeans and tried to brush them off without success.

While I packed snow between each layer, Evan rifled through his car and pulled a bag of candy out of his backpack.

"Sweet tooth?" I questioned when I saw the massive amounts of chocolate, licorice and jelly beans in the white paper bag.

"You could say that," he confessed with a grin.

We pulled red licorice and jelly beans out of the bag to create a face and waves of hair.

I took off my scarf for the finishing touch after he'd inserted excited stick arms that looked like they were reaching for the stars. We stepped back to take in our creation. I couldn't stop laughing.

Evan admired it proudly. "She has to at least smile."

"I hope so." I sighed.

Evan left to drive home as it started to flurry once again. I seriously had lost feeling in the majority of my body, and I desperately needed to thaw.

I took off most of my snow-caked clothes in the foyer, exposing pale legs that were now bright red. Sneaking up the stairs, I placed my crystallized clothes in the bathtub, readied for bed and snuggled in under the blankets, shivering.

I looked across at Sara's bed. She looked so peaceful, like nothing in the world could possibly be wrong. I just wanted her back.

My phone beeped next to my head, and I picked it up to read, Don't worry. We'll make her better.

10. DISTRACTION

When I awoke, Sara's bed was rumpled and vacant. I found her in the rec room, scowling over a bowl of cereal, watching a syndicated reality television show. I left her to fester, assuming she hadn't seen the snowman yet.

I walked down the stairs and peeked out the window overlooking the front lawn. As I was about to walk to the kitchen, what I had seen struck me. I opened the front door and stared at the sad image. Shutting the door with a grunt, I stormed up the stairs.

"What did you do to the snowman?" I demanded from atop the stairs.

"I kicked it in the face," she answered, continuing to watch the television without a blink.

I went into the bedroom and got dressed, grabbed my things and left without a word. I couldn't look at the pathetic decapitated head lolling on the ground as I backed out of the driveway. I clenched my teeth as I drove away.

I couldn't respond to Evan's So what happened? text. I just wanted to get away from the miserable girl who had overtaken Sara's body.

The front door was unlocked when I arrived home, but there didn't seem to be anyone there. My mother's car was still in the driveway, covered with a dusting of snow, and the kitchen light was on, but the house was quiet as I kicked off my boots and shed my jacket.

I froze when I pushed my door open and found Jonathan at my desk. The squeak of the hinges made him spin around with a start.

"Emma, hi." He greeted me with an inflated smile, like he'd just been caught doing something he shouldn't.

I was so shocked to find him in my room, I couldn't say anything.

"You scared me," he said with a laugh, recovering, and then explained nonchalantly, "Rachel said to use your computer to check my e-mail. Sorry. I obviously freaked you out."

His words shook me from my gaping expression. "It's okay," I assured him slowly, my cheeks warming at my overreaction.

"Are you sure?" he asked with a grimace. "You don't look okay."

"Really, it's fine," I repeated, easing the tension in my shoulders.

"So, did you check it?" I finally asked.

"What?"

"Your *e-mail*," I emphasized with a laugh, recognizing how ridiculous we were both acting.

"Oh, yeah. I did." He faltered, folding down the laptop before standing up. "I was about to leave but noticed the pictures. You play soccer too?"

"Yeah. I'm better at it than basketball," I replied, setting my backpack on the floor at the foot of my bed.

"You were quite amazing last night," he said, making me shift uncomfortably. "So if you're better at soccer, then I would definitely want to see that."

"Well, it's paying for me to go to Stanford," I admitted, embers lighting up my cheeks.

"Do you always turn this red?" he asked, examining my face.

"Usually," I admitted, my eyes drifting toward the floor.

"Sorry," he chuckled. "It's...cute."

My breath faltered for a second.

"Thanks for letting me use your computer."

"Anytime." I nodded, still unable to meet his gaze without my face flaming up.

He paused before continuing. "I've been meaning to say something, but..."

"What?" I asked, suddenly nervous.

"I'm really sorry about the first time we met. Rachel said you were going out and to just come in. I really didn't mean to walk in on you like that. I don't want you to feel uncomfortable around me."

And just like that, it was *even more* uncomfortable. I nodded, not sure what to say, wishing he'd never brought it up.

"I just made it awkward, didn't I?"

Of course my glowing cheeks gave that away.

"Umm…a little," I admitted with a half grin.

"Sorry." He grimaced again. "That's not what I wanted to do. Wow, I'm usually not so bad at this."

I couldn't help but smile at his faltering confidence. With that one sentence, he had just become a little more, well, like me.

"What?" he asked, his eyes searching mine. "Did I say something wrong again?"

"No," I answered, connecting with his dark brown eyes with a slight smile, making the corners of his mouth curve as well.

"Can you give me a hand?" my mother called from downstairs. When Jonathan and I emerged from my bedroom, she cocked her head to one side at the sight of us. "Uh, hi. What are you guys up to?" Her words came out hesitantly, with a hint of unease.

"I was checking my e-mail," Jonathan explained casually. "Remember, you said to use Emily's computer?" I looked over at him, surprised to hear my formal name. But then again, seeing my mother's questioning eyes, it was the right choice.

"Oh," she said, suddenly remembering. "Thanks for letting him use your computer." And instantly, all was right with the world.

I shut myself up in my room for the rest of the day, reading, studying and listening to music. I wasn't an expert at occupying my time. I actually preferred not to be alone for too long—that's when the thinking began.

And that's where I found myself late Saturday night, lying in my bed, staring at the white above me. I ran my hand along my neck, and a chill ran through my body. An image flashed through my head as fast as the snap of a picture, but the panic and fear wrapped in it forced me to sit up in bed. I shook off the remembrance that had forced its way to the surface—her frigid hands and my silent pleas for help. And then it was gone. I was alone in the house once again.

I searched the kitchen for something to eat, but there were scarce pickings. My mother and I kept missing each other for dinner, so I'd stocked up on microwavable anything to keep me nourished. But my supply was dwindling.

I called to order a pizza, and decided to pick up a movie along the way. As much as I wished I could hibernate for the winter to avoid the bone-chilling cold, I sucked it up and drove toward the commercial side of town, where the neon was allowed to glow, far away from the homes that paid for their quiet.

I pulled in to the gas station that had a movie rental machine. A few carloads of Weslyn students were lingering inside, trying to decide where to go—whose party to crash. I didn't make eye contact as I waited behind an older man to pick out a movie.

"Hey, Emma." One of the girls had recognized me. I looked over at the soda cooler, where she and two other girls were choosing forms of caffeine. I smiled politely, trying to place her. She may have been in my Art class, but I was pretty sure she was a junior.

"Great game last night," one of the guys said.

"Thanks," I replied in a low voice, stepping up to take my turn at the movie machine.

"Do you want to go to a party with us?" another girl asked.

"No, that's okay," I replied, trying to decide quickly on a movie. "I'm staying in tonight."

"See you around."

I made my way out of the gas mart and waved with an awkward smile. It was strange being recognized outside school without Evan or Sara. But at the same time, it felt kinda good. It was like waking up to discover that I was my own person, and people actually wanted to hang out with me. I grinned as I started my car.

I returned to the house, prepared for my solo night, with a new-found sense of confidence. I was somewhat disappointed to see that Jonathan's truck had returned. It was barely nine o'clock.

I pushed open the front door and heard the buzz of the TV in the living room. After abandoning my shoes at the door, I brought the pizza into the room. Jonathan was sitting alone, and seemed surprised to see me.

"You're back early." I set the pizza on the coffee table.

"Rachel's sick," Jonathan explained.

I nodded in understanding.

"I thought you'd be out."

"Staying in," I replied. "Hungry?"

"Uh, sure." Jonathan got up from the couch and crossed over to the kitchen. "What do you want to drink?"

"Diet Coke, please," I answered, looking around for my mother. I hung up my jacket, and Jonathan came back over with drinks, paper plates and napkins. "Is she in bed?"

"Yeah. She drank a little too much cough medicine," Jonathan explained, sucking in air through his clenched teeth. He handed me the soda bottle. "And then had a couple glasses of wine on top of it. I wouldn't be surprised if she's out 'til Tuesday."

"Great," I said with a shake of my head.

"What movie did you get?" he asked, eyeing the plastic casing.

"You know what? I have no idea," I admitted, pulling it open. "I was in a rush and just picked a new release. Do you want to watch it with me?"

"Sure."

I looked at the title and groaned. "Oh great. It's a horror flick. Exactly what I don't need."

Jonathan laughed. "We'll keep the lights on while we watch it."

"Did you think for a second I'd let you turn them off?"

He laughed again, taking the movie and inserting it into the DVD player while I doled out pizza on the paper plates.

There wasn't really a point to the plot, except maybe to sear my brain with lifelong nightmares—but then again, I already had those. I watched the entire movie with my knees pulled into me and a pillow clutched to my chest. I'd shove my face into the pillow whenever the music chimed in warning. Jonathan would talk me through what was happening and then let me know when it was safe to look again.

By the time the credits rolled, I wasn't sure if I was ever going to sleep again. Jonathan changed to the sports channel, where talk of the Super Bowl helped to dispel the disturbing images.

"What are you doing for the game tomorrow?" Jonathan asked, tucking in the lip of the pizza box and stacking the crust-laden plates on top of it.

"Oh, uh, nothing. I mean, I'm watching it, but I don't have plans."

"I'm sure there's a few Super Bowl parties you could go to."

"Maybe," I admitted, not having given it a second thought. "But I think I'd rather *watch* the game. You know?"

"Yes," he agreed. "We're going to a party with some of Rachel's friends, and I have a feeling the game's going to be background. I'd actually like to watch it too." He shrugged and carried the box into the kitchen.

It felt like I hadn't moved the entire movie. I stretched my legs and stood to go to bed.

"Are you sure you'll be able to sleep?" Jonathan asked when he saw me head for the stairs.

"Probably not," I admitted, "but that's not different from any other night."

He gave me a questioning look, but didn't say anything.

"Good night."

"Good night, Emma," Jonathan replied, watching me enter my room.

"Emma—" The dark beckoned. A banging followed. I fought to hold on to the bed, but the sheets were slipping. The room continued to tilt, determined to dump me into the black hole at the end of my bed. Horrific screams called from the abyss.

"Emma," the dark called out again.

I kicked my feet to work my way farther up the mattress.

The banging grew louder, and I shot up in bed. My sheets were tangled around me, and I was breathing so fast, I was practically hyperventilating. I turned on the light next to my bed.

"Emma?" came from the other side of the door. "Are you okay? Will you open the door?"

It was Jonathan. I inhaled deeply to calm my nerves. "I'm fine," I answered, sweeping strands of sweat-soaked hair from my face with a shaking hand.

"Please open the door?" he requested again.

"I'm okay, really," I responded, unraveling the sheets around my legs.

"Please," he pleaded. "Just open the door, okay?"

I hesitated and stared at the door. "Fine. Just a minute."

I crawled out of the bed and flipped the comforter over the top to hide the mess beneath. I tied my hair back in an elastic and pulled on a hoodie before unlocking the door and slowly opening it.

"I'm okay, see." I looked up at him, shoving my shaking hands in the front pocket of my sweatshirt. His eyes softened as he took me in. "It was just a dream. Sorry I woke you."

"You shouldn't go back to bed," he advised calmly.

"Huh?"

"When you have a nightmare like that, you need to get out of your bed, to clear your head," he explained. "Get a glass of water, watch television, something to clear your head. That way, when you go back to sleep, the nightmare's not still there, waiting for you."

I remained quiet, taking in his words. His eyes were soft and empathetic. "Come on. Let's watch TV for a while, okay?"

"Sure," I agreed, surrendering. "But you don't have to stay up."

"Don't worry about me," he responded. "Let's go see what they're selling at this hour."

I followed him down the stairs and curled up on the couch under a blanket while he sat on the love seat, flipping through the channels. I glanced over at him as the soft light of the television lit the lines of his strong jaw.

I would never have predicted that he'd know anything about needing to escape nightmares. He seemed impervious to fear, so confident and assured.

"The infomercials can be addictive," he noted, glancing over at me. I flipped my eyes to the TV, my cheeks peaking with color, having been caught staring. He continued as if he hadn't noticed. "You need to stay away from them because the next thing you know, you're watching the sun come up, convinced that a six-inch cloth can wash your entire car and still be clean enough to wipe the windows."

I nodded, not completely paying attention; a part of me was still trapped in the dark.

"It gets better," he promised, observing me intently. He sounded so sure of his words.

"How would you know?" I peered into his dark brown eyes, trying to look past them for answers, but he wouldn't let me in.

"Believe me, it does," Jonathan whispered, looking away. In that quick moment, the confidence in his eyes faltered, giving way to something else. I wasn't quite sure what I'd seen, but I inadvertently shivered when I caught a glimpse of it.

11. ALL BETTER

How are you feeling?" I asked, when my mother slumped down the stairs the next morning. Her nose was raw and red around the edges; her eyes were watery and puffy. She looked miserable—I shouldn't have even asked.

"I think I'm dying." She snuffled.

"You should go back to bed. Tell me what you need, and I'll get it for you."

"Tea," she requested pitifully. "And some flu medicine, so my head doesn't feel like it's going to explode anymore."

"I'll get that," Jonathan offered, appearing at the kitchen entrance, showered and dressed.

"Thanks," she said in a nasal voice, before sneezing into the balled-up tissue in her hand. "I wish you weren't seeing me like this."

"Don't even go there," Jonathan consoled her with a warm smile. "You're sick, and even sick, you're beautiful." He wrapped his arms around her as she flopped onto his chest. He held her and smoothed the damp strands of hair stuck to her feverish face. He was braver than I was. I was afraid to go within three feet of her. She was oozing from every orifice.

"I'll bring the tea up in a minute," I told her as Jonathan escorted her back up the stairs.

"I'll be right back," Jonathan announced a few minutes later on his way out the door.

I took the tea to her room and set it down on the nightstand. She had her eyes closed and the blankets pulled up to her nose.

"Do you like him?" she asked as I was walking toward the door.

I turned back toward her. She propped herself up on her elbow and carefully sipped the hot tea.

"Jonathan?" I clarified, not expecting her question.

Before I could answer, she said, "I *really* like him, and I hope you do too."

"Um, yeah, sure. He's nice."

"Thanks for the tea." She nuzzled back into the blankets, closing her eyes with a grin on her face. Even in her sickness, she was still a love-struck teenager.

"Looks like you'll get to watch the game after all," I noted after Jonathan returned from the pharmacy. "Where are you going?"

Jonathan hesitated. "Actually, I told Rachel I'd stay here with her."

"I'm not going anywhere," I offered. "I can take care of her if you want to do something else."

"I'd rather stay here, if that's okay."

"Sure," I answered in surprise.

"Where are Evan and Sara?"

"Evan's at Cornell with his brother, and…I don't know what Sara's up to."

Jonathan looked over at me, hearing the change in my tone upon mentioning Sara. He didn't ask; he just nodded.

I offered to pick up football food while Jonathan tended to my mother. Especially since we were running low on…everything. I'd pretty much assumed the role of grocery shopper in the house. My mother would shop when she wanted to prepare a specific meal, but with our conflicting schedules, that wasn't very often.

I didn't mind too much. She'd leave me a twenty and a small list of things she needed. The list was usually more than twenty dollars, but whatever. I covered the rest with the money that was deposited into my account each month—money I hadn't had access to for years, but was now in my total control.

I'd gotten to know the aisles well enough to get in and out of the store quickly. Except for today—it was insane.

"I think every person in three towns was at the grocery store today," I complained to Jonathan, struggling with white plastic bags strung across both arms.

"Let me help you." Jonathan rushed from the living room, relieving me of half the bags. "Is that everything?"

"If it's not, then too bad. I'm not going back to that zoo." I slipped off my shoes and followed him to the kitchen.

"I meant, is there anything else in the car?" He smiled at my dramatic response.

"No, this is everything," I answered, embarrassed by my reaction. "How's Rachel?"

"Passed out," Jonathan responded, proceeding to empty the bags and put everything in its place. "I have to go out for a while. Would you mind covering for me until I get back? I'll be here in time for kickoff. If she wakes up, just tell her I went to buy more tissues or something."

"Sure," I replied. "You shouldn't need an excuse, you know." I knew I shouldn't have said it as soon as I did. "Sorry."

"No, you're right," he agreed. "I just feel bad leaving when she's not feeling great. Although I'm not sure I can do anything to make her feel better. But she keeps saying she wants me to stay."

"She always wants you to stay," I blurted—my filter apparently shut off.

"Wow." He absorbed my candor with wide eyes. "Am I here too much?"

"No," I replied quickly. "That's not what I meant. Sorry, I'm a complete idiot today."

"You're doing that honesty thing again. Don't worry about it."
He paused and added, "Don't ever feel like you can't say what you're
thinking, okay?"

"Are you sure?" I asked with a smirk. "You'll probably end up
hating me."

"Unlikely," he said with a bright smile, putting the milk in the
refrigerator. My cheeks warmed with his comment. "Oh, here's my
phone number"—he scribbled on a piece of paper on the kitchen
table—"just in case you do need something while I'm out."

"Okay. Thanks." I picked up the number as he walked out the
door and decided to program it into my phone—just in case.

My mother didn't stir the entire time Jonathan was gone, thankfully. I hadn't been looking forward to telling her he wasn't there.

I texted back and forth with Evan most of the afternoon.
He and Jared were at an all-day Super Bowl party off-campus. It
sounded like quite the spectacle, from the details Evan provided. I
let him go right before kickoff, wanting him to enjoy the game with
his brother and not worry about responding to me.

I kept checking my phone anyway, still not having heard from
Sara. I wanted her to be the first to reach out after the way we'd left
things, and it took everything I had not to text her as I grew more
anxious.

Jonathan returned five minutes into the game.

"Ah," he groaned, looking flushed and freshly changed. "I
missed kickoff."

"Don't worry," I consoled him. "Nothing's happened, really.
You look…different." It was hard not to notice.

"I had to tap back into my life for a while," he explained, sitting down on the couch next to me with his eyes fixed on the game.
"Got a haircut, went to the gym, made sure my place hadn't burned
down."

I laughed, not expecting his sense of humor. "Well, the hair looks good."

"Thanks." He flashed me a blush-inducing grin. I reached for a handful of chips to keep from saying something else outlandish about how good he looked. "I bought beer. You don't mind, do you?"

"Uh, no," I answered, surprised that he asked. "It's football. Isn't that part of the guys' book of conduct? That a beer must be in your hand while watching?"

He laughed. "Do you want one? I could overlook the fact that you're a girl for the night."

"No," I responded emphatically. "Not legal, remember?"

"Oh, that's right," he answered, feigning that he'd forgotten. "I'm supposed to be the responsible adult, right?" He shook his head like the thought were ridiculous, got up from the couch and went into the kitchen, coming back with a beer and a Mountain Dew.

"Perfect, thanks," I said, taking the bottle from his hand.

We watched football and ate overly greasy food while making fun of the overpriced commercials that fell flat and laughing at those that were worth the millions. And we'd take turns checking on my mother whenever we heard her moan.

In the middle of the third quarter, the doorbell rang. Jonathan and I peered at each other quizzically, neither expecting a visitor. I shrugged and got up to answer the door.

"Hey," Sara said, as soon as the door opened. She had a number nine written in gold on her cheek, with her red hair pulled back into a high ponytail. I let the door go so she could enter. She peered into the living room to find Jonathan.

"Hi, Jonathan." She gave a small wave.

"Hey, Sara," he responded. "Nice look."

"Thanks." She smiled.

Sara looked back toward me nervously. "I tried to call you," she said, pulling on the corner of her shirt.

"You did? I'm sorry, I didn't hear my phone." I groaned inwardly, frustrated that I'd missed it—most likely I'd been checking on my mother when she'd called.

"Can we talk?" she asked in a quiet voice, flipping her eyes from the floor up to me. "I mean, if you guys are watching the game, I can come back."

"Seriously?" I stared at her incredulously. She pressed her lips into a small smile. "Let's go upstairs."

I closed the door behind us and sat at the end of my bed, expecting her to sit next to me, but she began pacing.

"Sara, what's wrong with you?" I demanded. "You know you don't have to worry about what to say to me. You never have before."

"But I've never been such a bitch to you before either," she blurted out. She stopped pacing, realizing what she'd just confessed. She looked at me, and I started to laugh. I knew the honesty would find its way to the surface eventually. She smiled in return.

"What happened?" I asked. Sara sat down next to me. "Did I do something wrong?"

Sara sighed. "No. I just…I'm an idiot really."

That didn't explain anything. "You're going to need to be more specific."

"I think I was a little jealous of you." She kept her eyes on the floor.

"Of me?" I questioned in disbelief. "That doesn't even make sense."

Sara took in an audible breath. "I know it's stupid. And it's going to sound even more pathetic when I say it, but I'm jealous of the way you and Evan are together. I mean, I want to find that—that guy who looks at me the way he looks at you. You don't have to even touch— he could seriously be at the other end of the house, but you have that connection, no matter where you are. It's crazy. And I want it."

Wow, I mouthed, stunned.

"I know. It's so stupid, and selfish, and pathetic. And totally my issue. So I should never have taken it out on you. I'm sorry."

I couldn't form words. I didn't even know what to say. It was unfathomable that Sara McKinley, the girl every guy wished would give him the time of day, the girl who had everything, wanted the one thing that I had. There had to be someone who made her feel...

"But you do," I realized out loud.

"What?" She looked at me like I'd been having a conversation without her, which I pretty much had.

"Sara, you have to give Jared a chance," I urged. "He's the only guy who's ever made you feel truly amazing. I mean, you like him so much you wouldn't even have sex with him."

"Hey." She gave me an offended shove, but a smile emerged on her face. Then it disappeared in the next breath. "Em, I can't. It doesn't make sense."

"Yeah, it does," I countered. "Why don't you just try? What do you have to lose?"

"My heart," Sara answered without pause. She took a breath and rested her head on my shoulder. "Do you forgive me?"

"Sara, I just want you to be okay. I'm not sure how to make you feel better, but I'll try."

"I have an idea." She grinned deviously. It was almost like I'd set her up to tell me, "You can help me throw a party next weekend."

"A what?" I questioned, afraid I'd just heard her ask me to help her with a *party*.

"It will be the best way to take out all of my frustration," she explained with a devilish gleam in her eye. "It'll have a theme and everything."

"I'm afraid to ask."

"It'll be my Love Stinks party," she boasted, like it was the best idea ever. "And it can even have rules."

"Rules?" I questioned in disbelief. "Since when do parties have rules?"

"Mine will," she stated proudly. "Since it's a Love Stinks party, no one will be allowed to touch the opposite sex. So, no hookups, kissing, or hand-holding."

I stared at her with my mouth open. "That's...cruel."

"Are you going to help me with my party and enforce my rules or what?" Sara demanded with a tilt of her head. "You said you wanted me to feel better. *This* will make me feel better."

"Torturing everyone else on Valentine's Day?"

"Yes." She smiled smugly.

"Fine," I caved, dreading this already. "How are we going to enforce your rules?"

"I haven't decided yet." She pondered, giving it serious consideration.

"Great. This is going to be ranked the best party of the year."

"It better be," Sara replied seriously. I shot her a skeptical look—she ignored me.

Sara stood up. "Wanna watch the rest of the game?"

I'd almost forgotten we'd left Jonathan in the living room, watching the game by himself. I stood to join her.

Before opening the door, she said, "I'm sorry for kicking your snowman's face in." She was trying to be sincere, but the apology sounded funny, and we both couldn't help but laugh.

"And I'm sorry I called you a bitch," I replied once we stopped laughing.

"Don't worry," she assured me, "I'll be fine. I'll snap out of it. This party will help."

She was about to turn around, but then added, "I hope you know how lucky you are to have Evan. He would give up everything for you. You have no idea. So if you ever do anything to screw it up, I'll never talk to you again, got it?"

"Uh, yes," I responded, afraid that if I answered differently, she'd kick my ass. She smiled, her vibrant smile instantly mending us.

We joined Jonathan for the fourth quarter. Sara took him up on his beer offer. The volume of the cheering rose to a whole new level with Sara as a spectator, so much so that my mother made a point of shutting her door. We looked at each other guiltily, but were dragged right back into the game moments later.

My mother had to miss two days of work to get over her illness, and right around then Jonathan disappeared, having contracted the flu himself. He stayed at his place as he fought through it. My mother was a bit of a wreck the rest of the week, until that Friday, when Jonathan finally emerged from the land of the dead—right around the time I was about to enter it.

I spent the weekend at Sara's to prepare for the party, and to give my mother and Jonathan time to make up for lost…I didn't really want to think about it. It was hard to be all romantic and sentimental when thinking about my mother and her boyfriend—and while hanging torn hearts and blood-dripping arrows.

12. "F" VALENTINE'S DAY

This is a little Goth, don't you think?" I questioned as Sara heavily lined my lids in black.

"Exactly." Sara smirked. "Here, just put this on, and you'll be all set."

"You want me to wear black lipstick? I didn't realize this was a costume party."

Sara rolled her eyes. "Just put it on. I know you won't be kissing Evan if your lips are black." I scowled and grabbed the lipstick from her hand.

I finished getting dressed while Sara was in the bathroom. She hadn't shown me what she was wearing, and I just about fell off the bed when she emerged from the bathroom.

"How are guys not going to want to grope you dressed like that?" I gawked at Sara's skintight wet black leather pants and black corset top that accentuated…everything.

"I didn't say I had to play fair, did I?" Sara grinned, her lips glossed brightly in red. I shook my head, feeling like a henchman to her goddess in my girly black outfit. She handed me a red plastic gun. "Here."

"And what am I supposed to do with this?" I asked, tilting it in my hand.

"Any contact between a guy and a girl, squirt them," she instructed.

"Sara, I can't squirt people with water for touching!"

"Emma, come on—you promised!"

"I'm going to die," I groaned, plodding down the stairs in my black knee-high go-go boots. Sara stayed upstairs to lock everything up, so people couldn't wander into bedrooms to defy the rules— and be inappropriate on her parents' bed.

"Is this night over yet?" I grunted upon entering the McKinleys' entertainment room, where Evan was programming the music.

"Wow!" He gaped, eyeing me from head to toe, swallowing hard. "How am I supposed to *not* touch you dressed like a Goth schoolgirl? Sara's sick."

"What?" I balked at the thought. "You *like* this?"

"I'd have to be dead not to think you looked hot"—he grinned—"and even then..."

"Omigod. Are you kidding me?"

Evan slid his hands around my exposed waist and ran his lips along my neck. My head swirled as I released a defenseless breath. I wanted nothing more than to kiss him back, but I was a prisoner to Sara's black lipstick. He ran his hand along my stomach and breathed in my ear, making my knees weak.

I needed to escape before I melted. "I think I need to walk away, or I'll throw *all* Sara's rules out the window."

Evan grinned. "Rules end at midnight," he proclaimed as I entered the kitchen.

"Who says?" I yelled back.

"I do."

I smiled.

Sara *was* sick! Unbeknown to me, she'd put the message out to the girls to dress as vixens, all in black—but had neglected to warn the guys. So not only was this a look-but-don't-touch party, but she was playing dirty.

Let's just say that as soon as the guys saw what was waiting for them, there were a lot of refills at the keg. That was the other rule: If you drank, you had to spend the night, and your car keys were collected.

The guest list was extensive but exclusive. Cameras and cell phones were banned and collected, along with keys. Picture taking was strictly forbidden. Underclassmen were not allowed, although some tried to crash. Evan and Kyle, Jill's boyfriend from Syracuse, manned the door, filling the bouncer roles perfectly. They broke a lot of freshmen hearts, shutting the door in their faces after the pathetic creatures got a glimpse of what they *weren't* going to be a part of.

Jill, Sara, Karen and I were armed with water guns. Casey had one for a while, but Sara revoked her privileges when she found out Casey'd filled it with a mixed drink and was squirting it into her mouth.

Jill's was later handed off to Mandy when Jill ran her hand along Kyle's back. Sara told her that if she couldn't obey the rules, she had no right defending them, and proceeded to give her a quick squirt to the gut. I couldn't help but laugh when Jill looked truly heartbroken at her demotion.

I patrolled as instructed, but everyone was well behaved. Then again, the party had only been going on for an hour. The first floor was open to the partygoers, decorated morbidly in dead flowers and crushed chocolate strawberries, then set aglow in red—it had taken quite some time to change the lightbulbs.

The entertainment room was set up as the dance floor, since it was the largest, most open space. The television screen was retracted into the ceiling, and the couches that lined the back walls had the cushions removed to keep people from getting lost in the dark to make out. That room remained vacant for the most part, since no one was ready to dance—or they couldn't figure out how to dance without touching each other.

Besides, the music was pretty angry. It was a compilation of aggressive songs, featuring Five Finger Death Punch and Disturbed— not exactly grinding music.

Things started to get a little more interesting during the second and third hours—right around the time the alcohol took effect. Sara had to refill her water gun twice, being the most prominent enforcer of the rules. I thought it was going to piss people off, but she seemed to be aiming for the guys—and they didn't have a problem being sprayed with water by a girl dressed like Sara.

It was innocent enough. Talking a little too close, then a hand slipped to the hip. One of the girls sitting down on her boyfriend's lap while he was playing cards at the kitchen table. The first kiss happened around ten thirty, and Sara and Mandy went ballistic, drenching the guy who thought he was finally hitting it off with one of the girls from the basketball team. As horrified as he was, there were plenty of people laughing—I mean, it *was* pretty funny.

"Sara, there's someone at the door for you," Evan hollered when the doorbell rang.

"You can answer it," Sara returned, taking a sip of her red martini.

"No, this one's for you." He walked toward me, careful not to touch as he leaned against the wall beside me. "Things are about to get very interesting."

Sara approached the door. I watched her lips form, "Oh, no," when she finally opened it. At the same time, Jared's eyes just about fell out of his head. "Hi," he choked. "That's quite the anti–Valentine's Day attire."

"What are you doing here?" she responded, her cheeks a brilliant shade of red.

"Fuck Valentine's Day," Jared exclaimed, handing Sara a dozen dried black roses. "These are for you."

"Aren't you going to let him in?" Jill scolded her, pulling Jared in by the arm and closing the open door that was making most of the scantily dressed girls shiver.

"Thanks," Sara responded blankly, taking the dead flowers—obviously in shock.

I looked to Evan, who wore a devious grin. "You don't play fair either, do you?"

"It's Valentine's Day!" he said defensively. "I kinda want to kiss my girlfriend."

I smiled brightly, admiring his strategy. Sara spotted Evan and shook her head, shooting him a tight-eyed glare. She knew that Jared's presence was his doing. Evan laughed.

Jared had a guitar case strapped to his back. "What's that for?" Sara inquired, leading him to the help-yourself bar on the sunporch.

"Later," Jared replied, grabbing a beer from the galvanized tub.

Without Sara realizing it, Evan switched the music to more popular dance songs, and the room started filling with bodies. She slacked on her patrol and handed her water pistol to another enthusiastic enforcer, who took to the dance floor with a vengeance.

About an hour later, we were running low on ice, and I didn't have the key to the basement, where the freezer was stored. I searched among the flashing lights and teasing bodies in the entertainment room, but didn't find Sara. After lapping the first floor, I decided to try upstairs.

The door to Anna and Carl's sitting room was slightly ajar. The crack allowed me to see Sara sitting on the love seat, leaning forward and completely mesmerized. I was just about to push the door open when I picked up on the strums of the guitar. I barely touched the door to open it an inch farther and found Jared sitting on the ottoman across from her, strumming the guitar. He was singing. I was too stunned to move.

"Be my, be my valentine," he sang as he strummed the upbeat chorus.

"I think I'm in love," Jill crooned drunkenly beside me, throwing her arms around my neck and laying her head on my shoulder.

"Do they breed them to be like that?" Casey cooed on the other side.

I hadn't even noticed they'd followed me. I quickly closed the door and knocked hard to warn Sara of our presence—but I think she may have heard us.

"Sara, you need to get out here," Casey yelled obnoxiously, knocking harder. "Jill's breaking the rules big-time."

Sara opened the door wide enough to be seen, but kept Jared concealed in the background.

"Shoot her," Casey demanded in her intoxicated enthusiasm, pointing to Jill. "She's breaking the rules. Shoot her right in the face." When Sara only looked at her in confusion, Casey grabbed my gun and shot a stream right in the middle of Jill's forehead. Jill let me go and screamed.

"I'm going to kill you," she bellowed, sending Casey down the stairs in a fit of laughter with Jill in pursuit.

Sara and I looked at each other, shaking our heads. "Hey," I finally said as casually as I could, "we're out of ice. Do you have the key to the basement?"

To my surprise Sara replied, "Yes. Let's go." She shut the door behind her and led me down the stairs. I clenched my teeth in a grimace, glancing at the door and hoping Jared didn't think she was rejecting his Valentine's ballad.

We filled up the tubs with ice, and Sara noticed the music change. She pointed to Evan accusingly, ready to pounce. He held up his hands, feigning innocence with an adorable grin on his face.

"You were in charge of the music," she spat.

"And look"—he pointed to the swaying bodies—"they're danc-ing. Not a bad job, if I do say so myself."

Sara rolled her eyes and disappeared upstairs. Evan yelled, "You're welcome," after her, and she flipped him the finger—which made us both laugh.

"It's almost midnight," I said, walking past him, wanting to touch him so bad it hurt.

"Don't worry," he promised, "it'll happen." I grinned and kept walking into the crowd.

The rule that Sara was most adamant about enforcing was that no one was allowed on the deck that overlooked the enclosed pool and hot tub. They were deemed instant aphrodisiacs, with the waterfall built into the rocks at the far end of the pool and the roll-ing bubbles of the hot tub. She kept the lights off, so as not to tempt the hormone-driven drunkards.

I caught a glimpse of light from the forbidden space and groaned in frustration, not wanting to be the person to kick them out. I waved Evan over and continued on to the deck as he cut through the dance floor to follow me.

The pool was surrounded by what resembled a greenhouse, panes of glass arching over a cut stone floor. In the summer, the glass covering retracted to open the pool to the outdoors. In the winter, it kept the pool in use, even though the glass was frosted over and there was snow piled up against the exterior.

I stepped out into the balmy air to find the potted trees around the pool lit with small lights, creating a romantic setting. By the pool's edge were Sara and Jared, kissing. I wanted to scream!

"No way," I fumed at the sight of them. I stormed down the stairs. She was the one who made up these asinine rules, and within an hour of Jared's arrival *she* was going to break them?! Not on my watch!

Before Sara even realized I was there, I exclaimed, "Rule breaker!" and shoved her. Jared tried to recover their balance, but it was too late; they plummeted into the blue water. Sara came up for air, gasping.

"What the fuck?" She stared at me in shock, her hair slicked back and her red lips smeared.

Evan started laughing, which made Jared do the same. A smile crept on my face, and I joined in. The commotion brought spectators out onto the deck.

"You are so dead," Sara threatened without sincerity. Before she could lift herself out of the pool, Evan swept me into the water alongside him. This set off a chain reaction, and bodies began plunging in after us.

When I surfaced, I found Evan in front of me, smiling proudly. He pulled me toward the rocks, away from the splashing and jumping. I held on to the side of the pool, my weighted boots threatening to pull me under as Evan wiped my lipstick off with the sleeve of his shirt.

"Told you I'd kiss you by midnight." He grinned, pulling me toward him. His lips encased mine. I could taste the chlorine of the water and feel the warmth of his breath. I gripped his shirt and pulled him closer, feeling his hand glide along the skin of my back. He turned me so that my back was against the pool's wall, placing his hands on either side of me, pushing himself against me. I wrapped my legs around his waist, and his hand ran along my thigh. My heart raced, and I couldn't breathe.

Before I knew what was happening, I was under the water again. The submergence separated us, and I resurfaced breathing heavily.

"Now who's breaking the rules?" Sara gloated while Jared trod water with a grin behind her.

"I hate your rules," I declared, splashing her in the face. She hollered and splashed back. A water war ensued. Among the splashing and dunked bodies, I caught sight of Sara again, her arms around Jared's neck as he kissed her cheek—and she was smiling.

I blinked my eyes open, the chiming ringing in my ear. The room was dark, and I could feel the weight of Evan's arm around my waist. There was a beep, then silence. I started to close my eyes again, sleep pulling me under. The chiming started back up. My eyes shot open.

I rolled over and picked up my phone from the nightstand. Without looking to see who it was, I answered, "Hello?"

"Where are you?" my mother demanded in a panic.

I sat up, jolted awake by her desperation. My sudden movement disturbed Evan, but he just rolled over and remained asleep.

"What?" I tried to register what was going on.

"Where the fuck are you? Why aren't you home?"

"I'm at Sara's," I replied, my heart racing. She was so upset. I tried to remember if I'd told her—but I knew I had. Doubt coursed through me anyway. "Remember, she had the party tonight?"

"You don't want to live with me anymore, do you?" she cried. I knew she was drunk—her words weren't forming properly—but I was too shocked to make sense of why she was saying this.

I felt Evan move beside me, but my back was toward him as I sat on the edge of the bed, tears forming in my eyes.

"You hate me. I know it." She'd reached the point of hysterics. "That's why you never sleep here. You're going to leave me too, aren't you?" I gasped at the agony in her voice, a tear escaping down my cheek.

"Rachel, what are you doing?" I heard in the background. "Who are you talking to?"

"She doesn't love me anymore," she sobbed, the pain smothering her words.

"Who?" Jonathan asked, sounding groggy. "It's three o'clock in the morning. Give me the phone."

"Why doesn't she love me?" she bellowed, the phone moving farther from her mouth.

"Emma?" he asked softly. My mother's drunken rant continued in the background. "Are you there?"

"Yes," I whispered, barely able to speak over the knot lodged in the back of my throat. It was silent. He must have left the room, closing the door to block her out.

"Are you okay?" he asked gently.

"No," I breathed, a whimper escaping. I put my hand over my mouth to contain it. Tears streamed down my cheeks, cascading over my fingers. A warm hand pressed against my back, but I didn't turn to face him. I just listened.

"She had too much to drink tonight," he tried to explain. "And we got in kind of an argument, so it's not you. I'm so sorry."

I breathed in deeply through my nose, removing my hand and wiping my cheeks before Evan could see. He scooted over to sit next to me.

"Emma? Are you still there?"

"Yes," I replied. "I'm okay." I took another breath to calm the twisting nerves strangling my chest, wiping my cheeks dry. "I'm okay," I repeated in a whisper, convincing myself.

"Go back to sleep," he murmured. "It'll be over in the morning."

"Okay." I hung up the phone and set it on the table.

Evan pulled my quivering body in to him, wrapping me tightly.

"Is everything okay with your mother?"

"Yeah," I breathed. "She forgot I was staying over at Sara's, so she was upset. She thought something had happened to me."

Evan didn't say anything. He held me tighter while gently rocking me and pressed his lips against my forehead. He moved back down on the bed, and I followed, lowering my head onto his chest. I pressed my ear against his heart to hear its rhythmic beats. Eventually, his breaths lengthened, and I knew he had fallen asleep. A tear ran over the bridge of my nose and dripped onto his smooth skin.

I listened to his calm, wanting it to capture me as well, but the storm inside me wouldn't rest.

13. OVERREACTION

I snuck out of the guest room before Evan woke. I could hear whispers and movement farther down the hall, although it was barely dawn. I suspected there was a need to escape before the sun shed too much light on faces that didn't want to be seen.

I found a few girls searching through the basket of clothes that they'd pulled out of the dryer, picking out items that belonged to them, stuffing them in their overnight bags.

"Emma," a petite blonde beckoned. "Could you get us our keys and phones so we can go?"

"Sure," I answered. I took out the bag that we'd hidden in the back of the hall closet and started laying out the Ziploc bags labeled with each person's name. They took their possessions and left. Most of the girls and a few of the guys were gone by the time Sara dragged her feet down the stairs, looking like she was still in need of a few more hours of sleep.

"Whatcha doin'?" she asked, stretching her arms, her hair twisted in a pile on the top of her head.

I tied up a trash bag filled with cups, bottles and stale chips and set it next to another full bag. She looked around. The kitchen was beginning to resemble itself again, since I'd already peeled back a layer of party leftovers.

"Thanks for picking up." She sat down on a stool, rubbing her palms over her eyes. "The cleaners are coming around noon, so we don't have to go crazy."

"How are you feeling?" I sat down next to her.

She propped her head up on her hand and yawned wide. "Tired. You?"

"Tired," I concurred. "Almost everyone's gone. I think there are a few guys sleeping on lawn chairs by the pool, a few more on the couches. Mandy, Casey and Jill are upstairs in the rec room."

"Alone?" she stressed.

"Kyle may be up there too, but Jill was luggage last night, so I don't think you have anything to worry about."

She groaned, "I hope not," then collapsed her head into her arms, "I think my head is going to fall off."

I smiled. "Are you going to tell me what happened between you and Jared last night?"

"No," she answered, her voice muffled from within her arms.

"What?" I shot back. "You want me to tell *you* everything."

"But you don't," she retorted, lifting her head up. "Honestly, we just passed out."

"And now what?" I pushed.

The tiredness disappeared from her eyes with the emergence of a smile. She lifted her shoulders in a knowing shrug. I knew exactly what that meant.

"Looks like you'll be putting some miles on your car, huh?"

"Yup." She beamed.

"So, just like that?" I asked curiously. "He shows up at your party, and that's all he needed to do?"

"Not exactly," she confessed guiltily.

I waited for her to continue.

"He wanted to keep seeing me after New Year's." I raised my eyebrows at this revelation. "I just couldn't see it working out. But he called and e-mailed a couple of times, trying to convince me. Then he stopped, and that's pretty much when I became a stupid girl. So when he showed up last night…" She paused and grinned. "I knew I couldn't say no again. You're right. I have to at least try."

"Good morning," Evan said from behind us. "Wow, we have some work to do before we leave, huh? Sara, what time's your flight?"

"Three," she answered, sliding off the stool to begin tearing the hearts off the wall. She was heading to Florida for February break, and Evan had skiing plans in Tahoe with the California guys—leaving me alone in Weslyn. They had both invited me to go, but I felt I should spend the week with my mother, since that had been the point of moving in with her in the first place.

"Do you want a ride? My flight's at three fifty." He came up behind me to wrap his arms around my shoulders, kissing me on the top of my head.

"That'd be great," she agreed. "Except my parents aren't coming back until Sunday."

"I thought you were too?" I questioned.

"Umm...no," she answered with a smirk.

"I'll pick you up on Friday," Jared's voice answered before he came into view on the stairs. Of course. It all made sense now.

"Perfect," Sara replied, color returning to her face and her hangover miraculously disappearing.

Jared and Evan woke the rest of the guys. A few helped put the pool furniture back in place, but the other pale, grumbling faces took their possessions and dragged themselves out the door.

The girls slunk down the steps once Sara turned on the music. If she was up, then everyone else had to be too. Aspirin and sodas were passed around as we tackled the repercussions of throwing a party. I stepped in something wet on the carpet in the family room in my bare feet, and every inch of me shuddered. I wouldn't even let myself think about what it might be.

When the cleaning ladies showed up, the house had been stripped of its anti-V-day decor, but it was obvious that the aftereffects still lingered in the air when they scrunched up their noses upon entering. Sara left them a huge tip before we headed out for breakfast.

"I still owe you a Valentine's Day," Evan stated in the car, after I'd stuffed my face with way too many blueberry pancakes.

"No you don't," I replied honestly. "I don't think anything will be able to top last night. It was pretty great."

"It was," he agreed, pulling down my street. "But would you be interested in going on a normal date? You know, adventureless? Dinner, movies, or something?"

I grinned at the thought of the two of us in a restaurant and nodded. "That would be nice."

"After I get back," Evan promised, turning into the driveway.

I only half heard him because I was staring at the cheerful yellow house, fearful of what awaited me after my mother's distraught phone call.

"Are you okay?" Evan asked from beside me.

"Huh?" I answered, pulling my eyes away to look at him.

"Is everything all right between you and Rachel? You were really upset last night."

"I just felt bad that I worried her, that's all. Just a miscommunication," I explained lightly, not wanting him to hear the guilt beneath the sugar coating. "We're fine." When he didn't look convinced, I insisted with a smile, "Really."

"You'd tell me, right?" Evan looked into my eyes, trying to read the truth. I blinked away, turning my eyes to the floor.

"Of course," I answered, opening the door. I leaned over and pressed my lips to his, begging him to believe me. "Have fun in Tahoe with the guys. I'll see you on Sunday."

He pulled me toward him and gave me a kiss that would be sure to tide us over for the entire week. Barely able to stand, I staggered toward the door, turning once to wave before he backed out of the driveway.

I took a deep breath, sobering instantly when I clasped the cold door handle. I pushed it open with my pulse racing, not sure what was about to happen. I quietly shut the door behind me, and froze when I heard laughter coming from the kitchen. Not at all what I was expecting.

"Emily," Rachel exclaimed, still giggling, from within the kitchen. "How was the party?"

The radio playing in the background was suddenly cut off by the high-pitched sounds of a blender.

"Don't let it get too thin," my mother instructed. I walked to the doorway to find the counters covered in food in different stages of preparation. Tomatoes were diced on a cutting board; garlic skins littered the table; lime slices lay squeezed and abandoned. The entire kitchen smelled like a Mexican restaurant.

"Hi," I greeted them hesitantly.

"Hey." Jonathan smiled, appearing completely relaxed. "We're, umm..."

"Preparing for Margarita Call Out of Work Day," my mother explained. That's when it struck me that they were supposed to be at work, it being Monday. "We're going to Heidi's to play cards and pretend we're in Mexico."

"Oh," I responded, thrown by her exuberant mood. "Sounds fun."

"Yes, it does," she answered excitedly. "I figured Jonathan could handle making salsa." She examined the contents of the blender. "Maybe I was wrong. Sweetie, just go start packing the bag, and I'll fix this, okay?" She kissed him on the cheek when he grimaced apologetically.

"He can't cook either," she explained with a comical shake of her head. "So, how was the party?" she asked again once Jonathan had passed me to get a bag out of the coat closet.

"It was fun," I answered, wondering if I'd dreamt the phone call. "But I didn't get a lot of sleep. I think I'm going to crash for a while."

"That happens—means it was a great party." She smirked knowingly. I hesitated, examining her. She looked perfectly fine, not at all devastated, as she had been on the phone last night.

"What?" she questioned when I lingered too long.

"Have fun in Margaritaville," I said with a smile.

She laughed at my reference and declared, "Oh, we will."

"Where are the mixers we bought?" Jonathan hollered from the living room, placing bottles and glasses into a reusable shopping bag.

"Upstairs in my room," my mother responded. Jonathan was a few steps behind me as I dragged my body up the stairs.

"Hey." He beckoned quietly before I could enter my room. I turned to face him. "How are you?" That one question, combined with the anticipatory look in his eyes, confirmed I hadn't imagined anything.

"Confused," I answered honestly, opening my door.

"I don't think she remembers," he explained. "I kinda screwed up last night, so she took it out on you. My fault, and I'm sorry."

"What do you mean?" I asked, the confusion still looming.

"I mentioned that I hadn't slept at my place in a while, and that I should probably stay there a few nights this week." He hesitated before admitting, "It wasn't the best thing to say on Valentine's Day."

I pressed my lips together and shook my head. "She thought you were breaking up with her, didn't she?"

Jonathan sighed and nodded. "We talked it over this morning, and she understands. So I won't be over much this week. I just need to…breathe a little, I guess."

His choice of words alarmed me. I suddenly understood my mother's distress. "Wait. *Are* you breaking up with her?"

"No." He shook his head emphatically. "She and I are having a lot of fun together, honestly." He was about to say something else when my mother interrupted from the kitchen, "Did you find them?"

Jonathan looked at me and then down to the kitchen. "I found them," he lied, not making a move for her door. Then he returned to me and quickly said, "I just wanted to explain, since you might not see me around for a bit. I'm still here; I just need to back off a little." Then he went down the stairs and into the living room.

I stepped into my bedroom when my mother came into sight, carrying a sealed glass container of salsa. I realized he'd never intended to get anything from her room; he just wanted to check in on me, to explain things. He hadn't explained much, in all honesty. I knew that he hadn't told my mother half of what he'd just told me, or else she wouldn't have been smiling that way.

Someone had left a red heart-shaped box filled with chocolates on my bed. There was a heart drawn on top in marker, with an *R* scrawled underneath. I held the box in my hand and stared at it. I didn't want to be the person who made things harder for her.

I lay on my bed with my hand on the heart, considering if my being there was what was best for her. How was I supposed to decide that? She'd sounded so hurt last night, convinced that I didn't want her. The irony was that I'd been afraid she was going to say the same thing to me.

I eventually fell asleep on top of my covers. The house was dark when I woke a couple hours later, but it wasn't exactly quiet. This house never rested. I turned on music to mask the house's distress, so I wouldn't jump at every little noise.

I was searching for a shirt to wear when a loud bang suddenly drew my attention. I shut off the music, remaining perfectly still and holding my breath, convinced I'd heard a cabinet slam shut in the kitchen.

I crept to my door. The hinges creaked as I slowly opened it. I listened intently and jumped when the radiator rattled on. I took a breath and rolled my eyes at my overreaction, turning the music back on.

I gathered a pair of sweats and a long-sleeved shirt in preparation for a shower, so I could feel a part of the human race once again and rid my hair of the chlorine smell. I had texts waiting for me from Sara and Evan when I emerged, clean and revived.

I turned each light on as I walked through the house, making my way to the kitchen to microwave a frozen macaroni and cheese dinner. I poured a glass of milk and brought the plastic tray into the living room. I wasn't sure I'd ever feel comfortable being alone, at least not in this house.

I got sucked into a pathetic reality television show with explosive drama and so many words bleeped, the sentences didn't even make sense. After wasting an hour of my life, I found a black-and-white movie I'd seen enough times to know just about every other line.

"Emma, you should go up to bed," the voice whispered. "Emma."

"Yeah?" I answered, not sure if I was talking in my dream.

"It's late," the voice responded.

I pulled the cover up under my chin, slowly realizing I wasn't in my bed. I pushed my eyes open to find the television playing highlights of a basketball game. I blinked heavily, waking in the dark with the lights extinguished except for the television.

"Sorry to wake you," Jonathan said from his seat across from me. "But I figured you'd be more comfortable in your bed."

"What time is it?" I asked, trying to focus on the glowing clock of the cable box.

"After two," he answered.

I pushed up to sit, slowly coming to the surface.

"You should go up to bed," Jonathan encouraged again.

I took a breath, "Okay." But I didn't move. My brain started functioning, and I looked at him quizzically. "What are you doing up?"

"Needed to step away from a dream," he answered vaguely, but with words I could understand.

Then it struck me. "Wait, I thought you weren't staying over this week."

"I'm not," he confirmed, then corrected with, "I wasn't supposed to. I had to drive her home; then she asked me not to leave her. I just..." He pressed his lips together, not finding the words to support his decision.

"You know she's always going to ask you to stay."

"And that's the reason I shouldn't."

I was confused by what he said, and slightly alarmed. But I let him decide if he was going to explain what he meant, and he eventually said more than I expected to hear. "I've sent out applications to graduate schools, and the closest one is in DC."

"Oh," I breathed, starting to understand, and not liking where this was headed.

"I like being with her. She's a lot of fun, and has the craziest perspective on the world. She doesn't ask questions about me or where I came from; she only cares about who I am now and just wants to be with me."

"And that's good, right?" I asked, suddenly curious why keeping his past hidden was important to him. But then again, I was the last person to want to talk about mine.

"Yes, not talking about my past is a relief, honestly," Jonathan replied. "But I don't want her to need me like she does. I just want..." He searched for the right words. "I don't want any pressure."

"She's always needed someone," I blurted. I hadn't planned to say it, but as soon as I did, I knew it was true. I looked up at him, my honesty shrouding me with guilt. "I didn't mean it like it sounded..."

"You're probably right," he interrupted. "I'm not sure it's *me* she needs, exactly."

I started pulling at a thread on the blanket.

"I shouldn't really be talking about my relationship with you anyway," he suddenly said. "Sorry, I'm sure it's weird."

"A little." But my conclusion started to make sense, looking back over the years. She'd never been without a man in her life, even for short spurts of time. I'd always believed it was her desperate way of replacing my father.

I looked over at Jonathan and wondered what she'd seen in him that reminded her of my father. Maybe it was his smile. When it spread across his face, the edges of his eyes would crinkle into a smile too. My lips curled up just thinking about it.

"What?" he asked, catching me in my memories.

"Nothing," I answered quickly, adjusting the blanket around me uncomfortably. "I was just thinking. I can understand why she'd want you to stay."

"Then does that make me a horrible person for needing some space?"

"No," I answered. "I'm just not sure how *she'll* do with the space. She really likes you."

"I like her too," he admitted with a sigh. "But you'll be here with her."

I let out a short laugh. "It's not the same."

Jonathan grinned, his eyes locked with mine. My smile faltered for a moment when I couldn't look away.

"I guess I should go to bed." I blinked, pulling the blanket off me. Before I got to the stairs, I turned to him and said, "Jonathan?"

"Yes, Emma."

"Please don't hurt her," I begged, my voice soft and edged with emotion. "I don't want to see her hurt again."

He paused for a moment, scanning my face thoughtfully. "I don't want to hurt her either." He offered a consoling smile before I turned away and walked up the stairs, not sure if he'd promised what I asked—fearful that he hadn't.

14. UNDER THE SURFACE

Jonathan wasn't in the house in the morning. Neither was my mother, who was once again fulfilling her obligations as executive assistant at the engineering firm. We didn't see Jonathan for the rest of the week either, and she *appeared* to be adjusting to the separation.

I tried to keep her busy. I even suggested a cooking lesson one night, but after the smoke detectors went off and we had to open every window in the house for ventilation, we opted to eat out. She worked late a couple of nights, coming home after I'd eaten and joining me on the couch to watch television.

"I hope he doesn't leave me," she uttered one night with a glass of wine in her hand. She'd kicked off her work shoes under the coffee table, and her blouse was untucked from her skirt. She was staring at the TV, but her thoughts were obviously with him.

"He cares about you." I tried to sound encouraging, but it fell flat.

"When does Evan get back?" she asked, changing the subject. Her gaze readjusted to the present, and she looked over at me with bright eyes.

"Sunday," I answered slowly, not prepared for the On switch to her personality.

"Wouldn't it be nice to take off to wherever you wanted, just because you wanted to?" She said this with an equal measure of envy and possibility. "We should have him over for dinner soon."

"Uh, okay."

"I'm going to bed," she announced. I watched her climb the stairs and hoped that whatever Jonathan was doing, it wouldn't leave her devastated in the end. I didn't think I could handle watching her heart break.

———

I met up with Jill and Casey the next afternoon; we ended up going to a movie that night. After a half day of incessant giggling, combined with soda and Jujubes, my teeth hurt from all the sugar. I could only take the two of them in small doses, and I'd OD'd today.

I had barely taken off my jacket when my phone rang. I pulled it from my pocket to see *Rachel* on the screen.

"Hi," I answered.

"Is this Emily?" a deep voice asked. Not answering, I looked at the phone again to make sure I'd read it correctly. It had my mother's phone number as the caller. I put the phone back to my ear, my stomach clenched.

"Hello?" he bellowed over the voices and music clashing in the background.

"Yes," I replied, my heart picking up its pace. "This is Emily."

My brain flashed through a thousand different images of what might've happened to her, inciting panic.

"You need to come pick up Rachel. I can't let her drive home."

"Um, okay," I responded with a heavy heart. I should have been relieved that she was okay, but then again, she really wasn't. "Where is she?"

"Mick's Place, on Route 113 in Stenton."

"Alright. I'll be there soon." I sank onto the steps with my phone in my hands, bowing my head in dread. I shouldn't have been surprised that she was drunk once again. It was what I'd become accustomed to as a child, but I'd hoped I wouldn't have to deal with it this time around.

My entire body hollowed with the acceptance of her condition, shutting off the emotion that threatened to take over. I just needed to focus on getting her home, and then I'd figure out the rest later.

I tried to locate the bar on the GPS on my phone, but nothing came up. I had no idea where she was. That left me with only one choice. I shook my head and groaned, "Shit," not liking what I was about to do, especially since he was probably the reason she was drinking.

I dialed the number and held my breath as it rang.

"Hello? Emma? Is everything okay?" The urgency in his voice made it clear that he was expecting the worst.

"Um...not really," I replied softly. "Can you help me?"

"Of course. What's going on?" he responded in a rush.

"I need to pick up Rachel, but I don't know where she is."

"I'll be there in fifteen minutes, okay?"

"Okay," I exhaled.

Jonathan's truck pulled in to the driveway, and I stepped onto the porch to lock the door behind me.

"Will you drive my car?" I asked, before he'd said a word.

"Sure," he responded, taking the keys with a questioning look.

"I think she's going to need to lie down," I explained glumly.

He took in my drawn expression. "It'll be okay. We'll pick her up, and everything will be fine."

"Yup," I answered, not believing a word.

I told Jonathan where she was, and his brows pulled together in concern.

"What?" I demanded nervously.

"It's not the best place to hang out," he noted with a heavy breath. "You should stay in the car while I go in and get her, okay?"

I closed my eyes and nodded, trying to hold it together.

When we arrived, I understood why he didn't want me to go in. The bar was a single-story box with neon lights nailed to its roof. Several of the letters were dark, and the end of PLACE was flickering red, fighting to stay lit. The small slots that were presumably windows were covered with glowing neon beer signs. The building was a dingy shade of white that the years and lack of care had rotted away. There were shingles missing in some spots or broken in others. It looked like a strong wind could bring the entire place down.

The dirt parking lot was poorly lit. A single spotlight hung from the corner of the building, casting more shadows than light. The lot was covered in patches of ice. It was a hazard to walk on while sober, forget about after drinking until you could barely stand. A group of rough-looking men with dark, stubbly faces stood outside, smoking cigarettes and making comments to the patrons coming and going. I was convinced they hadn't showered in days. A line of motorcycles would undoubtedly be parked in front of them if it weren't the middle of winter. They blended with the dilapidated background perfectly—the sight of them made me squirm in disgust.

"Stay in the car. I'll be right out," Jonathan instructed me, shutting the door behind him.

I sank into the seat with my arms crossed, watching one of the men in leather shake the hand of another who approached from a Camaro. The guy from the Camaro had a shaved head and broad shoulders, and wore a pair of black sunglasses, even though it was nearly midnight. Creepy characters flocked to this place, making me wonder why my mother would ever stop here.

One of the smokers glanced in my direction, and my heart started racing. I quickly looked down, hoping he couldn't see inside the car.

"Keep your fucking hands off me, John," a woman threatened, redirecting my attention.

The men were laughing as a woman with tight jeans and a cropped leather jacket thrust the door open to enter, glaring at them. The man with the leather trench coat and a long, thick mustache was still watching me. I shuddered and tried to sink farther into the seat. He nudged the tall guy with the heaving waistline next to him, nodding toward me and saying something. The guy laughed and nodded his head.

"Jonathan, where are you?" I whispered, anxiously staring at the black door, begging him to come through it. I looked back, and the mustached cretin grinned at me. My heart spasmed and my hands started shaking. I quickly flipped my eyes down, hoping he'd lose interest.

"Come on out of the car, sweet thing." He beckoned, making the rest of the men take notice. "Let me buy you a drink." There were laughs and sinister grins in reaction to my panic-stricken face. I made sure the doors were locked and silently pleaded once again for Jonathan to appear with my mother.

The scruffy man made a move toward the car, and my breathing faltered. I was trying to decide what to do when the black door thrust open, stopping him in his tracks. Jonathan emerged, carrying my mother passed out in his arms. I exhaled in relief, unlocked the doors and jumped out of the car to open the back door for them.

Jonathan gently laid her across the backseat. I threw a sideways glance at the man standing at the front of the car. The grin on his face was abhorrent. I couldn't keep my hands from shaking while I waited for Jonathan to adjust my mother. I just wanted to get away from there as fast as possible.

"Hey, buddy," the man hollered to Jonathan. I remained frozen by the door. Jonathan shut the back door and started to walk around the back of the car, not paying attention. "Hey, you." Jonathan stopped, recognizing that the burly man in the trench coat was talking to him. "Why don't you let me take one of those girls off your hands? I could show this one a good time." I cringed as he molested me with his eyes.

"Are you talking to me?" Jonathan demanded, his threatening tone making my eyes widen in alarm.

"Yes, I'm talking to you," the man growled. "I want a taste." His mustache-covered mouth spread into a detestable smirk, and he started in my direction. I pressed against the car, blindly feeling for the door handle while keeping my eyes on him. I was fearful of provoking him with any sudden movement—*move slow, and he won't attack.*

"I wouldn't do that if I were you," Jonathan's deep voice warned through clenched teeth. I flipped my eyes toward Jonathan, shaken again by the edge in his voice. The rest of the men became quiet and squared off toward Jonathan, whose hands were slowly flexing into fists by his side.

The man crept toward me until he had me in his direct sight, not taking any notice of Jonathan.

"I think you'd taste good." His cigarette- and alcohol-laden breath coated my face. I closed my eyes and swallowed hard, paralyzed. Fear held me hostage as he leaned in. The car rocked, and I opened my eyes to find Jonathan gripping the man's collar, pinning him against the car.

"Don't you fucking touch her," Jonathan grunted. The guy was taller than Jonathan, but Jonathan was broader. Jonathan glowered inches from his face. The crowd shuffled forward, prepared to join in if necessary.

The two men stared at each other for a second before the cretin snarled, "What are you going to do?"

Jonathan raised his fist.

"Jonathan, don't," I begged, released from my paralysis when I realized what was about to happen. "Please, let's just go." The crowd was prepared to brawl. My entire body shook as the tension mounted.

Jonathan caught sight of me out of the corner of his eye. His face was hard and full of rage, but his expression flickered when he saw the fear on my face. His eyes softened, and he slowly lowered his fist.

Jonathan was about to let him go when the man warned, "Listen to the girl. Why don't you just get the fuck out of here before I have to mess up that pretty face of yours." Jonathan narrowed his eyes at the threat, his jaw flexing. I inhaled sharply.

"Please, Jonathan," I begged, reaching for his arm in desperation. His muscles eased up at my touch, and he slowly let the man go, backing away.

"Get in the car," Jonathan ordered gruffly. He opened the passenger door, and I crawled in. He slammed it behind me, not taking his eyes off the guy, who was smoothing the crinkles out of his jacket with a malevolent grin. I watched the silent showdown as Jonathan crept around the car, prepared to attack if the stubbly-faced man made a move for my door. My heart was pounding so hard, my chest was about to explode.

"If she weren't here..." Jonathan began as he opened the driver's door.

"Then we wouldn't even be talking, now would we?" the man interrupted. "Don't come back unless you're willing to back that up."

Jonathan slid in and shut the door. His eyes were hard coals, fixed on the man standing at the front of the car, who was focused on me. He moved his lips to form a kiss and then challenged Jonathan with a snarky grin. My whole body convulsed in disgust.

"Let's just go," I repeated urgently. Jonathan gripped the steering wheel so tightly his tendons stood out along his forearms. He backed out of the space with such speed I had to grab the handle above the door with both hands. The tires squealed when they made contact with the road. A cloud of dust blew up behind us as we tore out of the parking lot.

Except for my hands, which were shaking on my lap, I couldn't move. A few miles down the road, Jonathan finally slowed and darted his eyes in my direction. His dark eyes were released from the rage that had possessed him. I let out a quivering breath and blinked away the tears clouding my vision.

"I'm sorry about that," he said softly, darting sideways glances in my direction while he drove. I stared out the window, trying not to cry.

He veered to the shoulder of the road and stopped the car. "Emma."

I slowly faced him, swallowing against the tightness in the back of my throat.

"Are you okay?"

I could only nod. His eyes searched mine. I pulled away from his probing, too vulnerable to let him see how shaken I truly was.

My mother groaned, deflecting his attention to the backseat.

"What's going on?" she mumbled, blinking but unable to sit up.

"We're taking you home," Jonathan answered, pulling the car back onto the road.

"Jonathan?" she rasped.

"Yes."

"I called you," she whimpered. "I called you," she repeated in a slur.

"I know," he said to pacify her, staring at the road.

I turned toward her, and she tried to focus on me.

"Emily?" she asked as if uncertain. "Oh, you're not supposed to be here." She sounded so sad, I had to turn away.

I followed Jonathan up the stairs when he carried my mother to bed. After removing her shoes and covering her with a blanket,

I looked down at her calm face with a broken sigh. I left the room and collapsed on the couch in the dark living room, drained. My hands were still shaking, and my chest ached.

"You should get some sleep," Jonathan said from the entryway. I looked up at him, dazed.

"I don't think I could if I tried."

He came over and sat next to me on the couch. We listened to the silence, letting the stillness settle in around us. My mind searched for understanding, unable to find solace among my thoughts.

"I don't know what to do," I uttered in defeat. "I really wanted it to be different."

"This is my fault. I should have called her back."

I knew his need for space had triggered this catastrophe, but this was how my mother handled things when she was upset. Unfortunately, that hadn't changed as much as I'd hoped.

"It's not your fault," I assured him. I thought of my mother in her bed and wanted to believe this was just something she was going through, that she'd adjust and get over it. I wasn't certain how far *hoping* would get me.

"What are you thinking?" he asked when I was quiet for too long.

"What was she even doing there? That place was *awful.*"

"I don't know," he replied, just as confused.

The night replayed itself in my head: the phone call, the sketchy bar, the confrontation with the creepiest guy on earth.

"Were you—" I began, just as Jonathan asked, "What did—"

We both stopped, and he encouraged me to speak. "Go ahead."

"Were you really going to hit that guy?"

Jonathan pressed his lips together, like he was considering his words carefully. "You mean, if you hadn't stopped me?"

I nodded.

"Definitely," he answered without hesitation. My eyes widened at his bluntness. He looked down and rubbed his hands together. "It's a part of my past that I don't like to talk about." He raised his head. "But that's never happened before."

"What?"

"No one's ever been able to stop me. I usually lose it, and there's no holding me back."

"You're a fighter?" I asked, not expecting the confession. For the first time I noticed a thin scar under his chin, and another above his right eyebrow, both barely visible.

"Used to be," he corrected. "My past, remember. I haven't gotten that angry in a long time. It scared me."

"It scared me too," I admitted.

He stopped rubbing his hands together, troubled by my admission.

"The whole thing scared me," I said, still feeling the aftereffects trembling beneath my skin. "Let's just say tonight sucked all around."

"Yeah, it did." He sighed. Jonathan leaned toward me to make certain he had my attention. His dark brown eyes focused on me, pulling me in when he said, "I don't ever want to scare you again." I couldn't say anything. The conviction of his words poured into me, and I could barely breathe.

He leaned back against the couch, releasing me from the connection. I took a deep breath to ease the pounding in my chest.

"What were you going to ask me?" I was finally able to get out.

"You said you thought it would be different. What did you mean?"

"I haven't lived with her for almost five years," I explained evasively, staring out the window into the night. "She's been hurt before, and I don't want her to go through that again. I just want it to be different for her, for us."

"Where were you during those five years?"

"In hell," I breathed, resting my head against the couch. He was quiet. I continued to stare into the dark, eventually breathing myself to sleep.

———

When I opened my eyes, the room was a warm gold as the sun filtered through the trees. My heavy lids closed again, and I pulled the blanket over me. I was about to drift off when I set my hand down and felt the hard lines of his thigh beneath it. My eyes stretched wide. My instinct was to jump up from the couch, freaked that I had fallen asleep with my head on his leg. But I didn't want to wake him, so I sat up slowly. Jonathan remained seated on the end of the couch, his head lolling to the side, breathing deeply.

I found my jacket draped over the arm of the rocking chair and my shoes placed beneath it—though I knew I'd had them on when I'd fallen asleep. I rubbed my eyes to ward off the remaining drowsiness and carefully rose from the couch. A floorboard creaked when I stood. His head rocked in response, and his eyes blinked open.

"Sorry," I whispered, my heart beating quickly. I'd really wanted to be gone by the time he woke up.

"What time is it?" he asked, squinting as he read his watch. "I should get going." He yawned and stretched his arms over his head.

"You're not staying?"

"Um…" he stalled, not expecting the strain in my voice. I bit my lip, realizing how I sounded.

"I mean," I fumbled, searching for a way to fix it. "I thought that—"

"I can stay," he interrupted. He sighed as his eyes climbed the stairs.

"You don't have to." I could tell he was unsettled by his decision.

"I don't understand what happened last night," he said, resting his head on the couch and searching the ceiling. "I've seen her drunk, and I've seen her get emotional. But I've never seen her that bad before."

I hesitated, taking in his troubled face—debating if I should just go up to my room. He was obviously concerned about her, and so was I.

I sat down on the couch, with one leg folded under me so I could face him. "She was upset." He rolled his head over to look at me. "I'm sure it's been hard having me move back in, too. I remind her of my father, and that… hurts her. I want to fix us, but I don't know how if I'm the reason she's in pain."

Jonathan studied my eyes, as the truth of my words swallowed me.

"You didn't do this to her," he said soothingly. I averted my eyes. "And as much I feel guilty for not calling her back, I didn't do this to her either."

We sat in silence for a minute. I tried to convince myself that what he said was true, and I *knew* it was. But I couldn't help feeling that if I hadn't forced myself back in, she wouldn't be forcing herself to forget.

"Can I ask you something?" Jonathan inquired hesitantly.

"Sure." I turned back toward him, waiting.

"What happened to your ankle?" He eyed the scar on my right foot, which was curled under me. I pressed my lips together, not prepared for the question.

He'd opened his mouth to say something when I answered, "A going-away present."

He was quiet a moment. "From hell?" I raised my brows in confirmation, not expecting him to get it. "I have one of those." Before

I could react, he lifted the right side of his shirt to reveal a long, thin scar that ran under his ribs. "Lived there once too."

There were so many questions I wanted to ask him, but shock stole them from my tongue. I eventually excused myself to go to my room.

Jonathan remained on the couch, not leaving as he'd promised—but not making any attempt to go to my mother's room.

Despite being exhausted, I couldn't fall back to sleep. I wondered if he was downstairs, lying awake as well, trying to figure out what might have happened to me. I couldn't even imagine how to begin to ask him to reveal his nightmares.

15. ANOTHER CHANCE

Jonathan, I'm so sorry. I promise I'll be better."

My eyes blinked open, only moments after they'd finally shut. I remained still, listening.

"Please don't leave me." Her words were broken with emotion. Footsteps creaked down the stairs. Cries filtered through my door. I didn't dare move, fearing they'd know I could hear them.

"I won't leave," he stated from the bottom of the stairs. His voice didn't hold signs of promise, but consoled with a defeated breath. "I need to clear my head, okay? But I'll come back tonight and we'll talk about it."

"You promise?" she asked, in an elevated voice that sounded desperate. His answer wasn't verbal because the next thing I heard was the door shutting, followed by gasping sobs at the top of the stairs.

It was difficult to listen to her. My insides ached, wanting to take away the hurt—but I didn't. I curled into a ball and waited. Waited for her to find her breath and put herself back together. Her whimpers only quieted with the click of her door.

I crawled out of my bed and dressed in running pants and a long-sleeved running shirt, pulling a fleece over it. I needed to get out of the house, away from the consuming emotions. I tied my sneakers and slipped on gloves, hiding my hair under a baseball cap. The brisk air filled my lungs as I stepped out the door.

The sun was out, and the temperature was above freezing, melting away the icy edges along the shoveled sidewalk. I eased into a jog and breathed deep, releasing the tension in my shoulders as I followed the concrete squares beneath my feet. I'd forgotten my iPod, which would have been ideal to distract me from playing the previous night over and over in my head. Instead, the racing thoughts remained trapped.

I explored the intertwining neighborhood, finding a park a few streets away. It was filled with kids in snowsuits jumping off whatever they could into the thick mounds of snow. Their laughter and squeals were a welcome contrast to the cries that echoed in my head.

As I rounded the corner of the park, my jogging slowed at the sight of the blue pickup. When I saw Jonathan sitting on a bench staring at nothing, I stopped. I considered turning around and running in a different direction, pretending I hadn't seen him. But then he spotted me, and I wasn't going anywhere.

I walked toward him, tucking my hands in my fleece pockets.

"Hey," I said, standing in front of him. "It's not bad out today. It's not California, but it's not bad."

Jonathan nodded lightly. His eyes remained troubled. I sat down next to him on the wooden bench. Neither of us said anything for at least a minute.

I was contemplating getting up to continue my run when he spontaneously confessed, "My father didn't like me very much. I wasn't submissive like my mother. I didn't worship him like my younger brother. I didn't let him control me, so he'd do anything he could to break me. My life's been complicated, and I can't..." The words trailed away, and he stared into the distance.

"I can't do this. This...drama." He took a breath and finally looked over at me. "I need my life to be simple. I need to know what's coming, to be in control. I don't handle the unexpected very well." He dropped his gaze.

"I understand. So does that mean you're done? That you're leaving?"

"Why? You think I should?" He waited for me to answer.

"I don't think I'm the person to tell you what to do. But I don't want her to hurt either."

"Emma, I promise that I don't want to hurt you…I mean, her." I turned toward him, confused by his stuttering sentence. His eyes flickered in apology. "I don't want to hurt Rachel," he emphasized. "You believe me, right?" His dark brown eyes delved into me the way that they did, invading my thoughts and leaving me too vulnerable to resist. He held me captive until I was able to pull away with a shiver. "Right?"

I nodded, staring down at my lap.

"My aunt didn't like me very much either," I blurted out of nowhere, redirecting my gaze toward the house across the street. "Actually, I'm pretty sure she hated me. I mean, you don't strangle a person if you like them even a little, do you?"

Jonathan's eyes widened in surprise. I guess he hadn't seen that coming.

"Wow, that was kind of a messed-up thing to say," I admitted with a nervous laugh.

"Yeah, a little," he said with a slight chuckle.

"I can't believe I just told you that." I shook my head in embarrassment. "You'd think that I'd be over it by now. I mean, she's in jail. But I can't seem to let it go."

"Believe me, I understand. My father's been dead for years, and he still gets to me."

Any remnants of a smile fell from my face. "I'm sorry."

"I'm not." I was taken aback by the conviction in his voice. His face was emotionless and smooth. And in that moment, I was envious. I shifted uneasily, struck by guilt for wishing she were dead for even that one second.

Jonathan exhaled audibly. "Wow, we're depressing as hell, aren't we?"

I laughed at the tension breaker. "Pretty pathetic."

"So, what are you up to today?" he asked, averting the heavy topic that threatened to devour us.

"Well, I guess I'm going to finish this run," I answered. "Then... I don't know. And you?"

"Exercise sounds good," he agreed. "Maybe I'll go for a swim. Then I guess I'll be back over."

"What are you going to do?" I asked, fearing his motives for returning.

"Don't worry," he assured me, "no more drama. Despite what happened, I don't freak that easy. I'm not going to break it off."

"Good." I smiled lightly, finding myself hoping my mother wouldn't continue with her liquid therapy and end up pushing him away for good.

I left him on the bench with a promise of seeing him later and returned to my run. I had a hard time making sense of what was happening, connecting with someone through shared misery. I didn't get it, but I wasn't ready for him to leave either.

I returned to the house cleansed with sweat, and discovered that I'd missed a call from Casey. After stripping off the layers and guzzling a glass of water, I called her back.

"Will you go to a party with me tonight?" she asked, straight to the point.

"Uh," I stumbled, not expecting the question. "I don't know."

"Please, Emma," she begged. "Jill and Sara are away, and this party is supposed to be amazing. I don't want to go by myself."

I sighed, having a feeling I was going to regret saying, "Fine, I'll go."

"Yes!" she exclaimed loudly. "I'll pick you up at nine, okay?"

"Sure," I agreed. "Where are we go—" She'd hung up. I supposed it didn't matter. They were basically all the same anyway.

"That's a cute sweater," my mother noted as she watched me concentrate on brushing my lashes with mascara. It was the first time I'd seen her. She'd stayed in her room most of the day.

"Thanks," I responded, twisting the tube back together. "It's really warm though, so I hope I don't get too hot."

"Cashmere does that. Wear a nice tank top underneath. I have a white one that would look great if you needed to take off the sweater."

"Okay, thanks," I replied, glancing at her reflection in the mirror.

She hesitated and said, "I keep fucking up, huh?" I turned to face her as she let out a disheartened sigh. "I'm sorry."

Before I could respond, she went to her room and returned, holding a ribbed tank top with a sweetheart neckline.

"Thank you," I said, not sure how to recognize her apology. I pulled off the hooded green cashmere sweater and slipped on the tank.

"Fits perfectly," she said, then asked, "Where's the party?"

"Not sure exactly," I admitted. "Do you want me to call you?"

"No," she replied with an indifferent shrug. "You're not the troublemaker kind, too much like your father." She smiled gently and turned to walk away.

"Mom," I beckoned, "I mean, Rachel." She turned back toward me, her face worn and sad, even though she was trying to hold a semblance of a smile. "Are you okay?"

My mother blinked away the tears that formed in her eyes. She cleared her throat and tried to laugh. "I can't believe I'm acting like this." She swiped a hand over her lids. "I'm behaving like a sixteen-year-old." Then she quickly added, "No offense."

I smiled.

"I knew he was younger. And I know that I get attached easily," she explained. "I shouldn't be surprised that I freaked him out." She appeared distraught as she confessed with a pained voice, "I just like him so much, Emily."

"I know." I smiled in sympathy, absorbing the crushed look in her eyes. I wanted to tell her that it would be okay, that he wanted to be with her too—but I wasn't convinced that was the truth. So instead I told her, "You're stronger than this."

My words left her without any of her own. She appeared surprised, and a tear slid down her cheek.

We were interrupted by a honk.

"Oh, that's Casey," I said. Then I paused. "Do you want me to stay?"

"No." My mother smiled, smoothing her damp cheek with a shake of her head. "Go. Have fun. Besides, he should be here any minute."

Jonathan was on the walkway as I headed to Casey's car.

"Party?" he guessed.

"Yup." I shrugged. "See you later. Oh, and be good to her," I said quietly as he passed me. I turned away before he could answer.

When I opened the door to Casey's Mini, electronic beats were released into the quiet neighborhood.

"Hi," she yelled, not making an effort to turn down the music that reverberated through my chest. I just nodded in return.

Casey wasn't a nonstop talker and messenger of all things gossip like Jill. She usually got the stories mixed up or completely wrong, so she'd listen and repeat what she didn't understand—which was most of it. She was genuinely a good person, but carrying on a conversation would take patience I didn't possess at the moment—so I just let the music do the talking.

We zipped through the winding dark roads of Weslyn, venturing into a neighborhood lined with iron gates. The hidden houses were set within the hills, displaying all their grandeur while overlooking the rest of us below. I knew this was going to be quite the party.

Casey turned the music down as we entered a long drive. The electronic gates slid open when we pulled in front of them. She eyed me in expectation.

"Are you mad?" she asked, biting her lip—preparing for my reaction.

"Uh, no," I replied, eyeing her suspiciously. "Why would I be mad?"

"You've never been here?" she questioned in surprise.

I watched the stone castle emerge before us as we crept up the wide circular drive filled with cars. It even had a tower in the center, with wings upon wings spread out on either side. The flawless structure had been built with large round stones. It was impressive, but emitted a cold façade.

"I would remember this place." I gawked up at it. "Who lives here?"

Casey stopped the car for the valet and put it in park. "Drew."

Before I could react, she was out of the car and taking a number from the guy in the black jacket.

Now I was mad.

"Why are we at Drew's? What made you think this was a good idea? And why would you invite me to come with you?" I shoved my car door open.

"Geez," Casey sulked. "He never has parties, and I really wanted to see the inside of his place. We'll leave in an hour, okay?" She looked like a pathetic puppy who'd been scolded for chewing on the furniture, her blue eyes big and her brows tilted down. I released an annoyed sigh.

"Fine, an hour," I grumbled. "But don't lose me, okay?"

"I promise," she chirped, all perked up again. I almost expected her to jump up in the air and clap.

I followed her through a large wooden door with a cast-iron knocker as large as my head. We entered the open-ceiling foyer, where a large table displaying an enormous floralscape was centered in the space.

There wasn't much of a crowd yet. The people we passed could have come from anywhere, since most were unrecognizable to me. Casey paraded through, handing her jacket to someone behind a closet door. I followed her loose bobbing curls, but she made a turn down one of two halls and disappeared.

I turned the corner, and the space opened into what must have been the family room. There were dark brown leather couches pushed against one wall. And a sleek, handcrafted twenty-foot bookcase climbed up another wall, displaying books and artifacts of various shapes and sizes. Large arching windows spread across two sides of the room, and at the far end, lights were suspended on poles, flashing on a dance floor. Tall, thin speakers framed a guy standing at a computer with large black headphones on his nodding head.

The room was scarcely populated—a few people sat on the couches, and a few more stood around the perimeter, talking. But Casey was nowhere to be found.

"Where's the bar?" I asked the first random person who passed me.

"Down those stairs," the girl pointed, then followed after her friends.

There was an arch in the wall, barely noticeable as the hall rounded a corner. I entered to find wide curving stairs—leading down to the dungeon, I presumed. I followed the polished wooden steps around the bend, into the largest rec room I'd ever seen. There were several pool tables, two bars, couches, televisions, foosball tables and a basketball shooting game. Soft lighting filtered through sconces around the perimeter of the stone walls.

There were more people down here than upstairs, but it still wasn't crowded—or maybe the space was so large it didn't feel like it was. I thought I spotted Casey at the bar at the far end of the room, and I passed several groups of people to get to her.

"Emma Thomas?" a girl asked behind me. I turned to find a group of girls in glittery tops holding martini glasses, gawking. "I *never* would have expected to see you here. This is crazy."

I looked from one to the other, not recognizing any of them.

"We graduated two years ago," the petite brunette stated when it was evident I didn't know who they were.

"Oh, hi," I said, not coming up with anything better to say.

"How've you been?" the girl with black curly hair and full red lips asked.

"Um…" I stumbled, not really believing that they cared, but decided to answer with, "Great, thanks. I'm actually looking for Casey Straus. Have you seen her?"

"No," she replied apologetically. "We should totally catch up later though, okay?"

"Definitely." I forced a smile as they waved and walked away. What had I gotten myself into?

I turned toward the bar again, but the blond curls had disappeared. I collapsed onto one of the stools, not wanting to chase after her all night. I figured after the hour was up, I'd text her and meet her wherever she was.

"What can I get for you?" the guy in the white oxford asked from behind the bar. I couldn't believe there was an actual bartender, but then again, there was valet parking.

"Something with caffeine," I requested. As he reached for a liquor bottle, I specified, "Nonalcoholic." He nodded and handed me a Mountain Dew.

I looked past him to the screen suspended behind the bar and occupied myself with basketball highlights so I wouldn't have to make conversation with people I didn't know. Or people I did…

"I told him, 'You're a douche and you're going to wish you were dead.'"

I don't know why I turned around. Perhaps it was because he had one of those obnoxious voices that carried through a crowd, attracting attention. It was almost an instinct, like hearing a car horn and turning to see who was honking as the car's about to hit you.

Jay's mouth dropped open. "Shit, Emma. I didn't know you were here. Sorry. I didn't mean anything by it."

It took me a moment to understand what Drew's annoying best friend was talking about. When it connected, I rolled my eyes with a groan and slid off the stool—walking past him and the awed eyes that surrounded him.

There was a steady stream of people flowing down the stairs, so I continued to the other side of the room, keeping my head down. I found a sliding door leading to a stone patio next to the other bar. I unlocked it and slipped out before anyone could say anything else to me.

I wasn't sure why I bothered to keep coming to these parties. I blew out a cloud of frustration into the frosty air and shoved my hands in my pockets, trying to decide my next move.

I pulled out my phone, realizing that I still had an unbearable forty-five minutes to go. I searched the dark, trying to spot a path that led to the front. Maybe the valet would let me sit in Casey's car while I waited for her.

The patio connected to a stone walkway that was cleared of snow. It branched out; one way led to a pool covered in a snow-crusted blue sheet, and another to a long building with a dark wood finish. Light spilled from the small windows that lined the top of the tall walls.

I approached the door, just to peek in, but when I opened it I was drawn inside. The distinct scent of freshly waxed floors with a hint of rubber filled my senses. I wasn't exactly surprised to find an indoor basketball court in Drew's backyard, but I couldn't understand why he'd never told me about it.

The court was empty, creating the perfect haven in which to hide for the next half hour or so. I unzipped my jacket and dumped it on the bench. Perfectly painted black lines framed the court, and two benches for the competing teams bordered one side. A professional scoreboard hung high on the wall at one end of the court. There was even a door leading to a locker room in one of the corners. I laughed, shaking my head. This was unbelievable.

I took off my black-soled shoes and strode onto the court, eyeing the rack of balls along the baseline. I pulled one off and started dribbling toward the foul line. Squaring up to the basket, I released the ball, bouncing it off the back rim and through the orange hoop. I slid my feet along the floor for the rebound, then dribbled back for another shot.

I continued to work my way around the perimeter, watching the minutes tick away on the caged-in clock behind the basket. When the door banged shut I stopped with the ball poised in the palm of my hand. I spun around.

"I thought I'd find you in here," Drew said with a soft smile, his dimples slightly creasing. "Then again, I wasn't expecting you to be at the party at all."

"Sorry," I apologized, my entire body breaking out in a nervous sweat.

"No, it's okay," he assured me, walking toward me. "Just surprised when I heard you were here, not a big deal."

Drew wore a light blue sweater that played off the color of his eyes, making them look like reflective pools of water. His black hair was swept to the side, more tamed than the surfing style I remembered, but it could have easily been mussed to resemble it.

"Where's Sara?" he questioned.

"Cornell," I responded.

"Then who are you here with? Because I know it's not Evan," he mocked.

"Casey," I shared, picking up on his teasing tone. He nodded.

I balanced the ball on my hip, trying to figure out the best way to leave without it being any more uncomfortable.

"Wanna shoot?" he proposed, holding up his hands in expectation.

"Why not." I tossed him the ball with a shrug. I thought I might as well, since I had to leave in a few minutes anyway.

He dribbled in closer and pulled up for a shot, the ball sliding through the net with ease. I shuffled to collect the ball and tossed it back to him for another attempt. He took a few steps to the right and landed the shot.

"Congratulations on winning States for soccer again this year," Drew said, accepting the ball again.

"Thanks," I responded, focusing on the rebounds so my nerves wouldn't get the better of me.

"Heard the girls' basketball team is pretty decent too," he continued, hitting every shot he took.

"Yeah, we have a good team."

He tossed the ball back in my direction, allowing me to take some shots. I dribbled out to the three-point mark and let the ball go, nailing it.

"Nice." He bounced the ball to me. I stepped up to receive it and set up for the shot; it bounced off the backboard and into the basket.

"Syracuse ball, huh?" I concentrated on the basket, not looking at him as I spoke. "How come I never knew they picked you up? That's pretty huge."

"No one really did," he responded. His indifference caught me off guard. I hesitated, flashing him a quick glance, before taking the shot. "I didn't want to make a big deal about it. My dad brags enough for the two of us. Besides, I'm redshirted this year, so I don't play much."

"Right." I nodded, still not understanding how the entire school hadn't known he was a prospect when they scouted him during his junior year. It made me wonder just how important basketball was to him, since it was obviously a huge deal to his father. I squared up to shoot. Drew moved in quickly, intending to tip the ball out of my hands. I pulled it down, and when his hand sank, I popped back up to hit the shot.

"Nice try," I taunted, rushing in to gather the rebound. Drew hurried after the ball, bumping alongside me. He was quicker, having the shoe advantage.

He grinned cockily and dribbled the ball back out. I took a defensive stance in front of him. He made a move on the inside, and I followed in tight, jumping when he released it. But it sailed over my fingers into the basket.

"Lucky," I jeered.

My anxiety dissipated with each shot. Drew pulled off his sweater, revealing a grey T-shirt with a surfing logo. I was beginning to sweat myself, so I took off my sweater too and tossed it next to his on the bench. As I turned back toward the court, Drew shifted his eyes down the fitted white tank top. I ignored the slight grin on his face.

He checked the ball back out to me and I dribbled, deciding where to make my move.

"How come we never played before?" he asked, jabbing his hand in to attempt a steal. I turned to block him with my shoulder, letting out a wicked laugh.

"I don't know," I responded. I spun around to release a quick shot over him, slicing through the net. "How come you never told me you had a basketball court in your backyard?"

"Graduation present," he explained. I nodded my head in understanding, knowing we hadn't been exactly speaking, nor had I been in any condition to play ball, when he'd graduated last June.

"I can't play in socks," I decided after sliding after the ball. "Barefoot rule."

"Fine," Drew agreed, kicking off his shoes and stripping off his socks.

We continued with the one-on-one match, the game intensifying with each rebound and score. I shoved up against him to sneak in under the basket, and he elbowed me a few times to earn space to take a jumper. I couldn't say who was winning; we weren't exactly keeping score.

I went up for a jump shot inside the three-point line, and Drew came in late for the block, nudging me with his shoulder. I landed hard on my right foot, and my ankle gave out under the pressure. I stumbled to the floor.

I pulled my knee into my chest, grabbing my ankle and sucking in air through clenched teeth.

"I'm so sorry." He bent down beside me. "Are you okay?"

"Yeah," I grunted, inspecting the damage. "Just landed wrong."

"It would suck if I took out the captain of the team right before play..." His sentence trailed when his eyes connected with the scar. "Oh, Em. Are you okay? Really?"

"Yeah, I'm fine," I tried to answer lightly, downplaying the strain in my voice. He held out his hand, slowly pulling me to my feet. I tested my weight and limped to the bench.

"I'll get an ice pack." Before I could refuse, he was jogging to the locker room. He returned a minute later with a white plastic pack, twisting it to initiate the cooling process. I rested my leg on the bench, and he set the pack on top of my ankle.

"I'll be fine," I insisted, slightly embarrassed by his concern. "Besides, aren't you throwing a party or something? You don't have to take care of me."

He smiled. "The party takes care of itself. And I wish I'd taken better care of you when I had you."

His words stilled my chest as I remained silent.

"What I meant to say is that I'm sorry," he said softly, sitting at the end of the bench near my foot, holding the ice pack in place. "I was such an asshole at that party, and I wish I could take it back. So I just...I wanted you to know I'm sorry."

I swallowed, since it seemed to be the only thing that I was capable of doing. I met his eyes, sincerity glistening in their tranquil hue. I didn't know what to say. But I believed him.

My view shifted past him to the clock on the wall. "Shit. I'm late."

"What?" Drew asked, my panic unexpected.

"I was supposed to meet Casey about an hour ago. I'm such an idiot."

"She's probably still inside," he assured me.

I pulled my foot out from under his hand and shoved on my socks and shoes. My ankle was tender, but I'd been through worse. I grabbed my jacket and headed for the door.

"Wait," Drew called after me, grabbing his jacket and fumbling with his shoes.

I pulled my phone from my pocket to call her and noticed I had five missed calls, three of them from Casey, and a string of texts. I groaned

The last text read, Have no idea where you are, but I left. At another party across town. Call me if you're stuck.

"Great," I grumbled.

"What's wrong?" Drew asked, tying his shoes beside me.

"She left. Now what am I going to do?"

"Do you want to leave?" he asked, standing up and sliding his arms into his sweater before pulling it over his head.

"No offense, I'm sure it's a great party, but—"

"I get it. I'll drive you."

"You can't leave your own party," I objected.

"They haven't missed me yet." He smiled sardonically. "I haven't had more than one beer, and I can't say that for just about anyone else at this party besides you. Still don't drink, right?"

I shook my head.

"Then let me drive you home."

I took a breath to give me a moment to decide. "Fine."

I followed Drew to the house so he could grab his keys. We shuffled through the crowd, which had grown to raging proportions during our absence.

"Where've you been?" a girl with long, flowing blond hair and a fitted strapless top asked Drew as we neared the stairs.

"I've been here," he responded without really looking at her. "I'll be back." We passed by, and I avoided the daggers that followed me up the steps.

A man dressed all in black stood at the top of the stairs. He looked like he was about to stop us when he recognized Drew. "Good evening, Mr. Carson."

"Hi, Frank," Drew greeted him. "Anyone giving you a hard time?"

"No one I can't handle," the muscular figure responded. I noticed an earpiece in his ear, and he squeezed a small mic on his collar, conversing with someone.

"You take partying to a whole other level," I observed, continuing down the long, wide hallway.

"I know what can happen when it goes wrong," Drew responded, stopping at a door. I remained still when he opened it. "You can come in if you want."

"No," I answered quickly. "I'll wait in the hall."

Drew smirked and entered his bedroom. He re-emerged a few minutes later with a jacket on and keys in his hand. We retreated down another staircase at the far end of the hall, with another man dressed in black posted at the top.

"I'll be back in a while," Drew told the guard.

"Don't worry. Everything's under control," the man promised in return.

The stairs led to a hallway near a side entrance, away from the crowd. We disappeared without anyone noticing. His SUV was parked on the side of the house, making for an easy escape.

"Thanks for driving me," I said, securing the seat belt.

"No problem," he responded, starting the vehicle.

We were quiet most of the ride. I was afraid to say anything, not wanting to start a conversation I wasn't prepared to have. As we continued, I looked around in a sudden panic.

"Where are we going?" I demanded in a rush.

"To your...oh shit."

My heart was beating so fast, I couldn't catch my breath. Drew opened his mouth in aggrieved apology. He pulled the SUV into the parking lot of the closed coffee shop.

I closed my eyes, trying to pull some semblance of composure together.

"I can't believe I did that," Drew said, shaking his head. He pulled away, putting distance between me and the house. "Where do you live now?"

I gave Drew directions to my mother's house on Decatur Street, finding it easier to breathe the farther away we drove.

Drew pulled in to the driveway behind Jonathan's truck. He put the SUV in park and turned toward me.

"It was good to see you," he said.

"Yeah," I replied, unbuckling the belt.

"Hey," he said, stopping me from reaching for the handle. "I wish I had known." I faced him, letting him continue but knowing

I shouldn't. "You know, about what you were going through," he explained softly.

A twinge of nerves spiked through me. I closed myself off, determined not to let his words in.

"I know I was a dick at times, but I really did care about you."

Those words snuck in unexpectedly, and I felt a warmth rush through me. "I know."

"I tried to visit you," he confided, "when you were in the hospital. But the police wouldn't let me in. I really am sorry, Emma—for everything."

I smiled slightly. "Thanks, Drew. No one knew, so it wasn't just you."

"Do you think I could call you sometime?" he asked slowly. "You know, to keep in touch?"

"It was good to see you too, Drew," I said, without answering. "Thanks again for the ride." I got out of his car. He waited in the driveway until I opened the front door. I didn't look back, shutting it behind me.

16. READY?

I pulled the earbuds from my ears and set the magazine next to me on the bed when I heard the knock on my door.

"Hi." My mother smiled, easing the door open. "Can I come in?"

"Sure," I answered, not sure why she was acting so nervous. Then I noticed the frame in her hand.

"I wanted you to have this," she said, propping the frame on the top of my bureau, next to Leyla and Jack's framed Christmas card. I slid off the bed to get a better look. "I figured you should have it, since it's the only one that escaped my clumsiness."

It was a picture of my father balancing me on his shoulder, smiling proudly. I was laughing, wearing a soccer uniform and holding up a trophy. My mouth turned up at the sight of it.

"Thank you."

"He loved watching you play soccer," she recalled. I examined the picture, but couldn't place the moment. I appeared to be around five or six. Perhaps I was too young to remember. "You understand why I don't have pictures of him out, right?" she asked tentatively. I nodded. "Well, it doesn't mean you can't."

I wasn't sure what to say. It was obvious it had taken a lot for her to share this with me. And I wanted to tell her how much it meant to me. I probably should have hugged her. But we just stood there awkwardly, having difficulty even meeting each other's eyes, forget about touching.

"So how was the party?" she finally asked, breaking the emotional tension.

"It was a party." I sighed indifferently.

"Did anyone say anything about the sweater?" she pushed.

"Oh no!" I exclaimed, shaking my head.

"What?" she questioned in alarm.

"I forgot my sweater," I explained, upset with myself. "I can't believe I forgot it."

"Can't you just go there and get it?" she asked, not understanding my dilemma.

"Well…it was at my ex-boyfriend's house, so I'm not so sure that would be a great idea."

"Ex-boyfriend's?" my mother mused with raised eyebrows. "Does Evan know you went?"

I pressed my lips together guiltily. "No. And I'm not looking forward to telling him."

"Good luck with that," she scoffed lightly, with a shake of her head.

"Oh, thanks," I retorted, my stomach twisting at the thought of having to tell Evan that I went to Drew's, *and* that he drove me home. "That makes me feel better."

"Sorry." She chuckled.

"Ready?" Jonathan hollered from the hallway.

"For what?" my mother questioned in confusion, just as red and purple squirt guns landed on my bed.

Jonathan appeared in the doorway, armed with a blue one. "For this." He smiled wickedly and released a stream of water.

I ducked toward the bed when he shot at us again. My mother yelped in laughter.

"Oh, you are so going to get it," she squealed, snatching the red gun and chasing after him down the stairs, spraying the entire way.

I grabbed the other gun and pursued them, losing sight of Jonathan as my mother ran into the kitchen for cover. I led with the gun, pointing it into the living room, but he wasn't there.

I turned and crept back toward the foyer. My mother stuck her head out and nodded toward the dark hallway that led to the basement door. Before I could react, Jonathan emerged from the shadows and grabbed me by the arm, pulling me in front of him just as my mother popped out of the kitchen, aimed to squirt.

Jonathan pressed his arm across me, taunting my mother to shoot.

"You're using me as a shield?" I accused him as he waved the gun, flashing it from my mother to me—ready to squirt whoever made a move first.

"She's not going to shoot *you*," he explained, steering me farther out into the foyer as my mother attempted to circle around to get a clear shot.

"Sorry, honey," my mother said, aiming the gun at my head.

"Mom?" My eyes spread wide in disbelief. Then I noticed her eyes flip toward the floor, and in that second, I dropped out of Jonathan's arm and onto the floor while she squirted him. I spun around and began streaming water at him as well.

Jonathan held up his hand to protect himself while he shot back at us. None of us attempted to retreat, allowing the water to fall on us as we laughed, until there wasn't anything left in our guns.

"Time to refill," Jonathan proclaimed with his hands raised in surrender.

My mother took my gun as I sat on the stairs, wiping the water from my face, still smiling.

"Okay, we get a head start," my mother instructed me a few minutes later, handing back the filled water guns. "Jonathan, you have to stay in the kitchen for twenty seconds before you can come out. Ready, Emily?"

I nodded. Jonathan eyed us suspiciously before retreating to the kitchen.

"Quick," she whispered, "up the stairs."

I scampered up the stairs with her right behind me. Ducking into the bathroom, I hid behind the door as she lay on the floor of the hallway, ready to ambush him when he came up the stairs.

"Ready?" she asked, glancing back at me. I thought I heard a knock at the door, but I couldn't be sure from where I was.

"Wait, you can't go outside," my mother hollered when the door squeaked open. She popped up and started shooting in that direction before she was even on her feet. I stepped out of the bathroom to follow her. But she'd stopped. She stood frozen at the top of the stairs, her hand covering her mouth.

"I am so sorry," she gasped. I followed her horrified gaze to find Evan at the bottom of the stairs with water running down his forehead and over his nose, stunned and confused.

I opened my mouth in shock and then burst out laughing.

"What did you do?" Jonathan asked from beside the door. "That's not the best way to greet someone."

"Evan, I thought you were Jonathan trying to escape," my mother explained in a rush, her face bright red. I shook my head, still laughing as I went down the stairs.

Evan wiped the water from his face with the sleeve of his jacket. "It's okay. It's only water." He eyed me with his amused grin. "You're laughing? You think this is funny, right?" I recognized that look.

Before I could turn back up the stairs to get away, he had his arms wrapped around my waist and I was off the ground.

"No, Evan. Don't," I begged. I had no idea what he planned to do, but I knew I was in for it. Jonathan appeared entertained, but my mother scrambled after us.

"What are you going to do?" she asked, watching as he wrestled me into the kitchen.

"Mom, help—" My pleas were broken with laughter. I tried to squirm away when one of his hands released me to turn on the sink. "Evan!"

He squeezed the sprayer on the faucet and doused me over the head as I broke free. My mother and Jonathan hid behind either side of the doorway to get out of the way. By the time I was out of range, I was dripping wet.

"Now *that's* funny." Evan's laughter was echoed by Jonathan and my mother.

"Thanks for your help." I sulked, looking down at my drenched T-shirt.

"What? And be soaked like you?" My mother chuckled.

"Nice, Evan," Jonathan said. "Next time, you're on my team." I shook my head and dripped up the stairs.

I returned a few minutes later with a dry T-shirt and my wet hair pulled back. Evan was helping wipe up the water in the kitchen.

"You missed a spot," I teased.

He turned toward me and grinned, taking in my wet hair. "No, I didn't."

"Oh, you're so funny," I said with roll of my eyes. "Ready to go?"

"Where are you going?" my mother asked, taking the wet towel from Evan.

"To Evan's."

"Really?" Evan queried, obviously not aware of the plan.

I nodded.

"Okay, to my house then."

"I'll be back later," I announced, pulling my jacket out of the closet.

"Good luck," my mother said, making me hesitate before leaving, suddenly understanding what she meant. Maybe we should've stayed after all.

"Are you okay?" Evan asked when he saw my face drop.

"Yeah," I muttered. "I just thought I forgot something." I grumbled under my breath, walking out on to the porch, "But unfortunately I didn't."

"You didn't want to stay?" Evan asked when we entered the car. "Looked like you guys were having a good time."

"Yeah," I said, distracted. "But I haven't seen you all week, so I wanted to be alone with you." Or thought I did.

By the time we arrived at Evan's, my stomach had twisted to the point of nausea.

"Are you okay?" he asked again, examining me intently when we entered the rec room. I could only imagine how pale I was.

"No," I blurted out before I'd even taken my jacket off. I released a deep breath and confessed what I'd rehearsed a thousand times in my head on our way over. "You're going to hear this tomorrow, so I'm just going to say it." I twisted my hands as he leaned against the back of the couch, waiting. "I went to a party at Drew's. I didn't know we were going there, and I never would have gone if I'd known where we were going. I'm sorry."

I let the shock of it settle in, but his mouth curved up and the concern in his eyes disappeared.

"Why are you looking like that?"

"That's it?" he questioned, unfazed.

"Yes, I mean no," I answered guiltily, not understanding his comical expression. "He ended up driving me home because Casey took off, but nothing happened—I swear."

"I know," he answered casually, taking off his jacket and flinging it on the back of the couch.

I studied him, not understanding why he appeared so calm while the nerves in my stomach were about to devour me.

"You know?"

He stood in front of me with his hands on my waist. "Emma, I trust you. I'm not worried about what party you go to at whoever's house, even Drew's. Was he a dick to you?"

"No," I answered, still in shock.

"Good," he said, giving me a kiss on the top of my head. He continued to the pool table and began pulling the balls out of the pockets.

I shook my head. "Where did you come from?"

"What?" He laughed.

"How did I end up with you? I mean, my life's so messed up, and then..." I kept shaking my head in wonderment. "And then there's...you. I couldn't have made you up if I'd tried."

"I don't understand what you're talking about," he replied, racking the pool balls with a sparkling smile. While I was still gawking at him, he walked over and wrapped his arms around me. "Most of your life wasn't your decision. You didn't get to decide who your parents were, that your dad was going to pass when you were young, or that you'd end up with..." His jaw tightened slightly, and he couldn't finish. "Those weren't your choices.

"The things you do get to choose, you put everything you have into them—school, sports, protecting the people you care about. And you chose me."

Warmth fluttered through my chest. I had a hard time meeting his eyes.

"So your life *is not* messed up." Evan paused, placing his forehead on mine, demanding my attention. "You've actually done a pretty amazing job at living it." He kissed me gently and pulled me in to him.

"I love you," I murmured into his chest, holding him tighter. I tilted my head back and met his steel-blue eyes.

"That I know too," he smirked, causing my mouth to drop open.

"Nice," I shot back, pushing him away. He grabbed my hand and pulled me back against him.

"I love you too," he whispered before tilting his head toward me.

I closed my eyes and felt the warmth of his breath on my lips just before they pressed into mine. I inhaled deeply at the touch of them, flutters instantly rushing through my chest. He ran his hand along the back of my neck, his mouth slipping across my parted lips.

My heart raced and my breath quickened as I pulled him in to me. He unzipped my jacket and slid it off, dropping it on the table. The tease of his lips along my neck captured my breath as I hopped up onto the side of the pool table and wrapped my legs around him.

He slid his hands under me and picked me up, balancing me while walking toward the couch, our mouths frantically passing over each other's. My entire body was pulsing. He laid me on the couch and eased himself over me.

I ran my hands under his sweater, and he pulled back to remove it. I sat up to run my lips along the hard lines of his chest, before pulling my T-shirt over my head. Evan grabbed the blanket at the end of the couch to cover us as I reached for his waistband.

My quickened pulse stirred a heat that crept through my entire body. We eased across boundaries, unfastening bindings, slipping beneath fabric. Our lips brushed in a breathless exchange.

Our mouths pressed harder; our breath grew faster as our hands slid along curves. He inhaled quickly at my caress, his heart beating against my bare skin. His breathing quickened, and his muscles flexed along his back, the tension rippling through his entire body as he groaned in my ear. I gasped when he found me, closing my eyes. A flush swept across my skin at his gentle touch. I writhed under the growing sensation until I was released with an exhilarated breath.

Evan pulled the blanket tighter around us, exhaling deeply. "Wow."

"Yeah," I breathed, still unable to focus clearly. I tucked myself into his arm and rested my head on his chest, draping my leg over his. "Can I ask you something?"

"Anything," he said, running his warm hand along my back.

"When are we going to have sex?"

"Umm..." Evan laughed. "I wasn't expecting *that* question."

I popped my head up to look at him. "I'm not saying that I don't like what we just did, it's just—"

"I know," he smiled. "We will. It's a big deal, and I don't want to do it on the couch in the garage, or in the backseat of a car. I want it to be what it should be."

"What if it's horrible?" I rested my chin on his chest. "I have no idea what I'm doing. You want it to be this epic moment, and I'm afraid I'm going to fail miserably."

"You're ridiculous," Evan said with a small laugh. "I'm not worried." He released a calming breath and repeated, "Believe me, I'm not worried." He put his hand under my chin to pull me in for a kiss.

Despite Evan's lack of concern regarding my sexual prowess, I *was* worried. No matter how much I tried not to let it consume me, it was all I could think about. I'd only been waiting for it to happen, since, well...forever.

My phone rang as I lay on my bed later that night, waiting for Sara to respond to my text. I quickly pressed *Answer*.

"What's going on?" Sara demanded before I could say hi.

"How was Cornell?" I asked, suddenly regretting sending the text.

"Shut up, Em," Sara shot back. "Your text said you needed my help. What's going on?"

After gathering myself, I finally stated bluntly, "Sara, I want to have sex."

"Well, of course you do," she responded, like I'd said the most obvious thing in the world.

"But what if I'm terrible at it?"

Sara started laughing hysterically. I hung up the phone. She called back ten seconds later.

"Sorry," she said calmly. "You're serious. I thought you were having one of your delusional episodes."

I didn't say anything.

"Emma, you and Evan love each other, so there isn't a wrong way of doing this. But I'll give you some pointers if you want."

I let out a short, nervous laugh, the anxiety making my stomach squirm. "Maybe."

"Don't worry. I won't draw diagrams or anything. Oh, or maybe I should."

"Sara!"

"Emma, don't you dare act all embarrassed to talk about it," she scolded. "*I'm* not the one to be telling anyone to have or not to have sex, but if you can't even talk about it with me, then maybe you're not ready. I know this is huge for you, and you of all people need to be emotionally prepared for it."

"I know," I replied. "I mean, I'm ready—I think. What do you mean by 'emotionally prepared'?"

"Well, you don't trust…anyone, really. You barely trust me and Evan. And having sex is all trust. You can't take it back once you do it, and it leaves you completely emotionally vulnerable. You trust him totally and completely, right?"

"Of course," I answered automatically. How could I not trust Evan? Especially after everything we'd been through.

"Emma," Sara scolded, "do you? No matter what's happening in your life, however complicated and personal, you'd trust him with it?"

I wasn't sure why I hesitated, but a streak of panic flicked through me at the thought of being completely open with *anyone*, even Evan.

"Yes," I answered, without as much conviction.

"That's what I thought," she said, honing in on the waver in my voice. "I'm not saying don't have sex. I want you to. It's amazing. I just want you to go into this completely aware of what happens to you after you put your clothes back on."

"Thanks," I sighed, feeling a little deflated. "See you in the morning?"

"Yes," she replied enthusiastically. "I have so much to tell you!"

We said our good-byes and hung up.

I stared at the ceiling, contemplating trust. Evan was the most trustworthy person I knew. I believed in him, knowing he would never not be there for me. But when Sara asked if I trusted him enough to tell him my most personal secrets, I'd choked.

The vulnerability of letting someone, *anyone*, into the darkness I couldn't face myself was unfathomable. It wasn't because I didn't trust Evan. I didn't want to reveal it to anyone, not even myself. After all, they were secrets for a reason.

17. FREAKED

Sara looked like she was ready to burst with whatever it was she needed to tell me when I saw her the next morning. She was seriously glowing. But the first thing she did was swat me across the shoulder.

"Hey," I hollered. "What was that for?"

"For going to Drew's party and starting up the gossip chain when you let him drive you home."

"Oh." I shrank guiltily. "It wasn't a big deal. Nothing happened."

"I know that, but people in this school are stupid. If you don't want them talking about you, don't do something that will make them talk."

"It doesn't matter," I said with a shrug. "They'll talk about me even if I stand still all day."

Sara laughed. "You're probably right."

"Are we done with this?" I asked, slightly annoyed. "Are you going to tell me about your week, or what?"

Sara didn't hold back. What she couldn't fit in before our first class, she continued with at lunch. I don't think Evan was all that thrilled to hear her talking about his brother. He finally said something about needing to talk to his coach before the next period. I was pretty sure he just needed to escape.

"I'll see you in Art." He departed with a kiss on my cheek.

"What's with him?" Sara asked, noting his sudden need to leave.

"Sara, you're dating his *brother*. Don't you think it's kind of weird for him?"

She shrugged as if she hadn't considered it before. "I guess. I don't know." When she'd exhausted all things Jared, she blurted, "So what do you want to know about sex?"

My eyes widened, not braced for the question in the middle of the cafeteria.

"Tell me what you've done so far," she inquired, with all the seriousness of a therapist.

"Do we really need to talk about this now? You're the one who warned against giving ammunition to circulating rumors. This is definitely not something I want anyone overhearing."

"Fine," she replied. "Come over after practice tonight."

I hesitated. I wasn't embarrassed to talk about sex, I was just… okay, maybe I was, a little. It wasn't like I'd ever had The Talk. What I knew, I'd learned in health class, so I wasn't exactly well versed on the subject. Sara would share stories, but she'd never go into explicit detail, like auditory porn or anything.

"If you get any more red, I think you may catch fire," Sara observed with a shake of her head. "Just come over later, okay?"

"Okay."

When we returned to our lockers after lunch, Sara pulled a textbook from her messenger bag. "This will help."

I took the book, and my eyes spread wide at the title: *Our Sexuality.* "Omigod, are you serious?" I flipped through the pages and shut it quickly when I saw way more skin than I was anticipating.

"It's a college textbook," Sara explained casually. "Thought you might appreciate the technical explanations versus the *Cosmo* version—you know, the science behind it."

"Uh, thanks." I went to shove it in my locker, and it fell to the floor, spreading open with the spine up.

"Here," Evan said, bending down to pick up the splayed text-book. I scooped it up before he could touch it, my pulse racing so fast I couldn't talk.

"What was that?" he asked, when I stuffed it in my backpack.

"Just pointers on how to pleasure you," Sara whispered with a smirk before walking away. I about fell over. I looked up at Evan with my mouth dropped open. He arched a brow curiously.

"Really?"

"We're going to be late for class," I said, slamming my locker door shut. My heart was pounding so hard I was beginning to sweat. He let out an amused laugh and followed after me.

"You don't need the textbook," Evan murmured in my ear from his stool beside me.

"Evan!" I whispered, with wide eyes.

"Sara has no idea, does she?" he continued with a sly grin.

"We are not talking about this." I buried my fiery face in my hands. He chuckled.

"Good afternoon," Ms. Mier greeted us from the front of the class, setting a large piece of wood on an easel. "Today we are going to create visual art using nails." On the board was a profile of a woman created with various oxidized nails pounded into the wood at different depths and angles to create a three-dimensional work of art. I was fascinated by the technique—the way the nails created the slope of her cheekbone and tilt of her nose.

"I've laid out boxes of nails for you to work with. You can each select a plank of wood and a hammer to get started."

"I can guarantee I'll have a purple thumb by the end of this assignment," I commented, turning toward Evan. He nodded, not looking at me.

We retrieved the supplies from the front of the classroom. I was considering what I wanted to create while filling my bowl with nails.

When I got back to the stool, Evan had the hammer balanced in his hand—examining it like he'd never seen one before. He ran his eyes over it, appearing a million miles away.

"Evan?" I sat down and tilted my head toward him to look up at his face. "Evan, are you okay?"

He was pale and wouldn't focus on me. "Evan, what's wrong?"

Without a word, he set down the hammer and left the room. It took me a moment to realize that he'd just walked out. I rushed to the door to go after him, but he wasn't in the hall. I stood in the middle of the corridor, at a complete loss.

I returned to the Art room and slowly lowered myself on to the stool.

"Is everything okay with Evan?" Ms. Mier questioned when she came around and found his spot vacant.

I don't know," I answered honestly. I didn't make much progress with the assignment because I kept watching the door, waiting for him to return. He never came back.

Evan wasn't at my locker after class either. I took my phone out of my backpack and texted, Where are you? Are you okay?

I set the phone to vibrate and stuffed it in the front pocket of my jeans, pulling my sweater over it so my Calculus teacher wouldn't see it.

Halfway through class, my phone vibrated. I slipped it out and held it under my desk to read, Not feeling great—went home.

I read it again, baffled.

Want me to come by after practice?

Evan responded, No. See you tomorrow OK?

Nothing about this felt right. He hadn't seemed sick all day. I was obviously missing something, but I didn't know what else to think, so I typed, Okay.

"I'm going to go home after practice tonight," I told Sara as we gathered our things at the end of the day.

"Everything okay?" she asked, taking in my somber mood.

"I hope so," I answered before shutting my locker door. "I'll call you later."

"Alright," she answered, studying me as I skulked away.

I called Evan as soon as I got into my car after practice. He didn't answer. I was wrecked with worry by the time I got home, my stomach twisted into knots.

"Maybe he's really sick," Sara consoled me when I called.

"Maybe," I agreed, but I didn't really believe it.

"Don't start overthinking like you do."

"I won't," I assured her, but I'd already gone there—replaying everything he and I had said throughout the entire day. I still couldn't figure out what would've caused him to leave school so suddenly. Something must have happened in those few minutes I was away from him in the Art room. Maybe he got a text that I didn't see? Whatever it was, it was sudden, and he wasn't sharing.

"We'll see if he's in school tomorrow. Text me if your brain hijacks you and you need to vent."

After I'd hung up, I pulled my books from my bag. I needed to distract myself, and I was hoping homework would help.

I was interrupted from the miserable depths of political theory by a knock at my door. Before I could respond, my mother stuck her head in.

"Hi," she said, opening the door wider upon seeing me on my bed. "I wanted to see if Evan would like to come to dinner tomorrow night. I thought he might be up here with you."

I'd opened my mouth to answer when she picked up the textbook Sara had given me, which was peeking out of my backpack. I scrunched my face when she read the title out loud.

"What's this?" she asked, then started flipping through the book. "Wow, they're really teaching you everything in high school these days. I could have used this when I went to school."

Without thinking, I blurted, "It's not for school." My mother's eyes widened and her mouth rounded in sudden realization. I wanted to close my head in the book.

"This is for *you*?" she asked, the shock still on her face. "You're still a virgin," she slowly concluded, like she wasn't expecting that to be the truth. The mortified look on my face made it obvious that it was. "I would have thought that you and Evan..." I dropped my head face-first on my bed. This day could not get any worse. "Do you want to talk about it? I never thought I'd have to give The Talk, but I can if you want." My head shot up at her offer, and that's when I noticed Jonathan paused in the hallway—yup, it had just gotten worse.

"No...um, that's okay," I stammered, cringing inwardly.

"Really, you can ask me anything," she continued. I think she would have sat down on my bed to keep talking about it if Jonathan hadn't knocked on the open door, letting her know he was there.

"Are you ready?" he asked. I couldn't look at him. I wanted more than anything to disappear.

"Oh, yeah," my mother responded, brought back to what she was supposed to be doing before she crossed all mother-daughter boundaries. "Well, ask Evan about dinner, okay?"

I could only nod, my explanation of his illness lost in the back of my throat. When she set down the book, I quickly shoved it deep inside my backpack.

Jonathan held the door open to let my mother pass, then said, "Good night." I looked up, and he grinned widely.

"Good night," I returned, my entire body on fire.

A few minutes later, I heard the front door close. I tried to turn my focus back to my assignment, but kept finding myself checking my phone—begging it to light up with a message from Evan.

About an hour later, it did. Sorry I missed your call. I'm okay. Pick you up in the morning?

Yes, I texted back. I knew I wouldn't find the relief that his text was supposed to provide until I actually saw him.

Falling asleep in the restless house was never easy. Staying asleep was virtually impossible. I flipped on the light next to my bed with my heart thumping. I stared at the door. A moment ago I could have sworn there had been a hammer driving through it, trying to shatter it to pieces so she could get to me. In the light, the black door was intact and still.

I got out of bed and pulled on a sweatshirt before quietly tiptoeing downstairs to escape the panic that still shot around inside me. Exhausted, but knowing sleep was probably a good hour away, I settled on the couch with a blanket covering me. I found a movie that had more dialogue than action, the perfect plot to drone me to sleep.

About a half hour later, the creak of a step drew my attention. Jonathan cringed at the sound and paused before continuing down the stairs.

"Hey," he greeted me wearily, pulling the blanket off the back of the love seat and sitting next to me on the couch. "What did you find?" He motioned toward the television.

"Not sure," I whispered, not completely surprised to see him up. "I have no idea what's going on."

After watching the underwhelming drama on the screen for a few minutes, he asked without looking over, "Do you always have the same nightmare, or is it different each time?"

"It's different each time," I answered, with my head pressed against the pillow. "But they usually end right when I'm about to die."

Jonathan was quiet.

I turned my head to find him appraising me, his mouth bowed in sympathy. "I take it yours aren't like that, huh?"

He shook his head, redirecting his gaze toward the TV. "Mine are always the same," he answered in a low voice, his jaw tightening as he stared straight ahead. His eyes hardened as he muttered, barely audible, "They won't let me forget." The features of his face looked carved from stone as he pressed his lips together in a tight line. The dim light glinted off his dark, pupilless eyes. A chill ran through me.

I almost asked what it was that kept him up most nights, but then again, I wasn't sure I wanted to know what made him suddenly so...hateful. He looked like a different person—a person I didn't want to know. I pulled my legs in tighter to ward off the frigidness.

Jonathan faced me, his lips turned up and his eyes creased around the edges—instantly returned to being the guy who'd started a squirt gun fight. I wanted to shake my head, wondering if I'd just imagined the transformation. Maybe it was the lighting, and my lack of sleep, messing with me.

I pulled the blanket farther up under my nose. "I just want to sleep," I murmured, my eyes burning with fatigue.

"I know." Jonathan yawned.

We returned our attention to the movie. My lids were getting heavy, harder to blink open. I was thinking about going back to bed when he asked, "So, do you need any guy advice?"

Exhaustion vanished instantly as color rushed to my cheeks. "Don't even start," I threatened, sitting up and hitting him with the pillow. He held up his hands to ward off the blow and started laughing.

"You should have seen your face when your mother offered to give you The Talk." He chuckled. "I was trying so hard not to laugh." His chest spasmed with laughter.

"Oh, yeah, that was *hilarious*," I shot back. "Can we please not talk about one of the more humiliating moments of my life?"

Jonathan smiled widely, his perfectly straight teeth gleaming in the low light. "Sorry."

"Are those real?" I blurted out without thinking.

"What?" he asked, completely perplexed.

"Your teeth." I continued to stare. They seemed too white in this low light, and too straight. I couldn't stop looking at them. A true indication that I needed to go to bed.

"That was a rather bizarre change of subject," he noted in amusement. "And yes, they're real. After years of braces, of course, but they're mine." He shook his head, still grinning.

"What?" I demanded, not sure why I wanted to know what kept the grin on his face. But I asked anyway.

"Forget it," he said playfully, "you don't want to talk about it."

I rolled my eyes. "My personal life is not up for conversation."

"Not your *personal* life," he corrected, "your *sex* life."

"I don't have a *sex* life," I retorted quickly, my face flushing as soon as I said it.

Jonathan laughed again. "I know."

I buried my head under the pillow and groaned.

"Why is everyone making such a big deal about it?" I murmured from beneath the pillow.

"Because it is a big deal," Jonathan responded bluntly. His voice lost its humor. "But you're serious, right? You and Evan?"

I peeked out from under the pillow and found him waiting for me to answer. I nodded.

"And what's going to happen when you go to Stanford?"

"Hopefully he's coming with me," I answered, sitting up and smoothing the hair that was floating around my head.

Jonathan nodded. "He's as smart as you?"

"Pretty much. He also has some influence that I don't."

"Money," Jonathan concluded with a smirk.

I shrugged. "Part of it."

"And powerful parents," he added. He didn't even wait for me to answer. "Do they want him going to Stanford with you?"

I looked down, not wanting to think about Stuart's harsh words on New Year's Eve.

"Aahh," Jonathan surmised. "Not so much."

"It's his dad," I explained quietly. "He doesn't exactly approve of me."

"Not approve of *you?*" He laughed like that was completely ridiculous. "It's probably the money. I know *that* dad. But I went to college with her anyway."

His words caught my attention. He nodded guiltily. "I did it too. Fell in love with the rich girl. Her parents approved of me enough, until they realized how serious we were. But we went to Penn State together anyway, even though I really wanted to get as far away from this area as possible—and Pennsylvania was still too close." He took a deep breath. "I shouldn't have stayed."

"You broke up?" I asked, even though the answer was obvious, since he was now dating my mother.

"Something like that." He grinned, the smile not reaching his eyes. I could tell by his uneasiness that the emotion was still raw, even after all these years. "College is…different."

I waited, not sure if I should ask him to continue—but wanting to know the story.

Jonathan gripped the blanket and looked toward the dark foyer. I could tell he was thinking about it, what had happened between them.

"People change. I mean, you barely know who you are when you enter, and you spend that time figuring out what you want from life, and who you want in it. The next thing you know, the people you always thought would be there, aren't. And the person you thought you could trust with everything, isn't the person you knew at all."

His shoulders sank. "And then six years later, you have a fraction of the life you thought you would."

I was quiet. I wanted to say something to distract him from going back there, to the place that bowed his head and caved his chest. But he did it himself.

"I got into USC," he declared with a proud smile, dispersing the emotion with ease.

"You did?! Jonathan, that's so great. Congratulations." I was genuinely happy for him, but then it hit me. "Wait. You haven't told her yet, have you?" I closed my eyes in dread.

"I will." He sighed.

All of a sudden, I felt the air go out of me, like someone had just punched me in the stomach.

"Emma, what's wrong?" His voice was heavy with concern.

"He was supposed to know by now." I gasped, unable to catch my breath, consumed by panic. "If he got in…he was supposed to know."

"Evan?" he confirmed. I nodded, my chest squeezing. The entire day was starting to unravel. His needing to leave at lunch. And then right after, in Art, the look on his face. He couldn't look at me or even answer my call.

"He didn't get in." I couldn't breathe.

"Emma, don't do this," Jonathan said soothingly. "Don't start freaking out before you know for sure."

"Easy for you to say," I squeaked, feeling like my world was tipping upside down.

"What if he doesn't get in?" he challenged. I stared at him with huge eyes, like he'd just told me I'd lost everything. I shook my head, denying that it was possible. I couldn't imagine being in California without Evan. I didn't want to even think about it.

"Wow," Jonathan observed. "This is everything to you, isn't it?"

I sank back into the couch, trying to ease the pain in my chest.

"Ask him. Don't go crazy thinking about it until you've asked him."

I nodded. "Just like you have to tell her that you're leaving." I watched Jonathan's face fall.

"Just not sure how to do it," he admitted glumly. "Her birthday's in a few weeks, and I was hoping to be around for it. Is that bad?"

"So you'd rather break up with her after her birthday?" I questioned, not sure which scenario I preferred.

"It's just that...I'm not ready to go yet." He paused and concluded, "It *is* bad."

"It's not my call," I told him. "But she should know."

"I know."

"Wait." I narrowed my eyes, suddenly recalling his reference to how different his life was *six* years later. "How old are you?"

Jonathan cringed guiltily. "How old am I, or how old does Rachel think I am?"

"Oh." My mouth dropped open. "You lied to her about your age."

"She has a problem with the age difference as it is," he explained with a guilt-ridden smirk. "I wasn't about to tell her I'm twenty-four."

"You *are* bad," I said, shaking my head, but unable to keep a scornful face.

"You have no idea," he replied with a wry smile, making us burst out laughing.

"Jonathan?" my mother called from the top of the stairs. Guilt quieted our laughter.

She turned on the hall light and came down a few steps, enough to see into the living room. When she saw us on the couch, her face dropped and something flashed across her eyes. I wasn't certain if it was shock or anger, but it was so brief I could've convinced myself I didn't see it at all.

"Couldn't sleep?" she concluded with a sympathetic smile. I wasn't sure who she was talking to. I shook my head.

"I'll be up in a minute," Jonathan told her. She nodded and went back to her room, shutting off the light before closing her door.

"I should go to bed," I said, standing up and folding the blanket.

"I like this," Jonathan said suddenly, before I could walk away, "talking to you. I feel like I can tell you things…things that I usually keep to myself. Most people don't understand."

"I know." I hesitated before turning from him.

It was true. Until that moment I hadn't realized what was happening. I was able to share the demons that wrestled with me in the night, and Jonathan understood in a way that no one else did. He was fighting with them himself, and that had drawn us together.

The corner of his mouth turned up softly. For a moment I couldn't look away. I was trapped in the darkness of his eyes. They sifted through me, searching for what haunted me. I pulled away with a blink. "Are you staying up?"

"I'm not quite ready to sleep," he admitted, picking up the remote.

"Be careful of the infomercials," I advised, borrowing his words from the first time he'd rescued me from my nightmare. He smiled. "The next thing you know, the sun will be up."

I left him on the couch and slipped back to my room. I didn't sleep much, but it didn't have anything to do with the nightmare. I kept thinking about what I expected from my future, and hoping more than anything that Evan would be in it.

Jonathan was still on the couch, asleep, when I got up before dawn to use the bathroom. I thought about waking him to send him to bed, but he was sleeping. And that was, after all, a good thing.

18. STORY TIME

A soft knock drew my attention to the front door while I was rinsing my oatmeal bowl in the sink. Before I had a chance to answer, the door crept open and Evan stepped in.

"Hi." He seemed tentative, not his usual confident self.

"Hi," I replied, checking his face for any signs of illness. He looked tired and sullen, which only heightened my concern.

He smiled slightly, but the trouble that flickered in his eyes remained. I approached slowly, preparing myself for the news that he wasn't going to Stanford.

"Are you okay?" he asked, examining the stress lines on my face.

I couldn't mask the signs of sleeplessness that hovered under my eyes or the worry that weighed down the corners of my lips.

"Are you?" I asked in return, continuing closer until I was less than a foot in front of him.

"I worry about you," Evan stated, tracing every inch of my face. "Are you really okay?" He ran his hand along my cheek. I closed my eyes, soaking in its warmth.

"I'm okay." That's all I could offer, because on the inside I was a mess. I needed to understand why he was acting so strangely.

Evan leaned in and softly pressed his lips to mine, loosening the knot of worried tension that had held me captive since the moment he'd stepped out of the Art room.

"That's a little better," I murmured when he pulled away. "Are you going to tell me what happened yesterday? Is it Stanford? Did you not get in?"

He looked at me in surprise. Then a smile eased onto his face. "You think yesterday was about Stanford?"

"I don't know what it was about," I continued, not at all relieved by the amused look. "You were supposed to know by now."

"I did get the letter," he admitted.

I stopped breathing, anticipating the next sentence.

"But I don't know if I got in."

"What?" I asked, my shoulders sinking. "What does that mean?"

"Oh, Em." He shook his head. "I'm sorry I didn't tell you. My parents won't tell me which college I'm attending until all the acceptance letters come in. We're still waiting on Yale."

"Does that mean they get to decide for you?" I asked in horror, realizing that if Stuart had his say, Evan wouldn't be going to any school in California.

"No," Evan chuckled, wrapping his arms around me and holding me against him. "I write down my first three choices, and then my mother reveals which school I'm going to. She makes a big production out of it. We go to a nice restaurant, and then she hands me an envelope with the name of the college inside. Don't panic. You're not losing me, no matter what." He kissed the top of my head.

"Why does she do that?" I asked, completely baffled.

"It's something she came up with for Jared. Jared didn't get his first choice. He picked Dartmouth. So she conjured this 'celebratory reveal' to soften the blow. She thinks it's only right she does the same for me. You'll come to the dinner, right?"

"Of course," I replied. But I quickly reconsidered. I didn't know if I could fake excitement if he wasn't accepted by Stanford.

"Better?" he asked, inspecting me again. I nodded. He leaned down and kissed me gently. "Ready to go?"

"Just need to get my jacket," I answered. He released me so I could go to the closet.

I followed him out the door, and he took my hand after I'd locked the house behind us.

It occurred to me during our drive to school that he'd never explained what had happened to him yesterday. I couldn't keep from trying to read his thoughts as he drove. His eyes lacked the light that usually shone within them. I knew something was still troubling him.

"What's wrong?" I finally asked. "Because I know something is." He exhaled deeply, as if he'd been preparing himself for my question.

"Will you come over tonight?" he asked in return. "There's something you should know, and I want to explain it when we're alone." I stopped breathing *again*. His tone was too serious for it to be anything good.

I nodded slightly, my chest burning in a storm of panic.

Evan pulled into a parking spot and glanced at me, then did a double take. I knew the panic was evident—I wasn't even trying to hide it. "Em, I'm sorry." He tried to console me, "That sounded much worse than I meant it to. You don't have to worry, I swear."

I nodded.

He met me on my side of the car and pulled me toward him. "I love you," he said softly, his blue eyes filled with sincerity. "Know that before you spend the whole day freaking out. Okay?"

"Okay," I whispered.

Before he could lean down to kiss me, I heard, "And that's Evan and Emma, one of Weslyn High's power couples. Evan's gorge, but don't even bother looking—he won't see you."

I poked my head around Evan, astounded. Jill walked by with a petite blonde with big doe-brown eyes and pouty red lips. The girl's eyes darted away when they connected with mine, realizing I'd overheard them.

Evan took my hand and turned toward them, shaking his head in amusement. When he spotted the new girl, he spoke warmly. "Hi, Analise."

She quickly replied, "Hi, Evan," with an abashed smile, her cheeks turning rosy.

Jill dragged her off quickly, most likely to get the inside story on how they knew each other.

"How do you know the new girl?" Sara asked from behind us. I turned quickly, unaware of her approach.

"Good morning, Sara," I greeted her.

"Good morning," she replied before turning toward Evan and demanding, "So?"

"My mother hired Analise's mom to work for her new consulting firm," he explained. "They moved here from New York."

"I'm sure my parents will be taking hers out for dinner soon enough to welcome them to Weslyn." Sara sighed.

"It's just her mom," Evan noted. "I think we're supposed to have them over for dinner on Friday. In fact, I'm pretty certain your parents are coming too."

"That's not surprising," Sara returned with a roll of her eyes. "Is she a junior?"

"I think so."

As we walked past her and Jill in the hallway, I took a closer look at the new transfer who was receiving so much attention. She was very pretty in a pure and innocent sort of way. Her fair skin made her red lips and blushed cheeks that much more pronounced, reminiscent of a porcelain doll. Her blond hair tossed in waves, barely touching her shoulders; she nervously twisted a strand around her finger. She seemed shy, barely able to make eye contact with anyone, but she'd certainly found the best person to tell her the ins and outs of the social hierarchy at Weslyn High.

And for no reason I could explain, other than pure territorial insecurity, I didn't want to picture her having dinner at the Mathews' dining room table. I was ashamed of myself for even thinking it, but the guilt didn't change my mind.

"My mother's hoping you'll come over for dinner tonight," I told Evan before he departed for his locker.

"Are you feeling okay, Evan?" Sara asked, interrupting us. "You look tired."

"I'm trying to get over something," Evan admitted. I was instantly struck by his meaning, wanting to know more than ever what he was planning to tell me.

Then he responded to my invitation with, "Sure. We'll go to your house after practice." He kissed my cheek and walked away.

"And *you* seriously need to start wearing concealer." Sara shook her head as she looked me over. "You could probably count the number of times you've slept through the night on one hand, and it's doing a number on the circles under your eyes."

"Thanks, Sara," I huffed, stopping in front of our lockers. "It doesn't help that I live in the creepiest house in Weslyn. And as much as your black wall looks chic during the day, at night I swear it breathes."

"Maybe you should try the medication your doctor prescribed," Sara advised. When I didn't respond, she changed the subject. "How's Rachel? Or better yet, how's Jonathan?"

I smirked sardonically at the eagerness in her voice. "Fine. Although she did see your textbook last night and was ready to give me step-by-step instructions before Jonathan walked in and overheard. I wanted to die."

Sara laughed. "Did you read it?"

"No!" I shot back quickly, making her laugh harder. "I don't think I'm going to. You can have it back."

"Just thought it would help." Sara shrugged, giving me a sly grin.

"I'll falter through it on my own, I guess," I murmured, shutting my locker door with my first-period books resting in my arm.

The rest of the day was filled with a buzz of oohs and ahhs over Analise. Since she was a junior, I didn't have any classes with her. I could avoid most of the gawking that stalked her. But as luck would have it, I found her sitting on the stool at my table in the Art room, exactly where Evan should have been.

"Hi," Analise said tentatively as I sat down next to her.

"Uh, that's Evan's seat," I responded coolly.

"He won't be a part of this assignment," Ms. Meir said from behind us, causing us both to spin around. "So, Analise, you are more than welcome to sit there for the duration of this project. Emma, will you explain what we're working on?"

"Sure," I answered slowly, not getting past the sentence in which she'd said that Evan wouldn't be part of this assignment.

I must have come off as the most horrible person in Weslyn High to this girl. I provided an abbreviated explanation of what we were working on, and basically ignored her for the rest of class. I was too busy trying to figure out what Evan needed to tell me and why he wasn't in class, convinced the two were connected. I didn't give her the slightest bit of attention.

"It was nice meeting you," Analise's soft voice said as we put our things away. I felt wretched.

"I'm sorry I wasn't very talkative," I responded guiltily. "It's been a weird day."

"I've heard you keep to yourself," Analise stated. "I understand."

"I'll see you tomorrow." I tried to recover with a soft smile.

"Sure," she smiled back kindly before we parted ways.

Evan was waiting for me at my locker.

"Did you drop Art?" I questioned before he could say hi.

He hesitated, his lips pressed together. "No. I just asked to work on something else for a while, so Ms. Meir gave me a photography assignment."

"Oh," I responded, embarrassed by the paranoid thoughts that had raced through my head the entire class. This wasn't the first time he'd opted for a photography project. My shoulders eased down. "Yeah, that makes sense."

I opened my locker and started stuffing my books in my backpack.

"We're sharing the court today for practice," Evan told me, watching me gather my things. "So we should be able to leave together to go back to your house."

"Sounds great," I replied. He gave me a quick kiss and disappeared down the stairs to the locker room.

I lifted my eyes from my physics book when his thumb ran across my scar. Evan gently grasped my ankle in his hand as we sat facing each other on the couch, attempting to study before dinner. He absently smoothed the marred skin while remaining focused on his history book. A strange tingling spread up my ankle with each stroke.

He lifted his head and found me watching his hand, but he didn't remove it.

"Sorry we weren't able to talk," I said, resting the open book on my stomach.

"We still can." He paused, and I watched nervously as he gathered his thoughts, searching for the right words. "When I heard—"

"Do you like broccoli?" my mother yelled from the kitchen, the sound of water filling a pan in the background.

Evan pressed his lips into a smile. "Yes," he hollered in return.

I raised my eyebrows when he looked at me. "So...you were saying?"

He flipped his eyes toward the kitchen, where my mother was moving her hips to the classic rock music coming from the small radio in the window. "It can wait."

"Are you sure?" I tried to read his expression, afraid that waiting was only going to continue to torture him—and me.

"Yes, it can," he assured me, leaning over and kissing me. I put my hands around his neck, not wanting him to move away. He pressed in closer.

"Umm..." my mother cleared her throat. Evan pulled back, and my cheeks caught fire instantly. My mother's face was as red as mine felt. She darted her eyes toward the floor and announced, "Dinner's ready."

Just then, the smoke detector went off in the kitchen. I waved my hand and coughed as we entered. My mother forced the window above the sink open, while I grabbed a towel and fanned the screeching alarm. This had practically become routine for us. The alarm had gone off almost every time I'd attempted to cook.

"Stupid oven," she grunted, pushing the wooden window up a half inch at a time. "It must have fifty years of burnt food in there."

"Do you need help?" Evan asked, moving toward her.

"No, I've got it," she grunted, pushing the window up a bit more. She hopped down from the sink and smiled. "You can sit." The detector was silenced, and I sighed in annoyance.

I sat down at the small table in the spindly chair facing the wall. The legs shifted slightly as my weight settled on it. Evan sat to my right in the sturdiest of the three chairs.

My mother placed bowls of broccoli and mashed sweet potatoes in front of us, then proceeded to fork a chicken breast on to each of our plates.

"What do you want to drink?" I asked Evan, pushing my chair back, the legs slanting with the movement.

"Water's fine, thank you," Evan responded, fanning the smoke in front of him in amusement, while my mother and I acted like it was part of the dining experience. Well...it usually was.

As I poured us two glasses of water from the gallon in the refrigerator, my mother settled on the chair across from Evan with a large glass of red wine. I spotted the bottle on the counter, already two-thirds depleted, and eyed her nervously. She still seemed to be okay, although she was busying herself inserting utensils in the bowls.

"Help yourself," she said, encouraging us by placing a few stalks of broccoli on her plate.

I sat back down as Evan scooped a spoonful of sweet potatoes

"How's basketball?" my mother asked, ignoring her food to take a sip from her glass. Then she continued in a rush, "I love basketball. It took forever for me to convince Emily to play, since she was so obsessed with soccer because of her father. But she's actually pretty good at it. I never played, but I love watching it. Soccer seems so all over the place, and I can never keep up with where the ball is and why they're blowing the whistle."

She stopped, noticing we were staring at her. I had no idea she was nervous until this moment.

"Sorry." She grimaced.

"It's okay." Evan consoled her with a smile, giving me a quick glance out of the corner of his eye. I pressed my lips together in apology. He reached for my hand under the table and squeezed it. "Basketball's great."

"Did you make the playoffs?" I could tell she was trying to concentrate on one sentence at a time, taking a sip after the question. Her cheeks glowed red.

"Barely," Evan admitted, setting his fork down to answer her. "We have an away game Thursday, and if we survive that, we'll play at Weslyn on Saturday night."

"I have to see you play!" my mother exclaimed excitedly. "If you make it 'til Saturday, I'm there."

"Great," Evan replied politely, flashing me another glance as I remained still—trying not to show how disturbed I was to have my mother attend my boyfriend's basketball game.

"Emma's playing Friday," Evan revealed.

"That's if we win Wednesday," I stated.

"You will. Your team's favored for the championship."

"That would be so amazing," my mother burst out. "We'd definitely have to have a party." My eyes widened at the thought, making Evan laugh.

"What?" my mother asked, not understanding the impact of her suggestion.

"Emma and parties don't coexist well," Evan explained with a smirk.

"Come on, Emily," my mother begged. "It would be so much fun."

"Yeah, no." I shook my head obstinately.

"Well, I'm having a party for my birthday in a few weeks," she announced. "You'll be here for that, right?" She looked at both of us eagerly.

"Of course," I answered, not sure what I was agreeing to.

"Evan, did Emily ever tell you about the time she fell out of a tree?" She laughed lightly as I rose with my plate in my hand. My mother pushed her plate away, having barely touched it.

Evan began to stand. "I've got it. You can sit," I said to him, taking his plate. He looked to me for assurance. I smiled with a nod and took the plates to the sink.

"No, I haven't heard that one," he answered, lowering himself back in the chair.

I listened intently while I loaded the dishwasher, not sure if *I* even knew the story she was about to tell.

"Emily was always running around, climbing trees and covered in dirt. That's why we got her involved in sports, so she wouldn't kill herself jumping off rocks."

Evan chuckled at the image. I rinsed the dishes absentmindedly, trying to remember.

"We lived in the woods, surrounded by trees, bugs and whatever other creatures slithered out there—it was pretty awful." I turned to catch her shudder. "Sorry, I'm not a bug person."

Evan laughed.

"Anyway, one time, she climbed too far up this tree, and the branch broke under her. She fell, banging into branches the whole way. I heard her crying and found her hanging about twenty feet up. She'd managed to grab the last branch before she would've hit the ground."

I leaned back against the sink, absorbing a story that I couldn't connect with. Although there was something about it that opened a hole in the bottom of my stomach.

"Derek had to use a ladder to get her down." She laughed, like the sight of me dangling from the tree, needing to be rescued by my father, was humorous. "She didn't break anything but was covered with bruises from head to toe. And she never climbed a tree again."

Then she directed her attention toward me. "Are you still afraid of heights?"

I stared at her, recognizing that the void in the bottom of my stomach was triggered by fear. I swallowed and replied, "I don't love them."

"I didn't know you had a problem with heights," Evan noted, examining my pale face. "You did okay when we went rappelling last year."

"I was pretty convinced I was going to fall to my death," I admitted. "I wasn't about to tell you that. Besides, I didn't really have to look *down*, just for the next step. But we never did it again, right?"

"No, we didn't," Evan agreed. "I had no idea."

I could only shrug, since I hadn't known why I was afraid of heights until I'd been blindsided by the memory. I couldn't recall a single second of it—but the emotions were there. The fear and desperation. I knew her story was true.

My mother continued with childhood stories. I should've been embarrassed, but it didn't feel like she was talking about me. It became apparent that I didn't have a single recollection of my childhood, and it was unsettling. That time had completely escaped me, leaving me in the present without a past.

When the cleaning up was done, so was my mother's bottle of wine—she was a giggly mess.

"Want to go for a walk?" I asked Evan. He stood from the table, smiling at another unrecollectable moment about some haircut I'd insisted on when I was eight that made people think I was a boy.

"Sure," Evan responded. "Thank you for dinner."

"My pleasure." She grinned fondly.

After wrapping a scarf around my neck and pulling on my gloves, Evan and I escaped into the cool crisp air of the lingering winter. It hadn't snowed in a while, but what was left wasn't going anywhere fast.

I stared silently at the ground with my hands in my pockets.

"That bothered you." His voice drew my attention. "It wasn't that bad from where I was sitting."

I shrugged. "No, it was fine." And it was partly true. I wasn't really bothered by my mother's nervous chattering, even after a bottle of wine. Evan waited, but I didn't continue.

"Are you going to tell me what you're thinking?"

I breathed in deeply, sifting through what I wanted to say. "I don't remember our house the way she does." I paused in thought before continuing. "I remember loving it, but I don't remember anything about it at the same time. All I can picture is lots of sun and trees. I felt safe there, so it couldn't have been as horrible as she's making it out to be."

I directed us toward the park, and we followed a worn path to the playground. I sat on the chilled seat of a swing. The black plastic hugged my hips. "I didn't realize how blank that time was for me until she was talking about it."

"You were young," Evan responded.

"Not *that* young," I countered. "You'd think I'd remember something as traumatic as falling out of a tree."

Evan sat next to me, watching as I rocked the swing gently with my feet on the ground. I stared at the flattened snow, still troubled. I'd locked everything up, blocking out the good with the bad, leaving myself with not much of anything to hold on to.

"I do remember one thing," I said, gazing at him with a soft smile on my face.

"What's that?"

"My dad made me this swing out of a piece of wood that he hung from one of the trees. I would pump so high my toes would touch the branch above. I'd tilt my head back and close my eyes; it was the most amazing rush. I was convinced that's what flying must feel like. I spent hours on that swing."

Evan smiled affectionately. I allowed the warmth of the memory to fill the emptiness.

"Sometimes I wish I were back there, when everything was perfect and I was happy, swinging my life away."

19. WAITING FOR FRIDAY

D id I totally screw up last night?" my mother asked as she poured her coffee. "I did. I completely embarrassed you. I was nervous, and I drank too much wine, then told too many stories. I am so sorry, Emily. Tell Evan—"

"Mom—I mean, Rachel—" She looked up at me with her lips pressed together. "It was fine. I promise."

"You didn't look fine," she recalled, eyeing me nervously. "You looked mortified."

"I wasn't." I smiled in an attempt to make her feel better.

Her nervous guilt getting the better of her, she asked, "Are you sure?"

I didn't know how else to convince her, so I just nodded.

"I'm sorry I can't make it to your game this afternoon."

"I understand. You have to work."

"Do you mind that I invited myself to Evan's game? Was that a bad idea? I really want to see him play. I was honest about that."

"It's okay." I laughed, wanting her to take a breath before she fell over. "You were great. Really. And I don't mind if you go to his game on Saturday. You can bring Jonathan too, if you want."

Her eyes shifted away from me and fell to her coffee cup.

"What?" I pushed, noticing the pinch between her brows.

"I'm not sure what's going on with him," she murmured. "I think he's keeping something from me." I felt a pang at seeing her so distraught. "Does he say anything to you, you know, when you're up at night?"

I shook my head, not confident that I could answer her. After all, I would be lying.

"What do you talk about?" She asked it like she was being left out of a secret club or something.

"Not much really," I answered. "Sports, commercials, how we wish we could sleep."

"Do you know why he can't sleep?" She watched me closely. I shrugged and looked away. "He doesn't tell me anything. We don't really talk about our pasts. It's good, you know, because it hurts me to think about it, but I wish he could trust me enough to tell me *something*."

I nodded, my voice paralyzed with guilt. I felt like the worst daughter in the world. I should have told her that he was moving to California. That he had a painful past too that was hard for him to share. I should have let her know that it had nothing to do with her and that he really cared about her. But she'd probably wonder why he was telling me all this and not her. And then I wouldn't know what to say—especially since I wasn't sure how to explain why I'd talked with him about things I'd been avoiding with everyone else in my life. So I stayed silent, watching her face twist with uncertainty and doubt.

"When do you see him again?"

"Friday," she answered with a sigh. "I'll ask him about the game then."

"I'm sure it's nothing," I finally said, feeling even more horrible for trying to comfort her with a lie.

"Well, I should go," she said, looking at the microwave clock. "Text me the score, okay?"

I nodded, and as I watched her walk out of the kitchen, I could feel the heat turning in my gut. I was angry with Jonathan. Angry that he'd put me in this situation. Angry that my mother was being tormented by his inability to just tell her the truth.

I pulled out my phone and texted him, You have to tell her!

I received a response when I arrived at school, In NYC til Friday—I will, promise!

Friday couldn't come fast enough.

"Hey!" I heard when I opened the door that night. "So happy you won!" I found my mother on the couch, curled up with a wineglass in her hand, still in her work clothes.

"Hi," I responded solemnly, dropping my things by the stairs.

"That's an excited face," she noted sarcastically, leaning forward to pick up the wine bottle and empty it into her glass. "Everything okay?"

"Yeah," I replied unconvincingly. I wasn't up for talking about seeing Analise by Evan's side after the game tonight, and how miserable I was that he'd offered to drive her home when I was hoping to spend some time with him. I didn't want to feel this way…jealous. And there wasn't any reason I should. But the rationale didn't relieve the slithering in my stomach every time she looked up at him with her big Bambi eyes. So I deflected her attention. "How are you doing?"

My mother laughed humorlessly. "I'm fucking great."

She couldn't see my face as I closed my eyes and ground my teeth, picking up the intonation in her voice. She was drunk.

Instead of going to my room to work on my English paper as I had intended, I joined her on the couch, hoping to comfort her enough so she wouldn't keep drinking.

"It was my highest-scoring game," I told her, trying to assess just how far over the edge she was. Her head swiveled toward me, rocking slightly. She smiled lazily, the effort pushing her eyes into slits. She was pretty far gone.

"That's awesome, Emily," she praised me in her drunken drawl. "I wish I could have seen it." She took a long sip of her wine, keeping her eyes closed for a moment after she'd removed the glass.

"Sorry about this—" She gestured to herself. "I didn't have dinner, so it got to me."

I nodded, wanting to take the wineglass out of her hand. Instead, she drained it in two large gulps. I widened my eyes as she tipped her head back, determined to get every last drop.

"I'll take that for you," I offered, holding out my hand.

"Thanks." She smiled, her teeth tinged purple. She handed me the glass, and I took it into the kitchen, finding a second empty bottle on the counter. I sighed with a shake of my head and set the glass in the sink.

My phone beeped. Can I come over?

I hesitated, not sure how to tell Evan no without it coming across wrong. Trying to get this paper done. See you tomorrow, okay? I looked at the bottle again and pressed *Send*. I didn't want him to see this. To see her.

Okay, he texted back. I returned the phone to my pocket as I walked back into the living room.

"You must think I'm pathetic," she uttered, her heavy tongue making her words jumbled. She ran her hand across her face, clumsily pushing her hair behind her ear. "That I'm like this over a guy."

"I don't think that," I said calmly. I watched as she breathed in deeply through her nose with her eyes closed, having a hard time forcing them open. "Why don't I help you upstairs to bed?"

"Yeah," she breathed. "Getting tired. Should've eaten."

I offered her my hand to help her from the couch. She grabbed on to it and hoisted herself up, swaying slightly. "Whoa, head rush."

I shut everything off—the disappointment, the frustration, the anger—and just focused on getting her up the stairs without wiping out. She crawled into the bed, and I removed her shoes before covering her. She pulled the blankets under her chin and looked up at me guiltily.

"It's not because I like him so much," she explained. "That's not it. I mean, I do like him a lot." She took a deep breath, her eyes watering. I swallowed hard, stung by the sadness surfacing in her eyes.

"I don't want to be alone." Her lower lip quivered, and she rolled away from me.

Her words punched me in the chest. Her back shook as she began to cry. I bit my lip and hesitated, tempted to touch her, to try to console her. But I quietly walked out the door, shutting it behind me.

My mother's sobs could be heard through the door. Still incapacitated by her words, I slid down the door frame and hugged my knees into my chest. The anger and disappointment were replaced with heartache. Tears slid down my cheeks as I listened to her cry.

I'd done this before. *We'd* done this before. I'd spent most of my childhood listening to her cry. Her cries haunted me, still echoing through my head when I tried to sleep that night.

———

"Are you okay?"

"Huh?" I shook myself out of my stupor to find my locker door wide open and Sara staring at me.

"You've been staring into your locker for forever and haven't touched anything. What's going on?"

"Didn't sleep much," I replied. My mother's cries were still ringing in my head. Half-forgotten memories pulled at me, the nights of tantrums, full of rage and pain—I used to hide under my covers, shaking. I blinked to force myself back into the bustling halls.

"What else is new?" She grinned, bumping me with her shoulder. "Want to sleep over tonight?"

I opened my mouth to say yes, but I didn't. Jonathan wouldn't be back until tomorrow, and I wasn't so sure it was a good idea to leave my mother home alone.

"How about Saturday?" I suggested instead.

"Okay." Sara closed her locker and headed to class. I grabbed my books and went to the computer lab, skipping Political Theory to get my English assignment done—the assignment I'd never touched the night before.

I fought through the rest of the day and faked pleasantries with Analise in Art, wishing the nail assignment was done already so Evan could take back his place next to me.

"Are you staying for Evan's game tonight?" she asked, bright and eager.

I nodded. I didn't bother to ask if she was staying, because I already knew that answer.

"Maybe we can sit together," she chirped happily.

"Maybe," I forced myself to say pleasantly, not looking up from aggressively hammering the nail into place.

Her sunshine-and-rainbows smile was too bright for my emotional hangover. I was afraid I'd have to squint to look at her, so I kept my head down—making it look like I was concentrating on my work. She let me be for the rest of class.

Evan was waiting for me at my locker with his backpack over his shoulder.

"Hi," he said with a smile that shook me from my funk.

"I'm so happy to see your face right now." I sighed, throwing my arms around his ribs and burying my head in his chest. I inhaled and let his clean scent release the tension in my shoulders.

"Uh, okay." He laughed and squeezed me back. "Bad day?"

"Something like that." My face was still pressed into him, muffling my words.

"What are you doing after my game?"

I looked up, my arms still wrapped around him. "I have practice."

"That's right," he remembered. "We're getting something to eat after, and I was hoping you would come."

"Sorry," I replied with a grimace, finally releasing him. "But I'll see you tomorrow night after my game, right?"

"Of course." He smiled. "It's our date. Are you going home first to change, or are you doing that here?"

"I was hoping to shower at home. Is that okay? Or will that make us late?"

"No, that's not a problem. I need to do the same thing anyway. That should give you enough time, don't you think?"

"Yes," I responded, finally finding a reason to smile for the first time all day. "That sounds perfect." It was still all about waiting for Friday—for my date with Evan, and for Jonathan to come home to…tell my mother he was moving to California. But I refused to think about that part. I would deal with the repercussions of his talk with her *after* my date with Evan.

I kept Jill and Sara in between Analise and me during Evan's game. But it was hard to ignore her gleeful yelps whenever he blocked a shot or rebounded the ball. Sara cocked her head toward Analise after a particularly enthusiastic round of cheering. She looked to me, about to say something, but I shook my head with a roll of my eyes. Sara laughed, reading my thoughts without a word.

"Are you coming with us for pizza?" Analise asked me as we made our way down the bleachers.

"I have practice," I told her, not thrilled that she was a part of the "we" Evan had mentioned.

"Don't worry, I'll be there," Sara gushed, her smile a little too forced.

"Oh," Analise replied, her joy faltering slightly. "Great."

Sara turned to me behind Analise's back with a wide mimicking smile. "Great."

I laughed and swatted her arm. "Don't be mean."

"Yeah, you're right." She groaned like it was difficult. "I'll be nice, I promise."

Sara was the easiest person in the world to get along with, and most people loved her instantly. But if she didn't like you... she could be vicious. She and I both knew that there was nothing particularly unlikable about Analise, but for some reason, we both found ourselves not exactly fond of her. I was actually kind of relieved that I wasn't the only one to harbor these inexplicable feelings toward the spritely girl who was eternally smiling.

"Evan, you were amazing," Analise praised him merrily.

"Thanks," he responded. Finding me behind her, his eyes locked with mine. I squeezed past her and kissed him on the lips, despite the sweat that pressed against my cheeks. He exhaled slowly when I pulled away. "Thanks." He grinned, squeezing my hand.

"I should get ready for practice," I told him. "See you tomorrow?"

"I'll wait for you in the lobby," Analise told him, interrupting us.

"Okay, sure," Evan responded, glancing at her quickly. "I'll be a few minutes, but I'll find you."

I looked from Analise's blond curls to Evan.

"I drove her," Evan explained, noticing the confusion on my face. I could only nod, afraid of what might spew out of my mouth if I opened it. He leaned down and kissed me again, "I'll see you tomorrow."

When I walked toward the locker room, my phone beeped.

Pathetic me going out with the girls after work. So so sorry about last night. Jonathan's back tomorrow—Yay! Promise to be good tonight!

Yup. Friday couldn't come fast enough.

20. NO SUCH THING AS "NORMAL"

Nothing was going to keep me from enjoying every second of our date—nothing. Not Analise and her adorableness, or the fact that she'd *had* to sit next to Evan throughout my entire game—yes, I'd noticed. Not the fact that I hadn't slept last night because I'd stayed up listening for my mother to come home. And when she finally did, she was staggering and giddy. And not even the fact that I was running late because I'd left my lights on in the parking lot and Jill had to jump-start my car. I was *determined* to have an amazing night.

I jiggled my key free from the front door and slammed it behind me, barely noticing as I raced up that my mother had left the lights on at the top of the stairs. I flipped off my sneakers and flung them across my room, peeled off my socks and left them on the floor, then threw my sweaty game jersey in the hamper. I was struck with déjà vu—recognizing how similar this felt to the night Evan took me to the concert. All that was missing was Jonathan walking through the door unexpectedly.

I ran to the bathroom in my shorts and a sports bra, pushing open the door and shutting it behind me in one swift motion. And then I stopped in my tracks. Irony punching me in the face...

"Hey?" Jonathan stood in front of me, gripping the waistband of his running pants, his dark brown eyes staring at me in shock.

"Uh, sorry." I gaped, instinctively crossing my arms over my chest as I stood immobilized in front of the door. Sweat ran down the side of his face, along the tendons of his thick neck and over the grooves of his broad shoulders and sculpted chest. His face was still flushed, and his sweaty T-shirt was crumpled on the bathroom floor. I clamped my mouth shut—it had inadvertently flopped open. "I didn't know you were here."

I quickly turned around and gripped the handle of the door. I had started to open it when Evan called out, "Em? I'm here."

I clicked the door shut. "Shit," I said through clenched teeth, banging my forehead against the frame. "Uh, I'm running late," I hollered through the door. "I'll be down in a little bit."

"Okay," he responded.

I breathed with my head still pressed against the wood, trying to figure out what to do.

"Wow," Jonathan breathed behind me. "This is awkward."

I spun around and glared at him. "You think?"

"So...you have a date?" he asked casually, like we weren't standing in front of each other half naked and sweaty.

"Jonathan!" I scolded him with wide eyes. "What am I supposed to do? How do I explain you coming out of the bathroom while I'm supposed to be taking a shower?!" I was on the verge of hyperventilating.

"It's okay," Jonathan said soothingly. But his comical expression lingered. "Just take a shower."

"What?!" I snapped, a little too loudly, then covered my mouth with my hand and listened, praying my voice hadn't carried downstairs. I heard the squeak of the front door and the rattling of the glass when it closed.

"Evan?" my mother acknowledged. "How are you? Where's Emily?"

My eyes couldn't stretch any wider without popping out of my head. Jonathan let out a small laugh, and my mouth dropped open in disbelief.

"She's taking a shower," he told her. "I guess she got held up after the game and she's running late."

"Emily!" my mother bellowed, the creaks of the stairs drawing closer. "Are you almost done?"

The handle jiggled, and the door started to open. I thrust my back against it, slamming it in her face.

"Hey!" she cried out.

"Sorry," I grimaced, latching the door so she couldn't open it. "I'm about to get in the shower. Do you need to get in here?"

"I can wait," she told me. "Have you seen Jonathan? He was supposed to be here by now."

I stared across at him as he pressed his mouth into a smile to keep from laughing. I was so annoyed I wanted to throw something at him.

"Uh, no," I replied, "but I didn't really look for him either."

Jonathan couldn't hold back and let out a constrained, breathy laugh.

Stop! I mouthed, my brows pulled together in warning. He only smiled wider.

"Okay, well, Evan's waiting for you."

"I know. I'll hurry." I closed my eyes and shook my head, knowing I had no choice. When I heard her walk away, I whispered, "Fine. I'll take a shower, but you have to stand by the door."

"Don't worry." He smirked. "I won't peek."

"Funny," I snapped sarcastically. "We have to switch spots so I can get to the shower. Please don't make this any more awkward than it already is."

In order to exchange places in this closet of a bathroom, I had to shimmy past him, pressed between the bathtub and the sink.

I turned my head to the side, inching past him with my stomach sucked in to avoid touching him. I could feel his hot breath on my neck and inhaled the mix of sweat and a crisp cologne that reminded me of the ocean. His slick skin slid across mine, despite my efforts to be as small as possible.

Jonathan chuckled from above me. I tilted my head up, our faces inches apart. "We have to stop meeting like this," he teased. I pulled past him quickly, my heart racing.

I picked up his damp T-shirt and threw it at him, making him laugh even more. I shook my head in exasperation and stepped into the tub just as Jonathan turned toward the door. I secured the shower curtain and stripped off the rest of my clothes, my heart beating so fast I was still sweating.

I cracked the curtain open enough to drop my damp clothes in front of the toilet before turning on the water. It was the fastest shower of my life—and I'd been forced to take some pretty quick showers. I somehow managed to wash my hair and body at the same time.

When I'd turned off the water, I peeked out from behind the curtain, but Jonathan was gone. The door was closed, but the latch was undone. I took a deep breath and grabbed the towel.

"Jonathan?" My mother's confused voice floated up the stairs. "You've been here this whole time?"

Realizing I hadn't brought any clothes into the bathroom with me, I took my mother's bathrobe off the hook on the closet door and secured it around me.

"I was using Emily's computer," he explained calmly. He was a very convincing liar; I almost believed him. "I was on a video chat with the office, so I couldn't get off when you came in. Sorry."

Without waiting to hear whether my mother bought his story, I opened the door and scurried to my room, catching a quick glimpse of Jonathan watching me out of the corner of my eye. I thought I noticed him grin. My face continued to radiate heat.

"I'm out of the bathroom," I called behind me, shutting my door.

"I'm going to take a shower, okay? I didn't get to after my run," I heard Jonathan tell my mother from outside my room.

I plugged in my hair dryer and let the hum block everything out—the lying, the hint of suspicion in my mother's tone, the racing beat of my heart that hadn't quite recovered from being stuck in the bathroom with Jonathan.

I could hear music playing downstairs when I turned off the hair dryer, and the water was running in the bathroom. I gathered my hair and pinned it into a bun at the nape of my neck—the only style of Sara's I was able to replicate fairly well. I retrieved the dress from the back of my closet and removed the plastic cover with a smile. I knew this was going to be perfect for our *normal* date.

I took a deep breath, inspecting myself once more in the full-length mirror, swishing the hemline of my red empire-waist dress as I turned from side to side. I tried to find the calm that would return the shade of my skin to its natural tone. As long as I didn't see Jonathan before we left, I thought I should be okay.

I finally emerged from my room, somewhat composed. I could hear Evan and my mother talking in the living room, where the music was playing. From the sounds of it, she was recounting animated tales of the bands she'd seen and the insanity that had ensued.

The skirt of the dress brushed against my thighs as my hand slid along the railing. Hearing my footsteps, Evan stepped into the foyer. His eyes lit up, calming me instantly. Then I heard the sound of the door opening behind me. I refused to turn back, fearful of being enveloped in flames.

"You look so beautiful, Emily," my mother sang with a smile on her face.

"Yeah." The comment wafted through the air, barely audible. I'd expected it to come from Evan, but the word drifted down the stairs, and I almost faltered on a step.

Evan reached out, prepared to catch me, but I steadied myself again and offered an embarrassed smile. "Still not the best in heels."

"I won't let you fall," Evan promised, taking my hand when I reached the bottom. I smiled, knowing he wouldn't.

"Hello, you," my mother said excitedly as she scrambled up the stairs toward Jonathan. My cue to get my jacket.

Evan helped me put it on, and when I turned to say good-bye, my mother had both arms around Jonathan, holding him tightly like he might float away. He stood watching us, his arm casually draped over her shoulders.

"Bye," we both called. I turned and was out the door before they could respond. I heard my mother say, "Have fun," before Evan shut the door.

"That's one of my favorite things," Evan said out of nowhere, backing out of the driveway.

"What's that?" I asked, pulled from replaying my mother's giddy excitement and Jonathan's ambivalence. I couldn't help but be worried for her. I pushed thoughts of them away, turning my attention to Evan.

"Watching you come down the stairs." He rested his hand on mine, thrusting my heart to life in a whirling flutter.

We drove to a restaurant a few towns over along the waterfront. I practically floated in, tethered by the warmth of Evan's hand. We were seated at a corner table overlooking the water. I was beginning to like "normal" dates.

"What happened after the game?" Evan asked after we'd placed our drink orders.

"Oh, I left my lights on and my battery was dead. Jill had to jump-start my car. I should have called you to tell you I was late, but I was too focused on getting home to change. Sorry about that."

"It's not a problem," Evan assured me warmly. "I learned a lot about your mother's concertgoing experiences while I waited." He let out a quick laugh, but I could only nod—not finding her adventurous life all that amusing, especially when it had taken place after she'd abandoned me.

The server returned with our drinks and we placed our order. The harmonious notes of a quartet swirled through the air, enveloping the hum of conversation. I could've easily been convinced that we were the only two in the restaurant. The candles' glow softened the angles of Evan's face and reflected in his eyes. He reached over the table and took my hand, giving it a small squeeze that I felt in my chest.

"You know, I don't know that much about the guys in California," I said, after I was able to form sentences again. "Will you tell me about them?"

Evan smiled at the request. "Sure." He paused for a moment, then started with, "Well, there's Brent. He's very…easy to get along with. He thinks he's better with the girls than he is, and always wants the best outcome in every situation.

"Ren is the most laid-back guy I've ever met. He lives and breathes surfing, and I'm convinced he'd sleep on the beach on top of his board if he could. He would do anything for anyone, doesn't matter if he knows them or not—if he can help out, he will. I'm lucky to know him.

"Then there's TJ." Evan paused with a wry smile, deliberating on how to describe him. "He's a lot to take, but he's always entertaining, and some of the things he gets away with make us laugh for days. But he's still a good friend, regardless of how many times we'd like to throw him in the ocean.

"And that leaves Nate. Nate's my best friend. I trust him with… well, everything. I'd trust him with you if I ever needed to." His eyes connected with mine, and a pang shot through my chest, suddenly realizing what he meant. "That's where we were going to go. Where we should have gone. His family has a summer place in Santa Barbara that they hardly ever go to, even in the summer. The guys basically take it over after school's out. I'm hoping we can spend at least a week there before you need to be on campus for soccer."

"I'd like that," I replied, just as the server set the entrees in front of us. "I wish—"

My words were cut off by, "I will not lower my voice."

We located the source of the outburst across the room, where a man in a dark suit was arguing with the maître d', who was bent over and speaking quietly to him. The woman across from him darted her eyes around the room in embarrassed apology. She handed the server the check and gathered her purse.

"Come, Roger. It's time to take me home," she implored him. All movement and conversation ceased as the other diners watched the spectacle.

I turned my back to the couple, empathizing with the woman, who looked like she wanted to crawl under the table. "I guess I'll never understand it," I mused under my breath with a shake of my head.

"What's that?" Evan asked.

I lifted my eyes, realizing he'd heard me. "Why people drink, I guess. It just seems to make them stupid. They end up saying something they regret or acting like idiots. I just don't get it."

"Well, there is such a thing as moderation," Evan said.

I nodded, recalling seeing Evan drink without acting out of control. "Have you ever been drunk?"

Evan laughed. "Yes. I have. And it's not pretty either. I'm sure I've qualified as the idiot a few too many times."

"Really?" I was surprised by his answer. I couldn't even imagine it.

"It doesn't happen very often. I actually haven't been drunk in a while. I don't really like how it makes me feel, especially the next day. Have you ever had a drink?"

I shook my head. I didn't want to recount the sips I'd taken at the parties my mother threw. I'd been too young to know better, so as far as I was concerned, they didn't count. "Don't think I ever will. Besides, I have no desire to have my face splattered across Facebook, doing something humiliating. I already get too much attention."

Evan let out a short laugh.

"What do you want to do on Sunday?" I asked, changing the subject.

"Want to go hiking?" he suggested. "It's not supposed to be cold, and it's better to go now while there's still snow, before it gets muddy."

"Sure," I responded. Fresh air and the calm of the woods would be the perfect escape from everything and everyone in Weslyn. I just needed to survive the next night's basketball game, alongside my mother, before I could get there. "I'd like that."

When we returned to Evan's car after dinner, I offered, "Do you want to go back to my house to watch a movie? I'm pretty sure my mother and Jonathan will be out."

"That sounds perfect," Evan replied.

We stopped at a movie rental machine on our way, and arrived to a dark house as I'd anticipated. Not bothering to change, I just took off my shoes and settled in under Evan's arm. We kept the lights off. The action movie cast a flickering light in the dark room.

Halfway through, we heard a car door shut in the driveway. I glanced at Evan in surprise. "They're back early."

That's when we heard the yelling. I tensed at the sound of my mother's elevated voice, not wanting Evan to see her like this. I could hear Jonathan calling after her.

She rushed through the door. "Then explain it. Go ahead, I want to hear it." She held something in her hand. Evan pulled me closer as my entire body went rigid. "How the fuck did her sweater get in your truck?"

Jonathan stepped in and looked from my mother to us, sitting on the couch. That's when it hit me. She was holding the sweater I was certain I'd left at Drew's. "I thought it was yours," he stated quietly, shifting his eyes between me and my mother.

My mother turned toward us, realizing we were watching the entire scene. Her jaw was tight and her eyes enlarged, symptomatic of a full-out fit. I had a split second to evaluate her. If she was drunk, everything was about to explode.

She shook the green sweater at me. "I thought you said you left it at your fucking ex-boyfriend's." It wasn't a question. It was an accusation.

I couldn't move. I had no idea what to say. I could feel Evan looking at me, waiting for me to answer. Jonathan kept his eyes on me as well, attempting to silently apologize. I was still trying to make sense of what was happening, and how he could possibly have my sweater.

"I know there's something going on." My mother glared at us accusingly. "I'm not stupid." When we could only stare at her speechlessly, she screamed, "You can all go to hell!" stomping up the stairs and slamming her door so hard I wouldn't doubt it cracked.

"I'm really sorry," Jonathan said. "We had...we had a bad night, so she's not thinking clearly."

My chest caved. He'd told her. He had to have told her he was leaving, and that was why she was so upset. It didn't explain the sweater, but it explained enough. Jonathan disappeared into the kitchen.

"Do you want to go?" Evan asked in my ear. I nodded. We stood, and I slipped on my shoes while Evan retrieved our jackets. He held my hand as we walked out the front door.

My chest hurt, and I was having a hard time forming thoughts. As we neared his car, I started to worry. I couldn't tell exactly how drunk my mother was in her tirade, but I knew she was hurt. And when she was hurt...

I stopped. "I can't go."

"What do you mean?" Evan was completely confounded.

"I have to stay," I told him with a grimace. "She's upset, and I need to be here for her."

"She needs to calm down," Evan explained, not following my logic.

"Yeah, you're right. But I need to be here for her when she does."

Evan studied me for a moment. "I don't really know what just went on in there, but it wasn't good. Are you sure you don't just want to give them time to sort it out?"

"She needs me." It was all I could think, and I couldn't leave knowing she might get worse in my absence.

"I'll stay with you," he said, squeezing my hand.

"No," I countered, causing him to cock his head. "It's complicated. Besides, you don't need to see this. I'll see you tomorrow, okay?"

Evan didn't say anything. It was obvious he was completely disturbed by the entire scenario, and I knew he didn't want to leave me.

"It'll be fine, I promise," I assured him with a faint smile, then attempted to downplay it. "It's a girl thing. She's having boy trouble, so...that's it. She's going to need a girl to talk to, okay?"

Evan took a breath and nodded reluctantly. "Alright. Call me if you need me for anything, okay? Even if it's in the middle of the night and you just need to talk."

I leaned up and kissed him. "I will." I was about to walk away when he pulled me back toward him and kissed me again, gripping me tightly like he was afraid to let me go. "I'll call you, okay?" I whispered, out of breath. He nodded and I walked back toward the house.

I pressed my back against the door when I'd shut it behind me, staring up at her room in deliberation.

"She's drunk," Jonathan stated from the dark of the living room. "She's probably passed out already."

"Great," I grumbled, wanting to slide down to the floor—emotionally drained from my mother's tirade. I pulled off my shoes. "I'm going to bed." I had a thousand questions for him about what had happened tonight, but I was too deflated to talk about it. Whatever had happened, it had brought out a side of her that was angry and spiteful. A side that made my insides shudder. All I wanted was to shut it out with the blanket pulled up over my head.

"She told me she loved me." Jonathan's voice broke through the stillness. I turned toward him. "She told me she loved me, and I told her I was leaving."

I sank onto the bottom step, absorbing what he'd just said. He walked over and sat next to me. I continued to stare at the floor.

"She was upset at first. She wanted to know how long I'd kept it from her, if I was just using her. She started drinking...a lot. Then she started to cry." He paused. "When she calmed down, we talked and decided that we still wanted to see each other, and would try it until I had to leave."

I turned toward him. "Why did you do that?" My voice was sharp and angry.

"What do you mean?" His face twisted in confusion.

"You're only making it worse by leading her on," I accused him harshly.

"I'm not."

"Yes, you are," I insisted, agitated. "Can't you see how messed up she is? You can't give her something and then tell her she can't really have it."

"That's not what's going on," he said defensively, his voice growing stronger.

I shook my head, then dropped it to my chest.

"I'm sorry, Emma," Jonathan murmured softly.

I was too angry to hear him. I stood up and climbed the stairs to my room without looking back. I turned on the light, and my stomach clenched at the sight of my green sweater lying on my bed, cut up into shreds.

21. DRAMA

Jonathan wasn't around in the morning. Neither was my mother. I was still too upset to face either of them.

My mother returned around noon with a shopping bag in her hand.

"I'm really sorry," she said, unable to meet my eyes as she set the shopping bag on the couch next to me. She hesitated a moment, fidgeting with her hands and shifting uncomfortably. Without saying anything more, she turned and went up to her room.

I watched her until she disappeared, then opened the bag and pulled out a green sweater. It wasn't the same one. But that wasn't the point.

"Thanks," I said from the entrance to her bedroom as she folded clothes from the laundry basket and stuffed them into her drawers.

"Are you mad at me?" She sounded small and fragile.

"No," I replied with a small smile.

"Can I still come to the game tonight?" Her blue eyes were big and sorrowful; her lower lip stuck out in an exaggerated pout.

"Yes." I laughed lightly at her comical expression—reminiscent of a child getting caught coloring on the walls.

"Great! What are you doing after the game tonight?" My mother asked, her voice suddenly peppy and excited.

"Uh, I'm not sure," I fumbled, still not used to the quick flip of her moods. "Jill and Casey were talking about going to a party;

Sarah's at Cornell again, visiting Jared. But Evan and I haven't made any commitments."

I leaned against the door frame.

"You can come in," my mother encouraged me, hanging up her clothes in the closet.

I hadn't really seen my mother's room before. It had always been dark when I'd entered to help her to bed. It was simply decorated, with white curtains hanging on the windows. The leaf-patterned comforter splayed across her bed was still rumpled, as if she'd made it by pulling the comforter over the distressed sheets.

A dresser with a mirror sat across from the bed, with necklaces dangling from the mirror's edges. Perfume bottles and rings were scattered on its scratched surface. A framed picture caught my eye.

"I'm not sure what to wear tonight." She sighed.

"It's just a basketball game, so jeans work," I advised her, picking up the frame to examine it more closely. It wasn't a picture at all, but a drawing done in pencil. The shading and detailing were phenomenal. I brought it closer to inspect the strokes of the artist's work.

"Yeah, but I'm hoping—" She stopped to watch me. I quickly set the portrait down, afraid that I'd upset her by touching her things.

"You can look at it," she told me.

I picked up the frame again and looked from the drawing to her, realizing it was my mother captured in a laugh, done before the stress lines around her eyes and mouth had formed. Her happiness was evident. I couldn't help but smile looking at it.

"You don't remember that drawing, do you?" she asked, studying me. My eyes twitched, puzzled by her question. "Your father drew that, back before you were born. You used to stare at that picture all the time when you were little."

"I did?"

"Derek drew pictures for you too. You'd sit at the kitchen table and he'd ask what your favorite part of the day had been, and then he'd draw it for you. You had his drawings plastered all over your room. Don't you remember?"

I scanned the floor, searching my memory, wanting to recall the moments she spoke of. I could hear laughter, and catch a glimpse of his face, but the memories refused to form. I shook my head, knitting my brows together in frustration.

"Do you remember *anything*?" my mother inquired, her tone careful. She examined my confused face, like she was just as confounded. "You mean you don't...remember...What I went through when...Why you had to go..."

I was unable to follow her cryptic sentences. She shook her head slowly and stared into the distance, or perhaps the past. She closed her eyes and swallowed, then composed herself easily, not a trace of distress left upon her face.

"Want to go out to dinner before the game? It's at seven, right?"

I couldn't answer for a moment, completely confused by what I'd just witnessed. "Yes, it is. And sure, why not." I tried to smile but faltered, still disturbed by the sheen in her eyes that she was trying to smile away. I decided not to ask what I should be remembering. Not today.

"I should get some homework done, since Evan and I are going hiking tomorrow. Let me know when you're ready to leave."

"Okay," she replied, going back to her closet.

I closed my door and sat on my bed, replaying the stunned look on her face when she realized I couldn't remember anything. I'd never been aware of how little I could recall from my childhood. I was always so determined to focus on my future and getting out of Weslyn. I'd held on to the feelings of being safe and happy for so long. That had always been enough for me. But now, I wanted to remember. Somehow it was important that I figure out what had happened in the blank spaces of my life.

I opened my closet and reached for the stack of pictures under my sweatshirts on the shelf. I laid them on my bed and returned to my door to slide the lock in place, concerned about how my mother would react if she saw I'd kept the pictures she'd smashed at the bottom of the stairs.

I sat on my bed and slowly flipped through the images. There was a photo of my father holding me right after I was born; another of me on his lap while sitting on the rocking chair, holding a book. I ran my finger along his cheering face, as we kicked a soccer ball back and forth. He looked so happy. *We* looked so happy. My mother wasn't in a single picture. I could only assume she was the one taking them.

There were others of the two of them, laughing and obviously in love. I'd expected to see a wedding picture, but there wasn't one. I figured she'd kept those safe somewhere, or I hoped so anyway.

After examining every detail of each photo, I lay back on my bed and shut my eyes. I tried to conjure up an image, begging for the vault to open. But nothing came—not a single moment. I sighed in frustration and slid the photos back under the sweatshirts.

I went downstairs and turned on the television, but my focus kept drifting toward the rocking chair. I *did* remember the chair— that was something. I thought of the picture of my father reading to me in it, and tried to picture the actual moment. Nothing.

"Ready?"

I jumped, suddenly pulled out of my head. My mother slid her arms into her coat, studying me oddly.

"What are you thinking about?" she asked, trying to read my face.

"Nothing." I shook my head. Maybe it was better not to remember.

I noted my mother's choice of a tight denim miniskirt with leggings. She *had* taken my advice to wear jeans, but not quite in the way I'd hoped. Considering her daring attire, I hoped I could convince her to sit in the parents' section, although that wasn't exactly a gossip-free zone either.

For dinner, we ended up at a small, crowded pub, where college basketball games on the screens incited spontaneous hollers from the patrons.

"I don't know if Jonathan's coming tonight," she told me after ordering a beer from the overly friendly server. Her face was drawn as she stared at the menu. "I was so awful last night."

"He told me about going to USC in the fall. I'm sure that was hard for you. I know how much you like him."

"I thought I'd fallen for him," she admitted, setting down her menu with a sigh. "I don't know. I'm so confused. A part of me wants to end it and move on, since it's going to end anyway. But the other part knows how much I'll miss him, and if I can still be with him for five more months, then why not?" She looked to me in expectation. "What do you think I should do?"

I hesitated, not sure what to say. "Whatever will make you happiest," I finally suggested.

"That sounds easier than it is." She sighed. "It's going to hurt either way. I hope he comes tonight. I apologized to him like a million times today. He said he'd try, but he has a project due at work, so he wasn't sure if he could make it.

"And I'm sorry about accusing you of…you know."

I took a sip of my water, hoping we were going to avoid that part of last night.

"It's just that I know you two get along. I hear you talking and laughing in the middle of the night. Sometimes I think he waits to hear you get up before he goes downstairs—like he doesn't even try to sleep. I know that sounds paranoid and crazy. I mean, you're my daughter, and—"

"He wouldn't do that," I consoled her, freaked by her jealous thoughts. "Besides, we really don't talk about anything interesting, I swear. Maybe you should ask him…you know, about his nightmare."

"I've tried." She paused to let the server set our burgers in front of us. "Does he tell you what it's about?"

I shook my head.

"He's been distant lately. I think I screwed up and he's not going to want to be with me, not even for the short time before he leaves. I mean, we haven't had sex in over a week."

I just about choked on the bite of cheeseburger I'd just taken.

"Sorry." She grimaced. "That was probably too much information."

"A little," I admitted with a cough.

When we arrived at the school Jonathan wasn't there, as my mother had anticipated. I couldn't bring myself to ask her to sit away from the students' section after watching her face drop when she received Jonathan's text.

"He's running late," she muttered, dropping her phone into her purse. "I know he's not coming."

"Maybe he hasn't finished what he needed to do for work yet," I said, trying to cheer her up. My words bounced right off as if they'd never been said.

We bought sodas at the concession stand and made our way to the bleachers.

"Hey, Rachel!" a few voices hollered.

"Hi, Mark! Hi, James!" she yelled back with a bright smile, her sullen mood masked instantly.

"You know people?" I asked in disbelief.

"Where do you think I sit during your games?"

Oh, I mouthed, never having considered it before. I was shocked when more faces recognized her. She knew more people in my school than I did.

"Hi, Rachel," Casey burst out, cutting across the bleachers to get to us, with Jill right behind her. "What are you doing here?"

"Watching Evan," my mother explained. Casey nodded like it made sense.

"Hey, Emma," Jill greeted me, sitting next to Casey, who opted to sit next to my mother. I was starting to feel like a stranger even among my friends—who evidently preferred my mother to me.

"Where's Jonathan?" Jill asked, making my eyes widen.

My mother shrugged evasively, not looking away from the court as they were about to tip the ball. The cheering erupted around us as the ball flew into the air.

She chanted along with the rest of the school, like she were just another student. I was a spectator, not only to the game but to my mother's popularity—it was beyond strange.

As the half progressed, she became more boisterous, making remarks that sent those around her into fits of laughter. I grew suspicious as she became more animated. Something was off. Her popularity grew the more vocal she became. The boys scooted in around her. I would have been nudged out of my position next to her if I hadn't been her daughter.

During halftime, my mother disappeared into the bathroom with Casey and Jill. I followed a few minutes later to find her dumping the contents of her flask into their fountain sodas. Her flagrant behavior suddenly made sense—I should've known better.

"Casey, you were supposed to lock the door," Jill scolded her with a huff.

"Sorry," Casey responded guiltily. "But it's just Emma."

My mother watched for my reaction. "You're not mad, right?"

I looked from one face to the other as they waited for me to say something. I shook my head and stepped into the first stall without a word. I leaned against the wall and listened as they giggled and Casey gushed about some cute boy sitting behind them.

"Do you want us to wait for you?" my mother called out.

"No, it's okay," I responded, trying to keep my voice steady. My insides were a slithering mess. I couldn't believe I'd caught my mother feeding my friends alcohol so they could get drunk together. I took a breath and tried to clear my head, to think of how to keep this from escalating out of control.

I pulled out my phone and sent Jonathan a text, Are you still coming?

If Jonathan didn't show up, then I knew my mother would just keep drinking, and the more she drank, the more unpredictable she'd become. This was going to be horrible.

My phone beeped. On my way. There in 15.

I contemplated waiting for him so I wouldn't have to return to the bleachers alone. In the end, I trudged back to my seat beside my inebriated mother and her giggling clique. I kept glancing over at them, watching as they laughed and gossiped.

Finally I saw Jonathan along the sideline, scanning the bleachers to find us. My mother stood and waved frantically, making her easy to spot. He climbed the steps closest to me and excused himself across the row. I scooted over so he could sit between me and my mother.

Before he could say anything, she leaned over and kissed him. He pulled back in surprise.

"What?" she snapped as he pulled his brows together.

"Are you drunk?"

She shrugged with a smirk.

"At a high school basketball game? Really, Rachel!" Jonathan didn't even try to sugarcoat his disapproval.

My mother huffed with a roll of her eyes. "What happened to you? You used to be fun." She turned her back to him and started cheering along with the girls.

Jonathan turned toward me. "So, what happened?"

I shrugged. "She's afraid you don't care about her anymore."

"Why?" he questioned emphatically. "Because I had to work?"

I didn't answer, and sank farther into the bleachers—not sure how to make this whole thing go away.

My mother reached into her purse and took out her mini Altoids tin.

"Are you serious?" Jonathan accused her as she popped a pill in her mouth.

"Well, if you're not going to be any fun, then I need something to make me happy."

"What was that?" I asked, having seen her pop the little white pills too many times to count, without really knowing what they were. Jonathan only shook his head in disgust.

He observed her silently as she grew more and more enthusiastic, drawing more attention. His jaw set and the tendons in his neck tightened.

About five minutes later he muttered angrily, "I'm sorry, Emma, but I can't—I can't do this." Jonathan stood up and passed by me toward the steps.

"Where are you going?" my mother yelled after him. He didn't look back. I could only watch after him in shock as he paced down the sideline and out the gym doors.

"Where is he going?" she demanded in a panic.

"I don't know," I replied uneasily.

"Make him stop," she pleaded, about to cry. "Please, Emily, you have to stop him from leaving."

She sniffled and her eyes flickered, coated with tears.

"Okay, okay," I said desperately. "I'll stop him."

Jill turned toward my mother, and her smile changed to a look of concern. "Rachel, what's wrong?"

"Please help her calm down," I begged Jill before I rushed down the steps and out of the gym. Jonathan was nearing the exit when I caught up with him.

"Jonathan!" I called after him. He turned at the sound of my voice. "Where are you going?"

He waited until I was near before he said, "Emma, I can't do this anymore. I don't want to be responsible for her every time she gets paranoid and emotional." He sounded defeated, releasing a heavy breath.

"Please don't leave," I begged him. "If you do, I am so afraid she's going to make a huge scene, and I don't know how to handle that."

Jonathan hesitated, deciding what to do. My stomach was a mess just thinking about the potential breakdown my mother was on the verge of having in front of the entire school.

"Are you leaving me?" my mother asked from behind us. "I knew you were."

"Rachel, stop," Jonathan stated firmly. "Not here."

"Then where? What does it matter where it happens? I know you don't want to be with me anymore, no matter what you said last night."

"Mom, let me drive you home," I urged her. "I'll get our jackets."

"Don't call me that," she snapped, stumbling slightly as she took a few steps toward Jonathan. I remained still, frozen by her harsh tone. Her eyes watered as she took another step in Jonathan's direction. "Please don't leave me. I can't lose you too."

"Let Emma drive you home," he requested somberly, glancing toward me to make sure I was still okay with driving her. I nodded slightly. "I'll meet you there and we'll talk. Okay?"

"Why can't I leave with you?" she sulked, starting to sniffle.

"I know you'll want to talk as soon as we get in the truck, and I can't. I'll meet you at the house where we can sit down and talk." Before she could say another word, he left. Tears started seeping from my mother's eyes. I sighed and tried to remain composed, despite the crushing feeling in my chest.

I texted Jill to ask her to hold on to our jackets. I'd get them from her later.

"Come on," I encouraged my mother softly, not sure if I should touch her or not. "Let's go."

She trailed after me to the car. Her legs lazily crossed in front of each other as her balance wavered.

My mother stared out the window the entire ride to the house. I kept my eyes on the road, not wanting to watch her suffer beside me. Jonathan's truck awaited us in the driveway when I pulled in. I hesitated to get out of the car, watching her stumble up the steps.

I really wanted to leave, to not witness what was about to happen. But I couldn't. I had to be here for her, no matter what happened. I pulled out my phone to text Evan, Had to drive my mother home. Sorry I missed you—call me when you can.

The cold started setting in around me, so I took a deep breath and headed into the house. As soon as I'd opened the door, I wished I hadn't.

"This isn't going to work," Jonathan told her. "How do you expect me to talk to you if you're going to continue to drink?"

"Fine," my mother yelled, throwing the wineglass on the floor, shattering it and spraying red wine all over. "I won't drink."

The shattering glass paralyzed me with the door handle still in my grasp.

"Rachel!" Jonathan hollered. "What the hell is wrong with you?"

I quietly shut the door behind me. But I wasn't quiet enough.

"*She's* what's wrong with me." My mother pointed at me. My eyes widened as I looked from my mother's finger to Jonathan's disgusted stance, his hands on his hips. I opened my mouth in confusion, not understanding what I'd done to warrant the spiteful look on her face.

"This has nothing to do with Emma, so don't even start."

"Why do you keep calling her that?" she snapped. "Her name is *Emily*. And she's going to take you away too, just like him." Her words cut into me like barbs. I had no idea where the hostility was coming from, but it was incapacitating. I remained frozen, unable to find the words to soothe her or defend myself.

"You're not making any sense," Jonathan argued. "I'm not staying here to listen to this." Jonathan walked toward the door.

I had nearly made it to the top step when more glass shattered in the kitchen.

"What the fuck, Rachel?!" Jonathan turned quickly at the sound. "Don't throw a fit every time you don't get your way."

"Don't leave," she whimpered, followed by the sound of glass crunching.

"Don't move," he urged her. "You're stepping on glass."

Jonathan disappeared into the kitchen and emerged carrying my mother in his arms, her head resting on his chest and her face slick with tears.

"Will you stay?" she slurred. Jonathan didn't answer, but continued up the stairs and into her room.

I exhaled, my chest tight from the tension that consumed the house. I considered following after him to help her into bed, but I couldn't bring myself to face her. Instead I crept down the stairs to investigate the mess. I stopped in the doorway, scanning the kitchen with a shake of my head. Trying to avoid the wine that covered most of the floor, I carefully stepped over the shards of broken glass and pieces of the wine bottle. As I reached for the broom, my phone rang.

I pulled it out to see Evan's name displayed. I took a deep breath before answering, "Hi."

"Hey. Got your text. Is everything okay?"

"Oh, yeah," I replied, trying to sound as casual as possible. "My mother and Jonathan got into another fight, so I had to drive her home. She was overly dramatic as usual, so I had to listen to her go off for a while. Sorry I didn't get to see you after the game."

"Are you sure you're okay?"

"Yeah, I'm fine. She's about to go to bed now anyway, all talked out." My stomach turned at my lie. "Can I meet you at your place in a little bit? I'd really love to see you." I wanted nothing more than to be released from the consuming emotions, and being in Evan's arms was exactly what I needed.

"Ah, I um…" Evan stumbled; a few voices hollered in the back-ground as he stalled.

"Are you ready?" I heard a girl ask, sounding closer.

"Just a second," he answered her. My heart skipped a beat, knowing exactly who she was. "I just, uh, promised Analise that I'd take her to Jeff's party. It's her first one, and she doesn't know many people yet. But I can see if she can go with someone else or something. Let me—"

"It's okay." I tried to sound unaffected, despite the pain twisting in my chest. "You go. I'm pretty tired anyway."

"Em, are you sure?"

"Yeah, I'm fine," I said, swallowing against the tightness in my throat, forcing the emotion out of my voice. "It's been a stupid night, and I'm really exhausted. I'll see you tomorrow?" My voice shook despite my efforts. I closed my eyes to fend off the tears.

"Okay," he answered, and before he could say anything else, I hung up the phone. I stood in the middle of the kitchen with the broom in my hand, trying to breathe against the swelling in my chest.

I took a deep breath before opening my eyes, turning everything off until I felt nothing. Then I began sweeping up the aftermath of my mother's fit.

"Let me help you."

I turned to find Jonathan in the doorway. I didn't answer as he filled the mop bucket with soap and water and began wiping up the wine that had run down the cabinets. We remained silent while we cleaned.

After bringing the bag of broken glass outside to the trash, I collapsed on the second step in the foyer, covering my face in my hands with my elbows propped on my legs, emotionally drained. Jonathan shut off the kitchen light and sat next to me.

"What's going to happen now?" I asked without looking up. "Did you end things with her?"

"I wasn't about to do that in her condition," he explained quietly. "I'm sorry you had to see any of that. It really wasn't about you."

I lifted my head. "I have no idea what happened tonight, but she was so...angry. I think she does blame me, but I don't know what I did."

Jonathan shook his head in contradiction. "This is between me and Rachel. It has nothing to do with you."

"But you are going to leave her now, aren't you?" I concluded dryly.

Jonathan was quiet for a moment. "Do you want me to stay?"

My eyes tightened; I was not sure how to answer. I didn't know exactly what he was asking.

"If I left right now, would it be worse for you...to live here?"

"Don't worry about me," I assured him without much conviction. "That wouldn't be the right reason to stay anyway. It would only be worse in the end, for everyone. She'll just have to get over you."

"I'm sorry, Emma," he said in a hushed tone.

"Me too," I breathed. He peered at me with sympathetic eyes, pulling me in. It took me a moment before I was able to break away. "I think I've had enough drama tonight, so I'm going to bed."

"And I should go," he responded, standing with me. I paused in my ascent when he opened the door.

"Good-bye, Jonathan."

"I'm not leaving *you*, Emma," he assured me. "If you ever need me, I'm here."

"Thanks," I answered, exhaustion heavy in my voice. I watched him disappear behind the closed door and continued to my room.

As I pulled the blankets over me, my phone beeped. I'm coming over appeared on the screen.

I'm in bed. I'll see you in the morning, I typed back.

10am, my house?

OK

I sank under the blankets, not looking forward to seeing any-one in the morning—not even Evan.

22. INSIDE OUT

I didn't remember sleeping. But the next thing I knew, it was morning. It seemed unlikely that I'd made it through the night without a nightmare, especially since I was still exhausted when I pulled the covers back—but I couldn't remember that either.

It was eerily quiet while I got ready, other than the house's occasional groans. There still wasn't any movement when I shut the front door behind me. I sat in my car for a minute before starting it, gripping the steering wheel with my eyes fixed on the house like I was expecting it to tell me what to do—how to make everything better. It just remained still, staring back at me.

"Sure," I whispered, "now you're silent." I drew in a breath and started the car.

I pulled into the Mathews' driveway to find more cars than usual. Along with Vivian's and Evan's BMWs and Stuart's Mercedes were a black Lexus and a blue Prius. I parked in the middle of the long driveway, blocking them all in—figuring we'd be leaving as soon as Evan put on his jacket.

I knocked. No one answered. I knocked again and waited longer—still no one came to the door. I turned the knob and slowly let myself in, cautiously scanning the kitchen.

"Hello?" I called out, creeping farther into the large kitchen. That's when I heard laughter. I stopped to listen and then moved toward the voices down the hall.

One of the doors along the long hallway, a door that was always shut when I visited, was cracked open. I could hear the voices coming from inside. I recognized Evan's.

"You are far from awkward," he said.

"Believe me, he knows awkward," Stuart teased with a light laugh.

"Dad!" Evan scorned with a playfulness in his voice. "She's not awkward either."

"She's something else entirely." Stuart chuckled.

"What do you mean?" she asked. Analise—of course.

I knocked. All conversation ceased as I became visible at the entrance.

"Hi." I scanned each surprised face and noted the stacks of envelopes piled on the large conference table where they were sitting.

"Hi." Evan acknowledged me with a dazzling smile. "It's ten?" I nodded. "Sorry. Lost track of time. Do you want to help? I promised my mother we'd stuff all these envelopes before we left. We're almost done."

"Oh." I glanced from Analise's bright eyes to Stuart, who wouldn't look at me at all. "Um, I need to get my things together for the hike. I just kinda threw them in my car so I could get here. I'll meet you outside, if that's okay."

"Okay, sure," Evan replied hesitantly. "I won't be long." I nodded and slowly walked away.

I'd obviously interrupted something, and I wasn't about to ruin it with my *awkwardness*. I couldn't believe I'd heard Stuart *laugh*. I'd never even seen him smile. I closed the kitchen door behind me, shutting out the voices and laughter with it.

I walked toward the garage instead of my car, leaving my expertly packed backpack resting on the backseat. I made my way up the stairs to the rec room, plopping down on the couch.

I lay there, staring at the beamed ceiling.

My phone beeped. How are you this morning? lit up the screen.

Tired. And you?

Same, he answered. I'm really sorry about last night. How is she today?

Didn't see her.

I'm going to talk to her. Going to be honest.

I stared at the last text, not sure what part he planned to be honest about. Before I could respond, I heard, "Here you are." Sara stood at the top of the stairs.

"Hi." I sat up in surprise. "What are you doing back?"

"We're going hiking with you," she said zealously.

"Great," I responded, but my voice fell flat.

Sara eyed me suspiciously. "Do you not want us to? Did you want to be alone with Evan?"

"No, it's great." I smiled weakly, truly not concerned with the added company.

"You're not right," Sara observed, coming around to sit next to me on the couch. "Spill it."

"It's nothing, really. Just tired. My mother and Jonathan had a fight last night, and I thought they broke up..."

"I heard," Sara exclaimed. "I thought Jill was exaggerating."

I groaned. Of course. Jill had had a front-row seat for most of the debacle. "Did Jill say anything else?" I asked, suddenly concerned that the drinking part had been leaked as well.

"No," Sara returned. "Why? Is there something else?"

"No," I lied. "That was enough drama for one night."

"That's why today is exactly what you need," Sara beamed before jumping up and pulling me to my feet. "Fresh air with your best friend and your boyfriend. And, of course, my boyfriend too. I've missed you. We all need this."

"True," I agreed, a smile eventually taking shape without effort.

I followed Sara down the stairs. Anna's SUV was parked behind my car, and Jared was tossing two backpacks into it. I added my backpack to the pile and eyed the bags, coming up with one too many.

"She's what?!"

Sara stood on the bottom step, eyeing Analise, who was standing next to Evan on the porch, all bubbly and excited. At Sara's reaction, Analise's smile deflated. I walked closer to hear what was going on.

"Come on, Sara," Evan countered. "What's one more person?"

I realized what they were discussing, and my shoulders sank. Evan looked to me for support. I forced my cheeks up and cheerily called, "Analise, you're coming with us, right?"

"Is that okay?" she questioned, looking from me to Sara. Sara tightened her eyes in my direction, not appreciating my betrayal. Then she turned back toward Analise with a sugary smile.

"Sure," Sara exclaimed with forced enthusiasm. "It'll be great." I couldn't help but smile wider at her exaggerated reaction. "Jared, why don't you drive? That way Emma and I can get to know Analise." She tossed him the keys.

After moving my car on to the street, I jumped into the backseat of the SUV and we headed north along the Connecticut–New York border into the mountains.

For ninety minutes, Sara interrogated Analise. Of course she did it in her own Sara way, laughing and getting excited when they liked the same things. But every so often, she'd shoot me an are-you-kidding-me glance that kept a smirk on my face.

We headed out along the trail, adorned with backpacks. Analise kept up alongside Evan and Jared, allowing Sara and me to follow behind—evidently she'd had enough 'girl time.'

"What's with her?" Sara asked, watching as Analise giggled and swatted at Evan's arm. "She seems nice enough, but I just…I just don't like her."

I laughed—probably louder and harder than I should have, making the trio turn back toward us.

"Emma!" Sara scolded, chuckling. "Stop. She's going to think we're talking about her."

I continued to smile, keeping enough distance between the two groups so we wouldn't be overheard. "I'm sure she *knows* we're talking about her."

"She's way too excited for my taste. Like a pathetic puppy dog."

"If she's too excited for *you*, then that's an issue."

"A *huge* issue." Sara laughed. "And if she touches Evan one more time, I think I may have to take her out for you. Why aren't you bothered by it?"

"Oh, I am," I told her. "I just thought I was being a stupid, jealous girlfriend."

"You're not," she assured me, but that only made me feel worse. "She needs to take those big brown eyes of hers and back the fuck off."

"Sara! Omigod!" I laughed. Sara joined me.

"What's so funny?" Evan asked, stopping to wait for us to catch up.

"Sara," I stated with a smile, like that was the only explanation needed.

Evan grabbed my hand, and Sara quickened her pace to catch up with Jared, sliding her arm through his. Analise, being the odd person out, continued along the trail, feigning interest in the tops of the trees to avoid looking at us.

Evan slowed down as we neared a bend, allowing the rest to disappear before stopping completely. "Hi." He smiled, vanquishing the jealousy that seethed under my skin. He leaned down and sent my heart into convulsions with the touch of his lips. "I've wanted to do that for way too long."

"I've *needed* you to do that for way too long," I breathed.

"How are you after last night? I heard about the argument at the game." He studied me intently.

"It's hard to watch," I admitted. "I have a feeling they're on the verge of breaking up, and I don't want her to get hurt."

"I know," he said, kissing me softly. "Well, it's good to get away from the tension, then." I nodded. Evan squeezed my hand, and we continued along the trail. This *was* exactly what I needed, despite Analise's presence.

"Can I ask you something?" Evan climbed up next to me on a rock after handing me our lunch.

"Sure," I answered, unwrapping the sandwich.

"What was that sweater thing all about the other night?"

I stopped midbite, not having considered how it may have looked to Evan. I pulled the sandwich away and said, "It was a misunderstanding." I took a bite, and Evan waited for me to continue. Before I'd even thought about what I was saying, I added, "It wasn't my sweater."

"Oh," Evan replied, dismissing the subject as he unwrapped his sandwich and began talking about how we both had one more game next week before the championships.

I forced myself to take another bite out of the sandwich, having lost my appetite. Lying made my stomach volatile. I didn't know why Jonathan had had my sweater. But for some reason, I couldn't bring myself to tell Evan that.

We returned to the car just as the sun was hiding behind the trees. Evan and I sat in the back with Analise. I made certain to sit in the middle. She really was nice, truly. But it was so very evident that she had a thing for Evan, and I wasn't going to pretend to be oblivious.

I nestled in under Evan's arm, resting my head on his chest. I breathed in his clean scent, swirled with the mustiness of the outdoors, and closed my eyes. He kissed the top of my head and played with my fingers, running his through mine and lightly drawing circles on my palm. I let the tingling of his touch lull me to sleep.

I looked at his face as he held my hand, walking with me along the beach. He hadn't shaved for a few days, making him look like he should be camping, not collecting seashells with his daughter. The ocean air ruffled his dark brown hair but his smile was permanent, making the lines along his eyes crease, like they were smiling too.

I held the pail in my hand, swinging it lightly. My eyes flitted everywhere except the ground—the birds darting along the shoreline pecking at the sand, the dark rolling water crashing into the rocks, then back to my father's face, which looked so relaxed and peaceful.

"There's a good one," he said, stopping to bend down and pluck a pearly white shell from the sand. "What do you think of this one, Emma?" He held it up for me to inspect.

I took the shell in my hand and ran my fingers over its smooth surface.

"It's perfect..." I looked up, but he wasn't there. I turned around, searching, but I was alone.

"Emma?" the smooth voice whispered in my ear. "Emma, we're home."

I blinked my eyes open in a panic. I was still wrapped in Evan's arm, but the empty car was quiet and dark. I inhaled deeply, and stretched to sit up.

"I wish I could've let you sleep," Evan said softly, still holding my hand in his. "You looked so peaceful. You haven't been sleeping much, huh?"

"Not really," I admitted. "I can't believe I slept the entire car ride. Did everyone leave?"

"Sara and Jared are inside."

He opened the car door and held it open until I stepped out.

"Wanna sleep over tonight?" Sara asked when Evan and I entered the kitchen door.

"Of course," I answered, deciding I'd already witnessed way too much strife between my mother and Jonathan, and I didn't want to be there for whatever was about to happen tonight.

After we'd said our good-byes, Sara followed me to my house. Seeing Jonathan's truck in the driveway, I parked along the street, since I planned to leave my car at the house. I just needed to run in to grab my books and clothes for the next day. For a moment, I considered jumping in the SUV with Sara and forgetting about my things—having no idea what I was about to walk in on—but I had assignments due that I couldn't leave behind.

"I'll be right out," I told Sara before jogging up the walkway. I stopped at the front door and hesitated. I couldn't hear voices; I could only hear music. I assumed they were in her room, since the downstairs was dark.

I took a deep breath and slowly opened the door, planning to slip in and out so they didn't even have to know I was there. I closed the door and concentrated on the stairs. I just need to get my things and I'll be gone, I kept thinking over and over.

I clenched my teeth as the loose board squeaked beneath my foot halfway up the stairs. I froze, listening. A caressing voice came from the speakers, filling the entire house, but then I heard…a moan? I held my breath as I slowly turned on the stairs.

The breathing became louder. There was movement on the couch. I focused in the dark, and my mouth dropped as intertwined legs came into view. I remained frozen, unable to look away, scanning the length of his body. His muscles rippled as she gripped his back. Her eyes were closed as her mouth rounded.

A moan escaped him, releasing me from my paralysis. I practically flew down the stairs and out the front door. I ran to Sara's SUV and slammed the door behind me, panting.

"What's wrong? Where's your stuff?" Sara asked in a panic.

"I couldn't..." I panted, trying to catch my breath, the image seared into my brain. I tried to shake it away, but I couldn't.

"Are they fighting?" Sara asked, her tone anxious.

"No," I replied emphatically. "They are *not* fighting."

"Omigod," Sara gasped. "No way. You didn't just walk in on..." She started laughing in amazed disbelief.

I flopped my head against the headrest. "Yup," I breathed, "I guess they didn't break up." Sara laughed even harder. I looked back at the house as we drove away, an uneasiness washing over me.

23. BOUNDARIES

F eeling any better?" Sara asked at breakfast the next morning. Her parents had already left for work, so it was just the two of us.

I shook my head, still haunted by the compromising position I'd caught my mother and Jonathan in the night before.

"I don't know how I'm ever going to look at either of them again," I said, groaning. Sara laughed, overly amused by my trauma. "Sara, I saw his *ass*, his *naked* ass—on top of my mother! I may seriously need to go back to therapy after seeing that." I flopped my head onto my folded arms.

"I bet he has an amazing ass," Sara mused dreamily, the smile consuming her entire face.

I peered up at her, appalled, my cheeks scarlet. My reaction only made her laugh harder.

"I don't think I've laughed this hard since you tripped in front of those college guys in California." Sara held her stomach.

"You love seeing me tortured and humiliated," I said, sulking. "Great friend you are!"

"Stop." Sara chuckled, unable to hide her smile. "It is funny, really."

"Walking in on my mother and her boyfriend, sure, it may be horrifyingly hysterical. But he was supposed to break up with her. This is so not good."

"They made up," Sara offered with a shrug. "Couples fight and make up all the time. What's the big deal?"

"He's leaving to go to grad school at USC," I explained. "My mother's in love with him."

"Does she know?"

"Yes," I told her, "but she wants to be with him until he leaves."

"Why is that so bad?" It was obvious she didn't understand my concern.

"I'll be gone when he leaves," I continued.

"And you're worried about her being alone?"

I nodded, biting my lip to keep the tears from forming. Fear ate at the pit of my stomach, as I wondered what my mother would do in her isolated misery. I didn't want her to have to go through it without me.

Sara and I stopped by the house first thing in the morning to pick up my books. Thankfully, the house was empty. I avoided my mother and Jonathan that entire day.

And I thought I'd timed it perfectly when I left for school the next morning, emerging from my room right after my mother had pulled out of the driveway. But as I headed down the stairs, I heard the refrigerator door close and realized Jonathan was still home. I paused in frustration—he was never home when I left for school.

I kept walking down the stairs and straight out the door, shutting it behind me just as I heard him call, "Emma!"

I picked up my pace, not wanting to see him, forget about talk to him. Jonathan stepped out the front door with a coffee in his hand and a laptop bag hanging from his shoulder. He glanced in my direction as I unlocked my car, hesitating slightly. When I avoided eye contact and slipped into my car, he continued to his truck.

I turned the key in the ignition and…nothing happened.

"No way," I grunted, pumping the gas and turning the key again. The car didn't even make an attempt to start. I collapsed in my seat, banging my hands on the steering wheel.

Jonathan braked at the end of the driveway. I remained in my car, ignoring him, grumbling profanities under my breath. This was the last thing I needed this morning.

He tapped on my window, forcing me to roll it down. "You okay?"

"No," I huffed, still unable to look at him. "My car won't start."

"I'll give you a ride," he responded. "Then I'll take a look at it later."

I hesitated, glancing at my watch. I knew Sara and Evan were already on their way to school, and it didn't make sense to have them come all the way out here to get me.

"Please, just let me drive you to school," Jonathan repeated when I didn't answer.

"Fine," I grumbled. I opened my car door and slammed it in frustration. I tossed my book bag on the passenger-side floor of his truck before pulling myself up onto the seat. I shut the door and fastened my seat belt, determined to ignore him.

We drove down the street and out of the neighborhood without a word.

"Can we talk about it?" Jonathan finally pleaded, turning down the radio when the tense silence became too much.

"No," I snapped. "I definitely *do not* want to talk about it."

But after only ten seconds, I turned toward him and practically yelled, "Why are you doing this to her, Jonathan? I don't understand!"

"I...I know," he stuttered. "I couldn't end it. I knew it would make things worse."

"So you'd rather torture her by making her fall more in love with you so you can dump her right before you leave. That's real great!" I shot back, my anger rising with each word.

"Emma, please don't be mad at me," he begged. "That's not what I want, really. I just…wasn't ready."

"Prolonging the inevitable isn't helping her," I lectured sternly. "It's torturing her. You can't protect her forever. You're coddling her."

"And you aren't?" he rebutted, glancing at me out of the corner of his eye. I opened my mouth to defend myself, but nothing came out. In truth, I didn't really know what he meant. He continued, his voice growing stronger, "Emma, you clean up after her when she throws a fit; you comfort her when she's irresponsible, and the other night she basically accused you of ruining her life. You're protecting her as much as I am."

I continued to stare.

"I'm sorry," he said, his tone softening. "I shouldn't have said that."

I let his words sink in. He pulled into the parking lot of the school, stopping alongside the walkway that wrapped around the building. Putting the truck in park, he turned toward me. His brown eyes were heavy with apology.

"So how do we fix this?" I questioned glumly. "Besides having *sex* with her." The words flew out of my mouth before I could catch them, delivered with a bite that I didn't anticipate.

"Uh," Jonathan stammered, shock flashing across his eyes. "You should never have seen that. I'm so sorry."

I clenched my teeth and stared at the floor, more disturbed by his actions than I could rationalize as heat rushed through my chest. "So now what?"

"You're right," he answered firmly. "I have to end things with her."

I flipped my eyes toward him, not convinced he meant it.

"Should I still wait until after her birthday?"

I groaned. I hadn't thought of that. "I don't know."

Our eyes connected in deliberation until I realized I was lingering too long and blinked away.

"Thanks for the ride." I reached down to pick up my backpack, and it struck me. "My sweater."

"Huh?" Jonathan didn't follow.

"What were you doing with my sweater?" I demanded.

Jonathan took in my expression. "I found it on the chair on the front porch when I was leaving for work a while ago. I thought it was Rachel's. I'd honestly forgotten I had it."

"Oh," I replied, my cheeks reddening at my accusatory tone. What was I really insinuating anyway? Maybe all this drama was making me overreact. I reached for the door handle, spotting Evan a few rows away, shutting his car door. I smiled at the sight of him. Then Analise appeared, shutting the passenger door. My heart froze and my smile disappeared.

"Are you okay?" Jonathan asked, noticing the change. I remained motionless, at a loss for words. "Emma?"

"Yeah, I'm fine," I choked, gripping the strap of my backpack. I opened the door.

"Emma." Jonathan stopped me before I could hop down. His eyes held me captive long enough to confess, "She's not the reason I decided to stay."

"Emma?" Evan hollered as I was about to ask Jonathan what he meant. I hesitated for a second, but knew I had to leave.

"Thanks," I choked, barely able to form words. I hopped down from the truck and shut the door behind me.

As Jonathan drove off, Evan emerged from behind the truck.

His eyes tightened. "Was that Jonathan?" He found my hand and securely laced his fingers through mine.

"My car wouldn't start," I explained, trying to ignore Analise on the other side of him.

"Want me to take a look at it later?"

"That's okay," I replied. "Jonathan said he would, but thanks." Evan nodded slightly, his eyes following Jonathan's truck as it pulled onto the street.

"Hi, Emma," Analise chirped, poking her head around to flash me her blinding smile.

"Hi, Analise," I replied, acknowledging her impassively. "Where's *your* car?"

"Evan and I are doing some work for Vivian after school, so we thought it made sense for him to drive me," she announced. As I listened, my feet faltered. Evan clearly saw the stunned expression on my face.

"That's great," I replied flatly. Analise went her separate way toward the junior lockers as Evan continued toward mine.

"You're upset," Evan noted as soon as Analise was out of ear-shot.

"No," I mumbled, not looking at him. "I'm just flustered because of my car."

"Good morning," Sara interrupted. "How are you—" Her eyes flipped from me to Evan, and she pressed her lips together. "Um…I see that you're not into mornings. I'll talk to you later." She nodded knowingly and took off to class.

I pulled my books from my locker, unable to face Evan without giving away just how much his time with Analise bothered me.

"Em, you don't have to—"

"I have to go to class," I muttered, brushing past him quickly. This morning sucked. I just wanted this day to be over, and it had barely begun.

Sara was waiting for me around the corner. "I'm coming over tonight. We're talking about this whole Analise situation."

"Okay." I sighed, knowing I needed it.

The day didn't get any better when Analise plopped her fluffy ass down at our table for lunch. Sara eyed her in disbelief, like she'd trampled over all sorts of boundaries. Sara opened her mouth to say something, but I shot her a pleading look and begged in a whisper, "Don't."

"You sure?" she questioned incredulously. I nodded just as Evan sat down between me and Analise.

The awkward silence lingered until Analise broke it with, "This food looks better than Mrs. Timmins' dinner last night, huh?" She let out a light laugh. "That was the strangest version of chicken I've ever seen. You should have seen it, Emma. I think it was grey. Right, Evan?"

I couldn't move. I knew Evan was watching me, but I remained still.

"What dinner?" Sara instigated, staring at me, silently begging me to speak up.

"Oh one of those business dinner thingies," Analise gushed with a nervous laugh, realizing she must have said something wrong.

"What did you think of it?" I asked, feigning curiosity with a strained smile.

Analise hesitated. Probably trying to decide if I was sincere or about to rip her head off. "It was actually pretty nice. Stuart and Vivian are so sweet, so they made it easy. And Evan can talk to anyone, and he introduced me to a lot of people, so it wasn't as bad as I feared it would be. We ended up having a really great time."

I stood from the table and stormed out of the cafeteria. I'd barely made it to the hall when Evan caught up with me.

"It was just a stupid dinner for my father's firm," Evan explained in a rush.

"Yup." I responded flatly and kept walking, not caring if he was next to me or not. I remained stoic on the outside, but my insides were squirming—I thought I was about to be sick.

"Em, stop," he begged. "Please, just listen."

I turned abruptly and gave him my full and cold attention. He drew back when he saw the disconnect in my eyes.

"My mother wanted Laura to meet some potential clients affili-ated with my father's firm," he explained calmly. "Analise just came along with her mother. It's not as bad as it sounds."

I turned and started walking again, choking on the fumes of anger that cut off all logic and rational thought to my head. I could only feel, not think—and I was afraid that if I opened my mouth, I would regret anything I said.

"Besides, you hate those dinners," Evan hollered after me.

I spun around. "So did *you*," I bit back and rushed off, leaving him behind.

"Hey, Emma," Jill said from beside my locker as I forcefully pulled the books from the top shelf, grumbling to myself about how I couldn't believe Evan had taken Analise to a firm dinner. "How's Rachel?"

I whipped my head to the side. It took every ounce of will-power I had not to snap at her. To tell her to mind her own business. But I swallowed the anger and said, "Fine."

"We never told anyone about the drinking," she assured me. Her voice was low; she was careful not to be overheard. Her words struck me as odd. My eyes twitched, questioning. Her face filled with sympathy.

Then it hit me. *Omigod. She thinks my mother's an alcoholic.*

"Thanks," I replied quickly, needing to look away as the heat crept across my face.

"We shouldn't have done what we did," she continued. "Casey and me. I'm sorry about that."

"Yeah, sure," I muttered, my stomach twisting in knots.

"If you ever need to talk…" she said consolingly, making me want to turn from her and run as fast as I could.

"Yup," I answered shortly. "See you in practice. I have to get to class."

"Oh yeah, sure," she replied uncomfortably, her cheeks slightly pink. I walked away with my head down, so people wouldn't notice how red I was.

I couldn't live in denial any longer, and it took Jill's words of solace to snap me out of it. Despite my mother's assurances that she was fine, she wasn't, and it was time I faced the truth. I had wanted to believe her so much that I'd convinced myself that she only drank to excess when she was upset or sad—and that was okay. That was *okay?!* What was wrong with me?

"Hi, girls," my mother greeted us cheerily from the kitchen when Sara and I arrived after practice.

"Hi, Rachel," Sara replied, setting her bag near the bottom of the stairs and walking into the kitchen. I followed her, suddenly afraid to face my mother. It was like I was seeing her for the first time—noticing the wineglass next to her on the counter as she cut vegetables. The sight of it made my chest hurt.

She picked up the glass and took a sip. "Are you staying for dinner?"

"I'm not staying long," Sara told her. "I gave Emma a ride home, and we're just going to talk for a while before I go."

"Oh, okay," my mother responded. "Jonathan went to pick up a new battery for your car."

"Great," I answered in a flat tone. "Well, we'll be upstairs."

"Um, Sara," my mother called as we were about to leave the kitchen. "It's my birthday on Saturday, and I'm having a few friends over. I thought it would be nice if you came over too, you know, for Emily. I think we're just going to play poker and listen to music."

"Sure, that sounds great."

"Really?" My mother's eyes lit up. "I'm happy you'll be there. I really want it to be fun."

"It will be," Sara assured her. "If you want me to bring any-thing, or do anything to help, let me know."

"I will." My mother beamed. It became evident to me just how important this party was to her, and with everything that had gone on the last few days, we hadn't really talked much about it. Despite everything, all I really wanted was for her to be happy.

"I think Evan has a poker table we could borrow," I added.

"That would be amazing," she said, glowing. "Thanks."

"Sure," I replied with a small smile before following Sara up the stairs. As I entered my room, I texted, Wait til after her birthday. And don't worry about me.

I unzipped my jacket and tossed it on the chair at my desk while Sara shut the door and settled on my bed. My phone beeped, and Jonathan responded with, Okay. But I do, can't help it. My cheeks flushed with heat, and I stuffed the phone in my jacket pocket.

"Okay. So, you have to say something to him," Sara began before I could even sit down. "You have to tell him that he can't hang out with her anymore."

I started to worry about what potential disasters awaited us at my mother's party. How Sara and Evan would react at the sight of it. Maybe she'd just get giddy drunk, like she sometimes did, and talk too loudly, spewing semi-embarrassing comments. I could live with that.

"Emma!"

"Uh, what?" I redirected my focus.

"The invasion of Analise," Sara stressed. "What's going on with you? Have you heard a single word I've said?"

"Yes," I replied. "I need to set boundaries."

"No," she corrected me sternly. "*Evan* needs to set boundaries. He can't have an obsessed girl doting on him all over the place and expect you to be the loving girlfriend who's pretending nothing's happening."

"Right," I agreed, without the gusto Sara was looking for. She gawked at me disapprovingly.

"But what if I'm overreacting?" I asked quietly, lying on my bed next to her.

"Overreacting? Um...the whole school is talking about *them*. They went to a party together last Friday. She's over at his house all of the time, and he drives her to school. They look more like a—"

"Okay," I interrupted, not needing the detailed visual. "I get it. I'll talk to him."

"Why do I feel like I'm talking you into this? Do you not remember being blindsided at lunch today? I saw the look on your face when she brought up the dinner."

Just the mention of it made me clench my teeth. "Yes. I'll talk to him."

"Okay. I have to go. My mom's waiting on me for dinner. I'll see you tomorrow," Sara said, grabbing her things and opening the door.

Evan appeared at the top of the stairs. Sara stopped short. "Uh, hi, Evan."

"Hi, Sara," he replied. She scooted past him and flashed me a teeth-bared good-luck look as she disappeared down the stairs.

Evan remained outside my room, hesitating at the sight of me.

"Hi," he said quietly, shutting the door behind him.

"Hi," I replied, barely audible. I sat against the headboard, pulling a pillow on to my lap.

Evan sat down on the end of my bed. The strain between us was suffocating me.

"I should have invited you to the dinner," Evan began. "I guess I know how much you hate them...but I should have given you the choice."

"It's not just the dinner," I returned, letting out a distraught breath. "You've been spending a lot of time with her, and I...I don't like it. It's that simple."

"Em, I don't see her like that, I swear. She's like a little sister to me." He silently pleaded for me to believe him.

"You may feel that way about *her*, but Evan, she has a thing for *you*. You have to know that."

"I know," he sighed. "It's not what I meant to happen. I just wanted to make her feel welcome, being new and everything. I know how hard it can be."

His words drifted through me and swelled my heart. I knew he meant it, because that's exactly who he was. "Evan, you're the most thoughtful person I've ever known, and I love you for that. But you need to set boundaries with her."

"I will," he agreed, moving closer. "So, did you just say that you still love me?" he teased, continuing to scoot along the bed until he was next to me.

"Yes." I battled to hide my grin. "Some sunshiny sprite is not—"

"Emma!" Evan looked at me in surprise.

"Sorry." I smirked. "She's nice. I just..."

I was interrupted by the warmth of his mouth pressed against mine. And suddenly she wasn't important anymore. I wrapped my arms around his neck and pulled him toward me, sinking down along my headboard so that I was lying on my back as he pulled the pillow off of my lap.

Evan continued to find my lips, trailing his mouth along my neck and sliding his hand across my stomach to the small of my back, positioning himself over me. I relaxed my knees as he lowered himself on to me, my legs wrapping around him.

Our breathing quickened as our kisses became more frantic. I ran my hands along the tight, lean muscles of his back, gripping the end of his shirt, sliding it up.

My door squeaked open. "Your car's..."

Evan rolled over quickly to sit. I pushed myself up, smoothing the back of my hair, staring at Jonathan's wide eyes and open mouth.

"Sorry, should've knocked," he said in a single breath and shut the door.

"Uh, boundaries?" Evan stressed from beside me.

"Yeah," I breathed, staring at the door.

24. HAPPY BIRTHDAY

Should I be worried?" I asked under my breath as my mother danced around the kitchen, pulling bowls on to the counter—dumping bags of chips and spooning containers of dip into them.

"Honestly?" Jonathan asked from beside me, watching the same spectacle.

"Of course," I replied, feeling stressed.

"Probably." His honesty made my stomach churn.

"That's what I thought." I exhaled in defeat.

"Hi," Sara greeted me joyfully as she opened the front door. I turned toward her, covering the worry with a smile.

"Hi," I responded.

"Sara!" my mother exclaimed, brushing past me to give Sara a hug.

"Happy birthday, Rachel," Sara said, hugging her in return while eyeing me in shock over her shoulder. I shrugged in response.

"I brought you something," Sara told her upon being released. She opened her bag and pulled out a neatly wrapped package about the size of a deck of cards.

"You're so sweet." My mother opened it without hesitation and removed a necklace from the box. She held the delicate silver chain in front of her. "It's beautiful. Thank you."

"You're welcome," Sara replied, taking off her jacket.

"Sara, you must know how to cook," my mother insisted, fastening the chain around her neck.

"Not really," Sara confessed. "My mother's tried to encourage it, but it hasn't taken yet."

"What's with you guys?" My mother shook her head. She returned to the kitchen, where she proceeded to pull ingredients out of the refrigerator. "I'm going to have to give Anna a hard time about this. What are you going to do when you go to college?"

There was a knock at the door. Jonathan went to open it as Sara and I took the bowls of chips into the living room. Jared entered, carrying a bottle of wine with a bow around it. I stopped short at the sight of it.

"Well, hello," my mother greeted him, smiling.

"Rachel, this is Jared," Sara said, introducing him and slipping her arm through his.

"Happy birthday," he said, presenting the bottle to my mother.

"My favorite," she gushed, taking the bottle from him. "Thank you."

"Where's Evan?" I asked, scanning the driveway. When I didn't see any sign of him, I shut the door.

"He drove separately," Jared explained, following my mother and Sara toward the kitchen. "He should be here any second."

I remained in the foyer, hoping Evan would arrive soon—and not wanting to go anywhere near the kitchen in fear that I'd be recruited to cook something.

"Are you friends with Evan?" my mother asked, laying tortillas on a griddle.

"He's my brother," Jared explained, standing in the kitchen doorway.

"I would have never guessed that," my mother replied, eyeing his broader frame and blond hair, flipped out around his ears. "You look as much alike as Emily and me." She let out a laugh, making Jared smile. "So *you* must know how to cook."

"Not at all," Jared confessed, glancing at Sara—obviously not sure what to make of my mother. "My brother and I are pretty opposite in just about everything. Is there anything else I can do to help?"

"Do you know how to make margaritas?"

"That I can help with," Jared replied, continuing into the kitchen.

"Great," I muttered under my breath.

The door opened with a knock, and Evan entered with the poker table.

"Let me help you with that," Jonathan offered, appearing from the living room to take the table. Evan followed him with folding chairs in each hand.

"Finally!" my mother exclaimed. "Evan, please come help me cook these quesadillas. You and I appear to be to be the only ones who have any talent in the kitchen."

"Jared has talent," Sara said defensively. "It's just not in the kitchen, that's all."

"Oh, so what room are we talking about?" My mother smirked. "The bedroom?"

"We did not just go there," Jared blurted in disbelief, looking from my mother to Sara. Sara started laughing, and I stared, wide-eyed, in shock at my mother's inappropriate candor—wondering if she'd already started drinking.

Evan returned to the kitchen after hanging up his jacket. "Uh, okay. So, what do you want me to do?" he asked, having no idea what he'd just walked in on.

"Flip them when they're ready," she instructed, handing Evan the spatula. "Want a drink?"

"I think *I* might need one," Jared interjected. My mother pulled two glasses from the cabinet, filled them with ice and held them out for Jared to fill with the margarita blend he'd created.

She handed one glass over and held up hers with a smirk, "To being talented."

Jared raised his eyebrows in shock and clinked her glass.

"Hey, I want in on this," Sara insisted, filling another glass to tap with theirs. I tried to keep from having heart failure as I watched my mother quickly drain half of her glass. I realized I had to prepare myself. This was about to happen.

"You okay?" Jonathan asked, passing me as he carried in more folding chairs from the porch and set them around the poker table.

"Not until tomorrow morning," I muttered, deciding to follow him to help set up the chairs.

"Emily, would you put on some music?" my mother hollered from the kitchen, although there was no need to yell, since I could hear every word they were saying.

"Sure," I replied. I flipped through the CD collection, not finding anything I would deem party worthy.

"Here," Jonathan offered, handing me his iPod. "There's a playlist on there for Rachel's party."

"Thanks," I said, accepting the iPod and plugging it into the wire attached to the stereo. I scrolled to the Rachel's Party playlist. My mother hollered in excitement from the kitchen when the first song came on.

"Perfect, Emily," she praised.

I was about to explain that it wasn't my selection, when Jonathan stopped me. "Just let her think it was you."

"Okay." I shrugged, not understanding why it mattered.

About half an hour later, the door opened and six people let themselves in, carrying brown bags filled with alcohol and snacks.

"Is this where the party is?" a guy with a tightly trimmed beard asked, peeking into the kitchen. He opened his arms when my mother squealed in excitement and rushed toward him, wrapping her arms around his neck while kissing him on the cheek. "Happy birthday, Rach," he said, kissing her cheek in return. She hugged each person, directing them all to hang up their coats and place their beers in the cooler on the porch. She was so excited. I tried to let the worry go and be happy for her. This was her birthday, after all.

"We brought the other poker table and chairs," one of the guys announced, popping open a can of beer after returning from the porch.

We had to introduce ourselves, since my mother was too preoccupied pouring margaritas for the two women she'd dragged into the kitchen.

"Wow, Emily," a woman named Sharon noted upon meeting me. "I can't believe how much you've grown up."

"Thanks," I responded, studying the woman, who obviously knew me. Her voice was crackly from too many years of smoking, and her face was etched with lines from a life that had not been kind to her. She wore her curly black hair long over her shoulders. Her dark eyes were heavily lined in black and layered with mascara.

"You still look just like your dad," she continued.

"Right?" my mother chimed in from behind Sharon, holding out a glass for her to take. "I swear she's not mine." She laughed playfully.

Sharon cackled. "You've been trying to get away with that one for years. But I was the one who drove you to the hospital when you went into labor, remember?"

"I couldn't exactly drive myself," my mother huffed.

"The bottle of wine may have had something to do with that," Sharon added, her laugh turning into a cough. I narrowed my eyes and looked from her to my mother.

"Relax, Emily." My mother chuckled. "She's only joking." I nodded with an awkward smile. Sharon clamped her mouth shut to keep from laughing, causing her to convulse in a coughing fit.

"Can I smoke?" Sharon asked in a rasp, pulling a pack from her pocket.

"Porch," my mother instructed. "I'll come out with you."

My mother and Sharon disappeared out the front door.

Evan finally emerged from the kitchen with several platters of quesadillas. Jared and Jonathan were helping two of the new arrivals move furniture to make room for the additional poker table. Sara and I brought in pitchers of margaritas and set them on the coffee table.

"I know, right?" my mother said to Sharon as they entered from the porch, the smell of cigarette smoke swirling around them.

"Evan, you can have a beer," my mother insisted. "It's my birthday. Besides, you're staying over, so you don't have to worry about driving." She smiled and handed him a freshly opened bottle.

"Thanks." He accepted it and placed his hand on my back, probably sensing my uneven breaths. I watched as my mother poured herself another drink. Closing my eyes, I exhaled quickly, trying to remain calm.

"You okay?" Evan bent down to ask in my ear.

I played off my worried expression. "I'm not so sure I know what I'm doing with poker."

"I'll help you," he assured me. "I'll give you a cheat sheet so you know what hand beats what."

"Okay," I replied, trying to appear relaxed. I met Jonathan's eyes across the room. He looked from my mother to me and shook his head. He was expecting something to happen, and my gut twisted in a knot, knowing it too. I looked away and tried to shake it off.

"Let's play," my mother announced, herding everyone into the living room.

As she drank more and more, my mother played less and less. She finally declared that whatever Jonathan earned would be her winnings. She hopped from table to table, initiating conversations;

then she'd jump up to select songs on the iPod and dance around with whoever she could pull away from the game.

And I played poker, or at least tried to. I had no idea what I was doing. I kept glancing at Evan's cheat sheet to decide if my hand was good enough to place a bet. We had to buy chips, so the betting was real—at the birthday girl's insistence. This kept a few of the guys a little too serious, considering it was supposed to be fun.

A few margarita pitchers later, my mother was a giggly mess, sitting on Jonathan's lap with her arms draped around his neck.

"Come on, baby. You need to bet big on this hand," my mother urged, kissing him on the cheek. With that statement, one of the guys folded.

"Thanks, Rachel," Jonathan replied, placing his bet.

"No, you should bet more than *that*," she garbled, pushing a few more chips in. "We're winning this hand." She stuck her tongue out at Sara and the other guy who hadn't folded. Sara laughed at her, taking a sip of her margarita.

"Sara, I like you," she spontaneously confessed, the effects of the tequila showing.

"Thanks, Rachel," Sara replied with a smile. "Happy birthday." She raised her glass for my mother to clumsily tap.

"Come dance with me," my mother insisted, popping up from Jonathan's lap and grabbing Sara's hand.

"But I'm still playing," Sara argued feebly. My mother grabbed her hand and pulled her from her chair, making Sara abandon her cards on the table.

My mother twirled herself under Sara's arm as she held her hand above her head.

I watched from the other table as Jared shuffled the deck.

"You don't say much, huh?" the woman with bleached blond hair noted. I thought her name was Sally, but maybe it was Ally.

"Not really," I replied, keeping my eyes on the cards as Jared placed them on the table in front of me.

"Don't drink either, huh?" she slurred, holding her head up on her hand.

"No, I don't," I answered.

"You used to make us drinks when you were little," she told me, making me pause before picking up my cards. "You were so cute, getting us beers. Rachel always had the best parties."

I studied my cards intently, knowing Evan and Jared were watching me.

"I'll take two cards," I requested, pretending not to be fazed by the glimpse of my previous life with my mother.

In truth, it was appearing to be not too much different than it was now—except I didn't take sips from the beer cans anymore. Our life was full of emotional waves, and had been even more so when I was young—laughing one minute, crying and screaming the next. There was always music playing, and there seemed to be a constant flow of people in the house. But despite the bodies, I was very much on my own. That's when my focus became school and sports. Despite my mother's lack of interest in my academic achievements, she'd always made certain I had soccer and basketball—even if she was incapable of driving me to the practices and games herself.

My mother's and Sara's laughter drew our attention. My mother bumped into the side table, knocking over a few pictures. Sharon joined them from her post on the porch, trailing cigarette fumes in with her.

"What do you do, Ally?" Evan intervened, taking a sip from his beer bottle.

"I'm a bartender," she replied, directing her attention toward Evan and lingering a little too long. "Can't believe you're still in high school. And wait..." She looked from me to Evan. "You two are dating, right?"

Evan nodded, before requesting two cards from Jared.

"I miss high school." She sighed, taking a gulp from her glass.

"No you don't," my mother countered, plopping down in the vacant seat next to Ally. "You hated high school."

Ally started laughing. "That's true. But we sure did get away with a lot of shit."

"Definitely," my mother recollected with giggle.

"Do you remember when you convinced Mr. Hall to let you skip that test because you told him you had wicked bad cramps, and then we went into the woods to get high?"

My mother laughed hard in remembrance, causing her eyes to water.

In between hysterics, Ally added, "And the time you gave Emily that Crown and Coke and we videoed her bumping into the wall for like an hour."

My mother held her stomach as she rolled in laughter. The guy next to Ally chuckled. "I remember that. You were hysterical."

I forced a chuckle, like I remembered it fondly, then folded and made an excuse about needing to go to the bathroom. But when I opened the bathroom door to leave, my mother was waiting to get in.

"Emily!" she declared happily. "Are you having fun?"

"Yeah, it's great," I told her, trying to smile. "Are you having fun?"

"I'm trying," she said, passing me to go into the bathroom. "It would be better if he would stop staring at you." And with that, she shut the bathroom door, leaving me outside, stunned. Who was she talking about?

I turned toward the stairs as Jonathan was reaching the top.

"Hey," he greeted. "Are you in line?"

"No," I replied, heading toward the stairs, still shocked by what my mother had said before shutting the door.

"What's going on?"

I shrugged, completely mystified.

"What?" The door opened behind us and my mother emerged. We both whipped around.

"Aahh," she said, as if she'd caught us. "And there you two are. You know I know. I mean, it's so obvious. But can't you wait at least until you're in California? C'mon, it's my birthday. You don't have to shove it in my face."

"Rachel, what are you talking about?" Jonathan laughed uncomfortably.

"Whatever," she said, dismissing him. "I'm over it."

I continued to gawk at her. "You can't think there's anything going on between us?" I insisted.

"Maybe," she shrugged and trod down the stairs, leaving us staring after her. I took a deep breath and followed her as Jonathan went into the bathroom.

The rest of the night, we didn't even look at each other. Or at least I didn't look at him. I refused to fuel my mother's drunken delusions, and I really didn't want her saying anything in front of Evan.

As the money dwindled, so did the participants. Jared and Sara were the first to leave.

"I think I got a little drunk," Sara said in my ear, laughing, as she clumsily hugged me good-bye.

"It's okay," I told her, patting her awkwardly on the back as Jared waited to help her put her jacket on. "I'll talk to you tomorrow."

Not long after, the other poker table and chairs were folded up as one of the carloads decided to head out as well.

"But you can't leave," my mother begged them, hugging Ally.

"Happy birthday, Rach."

My mother walked out to the porch to see them off.

"Who wants a shot?" she asked upon closing the door. It was a question that she didn't expect an answer to; she lined up the shot glasses on the coffee table, filled them with tequila, and began handing them to everyone, including me.

When she set the gold liquid in front of me, I cringed and glanced across the table at Jonathan.

"To being forever young," she declared, holding her shot glass in the air. "Come on, Evan, pick it up."

Evan raised his shot along with everyone else, slinging it back with a grimace. I didn't touch mine. Jonathan slid it surreptitiously across the table and drank it down before sliding the glass back in front of me.

"Thatta girl, Emily," my mother praised me, collecting the glasses.

While she was in the kitchen, Evan leaned over and asked, "Want to stay or go?"

I bit my lip in consternation. Before I could make a decision, the bearded guy folded his hand and declared, "Well, I think I'm broke enough. Sharon, we're going."

"No," she mumbled from her slouched position on the couch.

"Yeah, you're about ready to pass out," he noted, standing up from the table.

"Not you too," my mother sulked when she found him retrieving their coats from the closet.

"Your guy took all my money," he told her. "So happy birthday. Don't spend it all at once." She gave him a hug and a brief peck on the lips.

With it just being the three of us, and my poker chips down to a handful, Jonathan suggested, "Cash out?"

"Sure," I answered, standing up from the table. Evan remained to help Jonathan put the chips back in their silver case. I headed into the kitchen to begin picking up.

My mother came in from the porch, shivering. "It's just us, huh?" She observed the guys in the living room and me in the kitchen. "I *did* have fun," she said from behind me.

"Good," I answered, dumping the half-full glasses in the sink.

"I'm sorry about upstairs, you know, with Jonathan. I can be pretty stupid sometimes."

I could only nod, not knowing how to respond.

Then out of nowhere she asked, "So you don't remember, right?"

I turned around and tightened my eyes in confusion. "What? About your parties when I lived with you? I remember."

"I was just thinking," she said, ignoring my answer. She settled down on the kitchen chair—probably because she was having a hard time standing. "I've had to relive that day for all these years, and you don't remember it." Her face was smooth and emotionless as her eyes lazily flipped up at me.

I opened my mouth to ask her what she was talking about, but then I realized—she was talking about the day my father died. I closed my mouth and averted my gaze.

"You always had to wear pink," she remembered, lost in the past as her eyes glazed over. "He bought you a new pink dress every year."

I was held hostage by her words, unable to tell her to stop. My heart started to beat faster.

"You were waiting for him by the window, wanting to know why he was late. You kept asking where he was every five minutes." Sorrow flooded her face. "It's not fair that you don't remember the day I can never forget. When was the last time you celebrated your birthday, Emily?" Her question sliced through me.

My chest froze, and I had to force air into my lungs. All of a sudden, I wasn't in the room anymore. I was in my pink frilly dress, staring out the window.

"He would drive home early from work to hang those stupid colored lanterns in the backyard," she recalled impassively.

For a second I saw them. They were different shapes and colors, strewn in crisscrossing lines across the backyard. My stomach was swallowed by coldness, and I couldn't move.

"He'd bring home your cake, made by that ridiculously expensive bakery in the city. It always had to be chocolate with raspberry filling."

"When's Daddy going to be home?" I asked, the curtains spread so I could keep watch.

"He shouldn't be long," was what I was told each time. It wasn't my mother who answered me, but another woman. I looked over my shoulder to see her pulling a pan out of the oven.

"But it's getting dark, and he never comes home in the dark," I argued, continuing to stare out the window.

"Anything yet?" she asked, concern resonating in her voice as a man entered the room with a phone in his hand.

"No," he answered. "They said he left the office hours ago." The man looked familiar, but I couldn't place him.

"Rachel!" he hollered.

"What?" she called back from upstairs.

"I think we need to make the call."

Before she could answer, the phone rang. She rushed down the stairs as the man answered. "Who is it?" she demanded before he'd even said hello.

The anxiety in her eyes made me nervous. I kept watching her, unable to look away from her distressed face. It changed from worry to despair when the words spilled from his mouth after he hung up the phone. "There's been an accident."

"You took him from me," she murmured, not removing her eyes from mine.

"Rachel? What did you do?" Jonathan sounded like he was talking through a tunnel.

My vision blurred with tears. Her eyes widened in recognition. "Oh," she breathed. "You remember."

Pain flowed through my body like venom. I opened my mouth to cry out, but nothing happened.

"What did you do?" Jonathan demanded again more urgently. "Emma, are you okay?"

"Emma, what's wrong?" Evan's muted voice was etched with concern.

I looked into her eyes again, and swore I saw loathing. I winced.

I couldn't be there any longer. I needed to get out. But I couldn't move. My legs refused to cooperate. I choked on the sobs that were suffocating me. My body was on fire, searing in pain. I had to get away from her.

Before I knew what I'd done, I was out the front door—the legs that had failed me moments before were now carrying me in a run down the street. But no matter how hard I ran, I couldn't escape the ache that was crushing my chest. I breathed in, but I couldn't get enough air.

I ran down random street after street before collapsing on the damp, muddy ground, gripping my chest. It felt like it was about to burst open. I screamed in pain.

It all came back to me in a rush. The call. My mother yelling out in denial. I watched as if I were a spectator at a play. I didn't understand, but at the same time, I understood too well. He wasn't coming home. He was never coming home again.

I don't know how long I lay on the cold, wet ground, consumed by grief. I was pulled back to the surface when a warm hand brushed across my cheek. He gently propped my head on his lap as he soothed me with comforting words I couldn't quite make out.

"It's okay," he whispered.

"It hurts so bad," I gasped, my body tense. "*Please* make it stop." The tears continued down my cheeks.

Evan pulled me off the ground and carried me to the car. He gently set me down on the passenger seat, bending to kiss my forehead. I curled up in a ball, still clutching my chest—afraid that if I let go, I would fall apart.

I began to shiver, the cold earth having seeped into my bones. The warmth of the car did little to ease the shaking. Evan draped his jacket over me, and I burrowed my nose into the collar, breathing in his scent.

I fought for each breath, my jaw quivering. I was consumed by the pain, unable to escape it. It was crushing me.

I was trapped in my grief, barely aware of where we were when the car stopped. I think he may have tried to talk to me, but I couldn't hear what he was saying. His voice was muffled and distant. I closed my eyes and pressed my face against his chest when he lifted me from the car.

I remained still as he lay me on his bed. I felt my shoes slide off my feet and my jeans glide over my legs. I couldn't focus, but my eyes were open. I could only feel, and I didn't know how to shut it off. I couldn't push it back down to the hidden depths of darkness where I'd been protected from it for so many years. I was losing him all over again.

Warmth pressed against my back, and he pulled me into him. I gripped his hand, holding it tightly, keeping myself tethered to the present just enough so that I could regain perspective of where I was, lying on Evan's bed.

"I'm here, Emma. I'll never let you go," he whispered in my ear, holding me tighter.

My frame shook as I cried, releasing the torment that had been trapped since that day ten years ago. I found reprieve sometime in the early hours of the next day, when exhaustion shrouded the pain and I drifted into a sleep filled with vivid images of my father.

25. ALL OVER AGAIN

Before I opened my eyes, I heard music playing softly in the background. I couldn't quite figure out who was singing, but his voice was calming. I breathed in, letting the melody float over me before deciding to open my eyes. They didn't open very wide.

My eyes were swollen and puffy, and my entire body ached, especially my chest. I eased myself out of the curled position I'd locked myself in throughout the night. Though he wasn't in the room, Evan had left behind the comforting lyrics flowing through the speakers.

I sat on the edge of the bed and inhaled deeply. I felt empty, like everything inside me had spilled out, and there was nothing left. I rose from the bed and went into the bathroom, not bothering to look at myself as I passed the mirror, having seen the vacant look one too many times.

I stripped down and climbed into the shower, allowing the hot water to beat against my skin. The exhaustion held tight, even after the long shower. A pair of sweatpants and a T-shirt were set on the floor in front of the door when I got out. Evidently Evan knew I was awake.

I dressed in the T-shirt, which hung past my hips, and folded the waistband of the pants over so I wouldn't trip on them. I braided my wet hair before stepping back into the room. He was waiting for me, sitting up against the headboard, flipping through the channels with the television on mute.

Evan clicked off the TV when I slid onto the bed and curled up on his chest.

"How are you doing?" he asked gently, wrapping his arms around me.

"Okay," I rasped, my throat raw from the strain of emotion.

He squeezed me against him before asking, "Can you tell me what happened last night?"

I swallowed hard. Tears filled my eyes at the thought of saying it out loud.

"If you can't—"

"It's okay," I said, choking. Sitting up, I took another cleansing breath and met Evan's smoky blue eyes. Worry forged a line between them. I knew I had to try to explain.

"My mother blames me for my father's death." Just hearing those words spewing out of my mouth suffocated me.

His back stiffened. "How?"

"He died on my birthday," I explained. "On his way home from buying the cake."

"How is that your fault?"

I shrugged. "Logically, it's not. But…she hurts, and I give her a reason for her pain. I ruined her life."

"Emma, you *didn't*. She's an adult. She should realize that accidents happen. *You* can't believe that it's your fault."

"I…" I couldn't find the words to say what he wanted me to—that I knew I wasn't at fault. Guilt captured the words off my tongue before I could say them. I understood what was true, but I couldn't deny how devastating it was to be the reason he had been on that road, at that moment.

Logic didn't matter when the person I loved most had been taken from me. I finally understood why my mother needed me to feel her suffering. It hurt her too much to keep it inside. For her to be the only one to miss him like she did.

"I couldn't remember him," I told Evan, running my eyes along the lines of the comforter, allowing the images of my father to run freely through my head. "Remembering him would mean that I knew I'd lost him, and the grief that went along with it. So I didn't. I didn't remember, any of it—until last night. And it hurt..." I choked out the last word as tears flooded my eyes.

Evan pulled me against him and held me tight.

"It hurt so bad I couldn't breathe." Warm tears streamed down my face. "I felt it, all of it, as if it had just happened, and..." I swallowed back a sob.

"It's okay," Evan soothed me, kissing the top of my head. "I understand." I stayed in the comfort of his arms until I could move again.

I sat up and wiped my wet cheeks.

"Can we just lie here?" I asked, sniffling. Evan handed me a much-needed tissue.

"Of course."

I rested back down on Evan's chest, listening to the beating of his heart. He pulled the blanket over us and embraced me as if the strength of his arms could ward off the sorrow.

The music faded and the television turned on. Evan selected a movie for us to watch, but I didn't last long, still so drained from the emotional beating I'd taken.

When I opened my eyes again, the room was darkening. Evan was on his side with his arms locked around me, breathing heavily in a restful sleep. I inhaled his scent with my face pressed against his shirt and leaned up to kiss his neck.

He stirred and hugged me closer. I ran my mouth along his neck, feeling the warmth of his pulse under my lips. A smile formed on his face while his eyes remained closed. I found the spot under his ear and kissed him again.

"Hi," he murmured with a wide smile, slowly opening his eyes and inhaling deeply.

"Hi," I whispered in his ear, tracing his jawline with my lips, making my way to his mouth. He parted his firm lips to receive me. I breathed him in and pulled myself against him, kissing him harder as his hands moved under my shirt, along my back.

Our bodies moved together, easing over each other. His warm hands pressed against my bare skin, inciting a flutter throughout my body that made my heart convulse. Our breathing quickened, and his touch trailed down to the waistband of the sweatpants, teasing along the elastic. I lifted his shirt and he pulled back to allow it over his head, revealing the smooth lines of muscle beneath.

I ran my hands over the definition of his chest and grooves of his stomach, kissing along his shoulder to his neck.

I went to remove my shirt, but he propped himself up and pulled back, his eyes scanning mine.

"What?" I asked in confusion, not sure if I'd done something wrong.

"Not yet," Evan explained. "Not like this."

I collapsed against him, my body pulsing. "Okay," I breathed in disappointment.

"You understand, right?" He tucked my hair behind my ear.

"I do," I answered, unable to look at him. Of course I understood. Our first time shouldn't happen after I'd spent the day mourning the loss of my father. But I wanted to feel him, *needed* to feel him, to be close to him—to mend the fissure that had split open overnight.

"Do you want to stay over again tonight?" he asked, breathing in my hair as he pressed his lips against my temple.

"I should go home."

"To Rachel's?" he questioned in surprise. "I didn't think—"

"Yeah, I should," I interrupted. "It's okay. I want to talk to her. I understand now, and I didn't before. Maybe…maybe we can really fix us."

"Em." Evan waited for me to look up at him. I tilted my head and absorbed his troubled expression. "It's not your fault. No matter what she says, or believes, *you* have to know that, okay?"

"Okay," I answered in a whisper, kissing him gently.

The house was dark when we pulled into the driveway, and my mother's car was parked at the end. I hesitated before opening the car door, staring at the black windows.

"Want me to come in with you?" Evan asked, putting the car in park.

"No," I replied without taking my eyes off of the house. "I'll be okay."

"Call me later, alright?"

"I will," I answered, slipping out of the car and shutting the door behind me. I inhaled through my nose, preparing for whatever awaited me in the dark. Evan didn't move out of the driveway; he kept watch until I disappeared through the front door.

I flipped on the foyer light and listened. The house remained uncharacteristically still. I walked into the living room and watched through the window as Evan slowly backed out of the driveway. I turned on the lights and found the poker table still in place, half-eaten bowls of chips and empty shot glasses scattered about. I began collecting the remnants of the party and carried them into the kitchen.

Once I'd cleaned up and put everything back in its place, I climbed the stairs, having spent the past hour summoning the courage to do this. As I neared her door, I could hear her crying.

I froze, my insides squirming. Before I could back away, I tapped lightly on the door. The sobs ceased.

"Yes?" she answered, barely audible.

With my heart beating frantically, I slowly opened the door and stepped in.

"Hi," I said lightly.

My mother was lying on her bed, her eye makeup smeared with tears, her hair tangled and sprawled on the pillow. The red face and swollen eyes were all too familiar. She still wore the same clothes from the night before.

I sat down on the edge of her bed farthest from her.

"I thought you'd left me too," she rasped, pulling a tissue from the box next to her bed.

"No," I explained. "I just needed some time."

"So, you're…you're staying?" She took short breaths, recovering.

"I'm staying," I confirmed faintly.

My mother rolled away from me. I could make out small gasps as she continued to cry. My hand hovered over her, shaking slightly, hesitant to touch her. I let down the wall, the one that protected me from everything that hurt. I opened myself up and felt her pain, my pain, and became her daughter, resting my hand on her back.

I felt her chest expand as she inhaled a sobbing breath. I waited for her to surface, sitting beside her, letting her know I hadn't abandoned her.

After some time she became quiet. I took my hand away when she shifted on to her back to face me with reddened eyes.

"Do you want to watch a movie and eat a pint of ice cream with me?" I asked gently.

She attempted to smile. "Sure."

My mother slowly sat up, wiping the makeup and tears from under her eyes. "I'm going to take a shower." Before she left the room, she turned to me and said, "I'm glad you didn't leave me."

My mouth twitched into a fragile smile.

On her way to the bathroom, my mother yelled back, "Nothing romantic and sappy—I may throw something at the TV."

I laughed as she shut the door behind her. I went to my room to retrieve my wallet and keys. The red light was blinking on my phone, so I grabbed it on my way out the door.

After flipping through Jonathan's and Evan's missed calls and texts from the night before, wondering where I was and if I was okay, I deleted them all.

I got up the nerve to call Jonathan when I pulled into the grocery store's parking lot, not exactly sure what I should say.

"Hi," Jonathan answered after only a couple of rings. "How are you?"

"I'm okay."

"Are you sure? You didn't look okay last night."

"I will be," I assured him, running my fingers along the steering wheel.

"I can't believe she did that. I wanted to go after you, but Evan was already out the door, and she started screaming at me. Sorry. I should have gone anyway."

"No," I stressed, confused by his words. "I understand."

"Where are you now? At Sara's?"

"No, I'm back home," I answered quietly.

"You are?" He sounded surprised. "Why?"

"Umm..." I began, flustered by his disapproval. "Because she's my mother, and I don't think she should have to go through this alone anymore."

"Emma, what she did was horrible. How—" He stopped. I could hear him exhale, as if to calm himself. "I don't understand how you can let it go like it wasn't a big deal."

"I'm not...exactly," I replied weakly. "I just think I understand better now, that's all."

Jonathan was silent for a moment before he added, "I couldn't let her treat you like that. I had to end it. You understand, right?"

"I knew it was coming," I answered. He remained quiet. "I should get going," I finally said when the silence became too uncomfortable.

"Call me," he said in a rush before I could hang up. "If you need *anything*, even just to say hi, okay? Just call me." His voice was heavy with worry and made me pause.

"I will," I promised, not truly certain if I would—or should.

When I returned home, my mother was showered and on the couch with a blanket over her lap. She didn't have any makeup on to conceal the lines etched around her mouth and the creases at the corners of her eyes. She looked...worn. Defeated.

She tried to smile when I walked in carrying the movie and two pints of ice cream, but her eyes remained dull and distant.

I put the movie in and sat next to her on the couch. We ate our ice cream and watched the movie in silence, until her voice broke the stillness with, "I can be such a bitch, can't I?"

I didn't know what to say. I was actually afraid to look over at her, hoping she wasn't really expecting an answer. So I scraped my spoon along the top of the ice cream and waited.

"I don't know what happens," she finally continued. I glanced over at her out of the corner of my eye. She wasn't looking at me, but staring down at the floor, consumed by her thoughts. "It's when I drink too much. I get...I say things I shouldn't. I'm a terrible person."

"No you're not," I said automatically. She peered up at me, her blue eyes heavy with guilt. My mouth softened into a small smile. "I didn't understand what you were going through. I didn't know."

"It takes the edge off," she continued. My brow twitched, uncertain what she meant. "The alcohol," she clarified, "makes the pain bearable. I'm not as strong as you. You can shut it off and block everything out. You were able to do that even as a little girl. You didn't even cry at…at his funeral." Her voice broke.

My mother's eyes welled up, and her lower lip quivered. "I miss him." Tears slid down her cheeks as she gasped, "I miss him so much, and I don't know how not to." Her shoulders slumped forward as she gave in to the pain.

I set down my ice cream and scooted closer, putting my arm around her shoulders to comfort her. She collapsed against me, and I gripped her tighter as she cried.

I couldn't exactly say why, but I didn't cry. Maybe I had hurt enough and I just needed to shut everything off—like she'd said I would. I continued to console her without allowing her sadness to seep in. I couldn't recollect a time we'd ever shared an affectionate embrace. But in that moment, I could barely feel her against me. So detached and outside myself, I was anything but *strong*.

I remained by her side and ran my hand over her dark hair, soothing her with comforting words, assuring her that it was okay to miss him. That *she* would be okay.

My mother finally raised her head, wiping the tears from her face. "Thank you." She tried to smile, but it was as if her cheeks were too tired and weak to lift. She took a deep breath and sat up on her own. "Birthdays suck in this house, huh?"

I raised my eyebrows, not knowing how to react.

She followed with, "I think I'm going to bed. I didn't sleep much last night, so I'm exhausted. See you in the morning?"

"Of course," I answered, watching her stand. I continued to watch her as she walked up the stairs to her room. I lay down on the couch and pulled the blanket over me, not ready to sleep yet.

A loud banging caused me to bolt upright with a start. It was silent in the dark. Perhaps I'd imagined it. Then the banging erupted at my door, making me jump. My heart beat in panic.

My room was so black, I couldn't even see the door. I blinked but still couldn't focus on a thing. I remained frozen in my bed.

A frantic voice yelled from the other side. It sounded like a child, a little girl. I fumbled with my blankets at the sound of her panicked voice. I stepped into the dark and felt the cool boards beneath my feet.

I couldn't make out what she was saying. Her pounding blocked out her words. I thought she was saying, "Get me out." She sounded so desperate. I needed to get to her.

I blindly searched for the door, my hands reaching out in front of me. I felt the hard surface with my fingertips. The wood shook violently beneath my hands as her small fists slammed against it. That's when I heard her scream, "Get out!"

I gasped. My eyes shot open. The television was on, and I was lying on the couch. My heart pounded in my chest. The fear in her voice still reverberated in my head. I sat up with my hands shaking.

I eyed the stairs, considering going to bed, but knew I wouldn't be able to sleep. I picked up the remote and started flipping through the channels, though her plea still echoed through my head, sending a chill throughout my body. I wrapped the blanket around me tighter.

I picked up my phone, not really thinking about what I was doing, but needing another voice in my head other than the little girl's.

Almost instantly I heard, "Hi. Can't sleep?"

My lips curled into a half smile at the sound of his voice. "No. You either?"

"Nope. What are you watching?" Jonathan asked.

26. DISAPPOINTMENT

So, how's Rachel?"

"She's okay," I said, sitting on my bed, running my fingers along the pattern of my bedspread. "She's been lying low the past couple of weeks. She's focused all of her energy on teaching me how to cook—which is…disastrous. And I've been trying to teach her how to play basketball—which is even *more* disastrous."

He laughed. She'd lose control dribbling the ball every time she lifted her head. Just thinking of her chasing after it made me smile.

"It sounds like the two of you are figuring things out."

"We're trying," I admitted. "It's not always easy. There are still tears every so often, but nothing ice cream can't fix." I paused and then added, "She misses you."

"I'm not so sure she misses *me*," Jonathan replied. "I think she misses being with someone."

"Whatever," I said. "I'm not going to argue with you. But I'm pretty convinced it's you."

He let out a breathy laugh, knowing I'd argued with him anyway.

"Sorry you didn't win the championship. It was a close game."

"Yup." I sighed, having replayed the last two minutes of the game in my head repeatedly over the last week and a half.

"That foul was a bad call."

"Wait. You were there?"

"Uh, yeah," he confessed slowly. "I had to know how it would end."

"Well, it ended, that's for sure. I wish you'd said something to me."

"I thought it would be awkward, you know, with Rachel."

"Yeah, maybe," I admitted reluctantly. "It's just been a while since I've seen you."

"Maybe we should do something about that."

"Maybe."

"We should hang out sometime. Just...do something."

"Oh, yeah, *something* sounds fun," I teased. "I do that a lot, and I always have a blast."

"You're hilarious. But really, I'll pick a day and you'll just have to come along, to do whatever *something* I choose."

"Bring it," I taunted, making him laugh.

"So, tonight's the Big Night," he said with exaggerated enthusiasm.

"Don't make fun," I threatened lightly. "It *is* a big night."

"Only because you're making it that way. Emma, let whatever's supposed to happen, happen."

"Great pep talk, thanks," I snapped sarcastically. "I don't want to talk about it; I might throw up on my phone, and I like this phone. I would hate to have to replace it."

Jonathan laughed again. "Fine. We won't talk about it. But don't let his dad get to you, no matter what."

"I won't." I sighed, knowing that Stuart Mathews was the most intimidating man on the planet—there was no way I was *not* going to let him get to me. He scared the crap out of me!

"Tell me what happens. The suspense is already killing me," he taunted, sounding overly dramatic.

"Ha ha," I jeered. "I gotta go. Don't be surprised if I call you at three a.m. with a nightmare about being stepped on by a giant men's dress shoe. I'd name a brand, but I have no idea what men wear."

"I'll be waiting." Jonathan chuckled. "Bye, Emma."

I watched as *Call Ended* flashed across my screen, trying to summon the courage to prepare for dinner with Evan and his parents. It would've been better if Jared could have helped deflect the tension—he always seemed to know what to say to make the most serious situations seem light and uncomplicated. But he couldn't drive down from Cornell in the middle of the week.

"What are you wearing?" my mother asked from my open door. I looked up in surprise, wondering how long she'd been standing there.

"Uh, I was thinking the grey pants with the white blouse," I answered, motioning toward the two items hanging at the back of my closet. The pants were serious, like I was going to interview with a law firm serious. But the short-sleeved blouse with the puffy capped sleeves was light and airy, keeping it a little more fun.

"Pants?" my mother questioned.

"I'm going to be so nervous. I'll be sweating like crazy. Do you know how uncomfortable it is to sweat behind your knees with a skirt on? It's pretty disgusting actually."

My mother laughed. "Don't be nervous. I'm positive everything will work out for you both."

"You've never met his father," I groaned.

"Well, he can't be any worse than your grandmother," my mother countered with a roll of her eyes. I stopped and looked at her. I had no idea I had a grandmother. Carol and George had never mentioned anyone, nor had my mother until this second. I had always been under the impression that my grandparents had passed away before I was born. Maybe that's what she'd meant—past tense.

She didn't notice my stunned face. Or perhaps she chose to ignore it.

"Are you going to take a shower? It's getting late."

"Oh, yeah," I answered, jumping up from my bed, abandoning the phone that I still grasped in my hand on the bedspread. I gathered what I needed for the bathroom and moved past my mother down the hall.

After styling my hair in soft curls and dressing in my serious, but not too serious, attire, I was ready. Or at least, I *looked* ready. Sara would've been proud.

My phone beeped. I turned toward my bed, but it wasn't where I'd left it. Scanning the room, I found it on my dresser. I cocked my head curiously and picked it up to see, On your way?

Leaving now, I texted back before rushing down the stairs.

"Good luck," my mother said from the top of the stairs, dressed in a short skirt and camisole.

"Going out?" I deduced.

"I'm overdue," she replied. "No reason to stay in on a Thursday night." Her voice sounded off, a little strained. She smirked and added, "Besides, it's April Fool's Day. What could possibly go wrong?"

Everything, I thought to myself before saying, "Well, have fun," out loud. She turned and went back in her room. I paused in front of the coat closet, wondering if I should be concerned that she was going out. I took a breath and decided to focus on one nerve-racking situation at a time. I grabbed my coat and headed out the door.

When I arrived at the Mathews', Vivian was stepping onto the porch, wearing a long white coat and holding a small black clutch.

"Perfect timing, Emily," Vivian said in greeting, taking a key out of her purse. "Evan, we're ready."

Evan appeared, looking very polished, his overcoat covering what I assumed was a suit. I smiled at his shiny dress shoes, recollecting my nightmare prediction.

Dinners with the Mathews always made me nervous—fearing I'd say the wrong thing or embarrass Evan with my lack of social skills. But tonight I was a wreck. I was convinced I wouldn't be able to eat at all.

"Evan, would you mind driving?" Vivian requested, handing him the key to her BMW.

"Sure," Evan replied. Before heading to the car, he walked over and wrapped his arms around me. "You look amazing. A little pale, but still amazing. You can breathe you know."

"Not yet," I murmured from within his coat. He kissed the top of my head before opening the car door for me.

"This is such an exciting night," Vivian said from the passenger seat as we drove to the restaurant. "I hope we don't have to wait too long for your father to arrive."

"It doesn't matter if he's there," Evan told her. "He's not going to like where I'm going unless it's Yale."

"Evan," Vivian warned, "don't be that way. He only wants what's best for you, and he will come around to accepting your decision. He may need more time, that's all."

"Yeah, four years," Evan mumbled, loud enough for us to hear.

"Wait. You already know where you're going?"

"I already know where I *want* to go," Evan corrected. "I just need my mother to tell us if I'm going there or not. She's really great at keeping secrets, even from my father."

"Well, if he knew where you were going, then this wouldn't be nearly as exciting," Vivian smiled. "I'm the only one who knows for a reason."

I didn't understand her tactics, keeping his acceptance letters from him until tonight. Why did she need to let the suspense build? I thought I was about to pass out; I wanted to scream, "Just tell us already!" But of course I didn't. I remained still in the backseat, barely breathing.

When we arrived at the restaurant, we were escorted to a table in the corner with a little more privacy. Evan assisted in removing my jacket before taking off his own. My mouth crept into a big smile when he revealed what he was wearing.

Beneath his tailored suit jacket, he wore the Stanford T-shirt I'd given him for Christmas.

"I didn't want there to be any misunderstandings about my choice," Evan explained with a smirk when he saw me beaming.

"Very clever," Vivian stated in admiration with a shine in her eyes. "I'm not sure your father will appreciate your sense of style, but I adore it."

"Me too," I added, feeling a little more confident at the sight of him wearing the T-shirt, like he already belonged at Stanford.

Vivian insisted we order while we waited for Stuart. I selected the dish she recommended, knowing I wouldn't be eating much of it. I had a feeling that regardless of where Evan wanted to go and which college accepted him, his father was going to have the final say. After all, it was his money that was putting Evan through college.

And then we waited.

Vivian drove the conversation without pause, but she couldn't keep Evan from checking his watch every few minutes. I remained quiet, listening and nodding—glancing over as Evan's face became tighter with each minute that passed. By the time our entrées were cleared, with more left on the plates than eaten, Evan was straining every muscle in his body to remain composed.

Vivian excused herself from the table, taking her cell phone with her.

"He's not coming," Evan concluded dryly under his breath. "He wants to make it perfectly clear he doesn't approve and won't support my decision."

I wanted to say the right thing to make him feel better, but I didn't. His father had deserted him on one of the most important nights of his life. What was there to say? Instead, I held his hand as he gripped it firmly, allowing me just to be there for him.

Vivian returned and smiled tensely. "Well, it doesn't appear that your father will be able to make it. I apologize. So there's no use in delaying the suspense.

"Evan, you chose Stanford, and they also chose you. Congratulations." She tried to appear happy for him, but Stuart's refusal to attend had cursed the entire evening.

"Thank you," Evan accepted graciously, but his face still looked as though he'd bitten into something sour. I kept a worried eye upon him, feeling his hand tighten around mine.

I tried to smile as well, looking toward Vivian for reassurance—but I couldn't find any in her troubled eyes. Evan's choice to attend Stanford had divided their family, and that wasn't worthy of celebration.

I returned home that night deflated and confused. The one thing I wanted more than anything suddenly felt so selfish and wrong. And I wasn't sure how to make it right.

The house was dark when I entered. I flipped on the foyer lights and searched for signs that my mother had returned. Her car wasn't in the driveway. Her jacket wasn't in the closet.

I glanced at the clock and realized it was still early, so there wasn't any need to worry…yet. I went upstairs to change and brush my teeth before returning to the living room and curling up on the couch to wait for her.

My eyes blinked open, and I pulled my head off the pillow, listening. I squinted to make out the glowing time on the cable box. It was after three in the morning. I quickly swept the blankets off to peer out the window, finding my car the only occupant of the driveway. I ran up the stairs and opened her door. Her bed sheets were still crumpled after her halfhearted attempt to make her bed. She wasn't home.

I was trying not to panic, but I kept thinking of the night when Jonathan and I had to pick her up at the bar. What if something had happened to her? What if she'd tried to drive home? My heart pounded with each racing thought, flashing through all the horrific possibilities.

I paced the foyer, trying to decide what to do, then instinctively picked up my phone.

"Was it a shoe?" Jonathan teased on the other end.

"She's not home," I burst out. "It's after three in the morning, and she's not home yet. What if something happened to her? What if—"

"Emma!" Jonathan raised his voice to get my attention. "What are you talking about?"

"My mother," I explained, my voice edged with panic. "She's still not home, and I don't know what to do."

"Did you call her?"

It seemed so obvious a question. I closed my eyes and shook my head in embarrassment. "No."

"Call her and then call me back, okay?" he instructed calmly.

"Okay." I hung up and immediately called my mother's phone. I didn't know why I hadn't thought to do that originally. I guess the image of her in a ditch, bleeding to death on the side of the road, distracted me from thinking clearly.

The phone rang three times before someone picked it up. "Hello?"

"Hi, this is Emily," I answered, not recognizing the woman's voice. "I'm looking for Rachel."

"Oh," the woman croaked; obviously my call had woken her. "She's here, passed out."

"Um," I faltered, "where's *here*?"

"This is Sharon."

"Sorry," I blundered.

"Do you need to talk to her?"

"No, I'll see her in the morning." I hung up the phone and plopped down on the couch. I wanted to be relieved, and I was... mostly.

I called Jonathan back. "She's at Sharon's. Sorry that I freaked out like that. I should have called her first. I wasn't thinking straight."

"Don't worry about it," he assured me. "Are you going to be okay? Do you want me to come over or anything?"

I paused, not expecting the offer. "Uh, no. I'm just going to bed. I have school in the morning."

I did go to bed. But I didn't sleep.

27. LINES BLURRED

"Did you remember your bathing suit?"

"Huh?" I turned toward Sara, who was awaiting my answer with her shoulder against her locker. She'd caught me staring at nothing again. Thinking about my mother and wondering why I hadn't seen her this morning. I'd expected her to come home to get ready for work. Maybe she'd borrowed something from Sharon. From what I knew of Sharon, the choices must have been limited.

"You brought your bathing suit, right?" Sara repeated with her brows scrunched. "For Jill's party tonight."

"Yeah," I answered. "Are we staying at her place or going back to yours?"

"Not sure yet," she replied, walking next to me until we had to go our separate ways. "See you at lunch." I nodded and headed downstairs.

I felt like I was sleepwalking the entire day. Voices were incoherent murmurs. I jotted down notes without really understanding what the teacher was talking about. Everything around me went by in a blur, but I was moving in slow motion.

I expected Sara and Evan to say something, but they didn't. It struck me that perhaps they weren't surprised by my glazed stare and lack of contribution to their conversations. They always looked at me like they were worried, so today was apparently just like every other day. But it felt…off.

I wasn't sure I could explain it, but there was something that didn't feel right. I knew I was exhausted, not having slept more than a couple of hours, but it was more than that. There was a queasiness in the bottom of my stomach, like I had forgotten to turn off the iron or something—but much worse.

I drove to the soccer field after school. The rest of the soccer team hadn't arrived yet, since practice didn't start for forty-five minutes. I usually did homework and changed at school, but today I'd driven straight here. I reclined my seat and stared up at the clouds, waiting. I figured I'd change as the rest of the girls started to arrive.

My lids became heavier the longer I stared. I closed them, convinced I'd wake when the cars began pulling in.

> *"Do you have your cleats?"*
> *"Yup," I answered, picking them up by their laces.*
> *"Do you have your shin guards?"*
> *"Yup." I stuffed them under my arm.*
> *"Do you have your coach?"*
> *"Daaad." I laughed. "Stop being silly."*
> *"I just wanted to make sure you had everything," he teased. "Guess I'll be in charge of the soccer star." He scooped me up in his arms and tickled my belly, making me squirm and squeal in delight. Then he pulled me in to kiss me on the cheek.*
> *"We're going to win today," I told him, my voice proud and confident.*
> *"We're going to have fun today," he corrected, rubbing the top of my head as he carried me to the car.*
> *When we arrived at the soccer field, I raced ahead to join my friends while my dad unloaded the soccer balls out of the trunk.*
> *But as I got closer, the kids' laughter grew quiet, and the wind picked up. I squinted against the bright sun, spinning in a circle. Everyone was gone.*

"Dad?" I called out, searching for him. My hair whipped in my face. I clumsily pushed it out of my face, trying to see. "Dad!" I yelled, becoming more and more frightened. I spun around again, but I was alone. "Dad!" I screamed.

"Emma!" I opened my eyes and shot up in the seat, blinking around in surprise, disoriented by the sun setting behind the trees. There was a knock on my window.

"Emma, have you been in your car the entire time?" Casey asked from outside. She was sweaty, and her face was flushed. I opened my door and swung my feet onto the dirt parking lot, trying to catch my breath. "You missed the entire practice."

"I did?" I shook my head, trying to pull away from the dream completely. "I can't believe I did that."

"I hope Coach will let you play in the game on Sunday."

"Is he still here?" I asked, searching the almost empty lot.

"No," Casey replied. "I was about to leave when I saw your car. Are you okay? Are you sick or something?"

"No," I shook my head. "I got here early, and guess I dozed off. I still can't believe I slept that long. Wow."

"Are you going to Jill's tonight?"

"Yeah. I should get to Sara's. I'll see you there I guess."

"Okay," she replied with an unsure smile. "You'll be at practice tomorrow, right?"

"I will," I promised, hoping that missing practice hadn't jeopardized my starting position for Sunday.

The team was part of a traveling spring soccer league. It wasn't affiliated with the school district, and there were strict rules about missing practice—especially since we only practiced a few days a week. Coach wanted to make certain every player was serious about being there. He was more than willing to replace anyone who slacked. I needed this league to get into shape for Stanford, and I didn't want to jeopardize it by falling asleep in my car.

When I arrived at Sara's, I found her and Anna laughing in the kitchen. Sara was taking bites from a slice of red pepper that she'd plucked from a board where Anna was cutting up ingredients for a salad. I felt like I was intruding, and it struck me that I hadn't knocked. Maybe I was supposed to, now that I didn't live here.

"Emma," Sara exclaimed when she saw me. "Perfect timing. You can tell my mother that she is wrong about Kyle, and that he's not going to bring his college friends to this party tonight."

"Um," I began, trying to catch up. "No, Kyle's not like that."

"Oh, because he likes hanging out with high schoolers, even though he graduated last year," Anna replied with a smirk. "I'm sure he's going to bring some friends from Syracuse."

I shook my head when she said it, realizing who that could mean. "I hope not."

Sara started laughing, sensing my dread. "That could mean Drew. Em, that would suck so bad. I have to call Jill." She disappeared upstairs before I could say anything, even though her phone was in the front pocket of her jeans.

"It's great to see you, Emma," Anna said, mixing the contents of the salad in a bowl. "I feel like it's been awhile since you've been over. How is everything going with your mother? I just had lunch with her the other day. She seems so happy."

"Really?" I tried not to sound so surprised. "Everything's really...good."

"I'm glad to hear that. She and I talk a few times a week, so I get the updates on your busy schedule. But we've missed having you around."

Before I could react to her comment, the front door opened and Carl bellowed hello.

"Hi, Dad," Sara said as she came down the stairs. They appeared around the corner together.

"Emma, I'm glad you're here," Carl told me, setting down his briefcase. "How've you been?"

"Great," I replied automatically.

"I spoke with your Stanford coach today, and I have your housing information. I think we should look into booking a flight soon."

"Uh, yeah, sure," I replied, hit with the realization that graduation was only two months away. "I'm staying the night, so maybe we can do it tomorrow."

"Sounds good," he agreed. "I'm going to change before dinner." He kissed Anna on the cheek. "Do you need me to do anything?"

"No. Dinner's ready whenever you come down."

When Carl was out of earshot, Sara told us, "Jill said Kyle was bringing a few friends, but she wasn't sure who they were. But it's not going to be a crazy college party or anything, Mom."

"I just want you to be smart," Anna warned. "Call me if you need a ride home, okay?"

Sara smiled, her eyes twinkling, "Of course." I knew what she was thinking, that this party was just like any other—including the one we'd had here in their house, the one they still had no clue about.

We arrived early at Jill's, as promised. Jill needed our approval of her outfit—or I should say, *Sara's* approval. Casey was already there as well, along with…Analise.

I tried to keep smiling when I saw her, but I knew I'd failed when Sara elbowed me in the ribs. "I forgot she was coming," she whispered beside me. "I'd better not drink too much. I might get too honest."

I smirked, actually curious what Sara would say to Analise if she weren't filtered.

"But if she mentions Evan *once* tonight, I may not be able to hold back, sober or not."

"Sara—" I laughed. "He talked to her. It's been a little better the last couple of weeks."

"I suppose," she admitted with a sigh. "When's Evan getting here anyway? Who's he coming with?"

I pulled out my phone to check if he'd texted me. There was a missed call from an unfamiliar number, along with a new voice message. My stomach flipped. "I can't remember," I admitted, suddenly distracted.

"You're more out of it than usual today," she noted.

"I know." I sighed. I was about to make an excuse to go to the bathroom, so I could listen to the message, when I was interrupted by a scream.

Sara and I rushed into the room, where the scream was now followed by yelling. "You fuck!" Jill screamed. "I can't believe you spilled a drink on Dad's leather couch. The party hasn't even started yet, and you're already making a mess. Get out of here! Get out!"

The young guy with the bright red face and curly dark hair was trying to wipe up the mess with a piece of paper from the printer, which wasn't doing anything except spreading it around.

"Stop it," Jill scolded him, "you're making it worse. I'm pissed that you even have to be here at all."

Casey squeezed past us with a roll of paper towels.

Sara pursed her lips to keep from laughing. "Glad I'm an only child."

That's when I recognized the guy from a family picture hanging on the wall in the dining room. He was Jill's younger brother.

"How old is he?" I asked, walking away from the drama and into the kitchen.

"He's a freshman," Sara told me. "I guess he threatened to tell Jill's parents about the party unless he and a few of his friends could stay. She was so pissed. Don't you remember her telling us this at lunch?"

"Uh, no. Another blackout moment, sorry."

Sara scrunched her eyes. I knew she wanted to ask me if I was okay, but then she knew what my answer would be.

I looked at the clock and wondered what my mother was doing tonight. I'd texted her to say that I was staying over at Sara's, but she'd never responded. I still couldn't shake the feeling that something was wrong.

"I'll be right back," I told Sara. "I'm going to use the bathroom while I still can." She nodded, and I walked down the hall and into the floral-inspired bathroom.

I locked the door and pressed the code on my phone to listen to my message. It wasn't what I expected at all. "Hello, Emily. This is Vivian. I was hoping you were available for brunch on Sunday morning at eleven. I have someone I would very much like you to meet. You are welcome to call me back at this number. I look forward to hearing from you."

I removed the phone from my ear, completely taken by surprise.

Within an hour, the house was starting to fill with juniors and seniors, and the handpicked five or so freshmen who were friends with Jill's brother. Evan arrived with a couple of guys from the baseball team. When I saw their faces, I vaguely remembered him mentioning that he was coming with them.

I smiled at the sight of him cutting through the crowd. He was easy to spot, since he was taller than just about everyone, and I'm certain we were easy to locate, with Sara's fiery red hair standing out in the crowd.

"Hi," I said, glowing. He bent down and kissed me.

"So how's the party so far?" he asked, resting his hand on my back.

"It's actually pretty great," Sara intercepted before I could shrug it away as any other party. "Did you bring your swimsuit? Jill has a huge hot tub on her parents' deck that she's only allowing a few of us to use later."

"I didn't," Evan replied. "I may have shorts in my car though."

"That's great," a chipper voice said from beside us. I hadn't noticed Analise hovering until now. How long had she been standing there?

Sara squeezed my arm at the sight of her. I was beginning to get the impression that Analise got to Sara more than she got to me—if that were possible.

"Do you mean she told you about it, too?" Sara asked Analise, not hiding her detestation.

"Yeah," Analise replied, unperturbed. "She said it fits like twenty people or something. I guess Jill's parents have parties all of the time."

"That's what I heard," Sara nodded. Then she mumbled, "Let's hope they put extra chlorine in it."

I eyed her in confusion as Evan chuckled and said, "Nice, Sara. That's pretty gross."

I scrunched my face in disgust. Sara rolled her eyes at me for taking so long to understand what she was insinuating.

"Don't you dare try to get out of it," Sara threatened. "If I'm going in, so are you."

"Great," I groaned, completely disturbed by the thought of what potentially had gone on in the hot tub.

Kyle arrived with a keg and some guys from college. I moved away from the crowd of people rushing toward the free beer, so I had no idea who came in with him. I was pretty certain that if Drew were one of them, I'd know soon enough.

I tried to be sociable, truly I did. But I kept looking at my phone to see if my mother had called or texted me. I wanted to ask where she was or even *how* she was, but I was afraid it would seem like I was checking up on her. Well, I *was* checking up on her.

"Let's get our suits," Sara suggested, returning from refilling her glass with some red drink Jill had concocted.

"Where's Evan?" Sara asked as we made our way to Jill's room.

"Not sure," I answered. "He went to get a drink and then to look for his shorts, I think. I guess he'll find us."

Sara knocked on the door. "Who is it?"

"Jill, open the door. It's Sara and Emma."

The door opened cautiously, a pair of eyes peeking through the crack. Sara rolled her eyes and pushed the door open, making the girl behind it stumble backward. There were several girls in the room, adjusting their bathing suits and double-checking their appearance in the mirror. Sara grabbed her suit and began changing, not caring who saw her. I waited my turn for the bathroom. I had never been comfortable changing in front of anyone—even after years of being on sports teams and having girls change in front of me without a care. I usually had too much to think about, like where my bruises were and who would see them. Now I supposed it was just a habit that I couldn't quite break.

Before I left the bathroom, I examined my back one final time to make sure the striations were barely visible. There were only a few of them where the belt had cut deep enough to leave a scar, but they were still there—even after a year. I convinced myself it would be too dark to see them, and besides, I'd be in the water.

I emerged wearing a white bikini top with orange polka dots and shorts covering the striped bottoms. I secured my hair high on my head to keep it from getting wet and folded a towel over my arm.

I wanted to ask Sara if the marks were noticeable, but I didn't want to draw attention to them. Instead, I pulled a tank top on until we were in the dark. I followed as we were led out a sliding door onto a private deck. The deck wrapped around the back of the house, where the hot tub was letting off billows of steam into the cool April night. It had rained most of the day, so the wood was wet and cold under my feet. I didn't have the numbing power of alcohol to make me oblivious to the cold, like most of the girls.

There were already four or five people in the hot tub. I noticed Evan was one of them, and next to him was Analise. The predictability of that was nauseating. Worse than that, sitting next to her was Drew. I stopped abruptly. One of the giggling girls behind me bumped against my shoulder.

"Sorry," she said as she passed.

"Oh, shit," Sara breathed from beside me. "Where did he come from?"

Evan caught my eye and smiled, then saw my face and shrugged dismissively. If he could get over it, especially after having gotten into a fight with Drew last year, then I could too. The tightness in my stomach indicated otherwise. This could not get any more awkward.

I stripped off the shorts and tank top and slipped into the water. The heat of the water instantly warded off the goose bumps that had erupted while I was walking across the cold deck in my bikini.

I waded across to the other side and slid next to Evan. He draped his arm behind me. The water foamed and bubbled up over my chest as I sank into it, relaxed by its warmth.

"I like the suit," Evan leaned over to say into my ear. I grinned.

"That's right," I noted, "you've never seen me in a bathing suit before. This is actually the first time I've worn it." We'd gone to the beach a couple of times last summer, but I'd still been in a cast. I'd ended up wearing shorts and a tank top, since I couldn't go in the water.

"We'll definitely be going to the beach this summer." Evan smiled. I couldn't help but look past him at Analise, who was watching us, her eyes darting away quickly when I caught her. And I knew Drew was watching as well, with his elbows out over the sides and a beer in one hand.

"Hey, Emma," he said, raising his bottle in the air. I nodded with a small smile before looking away.

Sara was across from us, talking to Jill and Natalie. She called Analise over to join them. Analise couldn't refuse, and I knew Sara had done it on purpose. Thankfully a few more people entered and sat between Evan and Drew.

"I think I need to convince my parents to get a hot tub," Evan said, running his hand over the top of my thigh, causing me to inhale quickly, though no one noticed. They couldn't see under the water. "They can put it out by the pool that we never use."

"That's right, I've never actually seen your pool uncovered," I replied, taking hold of his hand, which was teasing the inside of my thigh. My face couldn't have been any redder, but that wasn't noticeable either in these conditions.

"Evan," I scolded under my breath, squeezing his hand.

"Sorry, it's the bikini." He defended himself with an amused grin. "It's too tempting." He leaned over and gave me a soft kiss, his wet lips sliding over mine. It was brief, but enough to incite a stutter in my chest. I almost forgot we weren't alone for that one second. Then I opened my eyes and saw Drew over Evan's shoulder and sat up a little straighter.

"Analise isn't watching you anymore after that," Sara said in a low voice. I hadn't noticed that she'd moved next to me. "You're making it steamy in here." She laughed and nudged my knee with hers.

"Did everyone see that?" I asked her, suddenly very aware of the number of people around us.

"No, just those who shouldn't have been watching."

I let Evan keep his hand on my knee, and I refrained from kissing him, despite how tempting it was as the moisture clung to the smooth, sharp lines of his face, down his straight nose and over his slightly parted lips. I had to keep reminding myself that we had an audience, even though the steam made it difficult to see across to the other side.

His thigh brushed against mine, and my breath faltered. He squeezed my knee, and I looked up at him. "This is torture," he said, leaning in closer. "Maybe we should get out of here. My parents aren't home."

My heart fluttered, and I smiled. "Really?"

"Really," he said, his breath tickling my lips. "Let's go."

"Okay," I said, biting my lip, wanting to lean in a little closer to taste the water running over his mouth.

"You go first. I'll meet you by the door." He leaned back, and I had to gather myself for a moment before turning toward Sara, who was talking to a girl on the other side of her.

"I'm going to leave with Evan," I informed her. "I'll text if I'm coming to your house, okay?"

"*If,*" she stressed with a knowing look. "Water too hot for you?"

"Something like that." I grinned widely, standing up and moving toward the steps. I couldn't look back because I knew my thoughts were transparent, and no one needed to see what I was thinking.

"Leaving?" Drew asked from behind me as I wrapped the towel around my chest, the heat from the hot tub evaporating into the cold, damp night.

"It's getting kind of crowded," I answered, barely giving him a glance.

"Did you get your sweater? I left it on your porch."

"Uh, yeah, thanks," I said vaguely, catching sight of Evan approaching behind him and hoping he hadn't overheard Drew.

Drew noticed Evan as well and said, "It was good seeing you again," before walking through the sliding glass door that led into Jill's parents' bedroom.

"See you in a little bit," I told Evan over my shoulder before heading toward Jill's room. I gathered my clothes and entered the bathroom, my heart beating so fast I was lightheaded. I tried to take calming breaths, but I was too nervously excited.

My phone fell out of my pocket when I picked up my jeans. The red light was flashing to indicate I had a message. I picked it up from the floor and slid my finger over the screen. The excitement drained away instantly when I saw the missed call and voice message from my mother.

I entered the code and listened to the recording. "Emily? Emily, you there?" Her words were slow and barely audible. "You with him? Fuckin'...You are." Then there was silence. She was a mess. My stomach flipped and my jaw tightened. I wasn't sure if I wanted to scream or cry. Instead, I took a breath and shut it off.

After I'd dressed, I went back out on to the deck to find Sara. "Are you going to stay here tonight?"

"I think so," Sara replied. "Why?"

"I was going to take my car," I explained. I had driven so that Sara could drink.

"No problem," she shrugged and then smiled. "Details."

I forced a smile, knowing there wouldn't be any details to share tonight.

I found Evan at the front door holding our jackets.

"Change of plans," I told him, more crushed than I could stand.

"What's wrong?" Evan questioned in concern.

"Umm, I'm not feeling all that great," I explained, my pulse quickening with my fabrication. "I think I'm going to head home instead."

Evan's eyes tightened in uncertainty. "What?"

"Uh," I faltered, recognizing he wasn't buying my illness. "I think I need to go to bed. Maybe the lack of sleep is getting to me."

"You were fine a couple minutes ago," he countered skeptically. "I don't understand. Did something happen?"

"No," I said, a little too adamantly. Evan arched his eyebrows. "I'm sorry. I'm tired. Okay?"

"No, it's not okay," Evan replied. "I know there's something going on. But if you're not going to tell me—"

"Evan, I swear, I just really need to go home," I explained softly, my eyes large and pleading.

Evan nodded, his lips pressed in a straight line.

"Talk to you tomorrow?" My stomach clenched as the disappointment resonated on his face.

"Text me before you go to sleep?" he requested, leaning down to barely brush my lips.

He stood at the door, watching me rush to my car. My stomach was nauseous with the lies I'd spewed, especially since I knew he'd seen right through them. I'd have to deal with that tomorrow.

I gripped the steering wheel tightly, now focused on finding my mother. I tried calling her, but it went to voice mail. I decided to start at home and then go from there. I didn't have Sharon's number, but maybe I could find it in my mother's room. I wasn't sure where else to look after that. Maybe Jonathan would know.

I didn't call him. It was eleven o'clock; it wasn't late. But I didn't want to involve him if I didn't have to. If I could fix this myself, then I would.

My thoughts continued to race, and my stomach churned with worry all the way to my house. When I saw her car in the driveway, I released an anxious breath. I pulled in behind her and noticed that the driver's door was still open and the front tire was on the lawn. When I got out of the car, I could hear chiming, indicating the key was still in the ignition. That's when I realized the engine was still running.

I looked around the car, confused. My heart pounded. I shut off the engine and closed the door. Then I spotted her, sprawled motionless on the top of the steps with her head and arms splayed on the porch. I rushed to help her.

She didn't have any shoes on, or a jacket for that matter. I knelt down beside her to see if she was hurt. Her knees were scraped and bloody from the fall, and there was a bump on the top of her forehead where it was pressed against the porch. I collided with her alcohol-saturated breath, wafting in the breeze within three feet of her.

"Mom." I sat on the top step and lifted her head up. "Mom, you need to get up." I tried to roll her so I could prop her up to sit. She groaned, but otherwise she wasn't moving. I leaned her into me in a seated position. "Mom. Rachel." I raised my voice to sound more commanding. "Wake up. Let's go. You need to go inside, then you can sleep all you want." I shook her shoulder, but nothing.

I tilted her head toward me. And she threw up. Before I could turn her away, the warm liquid was running down the front of me and soaking into my jeans.

"Shit!" I exclaimed, leaning her toward the side of the stairs as she heaved again. She didn't wake up, even after vomiting all over me, herself and the stairs. I looked down at the sour, potent mess. My throat tightened in disgust, and my stomach rolled.

There was no way I was going to be able to carry her. She was dead weight. I could've dragged her in, but then what? I couldn't leave her covered in puke in the foyer. It appeared I'd reached my last resort.

28. TO THE EXTREME

I sat on the steps and waited for him to arrive. I was tempted to unroll the hose to spray us and the stairs down before he got there, but I had no idea where it was. I was afraid to leave her alone long enough to change and get cleaned up, so I just waited.

I was trying so hard not to cry when he pulled into the driveway. I was frustrated, sad, even a little angry that I was in this predicament. Oh, yeah, and extremely humiliated—especially when I saw him emerge from his truck in a suit.

"Oh shit," I murmured when he neared. "You were out. You had plans. Jonathan, I am so sorry. I shouldn't have called you."

"Yes, you should have," he countered without hesitating. He took us in with his hands on his hips. My mother's tight dress was pushed up, revealing her underwear. Her knees were bloody, and her hair was matted with the vomit that was smeared across her cheeks and oozing down her chest. She was collapsed to the side, completely unmoving. At first sight, she appeared not to be even breathing, but I knew that she was because her breath reeked of alcohol and puke.

And then there was me. Slumped and broken, covered in dark-red vomit, like someone had just heaved their innards all over me. I couldn't move. The cold, slimy, vile substance made me cringe in disgust, sliding across my skin with the slightest movement.

"Bad night?" he observed with a shake of his head.

"Whatever gave you that idea?" I groaned sarcastically.

He took a deep breath and asked, "Is the door unlocked?"

"We didn't make it that far," I told him, handing him the house key. He crept carefully past us and placed his shiny dress shoes on the unscathed sections of wood. Opening the front door and flipping on the foyer lights, he disappeared into the house and re-emerged a moment later wearing a fitted T-shirt and the dress pants.

"Go ahead upstairs and get the shower ready for her." He looked me over and added, "And you."

I shuddered when I stood up, my wet jeans sliding along my thighs.

"Don't think about it," Jonathan instructed when I cringed.

I laid down a towel to kneel on and pulled the shower curtain out of the tub. Jonathan was a minute behind me, carrying my mother in his arms while trying to keep a distance between her and him. He wasn't successful. The dark-red vomit from her cheek smeared across his T-shirt as he laid her in the tub.

I grabbed a garbage bag for her clothes as we slid them off her. I should have been uncomfortable seeing my mother in her under-wear with Jonathan beside me, but I'd moved beyond that embarrassment. All I cared about was getting her cleaned up and into bed, so that I could do the same. We sprayed her down with the handheld shower, doing our best to wash her and rid her of the putrid smell.

Jonathan removed his shirt before he carried her to bed, not wanting to get the puke on her clean skin. I helped him rest her on her side, placing the bathroom's empty trash bucket below her. It wasn't like she would aim for it. She hadn't moved a mus-cle the entire time. She just breathed heavily and groaned every so often.

"Go ahead and clean yourself up," Jonathan said. "I'll stay with her in case she gets sick again."

Nodding silently, I went to my room to get clean clothes. I numbly removed my soiled items and dumped them in the garbage bag, tying it tightly to contain the sour odor. Then I lingered under the hot water, scouring the stench from my body. I didn't realize I was crying until I'd turned off the water and the hot tears kept streaming down my face.

I sat down in the tub, pulled my legs in to me and continued to cry into my folded arms.

"Emma?" Jonathan's voice called to me from outside the door, interrupting my tears. "Are you okay?"

"I'll be out in a minute," I replied, trying to sound as normal as possible. But I know I didn't.

After dressing and rinsing my face with cold water, I grabbed the trash bag and opened the door. Jonathan was sitting on the floor outside my mother's room, his back pressed against the wooden spindles that lined the top of the stairs. He wore the white dress shirt untucked over his dress pants.

I tried to smile, but it was no use. "Thank you," I said quietly, setting the trash bag on the top step to throw out—deeming its contents unsalvageable. "I'm really sorry for interrupting your night. Please don't tell me you were at a business dinner or"—even worse—"on a date."

Jonathan smiled warmly. "I told you to call me anytime you need me. And I meant it."

I sat down against the frame of my mother's door so I could see her and face Jonathan at the same time.

"What was this about?" he asked, motioning toward my mother with his thumb.

"I have no idea." I sighed. "She left me this weird message after she was already drunk, but I don't know what happened. Everything's been so great lately. We were talking more. I haven't seen her drink in a while, not even a glass of wine after work. She hasn't gone out, well…until last night.

"I just knew something was wrong today. I just knew it." I rubbed the palms of my hands over my eyes. "I don't know what to do anymore."

"You have to talk to her tomorrow. Find out what's going on. She can't keep doing this to you."

I nodded, not having the energy to think about what I was going to say. I'd hit a wall, and I was exhausted.

He observed my worn face. "You should get some sleep."

"I don't want her throwing up and choking in her sleep." I peered in at my mother, her mouth hanging open, the pillow damp under her wet, dark hair.

"I'll stay with her in her room," he stated. "I'll lie on her floor and keep an eye on her. I'm a light sleeper."

"You don't have to. I can do that."

"You look like you're about to fall over. I have a feeling that when you fall asleep, you wouldn't wake up for a tornado."

I knew he was right. I was so tired, I could barely stand up.

"Thank you again," I told him before shuffling to my room. I didn't bother closing my door, hoping I could help him if needed. I collapsed in my bed and fell asleep instantly.

"Emma." I could hear his voice. "Emma." The side of my bed caved in next to me. "Emma." He ran his cool finger along my cheek, brushing the hair from my face. "Emma, open your eyes."

I pushed them open and Jonathan was above me, sitting on the edge of my bed. "I'm going to leave." I glanced at the clock. It read a little past seven. "I don't think I should be here when she wakes up. She's going to have a pretty miserable day already. Call me later?"

"Okay," I grumbled into my pillow, my eyes barely open. I heard the stairs creak and the glass rattle when he closed the front door behind him. I shut my eyes and fell back to sleep.

I opened them again, what felt like a minute later, to the buzzing of my phone rattling on the table next to my bed. I put it to my ear.

"Where are you?" Casey demanded from the other end. I bolted upright and looked at the clock, which now read after ten. I was supposed to be at soccer practice. Panic flashed through me, and I whipped back the covers, prepared to rush to the fields, but they were a good half hour away.

"I'm sick," I lied, flopping back down on my pillow. "Sorry."

"That's why you left the party last night, right? That's what Evan said."

"Yeah," I replied, thankful that my lying to Evan was paying off, sort of. "I should have called, but I'm in bed." Which was technically true.

"I'll tell Coach," Casey said. "He's going to yell at me for being on the phone. I should go." Then she added quickly, "If you feel better, you should come to the game tomorrow. He may still play you."

I knew that was wishful thinking. Missing two practices in a row—I'd be lucky if I started next week, forget about playing tomorrow. I blew out the frustration with a heavy breath and stared at the ceiling. I'd never missed a commitment before, and the thought of disappointing my coach or teammates caused guilt to slither through me. I would go to the game tomorrow, supported by the lie that I'd been sick, and hope they wouldn't see right through me.

I might as well get up now, I thought, and rolled out of bed.

My mother's door was open. She was still asleep when I peeked in on her. The bucket next to her remained empty—which made me think of the porch. I cringed at the thought of what it was going to look like in the daylight.

I shoved my feet into a pair of old sneakers and went downstairs, noticing that the garbage bag was gone. I'd been prepared to toss it in the trash when I went outside. I dug around in the kitchen and found the acrylic pitchers used for the margaritas and filled them with hot soapy water. Then I braced myself and opened the front door—but there was nothing there.

I stepped out onto the porch to investigate further. There was no trace of the putrid mess other than wet, stained boards. I noticed the hose on the side of the garage—of course I'd found it now. Jonathan must have sprayed off the stairs before he left.

I didn't bother to return to bed, but curled up on the couch, pulling a blanket over me. My phone had a text from Evan and a missed call from Sara. I replied to both of them with a text promising to call them later. I wasn't sure I'd be a very convincing liar at that moment, and I needed time to decide what to tell them. But I wasn't ready to tell them the truth.

I returned Vivian's phone call, since it was time sensitive, and left her a voice message saying that I'd be happy to meet her for brunch in the morning. I could pull myself back together and be presentable by then...I hoped.

I closed my eyes and fell asleep. I was still so tired. I felt like I could sleep for three days straight.

The creaking stairs woke me. The room was bright, with the afternoon sun pouring in the windows. I squinted, trying to focus.

My mother had emerged, dressed in sweatpants and a T-shirt, stumbling down the stairs, her eyes slits and her hand holding her head. I sat up. She looked at me and held up her hand.

"Don't want to talk about it right now," she groaned, the anticipation evident on my face.

"Want me to get you something?"

"Aspirin, coffee and please cut my head off," she croaked.

I followed her into the kitchen and found the aspirin in the cabinet above the sink. I set two tablets in front of her with a glass of water while I started brewing the coffee. She rested her head on her folded arms on top of the kitchen table. She made careful movements to take the aspirin, grimacing when she swallowed them down.

I set a cup of coffee in front of her and sat across from her, waiting. She took a sip of the coffee and reluctantly looked my way.

"You want to talk about it, don't you?"

"I think we should," I replied, anxiously picking at my thumb. "Before you say anything, though, I have to ask you one thing."

"What's that?" The pain from her hangover was evident in her glassy, bloodshot eyes. She could barely open them.

"Don't ever drive again if you've been drinking," I told her. I meant it to be a request, but it came out harsher than I'd intended. She picked her head up at my tone. "If something had happened to you...or someone else..." I shook my head, unable to say it. My jaw tensed just thinking it.

"I won't," she whispered. "That was stupid. I shouldn't have driven home."

"You can always call me."

My mother let out a laugh that sounded more like a cough. "Not last night. I was so mad at you. There was no way I was going to ask you for anything."

I sat back in my chair, stunned by her words. "Why?"

"Don't pretend you're innocent," she accused, her eyes boring into me. "I hear you talking to him in the middle of the night. I saw the texts on your phone. Why are you still talking to Jonathan, like every day?"

She was *still* angry with me. It was evident in her glare. But the crack in her voice made it obvious that she was hurt too. I lowered my eyes, wringing my fingers under the table.

"I didn't mean to hurt you," I told her, not sure how to explain my friendship with Jonathan. "We just talk...that's all."

She shook her head. "Didn't you even think for one second how much that would hurt me? Emily, I was in love with him. I thought I'd finally found the person that would help me move on.

"I knew he was leaving, and all I wanted was the summer. I'd hoped by the end he'd consider asking me to go to California with him. Why wouldn't I want to move? He'd be there, and so would you. But..." She paused and pressed her fingers across her eyes.

"He was more concerned about *you* the night of my birthday," she continued in a low, shaky voice. "He didn't even care that I was upset too. You forgave me. I don't understand why he can't. So, don't you realize how much you hurt me by still talking to him? It's like you don't care about me." She sniffled and closed her eyes. My mouth hung open in silence. I felt like I'd been punched in the stomach and all of the air was forced out of me.

She stood with her coffee cup in her hand and walked out of the kitchen.

I'd never really thought about how my friendship with Jonathan would affect anyone around me. It wasn't like I was intentionally keeping that relationship a secret.

I sat in the empty kitchen, staring at the chair across from me, finally admitting that I *had* kept him a secret. And I'd refused to consider how it would make her feel if she found out. He was the only one who understood that dark part of me, and I could tell him things I couldn't tell anyone else. Selfishly, I didn't want to give him up.

I covered my face with my hands and breathed in. Guilt devoured my insides like acid. I felt like I was going to be sick.

"Are you kidding me?" she screamed from the top of the stairs. I rushed into the foyer to find her clutching his white T-shirt. "He was here last night? What the fuck, Emily?!"

"I couldn't carry you," I choked, my lower lip quivering. "I didn't know what else to do. I'm sorry."

"I can't believe you." She seethed, shaking her head, infuriated. "I can't believe you."

She turned her back to me. My heart beat erratically with the suffocating fear that I had finally made her not want me. I ran up the stairs and blurted desperately, "I won't talk to him anymore, I promise. But please don't be mad at me. I never meant to hurt you, I swear. I won't ever talk to him again, just don't be mad." I bit my lower lip, and my vision blurred with tears.

She stopped before entering the bathroom, absorbing my frantic pleas.

"It kills me to see you like you were last night. I don't want to do that to you. Please, don't be mad anymore, please?" My throat ached from holding back the tears. I swallowed hard and waited as she turned around.

Her eyes softened as she took in my tortured face. "Tell him you don't ever want to talk to him again, okay?"

"Okay," I sobbed, a tear rolling down my cheek as the pressure in my chest released. She walked in the bathroom and closed the door. I shut my eyes and took a deep breath, dreading what I was forced to do next.

29. FATHERLY ADVICE

There was no movement in the house when I left to meet Vivian on Sunday morning. My mother had pretty much been avoiding me, so I let her.

The guard at the gate checked me off the list, and I continued to drive farther down the road that split the golf course in half. I followed the signs to the clubhouse and parked in the lot outside a dark stone building with a wall of windows.

Vivian was in the lobby, talking to a group of women dressed for brunch. I was relieved I'd asked Evan what to wear when I spoke with him yesterday afternoon, because I would never have thought to wear a dress to brunch.

"Emily—" Vivian smiled brightly, reaching out with her arms to embrace me and kiss me on the cheek. "You look lovely, as always."

"Thank you," I replied, draping my jacket over my arm.

She addressed the women who lingered before her, "Ladies, this is Emily Thomas, Evan's girlfriend."

"Of course," one said with a smile. They each carefully looked me over, forming their own opinions of the girl from the headlines.

"Shall we?" Vivian prompted me. "It was so nice to see you all again." We walked past the ladies and into the dining room.

"Perfect timing," she whispered, "I was having difficulty continuing to be polite to that group of shallow human beings." I widened my eyes at her remark, and she grinned slyly. It was the first time I'd recognized Evan in her face. I smiled and followed her to a table by the large windows that overlooked the rolling green course.

"The woman I want to introduce you to is running a bit late," Vivian began after ordering a mimosa for herself and an orange juice for me. "So I thought this would give us time to talk about the other night."

My heart skipped a beat, fearing she was going to tell me that Evan wasn't going to Stanford.

"Stuart is very strong-willed. Evan shares the same spirit. So when they have opposing opinions, they will never reach a resolution. That's usually when Jared or I intervene, since we tend to be more open-minded and willing to compromise.

"Unfortunately, I'm not certain how to find common ground regarding this matter. Stanford is a marvelous school, and I am so proud of Evan for being accepted. However, Stuart has wanted one of his sons to attend Yale since they were born. Jared didn't quite have the grades to be accepted, despite Stuart's efforts. But Evan does.

"Evan is convinced that he didn't get accepted to Yale on his own merit, and Stuart won't admit whether he had any influence over the decision. But I do know that I've never seen Stuart so upset, and I'm trying to understand why."

"It's me." I said it so quietly that Vivian had to ask me to repeat myself. "Mr. Mathews doesn't approve of me, and Evan choosing Stanford is him choosing me over his father." I looked out the window, trying to calm the spasm in my chest.

"Why would you ever think that?" Vivian asked in complete bemusement.

"I overheard him telling Evan that I wasn't his future, the night of the New Year's Eve party," I admitted softly, the words still stinging.

Vivian was quiet. Her face was smooth, but her sharp blue eyes moved in contemplation.

"This is not about you," she said firmly. "This is between my husband and my son, and I'm so sorry that you were made to feel you had anything to do with it. Emily, I adore you, and I couldn't think of anything that would make me happier than for you to be my son's future.

"The only reason I was telling you this was to apologize for the tension the other night. I wish you hadn't had to witness my husband's silent defiance." She cupped my hands, which were clasped so tightly, my knuckles were white. "Please do not worry about this matter. I am quite certain it will work itself out."

"I want to promise you that I will never do anything to hurt Evan, and I will not come between him and his family. I love him, but I would walk away before I'd ever let anything jeopardize his happiness," I vowed passionately.

Vivian smiled adoringly. "I know, dear. That's why I wouldn't want him with anyone else." My heart swelled at her words, and I blinked away the sentiment with a smile. She laughed lightly at our emotional state, dabbing the corners of her eyes with a tissue.

"Oh, there she is." Vivian stood to greet her other guest.

A tall, slender woman with dark skin and big brown eyes approached us. She seemed so refined, in a light-blue dress with pearls strung around her neck. I stood with Vivian to be introduced.

"Emily Thomas, I am pleased for you to meet Dr. Michelle Vassar. She is an alumna of Stanford University, and was on their women's basketball team."

Dr. Vassar offered her hand. "Nice to meet you, Emily." I smiled and shook it firmly.

When we sat down, Vivian beamed and proceeded to gush about my acceptance by Stanford and my scholarship to play soccer for the university. I'd never had anyone so openly proud of me before, and at that moment I wouldn't have wanted it to be anyone other than Vivian Mathews.

After spending hours talking about Stanford, medical school and Dr. Vassar's professional experiences, I drove to the soccer field feeling lighter and more excited about my future than I had in months, replaying the entire conversation in my head.

I emerged from the bathroom dressed in my soccer gear and spotted Evan standing along the sidelines.

"Hi," I said, coming up behind him.

He spun around at the sound of my voice and his face lit up, making my heart falter. "Hi. How are you feeling?" I was relieved that he was over his skepticism regarding my feigned illness.

"Great! I had a really nice brunch with your mom."

"Good," he replied, pulling me toward him. I wrapped my arms around his chest and held him tight. He gave me a kiss and said, "Good luck in the game."

I grimaced. "Sorry, but I'm probably not playing today. You don't have to stay if you don't want to."

"I'll stay." His arms squeezed tighter around my waist. "Then we can do something after."

After benching me the first half of the game, Coach started me in the second half. I had a feeling it had more to do with us being down by one, and winning trumped upholding his policies. He announced that since I wasn't sick any longer, I could play. He conveniently didn't mention the two missed practices.

We came back in the second half and won by two. It was a good thing Evan had stayed after all.

"Do you want to follow me back to my house?" Evan asked. "Jared and Sara are there. They want to go bowling with us tonight."

"Bowling?" I questioned dubiously.

"Yeah," Evan chuckled in amusement. "You've never bowled before, have you?"

I shook my head, making him smile wider. "Yes, I'll follow you." I sighed.

"Emma"—Sara laughed—"you've already let go of the ball. You can't steer it down the lane like *that*."

I continued to lean to the right, hoping the ball would redirect itself and not veer so far left. My body movements didn't help. I only knocked down two pins.

"Sorry." I frowned. "I suck."

"It's your first time," Jared consoled me, trying to keep me positive. "We'll come back. Just try to keep your wrist straight so you don't spin the ball so much. Don't worry. Sara's not all that great either." He ducked away when Sara swatted at him.

It felt good to laugh. I hadn't done very much laughing lately.

After Evan had rolled a spare, Jared stood up and said, "I'll try to take it easy on you, Evan." Evan gave him a mocking smile. "Oh, are you coming to New York this weekend before you take off to Hawaii for April break?"

"I'm not sure," Evan told him, sitting next to me and draping his arm over the back of my orange plastic seat.

"You really can't come with me?" Evan asked me again while Jared selected the perfect ball.

"To Hawaii?" I laughed, like he'd just asked me to fly with him to the moon. "No way. I couldn't afford a trip like that. Besides I have to stay for soccer. It's the same reason I'm not going with Sara to the Keys."

"First of all, I told you, you wouldn't be paying for it. And secondly, you've already got into Stanford to play soccer. You can miss a week." He begged one more time, "Please, come with me."

I smiled, and before I could allow myself to even consider it, I said, "Sorry, I can't."

"I've tried, Evan," Sara interjected. "Believe me, I've tried. I think she's trying to soak in as much time in Weslyn as she can before you're off to Stanford."

"Yeah, right," I shot back with a horrified face that made her laugh. "I can't get out of Weslyn fast enough."

"Speaking of which," Jared chimed in after he'd motioned for us to admire his strike, which was flashing on the screen above our heads, "when are we going to officially celebrate your admission into Stanford? Both of you, actually."

"Graduation?" I suggested. I wouldn't be convinced I was going until I walked down the aisle with the diploma in my hand.

Evan considered this. "That's actually a great idea. We can have a huge graduation party in my backyard."

"Yes!" Sara exclaimed before rolling the ball down the lane.

"And your dad will go for that?" I questioned skeptically, knowing that he and Evan weren't exactly on speaking terms—kind of like me and my mother, but for extremely different reasons.

"Who cares?" Evan shrugged. "What's he going to do?"

Jared laughed. He widened his eyes, like he knew exactly what their father was capable of. Evan didn't seem fazed. But I couldn't help but shrink a few inches in my chair.

"Should I be worried about Evan and his father?" I asked Sara when I was driving her back to her house.

"Are you looking for insider information because Evan's making it seem like it's not a big deal?"

"Well, yeah," I answered uncomfortably. "Has Jared said anything?"

Sara was quiet, deliberating on what to say. She always got fidgety whenever she had to tell me something I didn't want to hear.

"Just say it, Sara," I demanded flatly.

"I promised Jared I wouldn't, so you have to swear that you won't mention it to Evan, no matter what." I just stared at her impatiently. "Fine. Mr. Mathews has threatened to cut Evan off if

he goes to Stanford. He said he could freeze his accounts, take away
his passport and even his car."

"Over choosing Stanford?" I struggled to get the words out.

"You know it has nothing to do with Stanford."

"Yeah," I breathed. "I do. I can't let this happen."

"It's not your decision to make, Emma," Sara warned. "It's Evan's."

30. UNEXPECTED FUTURE

My mother couldn't stay silent for long. It was against her nature. So whether she'd truly forgiven me or not, she was talking to me like she had.

"I may be a little late tonight," she informed me, rushing around as she tended to do most mornings before work. "Do you have practice today?"

"No, not today," I told her from my spectator position, on the couch with a bowl of cereal.

"Do you think you could cook dinner?" She paused and looked to me. "Or…maybe order out? I don't think I'll be out of the meeting in time."

I smiled and said, "I may go to Evan's for dinner."

"Great. I'll feel better knowing you're eating something that's not microwaved. But I won't be late, okay?"

"Okay." She'd been letting me know her schedule for the past couple of days. I was pretty sure it was her indirect way of apologizing for making me worry about her last Thursday night when she'd passed out at Sharon's without calling me.

She rushed out the door with a lightweight jacket over her arm.

This week had taken a pleasant rise in temperature. They were forecasting near eighty by Friday, which was unheard of in early April in Connecticut. I wasn't complaining.

With the increase in temperature and only eight weeks to go until permanent freedom, the seniors were having a hard time concentrating. Class was more chatty and the halls were bouncing with energy.

"Want to skip last class?" Sara proposed during lunch.

"I can't," I moped. "I have a paper due."

"What are you doing after school? You should come over."

"I don't think I'll have time. I have to get some laundry done before I have nothing to wear, and then I'm going to Evan's for dinner."

"This weekend then. I'm not leaving for Florida until Monday, so you can spend the weekend with me. Do you have a game?"

"On Saturday," I told her. "Yeah, I think we need some girl time."

Sara smiled. "Yes we do! I'm feeling a little disconnected from you lately, so we have some catching up to do."

"Agreed."

I'd decided even before this conversation that I needed to fill Sara in on everything that was happening with my mother. I didn't have Jonathan to talk to any longer, and Sara was my best friend. She was *supposed* to know these things. Now that we had actual time set aside for us, I somehow felt...better. Sara would know what I should do. Or at least have a very candid opinion on the situation.

With a promise of seeing Evan at his house after baseball practice, I drove home with my windows down. Spring was starting to stretch its arms, and I welcomed it after a frigid and snowy winter. The early spring flowers were in bloom, and the trees were in varied stages of budding or flowering, which meant in a few weeks they'd be filled with green leaves.

I knew this warm and sunny weather was a fluke in early April—they were already predicting cooler temperatures and rain by the end of the weekend. But today the heat from the sun felt good blowing against my face as I drove home.

There was a man standing on my doorstep when I pulled into the driveway. First impression—from his dark suit and briefcase—was that he was a salesman. He even wore a fedora on his head. But when I stepped out of the car, I realized his tailored suit was much too nice to belong to a door-to-door salesman. Besides, I didn't think anyone did that anymore.

"Can I help you?" I questioned as I approached him.

"Are you Emily Thomas?" the tall man asked, removing his hat to reveal thick white hair, brushed back to expose a receding hairline.

"Yes," I answered cautiously, still standing on the walkway, hesitant to get closer.

"My name is Charles Stanley," he explained. He stood erect on the porch, his perfect posture making him appear to tower a mile above me. "I'm the lawyer for the Thomas family. I am your father's executor."

"My father?" I questioned, unable to move.

"Yes, Derek Thomas," he answered patiently. "Is there somewhere private we can talk? Do you expect Rachel home anytime soon?"

"No, she's working late today," I told him, ungluing my feet and tentatively walking toward the door. "Do you have a card or something?"

"Of course," he replied, pulling out a silver cardholder from his pocket. He opened it and extended a card to me, confirming who he was. I didn't have any real reason to doubt him.

I unlocked the door and held the screen door open for him. "We can sit in the kitchen."

"Wonderful." He followed me into the kitchen and set his hat on the table. I kept my eyes on him, fearing that if I blinked he was going to disappear.

"Can I get you something to drink?"

"No, I'm fine. Thank you," he replied, sitting in the chair and unbuckling his briefcase to remove a file. I lowered myself into the chair across from him, my hands shaking slightly. "I'm sure you're wondering who I am and what I'm doing here, so let's begin. As I said, my name is Charles Stanley. I have represented the Thomas family most of my career, focusing mainly on estate matters and preparing their trusts and other financial concerns."

"I'm sorry," I interrupted, already confused. "You keep saying 'the family.' I don't understand. Who does that include?"

Charles nodded and began again. "Your father gave me permission for full disclosure, so I may reveal to you everything I know that pertains to him. Derek Anders Thomas was born to Laura and Nicolas Thomas. They lived in Lincoln, Massachusetts most of his life. His brother George Samuel Thomas was born three years later.

"Derek attended private schools through high school and went on to Cornell, where he studied architectural engineering and eventually graduated with a master's."

"Cornell?" I questioned in surprise, wondering why I'd never known this.

"Yes," Charles replied calmly, his smooth, deep voice devoid of emotion. Then he continued, "He decided to return to Massachusetts to be near his family, and took a position with the top engineering firm in Boston. This was where he met Rachel Walace." He paused. I swore I saw sympathy flash across his dark blue eyes for a moment before he returned to his emotionless report.

"She was a temporary replacement for their receptionist, who was on leave for a short time. From this point forward, the facts that can easily be researched are combined with your father's firsthand account and his own opinions. So unfortunately, I cannot substantiate much of what I'm about to tell you.

"Derek was under the impression that Rachel was older than she was when they first met. She indicated that she was twenty-six, and he at that time was thirty-two. They went out on several occasions, and he really enjoyed her company. She was different from most of the women in his social circle, and he described her as a 'breath of fresh air.'"

My insides were already chilled, because I knew how old my mother had been when I was born.

"In time, he discovered her true age to be twenty and broke off the relationship immediately. Your father believed in integrity and trust above all else, and she'd lied to him. She was distraught over the breakup, and made multiple attempts to regain his favor. Just when he thought she'd given up, she appeared by his car after work with the news that she was pregnant."

I exhaled and closed my eyes, my stomach turning to ice. I hadn't been planned. They weren't married. They weren't even technically *dating*.

"Are you okay, Emma?" Charles asked. "Can I get you a glass of water?"

"I'll get it," I said in a rush, pushing myself out of the seat. I needed a break from the story, from the truth of how I'd come into this world. It was so different than I'd ever imagined. I returned with a glass of water, and after taking a small sip, I said, "Go ahead. I'm ready."

"Derek agreed to restart their relationship, and to be there for you when you were born. Months later, he bought a house in Lincoln, where you were raised for seven years. Rachel chose not to live there after Derek's death; the house was not rightfully hers and became a part of his estate. Which brings me to why I am here today."

"Wait," I interrupted frantically. "Did they ever get married? Did he love her? What about his parents? Are they still in Lincoln?"

"I'm sorry. I am certain you have more questions than I am capable of answering. No, Rachel and Derek never married. He did care for her, and he was convinced that she loved him. But he admitted to me that he did not trust her. She was young and irresponsible, tending to be a bit excessive in her social habits."

I grimaced with a disgruntled shake of my head, knowing he was politely saying that she'd been a drunk even back then. This was how she'd always been. It wasn't a symptom of grief, a way for her to cope. It was as much a part of her as the lies she'd led me to believe all of these years. The lies that included a fairy-tale romance, a marriage that didn't exist and a love destroyed by a senseless accident. And where did I fit into her delusions?

My throat was tight. My insides were hollow. I thought my head might explode from all the conflicting emotions coursing through me.

"Your grandparents moved to Florida before you were born. They, your grandmother in particular, did not approve of having a child out of wedlock, so they disconnected themselves from Derek and Rachel, and therefore from you. Apparently your grandfather did not feel as strongly, and when he passed fifteen years ago he left a sizable inheritance to each of his sons—despite Laura's wishes.

"That inheritance is the foundation of your father's estate." He opened the folder and began displaying sheets with numbers and charts in front of me. I was too overwhelmed to understand them. They became a blur of ink before my eyes.

"What is this?" I choked, my hands trembling in my lap.

"This, Emma, is your future," he explained smoothly. "Your father invested wisely, and with his earnings at the firm, the sale of the house in Lincoln and his life insurance policy, on top of what he had inherited from your grandfather, his estate is quite impressive. All of these assets become legally yours when you turn eighteen in June.

"I decided not to wait until then to speak to you, since you have financial obligations with Stanford that need to be addressed more immediately. Congratulations on your acceptance."

"Uh, thank you," I replied automatically, staring at the figure at the bottom of the page—several commas floating before my eyes. "So this is mine? I can afford to go to college?"

"My dear girl, you can afford college, medical school and you'd still be able to open a clinic in Africa if you wanted." I looked up at his wrinkled face, and for the first time his lips gave a hint of a smile.

"I still don't understand," I uttered. "George never claimed to have money. I mean, I lived with them for years."

"George." Charles said it as if the name itself were an enigma. "George's choices were never made clear to me. All I know is that he was provided with an inheritance similar to your father's. What he chose to do with it, or to divulge to his wife, is not something I know anything about." He paused. His grave expression pierced me. "I can never express to you how sorry I am for what happened to you while you were in their house." My eyes stung with tears. I blinked hard to ward them off. "No one should ever have to go through what you were subjected to.

"But your father would be proud of the person you have become, Emma. You are strong and intelligent, and the fact that you are here trying to make amends with Rachel means you have a good heart. He would be *very* proud."

I nodded, swallowing against my closing throat. I averted my gaze, not wanting to cry in front of this man.

"You will continue to receive your monthly allowances, and they will increase once you turn eighteen. You will not have full control of your funds until after you graduate from college, or when you turn twenty-one. However, if you need anything, you may contact me at anytime, and I will make the proper arrangements for you, whether it is a computer, or a car, or an emergency situation. Your father has entrusted me to use my best judgment in assisting you."

"Thank you," I whispered, still not processing half of what he'd just said.

"Emma—" He beckoned. I looked up at the aged face that remained impassive despite the intensity flickering in his eyes. "You may call me *anytime*, for *any* reason. Please understand that. I know you do not know me now. But I hope to gain the same trust and respect that I earned from your father. In the meantime, I wouldn't advise alerting Rachel of this visit, or your inheritance."

"He never trusted her, did he?"

"No," Charles answered flatly. "He loved you more than anything, and wanted you to have both parents in your life. But he did not trust her with his finances, or with you."

"What?" I questioned with raised brows. "What do you mean, *with me*?"

"He hired a woman to care for you when he was at work. Concerned about Rachel's impulsiveness, he didn't want you left alone with her. Unfortunately, we weren't able to secure an alternative custody agreement, in case of his death, before the accident. He was trying to find a way around the legal rights of a birth mother so that you could be raised by someone who was better suited to care for and love you.

"In the meantime, we set up a portion of his estate to go to Rachel, along with the monthly allowances to care for you, which then became accessible to George and Carol when they took custody of you.

"This was never supposed to be your life, Emma. He wanted so much more for you, and I believe he would be happy to know that you will finally get it."

But I'd trade it all, every penny, to have him back, I wanted to say. I had a hard time raising my eyes to meet his, still too vulnerable with emotion.

We sat in silence for a moment before Charles picked up each paper and placed it in the folder. He handed it to me. I shook my head. "I think you should keep it. I don't want her to find it."

Charles nodded in agreement and inserted the folder into his case. "Then you should program my number into your phone and not keep my card."

I took out my phone and saved his number under the initials "CS."

"It was a pleasure to finally meet you, Emma," Charles said, standing and pushing the kitchen chair back into the table. "Do you have any other questions before I leave?"

"No," I answered quietly, my mind spinning with more thoughts than I could process.

"Please call me if you do."

I walked him to the door. He turned to me and placed his hat on his head. "Take care of yourself." He walked out the door before I could respond. I watched him as he continued down the walkway to the large, shiny black car awaiting him on the street. I shouldn't have been surprised when a driver stepped out and opened the back door for him.

I was still staring at the empty space when my phone vibrated in my pocket. I pulled it out and answered it.

"We're getting out of practice early," Evan announced excitedly. The lightness in his voice was a shock to my ears. I felt as if I'd just sailed through a hurricane. "Do you want to meet me at my house in an hour?"

I realized I hadn't even started the laundry. "An hour. Um…sure."

I hung up the phone and mindlessly went into the basement, sorting through the clothes to make sure I washed something to wear the next day.

Then I went to my room and sat on my bed, still in a daze. I eyed the drawing on my dresser that Leyla and Jack had sent me, and went to pick it up. As much as I missed them, I kept thoughts of them at bay so I wouldn't be tortured by my choices.

I inspected the woman in the picture. The one with the grey hair. My grandmother.

This family would never be mine.

And then it hit me.

I buckled over like I'd been punched in the stomach and slumped to the floor. I still couldn't comprehend everything that had just happened, but one truth slammed into me with such force I couldn't catch my breath.

I was never supposed to exist.

31. WHAT IF

I still hadn't completely pulled myself back together by the time I arrived at Evan's. He was sitting on the front porch swing, reading a textbook, when I pulled in.

"Hi," I said, sitting next to him, intoxicated by him immediately. It was obvious from his wet hair that he'd just taken a shower. "What are you reading?"

"Nothing interesting," Evan replied, closing the book and setting it on the porch below the swing. He lifted his arm, and I nuzzled in under it, resting my head on his chest, breathing him in. "I like this week."

I knew he was talking about the weather, and the fact that we were sitting outside in short sleeves in April, but my thoughts were somewhere else when I inadvertently laughed in contradiction.

"What, you don't?" he questioned, peering down at me.

"Oh, sorry." I shook my head, realizing he'd heard me. "Yeah, it's nice out."

"What were you thinking about?" Evan asked, knowing me too well.

I sat up to face him. My head was spinning, and I wasn't sure if I could verbalize what I was still trying to grasp myself, but I thought I'd give it a try. It took me a minute to open my mouth, but he waited patiently, watching my eyes flicker in thought.

"Not to sound too deep, but I've been considering how just one little thing can drastically affect so many different things. Cause and effect. Choices and consequences. Is there a reason behind it, or is it just chance? Randomness. Like one person bumping into another person. They date, have sex and the next thing you know—a baby's born. Whether that baby was supposed to be or not. Whether they loved each other or not. It happened. But...what if it was never *supposed* to happen?"

Evan was silent for a moment. "Where is this coming from?"

"I found something out this afternoon, and I'm not sure I'm ready to talk about it just yet."

"Do you want to go for a walk as we contemplate the meaning of life? Or we don't have to talk at all. We can just walk. But I have to insist on holding your hand—that's not an option."

"Okay," I answered, trying to smile so I wouldn't come across as so depressingly serious. "I'd like it if you held my hand too."

Evan led me around the back of the house, and we followed the cut section of the field that was his backyard toward the woods. We walked in silence for a while, letting the birds and the rustling of the breeze through the evergreens be the only sound. But my mind was not quiet, and it refused to remain calm.

"Will you do something with me?" I asked, mesmerized by our feet as they moved in unison.

"Uh...sure," he responded hesitantly.

"Let's consider *what if*. But don't read too much into it; it's just hypothetical."

"I can do *what if*," Evan agreed, taking my request seriously.

"What if...what if I didn't exist? As in, I had never been born."

"Em," Evan stopped me, pulling his brows together.

"It's hypothetical, remember? I'm not suicidal or anything, I promise," I assured him in a rush.

"Okay, fine," he conceded with a breath. "*What if* you had never existed? I think you've already considered this, so why don't you tell me."

"If I'd never existed, then my father would still be alive." I kept my eyes on the ground, because just saying that one statement out loud sent a shiver through my body and made my eyes tear up.

"If I'd never existed, then Leyla and Jack would have both of their parents." I struggled to keep my voice even.

"If I'd never existed, then my mother might actually be happy."

Evan stopped. We had reached the end of the path, right before it opened up into the meadow.

"And what about me?" he asked, his eyes steady and focused, trying to read my thoughts.

"Well, you and your father would be talking," I answered with false playfulness, trying to return it to the hypothetical game that I'd initially suggested.

Evan chuckled. "That is probably unlikely. We'd find some reason to argue...or not talk."

We were quiet as we walked through the meadow. It was starting to transition into the spring green that made it breathtaking. The brook was brimming from the recent rain. It rushed with force over the stones.

Evan sat down and I nestled next to him, facing the water.

"My turn?" Evan requested. "I'd like to challenge your what-ifs."

"Go for it."

"You don't know what would have happened to your father if he were still alive. I have a feeling he wouldn't have been half as happy as he was when he was with you. I saw the way he looked in that picture you have on your dresser; his whole face was completely alive just looking at you. You made him happy, and I would hate to have been the one to take that away from him, even if he couldn't have it forever." I smiled affectionately with my eyes glistening and leaned my head against Evan's shoulder as he held my hand.

"And unfortunately for Leyla and Jack, Carol would still have been the same whether you were there or not. You certainly didn't make her the way she is, and I can't talk about her more than that." I glanced up and noticed that his neck was tense, just thinking about her. I squeezed his hand in understanding.

"As far as your mother's concerned, I'm not sure I understand enough about her misery to be able to rebut your what-if. If you mean that your father would still be alive, and that would be what made her happy—perhaps. But she's harboring a lot more than just sadness. That was evident the night of her birthday. As I said, I don't understand what's wrong with her, but I'm very doubtful that it has anything to do with you." I didn't have the strength to convince him otherwise—but I knew I was critical to her misery.

"And I would absolutely not be the same person if you had never existed." I lifted my head and remained still with anticipation. "We can contemplate the meaning of your life all you want, but know that you're my meaning…the reason behind just about everything I do—and I would never want to change that." A smile stretched across my face, and a warm current rushed through my body. My chest swelled with love. I leaned up and kissed him gently.

"What about your father?" I prompted when I pulled away.

Evan produced a wry smile and said, "You don't have to worry about me and my father. My mother will never let him take Stanford, or *you*, away from me. He raised me to be the person I am today, so now he just has to let go and allow me be that person. This decision is mine, and he will have to learn to live with it." Evan's voice was strong but calm, not filled with the resentment or frustration I imagined he'd express when speaking of his father. I admired his maturity and restraint.

"So," he asked with a grin, "Do you feel better about existing?"

"Yes." I answered emphatically with a coy roll of my eyes. "You have a way of making a girl feel...significant."

"Good." Evan smiled and leaned over to kiss me. His words calmed me, and lulled the storm in my head to a hum. I was still troubled by everything I'd learned earlier in the day, but I knew here with Evan was where I belonged.

I spread out on my back, resting my head on his leg and closing my eyes to absorb the sun. "I like it here."

"Me too," Evan replied, playing with my hair. "The sun looks good on you."

I continued to lie on his lap, listening to the rush of the water beside us. The sun's warmth brushing against my face and his gentle touch made my skin hum with a delicate shiver. I wish I could've captured that moment and kept it safe in my pocket to experience whenever I wanted.

"I was told once that a girl needs time to prepare. So, Emma Thomas, would you like to go to prom with me?"

I sat up and gawked at him, my mouth open in a shocked smile. "It's...omigod, it's next month, isn't it?" He nodded. "Yes, Evan Mathews. I would *love* to go to prom with you." Then I muttered in dread, "Oh, no. That means I have to get a dress, doesn't it?"

"Or you could go nude. I hear that's the new pink." Evan smirked. I laughed.

"You would love that, wouldn't you?" I teased. "Oh, wait. Promise we won't have sex on prom night." Evan's eyes widened. "We can't be the couple who has sex on prom night." The thought of it made me cringe. That was absolutely *not* how I wanted to remember our first time. It was a bad movie in the making.

"We won't have sex on prom night," Evan promised, pursing his lips to keep from smiling. "How about the night before?"

"What? Really?" I studied his face, and he raised his eyebrows to indicate he was actually proposing the idea. "Are you serious about *planning* it?"

"Why not? The spontaneous thing isn't working out too well for us. We might as well set a date."

"Then, yes, I will have sex with you the night before prom," I vowed, sounding comically serious. "It's a sex date."

Evan laughed. "Can't wait." He leaned in and captured my breath with the touch of his lips.

When I arrived home, Rachel was just getting out of her car. It felt strange to call her that, *Rachel.* I let the word repeat in my head. That's what she'd wanted me to call her all along. And that's how Charles had referred to her. When he spoke of my parents, he said 'your father' and 'Rachel.' He never once called her my mother. I don't think that was an accident.

"How was dinner?" she asked, waiting for me before entering the house.

"It was nice," I replied. "Exactly what I needed."

"Good," she responded, looking a little confused by my answer.

"Did you eat?" We flipped on the lights in the foyer and the living room.

"We ordered takeout at the office."

She kicked off her heels and pulled her blouse out of her dress pants. I watched to see if she'd get a glass of wine from the kitchen like she usually did, but she didn't. Instead, she sat next to me on the couch and flipped on the television.

The whirlwind of thoughts in my head overtook me, and the next thing I knew I was asking, "Where are you from?" I kept my eyes on the channels as they flashed before me.

"What?" she asked, still continuing through the programs, obviously not expecting my question.

I had the opportunity to take it back, to not pry any further. But I decided I wanted to know. "Where did you grow up?"

She stopped, landing on a fishing program. I knew she hadn't meant to do that, so she must have heard me this time. I turned toward her, and she was looking at me like she didn't know me. I was prepared for her not to respond.

"Um, in a small farm town in Pennsylvania," she said slowly. "Why'd you want to know?"

"I guess because I never did," I explained bluntly. "Do your parents still live there?"

She was quiet. She looked from me to the television and back again—like she was trying to decide if she wanted to have this conversation. She obviously wasn't prepared for the questions, and maybe the shock of them was why she *did* answer. "My mother may, but I don't really know. I moved away with some friends when I was seventeen and never looked back. Never knew my father. He was a drunk and took off before I could remember him."

"How come I don't know any of this?" I questioned curiously. I wasn't completely surprised by the knowledge of her broken home life. It couldn't have been that happy if she'd never wanted to talk about it, or visit.

"I don't like living in the past. What's the point?" She redirected her gaze and began changing the channels again.

I found her words ironic, especially since she hadn't figured out how to move past my father's death. Or maybe she had, and his death was an excuse to be miserable. She didn't seem to be making any effort to be happy, except maybe with Jonathan—but even then, she had sabotaged it with her drunken tantrums. Perhaps she preferred wallowing in eternal sadness. I didn't understand why she wanted to live like that.

"Why don't you ever try to talk to me about what happened when I was with Carol and George?"

Rachel's shoulders pulled back; she was struck hard by my question. I realized I'd reached my limit, but I didn't hold back.

"Why was I there to begin with? Why did you leave me with them?" For years, this question had destroyed me; I always thought it was me—that I had been too much for her to handle. It's what had motivated me to be perfect, never to be a burden again. Perfection still left scars.

So now I just wanted to know the truth.

"I didn't leave you," she whispered. Her answer left me speechless. Before I could utter a sound, she stood up and walked out of the room. I watched as she went into the kitchen and gripped the refrigerator handle. She stayed like that for a moment, battling with the decision to open it or not.

I waited. She let the handle go with a shake of her head, appearing distraught and frazzled.

"I don't know why you want to talk about this," she said from the doorway, her voice shaky. "Why would you want to bring up things that have already happened? We can't change them, so let's just let them go, okay?"

I inspected her light-blue eyes as they darted around the room nervously, and I nodded.

"I'm going to take a bath." She disappeared up the stairs.

I had always been too afraid to question her. I wasn't sure where the courage had come from, but I was pretty certain Charles Stanley's visit had a lot to do with it.

I was prepared for her to be angry with me, and even yell. But that hadn't happened. Instead, she seemed nervous and uncomfortable. And maybe even a little…guilty.

32. IN THE WOODS

I didn't sleep that night, nor was I expecting to. I kept flipping my phone over in my hand, wanting to call Jonathan. I needed him to distract me with absurd conversations about a botched sci-fi movie, or the pillow that cured athlete's foot. It was hard not to call, to hear his voice waiting for me on the other end. But I had promised I wouldn't, so I didn't.

I heard Rachel's door open, followed by the pipes thumping into action for the shower. I viewed the clock and recognized that she was up early, which probably meant she wanted to be out of the house before I woke up. She was avoiding me again. Maybe I hadn't been the only one who couldn't sleep last night.

I waited to hear the front door close before getting out of bed. While in the shower, I considered apologizing to Rachel just so that she'd stop evading me. Or perhaps it would blow over by the time I returned from practice tonight, or maybe time away at Sara's would help. Or maybe I didn't care.

That last thought was unexpected.

I didn't know where it had come from. It didn't feel like me. But at the same time, it felt more honest than I'd been with myself for a long time.

I dressed in a fitted grey T-shirt and jeans, and opted for the pink checked Converses that I'd only dared to wear a few times. They drew attention, and I didn't usually want that. It was supposed to be nearly eighty degrees today, which was unheard of in Connecticut in April. I decided to grab my zipped sweatshirt just in case the morning air was still cool.

I hated the weather teasing with summerlike conditions, knowing it would only return to the rainy and cool norms within a day or two. It was torture to think summer and graduation were *that* close, yet still two months away.

I grabbed my backpack and soccer bag before heading out the door. As I walked toward my car, a black motorcycle came into view. I stood by my car as the bike pulled into the driveway and coasted to a stop beside me.

The rider had on a black T-shirt and jeans with a pair of black leather boots. His head was covered with a helmet reminiscent of a combat helmet—not much protection, if you asked me. The mirrored glasses covering his eyes reflected my dumbfounded stare. Then he smiled, and the creases around his mouth rocked me back slightly.

"Jonathan?"

"Good morning," he replied after shutting off the engine. "How are you?"

"Uh, fine," I answered, flustered. "What are you doing here? I thought we weren't talking to each other; that we decided it was the best thing to do."

"Not really," he countered, taking off his glasses. "*Rachel* decided we shouldn't talk, and she's not here right now. I don't think it's the best thing at all, do you?"

I was stunned by his defiance and continued to stare at him, not knowing what to think, forget about what to say.

"Let's do something," Jonathan demanded boldly, not at all a request.

I laughed. "I have to go to school, and shouldn't you be at work?"

"This is not the kind of day when you should be at school. And no, *I* should be right here," he stated. "Come on, Emma. You've already been accepted by Stanford. One skipped day of school isn't going to change that."

"I don't know," I hesitated, inspecting the shiny black Harley with chrome detailing—determining whether I was willing to even get on the bike, forget about ditching school.

"You agreed we would do *something*, so let's do it. Stop thinking so much and get on the bike, Emma." His directive was bold; he wasn't willing to hear another excuse. He slid on his glasses and jumped on the starter, revving the motorcycle to life. The deep guttural engine roared, calling for the road with a twist of his wrist.

I took a deep breath…and stopped thinking. I opened my car door and tossed my bags inside, grabbing my sunglasses and sliding on my sweatshirt. When I turned around, Jonathan was holding out a black helmet with a crooked smile.

I fastened the straps under my chin, then slid my sunglasses into place. He kicked up the stand, and I flipped my leg over the back. The leather seat slid us close together; the front of my thighs pressed against the back of his. I grabbed hold of his waist and closed my eyes in anticipation.

My brain might have been turned off, but my heart raced with adrenaline. I knew it would've been overloaded with panic if I'd taken a moment to think about the many ways this was not a good idea—particularly the gruesome death that was a possibility if he took one wrong turn. Maybe there was a benefit to not thinking.

Jonathan slowly backed the motorcycle up and then walked it forward to turn us around before accelerating down the driveway and out of the neighborhood. That's when the thoughts broke through, and I wondered what the hell I was doing. Skipping school to hop on the back of a motorcycle with my mother's ex-boyfriend and taking off to who knows where *definitely* was not a good idea. But before I could allow the voice of reason to penetrate too deep, I shut it off again. Instead I watched Weslyn slip away and closed my eyes to feel the wind whip against my face as the engine roared between my legs. I let the adrenaline rush through me and decided just to go with it, regardless of the consequences.

I had no idea where Jonathan was taking us. I never even considered what his *something* could be before the impulsiveness had hijacked me. We ended up on the highway at some point and continued west, deeper into Connecticut, until we entered New York.

We exited the highway and followed winding roads lined with woods. The houses were set deep within forested driveways, each marked with a mailbox on the road. We slowed enough for me to attempt to talk, or holler, "Where are we going?"

"There's something I want to share with you," he turned his head to the side to yell in return.

A few more twisting roads later, we slowed practically to a crawl. Jonathan veered down a road that barely resembled one. The tire-worn dirt tracks were filled in with weeds and splotches of grass. He weaved along the drive and pulled up in front of the skeletal remains of a house.

I took in the plot curiously, unfastening the helmet as Jonathan shut off the engine and kicked the stand into place. I dismounted, and my legs shook slightly from the long ride.

A fire had devoured the entire structure, leaving only remnants behind. A tall stone chimney remained erect among leaning beams and ash. On the far side of the house, a section of crossbeams stood defiantly, despite its black, scarred outer skin. It connected to what appeared to have been a porch. The stone foundation outlined the modest home, but the interior was unrecognizable, since it had been completely incinerated.

"Jonathan, why are we here?" I asked, turning around. But he wasn't looking at me. He was staring at the charred remains.

I had an ill feeling in my gut. I didn't like this place. There was something about the way the blackened structure was set in the shadows of the woods that made it appear haunted, like there was a dark tale to be told if you listened carefully.

"What are you afraid of, Emma?"

"What?" I practically jumped, convinced he'd read my thoughts.

"What is it that keeps you up at night? What is the source of all of your nightmares? What are you afraid of?"

The ill feeling in the pit of my stomach spread, and I didn't want to be there anymore. This was the place where bad things happened and nightmares took root. I shivered with the realization of where we were.

"This was your house, wasn't it?" I asked, barely audible, disturbed by the distant gleam in his eye. He continued to scan every inch of the ruins like he was putting it back together in his head. "What happened here?"

"I thought I would feel different. More afraid, I guess." Jonathan contemplated out loud, not really talking to me. "It's so much worse in my dreams. Fire's coming out of every window. Smoke blacking out the stars. And I can't get close because it's so hot; it feels like my skin will melt off." He walked closer, holding out his hand like he could feel the flames.

I watched as his nightmare unfolded in front of him. He wasn't here with me. He was in the presence of his past—reliving it again. I was too stunned to save him.

Jonathan crouched in front of the stone steps and reached out tentatively, prepared to pull back if they were hot. He ran his hand across the bumpy surface and shook his head.

"I just sat in the woods and watched. Watched it all burn away. But the screams…their screams all sound the same."

"What?" I questioned in shock, my chest tightening with his words. "Did someone die in the fire?" Then I remembered. "Your father. This is how he died."

"So did my mother and younger brother," Jonathan murmured, sitting on the bottom step and running his hands through his hair.

I cautiously walked toward him and sat next to him on the cool stone. "Did he set the fire?" Jonathan shook his head.

"Is this why you brought me here? To show me your nightmare—the one you keep having over and over again?"

"Actually, this was for me," Jonathan admitted, glancing at me. "I thought we should face our fears together. Especially since we're both leaving soon. Then we can officially start over, without our fears following us.

"But I'm not afraid. In truth, I'm angry." He clenched his fists and pressed them against his thighs. "That man took everything away from me the night of this fire, and there's nothing I can do about it. He's dead, and so are they." Jonathan's face was hard, his eyes cold and distant. Then he bent forward, covering his face with his hands.

I barely heard him say, "They shouldn't have been in the house. This shouldn't have happened to them. I keep hearing their screams over and over again. Reminding me I couldn't save them."

"It's not your fault," I soothed softly. "You didn't do this to them. Maybe that's what you have to do. Forgive yourself."

Jonathan lifted his head, a line creasing his brow. "Forgive myself." He repeated it like the words were unfamiliar to him. He took a breath, pushing away the distance in his eyes, returning to me. "I bet you're wishing you hadn't skipped school right about now, huh?" He grinned faintly, trying to rescue us from his nightmare.

"Let's get out of here and do something much more interesting. My fear doesn't exist here." Jonathan turned toward me, delving into me the way he always did. "Okay, Emma. What are you afraid of?"

"Oh no." I shook my head firmly. "We don't need to conquer my fear today. I'm sure there's another way to spend our day." He continued to wait until I finally buckled. "Fine. I'm afraid of heights."

"Done. But I know this has nothing to do with your nightmares, so don't think you're getting out of it that easily," Jonathan warned, standing up and walking toward the motorcycle. I remained on the steps, unmoving—not sure I was ready to follow him to my fear. *Knowing* I wasn't. I took a breath and pushed myself off the stone, conceding, as I always seemed to do when I was with him.

I climbed on the back of the bike and watched Jonathan's past disappear behind us, swallowed up by the surrounding trees as we drove away. Then I gripped him tightly and hid my face against his back, trying to prepare to face my fear. Which was not at all possible.

We didn't have to go very far to confront my fear. Within twenty minutes, Jonathan pulled off the road into a gravel inlet that could easily be missed.

"Where are we?" I asked, taking off my helmet and sweatshirt, starting to register the eighty-degree heat that had been promised.

"You'll see." Jonathan grinned slyly. I followed him as he led us along a path into the woods. Soon the rush of water reverberated through the trees, and I caught a glimpse of rapids twisting over rocks before dipping out of sight.

The air was a little cooler within the shadows of the trees as we followed the turbulent water that continued to evade full view. It sounded like it was running beneath our feet. And pretty soon, it was.

Jonathan stopped on a flat ledge that opened up in front of us. About twenty feet below was a pool of water, capturing a small cascade pouring into it from a little farther up. The path continued down to the water's edge, where a cluster of boulders rested in the water.

"This is a favorite swimming spot in the summer," Jonathan explained, and I could easily picture it—sitting on the smooth surface of the boulders to soak in the sun and cooling off in the clear water. I peered over the edge without getting too close, my pulse thrumming through my body. Angled slabs of rock lined the bottom of the crystal pool.

"Ready?" Jonathan asked from behind me.

I whipped around. "What? Ready for what?" Fear captured my breath; I knew what he was expecting.

"Do you want to keep your jeans on? They may weigh you down. But I would keep your sneakers on because the water can hurt from this height if you hit wrong."

"You're not serious," I challenged, my words coming out in a rush. "You can't be serious."

"I have a knife if you want to cut your jeans into shorts," he continued casually, ignoring my panic attack.

"No, no, no, no, no," I cried, moving to get off the ledge, but Jonathan stepped in front of me, blocking the way. "What are you doing?" I gawked at him with wide eyes, my heart beating so hard it actually hurt.

"Jump, Emma," he commanded, his voice stern but not threatening.

"No way," I practically yelled. "This is so high, and the water's not that deep. You can't make me do this. I won't do it."

"It's actually very deep, I promise you," he continued in his even, assertive tone. "Emma, you're either going to jump, or I'm going to push you." He stepped closer, making me back up toward the edge.

I searched for another way off the ledge, but it wasn't wide enough for me to get past him. "Please don't make me do this."

"Emma, jump or I'm going to push you," he repeated a little more firmly. He remained emotionless and calm, but from the intensity in his eyes, I knew he was serious. I wasn't leaving this ledge without going in the water.

I turned away from him and focused on breathing, since I wasn't breathing at all.

Breathing in, then out—in, then out. My chest moved up and down. In, then out. I swallowed hard and let my eyes fall over the edge to the water below.

Jonathan remained silent behind me. I didn't look at him.

I inched closer until I was about a foot from the edge. Becoming dizzy, I quickly looked up. I focused on the trees along the cliff on the other side of the water and grounded myself again. I closed my eyes and my heartbeat pulsed through my head. My breathing quickened, and my stomach rolled with nerves, and then a shot of adrenaline streaked through me.

Before the adrenaline could slip away, I took the step and leapt—just as I felt his hand press against my back. My stomach opened up, becoming hollow as the air rushed by me and my head buzzed with fear and excitement. A second later my feet slammed into the water, and I was consumed by the frigidity.

I kicked to the surface and expelled the small amount of air in my lungs, my chest frozen from the shock of the water. My muscles tightened as I gasped for air. I focused on swimming to the boulders. My jeans were heavy and slowed my progress. A spray of water hit me from behind with a loud splash.

I knew it was Jonathan, but I was too focused on getting out of the icy water to look back. I clambered up on a small rock and then over to a bigger one, my jeans sliding down a bit as I crawled into the sun, shivering uncontrollably.

I wrapped my arms around my chest, trying to control the convulsive tremors—waiting for the sun to warm me up.

Jonathan emerged from the water and pulled himself on to the rock next to me. I didn't acknowledge him, tucking my head into my arms. My muscles began to ache from shaking so hard.

"Whoa, that's frickin' cold." I glanced over at him and realized he'd stripped down to a pair of black boxer briefs. I darted my eyes toward the water, my cheeks warming quickly. He didn't look as miserable as I did with his legs out in front of him, propped up with his arms behind him. "The sun feels good though."

I eased my legs out and realized my jeans were the reason I was so cold, keeping the water pressed against my skin. "Can I borrow your knife?" I requested.

Jonathan narrowed his eyes. "Why? You going to stab me with it for making you jump?"

I smiled deviously, allowing him to think I was contemplating it. Then I laughed lightly. "No."

"It's up with my jeans," he nodded. He didn't show any inclination to get up, so I stood and faltered my way back to the ledge, my heels catching on my sopping wet jeans with each step.

I picked up his jeans and found the black-handled knife in the front pocket. I unfolded the blade and it snapped into place. I pulled the fabric from my skin and carefully stuck the tip through to make a hole, then began sawing around my thigh, letting the jeans leg fall to my feet. I instantly felt better as the warm air soothed the goose bumps.

I crouched to slide the knife back into his jeans pocket, and my eyes drifted toward Jonathan, lying on the boulder with his hands behind his head and his eyes closed, absorbing the sun. He appeared completely at peace. The muscles along his broad chest were relaxed, but the definition of his body was still evident, pressed against the stone. I quickly looked away and found myself inadvertently staring back over the ledge, at the water below.

I waited for the panic to set in. But it didn't. My heart beat harder, but it was adrenaline, not fear, that pumped through my veins. And it felt exhilarating.

I didn't give myself time to think before I leapt and braced for the cold that I knew awaited me. The thrill of the fall caught my breath before I was swallowed up by the heart-stopping water.

I let the adrenaline course through my body with a smile as I kicked toward the rocks—which was much easier in shorts. I picked a dry boulder and eased myself up, the warmth radiating through the hard surface and into my legs. I removed my shoes and socks and set them next to me.

I noticed Jonathan watching me with a comical grin.

"What?" I demanded impatiently.

"You're not afraid of heights."

"I know. You cured me, right?" My voice was heavy with sarcasm.

"Emma, your fear was never of heights." I scrunched my eyes, not following. "What were you thinking when you were looking down at the water? What was going through your head?"

"That there was no way I was going to jump."

Jonathan chuckled. "Besides that."

"That I was going to—" I stopped. He saw it in my eyes as the unspoken words caused my heart to falter.

"Emma, what are you afraid of?" Jonathan asked again, studying my face.

"I'm afraid of dying," I breathed. Hearing it out loud made my chest hurt and my eyes sting with tears. I blinked them away. Jonathan pressed his lips together and bowed his head.

The falls crashing into the pool in the distance filled the silence. Neither of us said a word. We both knew where this fear stemmed from, and I wasn't convinced there was anything that could be done about it. *She* was never going to let me feel safe again, even if she couldn't reach out and kill me.

33. CONSEQUENCES

Would you like a cherry on that?" the girl asked in a low, flirtatious voice.

"No, that's okay," Jonathan answered, not fazed by her ogling.

I stifled a laugh as I sat on top of the picnic table with my feet on the bench, watching the entire transaction. Jonathan returned with the two sundaes in his hands, and I could hear giggling behind him. Two of the girls working the ice cream stand couldn't keep their eyes off him, whispering and laughing as he walked away.

"You have a fan club," I teased, taking the sundae he offered to me. "They must recognize you from The Ads."

"Funny," Jonathan retorted with a sideways glance as he sat on the bench beside me.

"Or maybe they think you wet yourself," I laughed, nodding toward his jeans, where the wetness from his boxers seeped through.

He smirked. "That's probably it. You know you're going to leave a wet ass mark on the table when you get up, right?"

I leaned to the side to reveal the dark wood mark under my damp jeans. "Oh well."

"What time do you have practice today?" Jonathan asked before spooning in a mouthful of ice cream.

"Three thirty," I told him after pulling the spoon out of my mouth.

"We'll head back after this."

It was the first time I'd thought about returning to Weslyn, and a swell of nerves enveloped me. I should've at least texted Evan before I left. My phone was in my car, so that wasn't possible now.

"Are you worried?" he asked, reading my tense expression.

"I'll have some explaining to do," I sighed.

"To Rachel? She won't even be home."

"No. To Evan," I explained glumly. "He's probably been freaking out all day since I didn't show up at school."

"Oh," Jonathan pursed his lips and nodded. "What are you going to say?"

"I don't know." I shrugged. "The truth, I guess."

"And he'll be okay with that? That you spent the day with me?" Jonathan appeared shocked.

"Why wouldn't he be?" I responded, not at all concerned. "He trusts me, and it's not like you and I have a history or anything. I mean, we're…friends."

"Yeah," Jonathan smirked. "You're right. I guess I probably wouldn't be as okay with it if I were him. But I don't trust very easily either."

His last sentence echoed through my head, and it all suddenly became clear. "You have a hard time getting close to people, don't you?"

"Yeah," Jonathan answered, contemplating my question, "I suppose I do. No one really gets me, and I guess I'm afraid—" He froze. I waited for him to say it, knowing it was on the tip of his tongue. His eyes slowly hardened, and his jaw tightened. He wasn't going to say it.

Jonathan stood up and tossed his sundae in the trash before striding toward the motorcycle parked on the far end of the lot.

"Jonathan!" I called after him, but he didn't slow down. I threw my ice cream away and ran after him. "Jonathan!"

I caught up with him and grabbed his arm. "Jonathan, stop."

"We should get you back so you're not late," he said dryly.

"Look at me," I coaxed, still holding his arm as he kept his back to me. "Come on, please."

He took a deep breath and turned toward me, his eyes on the ground.

"You can tell me," I said, but Jonathan remained silent. "Jonathan, what is it? What are you afraid of?"

"You *know* what I'm afraid of," he countered defensively.

"Did you?" I questioned him. "I mean before now, did you know that's what it was?"

Jonathan raised his eyes to meet mine. They were soft again, but edged with pain. He shook his head. I realized my hand was still on his arm, and I slid it down to his hand and squeezed it gently. He looked down at the gesture and smiled faintly before I let go.

Instead of stopping at the bike like I thought he would, he continued to the wooden fence that lined the parking lot and leaned against the top beam.

"It makes sense," he murmured, resting his hands on the wood on either side of him. "I mean, I haven't been in a real relationship since Sadie, not until Rachel—and that wasn't supposed to happen the way it did. I mean, it was never supposed to be a relationship. That's probably why we couldn't stay together after she told me she loved me. I couldn't do it."

"You didn't love her?"

He shook his head, lowering his eyes.

"What happened with Sadie?" I inquired cautiously.

Jonathan didn't raise his head. "I proposed to her toward the end of our junior year at Penn State."

My heart skipped a beat, not expecting this revelation. "She said no?" I probed when he stalled for a moment.

"She said yes." His dark eyes rose to find mine. The sadness in them captured my breath. "Two weeks later, I walked in on her and another guy."

I didn't know what to say. But it was all making sense; this was the reason he couldn't get close to anyone, and for his need for a simple and predictable life. He feared loving someone and being hurt again. It explained the impenetrable confident facade that kept him at a distance.

"I'd lost my mother and brother. Sadie was the only one who knew how much it destroyed me. And after what she did to me...I never let anyone else in. I've never trusted anyone to get that close. Well, except..." Then he looked at me, and my cheeks reddened. "I mean, it's different," he corrected himself quickly. "You and I have this weird connection, it's not like..." He didn't finish.

"Of course," I said, nodding in understanding. "We get each other. That's all."

"Right," he agreed with a crooked smile. "Well, it looks like we *are* pretty pathetic, after all. We've spent a gorgeous day dwelling on unconquerable fears. You're never going to want to do something with me again."

"Sure I will," I laughed. "As long as you don't try to cure me again."

"Done." He smiled in return. "Wait. Will the school call Rachel about where you were today? I don't want to make things worse for you with her. I know how she can be."

"I can handle her," I told him. "She's kind of avoiding me right now anyway."

"Why do you put up with it? I have to be honest, I don't really understand your relationship."

"Neither do I," I answered truthfully.

"Emma, has she ever said anything nice to you, you know, like she's proud of you, or that she loves you for that matter?"

"I don't want to talk about her," I muttered, picking up the helmet. I was still confounded by all that I'd learned in the past twenty-four hours, and I preferred not to think about her until I had to. "We should get going so I'm not late for practice."

Jonathan nodded and picked up his helmet.

The closer we got to Weslyn, the harder it was to push away the questions that my mother had left unanswered. I still didn't understand what she meant when she'd said she didn't leave me with Carol and George. I was always told, and thought I remembered, that she shoved all of my things in a black garbage bag and dropped me off on their doorstep in the middle of the night. If she didn't do it, who did? And why didn't she come back for me?

That triggered Jonathan's question—had she ever told me she loved me? It should've been easy enough to remember, being told I was loved, especially by my own mother. Mothers told their kids how much they loved them all the time. Even Carol would gush over Leyla and Jack with affection, letting them know they were loved.

I may have had a hard time recalling my childhood, but I always knew my father loved me. I never doubted that for a second of my life. But did my mother?

By the time we arrived on Decatur Street, I couldn't think of anything else. Thoughts of who my mother was in my life and why I was trying to build any sort of relationship with her swirled in my head. I knew my efforts were driven by guilt. I didn't understand why she was set on trying.

Jonathan slowed drastically right before the house, causing me to look up. Rachel's car was in the driveway. My chest spasmed in panic.

Jonathan pulled to the sidewalk and stopped for me to climb off. "I'm so sorry, Emma," he offered as I took off my helmet. "Do you want me to come in with you?"

"No," I replied, hoping she wasn't looking in our direction. "That will just make it worse. You should go."

"Are you sure?"

I nodded.

"Call me if you need *anything*, okay?"

"I told you, I can handle her," I stated calmly, despite the churning that was devouring my insides. I wasn't sure what was going to happen, but I'd soon find out. I stepped back and watched him pull away. Then I took a deep breath and walked toward the house.

Rachel was sitting on a chair on the porch, and when I got closer, she stood and accosted me.

"Where have you been?! Who was that on the bike? Why didn't you call us? Do you have any idea what we've been going through all day?!" Her voice was elevated, and her hands were on her hips.

I slowly climbed the steps and gathered myself to try to explain, hoping she'd understand why I'd needed to get away for the day. I clasped my hands in front of me and looked from the boards up to her reddened face and opened my mouth to speak...

Her eyes grew wide, and her mouth dropped open. "Omigod, you were with him! That was Jonathan, wasn't it? I was right. There is something going on, isn't there? How could you do this to me?! Do you even care about me?!"

I pulled my brows together in disbelief. I took long, deep breaths to control the fire erupting inside of me.

"It's none of your business where I've been all day, or who I was with," I snapped, causing her to pull her head back in shock.

"What are you talking about?" she countered. "Of course it's my business. I'm your mother."

"No you're not," I scoffed, feeling the tendons along my neck tighten. "You never have been. Don't think you can be now."

"Why are you talking to me like this? What did he say to you?"

"This has nothing to do with Jonathan. This is about you. It's always been about you—what you want, how you feel, who you want to be with. Have you ever once thought about me and what I'm going through? Do *you* care?"

Rachel's mouth opened in shock.

"Do you ever consider what I go through every time you drink too much, or disappear to a bar to come home whenever you want with whoever you want?"

She stumbled back at my attack. The angry fire spread through my veins, consuming me. I remained unaffected by the stunned look on her face or the tears forming in her eyes. My voice grew louder. I was blinded with fury, and I couldn't have held back even if I'd tried.

"You've never thought about anyone other than yourself my entire life! Do you even love me? You probably never wanted me. That's why you left me with *them*. Do you have any idea what she did to me? Do you ever think about it? That would mean you'd actually have to stop thinking of yourself for one minute!"

I took a step toward her, and she shrank beneath me. The fear in her eyes fueled my rage. My hands shook as I clenched my teeth. I was unable to reel my anger back in.

My entire body was engulfed in flames when I yelled, "I don't understand why I'm here! You're not a mother, you never have been! I don't need you!

"Besides, you're too consumed with my father's death to care about anyone else. Why do you keep obsessing over a man who never loved you?"

The sound was loud, and the sting was hot on my cheek. My head rocked to the side with the force of her hand. I slowly lifted my head and stared at her, snapped out of my spiraling rage. Tears streamed down her face, and she looked like she was about to collapse.

My entire body trembled. I hadn't realized I'd been crying, but the corners of my eyes were raw from the flow of tears.

"Emma?" I heard behind me and spun around. Evan was coming up the walkway. "What's going on?" He looked more distraught than I'd anticipated. As he got closer and saw the red mark on my face and our stunned expressions, the worry turned to anger. "What happened? Did you hit her?" He glared at Rachel, who was still too shocked to speak.

I wiped my cheeks and faltered down the steps. "I have to go."

"What?" he questioned me in disbelief. "Emma, where have you been all day? Why didn't you call me? What just happened here?"

"I didn't have my phone, and I'm so sorry." My voice was shaky, the repercussions of my brutality starting to settle in. "I have to get to practice."

"Really? You don't look like you should be driving anywhere. You need to talk to me."

I stopped and took a breath. My eyes pleaded for him to understand. "I will, I promise, but I can't right now. I have to go. Don't you have a game?"

"Yeah, but—"

"Evan, go to your game. I can't explain right now. I'm going to be late for practice." My hands shook uncontrollably. I glanced up at the porch, but she was gone. "I'm staying at Sara's this weekend. Come over tonight, okay?"

I started to walk away, but he rushed up and blocked my path. "I can't let you leave like this. What happened?"

"We got into an argument," I explained, swallowing hard to keep the guilt at bay. I didn't want to think about it. If I did I might crumple right there on the driveway. "Please. Please, let me go to practice. You can follow me there if you don't trust me."

His eyes narrowed. "What?" he questioned angrily. "Emma, this has nothing to do with trust. I was *worried* about you. You've been more withdrawn lately, and yesterday you started questioning whether you should exist or not. I was afraid that something had happened to you today. That you..." He couldn't finish. The pain on his face captured his words.

I bit my quivering lip and closed my eyes. "I am so sorry," I muttered softly. "I can't believe I did this to you. I just needed to get away for the day, to figure things out. I should have called you. I'm so, so sorry, Evan." I wanted nothing more than to touch him, to wrap my arms around him and hold him against me. But I was afraid to reach for him, because it would've destroyed me if he'd pulled away.

"Okay," he mumbled, nodding, not making any move toward me. "Okay," he repeated, looking me in the eye, nodding again, like he was trying to accept my words and figure out what to do next. "Go to practice. I'll see you at Sara's tonight." He turned around and strode toward his car without another word, and without touching me.

I continued to my car, shutting everything off. I couldn't think. I couldn't feel. I just needed to get away from this, and I knew practice would distract me long enough to calm me down.

I backed out of the driveway before Evan was in his car. I glanced at the rearview mirror to see him standing by his door, watching me drive away.

I swiped at the tears and wrapped my fingers tightly around the steering wheel. This was my fault. This was all my fault. And now I had two hours to figure out how to fix it.

34. CONFESSIONS

Emma, what the hell is going on?!" Sara demanded fervently from the other end of the phone. "What happened to you today?"

I sat in my car coated in sweat, having pushed myself to the extreme during practice to distract and punish myself. I'd emerged prepared to make amends.

"I know, I was completely stupid today," I responded with a heavy breath. "And now everyone's angry with me. I just got out of practice, and I'll be over after I pick up clothes for the weekend. I promise I'll tell you everything, okay?"

"Yes, you will," she stated firmly, letting me know that she expected the extended version of the story. "I'll see you in a little while then."

I hung up and found a text waiting from Jonathan: You okay?

I have some major damage to fix, I answered.

I pulled out of the lot and headed to the house, not sure whether Rachel would be home or not. I wanted to prepare myself either way, unsettled by the thought of both scenarios.

My phone beeped while I was driving. I glanced over at it to find, It was my fault. I can try to explain if you want. I am really so sorry Emma. Mad?

When I pulled in to the driveway, I responded with, I knew what I was doing, not your fault. Not mad, but need time to make things better. Talk soon.

Just as I was about to open the door, my phone chimed again. My heartbeat picked up when I placed the phone to my ear. "Hi."

"Hi," Evan said, so quietly I could barely hear him.

"I'm at the house picking up clothes for the weekend. I'll be at Sara's soon," I told him, my voice soft and cautious.

"I don't think I'm going to Sara's."

My heart twisted, and I closed my eyes.

"Why?" I breathed.

"I think I need time away too," he explained in a quiet, even tone. My eyes filled. "Emma, I know you haven't been honest with me." A lump lodged in my throat. "I don't understand what's going on and why you can't tell me, but I know that you've been having problems with your mother. I knew when she called in the middle of the night at Sara's, and I saw how upset she was with you over that sweater. I saw what she did to you the night of her birthday, and I knew she was the reason you left Jill's party. And now this."

My breath shook as I listened to him, his insight crushing me.

"Emma, you're not letting me in…again. I can't…If I'm part of your life, then you can't keep shutting me out."

We were silent for a moment. Guilt strangled me, and I choked on every word that attempted to surface.

"I'll be back next Saturday. We'll talk then."

"Evan," I implored. But there wasn't anyone on the other end. I swallowed my tears and clamped my mouth shut to keep the hurt trapped. I couldn't contemplate an entire week without talking to him—and I still didn't know how to explain my motives.

I got out of the car and dragged my body to the house. Anything Rachel said to me now could never be as painful as Evan's silence.

I reflected on how this day had begun with promises of the summer to come. The warmth still lingered, and there was even the scent of a fire pit in the air. It was unfortunate that the most gorgeous day of the year had become the darkest.

The front door was unlocked, and the lights were off. The gold hues of twilight filtered through the windows and cast shadows along the floor. I walked to the stairs, deciding time might be what we all needed, and that I'd just get my things without seeking Rachel out.

"I tried," she murmured from within the living room. I turned toward her voice, and hesitated. "I really tried to like you. I wanted to."

I took a step closer, recognizing the signature slur. I was too broken to be wounded by her words, but decided I needed to hear them anyway.

Light from the front window spread along the floor to the coffee table, leaving the couch in the dark. Rachel lay on her side, supporting her head on the arm of the couch. A depleted bottle of vodka stood on the coffee table, next to a glass filled with ice.

Rachel grabbed the bottle and dumped the contents over the cubes, filling the glass to the rim. She picked it up, sloshing the vodka over the side on to the floor. She took a large sip and placed the tumbler back on the table.

I stood in the entrance of the room, watching her. Truly wondering if the vodka took away her pain. It seemed to always amplify her emotional state, not mask it. It released her secrets unfiltered, brutal and honest. I awaited the truthful assault.

"I thought he would love me more because of you. He was so happy when you were born. But you took him from me." She picked up the glass and took a larger sip before setting it down, half-consumed.

"You can't take them all away from me, Emily."

I wasn't sure what she meant. At first I thought she was talking about my father's death, but I didn't know who else she meant... Then it hit me. Jonathan. She thought he'd chosen me over her.

"Why didn't they love me? Why wasn't I enough?" She choked, raising her voice. "Why you?" Her head lolled slightly as she shifted to face me. Her eyes were heavy, but the hatred in them was unmistakable. "You." She shook her head lazily, closing her lids with the motion. "You. You should never have been born."

And just when I thought I couldn't hurt any more, her words left me incapacitated. I leaned against the doorway for support.

"Sharon left you, not me."

I was confused again, until she clarified. "I didn't leave you. Was in the hospital. Took too many pills." The more she talked, the harder it was for her to form words. The vodka was completely taking over. "Said I couldn't have you. But never wanted you. I can't." She breathed heavily, the effort to speak draining her. "Can't love you."

My head spun, and each breath was excruciating. She took another sip from the glass and almost missed the table when she set it back down with a hard thump. She laid her head on the arm of the couch and closed her eyes.

I stumbled out of the room, then stopped before I reached the stairs. I turned back around and realized there was something wrong. I scanned the living room in a panic. Where was it? What had she done with it?

Then I remembered the smell of burning wood when I came home, and spun around toward the back door. I rushed out into the small yard and practically collapsed on the stairs. It felt like someone had thrust their fist through my chest and was squeezing my heart.

In the middle of the yard was a heap of embers, still glowing red. A few spindles were recognizable among the ashes, but it was gone. She had set the rocking chair on fire, and now there was nothing left.

I clumsily lowered myself down on the steps while holding on to the railing, staring at the remains and shaking my head in grief, lost in the wafts of smoke.

Pulling myself up, I returned inside, empty and broken. My insides felt like they'd been ripped out and burned as well. I couldn't see straight. My eyes were glazed over as I made my way to the stairs.

I trudged up to my dark room without glancing into the living room. Flipping on the light, I mindlessly filled my bag with random clothes. I zipped the bag and fell back into darkness when I shut off the light. My hand slid along the railing as my legs numbly carried me along.

I gripped the doorknob to leave and hesitated, searching within the shadows of the living room. I couldn't see her. But I could hear her breathing.

Compelled, I walked to the love seat and sat down across from her. I folded my arms and stared at her silhouette, listening to her breathe.

I knew. I'd always known she didn't love me. I didn't know why I'd thought I could change that, even after all this time. It would never change. She couldn't even look at me for most of my life, forget about loving me.

I knew. But I didn't understand why she'd kept trying. She'd shown up at my sports games. And the letters she'd written…why? I guess that had been her effort—she said she'd tried. She couldn't convince herself to love me, any more than I could believe that she did.

I looked away and my eyes fell upon the glass, leaving a wet ring on the coffee table. Painkiller. Really?

I leaned forward and picked up the half glass of vodka. The ice cubes were melting into tiny stones. I brought it to my nose and smelled it. My mouth filled with saliva, and I cringed. I pressed the rim to my lips and tipped it back, taking a large sip.

I coughed and grimaced in disgust. The liquid set my stomach on fire as it crashed against its empty walls. I took a deep breath and shuddered. It was horrible, but so was aspirin if you let it touch your tongue—and that was supposed to take away pain as well. I held my nose and swallowed again, emptying the glass—wanting it to work, to take away my pain.

I held the empty glass in my hands, and my eyes filled with tears. What had I done? I clenched my jaw and breathed heavily through flared nostrils. What had I done? I shook my head, horrified.

I slammed the glass down on the table and stood up to leave. The sight of the vodka bottle filled me with so much fury, I wanted to scream. I picked it up and clenched it so tightly, I thought it might shatter in my hand. Shaking with rage, I threw it into the darkness. The glass shattered against the wall on the far side of the foyer.

I breathed a sob and rushed to leave. Grabbing my bag, I slammed the door behind me.

I didn't remember driving to Sara's. I probably shouldn't have been driving at all, blinded by tears, my head hazy. I pulled myself together as best I could when I turned into her driveway. Anna and Carl didn't appear to be home, thankfully.

Gripping my bag, I climbed the steps to Sara's front door. Sara opened it before I reached the top. "Where have you been? I've been..." Her sentence trailed off. Her aghast expression indicated that I was a bigger mess than I thought.

She held the door open for me, and I walked in, lowering my eyes as I passed her. I continued up the stairs to her room without a word.

I dropped my bag on the floor next to the bed I usually slept in and sat on the edge with my shoulders bowed. My head felt light and was spinning slightly.

Sara sat next to me and waited, knowing I would tell her once I found the strength.

After a few minutes of silence, I took a deep breath and said, "I wasn't supposed to live."

"What?" Sara gasped, sitting perfectly still.

"She killed me, Sara. I was dead. Why am I still here?" My voice was heavy. Tears filled my eyes.

"Oh, Emma," Sara breathed. "Don't think like that."

"I don't want to feel like this. This pain. I shouldn't have to feel it. I was supposed to be dead." A tear rolled over the rim of my lid and slid down my cheek.

"Emma, please tell me what happened," Sara begged softly. "You're not making any sense."

I took a stuttering breath and revealed, "My mother told me she never wanted me. That I was the reason my father never loved her. He left me everything, Sara." I connected with her large blue eyes. They glistened with sadness. I had to look away, unable to bear her pain as well.

"What do you mean he left you everything?" she asked patiently, trying to understand.

"A lawyer came to see me yesterday. My father had a trust set up for me. The lawyer told me the truth about my parents. They were never married, and my father only stayed with her for me. She blames me. She hates me. I'm pretty sure she even tried to kill herself because of what happened."

"What are you talking about?" Sara's brows tilted in confusion.

"That's how I ended up with Carol and George. She was in the hospital after taking too many pills. I think she tried to commit suicide." I spoke without connecting with my words. My whole body was a whirl of incoherence. I could no longer feel or think.

"When did she tell you this?" she asked, shaking her head like it was incomprehensible.

"Tonight," I stated flatly. "I should have told you. I should have said something about what was going on…her drinking…but I thought I could handle it. I thought I could fix her. But I can't."

"It's not your fault," Sara consoled me, taking my hand. Her words echoed through me, and I focused on her, drawn back to my exact words to Jonathan earlier in the day. In that moment, I recognized the impossibility of forgiveness when my insides were tangled in culpability. Guilt was lonely and isolating. I wondered how Jonathan had lived with it all of these years.

"I'm so tired," I told her, the ache in my chest sucking the will out of me. "I don't want to do this anymore."

"Do what?" Sara whispered, helping me up so she could pull back the covers.

"Hurt," I muttered, tears seeping between my quivering lips.

"You don't have to," Sara soothed, guiding me down on the bed. "Emma, it's going to get better. You don't have to do this alone. I'm here, okay?"

Sara lay next to me on top of the blankets and smoothed my hair away from my face. "You don't have to hurt anymore," I heard her whisper again as I closed my eyes.

35. EVERYONE HURTS

I thought I'd be up most of the night, unable to sleep, but when I opened my eyes it was midmorning and Sara's bed was empty. I lay under the covers for a while, not sure what the point was of getting up. But I couldn't suppress the need to use the bathroom, so I forced myself out of the bed.

Since I was already there, I decided to shower. I realized I'd never showered after my day trip with Jonathan or practice last night, and I desperately needed it. I remained hollow as I stood under the water, unable to feel anything stirring inside—not an emotion or a single thought. I was tempted to go back to bed when I came out of the bathroom wrapped in a towel, but Sara had already made it and was lying on top, reading a magazine.

"Hey." She greeted me with a smile. "Are you hungry? My mom's making pancakes."

I shrugged and started to dress, not caring if Sara saw my scars—she'd seen them at their worst anyway.

"So, where were you during school yesterday?" she asked casually, keeping her eyes on the magazine as she turned the pages.

"With Jonathan," I admitted softly, my voice hard to find.

This got her attention. "Excuse me? You were with Jonathan? Why…uh, what did you do?" It wasn't often that Sara had difficulty finding her words.

"We went for a ride on his motorcycle," I told her. She waited, but I didn't continue. There wasn't much more I could say without revealing his secrets, and I couldn't do that.

"What's going on between you two?" she questioned. "Anything I should be worried about?"

"No," I answered simply. "We get along. He understands what I'm going through, that's all."

"What does that mean, 'what you're going through'?" She sounded worried. I suppose I would have been if she'd said it.

"About Rachel's moods and stuff," I attempted to explain. "We talk. He understands. I mean…he dated Rachel, so he gets it. We've become friends through all of this."

"Okay," Sara said contemplatively. "I think. Did you explain this to Evan?"

"I didn't get to," I breathed, sitting next to her on the bed. "Sara, I totally screwed up. He's so upset with me he wouldn't even see me before he left." The misery of his call stirred in my chest.

"Yeah, I know," she comforted me. "He was so freaked when you didn't show up at school yesterday. Then when you didn't answer your phone, I thought he was going to lose it completely. I gave him Rachel's number when he asked, not like she was any help or anything. You really should've called or texted him or something."

"I know," I said, feeling ill. "I left my phone in my car. I wish I had called. But I was hoping we'd get to talk, so I could explain. I really never meant to worry him."

"What are you going to do about Rachel?"

I was quiet for a moment. "I can't live with her anymore." My voice cracked slightly, the emotions escaping despite my efforts to bury them.

"I know," Sara agreed, her voice sympathetic. "Want to go to Florida with me this week?"

"I can't," I answered automatically. "I really need to be here for soccer."

"I knew you'd say that, so I talked to my mom, and I'm flying down on Thursday with my dad instead of leaving with her on Monday. I want to be here with you."

"Thanks." I smiled faintly. "I want that too." And I did. I needed to be with the one person who wasn't angry with me, and didn't force me to explain every feeling that was coursing through my body.

"Can you tell me about last night a little bit?" she inquired gently. "It was a little confusing, but you were upset, so I decided to wait."

"Like what?"

"Who's this lawyer, and what did he tell you?"

I recounted my conversation with Charles Stanley and what he had revealed about my parents and my grandparents, and the trust I'd inherited.

"Wow," Sara mused after I was done. "That's crazy. That must be where Leyla and Jack are, huh? In Florida with your grandmother."

"I think so," I replied with a slight nod.

"Em," Sara began cautiously, "you said that you thought your mom may have attempted suicide. Why would you say that?"

I crossed my arms and bowed my head, picturing her on the couch, barely coherent and confessing what no mother should ever admit, no matter how true. Sharpness cut through my chest just thinking about her spouts of disdain.

Somewhere among the slur of words, she'd mentioned not being the one who'd left me with Carol and George. She said Sharon had left me. She was in the hospital. She took too many pills. I shared this with Sara, along with my deduction that she had overdosed.

"Maybe it was an accident," Sara suggested.

I shrugged in contemplation, but I doubted it. My mother had been so grief stricken by my father's death, I suspected she may have done it on purpose. I recalled my cutting words to her on the porch, and my eyes stung with shame. Regardless of her lack of feeling for me, I should never have said what I did. I had been cruel.

Anna called up to us when the pancakes were ready. I followed Sara downstairs, although I didn't feel much like eating.

I could tell by the way Anna looked at me, full of sympathy and concern, that Sara had told her. I couldn't expect Sara to keep anything from her parents after what had happened last year. I wasn't upset, but I wasn't sure I could talk to Anna about it.

But I also knew she wasn't the type of mother to leave it alone. She waited until after breakfast, when Sara was in the shower. I was sitting in the rec room, aimlessly flipping through the channels. Anna sat next to me on the couch, and I shut off the television. I waited for her to begin.

"Sometimes people hurt more than they can handle," she soothed, observing me. I had a hard time meeting her eyes. "And sometimes they don't know how to ask for help. They're so caught up in their own pain, they end up hurting everyone around them. I wish you didn't keep getting hurt."

I didn't respond, but she knew I wouldn't.

"I know you have commitments here and won't be coming to Florida with us. We'll help you get your things next week when we return." Anna placed her hand over mine. It was warm and soft. I tried to smile, but it never truly formed on my lips.

When she left the room, her sentiment kept floating through my head. I thought of Evan and everything I'd put him through. I began to wonder if I was the one being hurt, or the one doing the hurting.

"I want to call him," I told Sara while sitting in the mall restaurant. She had somehow coaxed me into shopping with her. I must have been completely distracted when I said yes.

"It's only been a day," Sara countered. "Give him some more time."

"I just..." I pushed the fries around on my plate, not eating them. "I want to apologize. He won't even have to say he forgives me. I just need him to know how horrible I feel."

"I'm not so sure that's what he's looking for, Emma."

I knew she was right. An apology was just words. Evan wanted me to trust him, to confide in him. That's all he'd ever wanted. He wanted to be the one I turned to when everything was falling apart. He wanted to be...Jonathan.

I had no idea when this had happened. When Jonathan became the first person I thought of, the first person I called when everything was miserable and complicated. He was the one I reached out to when I couldn't sleep at night, or couldn't carry Rachel to bed, or when I needed to escape her completely. He knew me in a way that Evan didn't, but in a way that Evan had always wanted to.

"Why does he want to know?" I pondered out loud. "Why does he want to know all the bad things, the things most people pretend not to see? Why does he want to know I hurt, or that my mother's never loved me? It's almost more important to him than knowing I'm safe and happy."

"That's not it at all," Sara countered with a crease between her brows. "Emma, Evan wants to know you and all that makes you, you. The good, the bad and the horrible. He needs to do some 'fessing up himself and not keep running away when he gets his feelings hurt. But you can't keep him in the dark when everything starts falling apart. You're not protecting him, you know. You're pushing him away."

"I guess I wasn't sure he'd understand," I confessed with a sigh.

"Like Jonathan does?" Sara finished the thought. I nodded. "Give him a chance."

My phone chimed. I looked at the screen and then to Sara with wide eyes.

"Who is it?"

"Rachel," I said, stunned. "Should I answer it?" Sara shrugged with a grimace of uncertainty. I missed the call.

She followed up with a text, Where are you?

I showed Sara the text. "She doesn't know you're staying with me?"

"I don't remember if I told her, or she may not remember. But why does she care?"

"I don't know," Sara answered, just as perplexed.

I decided to text back, At Sara's.

I left it at that, and she responded, OK. I shook my head in confusion.

"Okay, enough doom and gloom." Sara stood up. "We're going to check out prom dresses," she declared with a vibrant smile. She observed the dread on my face. "Don't worry. He'll forgive you before prom. Come on. I'll make it fun."

Sara pulled me from my seat. She excitedly led the way through store after store. She picked out the most obnoxious dresses and modeled them for me, determined to make me laugh. And I did. Exactly as she intended.

————

Sara jumped on the couch, attempting a split in the air while striking the electric guitar. I knelt on the ground, leaning back with the guitar raised above my head, letting the ear-splitting sound reverberate through the amp. The song we were supposed to be playing along to blared over the speakers.

Out of the corner of my eye I saw movement, and I turned to find Anna at the top of the stairs, screaming, "Emma!"

I stood and removed the guitar strap from around my neck. Sara noticed my change from rock star to worried girl before catching sight of her mom. She hopped down from the couch and shut off the amp and the music.

My ears were still ringing when Anna announced, "Your mom's on my phone." I froze midstep. "She's worried about you. My phone's downstairs in my room."

I followed Anna downstairs, glancing back at Sara's concerned face before I disappeared. We entered Anna's bedroom, where her suitcase lay open on her bed. She'd been interrupted while packing for the trip that she was leaving for in an hour. The cell phone was next to the suitcase.

Anna picked it up and said, "She's right here," to Rachel before handing it to me. She walked past me, closing the bedroom door behind her.

"Hi," I said cautiously.

"Emily?" Rachel confirmed in relief. "Are you okay? I didn't know you were staying all weekend. I haven't heard from you."

My brows crumpled in confusion. "What?"

"Did you tell me you were staying there?" she asked in her nervous rush. "Did I forget? I'm so sorry. I probably forgot."

"What's wrong with you?" I demanded. "Why are you all of a sudden worried about me?"

"Oh." She sighed, sounding disappointed. "Are you still mad at me? I'm so sorry I overreacted on Friday. I shouldn't have thought that you would ever do anything to hurt me. I was upset. Are you really mad?"

I pulled the phone away from my ear and stared at it, completely speechless. Who was this woman? Even if she didn't remember what she'd said to me that night because she was so drunk, she had to have remembered what *I* said to *her*—how much I hurt her.

"Emily?" she called out to me.

"I'm here," I answered, devoid of emotion. "I'm staying here this week. It's vacation anyway, so...I'm staying here." I couldn't tell her I was moving out. I wanted to. I meant to. But I didn't.

"Okay." Her voice sounded strained. "Well, I guess I'll see you next week."

"Yeah," I breathed before I hung up, too confounded to say anything else.

"Well," Sara demanded when I appeared at the top of the stairs. I didn't acknowledge her, too baffled by what had just happened. "Emma," she urged impatiently, "what did she want?"

"I have no idea," I murmured in a daze. I sat down on the couch next to Sara and told her what had happened.

"So she doesn't remember?" Sara questioned skeptically. "I really doubt it, Em. I bet she wants you to think that so you'll move back in again."

"But why would she do that? She doesn't even want me." It didn't make sense, but I'd come to the same conclusion as Sara.

"I have no idea," Sara agreed. "Maybe you should talk to her."

"You mean I should *break up* with her," I corrected. "I can't believe I need to have the 'we're over' talk with my own mother. How depressing is that?"

"She can't keep hurting you and using you like an emotional punching bag. It's messed up. How many times do you have to forgive her before she destroys you?"

I knew she was right. It was only a matter of time before she got drunk and did something devastating again. I just didn't understand why she kept pulling me back in, making me feel like she wanted me, when in her vodka-induced proclamation, she'd confessed that she wished I'd never been born.

"I'll come with you," Sara said from beside me. "I'm not going to let you do it alone."

———

Sara drove us to the house the next evening after my soccer game. I still hadn't figured out what I was going to say when we pulled in behind Rachel's car.

"You don't have to come in," I told Sara as I slowly unbuckled the seat belt, my heart beating so fast I couldn't think straight.

"Uh, no," Sara countered stubbornly. "I'm coming in with you."

I took long, even breaths as I approached the door, trying to remain calm. It was useless. I was a wreck. Sara stayed by my side and opened the screen door for me. The front door was locked, so I used my key to let us in.

We hadn't made it very far into the foyer before we both stopped. The house was a disaster. Sara and I scanned from the kitchen to the living room speechlessly. Plastic red cups and glasses were abandoned on just about every surface. Bottles littered the floor, along with bowls of chips and empty boxes of pizza. The stench of stale beer and old pizza made our noses scrunch in disgust. It was ten times worse than Sara's house had been after the anti-Valentine's party.

"Looks like Rachel had a party," Sara observed, stepping carefully across the cluttered floor and into the living room. "Or two."

"What the hell?" I muttered in disbelief, wondering when this had happened. I ran up the stairs, expecting to find her in rare, or not so rare, form in her bedroom—but it was empty. I turned to head back downstairs, and my mouth dropped open. "No way."

My door was open and my bed was unmade. "Oh, please, no," I shook my head. "I can't believe she let—" I was afraid to finish the sentence.

Sara appeared behind me. "We are so burning those sheets."

"It doesn't matter," I said with a heavy sigh. "I can't live here anymore."

"Uh, of course not," Sara scolded. "When between the car and entering the house did you decide that you were going to do that?"

"I didn't," I fumbled. "I just—"

"Live in a world of denial," Sara finished sternly. "Em, look around and open your eyes. She's not going to change."

"I know," I breathed, the disappointment heavy in my voice. I sank down on the top step and pressed my elbows into my knees. The little bit of hope I'd held on to after the conversation with Rachel yesterday had slipped away as soon as I'd opened the door.

"I'm sorry, Em." Sara sat next to me and leaned her shoulder against mine. "I don't mean to be so harsh. I just don't want you to get hurt anymore. She doesn't deserve you."

My eyes welled, and I nodded. I knew this was it. We weren't fixable. The disappointment made my chest ache as I swallowed hard. Giving up went against my nature—I'd never done it before. I could faintly hear the hopeful thoughts forming, that maybe she could change. I pushed them away before they got too loud.

"Let's go," I finally declared, standing with Sara.

The front door opened, and Rachel appeared in the doorway, laughing, with her arm wrapped around the waist of a guy with blond hair and a large smile.

She looked up to see us. "Uh, I thought you were going to be away this week."

"I am," I said, moving past her with my shoulders pulled back, barely giving her a glance. "I'll be back next week to get my stuff."

"Emily!" she called after me from the porch. "What do you mean? Don't be angry with me. I'll clean up, I promise."

Without looking back, I got into Sara's car. I held it together while Rachel could see me. Once we'd pulled out of the driveway and started down the street, I crumpled in half and cried. I knew I never was, and never would be, someone she loved. And whether she deserved me or not, it was still painful to admit.

36. RESTLESS

I was just thinking about you. Can't sleep?"

"No," I answered softly.

"I didn't want to wake you, so I was waiting to call you tomorrow."

"Well, it *is* tomorrow," I said with a slight grin.

"Barely." He laughed lightly. "I'm glad you called."

"I was afraid you wouldn't want to hear from me."

"Emma, I always want to hear from you. It's when I don't that makes me worry."

"I'm sorry. Really, I'm so sorry for not telling you what was going on with my mother. But I want to. I want to tell you *everything*."

"We'll talk when I get back, okay? For now, I just want to know you're all right."

"I'm better."

"The two a.m. call is convincing," he replied playfully.

A smile crept across my face. "I'll be able to sleep now that I've talked to you."

"So will I."

"Will you still call me tomorrow?" I requested, not wanting to sound too desperate.

"Yes, I will. You should try to get some sleep now."

"Okay," I whispered. Before I hung up, I called, "Evan."

"Yes, Emma."

"I love you."

"I love you, too."

I hoped I hadn't dreamt the call when I woke the next morning. It stirred, faint as whispers in my head, not seeming real. But when I looked at my call history and found his number at two eleven in the morning, I exhaled in relief.

"Wow, is that a smile I see on your face, Emma Thomas?" Sara teased when she walked into the room. "Did you actually have a nice dream for once?"

"Uh, no," I countered. "I talked to Evan last night."

"Really? What did you talk about?"

"Nothing much. It was late, but he promised to call me today."

"That's good," she replied with a smile. "He can't stay upset with you. He's kind of pathetic that way."

"Sara!" I balked. "He's not pathetic."

She smirked and continued to her closet.

"I can't wait for the next two months to be over," I sighed, lying on my back and looking up at the skylights with a pillow hugged to my chest. "Are you coming out to Santa Barbara with Evan and me this summer before school starts? I'm pretty sure Jared knows the guys we're staying with."

I waited, but Sara didn't respond. "Sara?"

She emerged from the closet with her mouth contorted. She couldn't look me in the eye, so I knew she had something that she didn't want to tell me. "Sara, tell me."

Sara took a deep breath and pressed her knees against her bed, her face already apologizing for whatever it was she was about to say. I braced myself.

"I didn't accept the offer to go to CCA in San Francisco." My eyes widened in shock. We'd been planning to go to college in California for what seemed like forever, and her acceptance by California College of the Arts was perfect. We'd be near each other while I was at Stanford.

"I'm going to Parsons."

"New York?" I uttered as my mouth dropped. The disappointment left me speechless. I'd never been without Sara since I'd met her, and being so far away from her for college was impossible to wrap my head around. I didn't respond for a moment, needing to get over the blow. Then I took a step back and released the part that was about me.

Parsons was closer to her family…and Jared. And it was one of the best fashion design schools in the world. She watched me carefully, waiting for my full reaction. I finally looked up at her with tears in my eyes and a proud smile on my face. "I'm going to miss you. But Sara, I'm so happy for you." The worry disappeared, replaced by a stunning smile that lit up her eyes.

"Really?" she asked, walking around the bed. "You're not mad?"

"Mad? I'm not going to lie. I'm sad we won't be together, but I want this for you. Parsons is amazing, and you deserve to go there."

Sara sat next to me and gave me a hug. It surprised me at first, but I wrapped my arms around her and held her with my face buried in her hair. She squeezed me tight, not making a move to release me. A tear escaped down my cheek as I kept holding on, almost afraid to let go. I couldn't imagine my life without her.

Her voice heavy with emotion, she murmured in my ear, "I'm coming out to California for the summer, until school starts." We slowly separated. Her eyes glistened with tears. "We'll see each other every break. And I'll e-mail you and text and Skype every day; it'll be like I'm there with you. And you'll have Evan, so you won't be alone."

I grinned at her assurances. "I know. We're always going to be friends."

"No. We're always going to be *sisters*." Sara smiled and wiped away the tears that moistened her cheeks.

"Besides, there's so much to look forward to in the next two months," she said jubilantly, trying to laugh away the sadness. "We have prom, senior week, graduation. Emma, I know right now it sucks for you, but everything's going to get better—especially now that you're moving back in with me. I know it doesn't feel like it, but you'll get through this—you always do. And you may even enjoy the last couple of months of your senior year."

I nodded, running my hand along my damp cheeks with my lips pressed into a smile. A mixture of emotions fueled the tears. I'd lost my mother (again). And now Sara...She truly was my sister in every way, and I was so proud of her. Everything was changing so fast. I hoped it wasn't going to change too much.

"That was quick," Sara noted when I returned from speaking with Evan, after having anxiously awaited his call all day. I sat down next to her at the kitchen table.

"He just wanted to say hi before it got too late," I explained quietly, using the tongs to lift the fettuccine out of the bowl and set the small mound on my plate. "They were on their way out to surf, so the guys were waiting for him."

"He's still a little off, isn't he?"

"A little," I admitted, poking at the pasta with my fork—not even considering taking a bite.

"He'll be back in a few days," Sara said encouragingly. "I'm sure it's hard over the phone. It will be different in person."

"I hope so." I sighed, playing back the awkward strain in our conversation as we searched for anything positive to say. There wasn't much to talk about until he heard what I hadn't told him over the past couple of months. The missing conversations separated us further than the physical distance between Connecticut and Hawaii.

"What should we do tonight?" Sara asked, trying to distract me.

"Don't you have to get up early to go to the airport?"

"We can make it an early night and just watch a movie," she suggested. "Besides, you could use the sleep." She smirked teasingly. There was no denying the repercussions of sleep deprivation, especially with Sara. She just had to look at me to know how long it had been since I'd slept—and it had been a while. With the buildup of drama and anxiety, sleep was a turbid mirage.

"Are you going to be okay staying here by yourself?"

"I was thinking about asking Casey if I could stay with her, since we have soccer together," I told her. "Evan's back Saturday, so it would only be for two nights."

"That won't be bad," Sara mused. Then she grinned wickedly and added, "You seem pretty positive that you're staying over at his house on Saturday night. You're not all that worried he won't forgive you, are you?"

I shrugged sheepishly. "I'm hoping I can convince him."

"Oooh, Emma." She chuckled. "I *have* rubbed off on you."

"Sara"—I gaped—"I'm not going to seduce him so he'll forgive me. Besides we're not having sex until next month."

"What?" Sara laughed in disbelief. "You've *planned* it?"

"Yeah," I admitted, my cheeks reddening. "We have a sex date for the night before prom."

Sara laughed harder. "You two kill me. How in the world can that be romantic, *planning* to have sex? Where's the lust and passion?"

"You don't know Evan," I replied without thinking, then turned crimson when Sara's mouth dropped open. "Okay, what movie are we watching?"

I closed my eyes and listened to the rhythm of her breathing from the bed next to me, hoping it would lull me to sleep. Sara inhaled and exhaled in long easy breaths. I could predict the next draw of air. But then it stopped. I waited, but she didn't breathe in again.

I opened my eyes and rolled over onto my back, listening intently. I inhaled quickly when the silhouette appeared next to my bed.

"Sara?" I questioned. "Is something wrong?"

She didn't move. Maybe she was sleepwalking. I propped myself up on my elbows, trying to focus on her and asked again, "Sara?"

When my eyes adjusted to the light, I realized it wasn't her. I kicked my legs to remove the blankets, but the more I kicked, the more tangled they became in the bedding. Then I couldn't see. I'd sunk beneath the blankets and everything was dark. I pushed at the sheets but they pulled tighter around me. Then she gripped my neck.

I choked and coughed, trying to pull her hands away, but they were too strong. I kicked and shook my head from side to side to get out from under her claws, but it was no use.

"You don't deserve to live," she grunted.

I grabbed on to her wrists and pried them loose, screaming, "You've already killed me!"

My hands were on my throat when I woke. My breathing was heavy and my heart was pounding fiercely. The room was dark, and I could hear Sara breathing in the bed next to me. I pulled back the blankets and crept out of the room. Sleep and I weren't going to find each other tonight, and there was no point lying there, staring into the dark.

I had my phone in my trembling hand when I sat on the couch in the rec room. I thought about calling Evan, but I knew it would just be another awkward conversation, and I didn't want to go through that twice in one day.

I clicked on the television and turned down the volume so Sara wouldn't hear it. I started scanning the channels and stopped on an infomercial for a microfiber cloth that claimed to be able to clean a car, computer, or boat by just adding water, "streak free." I almost laughed out loud. After a minute of being sucked into the enthusiastic sales pitch, I picked up my phone.

"I saw your infomercial," I said as soon as I heard him pick up.

"Just needs water," he replied, a smile in his voice. "Been wondering how you've been sleeping. Thought you might be cured after all."

"Hardly," I responded. "How about you? Been out on any dates lately?"

"Not yet." He chuckled. "Where are you?"

"At Sara's."

"That's good. You're not going back, are you?"

"No," I replied quietly. "I'm not. Some things aren't fixable."

"I thought when I didn't hear from you that he may have made you stop talking to me."

I was puzzled by his assumption. "Evan's away right now. We haven't had a chance to talk yet."

"Oh," Jonathan replied. "Then should you be talking to me?"

"Yeah, why not? We're friends," I replied, bewildered. "Evan has girls who are friends too. You're not the reason things are off between us anyway."

"Do you want to talk about it?" Jonathan asked hesitantly.

"No," I whispered.

After a moment of silence, he asked, "Do you want to hang out again?" Then he added quickly, "No cliffs this time."

I laughed. "Sure. We could do something tomorrow if you want. I have practice in the afternoon, but maybe after that."

"Yeah, I should be home from work by six. How about..." He paused for a moment. "How about we get dinner or something? And I kind of have something to share."

"Really?" I replied, intrigued. "Sure, just text me where to meet you."

"Okay. I'll see you tomorrow." When I hung up, I realized my lips were turned up into a smile, and my heart was beating a little faster.

37. INTO A NIGHTMARE

I thought you said you weren't very good," Jonathan teased as we walked out of the pool hall and into the cool drizzly night.

"I'm not," I retorted, pulling my hood over my head. "You're just worse than I am."

"Thanks," he shot back with a smirk. "So what next? Do you have to get back to your friend's?"

I checked my phone. Casey had promised to text me when she was on her way home from the party. In case she'd forgotten, which was definitely possible, I sent her a text asking where she was.

"I think she's still at the party," I told him. "Do you mind if I hang out for a while longer?"

"No, you're welcome to stay as long as you'd like," Jonathan assured me. "But I'm not sure what to do that's not a bar."

"I'd like to check out the band you were talking about, if that's okay."

"Oh, yeah, sure," Jonathan fumbled.

"We can do something else if you don't want to go back to your apartment," I suggested, his response making me feel a bit awkward.

"No, it's fine. I've honestly never had anyone at my place before. I'm trying to remember if I left it a mess."

"Really? You've *never* had anyone over?" I repeated in surprise. "Why not?"

Jonathan shrugged. "Umm, I don't really know. I usually meet people out, I guess. But yeah, let's go there." I followed Jonathan across the intersection and down a side street. The reflection of the water shimmered at the end.

"So Rachel's never been here?"

"No," he stated quickly. "I needed to take a break every once in a while. But she asked, trust me."

I nodded, imagining her agitation at not knowing where he lived. But I also remembered him disappearing a few days each week, and she probably wouldn't have let that happen if she knew where to find him.

We crossed the street at the end of the road and followed the water toward the marina.

"Why did you stay?" I decided to ask, considering how long he'd put up with her, and recognizing how often he'd needed to be away from her.

"Uh, what?" Jonathan questioned in confusion. "You mean with Rachel?"

"You had every right to get out way before you did. What made you stay?"

"I thought we agreed not to talk about her or anything else depressing." Jonathan replied, avoiding the question as we approached an old white brick building along the wharf.

"You're right," I conceded. I eyed the worn structure warily as Jonathan slid his key in the black metal door.

"Don't judge it by the outside," Jonathan advised. "They completely gutted it." When he opened the door, he flipped on the lights, illuminating a metal grated staircase that led to an opening above.

"I guess they did," I said, admiring the contemporary space at the top of the stairs. White walls stretched about twenty feet to an exposed beam ceiling. An entire wall was lined with brick and mill-size paned windows that overlooked the water. The floors appeared to be original, but the thick planks were newly varnished. "This place is amazing."

"I was lucky to find it," Jonathan admitted.

I walked over to the small black table set in front of a window to view the few boats rocking on the water below. Across the wharf was a boatyard where more boats awaited warmer temperatures before returning to the seas.

"Want something to drink?" Jonathan asked from the kitchen area of the studio. It was sleek, with stainless everything and tall wooden cabinets suspended above a marble countertop.

"No, I'm fine."

Jonathan removed a beer from the fridge and flipped it open. He approached the entertainment unit set on a long black table against the wall. I found a seat on the sofa that was perpendicular to the kitchen and the windows, offering a perfect view of the entire room. The beige sofa was linear and modern in design, but more comfortable than it appeared.

As I sank into the cushion, I peered up at an open platform suspended next to the kitchen wall. Metal stairs led to what I assumed to be his bedroom, but it was too high to see from this angle.

His studio was so…clean. I didn't know why he was worried. It was almost *too* clean. That's when it struck me that there wasn't anything in it other than the furniture. No artwork or decor of any kind. Nothing…personal.

"How long have you lived here?" I asked, thinking that maybe he was still working on it.

"Since I graduated," Jonathan said, scrolling through his downloads to find the band he'd told me about while we played pool.

"Two years?" I confirmed, scanning the room again.

"Just about," he agreed. Acoustic guitar strums echoed through the room, followed by a woman's smooth voice. "I know. It's pretty… minimal. I wouldn't even know how to begin decorating it."

"Don't you have any girlfriends who can help you out?"

"I've discovered that having girls as friends just leads to complications. So, no, I don't."

"Complications?" I questioned curiously.

"Yeah. Someone eventually wants more, and it gets…*complicated*," he explained with a shrug before taking a sip of beer.

"Oh." I nodded, understanding. "Yes, that is true."

"So, you've experienced this?" Jonathan sounded interested as he sat in the chair next to the sofa.

"Firsthand?" I considered for a moment, then continued, "Well, yeah. That's what happened with Evan. We started out as friends, but that didn't take." My cheeks warmed as I reflected upon our "friendship."

"I have a feeling you weren't really *friends*, even at the beginning," he observed, looking at my flushed face.

My cheeks became hotter. "No, probably not. But I do know what you mean. He has a girl right now who's supposed to be a friend, and she definitely has a thing for him. It's, as you said, complicated."

"You don't care that he's friends with other girls, right? I mean, you have me," Jonathan countered.

"No, I don't mind. But you and I are different," I argued. "We're *not* complicated."

Jonathan challenged my words with a raise of his eyebrows. "Right. We're just messed up."

I laughed and nodded. I pushed off my shoes and curled my legs next to me on the couch. My phone beeped, and I pulled it from my pocket.

Still at party. Wanna come? It's a good one.

I grinned at Casey's message and texted back, No thanks.

"That your friend?" Jonathan confirmed. "Do you have to go?"

"No. She's still at the party."

"Good," he replied, making me look up from my phone. He tipped back the bottle to avoid my curious expression.

"I like this," I said, commenting on the band and letting his remark slide. "They have a nice sound."

"Yeah, it's just a guy and a girl," Jonathan explained. "They're pretty incredible."

Their voices chimed in unison. I was enchanted by the lyrics as we sat quietly, letting them speak for us. I closed my eyes, allowing the music to float through me.

"Emma?" Jonathan called to me. I pulled my lids open, which was harder than I expected. I must have started to doze off. "Are you okay?"

"Sorry." I shook my head and sat up straighter to ward off the bout of sleep. "I'm just tired."

"Really, are you okay?" he asked again, studying my face intently.

I shifted away from his delving brown eyes and nodded. "I haven't been sleeping much."

"Or eating," Jonathan reproached me.

I shrugged guiltily. "That obvious?"

"Uh, yeah," he confirmed with a firm nod.

"It's been a crazy week," was my feeble defense.

"That's an understatement," he said with a wry grin. "I know we said we weren't going to talk about it, but we can if you want. I'm really sorry about everything that happened. I still feel like it's my fault."

"It's not," I stressed. "It really had nothing to do with skipping school and spending the day with you. In the end it was about the truth, and I just didn't want to see it."

"What do you mean?"

"She doesn't love me. She never did. There's nothing that's ever going to change that."

Jonathan didn't respond. We were quiet for a moment before he asked, "What about you?" I glanced over at him. His voice was quiet and smooth. "How do you feel about *her*?"

I let his eyes search mine as I considered his question. "I don't know. I always thought I loved her. I mean, she's my mother. But…I don't know."

"What if you didn't think of her as your mother? Just as a person you know. How would you feel about her?" he coaxed.

"That I don't like her," I answered without hesitation. "She seems funny and nice on the outside, but when you get close enough, you realize she's selfish and manipulative and, well, a bit unstable. So I guess…maybe I don't love her either." I lowered my eyes as my words took hold. "Wow. That's messed up."

"Tends to be our unavoidable theme," Jonathan noted with a guilty grin. "Sorry. We can't seem to avoid the depressing, can we?"

"I think it's because we both understand what it's like. It's not easy to talk like this with other people because they don't know. They don't know what it's like to be hated by the people who are supposed to love you." I sank farther into the couch and allowed the bleak mood to settle within me, drawing on my weariness. I thought about leaving, but I just needed to rest for a moment. I laid my head on my arm.

"What is it like?" Jonathan asked, calling me back to meet his dark eyes. "For you, I mean, what's it like?"

I breathed out a humorless laugh and allowed the honesty to slip through. "It makes me stupid."

"What?" Jonathan questioned in alarm. "I don't understand how you can say that."

I focused on a distant light on the water, trying to find the words to explain what was starting to become apparent to me—having thought incessantly about what I'd done wrong over the past year. I had my mother to thank for clicking it all into place for me with her bouts of drunken candor.

"I close my eyes to the truth. I refuse to see what's happening, convinced that I can handle whatever it is—believing that I'm strong enough and will recognize when I'm not.

"But in order to really see it, the truth, I have to admit how much I'm hated. And who wants to think they deserve that much anger? To be despised so much…to have someone wish you'd never existed." I paused to take a breath.

"I shut it out. I *choose* not to see. I never ask for help. I even try to convince everyone that it's not a big deal. They don't know. No one really knows how bad it is because I won't let them." I paused and repeated, "It makes me stupid."

Jonathan silently absorbed my whispered words. Exhaustion rolled over me, and my head became as heavy as my heart. I felt outside of myself as my eyes burned with fatigue.

"How do you do it?" Jonathan asked. He sounded so far away. I tried to focus on him, but I couldn't. "How do you get through it?"

"By not feeling," I murmured, blinking heavily, lulled by the voices crooning in the background. This wasn't difficult to explain, since I'd done it so easily all those years living with Carol. "I shut it off. And I guess if it's really bad, I block it out completely. I didn't realize I did that until my mother showed me what I'd forgotten."

I shut my eyes. "She thinks I'm strong because I can push everything into the dark. But it leaves me empty. And the dark always ends up finding me in my sleep."

I felt the weight of a blanket being pulled over me. I opened my eyes and found him propped on the coffee table in front of me. He smiled gently, holding a pillow in his hands. I sat up enough for him to place it beneath my head and lowered myself down again.

"Sorry," I whispered, my eyes sliding shut again. "I'm so tired."

"I know," he replied gently. "You can sleep here if you want."

"I'm just gonna rest before I go," I muttered, blinking. My eyes were so heavy; it almost hurt to keep them open. Jonathan stood up.

"Jonathan?"

He squatted down in front of me. "Yes, Emma."

"Do you think you'll ever love again?" I murmured, not fighting against my lids any longer.

"I think so," he whispered, brushing the hair from my cheek. I shivered against his touch. "I'll see you in my sleep."

I pushed my eyes open one final time to find him walking away. "What did you say?"

"I said I'll see you in the morning. Get some sleep."

"I'm just going to rest for a bit," I slurred, closing my eyes again. I couldn't have kept them open if I'd tried.

My screams still echoed through the room when I sat up in a panic, trying to breathe.

"Emma?" Jonathan called out. The clang of the metal stairs echoed sharply in the dark. It took me a moment to focus on him when he crouched in front of me. "You're okay. It was just a dream."

I nodded, and my lips trembled. "I can't do this anymore," I choked, my eyes filling with tears. I was too exhausted and shaken to hold them back. "I'm so tired."

"I know," Jonathan said soothingly, sliding next to me on the couch and rubbing my shoulder.

I released a quivering breath and wiped my eyes with my sleeves. "I don't know how to make it stop."

Jonathan's brow creased with empathy.

"Can I please have a glass of water?" I requested, trying to recover from my emotional meltdown.

Jonathan nodded and stood to retrieve it. I sat up with the blanket wrapped around me and took a deep breath to calm the shaking. He turned on the canister lights above the island, providing enough light for me to look around.

"Where's your television?" I asked, not finding the postnightmare distraction.

"Oh, it's in my bedroom." He nodded toward the loft in the corner. "You need something to clear your head?" he surmised.

"Anything," I begged. "I can't keep thinking about her trying to kill me anymore."

"You can't let her control you. Emma, you're stronger than this. You just have to believe it." He handed me a glass of water and sat next to me. "Do you know what happened that night? Or did you block that out too?"

"I died," I answered bluntly. "So I have no idea what happened."

I felt the warmth of his hand encapsulate mine. The strength of it wrapped around my thin hand comforted me, but it also made my heart pound. I eased it away to hold the glass with two hands. He pretended not to notice.

"Emma—" He beckoned, making me look at him as I sipped the water. "Do you want to sleep better?"

I scrunched my eyes warily. "What do you have in mind?"

"Do you trust me?"

"Are you going to try to cure me again?" I questioned skeptically.

"Yeah." He grinned. "I think this might work, or at least help you. Will you let me?"

I paused a moment in deliberation. Jonathan's eyes were big and pleading, begging for me to trust him. I sighed in defeat and threatened, "If it doesn't work, I swear I will keep you up every night I can't sleep."

"I can handle that." He grinned in triumph. "Get your jacket."

"What?" I questioned in alarm. "We're leaving?"

"Did you think I was going to try to hypnotize you or something?" he chuckled.

I sighed in resignation and slipped my shoes on as he tossed me my jacket.

"So how's your triathlon training going?" I asked, cutting through the tense silence that had encapsulated us upon entering the truck.

"Really?" Jonathan laughed in disbelief at what I was asking him.

"Well, I need to talk about *something*," I defended myself with a groan. "From the looks of it, we're heading back to Weslyn. And if we're going where I think we're going, then we'd better start talking before I make you turn the truck around."

"Training's going great," Jonathan burst out. "I haven't been cycling lately because the weather's sucked, but so far—"

"Okay, that's not helping," I interrupted, glancing over at him apologetically. "Sorry, I do want to hear about it, but I'm about ready to have a heart attack, or anxiety attack, or something."

"Breathe, Emma," he urged. "Slow, deep breaths. Just breathe."

I tried to remember how. My heart continued to convulse, and breathing was becoming more challenging.

"Wait." It suddenly struck me. "How do you know where to go?"

I thought I heard him laugh. "It's not hard to find anything in Weslyn. All you have to do is ask, and people talk. Don't worry. Nothing's going to happen to you," he assured me. "I promise."

I buried my face in my hands as the world spun out of control. I couldn't watch as we turned down each road. The closer we got, the more I had to fight the urge to jump out of the truck.

"Come on, Emma." I was too wrapped up in my anxiety to realize we'd stopped.

"I can't," I whimpered, unable to uncover my face.

"Yes you can," he cajoled. "I'm here. Nothing's going to happen."

My hands shook when I lowered them. I kept my eyes closed and tried to calm the panic that was overtaking me. "I don't think I can get out."

His door opened and closed behind him. I stayed within the dark cab, paralyzed. My door opened, and his warm hand wrapped around mine. "You can do this."

I opened my eyes and looked into his. "Come on, Emma." I concentrated on his face. It was so sure and confident. I held tight to his hand as if it were a lifeline. I suddenly felt so small.

"Just look at me," he encouraged, as I stepped down from the truck. "Keep looking at me."

I nodded, unable to find my voice. I continued to focus on him, his eyes assuring me with every step.

"Okay, close your eyes," he advised, "I'm going to turn you toward it." My knees buckled, but he kept me upright with his hands gripping my shoulders.

"Why are we doing this?" I whispered, feeling the warmth of the tears on my cheeks.

"Because I can sleep," Jonathan answered softly in my ear, still holding me upright.

"What?" His words distracted me from my anxiety, and I tilted my head toward him. "What did you say?"

"I don't know if it was facing it, or sharing it with you, but I've been sleeping through the night. And I want you to be able to, too." He gently ran his thumb along my cheek to wipe away the tears. "Go ahead and look."

I reluctantly moved my eyes from his face to the house in front of me. It felt like there was a stone in my chest. I leaned against him.

"This is where it happened," he said in a hushed whisper, wrapping his arm around my shoulder. "This is where you died."

I nodded, unable to see clearly through the tears.

"Do you remember now?"

I blinked the tears free and stared at the grey Cape, sunken within the shadows of the neighbors' trees. A FOR SALE sign hung in the minuscule front yard. It looked so much smaller than I remembered. I got lost in the dark windows. So much pain lay hidden behind them.

"Where did it happen?" he asked, his voice faint like a whisper in my head.

"In my room," I rasped, my eyes shifting to the side of the house. Jonathan took my hand and guided me closer. My pulse raced with each step. He led me along the wooden fence that bordered the neighbor's yard.

"Where?" he asked again.

I pointed to the second window. "Here." I trembled beneath the white-framed window, her voice seething from the other side. *I am not losing my family because of you.* I shivered.

"Emma, what happened to you?" he probed, not letting me go.

Staring into the dark, I was swallowed by my nightmare. *Tugging at the restraints around my wrists.* "I couldn't move," I murmured. *The fabric upon my face.* "And I couldn't see." Jonathan's arm tightened around me. *Struggling beneath her weight.* "I tried to get away, but I couldn't. Then...then I felt her hands..." I blindly touched my neck, still able to feel her cold claws. I shuddered. "I fought so hard. There was...pain..." I breathed in quickly as it streaked through my body, "My ankle..." I clamped my eyes closed. *Banging and muffled cries.* "But then I just...I just gave up."

I bowed my head with a gasp and tears ran over my nose.

"But you didn't, Emma. You didn't give up. You're here."

"I don't want to be here anymore," I whispered.

"Okay," he said, his lips next to my ear. "Okay, we'll leave."

I stepped away without looking at him, and he let me go. I walked back to the truck with my head down, trying to release the crushing pressure in my chest. I'd just stepped into one of my nightmares. And I was fighting so hard to get back out.

38. COVERING UP

Good morning." Jonathan smiled from the chair across from me, where he sat with a blanket over his lap. "You slept."

I took in a breath and blinked. "Have you been there all night?"

"Do you mean, all morning?" he teased. "But you slept."

"You didn't sleep?" I questioned, pushing myself to sit up, the weariness still lingering despite the few hours of rest.

Jonathan shrugged without answering, but continued to wear a smug grin.

"Oh, don't start thinking you cured me or anything," I said, suddenly realizing what was behind the grin. "Just because I slept for a few hours, it doesn't mean the nightmares have vanished. We'll see if you deserve the pat on the back when I go to bed tonight. Besides, they don't happen *every* night, and you know that."

"You *are* really good at this denial thing, aren't you?" He laughed. "You have no idea what's going on until you can't ignore it any longer."

"Yeah," I huffed. "I *love* not sleeping at night, and just want to prove you wrong."

"That's not what I meant." He grinned wider, but before I could question him, he stood up, leaving the blanket on the chair. "Are you hungry? I have...cereal."

"Thanks, but I should get to Casey's," I replied, standing to stretch my legs with my arms extended above me—feeling the ache in my neck and back. "Your couch isn't very comfortable to sleep on."

"It's not meant to be slept on. I offered you the bed." He shrugged. I didn't respond. I hadn't exactly been comfortable with that offer.

I picked up my phone and slid on my shoes. I scanned through my missed texts from Casey, and the one response that wasn't actually from me. "Thanks for texting Casey for me last night."

"I didn't want her to worry," he replied, pouring cereal into a bowl. "She thought it was you. I don't think you'll have to tell her where you were."

I nodded, not sure how that explanation would've come out anyway. I still didn't know what I would say if she ended up asking. But then again, Casey wasn't the curious type, so I hoped to avoid the inquiry altogether.

"I have to stop by Rachel's to get my shirt for the game tomorrow," I remembered out loud with a groan, sliding on my jacket.

Jonathan paused, appearing concerned.

"Don't worry," I assured him. "She should've left for work by now. Speaking of which, aren't you going to be late?"

"I'm working from home today," he explained. "You have a game tomorrow?"

"Yeah."

"Would it be okay if I watched it? I've never seen you play, and I kinda want to see what the scholarship's all about."

"Umm, sure," I fumbled. "I'll text you where we're playing. I can't remember where it is right now."

"Great. Thanks."

I was about to leave when he called, "Emma."

I hesitated.

Jonathan leaned back against the island. His dark hair was disheveled, but the way the waves twisted, it looked like it was on purpose. His wrinkled T-shirt clung to him, hinting at the broad muscles beneath. Taking in his casual stance against the counter, I could actually picture him in the magazine, and recognized why he drew so much attention.

"I like this," he confessed. "Us. Being able to talk. I've never been able to do it before. Not even with…Sadie. I've needed it… you. And now you're here, and well…thank you."

A chill ran through me when I found myself caught in the depth of his eyes. I blinked away and nodded. "I like this too." My voice came out small and broken as heat spread across my cheeks.

Jonathan smiled. "I'll see you tomorrow then."

"Yeah," I replied with a faint smile. I suddenly wasn't so sure if his coming to see me play was such a good idea. Something felt different this morning—like my vulnerability last night had allowed him to get too close, closer than he'd already been. "I'll see you tomorrow."

When I turned onto Decatur Street, I slowed to a crawl, just in case. I came to a sudden stop when I saw her car in the driveway, and quickly put my car in reverse. I huffed in frustration as I backed away, knowing I needed my shirt by tomorrow morning. But the last thing I wanted was another confrontation, or a *Twilight Zone* conversation in which she pretended nothing was wrong.

As expected, Casey hadn't thought twice about where I'd spent the night. Instead, she went on about the great party I'd missed. I'd only had a few hours of sleep on Jonathan's couch, so I was pretty out of it most of the day. She didn't seem to notice.

I had every intention of returning to Rachel's that night, in hopes that she'd be out doing what she did best on a Friday night— but I never made it that far.

"Emma, you can sleep in the guest room," Casey's voice cut through my head. I opened my eyes to find her standing above me with the movie still playing in the background.

"Sorry," I said. "I'm so pathetic today, I know. I'm just really tired."

"It's okay," Casey replied. "I didn't expect us to go to a party or anything. Besides, I'm pretty tired from last night too. I'll see you in the morning?"

"Yeah," I told her, dragging my feet to the guest room. My phone chimed as I was about to slide under the covers. I didn't look to see who was calling as I put it to my ear. "Hello?"

"Hi," Evan said from the other end. My heart skipped a beat at the sound of his voice.

"Hi," I returned in joyous relief. "How are you?"

"Good," he responded, sounding a little surprised. Maybe I'd come across a little *too* happy to hear from him. "I'm at the airport in LA for my connecting flight, and I wanted to hear your voice. It's been really hard not talking to you."

"You have no idea." I exhaled. "When will you be home?"

"Tomorrow afternoon. Can I see you? I'll come straight from the airport."

"Um, why don't I meet you at your house? Will your parents be home?"

"My mother might be," he said, considering, "I don't think my father will be around. She mentioned a meeting in DC I'll see you at my house. I should be there between two thirty and three."

"That's perfect." I smiled.

"I should've called you, Emma. I'm sorry," he quickly added; the regret in his voice forced my pulse to quicken.

"You needed time," I stated quietly. "I deserved it."

"No. I should have called. That wasn't right, to do that to you. I'll see you tomorrow, okay?"

When I hung up the phone, I was filled with both elation and dread. I missed him so much I ached, but I knew what was going to happen when we saw each other, and I wished it were already over. I couldn't fast-forward the inevitable, so I accepted that we were about to have a long and difficult conversation and collapsed into bed, where exhaustion pulled me into a dreamless sleep.

———

I left a little early for the game so I could pick up my jersey on the way. I anxiously tapped my fingers on the steering wheel the entire drive, hoping she'd stayed at *his* place, whoever that might be.

"Shit," I grunted, when I saw the two cars in the driveway. I pulled up along the street and closed my eyes while gripping the steering wheel. Focused on running in to get my shirt and back out, I didn't bother to remove my keys from the ignition. I wouldn't acknowledge her if she said anything to me.

My heart beat frantically when I approached the front door. I hesitated before opening it, thinking I'd heard her yell. When I didn't hear it again, I continued inside.

Her agonizing cries stole the breath from my lungs. I stared in horror at the large man pounding his fist into my mother's side as she cowered on the floor in front of the couch, her hands over her head. She hollered in pain with each blow, trying to shrink away from him without anywhere to go.

"What are you doing?" I yelled, without thinking about anything except making him stop, despite the fact that he had a good five inches on me and looked enraged enough to take down a bull.

"This is none of your business," the guy growled at me. "Get the fuck out of here."

"Emily," my mother gasped. She tried to pull herself up on the coffee table. My mouth opened in shock when I saw the blood gushing out of her nose and the swelling enveloping her right eye.

He wasn't about to let her get back up, turning toward her as she stumbled to her feet. He raised his bloodied fist just as I screamed, "No!" The collision spun my mother around, and she teetered over the top of the coffee table. It collapsed upon impact. Her crumpled body didn't move, sprawled awkwardly on the splintered wood.

He turned to intercept me when I rushed to her, shoving me out of his way with virtually no effort. I landed hard on my side with a grunt.

"You want to make this your business?" the guy threatened from above me. I shrank into the floor. He snarled down at me as he breathed heavily through flared nostrils. His black eyes threatened to bore right through me. "Then you're going to get hurt, little girl. This is between me and Rachel, so I'm only going to warn you one last time. Stay the fuck out of it."

I tensed, prepared for him to hit me. But he moved past me, slamming the front door behind him. I scrambled to my knees and slid over to the collapsed coffee table, where my mother was starting to moan.

"Mom?" I called to her with tears in my eyes. "Can you hear me?"

She groaned louder and squinted with her good eye. "Emily? Is he gone?"

"Yeah, he's gone," I assured her, tenderly sitting her up. She whimpered with the slightest movement. "Can you get up? We need to get you to the hospital."

"I think I broke my wrist," she cried, holding her left wrist, the one she'd held out to break her fall.

"Easy," I coaxed gently. My voice was steady as I supported her to sit, but my entire body was shaking.

"I'm sorry," she gasped, fresh tears streaming down her face. "I'm so sorry."

I consoled her, dismissing her pleas. "Now let's see if you can stand." Supporting her under her arm, I helped her up.

She was crying uncontrollably by the time we reached the car. I took a deep breath when I sat on the driver's seat and tried to remember how to get to the hospital. I needed to remain calm so I could think clearly.

"It's okay," I breathed to myself. "Everything's going to be okay." I flipped my eyes toward my sobbing mother and said it louder for her to hear, "Everything's going to be okay."

Her cries dwindled to spastic breaths and sniffles as we neared the hospital.

"How are you doing?" I asked, afraid to take my eyes off the road, strangling the steering wheel.

"I'm sorry," she choked again.

"Okay." I dismissed her apology anxiously. "But how are you feeling? Can you see out of that eye? Does anything else hurt?"

"I think I'll be fine," she murmured, wiping the blood from her face with her sleeve-covered hand.

"Who was that guy?" I asked, now that she was starting to sound more coherent.

She just shook her head.

"Rachel," I demanded forcefully. "Who was that guy? Why did he do this to you?"

She swallowed audibly and released a quivering breath. "I owe him some money," she whispered faintly.

I pulled my brows together. "For what?"

She wouldn't answer. I didn't ask again.

I tried to remember if I knew what he looked like, for when the police asked. Besides being big and sleazy-looking, I couldn't remember anything about his face. Then I knew. There was only one reason my mother would owe a guy like that.

"He's your dealer," I concluded out loud. Rachel remained silent. I couldn't stand to even look at her. I clenched my teeth together and stared at the road as the anger built up in my gut, tightening every muscle in my body.

When we arrived at the emergency-room entrance, I demanded, "Give me your phone."

"What?" she squeaked. "Why?"

"I'm calling Sharon to pick you up," I told her, my voice edged with fury. "You should probably stay with her anyway until you can fix your mess."

"Emily," she pleaded desperately. "Please don't leave."

"I'm not staying here with you," I snapped coldly, unable to look at her. "I'll go back to the house to pack you a bag, and I'll leave it on the porch for Sharon to pick up."

"Don't," she sobbed. "Don't say anything, okay?"

I turned toward her with my face pulled tight in disgust. I couldn't believe she was actually asking me to lie for her. I shook my head in anguished disbelief.

"Please," she begged. "I'm just going to tell them I was robbed and he took off before I could see him." Her eye was practically swollen shut, and congealed blood lined her nose. Her one good eye continued to tear up as she breathed in spasms. She looked horrid. But I couldn't pity her. As she gibbered in front of me, desperate for me to protect her with another of her lies, I loathed her.

I seethed through clenched teeth, "Don't worry. I won't tell the police that your drug dealer beat you because you owe him money. It's none of my business, remember?"

She gasped in a sob and turned from me, carefully letting herself out of the car and leaving her phone on the seat. As soon as the door was closed, I pulled away without looking back.

The impact of what had happened sank in as I turned on to the main road, and I pressed my lips together to keep them from trembling. The anger kept back the tears, but my body shook despite my efforts.

I parked along a residential street and picked up her phone with an unsteady hand. After I'd left a message for Sharon, my phone rang.

I took a deep breath before answering.

"Emma?" Jonathan said when I answered with a strained voice. "Are you okay? Where are you?"

I closed my eyes and grimaced. He was at my soccer game. "Umm…I had to get my shirt," I tried to explain, my voice cracking.

"What happened?" he demanded urgently. "Emma, where are you?"

"I had to take Rachel to the hospital," I told him, trying to remain calm. "Jonathan…" I pressed my lips together. The anger was taking over, and I was about to lose it. I breathed in through my nose to ward off the tears.

"Are you okay?"

"Yeah." I exhaled, took another deep breath and explained, "There was some guy looking for money. He beat her pretty bad."

"What?" Jonathan practically yelled. "Did he hurt you?"

"No, I'm fine. But she's a mess." I bit my trembling lip and the tears escaped.

"Where are you now?" he demanded. "I'm driving back toward Weslyn. Where are you?"

"I'm going back to her house," I explained. "I have to pack a bag so she can stay at Sharon's."

"Emma, I don't think you should go back there."

"He's gone," I told him, wiping my cheeks.

"Don't go into the house until I get there," he instructed me firmly before hanging up.

I pulled back onto the road and fought for control over the nerves twisting inside me, tucking everything away, as I was so good at doing. I was numb but focused by the time I pulled into the driveway. Jonathan hadn't arrived yet.

The front door was still open from our hasty exit. I scouted the street in search of cars, but none were in sight. I was confident the dealer wasn't coming back.

I walked through the screen door and stood in the foyer, listening. The house remained silent, so I continued up the stairs. I was about to walk into her room when I thought I heard a board creak. My heart stopped. I turned toward the stairs, but there wasn't anyone there.

I exhaled, realizing I was holding my breath, and started toward her door. I caught sight of my open door out of the corner of my eye and froze. Something was wrong. I turned back, my heart racing. Lying on the floor inside my room was a small blue gift box—the gift box that held the necklace Evan had given me. The necklace that was supposed to be tucked under my clothes in my top drawer.

He *had* come back.

I raced across the hall. I was shaking my head, yammering, "No, no, no, no," when I slammed into his chest. Rocked backward, I cautiously stepped away while he continued out of my room. He revealed a snarky smirk. My eyes widened, fearing he'd hurt me as he had my mother. My heart thrust against my chest—I braced myself to run. That's when I saw the necklace in his hand.

"Oh no," I cried in a breath. Without considering the consequences, I lunged toward him and reached for it. He grabbed my hand before I could touch it, shoving me away.

"You should have listened," he grunted. The hardened glare in his dark eyes sent a chill through me. I knew that look. I instinctively began to raise my hands to protect myself, but the punch knocked me to the floor. Pain flooded through my jaw, and my eyes filled with black dots.

I scrambled to my feet, trying to find my focus, needing to reach him before he could make it to the stairs. I pulled at his hand. He turned back around, snatching the necklace out of reach, and exclaimed, "You little bitch. What the fuck are you thinking?"

"You can't have it," I cried. "Please, I'll pay you. But you can't take that from me."

He laughed and shoved me hard. I collided with the wall and grunted.

"Who the fuck do you think you are?" he sneered. He swung his arm and backhanded me across the head, knocking me to my hands and knees. My head pounded, but I willed myself to get back on my feet. Before I could, his boot crashed into my ribs.

I screamed out and fell to the floor, my arms wrapped around me as I curled into a ball, unable to catch my breath.

"Emma!" I heard from the bottom of the stairs.

I couldn't find my voice to warn him, to tell him to leave. Immobile in my curled position on the floor, I heard scuffling and grunts. I rolled over to see Jonathan shoving the guy against the wall and thrusting his fist into his stomach. The guy buckled over.

I used the wall to help me up, and leaned against it with an arm across my ribs. Every breath was agonizing. I wanted to yell out, but I could only gasp in broken breaths. I fumbled for my phone, but it wasn't in my pocket. I searched for it on the floor but couldn't find it.

The sparkle of the diamond caught my eye on the floorboards at my feet. I wrapped my fingers around it and clenched it tightly in my fist, feeling the stone digging into my palm.

Jonathan landed a punch to the side of the guy's head, causing him to stagger back. Before he could regain his balance, Jonathan followed with another to his jaw, and the guy teetered over, landing hard on the floor. Jonathan kept hold of his shirt, propping him up, and slammed his fist into his face. The guy's arms went limp by his sides, but Jonathan was relentless, swinging over and over again.

"Jonathan!" I screamed as blood smeared the man's face. The tendons in Jonathan's neck strained as he continued to pummel the mangled face, blood spraying out of the man's mouth and nose. His rage was insatiable.

I staggered over and grabbed the arm that was holding the guy up. "Jonathan!"

Jonathan's head snapped up. His eyes were dark and feral. I didn't recognize him with his lips pulled tight in a hateful sneer. I stumbled back, inhaling sharply.

It took him a moment to focus on me, for his eyes to soften. The stone disintegrated, but it was too late. I stood with my mouth open in abhorrence. His face contorted painfully when he saw the horror on my face.

Jonathan slowly lowered the guy to the floor and stood up, not taking his eyes off me.

"Emma," he breathed desolately. I shook my head, unable to comprehend what I'd just witnessed. I backed away and stared down at the unrecognizable figure on the floor. He wasn't moving. I couldn't even tell if he was breathing. His face was deformed and drenched in blood; he didn't look human.

"Emma, look at me," Jonathan instructed calmly, no longer dazed. "Don't look at him, look at me."

I pulled my eyes away from the blood-spattered face and focused on Jonathan. "Emma, keep looking at me. Are you okay?"

He moved to touch my cheek. "Your face." I pulled back sharply, forcing him to withdraw his blood-covered hand. I absently raised my hand to my mouth and winced at its touch. When I pulled it away, my fingertips were covered in blood. At first, I wasn't sure if it was mine. But then I tasted the tang of it in my mouth. I ran my tongue along the cut on the inside of my lip, where my teeth had punctured the tissue.

I was too numb with shock to recognize the pain. Everything moved slowly. I couldn't think. I couldn't breathe. I just stood in that spot and stared at Jonathan's concerned, blood-speckled face.

"Is he..." I rasped, but couldn't finish the question, my eyes drifting back down to the blood covering the floor.

"Don't look at him." Jonathan stepped toward me to block my view. He guided me to the stairs with outstretched arms, without touching me.

"What did you do?" The intensity in his hardened face flashed before me, and I shuddered. "You looked so...angry."

"I'm sorry you had to see that. But he hurt you. And I will never let anyone hurt you." There was a quiet strength in his voice. "Sit here, okay."

I grabbed the banister and slowly lowered myself onto the top step. I was still stunned, unable to form a coherent thought. I kept seeing the man's face explode, and feeling the spray of blood across my cheeks. But what truly disturbed me was the image of Jonathan, so cold and rigid with fury. I smudged the drying blood off my cheek with the back of my hand.

Jonathan sat down beside me and blotted my face with a wet towel. I stared at him blankly. His face was clean and smooth. He appeared calm and alert, although he kept examining me uneasily, like he was afraid I might fall apart.

I pulled back with a quick breath at the touch of the cloth to my mouth. "We'll put some ice on that when we get back." His brown eyes connected with mine, and he spoke to me softly. "Just sit here and look straight ahead, okay?"

I nodded. This didn't feel real. I started to wonder if I was dreaming. I couldn't move. This had to be a dream. But then the pain seeped through my ribs, and the side of my face throbbed. The taste of blood ran over my tongue.

I heard Jonathan shift the unconscious body, then the jangling of keys. I kept my eyes closed as Jonathan brushed past me down the stairs. My entire midsection screamed with every breath. I let the agony writhe through me, desperately needing it to keep me grounded.

"Emma," Jonathan called to me, redirecting my tortured reality. I opened my eyes to find him next to me. "I need you to get in your car. You're going to follow me, okay?"

I searched his calm face, slowly becoming more alert. "Where are we going?"

"Don't worry about anything. You just need to follow me." His dark eyes beseeched me to trust him, and I nodded.

I pulled myself up and let out a pained breath.

"Are you okay?" he questioned in alarm, putting his hand on my arm to support me. "How bad are you hurt?"

"I'll be all right," I grunted breathily, moving away from him down the stairs. I didn't want him to touch me. The unrelenting rage that had overtaken him still haunted me.

My car wasn't in the driveway. In its place were Jonathan's truck and a dark blue Charger. I looked around in confusion before locating my car on the street, closer to the neighbor's house on the corner. I slowly made my way to it, panting in pain with each step.

I sat with the engine running and waited, staring straight ahead. Eventually, the Charger pulled in front of me.

I drove behind him in a trance, focusing on the license plate with my right arm folded across my ribs, squeezing the diamond into my palm. We pulled into the parking lot of the bar outside of town where we'd picked up Rachel. Even though it was the middle of the day, there were still a few cars in the deserted dirt parking lot.

I watched Jonathan wipe down the handle of the car door before walking over and getting into my passenger seat.

"Drive," he ordered. I pulled away and merged back on to the main road.

When the bar disappeared from sight, he offered to drive.

I shook my head, needing to concentrate on something other than what we'd just done. We drove in silence until I pulled into the driveway. I shut off the engine and didn't make a move to get out.

"Jonathan, is he dead?" I asked in a whisper, turning my head to look at him.

"No," he assured me. "He needs to go to the hospital, but he's not dead. Someone will find him."

"Will he come after us?"

"No. You don't have to worry about him ever again. I promise." His eyes shone with conviction, and I knew he was confident in his words. I wasn't.

I got out of the car and Jonathan followed me to the house. He reached for the screen door to pull it open for me, and I stopped at the sight of his raw bloody knuckles. "Your hand," I gasped.

"Don't worry about it," he replied dismissively. "We need to get some ice on your face to help the swelling."

I shook my head. "You need to wrap that. I think we have something in the bathroom."

I climbed the stairs with Jonathan behind me and continued to the bathroom without pause, past the blood that still covered the floor. While Jonathan rinsed his hands, I rummaged through the closet and pulled out ointment and gauze bandages.

He blotted his knuckles dry. I gently balanced his hand on my closed fist to inspect the scraped skin that shone with blood. I was about to squeeze the ointment on his knuckles when he pulled it away. "I'll be fine."

"Jonathan," I implored him, looking up at him. My words were lost when I realized how close we were.

His dark eyes pulled me in. I couldn't move. He raised his hand, gliding his fingertips across my bruised face. I inhaled with a shiver at his touch. He slowly leaned forward. I held my breath, lost in his penetrating gaze. I closed my eyes just before his lips gently brushed against mine.

I squeezed my hand and the stone cut into me. With a shake of my head, I pulled away, my breath coming in gasps. Jonathan creased his brow in pained confusion. I rushed past him.

"Emma!" he called out as I scurried down the stairs. "Emma, please!" he called again, his voice urgent. I pushed through the door, leaving him behind.

39. BREATHE FOR ME

Evan?" I called into the kitchen as I pushed open the door, my eyes frantically scanning the room. I paused, but only heard my wavering breaths.

"Evan?" I called out again more desperately as I continued down the hall.

"Emma?" His eyes tightened in confusion, then widened when I came into full view from where he stood at the bottom of the stairs. "Emma!" he exclaimed. "What happened to you?"

The pained shock in his blue eyes incapacitated me. I opened my mouth to speak but only gasped, unable to find the words. His face twisted in panic when I faltered, sinking to my knees with my arms wrapped around my ribs.

I closed my eyes at the touch of his arms sliding around me and collapsed against his chest. I didn't cry. I didn't say a word. I just breathed jagged bursts of air. He gently rocked my quaking body with his cheek pressed against my temple. I could barely hear him breathe, "Oh, Emma, what happened to you?" I remained quiet and just let him hold me.

I couldn't keep the blood-soaked face from my thoughts, or Jonathan's hardened glare as he'd continued to punch it. The dark look in his eye when he finally turned toward me, then the shock when he saw my horrified reaction. His touch on my cheek, and the brush of his lips.

My head shot up, and I searched for Evan, gasping frantically.

"Emma?" His eyes darted across mine, tight and intense. "No
one can hurt you now. Okay?"

I nodded, and my chin quivered. I couldn't do anything except
breathe in spasms as my eyes blurred with tears. But I still didn't cry.
I couldn't. My entire body felt like it was about to burst apart, and
I was doing all I could to hold it together.

"Can you get up?" he asked, with his arms still encasing me. I
shook my head and rested on his chest, closing my eyes and concentrating on the quickened beats against my ear. "You won't stop
shaking, Em. Please tell me what happened to you."

I exhaled in a rasp, unable to speak. I felt like I was breathing
under water. I pressed my nose into his shirt and inhaled him, trying to fight my way back to the surface.

"Evan?" Vivian questioned in confusion. "Why are you…
Emily? What's happened?"

"I don't know," Evan replied quietly.

I opened my eyes at the touch of her cool, soft hand sweeping
against my cheek. Her bright blue eyes examined me sorrowfully.
"We're going to take care of you." I pressed my lips together to hold
in the ache and nodded. I closed my eyes again, and Evan cupped
the back of my head and squeezed me gently.

I heard her heels click on the floor as she said, "I think that will
be all for today. Thank you for your help, Analise. If you wouldn't
mind calling your mother to let her know that we'll reschedule that
meeting for another day."

Evan slowly pulled back to examine me. I met his troubled gaze
reluctantly. He gingerly tilted my chin to get a better look at the
side of my face. "Let me get some ice."

He started to move away and my eyes widened in panic. "No,"
I pleaded, grabbing his arm. "Not yet."

Evan drew me back into him, kissing the top of my head. "Okay," he agreed.

"What do you need?" Vivian asked from behind me.

"An ice pack," Evan told her calmly, not letting me go.

"Do you think she needs to go to the hospital?" Vivian asked.

"I don't know. She hasn't said more than a few words since she got here."

"Emma?" Vivian soothed. I opened my eyes at the use of my preferred name, never having heard her say it before. Evan loosened his hold. "Emma, what happened to you, dear?"

I looked into her sharp blue eyes as she patiently waited for me to explain. "He tried to take it." My voice came out quiet and shaky.

"Take what?" she coaxed gingerly.

Evan released me carefully when I moved my hand out from between us, unfolding my fingers to reveal the necklace. I heard her breathe in sharply at the blood coating my palm. I'd squeezed the diamond so tightly it had torn open my skin. I closed my hand back around it, numb to the wounds.

"Who was it?" she asked, her voice strong but tender.

"I don't know," I told her. "He was in my room when I got home."

She nodded and stood back up. "I'm calling the police."

"No," I begged, turning toward her. The pain in my ribs seared through me and I screamed, folding in half.

"Emma!" Evan called out, his arms back around me. "Where else did he hurt you?"

My chest tightened against the panting breaths, tears streaming down my face.

"Emma, we need to look, okay?"

I slowly sat up and carefully lifted my shirt. My side was dark reddish-purple where his foot had made contact. Evan winced and squeezed my hand. I quickly looked away, unable to witness his aggrieved reaction.

"I don't want to go to the hospital," I pleaded to Evan.

"Then I'm calling Michelle," Vivian retorted from beside me, drawing my attention. "We'll go to her office, and the police will meet us there." By the set look in her eye, I knew this wasn't a choice. She bent down next to us and put her hand on the side of my face, smiling affectionately. "Let us care for you, Emma."

It was difficult to face myself in the fogged mirror after stepping out of the shower. The right side of my jaw was deep red. My lower lip looked like it was still packed with gauze, even though I'd removed it a while ago, once the bleeding had stopped. A small cut ran over my lip where my tooth had torn into it.

I gingerly spread the clear gel over the swollen, discolored skin, cooling it instantly. I turned the tube over in my hand, wondering if the homeopathic medicine would really get rid of the bruising as quickly as Dr. Vassar said it would. There was no way I was going to school, or anywhere in public for that matter, until it went away.

I eased Evan's T-shirt over my head, holding my breath against the sharp pain triggered by simply raising my arms. Four to six weeks. That's how long it would take for the two fractured ribs to heal. I hoped the pain would subside in less time than that, considering breathing was a form of torture.

I walked into the guest room feeling as broken as I looked. I stopped at the sight of Evan pacing next to the bed, staring at the floor with his hands on his head, unaware that I was there.

Evan strode back and forth, lost in whatever torturous thoughts had overtaken him. He'd been so calm all day—holding me, comforting me, quietly watching as Dr. Vassar examined me. He listened silently while holding my hand when the police asked questions. Remaining by my side, strong and supportive, he'd hardly said a word.

But now he looked like he was coming apart. He flexed his hands, breathing in exaggerated breaths. Seeing him this disturbed paralyzed me. He raised his head and stopped abruptly when he noticed I was watching.

My brows twitched at the sight of his glassy blue eyes. He hid the despair under his lids and tried to regain his composure, but his jaw only became tighter and the tendons along his neck rigid.

"Evan?" I whispered, not moving.

He opened his eyes. They glistened in agony, and the line between them deepened when he looked at me. We remained still for a moment. His torment ripped through me.

"I promised no one would ever hurt you again." Despite his strained appearance, his voice was calm and strong. I looked into his eyes and was suffocated by the weight of their despair.

"What?" I shook my head in confusion.

Evan remained still, not moving toward me—the muscles along his arms remained taut, like he was in physical agony just saying the words. "That night, when you were lying there, broken and barely breathing, I promised. I promised to always love you and that no one would ever hurt you again."

My mouth opened in shock, but I was too stunned to speak. I moved to the bed, still trying to understand, and lowered myself to sit on the end of it, staring blindly at the floor. My first thought released through my lips: "What did I do to you?"

Evan knelt before me. It felt like the air was being crushed from my lungs.

"You were there?" This was one of the details I'd never heard, because I'd refused to learn what had actually happened to me that night. And he'd never told me.

Evan swallowed with a slow blink and nodded his head. "I knew I couldn't convince you to leave, so I stayed. I waited in my car, making sure nothing happened. But I fell asleep, and when I woke up, she was there."

"Oh my God," I gasped, having a hard time accepting what he was telling me, shaking my head. "No."

"George was already in your room, trying to get her off of you, but he couldn't. I pushed him out of the way and threw her off, but—" He stopped and closed his eyes. I watched his chest rise with a heavy breath before he continued. I wanted to make him stop. I didn't want to hear it. He wasn't supposed to be there, in my nightmare.

But I was too overwhelmed to ask him not to continue. I watched his lips move. "I couldn't believe what she'd done to you. You were cuffed to the bed, and there was tape over your mouth. You'd been crying, the tears were still running down your face. But...you weren't breathing."

"Evan," I gasped, my eyes blurred. I placed my hand on his cheek, and my body ached with every word. "You shouldn't have seen that."

He looked up at me with his eyes tight, shaking his head fiercely. "I was supposed to protect you, Emma."

A tear slid down my cheek.

"But I didn't." His eyes closed, he struggled with the words. I knew he was still tortured by the image of what he'd seen.

"You were so still and pale," he continued. His smoky blue eyes connected with mine, and he whispered, "I breathed for you."

"You?" The shock of his confession devoured me.

"I begged for you to breathe with every breath I gave to you. I kept pleading for you to breathe over and over again. And then... then you did." He blinked away the tears that flooded his eyes. "I promised—"

"Evan," I interrupted. "This isn't your fault." I couldn't even begin to imagine what he'd gone through that night. What he'd seen. What he had been forced to do. And then had had to live with while keeping it from me for nearly a year. "I'm so sorry," I softly cried.

"Emma, don't," he urged. "You don't have anything to be sorry for."

"But you," I stumbled, "But you shouldn't have..." I couldn't find the words to explain that he wasn't supposed to have been there. I chose to stay. It was my silence, my denial, my decision, that put us there that night.

"I shouldn't have what?" he challenged. "I *should* have called the police, or told someone long before that night. I know that now. And I have to live with that. But wanting to protect you, loving you...You will always be my choice."

His words pierced me, and I closed my eyes, letting the tears slip through my lids. Evan lowered his head on my lap and wrapped his arms around me. I ran my hand over his hair, comforting him.

I'd never wanted to hurt him. To damage him. But I had. And even now, my choices continued to destroy him—all I had to do was look in his eyes to see it.

Vivian didn't say anything when he stayed with me that night. We lay facing each other, with his hand covering mine. It was difficult to lie on my broken ribs, but Dr. Vassar had explained that it would help me breathe better, and it did. The tortured look on his face pierced my heart. I was having a hard time finding my breath.

"Will you please tell me about Rachel and why you spent the day with Jonathan?" he asked softly, not taking his eyes off mine.

"You knew?"

"Of course," he replied. "What happened in that house, Emma?"

I wanted to look away, but I couldn't. His impassioned blue eyes held me captive. My voice was soft and strained with emotion.

"I thought she would be different. But she hasn't changed. When she started drinking, I was convinced it was my fault—that I reminded her of my dad and I upset her. I wanted to help her, but she just kept drinking. And got worse. Each time she'd hurt me more. In the end…she doesn't love me. She never has."

Evan was quiet, gently running his hand over my cheek.

"And Jonathan?" Evan coaxed.

My eyes flickered, fearing he could see into me. "He was there. He knows how unstable she is, so he understands. He's become…a friend. We went for a drive that day, to get away from her. It wasn't planned. He just wanted to be there for me." I couldn't say more. It was evident from the tightness around his eyes that he was trying to understand, but that this was hard to hear. I kept the rest of what we'd shared to myself.

"Now I'm here for you," he whispered, holding my hand and kissing it gently. "Close your eyes, Emma. I'm not going any- where."

I closed my eyes. But I didn't sleep.

———

When I opened my eyes again, it was light and Evan wasn't next to me. Sara was.

"Hey," she greeted me with an endearing smile. "You slept a long time."

"I did?" I responded in surprise, since I didn't remember sleep- ing at all. Holding my breath, I gingerly pushed myself up and noticed it was almost noon. "What are you doing here? I thought you weren't coming back until tomorrow."

"Jared called," she explained. "I came back on the earliest flight I could get."

"You didn't have—"

"Don't even start, Emma," she scolded. "You know I'd do anything for you. Even sit next to an annoying guy who snored on my shoulder the entire flight." She grinned. But her grin couldn't mask her troubled eyes.

"Thanks, Sara," I replied sincerely. "Where's Evan?"

"Cooking something," Sara explained. Moving closer, she raised her hand to my cheek, careful not to touch it. "That's going to take some great makeup skills. Good thing you have me."

"Good thing," I agreed with a wry smile, wincing when I pulled myself up to sit, moving the pillow behind me. Sara's eyes tightened.

"Oh, I have these for you," she said, handing me two ice packs. "Evan has strict orders."

I took the packs to set on my bruises. Sara opened her mouth to say something, then stopped. Her brows pulled together and she listened intently. She walked to the door and opened it. I watched her curiously, and then I heard it too. It sounded like someone was calling my name.

Sara moved out the door quickly, and I scooted off the bed to follow. I couldn't make out who was saying it, but they kept calling for me.

"I know she's here," the muffled voice declared. "Emma!"

Sara was standing in the open doorway of the kitchen when I rounded the corner.

"Sara, don't let her out here, okay," Evan instructed from the porch.

"What's going on?" I asked, my pulse picking up when I caught sight of the hardened look on Evan's face.

Sara closed the door, and I could hear Evan continue sternly, "She's fine. You don't need to be here."

I looked out the window in the sitting room and saw Jonathan standing in the driveway. My heart faltered. He was clenching his fists, and his face was reddening.

"Just let me see her, Evan," he demanded, becoming more agitated and taking a step toward Evan. "At least tell her I'm here."

"Why *is* he here?" Sara asked from behind me.

"He just wants to know that I'm okay," I told her, heat rising to my cheeks. With Evan stonewalling him, I knew he was on the brink of losing his patience, and I couldn't let it escalate. I moved past her toward the kitchen.

"Where are you going?" Sara demanded urgently.

"He just wants to know that I'm okay," I repeated, my heart beating harder against my chest.

I opened the door, and Evan glanced at me quickly without realizing it was me. He turned back, stunned, when he did. "Emma, don't."

"It's okay," I assured him with forced calmness. "He just wants to make sure I'm okay."

Evan tensed when I walked past him, but he didn't stop me.

Jonathan's face softened when I approached, the confrontational glare instantly replaced by a subtle smile, but the anxious look in his eye remained.

"Hey," he greeted me quietly when I neared him. I stopped in front of him with my arms crossed protectively over my ribs.

"Hey," I replied timidly. "What are you doing here?"

"I'm sorry," he began. "I've been trying to call you. I was going out of my mind worrying about you. You left so fast after..." He paused, and my heart faltered at the remembrance. "I didn't know how badly you were hurt. I needed to see you."

"Oh," I responded, my cheeks reddening. "Um, I don't even know where my phone is. I should've called. I'm sorry I didn't." I could feel Evan watching us, and knew Sara was probably next to him as well. I didn't dare look.

"How are you?" he asked, but it was a loaded question, and I didn't answer until he clarified. "How badly are you hurt?"

"I'll be okay," I replied softly.

"I scared you, didn't I?" he said, his voice faltering. I looked up into his eyes, having avoided them since I stepped out of the house. I was struck by the sorrow in them. "I promised never to do that. I'm so sorry, Emma."

I swallowed hard, and nodded, unable to speak.

"I care about you," he explained. "I couldn't—" He glanced toward Evan without finishing, recognizing we weren't alone. "What does he know?"

"Um," I faltered. "I didn't say anything, really. Just explained how everything was a mess with Rachel. And I didn't tell the police you were there either. I told them I walked in on the guy and couldn't remember what he looked like."

"Okay," Jonathan accepted with a nod. "So he doesn't know about the nightmares, or your fears, or..."

I shook my head, dropping my eyes to the ground guiltily. I gripped my hands as the tension crashed in on us. I couldn't breathe. Jonathan reached to touch my arm, and I backed away with a shake of my head.

"I know," he said with a defeated sigh. "It's not right to put you in this situation."

I lifted my eyes to his. The remorse in his glistening gaze caused my heart to falter.

"Emma, please don't give up on me." His words spilled out in a desperate rush, leaving me speechless.

"Please," he begged again.

"I won't," I whispered. "I just need some time."

"I understand," he replied, bowing his head. "I'll go. But I'll hear from you...when you're ready?"

I nodded, evading his eyes. I turned away, my shoulders bowed, crushed with guilt. I continued past Evan and Sara, who were standing on the porch, watching our every move. But I knew they hadn't heard a single word we'd said.

Sara followed me inside while Evan waited for Jonathan to back out of the driveway.

"How'd he even know where you live?" Sara asked Evan when he closed the door.

"I don't know," Evan replied, his eyes following me carefully.

"It's not difficult to find anything in Weslyn," I found myself saying. "You just have to ask." They peered at me curiously.

"What was that about?" Sara demanded as I moved to leave the room. "He seemed so upset."

"He was there," Evan said before I could utter a word. My heart skipped a beat, wondering how he knew.

"What?" Sara spun toward him. She flipped her eyes from Evan to me. I looked down. That's all she needed. "He was. Why?"

"Why did you lie to the police?" Evan demanded on top of her question.

I took a deep breath and began. "The guy was my mother's drug dealer. I didn't want the police to know." I looked from one to the other for a reaction. They appeared surprised, but remained quiet. I shifted my gaze back to the floor and continued. "He beat her pretty bad because she owed him money. I found her when I went to the house to get my soccer shirt. I ended up having to take her to the hospital. Jonathan found out and didn't want me to go back to the house, but I figured the guy would be gone. I was wrong." I paused, deciding how to continue. "Jonathan showed up, and fought the guy off."

"That's what I thought. I saw his knuckles," Evan said with a slight edge to his voice. "So, he protected you?" I raised my head, struck by his tone. I nodded, and pain shot across his face, knowing Jonathan had done what he'd vowed to do—to protect me.

"So why did he come by here?" Sara asked, breaking our tense connection.

"I ran out," I explained quickly. I couldn't tell them how badly Jonathan had beaten the guy, and that I thought he might be dead.

Or the true reason I'd left in such a rush. I took a quick breath and repeated, "He just wanted to know that I was okay."

"That's it?" Evan asked skeptically, examining me. My face flamed up, fearing he'd seen more between us. I nodded, unable to hold his gaze for more than a second. "I know you explained that you and Jonathan are friends and that you can talk to him about Rachel. I get it. But why do I get the feeling he knows more than I do?" His voice became stronger as he spoke, more agitated. I opened my mouth instinctively to defend Jonathan, but stopped when I saw the challenging look on Evan's face. "Then the way he was out there…The way he was looking at you…" I shifted my eyes. He released a breath, and lowered his voice. "I'm sorry, Emma, but I just don't trust him."

And maybe he had good reason not to.

40. HONEST TRUTH

No matter how hard I tried not to, I kept thinking about what I'd witnessed. His dark eyes were so compelling and trusting, yet could turn instantly cold and hard. There was more hidden in their darkness than pain and torture. More than anger and loathing.

It seemed impossible that the same man who stayed up with me in the middle of the night, laughing at infomercials, was capable of bludgeoning someone into a grotesque, bloody mess. I shuddered at the remembrance, hugging the pillow against me tighter.

"What are you thinking about?"

I turned my head with a start. Evan stood in the doorway of the sunroom, the warm rays lighting up the breathtaking angles of his face. There was no darkness hidden in his steel-blue eyes. The disturbing thoughts were instantly brushed away at the sight of him.

"Hi," I greeted him happily. "How was school?" I closed the book that was resting on my lap and set it on the wicker table beside me along with the pillow I was mangling.

"The same." He shrugged, sitting down and resting my legs across his lap. "How was your day?"

"I helped stuff envelopes," I told him. "So exciting."

Evan laughed. He leaned toward me and ran his fingers over the vanishing bruise along my jaw, inspecting it. Then he leaned a little closer and gently kissed me.

"Aren't you supposed to be at practice?" I suddenly remembered when he pulled away.

"The coach had an appointment, so we have practice tomorrow instead."

"On a Saturday?"

"Unfortunately." Evan grimaced.

"Oh," I sighed. "I was hoping we could get my things tomorrow. Anna hired some guys to move the furniture out this weekend, so I need to pack up before they arrive."

"Is Rachel back?"

"I have no idea," I answered with a shake of my head. "I haven't heard from her, but I don't really expect to either. I'm hoping she's not."

"Do you want to go there this afternoon?"

A jolt shot through me just thinking about going back to the house. I knew we'd have to eventually, but I wasn't expecting it to be this afternoon. I thought I'd have more time to prepare.

"Okay," I answered, "let's do this," realizing there wasn't any way to prepare for it, no matter how much notice I had.

"You don't have to," Evan reassured me, picking up on my anxiety. "Sara and I could go when she gets out of track practice. Besides, she said she wanted to help."

"No," I countered, trying to sound confident, "I can do it. I'll text her and tell her to meet us there when she gets out."

"Are you sure?" he queried again, eyeing me skeptically. "What if she's home?"

I didn't know how to tell him that it wasn't Rachel that made me dread going back to the house. It was the fear that there would still be blood on the floors. But the police hadn't returned to question me further after searching the house, so I was fairly confident that Jonathan had cleaned it up and disposed of the broken coffee table. I had a feeling I'd see the blood even with my eyes closed.

"I can handle it," I assured him. Evan stood and offered me his hand. I took it and eased myself from the wicker chaise that was layered with pillows for my comfort. It didn't matter how many pillows it had, they didn't keep the pain at bay every time I had to breathe.

"I wonder how bad it's going to be," I thought out loud as we weaved through the back roads of Weslyn.

"What?" Evan asked with uncertainty.

"My room."

"How come you didn't go back with the police to see if anything was taken?"

"Because I knew there wasn't," I replied flatly, knowing the only thing he'd tried to take was hanging around my neck.

"Do you think he'll come back?" I could feel him watching for my reaction.

I shook my head and stared out the window, not wanting him to see the look on my face as I closed my eyes and tried to push away the bloody image that induced a shudder. *What did we do?* I mouthed to my reflection, resting my head against the glass, replaying Jonathan wiping away his prints on the car door. I wondered how careful he had been when ridding the house of evidence.

I was so wrapped up in preparing myself to face the mess that I really didn't give much thought to what it was going to be like to see my mother—if she was home. Her car was still in the driveway when we pulled in. But it had probably been there since I took her to the hospital. When we neared the house, music reverberated through the front door, confirming that she'd returned.

Evan stopped on the steps and turned to me. "Do you want to do this? We don't have to."

Despite the nausea in my stomach, I nodded. He eyed me warily, but didn't try to talk me out of it. Evan opened the screen door for me. I took a deep breath and walked into the house.

I didn't look for her. I continued up the stairs and Evan followed. I kept my eyes on each step and veered into my room without looking at the spot where his battered body had lain motionless. By the time Evan closed the door behind us, my heart was beating so hard I thought I might fall over.

We waited for her reaction. The music continued in the kitchen, allowing us to relax and breathe easier. I was just beginning to think we'd be able to leave without incident when I heard the door beneath my bedroom slam shut. She must have been out back. Evan stopped and looked toward me, awaiting my reaction. I shook my head with a shrug, trying to appear unaffected.

"Oh, Emma," Evan said under his breath.

I snapped my attention back to the room and my mouth dropped open. "What the—"

It was completely torn apart. The mattress was pushed off the bed. The bureau drawers were dumped and tossed in a heap. The clothes in the closet were strewn across the floor. The only things left untouched were Evan's pictures on the cloth-covered bulletin board and the stacks of clothes on the top shelf in the closet.

"My laptop's gone," I noticed, deflated. I walked closer to the desk and discovered the hard drive on the floor beneath the desk. I eased myself under to pick it up. "At least I still have this. I guess I can always buy another laptop."

"True," Evan responded, trying to sound optimistic. Then he questioned in confusion, "But I thought you said he didn't take anything?"

"He didn't," I confirmed. "She must have, or someone from one of her parties maybe." I absorbed the disaster with a disheartened sigh. "Okay, let's do this."

Evan set the suitcase and a large duffel bag on the box spring. He scooped the clothes from the floor and tossed them next to me so I could stuff them in the bags. There was no point in folding them.

The music stopped. Evan and I hesitated and looked at each other just as Rachel called out, "Emily, are you here?" We'd driven my car, since it had more space than Evan's two-seater sports car. She must have spotted it in the driveway.

My heart sped up at the sound of her voice.

"What do I do?" I asked him, not ready to face her.

"She knows you're here, Emma," Evan said. "You don't have to answer. Or you just say yes and leave it at that."

"Emily?"

I breathed out through pursed lips and then hollered, "Yeah, I'm here." Evan and I stared at each other and waited, but she didn't say anything. I swallowed and tried to relax my shoulders.

Evan picked up armfuls of clothes at a time and shoved them in the bag. I knew he was trying to hurry, since I was unable to mask the escalation of my anxiety. I tried to convince myself that she didn't bother me. That I could get through this without having to face her. But she *did* get to me, and I didn't see how we'd avoid her when we left my room.

"You don't have to talk to her," Evan advised quietly, probably reading the fretful thoughts that flickered across my face. "We'll just leave. You won't have to say anything."

I nodded and mindlessly tucked the clothes in the duffel bag that was already stretched to its limit. Evan struggled to zip the suitcase.

"I'll bring these to the car and get the boxes and my duffel bag. The rest should fit in them, and then we'll go." He hesitated. "Are you going to be okay while I'm gone?"

"Yeah," I murmured.

I didn't move as I listened for Evan to walk down the stairs. The bedroom door didn't close all the way behind him, so I heard when she said, "Evan! I didn't know you were here too. What are you doing?" She sounded surprised. My jaw flexed at the sound of her voice.

"Just getting her things," he answered casually and continued out the front door.

"Emily, what's going on?" she called up to me, her voice heavy with concern. "What are you doing?"

I didn't answer and remained motionless—hoping she'd give up.

"Emily!" she yelled louder. "What's going on?!"

I closed my eyes and clenched my teeth. The angry storm began to rouse in my gut. I breathed deep, trying to control it. The boards creaked on the stairs.

I focused on remaining collected when I stepped out of my room, stopping her midstep. "I told you I was coming back to get my things." My voice came out even and controlled, but my hands were clenched by my sides.

She appeared confused. I stood stoically at the top of the stairs and took her in. Her right eye was encircled with a greenish blue bruise, and her left hand was in a black splint. I could tell there was more damage to her body as she leaned into railing for support.

She didn't react to the sight of the bruise on my face. But I didn't expect her to.

"You're leaving me?" she whimpered with big eyes.

My pulse quickened, spreading the anger into my muscles. I couldn't control it.

"Am I leaving you?" I repeated, my teeth grating with each word. I pulled my brows together and scoffed in disbelief. "Am *I* leaving *you*?"

Her eyes watered as she pleaded, "Please don't leave me."

Evan appeared behind her in the doorway. I caught sight him as he assessed our positions. "Emma." I focused on him, trying to push away the fury that was overtaking me. He flipped his eyes to my room, and I nodded. Without looking back at her, I returned to the bedroom.

Evan entered a few seconds later, closing the door behind him. "What happened?"

I shook my head and started pacing. "I can't believe her. I seriously think she's delusional."

"Emma, what did she say?"

"How could she be surprised that I'm leaving?" I fumed, staring at the floor as I continued to pace.

"Emma." He beckoned calmly.

"She didn't even say anything about the bruise. Does she even care what happened to me? Of course not!"

"Emma!" Evan bellowed loudly, standing in front of me. I stopped and looked up at him as he set his hands on my shoulders. "She doesn't matter."

I pressed my lips together to stifle the emotion and nodded. "You're right. I'm sorry."

"Don't be sorry," he soothed, pulling me into him. "I know this is hard. We don't have to stay."

I took a breath. "It's okay. We're almost done."

Evan kissed the top of my head before releasing me. "We'll be fast, all right?"

I nodded.

Evan handed me a box, and I started taking down the pictures on the board and placing them and the other items from my desk into it while he finished packing the clothes from the closet.

It was uncomfortably quiet as we rushed to gather my things. I tried to shut everything off as I finished with the box, not wanting to feel anything. But I couldn't. I couldn't quench the anger that burned in my chest every time I heard her voice asking if I was leaving—like *I* was the one abandoning *her*.

"Emma, you're shaking," Evan noticed, taking hold of my hand.

"Sorry. She got to me." I grimaced with my face scrunched.

"Maybe we should just go."

"Everything's pretty much packed anyway," I agreed, taking a look around.

Evan slung the duffel bag over his shoulder and picked up the box I'd packed. "I'll just come back in to get the last box." He nodded toward the one containing my sweatshirts and the pictures of my father I'd hidden beneath them.

In my final scan of the room I noticed something was missing, my heart skipping a beat.

"Are you coming?" Evan asked as he opened the door.

"I'll be down in a minute," I told him, searching desperately. "I want to look around one more time."

"I'll be right back," he said, his way of telling me not to leave the room without him.

I carefully knelt down and peered under the bureau and then the bed. I picked up the comforter that was on the floor. The framed picture of me and my father that had been on my bureau was gone. There was no reason anyone would want that picture, except for her. The one thing she thought I had left of my father, and she had taken it.

Anger engulfed my entire body. My heart pounded so hard, it was difficult to breathe.

I didn't wait for Evan. And I didn't walk out the door to his car. I sought her out in the kitchen where she sat at the table, slicing a tomato while listening to the radio.

"Do you want to stay for dinner?" she asked with a warm smile when I appeared in the doorway.

"What the fuck is wrong with you?" I snapped vehemently.

"Excuse me?" she asked in shock. "I thought you might want to stay for dinner. I thought we could talk."

"About what?" I shot back. "How much you don't want me? How much you miss my father and that you blame me for his death? Or the fact that your drug dealer beat the shit out of us because you have *serious* issues? Yeah, that's great dinner conversation. I think I'll pass."

"Why are you acting like this?" she questioned quietly, standing up and walking to the counter.

"Are you serious?" I shouted incredulously. "Are you *that* delusional?"

She picked up a prescription bottle, emptied a few pills into her hand and tossed them in the back of her throat, rinsing them down with a glass of water.

"Oh, or maybe you're just high," I accused her spitefully.

"What? It's medicine for my wrist," she said defensively. "But why should you care? You're leaving me. You don't care about me." Her voice broke. I felt a slight twinge in my chest. There had been a time when it hurt to see her this upset, and I would've done anything to console her. Not now. As quickly as the empathy surfaced, it was swallowed up.

"No, I don't care about you. Just like you don't care about me," I fumed, my voice cold and inhuman. "You can take the entire bottle. I don't give a fuck."

"I don't understand what's wrong with you." She shook her head, tears seeping down her cheeks. "I'll try harder. Don't leave me alone. Please, Emily. I'm so sorry."

"No you're not," I screamed, making her flinch. I lowered my voice again, and shot each word at her with lethal precision. "The only thing you're sorry about is that I was ever born. Or don't you remember telling me that in one of your drunken stupors? You conveniently forget how much you hurt me over and over again. And I'm stupid enough to keep letting you. Well, I'm done.

"You never wanted me, and I never wanted this life. So as far as you're concerned, I *am* dead. And you won't ever see me again."

Rachel sank to the floor sobbing inconsolably. I turned my back to her.

Fury pulsed through my veins, blinding me. I almost ran into Evan, who stood frozen with the screen door open, silently watching. He avoided my eyes, and my shoulders slumped in disgrace.

I hurried past Evan toward the car. My entire body trembled. I released a broken breath as the tears flooded my eyes.

"Emma," Evan called after me, rushing to catch up and grabbing my arm.

"I can't," I pulled away. "I can't be here. We need to go. Please. We need to go."

I turned away from him and climbed into the passenger side. I closed my eyes to hold back the tears, taking long drawn breaths. My chest tightened with each pass of air, trying to release the rage that possessed me.

Evan slid in beside me and pulled the keys from his pocket.

"I don't ever want to see her again," I choked, shaking my head. I pressed my fingers into my forehead, rubbing it hard with my eyes closed. "I can't..."

"I know," Evan said, starting the car. "Try to calm down, Emma. Breathe."

The shame of what he'd seen hit me as we drove away. I pulled my brows together in distress. "I'm so sorry, Evan. I don't know what just happened. I was just so...angry. I couldn't stop."

"I've never seen you like that before," Evan said quietly. "You always keep everything locked up. It was hard to watch, but you'd reached your limit."

I looked over at him, perplexed. "Evan, I was awful. Worse than awful. You should be disgusted with me." The weight of what I'd done crushed me, and I felt wretched.

"I was shocked," Evan admitted, glancing over at me quickly. "I mean, you were…enraged, and I hope to never see that side of you again. But Emma, after everything she's put you through, you had every right to be furious. Except for you wishing away this life. That…that bothered me."

"I was upset," I whispered, still unsettled by his reaction, or lack thereof. "You know I didn't mean it."

"I hope not," he returned, flashing me a worried glance.

"Where are we going?" I asked, looking around as he turned on to a street that didn't take us back to his house.

"Somewhere that will help you," Evan answered, reaching for my trembling hand.

Then I recognized where we were headed. "We're going to the high school?"

Evan just grinned.

I eyed him curiously when we pulled into the school's parking lot. "I don't understand."

"Just come with me," Evan requested, getting out of the car.

The school was practically deserted. A few voices could be heard through the halls, but most clubs had disbanded, and the sports' practices dispersed.

When we reached the second-floor corridor, Evan turned to me and instructed, "Close your eyes."

"Are you serious?" I asked dubiously, not really in the mood for one of his surprises.

"It's not what you think," he assured me. "Just close your eyes."

I let out a resigned breath and did as he directed. Evan kept hold of my hand and guided me further down the hall. We stopped and he released me. I heard the jangling of keys and the click of a lock.

"Keep them shut," he ordered, taking hold of my hand again and leading me forward.

With the slightest inhalation, I instantly recognized the scents swirling in the air.

"Breathe, Emma," he coaxed, squeezing my hand. "It's okay."

"How'd you know?" I asked, overcome with emotion. I breathed deeply and eased the air through my chest, searching for the release I'd always sought in this room. I opened my eyes and found Evan gazing at me affectionately.

"Because I know you."

I closed my eyes and consumed the faint traces of paint, glue and cleaner, releasing the darkened fury with each cleansing breath.

I moved to him and put my arms around his chest, pressing against him. "Thank you."

He held me tenderly, being careful not to squeeze too tight.

"Hold on to this life, Emma," he whispered. "You're so much stronger than you think you are."

I looked up at him with glistening eyes. Evan bent down, and the warmth of his lips captured my breath, helping me find the calm I was unable to find on my own.

41. POWER OF SUGGESTION

"Where are you?" Sara asked when I picked up the phone. I groaned, instantly realizing we'd forgotten to tell her that we weren't at Rachel's.

"Oh, Sara, I'm sorry," I replied. "We're driving back to Evan's. Rachel and I got into a horrible fight, so we left. Are you there?"

"Yeah. Did you get everything?"

I considered, then recalled, "There's one box left, but we can get it another day."

"Why don't I just grab it now, since I'm here?" she offered casually.

"You may not want to do that," I cautioned. "She was a mess when we left. I was…I was pretty ruthless."

"And I'm sure she had it coming," she responded, unaffected. "I don't care. I'll just run in, get it and leave."

"You were warned. Call me if you need to, otherwise just come to Evan's."

Evan raised his eyebrows when I hung up. "She's going in?"

I shrugged. "Guess so."

"Wow." He grimaced. "This should be interesting."

Before we reached Evan's, my phone rang. "Uh-oh," I groaned when I saw Sara's name on the screen.

"Emma, you need to come back to the house," she spewed urgently.

"Sara, what's wrong?" Fear paralyzed my heart.

"Rachel. She's not moving," she said in a rush. "The ambulance is coming but...oh, God."

"Sara?" My eyes flickered as I listened, but it was silent. I pulled the phone away from my ear to find that we'd been disconnected. "Evan, we need to go back."

Without me realizing, he'd turned around as soon as he heard the stress in my voice.

The car sped up. "What did she say?" he asked, keeping his eyes on the road.

"That Rachel wasn't moving, and an ambulance was on its way. But then...then something happened, and I lost her. Evan, if anything happens to Sara..." My mind was racing, fearing that the drug dealer had returned to collect the debt, despite his injuries. Or maybe someone else was doing it for him. I couldn't sit still, wanting us to drive faster, although Evan's acceleration through the empty residential streets meant we were traveling at easily twice the speed limit.

"We'll be there soon," he assured me, as I gripped the handle above the door.

My chest hurt from holding my breath as we turned on to the street. An ambulance, fire truck and two police cars were out front, their lights flashing brightly against the black backdrop.

"Oh no," I breathed. A thousand horrifying images rushed through my head, making me falter on weakened knees when I rushed out of the car.

"Sara!" I yelled, running toward the house. I was intercepted by a police officer, demanding that I stay outside. He questioned me about the people who lived there. I wasn't listening. I tried to see around him, frantically searching for her, but I was restrained and couldn't move forward.

I just about collapsed when I saw the paramedics exit and rush to the ambulance to retrieve a stretcher.

"What's going on? Please, you have to tell me if she's okay!" I pleaded in a desperate sob. "Sara!"

"Emma?" I heard her rasp. She sounded like she was right inside the door. I tried to get to her, but the police officer held up his hand, and I was pulled back.

"Miss, you need to stay outside until they've removed her."

"What?!" I demanded frantically. "What do you mean?!"

The paramedics and firefighters came into view through the open door, carrying a board.

"No," I gasped, tears pouring down my face. "No."

But then I saw the dark hair, not Sara's fiery red. I froze.

I watched unblinking as they transferred Rachel to the stretcher and wheeled her past me with an oxygen mask over her face. All the emotion drained out of me. I stared after her in shock.

"Emma!" Sara called, rushing out of the house. Her face was red and streaked with tears.

"Sara!" I exclaimed, hugging her tight. I knew my ribs were supposed to hurt. They should have hurt a lot today, but I couldn't feel anything. Sara sobbed into my shoulder. That's when I realized Evan was behind me. He'd been holding me back, helping the police officer restrain me. "Sara, what happened?"

"I found her in her room," she choked. "Her door was open, and she was lying on the floor. There were pills and a bottle of vodka. She wouldn't move. Then she stopped breathing." She took a quivering breath and burst out, "I tried, Emma. I really tried."

"It's okay," I said soothingly, my heart aching at her distress. "It's okay."

Then the realization slowly began to sink in, and I heard myself say, "It's okay." But I wasn't really sure who I was talking to. Everything slowed down, and I felt like I was looking through a tunnel.

The police officers asked us to come into the house to answer some questions. I responded without really connecting with what

I was saying. I doubt I was coherent, and felt dazed through the entire interview. They said something about the ambulance and a hospital, and I nodded, not understanding.

"Thank you," I heard Evan say, and I watched the police officers return to their cars. There were people outside on the sidewalk. Neighbors gathered to catch a glimpse of my nightmare. That's what this was. I was trapped in a never-ending cycle of nightmares. Voices echoed around me, and I tried to focus on their faces.

"Emma, we should go," Evan said above me. My head felt heavy as I nodded. "Want to come with us?" He was talking to Sara, but I just kept nodding.

"Emma?" Sara called to me, taking my hand. I could still hear her sniffling. "She's going to be okay. I mean, she has to be."

Who? I wanted to ask, not following. Then understanding rushed in on me all at once, I was punched in the stomach with the flood of information, my brain translating it in an instant.

"No," I said strongly, drawing Evan and Sara's attention with a start. "No. I don't want to go to the hospital."

"What?" Sara questioned in confusion. "Your mother just overdosed..."

"I know," I interrupted. "I don't want to see her."

"Don't you want to know if she's okay?" Evan asked, his voice careful.

"No," I replied fervently. "I don't want to see her. She did this. She did this because of me, to hurt me. I won't let her. I won't let her."

"Emma, what are you talking about?" Sara demanded fervently.

Evan crouched in front of me and met my eyes. "Are you sure?" I nodded. He studied me intently for a moment and then nodded. "Okay. We don't have to go."

"Evan, what the hell are you talking about? What if she—"

"Sara," he cut her off before she could finish. "You weren't here earlier. It's probably not a good idea to go to the hospital. We should get you home anyway. It's been a crazy night for you too."

Sara shook her head, aghast. "I don't understand."

"I'll explain later," Evan told her. "Emma, let's go."

I was still a bit dazed. I took his hand and allowed him to guide me. He and Sara shut off the lights along the way, and he found the key on my keychain to lock the door. We continued to the car, and Sara crawled into the back while I sat in the passenger seat. We drove to Sara's in silence, or maybe I just couldn't hear them talking.

Anna was a wreck when we arrived. She'd been contacted by the police, since they knew Sara's father. She fretted over us when we entered, hugging each of us, running her hand over our tear-stained cheeks to examine us more closely. Evan did most of the explaining, since he was the only one composed enough to make sense.

My entire body ached, and my ribs burned with pain. I didn't want to talk. I didn't want to listen. I yearned to shut it all out, and crawl under the blankets. Eventually, once Anna and Carl were satisfied with what they were told, we were released upstairs.

Evan stayed with me as long as he was allowed, lying quietly next to me on the bed, watching me drift off. Sara ended up crawling into bed with me sometime in the night, probably unable to sleep. I'm not certain I slept much either. My eyes searched in the dark, blinking in and out of consciousness.

"I told her to do it," I whispered to Sara when she opened her eyes across from me, the dawn softly glowing above us.

She blinked wider, trying to understand.

"I told her I didn't care if she took the entire bottle. And she did."

"Emma," Sara breathed in shock, finally understanding what I meant. "You didn't make her do it."

"But I don't know if I would've stopped her either," I confessed in a flat tone.

"Don't say that. You would have."

"I hate her, Sara," I rasped, my eyes blurring with tears. "I hate her so much." My voice broke, and I swallowed against the truth. Tears ran over my nose and on to the pillow. "I didn't want to see her, because…because I don't care if she's dead."

"Oh, Emma," she cried, her blue eyes seeping in pain. "I don't believe that. You're angry. But I don't believe you'd want her dead."

I didn't say anything more. We lay silently, absorbing the torment in the other's eyes, eventually falling back into a restless sleep.

I felt responsible for what Sara had endured because of Rachel's selfishness. But I didn't feel remorse for what I'd told her. I really didn't care if my mother lived or died.

————

"Are you sure you don't want to come?" Sara asked again with the bag in her hand.

I looked at Sara and her mother from my kneeling position on the kitchen floor, scooping up the congealed tomato and throwing it in the trash. "I'm sure. I'll finish picking up. I still need to throw out the food in the fridge."

"We'll see you back at the house after we've been to the hospital," Anna told me with the last box from my bedroom in her arms.

"I won't be much longer."

After I'd picked up the salad ingredients Rachel had thrown all over the kitchen, I mindlessly washed the dishes and emptied the refrigerator.

I didn't look around when I left, just shut the door behind me and locked it. I tossed the trash bags in the cans on the side of the house and dragged them to the curb.

Instead of returning to Sara's empty house, I kept driving. I knew exactly where I was going, even though I wouldn't let myself consider why I was going there, or what might happen once I arrived.

I rang the buzzer and half hoped he wasn't home. My heart skipped a beat when the black metal door opened.

"Emma?" Jonathan scanned my face and instantly asked, "What happened?"

I took a breath. "Can I come in?"

"Oh, yeah, of course." He backed up to let me pass.

I climbed the stairs with him behind me. I sat on the couch and he took a seat in the chair, anxiously awaiting my words.

"Rachel tried to kill herself last night," I revealed without any intonation in my voice.

Jonathan slowly nodded his head and lowered his eyes. He looked back up at me and told me, "Don't feel guilty."

My eyes scrunched in confusion, not certain if I'd heard him correctly.

"For not caring…you shouldn't feel guilty."

My eyes instantly filled with tears, knowing the real reason I'd driven here—because he understood. My throat tightened.

"I feel so horrible. What kind of person am I? I mean, she's my mother—"

"No she's not. She never was," he countered softly. "Emma, she wasn't even close to being your mother. You have every right to hate her."

I bowed my head in my hands and sobbed, each gasp sending a wave of pain through my body. I wrapped my arms around my ribs, to no avail. I couldn't stop crying.

Jonathan moved next to me and wrapped his arm around my shoulder. "You didn't do anything wrong, Emma. It was her choice, not yours. You didn't make her do it."

"I told her to," I choked, tilting my head up at him.

"So," he responded, wiping the tears from my cheeks. "It was her pain, not yours, that made her do it."

"But I wish," I stuttered, "I wish she were dead. Then maybe she'd stop hurting, and stop hurting me." I tried to continue but couldn't catch my breath. "That's so horrible. I'm so—"

"No," he soothed, pulling me to rest my head on his shoulder, gently rubbing my back. "She hurt you, Emma, over and over again. You can let her go now. Don't let her hurt you anymore."

I fought for my breath in the crook of his neck, letting him comfort me in his arms. It wasn't until I was calm enough to think straight that I realized it was not where I should be. I lifted my head, and his hand was on my cheek, wiping my tears. And then his soft lips were on mine.

I jumped up and stumbled back, shaking my head. "I can't."

Jonathan bent his head with a slow exhale. "I don't understand."

He looked up at me, and his eyes connected with mine, so exposed and vulnerable. My heart ached at the intensity of their emotion. I wiped my cheeks, and shook my head again. "I can't."

"You should ask yourself why you can't, Emma," he said calmly, pulling his eyes away, making me want to crumble in misery. "Is it because you don't feel it? You're here, so you must feel something. You can't deny that, no matter how hard you try."

I shook my head, not in denial, but in confusion—not knowing why I was compelled to see him. I thought it was because I knew he'd understand. But I could have just called him. I didn't have to be here, to see him in person.

I couldn't think straight.

"You've been through a lot in the past week," he whispered, his dark brown eyes peering through me, seeing more than I ever intended. "So you should just wait. Wait until everything settles. Okay?"

I didn't say anything, not certain what he was asking of me.

"We have this connection, and it's crazy," he explained. "I don't know how to give it up, do you?"

I shook my head, unable to speak because I knew it was true.

"It's going to be okay, Emma, I promise. We'll figure this out."

"Okay," I whispered. I released a quick breath and said, "I should go."

"I know."

I approached the stairs, my knees weak. I turned back toward him and said, "Jonathan, thank you...for understanding."

"I'm always here for you, Emma." He smiled gently. I groped my way down the stairs, barely able to stand, not feeling much better than when I'd arrived. Then again, I wasn't sure what I was feeling at all.

42. SOMETHING TO HOLD ON TO

Y ou asked why I stayed when I had every reason to leave—I
stayed for you. I was drawn to you almost instantly without
really understanding what was happening. I will always be
here for you, Emma.

I thought I'd caught a glimpse of his blue pickup truck in the
bustle of the parking lot, amid the cars trying to position for spots
and bodies not getting out of their way. I stretched my head around
a group of guys in letter jackets to get a better view.

"What are you looking at?" Sara asked from a few feet ahead of
me, stopping when she realized I wasn't beside her. The guys began
walking toward the school, and what I'd thought was his truck was
a Tahoe. I released my breath and turned away.

"Nothing," I said, catching up with her.

Sara tightened her eyes skeptically. I tried to smile, but it felt
foreign, having not done it very much in the last couple of weeks.

"Do you know what we need?" Her eyes lit up at just the
thought.

"What?" I asked, not certain if I should encourage the mischievous glint in her eye.

"We need a senior skip day," she exclaimed as we spotted Evan
a few rows ahead of us. He raised his chin in recognition when he
saw us and waited for us to reach him.

"But don't we have one in two weeks?"

"That's *planned*. The entire senior class is skipping that day. What's the fun in that?" Sara scoffed with a shake of her head. "Emma, you're in need of some serious spontaneity. We have to pick a day sooner, to rid of the distractions and just have a good time. A *much-needed* good time."

"I could use that." I sighed. I'd been fighting with more distractions than I could handle, including the Sunday I'd gone to see Jonathan—which I couldn't stop thinking about. Or the text he'd sent the next day, which I'd read every day since. I was desperate to rid myself of that distraction in particular, and clear my head.

"What do you need?" Evan asked overhearing us. He slid his hand into mine.

"A skip day," Sara declared proudly. "Just the four of us!"

"Four?" I questioned.

"Jared," Sara explained. "How about this Friday? It's supposed to be so nice, and Jared will be here for Evan's birthday. We'll go to the beach."

"I don't know if it's quite beach weather," Evan replied.

"Who cares?" Sara shot back, already beaming at the idea. "We don't have to wear bathing suits. We'll have a picnic and build sand castles and play catch or whatever. Don't try to ruin our skip day, Evan!"

Evan chuckled and held up his free hand in self-defense. "Okay, Sara. Friday is our skip day. It'll be great."

"Of course it will."

I grinned at her enthusiasm as she almost bounced her way to our lockers. I turned to Evan as he was about to head toward his. He bent down and kissed me briefly. "Will you come over after my game today?" he murmured in my ear.

"Sure." I smiled, letting go of his hand and watching him walk away.

I was still relishing the tingle of his breath against my ear when I opened my locker to gather my books.

"I don't think you should wait until prom," Sara mused, eyeing me with a smirk. "The two of you *need* to have sex more than any two people I know."

"Sara!" I exclaimed, looking around in a panic to see who may have overheard.

"Just sayin'." She smirked again and walked away.

My cheeks flushed, I rolled my eyes and turned back toward my locker.

"I'm going to shower," Evan told me as we parked in his driveway. "Where do you want to wait for me?"

"I'll meet you in the barn," I replied, opening the car door. My phone chimed as I reached the steps leading to the rec room. I was about to press the ignore button, as I had for the previous three calls that day. Then it beeped twice indicating the missed call, followed by a text.

Emma, please talk to me. Please.

I stared down at my phone. His plea felt like a weight in my chest. I hadn't stopped thinking about him since I'd left him that day. But I didn't really know what it was I was thinking...or feeling. I kept avoiding him, afraid of the emotions his voice would conjure up. But I couldn't keep doing this to him...or to me.

I sat down on the couch and took a deep breath, listening to the phone ring on the other end.

"Hi," he answered quickly.

"Hi," I replied, my heart beating profusely. "I'm sorry I haven't called."

"I'm sorry I keep calling," he replied. "It's just hard, not hearing from you, especially after talking to you almost every day."

"I know. It's been hard for me too."

"I got a little scared. I thought maybe…maybe you didn't need me anymore. You know, now that Rachel's not around and—"

"Don't say that," I interrupted. "I've wanted to call, to talk to you, but…I didn't know what to say. What you expected me to say."

"Emma, I don't expect anything. I just want you to be honest, that's all." After a pause, my mind trying to understand what he was asking of me, he filled the silence with, "How have you been sleeping?"

I laughed lightly at the question. "Pretty well, actually. Maybe you did cure me, or I just don't care anymore. How about you? Is the nightmare gone?"

"It comes back every once in a while."

"So you've been sleeping too," I concluded.

"I wouldn't say that," he countered. "I keep waking up, afraid I missed your call. So…not sleeping that great."

"I'm sorry," I repeated, my voice heavy with guilt.

"It's okay." He dismissed it easily. "When can I see you? I think we should…talk. There's so much I need to say to you, and I don't want to do it over the phone."

"Uh…" I delayed answering as a streak of nerves shot through my chest. "I'm not sure." I jumped at the sound of the door closing at the bottom of the stairs. "I should go. Someone's coming."

"Emma," he called to me. I stared at the stairs waiting for Evan to appear, still listening. "I know you're confused right now, but I've missed us, you know, our talks—being able to share what no one else understands. I don't want to lose that, to lose you."

"I don't either," I murmured, watching the stairs. Then I heard the door close again. "And we will talk. I promise. But I should go." I hung up and sank into the couch, having a hard time catching my breath after hearing his voice. I missed talking to him. But I'd known ever since he kissed me, it wouldn't be the same between us. I never wanted this—for him to feel this way. It scared me.

After everything we'd been through, all the nights sharing and revealing what no one else knew, I couldn't deny that there was something between us. I'd felt it the first night he stayed up with me. Our horrific lives and recurring nightmares bonded us in a way that was difficult to explain.

But I also believed there was something more to what kept him up at night. Something he couldn't yet face himself. The source of all the fury that waited to be unleashed with the slightest trigger. The thought of it made my pulse race.

I closed my eyes to try to calm my thoughts and push it all away—the intensity in his eyes, the confidence in his words...the touch of his lips.

"Emma?"

I opened my eyes with a start to find Analise in the doorway. I hadn't heard her coming up the stairs. Her lips were drawn tight; she was not her usual bubbly self. I remained frozen, wary of her serious expression. From the grim look on her face, I began to wonder if she'd overheard our call. My face flushed at the thought.

"Evan's in the shower," I said, trying to sound composed.

"I know," she replied simply. "I wanted to talk to you."

I held my breath.

"I never told anyone about what I saw, you know," she revealed, taking a few steps into the room but not getting any closer. My eyes flickered in confusion, so she explained, "That night you were hurt. I was at the house, helping Vivian." I nodded, not wanting her to recount the entire story. "That was when I realized how much he loved you."

I swallowed hard and glanced down at my phone. I quickly shoved it in my pocket, as if it were branding my hand with guilt.

"I'd hoped he didn't," she stated flatly. I puckered my lips to ask what she meant, but she didn't let me speak. "You're not the easiest person to like. You're pretty depressing most of the time. I didn't think you deserved him."

Shock bolted through me; I had not expected her brutal honesty. I'd never considered she had it in her. "What's your point, besides letting me know how miserable I am?" I asked coolly.

Analise didn't seem fazed by my tone. "My point is…he loves you. I mean it's obvious to everyone how much he cares for you, but I was hoping he didn't really *love* you, not like that—not like I saw when he held you that night. Like your pain was his and he would do anything in the world for you, to protect you."

I looked down, biting at my lower lip.

"All I have to say is that he's the most amazing person I've ever met, and I'd give anything for someone to love me like that, so you'd better deserve him, Emma."

I looked up at her with my mouth open, speechless. She turned away and walked downstairs just as the door was opening.

I heard Evan's voice. "Hi, Analise."

"Hi, Evan," she chirped happily. Not a hint of the threatening tone she'd had a few seconds before.

I was still shaking off her words when Evan entered. He tightened his eyes at the sight of my stunned expression and asked, "Is everything okay? Did something happen between you and Analise?"

I shook my head, still recovering. I tried to smile and finally said, "No, she was just asking how I was feeling."

"Oh, that's nice of her," he replied skeptically. "You're still okay that she and I are friends, right?"

"Of course," I answered lightly, but for the first time, actually meaning it. "She cares about you, and everyone needs a friend looking out for them like that."

Evan drew his brows together like I'd just spoken in a foreign language. "Okay," he said slowly. Then a breathtaking smile spread across his face. "So I have something to show you."

My lips turned up at the excitement flickering in his blue eyes. "What is it?"

"Come with me and find out." He took my hand and pulled me from the couch. I released Analise's words of warning, and Jonathan's words of want, leaving them behind as I followed after Evan.

"Close your eyes," Evan requested.

I scrunched my face, "Do I have to?"

Evan released a breathy laugh. "No, you don't have to."

He held my hand and led me along the back of the house, eagerly awaiting my reaction. I wasn't sure what I was supposed to be seeing until we neared the large oak tree that sat on the edge of the property.

My eyes glistened as a slow smile spread across my face. "Evan," I breathed.

"I wanted you to have something good to hold on to. Something that would remind you of him, but also let you know that you'll always be here with me."

I smiled wider and turned to him, engulfing him in the tightest hug. "Thank you. I love it," I choked in a gasp of emotion.

I pressed up on my toes to reach him. He breathed into me, his firm lips sliding over my mine, making my entire body hum.

Evan pulled away and asked, "Aren't you going to try it?"

"Yes," I answered enthusiastically, turning back to the tree. "Did you make it?" I wrapped my hands around the ropes and pulled my body up onto the board, balancing myself as the seat tilted beneath me.

"I did," he revealed proudly. "Not sure how steady the board is though."

"It's perfect." I glowed, pumping my legs as I leaned back. My healing ribs tweaked uncomfortably as I gained momentum, but I dismissed the tenderness. Nothing was going to keep me from enjoying this moment.

I couldn't release the smile on my face as the branches above me grew closer with each extension of my legs. I closed my eyes and felt the rush of air on my face and the flitter in my stomach as I swung back and forth. My throat closed, and I captured the tears beneath my eyelids. I was so overcome with emotion, my chest felt like it might burst.

I opened my eyes and searched for Evan when I couldn't find him in front of me. He was leaning against the tree with his arms crossed, watching. A tear rolled over my smiling cheek as his eyes danced with glints of light.

I knew how much Evan loved me. And I knew I didn't deserve it. But I also knew he was the only one I loved. The only one I would ever love.

43. SPONTANEITY

This is a perfect beach day!" I declared sarcastically as we walked against the whipping wind that flooded my body with goose bumps.

"It's not *that* bad," Sara said defensively, her arms folded around several blankets. "The sun's out."

"Wish I could feel it," I griped, carrying a bag of food and another of "beach toys" that the guys had packed. Sara rolled her eyes and kept walking.

We were somehow able to spread out the blanket. The guys lowered the cooler on one corner to keep it from blowing away. I set the bags on two other corners, and Sara tucked the fourth in the sand.

I ventured toward the shoreline to take in the rolling waves with my arms tucked against my body, warding off the cold wind that blew my hair from my face. Evan wrapped his arms around me and spoke in my ear. "Want to get under a blanket with me?"

I turned toward him and smirked. "Are you propositioning me?"

"Maybe," he replied coyly, bending down to kiss me.

Evan grabbed one of the blankets and sat down with his arms spread wide, waiting for me to lower myself in front of him. I leaned back between his knees and he wrapped the blanket around us. My body temperature elevated instantly.

"Much better." I smiled, continuing to watch the waves crash before us.

"Really, it's not *that* cold." Sara shook her head at us.

"Do you know what would be great right about now?" Jared proposed. "Hot chocolate."

"Yes!" I exclaimed enthusiastically.

"Too bad," Sara shot back. "I didn't pack any."

"Want us to go buy some?" Evan suggested.

"No," I complained. "You're keeping me warm."

"Fine," Sara huffed, "if you really want some, we'll go." She stood up and waited for Jared before heading toward the boardwalk in search of a coffee shop.

Evan held me against him, and I got lost in the waves, mesmerized by their rhythm. Every once in a while I could feel the heat of the sun on my face, fighting through the gusts.

"It really isn't that bad," Evan said in my ear.

"Yes, it is," I countered, "but I'm good as long as you stay here." I pulled his arms tighter around me and snuggled under his chin.

"So I have the perfect night planned out."

"Really?" I questioned, knowing he meant the night before prom. "And why do you get to do all the planning? Maybe I wanted to."

"Umm, okay," he responded hesitantly. "How about we split up the weekend? I have the night before, and you have prom night."

"That's not exactly fair," I argued. "Your night is already going to be better than mine, since we're having sex."

Evan laughed. "We don't have to."

"Oh, yes, we do," I insisted. "Okay, fine. It's probably not going to be that great anyway, so you have Friday, and I'll have Saturday. And *mine* will be better."

"You're making this into a competition?" he mused with a chuckle.

"Yeah." I grinned. "And wait until you see me in my prom dress."

"But my night, I get to see you without anything on at all, so I'm pretty sure I'm going to be the victor of this competition."

I jabbed him in the ribs with my elbow. Evan released a groaning laugh and tilted me back so I was looking up at him. He wrapped the blanket tighter around us and kissed me. His cheeks felt hot against my cold nose. I slid my arms around his neck, and he enveloped us in the dark, pulling the blanket over our heads.

The sand shifted under me as he laid me down. Evan lowered himself beside me with his leg between mine. I pulled him closer, finding his lips again, the heat of his breath swirling through me with the touch of his tongue. My heart beat erratically as he pressed closer, his hand sliding across my stomach, underneath my clothes.

I ran my fingers through his hair, releasing a gasping breath as his mouth trailed along my neck. I could feel his body tense as I held him tight against me, breathing heavily. He pulled up, but I couldn't read his face.

"What is it?" The sun blinded me as Evan pulled back the blanket to peek out.

"I thought I heard them," he said, dropping the blanket again. He lowered himself back down to kiss me.

Before we could get too worked up, I interrupted with, "They will probably be back soon." The brief interlude made me realize we were in the middle of the beach, and despite how secluded it felt under the blanket, I could only imagine what it looked like to anyone walking by.

"Yeah," Evan groaned reluctantly, folding the blanket back.

I sat up and smoothed my hair into a ponytail. Evan ran his hand along my back as he remained lying on the blanket with his arm under his head.

"Two weeks." He sighed. I grinned.

"We don't have to wait until then," I suggested. "It doesn't have to be planned."

"But I *have* a plan," he returned. "So I can wait."

I smiled. "You're funny."

"Why?" he questioned, smiling too.

"All of your surprises," I explained. "You come across as spontaneous, but the truth is, you plan out *everything*. And Sara thinks *I'm* bad."

"I can be spontaneous!" he argued.

"Okay, then let's have sex right here, right now," I proposed.

"Here?" Evan scanned the beach. It was practically deserted, since any sane person would deem it too cold. But there were still a few crazy people walking along the shoreline, bundled up. "You want to have sex right now?" He watched for my reaction, to see if I was serious.

I caved. "Fine. No. But I was trying to make a point."

"I can be spontaneous," he repeated. "You wait."

"You can't plan to be spontaneous," I teased.

"Hey," Sara said, drawing our attention as they neared us. She set the tray of hot chocolate on the blanket. "It's not that bad out if you move around."

"Thanks for getting these," I replied, taking a hot chocolate. "But I'm still staying under the blanket."

Jared looked at Evan. "Football?"

"Sure," Evan agreed, leaving me with a quick kiss. The heat escaped with his departure. I pulled the blanket around me with a shiver.

"Your hair's a mess." Sara eyed me suspiciously. "What were you two doing while we were gone?"

"Keeping warm," I answered, my cheeks igniting as I took a sip of hot chocolate. We watched the guys toss the football and chase after it as it got carried away in the wind.

"Do you swear Evan doesn't know anything about tomorrow?"

"No, he has no clue," Sara promised. "He still thinks he's spending the day with his brother, hiking."

"Good." I smiled.

"I think you're going to pull it off."

"I hope so." My stomach churning with nervous energy just thinking about what I had planned for his birthday.

We turned our attention back toward the guys.

"Emma, if you ever want to visit your mother in the hospital, I'll go with you," Sara offered suddenly.

"No," I shook my head. "I don't want to see her. I can't."

"Alright," she replied, her voice low and careful. "Em, are you okay?"

I heard the weight of concern in her question. "I'm getting there," I assured her with a small smile. "Can't say my life's boring."

Sara let out a sharp laugh. "What? That's kind of a twisted thing to say."

I shrugged, accepting that it was true. But her comment made me think of Jonathan, and my shoulders sank. I hadn't talked to him since the day I'd called him from Evan's. We'd texted a few times, but each text felt strained. I knew I'd need to face him eventually. He'd said he wanted me to be honest. But I wasn't so sure that he was prepared to hear the truth, and I was afraid to tell him.

Sara pulled a blanket around her, giving in to the fact that it really *wasn't* warm. The guys jogged back to us, their faces red and hair disheveled.

Evan cuddled in under the blanket. "Omigod, you're freezing." I tensed away from his frigid touch.

"I know"—he pulled me closer—"I need you to help warm me up."

I squirmed under the blanket with a yelping laugh when he tried to put his frigid hands under my shirt.

"Okay, fine," Sara conceded with a heavy breath, "let's go back to my house where it's above seventy degrees and we can go swimming."

"Thank you." I jumped up to gather our things, wanting more than anything to get out of the relentless wind. We packed up and headed to the car.

"Do you want to come back to my place instead?" Evan asked me when we were in the backseat, on our way back to Weslyn. "I was hoping to spend some time with you before Jared and I head off for the hike tomorrow."

I grinned and nodded, unable to face him—afraid my grin would give away that I was hiding something. "I like that idea. Do you mind if I shower first, to get the sand and salt off?"

"Sure. You can just meet me at my place when you're done."

Sara didn't have an issue when I told her I was going to spend the rest of the day with Evan. I was pretty certain she wanted some alone time of her own with Jared. I found Evan in the backyard when I arrived, sitting under the oak tree, waiting for me.

"I can't believe we spent most of the day freezing," I said, pulling myself up on the swing. I soaked in the warmth of the lowering sun as I swayed back and forth. "It was beautiful here all day."

"The day's not over yet," Evan said, leaning in and gripping the wood to give me a push. "We can enjoy it 'til it's over."

"What does that mean?" I asked. "Isn't that what we're doing?"

Evan laughed. "It is. But how about you stay the night? It's supposed to be pretty nice tonight. We can sleep outside."

"Like camping?" I clarified.

"That's a better idea. I think I have a tent in the garage. We can sleep in the backyard, or we can go to the meadow. The sky will look incredible out there, away from the lights. What do you think?"

"Evan"—I grinned accusingly—"Did you plan this?"

He started laughing. "No, I swear. It just came to me when you were talking about missing out on today. I'm going to be gone all of tomorrow, so let me spend the rest of today with you."

"So you're being *spontaneous?*" I teased. He smiled and intercepted my swing, placing his hands on the board on either side of my hips. He leaned in and kissed me gently.

"Will you please stay over?" he whispered, brushing his lips across mine again.

"Yes," I replied in a breath with my eyes closed, leaning in for another touch that made my head spin. He kissed me a little longer, and I thought I was going to fall off the swing.

He pulled away. "C'mon, Emma." He held out his hand and I jumped off the swing to take it.

We gathered sleeping bags and the tent, along with firewood and other essentials from the barn. Evan packed us sandwiches and drinks. I grabbed marshmallows, making Evan smile. We strapped everything into the trailer on the back of the ATV.

"I like spontaneity," I announced as we headed into the woods. Evan grinned as he drove us farther along the trail toward the meadow.

As the sun tucked behind the trees, we set the tent up in the clearing, closer to the brook, where the grass wasn't as long. Evan pulled out a small shovel and dug a fire pit.

While he stacked the wood near the pit and prepared a fire, I set up the interior of the tent.

"You brought an air mattress?" I questioned when I pulled the sleeping bags out of the trailer.

"I thought it would be more comfortable," he explained. "I know you're still a little sore."

"Thanks." I grinned.

Evan lit the fire as the hues in the sky transitioned from orange to dark purple. The lingering warmth teased that summer was right around the corner, but still far enough away to make me yearn for it. Evan laid out a thick blanket in front of the fire where we sat to eat.

"I really do like it out here," I said with an easy smile.

"Me too," Evan agreed. "Does Sara know you're staying over?"

"Ooh, no," I said with a grimace. "I left my phone in my car. Do you have yours?"

"No, it's in my room," he said. "Do you want to go back to call her?"

"She knows I'm with you, so she'll cover for me. Anna and Carl trust you."

Evan grinned. "I'm sure they might hesitate if they knew we weren't sleeping in separate rooms tonight."

"No, I think they would still trust you."

After we'd finished eating, I lay back on the blanket. The sky was filling with stars as the darkness spread.

"Everything seems so possible when I look up at the sky and see the universe gleaming before me."

"It is," Evan replied, lying next to me to take in the same view.

"Wanna know something I've realized?" I continued without waiting for Evan to respond. "I've spent most of my life trying to make it to a future that still hasn't happened, or avoid a past that won't let me go. I don't remember when I've ever just stopped to live in the present, to hold on to the seconds I'm in."

"Well, your future's still unfolding, you'll just have to let it happen as it intends to. But what's keeping you from being free of your past?"

I thought for a moment. "Forgiveness."

"Do you forgive *me*?"

I shifted my head toward him with my brows knotted. "Why would I need to forgive you?"

Evan tilted his head to the side to look into my eyes. "Because I kept it from you...what happened that night."

"But I didn't want to know, so you did what you thought I needed." I turned back to the stars. We listened to the crickets chirp in the stillness.

"Evan?"

"Yes."

"Can you tell me one thing that I still don't understand?"

"I'll try."

"How did my ankle shatter?"

Evan was silent. I zoned in on a single star above me and waited. "She had a hammer. I saw it on the bed next to your foot." His voice was low and strained. I closed my eyes, the strangled words overtaking me.

"That's why you couldn't do that art project, isn't it? Why you had to leave the room that day?"

I reached for his hand. It was hot and tense. I laced my fingers through his, and he gripped them tightly.

"I forgive you," I breathed. "Now you have to forgive me."

"For what?"

"Not listening. For staying when both you and Sara begged me not to. For not telling anyone and convincing you to remain quiet too. For not asking for help. For—"

"That's enough," he cut me off. My heart pounded hard, thinking of the many reasons I needed to be forgiven that I still hadn't named. Evan raised my hand to his lips and kissed it. He rolled on his side and intercepted my view, his eyes glassy and full of emotion.

"I forgive you," he whispered. My throat closed, and I swallowed against the tears that pooled in the corners of my eyes. "I forgive you," he whispered again, running his hand along the side of my face. My eyes shut with the tenderness of his touch. "I forgive you," he breathed, his voice wavering. I opened my eyes to see the tear glisten as it rolled down his cheek.

I opened my mouth to speak. My lip quivered and the words remained choked in the back of my throat.

"Now, Emma, you need to forgive yourself."

I pressed my lips together and closed my eyes, the tears caught in my lashes. Before I could open them again, my breath was captured by the firmness of his lips. That kiss said every word left unspoken. It filled me with more emotion than I thought possible to contain.

I leaned toward him, and he wrapped his arms around me, fusing us together. His heart beat against my chest, thumping so hard it reverberated throughout my entire body. His mouth slid over mine. I could taste our tears, the salt lingering on his lips and over my tongue.

My heart ached with each kiss. I couldn't get close enough to him, pulling him into me. I needed him more than I needed to breathe.

I pulled back and slid my shirt over my head. His warm hands ran along my back, unclasping. Our mouths collided with such frenzy, we couldn't catch our breath. Evan lifted his shirt over his head. His taut muscles pressed against my bare skin. The heat of our flesh melded us.

Evan rolled me on my back and trailed his mouth down my neck and over my skin, triggering a swirl of heat that rushed through my body. We slipped out of our clothes, only separating long enough to toss them aside. I knew him, every inch of him, but never like this.

The tenderness of his touch captured my breath. My heart thumped with each burst of air escaping my lips. I pressed my eyes closed, my brows pulled together. He intercepted my staggered breath, his mouth engulfing mine. I could feel everything and nothing all at once, my body tensing. I clasped his hand, locking my fingers in his, arching up to meet his mouth again before exhaling and floating back to the blanket.

I lay motionless, caught in the recovery with my pulse thrumming. Evan reached into his pocket, removed the wrapper and returned to me. My heart stammered as he lowered himself, watching me intently.

I took in a sharp breath when he found me.

"Are you okay?" Evan asked, looking into my eyes.

"Yeah," I exhaled, wrapping my legs around him.

His rhythm was gentle and slow. My breath became drawn, and I closed my eyes. I ran my hands along his back, gripping him as his pace quickened.

I opened my eyes. His lips were parted and his breaths erratic. I reached up to taste him, his tongue slipping into my mouth. He pulled away with a rush of air. Looking into me. Seeing more than I ever thought possible. Vulnerable and exposed. Love and desire. My chest swelled with every imaginable emotion.

His chest was slick with sweat as he slid against me. I ran my mouth along his salty skin, my entire body pulsing. Evan clenched his eyes shut and his body became rigid, slowing until he melted on top of me. His chest thumped against my stomach as we surrendered to the calm. I kept my arms wrapped around him as he recovered in slow breaths, with his head on my chest.

"Am I hurting you?" he asked, and then clarified, "Your ribs?"

I shook my head, having completely forgotten about them.

"I like listening to your heart," he said, holding my hand. "It's beating so fast."

Evan lifted his head to inspect me, sweat trickling along his sculpted face and down his neck. "Are you cold?"

I shook my head.

"Can you talk?"

I shook my head again. He grinned, reaching up to kiss me softly. He eased away. The cool air wicked the sweat from my body with a shiver. He leaned over and grabbed the edge of the blanket, folding it over us, positioning me so I was on his arm as we both lay on our sides, facing each other.

"Are you okay?" he asked, his eyes twitching slightly in concern.

"Yes," I smiled brightly, making him smile in return. Then I started laughing.

"What's so funny?" he questioned, his eyes twinkling.

"I love spontaneity."

Evan smiled wider. He leaned over and brushed his lips across mine. "I love you, Emma."

44. IN THE END

The sun woke me earlier than I usually rose, but the melodic chirping and filtered light were a welcome transition into the day.

I smiled when his breath tickled the back of my neck as he slept with his arm draped across my stomach. I shifted back to cuddle into him. His arm instinctively tightened around me. I breathed in at the touch of his skin along my back, firm and warm. A swirling heat roused in me, and I took long drawn breaths, pressing against him. Evan began to stir.

The rhythm of his breathing deepened, and I knew he was awake. His hand slid along my side, over my hips. Although the feel of his fingers tickling my skin elevated my heart rate, my body was still in a bit of shock from last night, and I knew I wasn't prepared for it again this morning.

I gently eased forward and reached over for the backpack on the tent floor. I dug in the front pocket and pulled out the packet.

"Gum?" I offered, popping a piece in my mouth.

Evan laughed. "Yes, thanks." After he'd taken a piece, I rolled over to face him.

"Good, now I can kiss you," I declared and pressed my lips against his, the burst of cinnamon filling my mouth with the touch of his tongue. "Happy birthday," I breathed, my head swirling. His steel-blue eyes were vibrant and reflective. My heart stuttered at their intensity.

"Thank you," he smiled and then added, "for the perfect present." My cheeks warmed. Evan ran his finger along my blush, brushing the hair from my face.

"You're beautiful," he whispered, making my cheeks even redder. He swept his finger over my lips and followed the touch with a kiss, barely touching—stealing my breath.

"I love you," I murmured, lost in the depths of his eyes as they flickered in front of me like he was silently listening to my every thought. Evan pulled me against him and held me. I inhaled the sweet scent of his skin. "Do we have to leave here?"

"We should probably think about it."

My stomach growled, and I placed my hand over it. Evan grinned. "And it sounds like you need to eat."

"Fine," I conceded reluctantly, "we can get up." I sat up, holding the sleeping bag over me. "You know, I've never slept naked before."

Evan laughed lightly. "And I bet you've never roasted marshmallows naked either." He leaned over and kissed my shoulder.

"No, that was a first too." I nodded, making him smile. "Do you have any idea what time it is?"

"No, but I'm sure Jared's looking for me."

"That's right," I grinned, trying not to blow the surprise. "You're going hiking." I began searching under the sleeping bag. "Where are our clothes?"

"I think they're still outside," Evan noted.

"Oh," I responded with wide eyes. I unzipped the tent and a breeze of cool morning air swept in. The grass still glistened with morning dew. I spotted our clothes tossed in a small pile next to the abandoned blanket. I contemplated how cold the grass was going to be on my bare feet.

"I'll get them," Evan offered.

"No," I sighed, wrapping the sleeping bag around me to fend off the chill, "I'll get them."

I ducked out of the tent and scampered across the chilled, wet grass on the balls of my feet. I scooped up the pile and rushed back to the tent, tossing the clothes in before climbing in after them. "Oooh, it's cold out there," I said, shuddering. Evan laughed as he sorted through the articles of clothing.

"Well, you're not going to love this. Our clothes are kinda wet." He slid his jeans over his hips, fastening them.

"Great," I groaned, feeling the dampness against my skin as I pulled on my shirt.

"How are you feeling? I mean, are you…okay?" Evan asked cautiously as we dressed.

"I feel a little…different," I tried to explain, not sure how to describe the post-first-time-sex discomfort. Evan hesitated, not exactly following, so I added, "But I also feel amazing." And that wasn't at all an exaggeration.

"Good," Evan said, accepting my answer and giving me a quick kiss. "Let's go back to the house, and I'll make us breakfast and figure out what Jared has planned. And I can give you a dry sweatshirt to wear."

Jared was waiting for Evan in the kitchen when we walked in. He looked from one to the other—I could only imagine what we looked like, wearing damp, wrinkled clothes, our hair unkempt. He arched his eyebrow slightly, but then redirected his attention to the bowl of cereal. "We're leaving in twenty minutes."

"Cereal sounds good to me," I said, sitting on the stool next to Jared. He remained unperturbed by my discombobulated state. I was certain Sara wasn't going to have the same lack of reaction.

"Where have you been?!" she demanded when I called her from my car, having just left Evan and Jared to pack for their hike. "I've been trying to get hold of you for forever."

"I was with Evan," I explained, completely baffled by her over-reaction.

"I *know* that, but I needed to talk to you. My mother's having a dinner at the house tonight."

"What?" I practically shouted, my pulse quickening. "Sara, what am I supposed to do?"

"That's what I needed to talk to you about," she said, stressed. "Just get to the house and we'll figure something out.

My phone beeped as I said, "Okay." When I looked at the screen, my battery light was flashing. That was the least of my worries as I dumped it on the passenger seat and continued to the McKinleys' house.

When I entered, Anna was in the sitting room with a woman in a suit, reviewing some papers. She stood when she saw me. I was hoping to sneak upstairs, fearing "just had sex" was written all over my face.

"Emma, I am so sorry about tonight. I knew about the party at Evan's, but I didn't realize you were planning to have dinner here first."

"Oh, it's okay," I said lightly, creeping up a step at a time before she could get a good look at me. "We'll figure something out."

"If you want to take him to a nice restaurant, I would be happy to pay for it."

"That's very nice of you," I assured her, taking another step. "But it'll be fine."

"Emma?" Sara bellowed from the third floor.

I smiled awkwardly at Anna and turned to run up the stairs. "I'm coming!"

When I reached her, I found Sara folding the flaps of a cardboard box full of decorations.

"I have an idea," she burst out, standing up to face me. "You can..." She stopped. "Omigod. You had sex."

My entire body flushed, and no matter how hard I tried to stop it, a huge smile spread across my face.

"I can't believe it," she gaped, rushing over to hug me. Then she unleashed a barrage of questions, "Did it hurt? Did you...uh, bleed? Are you sore? How do you feel?"

"Um," I stared at her in shock before I fumbled, "Just a little... no...*yes*...and..." I smiled wide, with my cheeks aglow; I didn't even have to answer the last question.

She squealed proudly, "I can't believe you had sex! This is so amazing. It gets better, I promise." Then she rolled her eyes in frustration, "And I'm so mad at you right now because we don't have time for you to tell me all the details."

"I think I just told you more details than I ever expected to," I admitted, leaving out that it was probably the most incredible night of my life and that I wasn't sure how much better it could get. "Anyway, what's your idea?"

"Okay, here's your grocery list. Go shopping now. Then come back here. You can shower, and I'll do your hair before we leave to decorate the barn," Sara rattled off instructions, barely taking a breath.

"Jill, Casey and...Analise"—she said her name with a snarl, which made me laugh—"are meeting me here in a couple of hours, and then we're going to the Mathews' to decorate.

"You can bring the dress with you and change right before Evan arrives at seven. That should give you time for a couple of tries, in case you burn anything."

"Thanks," I shot back with a mocking grin, "but where am I going?"

Sara hesitated, her lips pressed together. "Decatur Street."

"What?!" I stared at her, certain she hadn't just told me that I was supposed to surprise Evan with a romantic dinner in the same house where I'd seen a man get nearly pummeled to death, and where my mother had tried to kill herself. I shook my head. "No way, Sara."

"I'm sorry," Sara said with a grimace, "but there isn't another choice if you really want to cook for him. Otherwise, you'll have to go to a restaurant. I mean, it's only a house, Emma. She's not going to be there. She was admitted into that program for the next six months. There's no one there."

"Oh, you've got to be kidding me," I groaned under my breath. I'd been planning this dinner all week. The logistics had been sorted out carefully. We were supposed to have dinner on the deck overlooking the pool while Sara and Jared set up the barn for the surprise party after. It was my turn to actually do something for him, but this wasn't part of the plan.

I considered just scrapping the dinner and taking him to a restaurant. But every time I thought of this night, it was more about the look on his face when he discovered I'd actually cooked for him than anything else. I didn't want to lose that over a... technicality.

"Fine," I huffed, "I'll cook there. But where should we eat? That kitchen is the least romantic place on earth."

"How about the backyard?" Sara suggested. I shook my head, feeling nauseous at just the thought of being near the ashes of the rocking chair.

"Umm, I can put the kitchen table on the porch, I guess," I suggested with a shrug.

"That's perfect," Sara exclaimed. "Let's look in the closet downstairs. I'm pretty sure my mom has a ton of tablecloths you can use to cover it up."

"How many people are coming?" I asked, following Sara down the stairs.

"Uh, everyone," Sara answered with a sarcastic tone. "You put me in charge of inviting, so of course they're all coming."

"But you just invited them yesterday," I stated in amazement. "That was the plan—to invite last minute so no one would ruin the surprise. We figured maybe half would come."

"Well…we figured wrong," Sara shrugged. "It probably has something to do with seeing the Mathews' place. No one's really been there before."

"True," I agreed. "But that's *a lot* of people."

"Yes, it is." Sara smiled. "And everyone is arriving at eight, so you and Evan should arrive at eight thirty."

"Okay," I replied, anxiety churning in the pit of my stomach.

Everything was going as planned when I left Sara's with my hair in soft waves down my back and the pink dress hanging in the backseat. I kept replaying my strategy for when I arrived at the house over and over in my head.

Move the kitchen table to the porch. Cut up the salad and fruit. Season the steaks and keep them wrapped in the fridge. Mix the brownies and stick them in the oven before I change. Then the finishing touches after, like set the table, light the candles and…oh, yeah, take the brownies out of the oven.

I could do this. It was going to go perfectly.

And despite the palpitations that made me fearful I was about to have a heart attack, and the jitters that kept my hands shaky, it was going exactly how it was supposed to. I kept glancing at my phone on the counter, hoping the battery wouldn't die before Sara called to tell me he was on his way.

In order to get him here, he'd have to know I had a surprise waiting for him. Sara was supposed to send him to me after he'd dressed at his house. Jared would make certain he didn't go anywhere near the barn. I could only imagine his reaction when he was told where he was to meet me. Sara's call was supposed to give me a twenty-minute heads-up.

I was mixing the brownie batter in the bowl, reading the back of the box for the hundredth time to make sure I hadn't missed anything, when my phone chimed. My stomach fluttered with nerves, fearing he was ahead of schedule.

I picked up the phone, sucking the chocolate off my finger. "Hello?"

"Emma?" Jonathan responded. My heart stammered. Without giving me time to react, he asked, "Where are you?"

I took a breath and tried to sound as casual as possible. "I'm at Decatur Street unfortunately, but it's the only place I—"

"Emma," Jonathan interrupted, "There's some—" A beep from the phone signaled in my ear at the same time as the smoke detector blared loudly.

"Shit!" I exclaimed, forgetting the stove had a tendency to smoke. "Hold on. I can't hear you." I set down the phone and the bowl I'd tucked under my arm, and proceeded to fan the alarm with the dish towel until it turned off.

"Stupid stove," I muttered, clambering up on the sink to push the window open with a grunt.

I picked up the phone again and said, "I'm sorry about that." But he didn't respond. I pulled back the phone and the screen was blank; my battery was dead. "Great. And just when everything was going so well," I grumbled.

I opened the front door and allowed the smoke to filter through the screen. It was a good thing we were eating outside. I continued back into the kitchen to pour the batter into the greased pan. I placed it in the oven and set the timer before I made my way up to the bathroom to get dressed, knowing Sara would be trying to call me any minute—although I wouldn't be able to answer. I wanted to shoot myself for forgetting the charger.

I tried to calm my nerves as I zipped the dress along my side. My hands were sweaty, and I needed to dry them off in order to seal the last inch. Closing my eyes, I took a deep breath, unable to get rid of the flutters overtaking my stomach.

I stepped out of the bathroom, disappointed I no longer had a full-length mirror to double-check the sundress for the chocolate that seemed to be everywhere.

I skipped down a few steps and stopped at the sound of a car door closing. He was early, and I wasn't ready.

"Shit," I breathed, rushing down the stairs in search of my shoes. Then I saw the mess I'd left behind in the kitchen and tried to decide what was more important. I picked up the chocolate-lined bowl and dumped it in the sink, filling it with water while I scraped the scraps of vegetables and fruit from the countertop into the trash.

I slid the trash can in place and rinsed my hands just as the screen door slammed shut.

"Emma?"

I froze, my heart hammering in my chest. I shut off the water and slowly turned around, wiping my hands on a paper towel.

I opened my mouth, but nothing came out.

Jonathan's eyes widened at the sight of me. "Wow. You look beautiful."

"Thanks," I choked.

But then his eyes tightened as he looked to the stove, the chocolate aroma filling the kitchen. "Are you *cooking*?"

"Um, I wouldn't really call it cooking." I laughed nervously. "It's just brownies."

"But you're cooking…for Evan." Jonathan appeared disturbed by his conclusion.

"It's his birthday," I explained feebly. "So…what are you doing here?"

Jonathan remained contemplative for a moment, unable to move past the scene he'd walked in on. "I need to talk to you. It's important." He turned toward the living room as the timer for the brownies sounded.

I removed the pan and shut off the oven. After seeing the perplexed, yet disappointed, look on Jonathan's face, I wasn't concerned with how the brownies had come out. Without inspecting them, I set them on the cooling rack and fretfully followed him into the living room.

Jonathan was staring out the front window with his arms crossed when I entered.

"What do you need to tell me?" I asked, tearing him from his thoughts.

"I understand why you're still with him," he began, turning toward me. "He really cares about you, and he's a good guy. It doesn't mean I like it, but I understand."

I needed to sit down for this. I slowly lowered myself on to the couch, preparing for where this conversation was headed.

"But, Emma, you and I have both admitted that we have this inexplicable connection between us, right?" He paused for me to respond. I could only nod slightly. "We trust each other with secrets no one else knows. I can be completely honest with you about everything. I've never been able to do that, not even with Sadie. Have you ever told Evan about your nightmares? Your fears?"

I swallowed audibly, knowing he was right. I'd never shared the darkest part of me with anyone other than him. I never wanted Evan to know that side of me. I shook my head, shifting uncomfortably.

"I've been where you are, remember? I thought Sadie was it. But in the end, they don't understand people like us. They never will, because they've never had to go through it. You and I are the same. We share a bond that's stronger than what you think you have with Evan.

"So...I'll wait. I'm not going to force you to decide, because in the end, I know you'll see it, too. I'll wait because I love you, and I promised to always be here for you—for whenever you need me."

The air seeped from my lungs. His words rushed through my head in a dizzying blur.

"Is that why you're here?" I rasped. "To tell me you'll wait for me?"

Jonathan approached the love seat and sat across from me. He pressed his elbows on his thighs, shortening the distance between us. I knew he wanted to touch me. He grasped his hands to contain himself as I subtly leaned away.

"That's not the reason I'm here. I didn't actually intend to tell you I loved you," he confessed, averting his eyes. "I wanted to wait until I knew you'd be able to say it back." He took a deep breath. His intensely troubled expression distracted me from his confession.

"Why are you here?" I asked, but was suddenly afraid to know. My gut twisted in nervous anticipation.

"The police came to see me today," he revealed, forcing my heart to skip a beat.

My body responded before I could completely comprehend what he was saying. "What? Why?"

"They found a partial print on the car, and matched it to me."

"Wait. What car?" I drew in a sharp breath when I realized, "Oh no. But why would..." My words were lost with the conclusion, "He's dead."

Jonathan eyed me carefully as I took it all in. "Yeah."

"Oh no. Oh God, no." I shook my head, still in shock. "What did we do?"

"You didn't do anything," he replied firmly. "He was hurting you, Emma. I'm not going let anything happen to you, I promise."

"I can't believe...he's dead." I kept shaking my head, unable to accept it. "Can't we just tell the police the truth?"

"We covered it up," Jonathan explained patiently. "I cleaned any trace that he was here. So no, we can't tell them the truth. They haven't charged me with anything; they're just asking questions right now. And I've spoken to a lawyer. It sounds like they don't have much to go on."

"What did you tell them?" I asked, the panic subsiding enough to allow some coherent thoughts to surface.

"That I noticed his car at Rachel's party the night before he was found, and that I'd stopped by here to talk to her so I may have inadvertently touched it."

I nodded slowly, consumed by a thousand thoughts and images all at once: what we'd done, the lies we'd told, the bloody mess left behind, what could happen to us if the police ever discovered the truth. And above all else, I couldn't stop thinking about the battered body we'd abandoned in the parking lot. A cold sweat ran down my spine with a shiver.

"Just stick to your story about not seeing the face of the guy who broke in, and they can't connect him to being here after the party."

"Okay," I breathed, my thoughts reeling. Something he'd said left me unsettled. I paused a moment to reflect, and then it occurred to me. "Wait. How did they have your print on file to match it?"

Jonathan's face dropped. When I peered into his dark eyes, I saw a vulnerability that made my heart ache.

"Jonathan, what did you do?" I asked fretfully, not taking my eyes off him.

"Emma, I've wanted to tell you," he began, running his hands through his hair, "but I was waiting until I knew you could handle it. Since I can barely live with myself, I was afraid you would—"

"What?" I begged. "Please, just tell me."

The distress in his eyes made my pulse thrum.

He stood up and began pacing in front of me, rubbing his hands together. I watched him anxiously. For a moment, I thought he wasn't going to speak, but then he stopped in front of the window. "They took my prints after the fire."

My eyes blinked in confusion. Then my mouth dropped. "No," I gasped, forcing him to face me.

"You have to understand. They weren't supposed be home. They had been at a basketball tournament, but Ryan got sick. I thought my father was home alone." He absorbed the shocked look on my face. I couldn't utter a sound, horrified. Jonathan quickly looked away and began pacing again.

"When I moved away to college, my father took everything out on Ryan. I couldn't let that happen. He wasn't as strong as me. I needed to protect him."

"They were your family," I breathed in abhorrence. Jonathan stopped midstep. "How could—" I shook my head, the words stuck in my throat. Tears filled my eyes as the black skeletal remains of the house invaded my thoughts. My stomach turned to ice, imagining their screams as they desperately tried to get out.

"You can't hate me any more than I hate myself." I looked up at his glassy eyes. Their tortured depths made my lip quiver. "They weren't supposed to be there," he repeated, consumed in grief. "I'll never forgive myself. But I want you to know everything, to know the truth." Jonathan bowed his head and pushed his palms into his eyes.

I closed my eyes, trying to understand what could've driven him to want to murder his own father. Then I recalled the twinge of envy I'd felt when he'd revealed that his father was dead, and how I'd wished that upon Carol. But I could never bring myself to do it. To kill her. Could I?

Then again, hadn't I just cried on his shoulder, wishing my own mother was dead? After encouraging her to end her misery with a bottle of pills? How different was I, really? Just because they weren't dead, didn't make me wish it any less.

"I don't know what to think," I told him honestly, running my hand across my forehead with my eyes squeezed shut, a tear escaping down my cheek.

"I know." He exhaled heavily. "It's a lot, and I'm sorry."

My head snapped up at the sound of the screen door slamming shut.

Evan looked from Jonathan to me. "What's going on?" I brushed away the tear. His eyes flickered in confusion, then alarm. "What did you do to her?"

I opened my mouth to answer, but Jonathan stood in front of me before I could utter a word.

"This has nothing to do with you, Evan," Jonathan explained. His voice was low, and it sliced with warning. "You're not a part of every moment of her life."

"What is that supposed to mean?" Evan demanded in the same tone.

"Jonathan, don't," I begged, fearful of what he would say next.

"Did something happen to Rachel?" Evan inquired, keeping his eyes on Jonathan without a glance in my direction.

"No." Jonathan laughed humorlessly. "This is between me and Emma. You're not the only one she confides in. You don't *need* to know everything."

I'd opened my mouth to interrupt the conversation when Evan returned with, "And she confides in you?"

"She does," Jonathan explained simply.

"Evan," I called to him in a rush, needing to ease the suspicion that gleamed in his eyes.

"No, I want to hear this," he interjected sharply. His harsh tone drove me back a step.

"Yeah, she tells me things that you wouldn't understand," Jonathan explained coolly.

"Please don't do this," I beseeched, reaching for Jonathan's arm. But he moved toward Evan, blocking my path. I was drowning in desperation, but neither of them responded to my pleas.

"What does she trust you with? What wouldn't *I* understand?" Evan inquired, clenching his jaw. Jonathan stepped over the threshold into the foyer. I tried to position myself next to him, to calm the growing tension that hummed between them, but it was as if I were invisible. My heart pounded against my chest.

"Don't worry about it," Jonathan returned cockily. "As I said, this has nothing to do with you."

Jonathan's arrogance was grating under Evan's skin, and the taut muscles along his arms made it evident.

"Evan, I can explain," I interjected passionately.

"I'd rather hear it from him," he snapped, making my stomach flip.

Jonathan produced a snide grin. "You really want to torture yourself, huh? Just let it be. I'm not taking her away from you or anything."

"Then what is it? What is it about you that makes her want to tell you things she can't tell me?"

Jonathan shrugged dismissively. "I get her in a way you never will. It's not your fault. You just don't understand. And I do."

Evan's shoulders drew back as if the words were razor sharp.

I knew Jonathan was walking along a dangerous line, but neither of them would listen to me. I couldn't keep him from pushing Evan over the edge.

"Jonathan, knock it off," I warned him, without effect.

"I'm there for her when the nightmares wake her in the middle of the night. I'm the one she calls when she needs someone to confide in about Rachel. She reveals the secrets you can't handle because she trusts me. And she knows I will always be here to protect her."

I screamed out in surprise as Evan's fist collided with Jonathan's jaw, knocking Jonathan back a few steps. I quickly sidestepped him as he stumbled for balance.

"You don't know anything about protecting her," Evan seethed. Jonathan straightened, wiping his mouth with the back of his hand. A streak of blood stained his skin.

In a sudden movement, Jonathan charged Evan, ramming him against the wall. The house shook around us, as though it was vehemently protesting the attack.

"Don't!" I yelled, rushing toward them. The violence of the exchange mounted as they grappled and threw each other around the foyer. Guttural groans escaped with each punch thrown. Blood spattered their faces.

I couldn't find a way to get between them. Their movements were so quick. They were oblivious to my presence, and I could easily have been swept up in the brawl. I begged them to stop over and over again, but they showed no signs of relenting.

My entire body shook as I shuffled around them, desperate for their attention. My cheeks were slick with tears as I fought to breathe. Each punch thrust directly into me, bludgeoning my heart.

I knew I'd done this. I'd created the tension between them that had erupted into this moment. Their anger and frustration had nothing to do with the person they were fighting. It had everything to do with me, and what I couldn't give them. Which was all of me. I felt my insides implode as they fell against the groaning walls.

I caught a glimpse of Evan's face and drew in a sharp breath at the sight of the gash above his right eye, blood trailing down his face. I couldn't stand by and watch anymore.

"Jonathan, don't!" I commanded loudly, grabbing for his arm. Impervious to my presence, he jabbed his elbow back and collided with my jaw, sending me sailing back. Unable to keep my balance, I collapsed with a cry.

Evan redirected his attention to my stunned face just as I landed on the floor. "Emma!"

The distraction left him open to a vicious blow to the temple.

"No!" I screamed, my voice echoing through the house. Evan's eyes left me and tilted back as his head lolled to the side like a ragdoll's. He crashed against the wall, and Jonathan pinned him upright, landing a ferocious blow to the side of his face.

I scrambled to my feet, driven by the adrenaline that accelerated through me. I squeezed in front of Evan and closed my eyes, bracing for the pain of Jonathan's crushing fist. My whole body tensed, pressed against Evan's slouched form.

Nothing happened.

Evan started to slide, and I quickly turned toward him, attempting to ease him to the floor. But his dead weight was too much for me to support, and he toppled over with a reverberating thump, his head knocking against the wood.

I collapsed beside him, and my chest shook with jagged breaths. "Evan!" I bent over him to examine his bruised and bloodied face. "Evan, can you hear me?"

I tried to reposition him, sliding him from his awkward angle against the wall, struggling to turn him on his back.

"Let me take a look," Jonathan said from beside me. He bent down and grabbed Evan's shoulders to lay him flat.

"Don't touch him!" I shouted, bending over Evan's body as if to shield him. "*You* don't get to touch him!"

"Emma." His voice sounded pained. He placed his hand on my back. I thrust against him forcefully, causing him to pull away with a jerk.

"Don't you dare," I threatened. My muscles quaked; I was fueled with rage. My eyes bored into him.

"Emma, please," he begged, his voice breaking with emotion as he swiped at the blood trickling down the side of his face. "I lost it. I didn't mean it. I'm sorry."

"No you're not," I shouted back. "Don't even say it. This is what you do. This is what *we* do. We hurt people." I choked on the words, forcing them out of my mouth.

The tendons along my neck strained as I screamed, "Look what we've done!" Jonathan flinched, his swollen eye watering. I hunched over Evan with a sob and gasped, "We've hurt so many people." I sniffled and gently caressed his bruised cheek. Evan remained still under my touch.

"Don't say that," Jonathan implored, his words coated with desperation. "We're the ones who've been hurt, Emma."

I released a vicious laugh. "No, Jonathan. We're just as bad as they are, with our lies and deceit. We destroy people's lives."

Jonathan opened his mouth to stop me, but I pierced him with my vile tongue. "And you. You've *killed* people. You're not any less of a monster than your father."

Jonathan's bruised face turned ashen as he released a strangled gasp, like he'd been stabbed through the heart.

"It was anger and pain that drew us together. That's our *bond*. Not love." My words shot out with lethal force, ripping his protests from his opened mouth. "I don't love you." His eyes flitted across mine, begging me to stop—but I continued, relentless. "*No one could ever love you.*" Jonathan's chest caved. He took several staggering steps before faltering to his knees, his confidence decimated.

Loathing corroded my veins and shriveled my heart. I watched as he cowered under my words, relishing his silent torture. "Don't *wait* for me. I don't want you to *be there* for me, not ever. Stay out of my life, and I won't breathe a word about what you've done." Jonathan closed his glassy eyes and bowed his head, clutching his chest.

I turned my back to him, unable to continue to bear witness to his devastation. I hid my shame behind my lids, tears continued to cascade down my face, dripping from my chin. My words wielded as much destruction as Jonathan's fists. I tore people apart with my lies and secrets, unleashing a verbal wrath that could alter a person's conviction. I wasn't worthy of being loved any more than he was.

I tensed when the screen door slammed shut behind me. I knew he was gone, and that I'd never see him again.

My chest spasmed in pain as I released heaving sobs, bending over Evan's unconscious body. I placed my hand on his chest, and he shifted slightly. I sucked in broken breaths, trying to relinquish the pain, but I knew that would never happen...not after today.

Evan moaned below me. My body shook in agony and my insides began to splinter. It was excruciating. I could barely breathe.

"Emma?" Evan murmured, his lids twitching.

"I'm so sorry." I released an impassioned cry, a tear dropping on his cheek. I leaned down, breathing him in with a brush of my lips against his—savoring his clean, sweet scent and the warmth of his firm lips before pulling away. "I don't know if you'll ever forgive me, but I won't destroy your life too." My heart fought for each beat as the pieces began to fall. "I love you," I breathed.

Easing his head on to the floor, I rose. My legs were unsteady as I balanced my broken frame. I faltered to the screen door and pushed it open. It took every ounce of strength I had to walk away.

"Emma!" rang through the darkness, shattering me into a thousand pieces.

EPILOGUE

I slid into the silent vehicle beside Sara, and Carl backed out of the driveway. I stared out the window the entire drive, allowing Anna and Carl to converse in the front without comprehending a single word. Sara's presence pressed in beside me, but she made no attempt to speak.

When we pulled up to the airport drop-off, Carl removed the suitcases from the trunk while Anna waited for me on the curb.

"I'll ship the rest of your things once you're in your dorm," she told me, smiling kindly. She examined my face and gently brushed my cheek. "You don't have to do this, Emma. You deserve to walk down that aisle on graduation day with everyone else. I wish you'd reconsider."

I smiled lightly, knowing she only wanted to console me, but I was beyond reach now. Everything was still and quiet inside me, impervious to the emotions that weighed on her face. There was nothing left. It had all shattered, leaving me hollow.

"I should get going," I replied, sliding one arm through the strap of my backpack. Anna hugged me and handed me my boarding pass.

"Call if you need anything," she urged, and I nodded.

"Your adviser will be contacting you after you arrive to arrange for your final exams," Carl explained, rolling the suitcase over to me and setting the duffel bag next to it.

"Thank you," I said sincerely. He hesitated before giving me a brief, firm hug.

"You know where we are," he said to me before getting in the car.

Sara remained still, leaning against the SUV. I paused, but she hadn't said a word to me since I'd booked my flight two days ago, and I wasn't expecting her to speak now.

I picked up the duffel bag and rolled the suitcase behind me, heading toward the check-in counter.

"Emma!" Sara yelled, jogging to catch up. I closed my eyes and exhaled in relief, stopping to wait for her. Her eyes were glassy as her brow scrunched in agony. "Don't do this. Please. This isn't what's supposed to happen."

I remained unaffected and smiled at her reassuringly. "It'll be okay."

"Emma, please!"

"I'll see you in a few weeks, right?" I confirmed, my eyes soft.

She swallowed and pressed her lips together with a nod. Then she grabbed my shoulders. Her words poured out passionately. "You're making the biggest mistake of your life. Don't do this. I know you're going to regret it."

I waited for her to let me go, and replied in an even tone, "I'll see you soon." I turned from her and walked away.

———

I pulled the key out of the door and tossed my backpack on the bed. I opened the small refrigerator to get a water, trying to ignore the fact that Lyle was in the room. Unfortunately, he was hard to ignore.

I froze with the door in my hand, recognizing the box on his bed as he shamelessly rummaged through its contents.

"What the hell?" I demanded, furious, slamming the fridge shut. I pulled the box off of his bed and inspected it.

"I was looking for a sweatshirt," he explained feebly. *His invasion of my things wasn't new. He'd done it a lot in the past few months, but this was crossing the line.*

"You're not going to find one in here." I scowled angrily. "Give me those." I snatched the pictures from his hands.

"Relax, Evan," he countered, flopping back down on his bed. "Who's the girl anyway? She's pretty hot."

"None of your business," I snapped, placing the photos back in the box, on top of the camera case I hadn't touched in months. I hesitated, removing the square envelope from the stack. I ran my fingers over my mother's name, written in her distinctive penmanship. A cold current filtered through me at the touch of the thick paper between my fingers.

The letter that had once been sealed in this envelope had changed everything. I never got to read it. But whatever she'd written to my mother kept me from following her, forcing me to stay on the East Coast while she escaped to California. No explanation. No good-bye. That letter had changed my life, and I never saw a single word of it.

I set the envelope back in the box and paused before closing it, taking in the image of her laughing. Her laugh was infectious, lighting up her caramel brown eyes, creasing them around their edges. She reminded me of the picture of her father she used to have on her dresser.

I had to look away. I knew I was only torturing myself. She'd left. She'd left me here.

Just before I closed the box, I realized something was missing. I looked around the room and spotted the sweatshirt hanging on the back of the chair at Lyle's desk.

"What the fuck, Lyle!" I bellowed, grabbing it.

"What would I want with a Stanford sweatshirt?" he said defensively with a roll of his eyes.

"If you touch my things again, I'll break your hand," I threatened. He didn't look up from his textbook, but I knew he'd heard me. Color flushed across his face.

I shoved the sweatshirt in the box and folded the flaps, hiding the image of her laughing at something I'd said. I slid the box into the bottom of my closet, next to the others.

"I don't get it," he muttered. "What's up with the boxes anyway?"

I closed the closet door, shutting away all of the reasons I was compelled to say, "I don't know if I'm staying."

ACKNOWLEDGMENTS

Writing may be a solitary venture, but publishing is not. There are so many people who are a vital part of the entire experience, whether it's providing emotional support and words of encouragement, or reading it through and freaking out when the ending is so far off the mark they virtually have a meltdown, or examining each sentence and every word until they are perfectly constructed. I may create on this tiny island, but I am surrounded by a vast ocean of friends whom I love, and I am in awe of their magnificence.

First and foremost, I must thank my ever patient and brilliant assistant, Elizabeth. She has been the perfect partner, polishing my words until they gleam with pride. We complement each other so well that my words became hers and hers mine. She has the kindest soul I've ever had the privilege to be touched by.

Faith, my ever present voice of reason. If I ever doubt, she is always there to provide her much valued honesty and insight. I will follow her advice down the darkest roads, knowing I will end up exactly where I belong, safe and sound.

Emily, my sunshine and warmth when I need assurance that all is truly wonderful in the world. And the one to reel me back in when I've veered too far off the path. I will never get lost with her in my life.

Courtney, my bright-eyed and even brighter-smiled friend, who can come up with the best one-liners that will keep me laughing for days. Attitude will get you everywhere, and by her side, we will conquer the world!

Amy, modestly brilliant, and I am thrilled that she was a contributor to our team, giving the story that something extra to make it spectacular.

The fabulous team at Trident Media Group for believing in me, especially my wonderful agent, Erica Silverman.

Tim Ditlow, for embracing my voice, and the entire editing team at Amazon Publishing, for making it that much better.

There were a select few who read *Barely Breathing* in varied stages from its infancy to its nearly finished progression. But there were plenty of others who were there to listen, praise, encourage and celebrate with me along the way. I thank you all!

Lastly, I want to thank my truly incredible fans who have enthusiastically embraced me since I released *Reason to Breathe*. Your enthusiasm will forever inspire me to create words worthy of being read by you!

ABOUT THE AUTHOR

 Rebecca Donovan, a graduate of the University of Missouri–Columbia, lives in a quiet town in Massachusetts with her son. Excited by all that makes life possible, Rebecca is a music enthusiast and is willing to try just about anything once.

Web: www.rebeccadonovan.com / Facebook: thebreathingseries / Twitter: beccadonovan